TRIPTYCH opens in the glittering world of baroque palaces in royal Saint Petersburg. It is there that Gregory and Sonya's enigmatic courtship, coloured by political and emotional distrust, leads to their tempestuous marriage. Sonya and Gregory are key players in a conspiratorial drama over which they have no control – one that catapults them out of their beloved Russia and on separate, arduous journeys to a new life in New York's bohemian Greenwich Village.

There, amidst immigrant poverty, Sonya uses the power of her beauty and womanliness – the very things she once scorned – to build a vibrant life. Part of that life is Delphi Stern, Sonya's remarkable daughter, whose parentage is unknown to Tolchin although she is the true inheritor of his spirit.

We follow her through poverty and notoriety in the freewheeling Paris of the 1920s, and then on to Berlin in the thirties, where we see her creativity blossom just as the shadow of war begins to spread over Europe.

TRIPTYCH is a story of many kinds of journeys: from generation to generation, from cause to cause, and through the dark terrain of the human heart.

TRIPTYCH

Elinor Landey

CORGI BOOKS

The authors wish to express their gratitude to Nan A. Talese and Morton L. Janklow for their advice and encouragement. They also wish to thank, for their patience, understanding, and love, Willy and Arthur Klein, Shere Detwiler, and Yummy, Nina, Anna, and Tony Lo Bianco.

TRIPTYCH
A CORGI BOOK 0 552 12381 1

First publication in Great Britain

PRINTING HISTORY

Corgi edition published 1984

This book is set in 10/11 Lectura

Corgi Books are published by Transworld Publishers Ltd., Century House, 61-63 Uxbridge Road, Ealing, London W5 5SA.

Printed and bound in Great Britain by
Hunt Barnard Printing Ltd, Aylesbury, Bucks.

For Each Other

Dates before 1917 are given in the Russian Julian calendar. This calendar was twelve days behind the Gregorian calendar, which was in use elsewhere.

triptych *n.* (Greek *triptukhos*, consisting of three layers) 1. A folding writing tablet in three parts. 2. A picture or carving in three compartments side by side.

Book I

1

In her palace on Nevsky Prospect, Princess Mariyenka
Nicolaevna Poliakov had been in labor since dawn. At the
first pains, she had woken her sister, Adele, who had come
from Moscow for her confinement, and had Adele send for
Vera Petrovna, the midwife. Now, four hours later, she
was sitting at her *table de toilette*, staring at her reflection
in the glass. She pushed back a loose strand of her
chestnut hair, ran her finger across her arched brows,
adjusted the bodice of her pink silk gown so that her
breasts, which almost burst through her pale skin, were
perfectly symmetrical, and smiled at herself.

Her dog, Pushkin, a fat Pomeranian, jumped from his
post by her feet and pawed her knees. 'You know, don't
you,' she said to him, leaning down and ruffling his fur,
'that there will be little time for you today.'

'I will never understand you, Masha,' Adele said,
watching Princess Mariyenka stand up with great effort
and smooth her gown over her bulging stomach. 'You will
not lie down, you will not put out that dreadful little dog,
and now you insist on walking through the halls to your
husband.'

'But I always tell Leon when a birth is imminent, my
dear. It has become a ritual, a ritual which has brought us
luck.' The princess took her blue velvet robe from the back
of the chair and draped it loosely around her. Carefully she
made her way down the carpeted hall, past the waiting
servants, to her husband's rooms, her dog yipping at her
ankles and cutting across her steps.

'You will be the death of me, little monster,' she chided
as he rushed at her, grabbing the hem of her robe, making
her clasp it to her before it fell at her feet. What a beauty
he was, his fur like the finest sable, his soft round eyes full
of love and mischief. Save for Pushkin, everything in the
house was quiet. The princess smiled. Soon no room or
corridor would be peaceful. There would be such activity,

11

everyone flying about like a flock of blackbirds in summer. She opened the door to her husband's apartment, walked noiselessly to his bed, and stared down at him. Tears came to her eyes. How handsome he was, and how he looked like a boy when he slept, curled up just as his child in her was curled. She stroked his dark auburn hair and beard. Could any other man's beard have been as soft as her husband's?

'How beautiful you are,' he whispered sleepily and then, pushing himself forward, held her face in the palms of his hands. 'Are you sure you shouldn't be in the hospital?'

'What do men know?' she teased.

'But I worry.'

'You always worry. I've had four healthy ones here at home. Why should there be complications with the fifth?' She touched his lips with the fingers of her right hand.

'What about this new business they are using there for the pain?'

'The pain of childbearing is quickly forgotten. The joy never is.'

'You are sometimes stubborn, Masha.'

'But I am right, my love. Vera Petrovna tells me that only last week Countess Rostova lost a perfectly healthy infant in the hospital. It is too unsanitary there.' She grimaced suddenly at an unexpected burning in her groin.

'Mariyenka!' Her husband was more startled than she. The dog jumped up on the bed and he roughly pushed him away, knocking him onto the carpet. 'Mariyenka, are you all right?'

'Leon! Pushkin is so frail!'

'It is not Pushkin who concerns me.'

'That was only a small warning. You see, it has stopped. I am going back to my chambers. And you,' she said, leaning awkwardly down to kiss him, 'must be kinder to Pushkin.'

Her husband put his arms around her and she allowed his embrace even though his morning smell nearly overwhelmed her with nausea. She excused herself and slowly made her way back to her room, breathing as deeply as she could to keep from becoming ill. Once inside, she walked to the double-hung windows, lifted the heavy velvet drapery back, and looked down into the street. Just to see the sleighs as they darted by, their runners fairly off the ground, cleared her head. That looked like Princess Irina's troika. Where could she be going so early on a Sunday? Princess Mariyenka missed the troika races on the Neva, all the marvelous speed, all the clamor of the crowd. Well, she thought, pulling the drape closed, it was almost over. Soon she would be outside again, feeling the damp Petersburg cold through her furs and the soft snow on her face, hearing the snorts of the horses and the curses of the likatches and vankas. What a bother to have her confinement during the height of the season.

A slight pain came and went, reminding her of the next few hours. At least she was not frightened. She had only scorn for those women who carried on during childbirth, fainting and screaming as if it were the end of the world. She closed her eyes for a moment to utter a silent prayer, the same one she had made every day for months, 'Please, most holy God the Father, let this be a daughter.' Not that she wasn't proud of her four sons, each one more handsome and hardy than the next, but she wished God might now provide her with the solace of a daughter. There were too many soldiers in her house. The boys were still young, too young, and already her husband had taught them the wonders of that most terrible of games, war. What Russian woman could think of war and not think of all she had lost, fathers or brothers or husbands or sons? Two of her brothers had died fighting the Turks before they were twenty. She sighed aloud and her sister, Adele, who had been sitting near her in the new blue damask chair, quickly got to her feet and rushed to her side. 'Are you all right, Mariyenka? Do you think we should call Feydor Vasilovitch?'

'Of course not. Vera Petrovna has safely delivered me four times, not to mention that she brought both of us into the world. I have every confidence that she has more experience in her thumbnail that all the doctors in Russia. Besides, the pain is not bad. I was sighing because I was wishing for a daughter.'

'You shall have one. I can tell. You have carried so low. It will be a girl.'

Princess Mariyenka sighed again. 'Really, Adyenka, that makes no sense whatsoever. Ask Vera Petrovna.' She turned to the ancient midwife, who sat knitting close to the stove. Except for her sinewy hands and her quick, clear blue eyes, Vera Petrovna looked at least a hundred. Her mouth had long since sunken into the space left by the loss of her teeth, and only a few strands of sparse white hair poked out from beneath her cap. Mariyenka smiled at the woman. She had never considered calling for anyone else despite Vera Petrovna's age. 'How many babies have you seen come, Verushka?' She spoke to the midwife in Russian, not in French, as she did to her family and friends. 'High or low, does it make a difference?'

'Of course not,' the old woman answered with great finality.

'You see,' the princess said to her sister. 'I told you. No, God gives us no signs. He must like surprises.'

'You will be the one to see,' Adele insisted. 'It will be a girl.'

'I hope so,' Princess Mariyenka answered, even as she clenched her teeth. The pain had started in the lower abdomen and then spread quickly outward, becoming stronger and stronger until it reached the top of her head and she thought she would surely lose consciousness. She leaned against her sister, and Adele held her tight until the pain receded back down, past her throat and neck, past her chest, returning to her womb, where it vanished.

'You must lie down, Masha, I insist. You carry on so.'

'If it is a girl,' the princess said, tucking Pushkin under her arm and letting Adele lead her to the flowered chaise, 'she is going to be very strong.' The chaise had been prepared for the birth with a rubber mat covering more than half of it, a large pillow at its head, and a thin crocheted blanket folded across it. On the table next to it were Vera Petrovna's instruments and a stack of freshly laundered towels. The princess preferred the hardness of the chaise to the softness of her bed. It had always seemed more suitable to have something firm beneath her in those last moments when she had to push the child out.

'It's more important that a girl be beautiful than strong,' Adele said somewhat wistfully. The princess felt momentarily sorry for her sister, for even she, who could find beauty in almost any child, was hard put to find it in her niece. As her pain began again, four-year-old Maya Sergeievna's image flashed in front of her, a little face as homely as a potato, a body like a bear cub's. The princess visualized her brother-in-law, with his nose nearly as large as the dome at St Isaac's Cathedral and his eyes smaller than raisins. She almost smiled to think of her husband's handsome face, and her own.

The princess took a great deep breath. Adele, blotting away the beads of perspiration forming on her sister's forehead and upper lip, nodded to Vera Petrovna. The midwife stood up and scuttled to the chaise and put her hands on the princess's swollen belly. Several seconds later she lifted up the thin silk gown, spread the princess's stiffening legs, and put a firm hand between them for an examination. Adele wet a cloth and put it on her sister's forehead.

'Leave that, Princess,' Vera Petrovna said. 'Please, make sure the hot water is ready, I shall need it soon, and see if Anna Markova is up from the kitchen. I may need her. It will be before the afternoon bells.'

'My goodness,' Adele said, dropping the wet cloth on the thick Aubusson carpet and running to the door of the bedroom. 'Everything happens too quickly. You. You!' she yelled at one of the blue-shirted peasants stationed outside the door. 'Get the hot water ready. Make sure it is boiling! And you!' She pointed at another. 'Go with him and make sure. And you,' she said to still another, suddenly racing back into the room and grabbing Pushkin, who yelped and tried to nip her, 'take this dog.' She fairly threw him into the man's arms.

'Adele! Pushkin!' The princess's voice was weak.

'Take him to the kitchen, and then find Anna Markova; tell her she is wanted here.'

On her chaise, Princess Mariyenka lay very still, her eyes closed, waiting for the next great invasion of pain, still praying for a daughter.

In his study, General Leon Poliakov took his third glass of tea from the samovar and walked back to his desk. He had been going over his papers and periodicals as was his custom on Sunday morning, and an article in *The New Times* by, of all people, his friend Alexei Sermayov had irritated him. His mouth tightened and little lines puckered his lips. Sermayov wrote favorably of the Loris-Melikov reforms, reforms that the czar was to sign that very morning. The general could not understand it. Why, they might as well declare Russia a constitutional monarchy, like England. The czar would be left impotent. The general found Melikov the worst kind of hypocrite, too dapper, and above all, too much of a westernized intellectual. He didn't trust that sort of fellow. At the core of every liberal lay the seed of revolution. Give them a slice and they would want the whole loaf, as the old saying went.

The general sighed and set his tea down squarely in the middle of his walnut desk. Enough politics. Upstairs, Mariyenka – he smiled at the thought of her – was giving him a child. He picked one of the gold-tipped cigarettes out of its silver case and lit it, then sat down in the brass-studded leather chair, the very same chair he had sat in as a boy when it had been behind his father's desk. He leaned back and watched the smoke drift out in layers across the room, finally rising up toward the mahogany-paneled ceiling. He much preferred this room to the study on the ground floor where he received his visitors. Here the deep browns of the wood and the muted blues and reds of the Persian carpet were as comforting to him as his face in the mirror. Across from him, his books filled the leaded-glass-fronted cases. Old friends, he thought, steeping himself in the peace that he could always find here. An ash from his cigarette dropped onto the navy cashmere dressing coat his wife had given him on his last name day, and he carefully scooped it up and reached across the desk to deposit it in the ashtray. He was, he knew, as fragile as that ash, as perishable as all of God's creatures, and yet he felt superior, solid and impregnable. His life was symmetrical, as evenly arranged as the silver frames, the lapis and malachite boxes, the pipes, the pens, and the collection of Fabergé animals that graced the top of the desk in front of him. Physically, as well, he was solid and symmetrical, and he prided himself on his carriage and his manner. He was large, yet graceful, exceptionally hand-some, with a high forehead and a strong, straight nose. His eyes were hazel, sometimes yellow, depending on his mood. He hated that womanish trait and was forever annoyed by friends and acquaintances who noticed it. Nonetheless, his eyes were his finest feature. Now the eyes were closed, the thick lashes making shadows on his cheeks. His cigarette burned on the edge of the rose and green cloisonné ashtray. The general had slipped into a reverie. He was dreaming of his life.

On the whole, Leon Ivanovitch Poliakov was quite pleased with himself. His life had been exactly as his father or his father's father might have planned it. He had attended the prestigious Corps de Pages, had been an officer in the Knight's Guard, had risen rapidly to the rank of general (his father, after all, had been a general before him), married the daughter of the immensely wealthy Prince Eryenkov, and had just been invited to join the most exclusive of St Petersburg's hundreds of clubs, the Imperial Yacht Club. He visited Paris for the fashions, Carlsbad for the waters, and Monte Carlo for the gambling. He attended performances at the theater or the opera as an intimate of the royal family, had four healthy sons, and adored his wife. Such good fortune! Sometimes, of course, the social aspects of his life were too demanding, and he often begged his wife to take her sisters in his place. Princess Mariyenka would laugh at him, her eyes twinkling, and shake her head. It was understood that the two of them could never be separated when it was possible to be together. A smile broke on his mouth. He was truly a contented man. His only complaint was that he never had enough time to read. At thirty-eight, he thought of himself as serious and wise, and he looked forward to the day when he would be fifty, and even wiser.

He rubbed his beard, still smiling to himself. With the birth of each child he had sat down in this place, alone, and taken stock of his life. He had yet to be disappointed.

The knock on the door had startled him and he sat up quickly, straight in his chair. 'Yes? Yes?'

His major-domo, Ivan Ivanov, pushed open the door respectfully. He was dressed in his morning livery. The

17

general noticed at once that his gloves were clean and his brass buttons polished but that his shoes were not. He scowled at him. 'What is it, man?' he asked sharply. They always found some reason to bother him. The more servants, the more interruptions.

'I'm sorry to bother you, sir, especially at a time like this.'

'What is it!'

'It's the groom, sir. His wife is here. He's been arrested, sir.'

'Which groom?' the general asked. The smell of his dying cigarette annoyed him and he snuffed it out. The sugar had congealed on the bottom of his glass of tea, and he stirred it up, but he knew it would be cold now and didn't drink it.

'The head groom, sir, in the country. They say he was drunk and attacked a young girl. His wife swears he was at home. She wishes you not to judge him until after his trial. She also asks for his salary. She has a large family to look after.'

'Damnation.' There was a silence.

Ivan Ivanov did not blink. 'She is quite hysterical. She traveled all night. I would not have bothered you otherwise,' he said finally.

'The boys are riding next week, am I right?'

'Yes, sir.'

'Do you know him well, this groom, I forget his name.'

'Boris Petrovitch, he is my cousin.'

The general was still scowling. They were always related. If he had not known better, he might have thought it was a conspiracy. All the cousins, uncles, brothers of peasant Russia conspiring to slow everything down, to produce mass confusion. It hadn't been that way when he was a child. No one was capable of anything anymore. And if they weren't stupid, they were drunk, lying about in the streets riddled with *kvas*. On top of it all, the police chief in the country was a rich man from all the money the general alone had given him. A groom or a cook was arrested every time the chief lost at cards. Would it never end?

'Tell the woman that her husband's salary will be used

to get him out of jail. Make arrangements to have him freed. And while we are at it, make sure that the horses are in shape for the boys. Anton was complaining about the gelding only last week. Also, the black mare here needs a new shoe on her right foot. She jerked the troika like a goat last night.'

A loud bell interrupted him. Fire, the general thought immediately, waiting for the next signal. Instead he heard shouts in the street, a high, piercing scream, then silence. Now there were more bells, farther away. Another shout. Peculiar noises that made no sense and belonged to no pattern. Someone was screaming something, but he couldn't make out the words. He left his chair and pushed Ivan Ivanov aside, running the length of the hall and down the marble stairs to the grand foyer. Ivan Ivanov followed close behind.

'Are you going out, sir?' It was the old footman, Petya. The butler, Tolya, was nowhere to be seen.

'What is that terrible noise, Petya?' They were both running toward the front door.

'I don't know, sir. I was down in the cellar. I just heard it.'

Down in the cellar stealing my wine, thought the general. 'Open the door,' he shouted.

'Your coat, sir, your coat, you'll catch your death.' Petya nodded at the young boy who stood at the entrance to the cloakroom, watching them. 'Hurry, stupid, the general's greatcoat.' The boy disappeared momentarily and came back, hardly visible beneath the heavy fur coat.

'Open the door,' the general commanded Ivan Ivanov and his valet LeFaux, who had come to see what the commotion was about. 'Careful,' he shouted at the boy and old Petya, who were helping him on with his coat.

'Yes, sir.'

'Yes, sir.'

The frigid air burst into the house, seeming to push everything out of its way. The general thought for a moment it might knock poor Petya over. With it came the sound of the streets, the shouts, the bells, the unusual activity, all the more clearly.

The general ran out. Everywhere, it seemed, everything

was rushing. The general grabbed the first man he could stop. 'What is it, man?' he demanded. 'What's happened?'

'Oh, my God, the saints protect us, they've shot the czar. The czar is dead, I hear. I hear, he's dead.' The man wept openly, crossing himself again and again. The general let him go. He was nothing more than a street vendor and reeked of drink. Obviously his word could not be believed. A mounted policeman came around the corner and the general ran to the center of the street, waving his arms. 'Ho!' he shouted up at the man as the horse snaked around him. 'Ho! It's General Leon Poliakov.' As if it had heard, the horse came to a rest some twenty feet down the street. The general ran to the policeman.

'Is that you, General? It is Sergeant Mirsky, from Prospect Station. I am at your service.'

'Yes. Yes. What has happened?' He frowned. The fellow had come to him once for a favor. He couldn't remember the connection.

'They say the czar has been mortally wounded. Blown to bits by terrorists. They have taken him to the Winter Palace. Either he is dead already or he will soon die. There is no hope.'

The two men looked into each other's eyes. General Poliakov crossed himself. He saw tears in the eyes of the young sergeant. 'If you will excuse me . . .'

'Of course, of course,' the general said, standing still in the center of the street as the sergeant slapped the reins, urging the horse forward across the icy street. What a fine horse, he thought, feeling all at once drained and yet fully alive, the way he had not felt since eighteen years before, when as a young captain he had led his troops into Poland. It could not be. It could not. And yet everything, the church bells tolling in the distance, the sergeant's tear-filled eyes, the cloud now passing in front of the sun, even the gait of the horse, convinced the general that it was. Poor Alexander. Ha! So much for reforms. So much for Melikov and his glossy beard. Ha! Just as he had thought – give them an inch and they would want a mile. Nothing was enough for them. How dare they kill the czar? How would such a thing look to the rest of the world? He felt anger rise in his chest and his neck, his veins fairly bursting from the rush of it. Damn them all, all the intellectuals, the anarchists and Jews. Damn them!

The general shivered, turned, and made his way back to the house. Where was his secretary? He would have to send the coachman to police headquarters to find out the details. Meanwhile, he quickly assessed his position with the future czar. Alexander Alexandrovitch was, unlike his father, a man of strong conservative convictions. He had been tutored by Pobedonestsev, a man the general greatly admired. He had seen Czarevich Alexander only last week. They had had a pleasant chat. The general's position would not be threatened, especially since he had always been on the side of law and order. Perhaps he could help stamp out all the radicals.

As the door closed behind him on the sounds of the street, he heard voices from upstairs and the sustained cry of a newborn infant echoing through the vast halls. Behind the sound came his sister-in-law, hurrying toward him, a great smile across her face.

'Congratulations, Leon Ivanovitch,' she said. 'You have a daughter.'

Eighty thousand people, among them General Leon Poliakov, witnessed what was to be the last public hanging in Russia, when the members of the Narondnaya Volya, the People's Will, were executed for the assassination of Czar Alexander II. Among those hung was their leader, Sofia Perovskaya. She was twenty-eight years old.

In July 1883, General Poliakov was named an aide to Count Dimitri Tolstoy, the Minister of the Interior, and in 1885 was named assistant head of that department.

2

Sonya's first clear memories were of her nurse, Marushka.
Marushka had been her mother's nurse as well. Had her
mother loved her as much as Sonya did? To eight-year-old
Sonya, Marushka was always like summer, as warm as
summer sun, as ripe as summer fruit. She was round, rolls
of flesh at her wrists like bracelets, a sack of fat at her
shoulders which bent her toward Sonya, a great swollen
bosom, softer than down. Her body shook when she
laughed and a dozen dimples would appear in her round
red cheeks. She seemed propelled by sheer exuberance, her
high spirits pulling her like wild horses. No, Sonya's
mother could never have loved her as much as Sonya did.

'If the sun appears in the middle of a rainstorm, quickly
pray to the saints or Russia will suffer.'

'I will, I promise.'

'You are a good little angel, my Sonya.'

'Tell me another, Marushka, tell me another!'

'When you are grown, avoid roses. Roses at the time of
the full moon can suck your breath out of you.' Marushka
put down the hairbrush. 'We have prayed, your hair
shines, now off you go to bed.'

'My Mama loves roses.'

'Get under the covers.' Marushka walked to the
window. 'I am closing the curtains.' Marushka's hand
released the woven gold cord that held the curtains, and
the light green brocade fell together in a great rush,
blotting out the pale summer light. Sonya crawled under
the pink and green quilt on the wide, high bed and looked
up at the canopy, its pink cloth embroidered with delicate
garlands of blue and gold flowers on long slender green
stems. It was like sleeping in the garden.

'Roses are beautiful,' Sonya said, lying back on the thick
pillows and smiling.

'Beauty can be the devil's instrument.'

'But I am beautiful. I must belong to the devil.'

'Shhh, little Sonya.'

'Tell me I am beautiful,' Sonya teased, crossing Marushka's fingers one over the other. 'Tell me or I shall knot up your hand.'

'Hush.' The old woman smiled, settling herself on the edge of the bed, making the mattress shudder and sink.

'My hair is the color of roses, and blood, too.'

'Your hair is orange, like a carrot. You had best be careful or a bunny will get you.'

'Will you tell me the story about the child who is born on the day the czar is murdered?'

Marushka fairly jumped up from the bed. 'What are you saying? I don't know what you mean!'

Sonya lifted herself up on her elbows and then pushed herself forward, grabbing Marushka and tickling her. 'I heard you tell Petya and Vladimir, and now you shall tell me!'

Marushka squirmed away from Sonya's hands. 'I don't know what you are talking about! Not a word, not a word. Your mama would have a fit if she knew we were talking like this. You must sleep, my treasure.'

'Tell me, tell me,' Sonya chanted. 'If you do not tell me I will never go to sleep. I know I was born on March first, 1881, the day Czar Alexander II was killed. It is no secret. I was born at the exact moment.'

'Who told you such a thing?'

'Bruno told me.' Sonya smiled, liking Marushka's discomfort, going on with her torment. 'And I heard you tell Petya and Vladimir that children born on a day a czar is murdered carried demon spirits and were in league with the devil and cursed by God. You said such children have nothing to fear, that they had blood for their companion.'

'I said no such thing!' Marushka crossed herself.

'Oh, yes you did! I heard.'

'Never. I never . . .'

'Oh, Marushka, that does not frighten me. It makes me feel strong! I am not afraid of anything, not even the shadows of strange men who come to my ceiling every night and speak to each other.'

'Strange men?' Marushka sank down on the edge of the bed again, worry making her face very long, like the icon in the niche across from them.

'Marushka, you know everything. You can tell me what they are saying. Tell me and I promise to go right to sleep and never ask you about my birthday again.' Marushka's eyes widened a bit and she shook her head up and down slowly as Sonya continued. 'Do you see there on the ceiling? There in the shadows way at the very top. There.' Sonya pointed. 'On the left side.' She watched Marushka's eyes go to the spot. 'Every night, after you kiss me, I see those men. Look, Marushka, there is a long skinny one who looks like my French tutor.'

Marushka was squinting up at where Sonya pointed. 'I see only the shadows from the glass icicles around the light, and they dance as the glass moves.'

'They talk to me, Marushka, and they talk to each other, only I don't understand them. I can't understand what they say. You know what they say. Tell me!'

The old woman looked at Sonya's anguished face and her eyes brightened, a smile forming and making the dots of her dimples appear above and below that smile.

Sonya pulled at her. 'You do know! You know what they're saying. Tell me!'

'Men have secrets that we women will never understand.' Marushka was playing with her.

'What secrets could they have I would not understand?'

'It is not your place to understand the secrets of men.' Marushka reached toward her but Sonya pulled away.

'Marushka, it is terrible . . . It is dreadful . . . I have never told anyone before.' She covered her mouth with her hands and then flung herself at the old woman and held tight to her. Shame burned through her, and she feared her burning cheek would scorch Marushka's challis dress.

'What is it, my sweet? Tell your old *nyanya*.'

Sonya took a deep breath and pressed her head against her nurse. 'I wish I were a boy,' she said and then threw her head back to catch the expression that crossed Marushka's face. 'Don't smile. Please don't laugh at me! It's true. I want to be a soldier like my brothers will be.'

'Oh, my little one, my sweet one,' Marushka said, grabbing her and pulling her down against her soft breast, stroking her hair, rocking her. 'You will forget about that.

You mustn't worry so. Sometimes little girls want to be boys, but that passes. Yes it passes.'

'No, it will not pass,' Sonya said. It was not what she wanted to hear.

'Yes, yes, it does. As your body tells you it is time to be a woman, you will forget about the shadows on the ceiling and wanting to be a man. You will be the most beautiful woman, like your mama. You will have so many suitors and admirers, but you will marry the handsomest man in all the world and he will make you very happy. And you will have beautiful children and certainly the most splendid palace in all Petersburg, and all the world will love you as I do.'

'But I do not want to be like Mama. I want to stay the way I am.' Oh, how she had prayed that the curve of her mother's hips and fullness of her breasts would not be her legacy. How she prayed that she might remain as she was, long and lean as her brothers.

'My child, how can you say such a thing? Your mother is one of the most admired women in this world!'

'I do not want to be like my mama. I want to be like Papa and like Bruno. I want to win battles, Marushka.'

'And so you will, my sweet fawn, so you will. You are so young now, you do not realize that what you want today is not what you will want tomorrow. A woman's battles are every bit as great as any man's, and you will win them all.' Marushka gently laid Sonya back on her pillows. 'Now you must sleep so that tomorrow you will be ready to fight.'

'Are you laughing at me, Marushka?' Sonya whispered.

'No, my little one. I am not laughing. I believe your shadows are there, but I know that soon they will leave you. Soon they will be gone.'

Sonya wondered as Marushka kissed her if the old woman could taste the salt of her tears. 'Close your eyes.' The old woman said, 'You must save the gift of tears for something worth their sweetness.'

She saw the gun before she heard the noise. 'Bang!' he screamed. 'I've got you! Bang!'

Down she went. He tiptoed over to look at her. 'No,' she yelled, grabbing him around the legs, 'I've got your horse now. You only shot me once, a minor wound. But I've got your horse and you're mine.' She pointed her finger at him. 'One in your arm. Bang! One in your leg. Bang! One in your heart. Bang!'

He fell on top of her, squeezing the breath out of her and then tickling her until she was exhausted from her laughter. 'No fair,' she gasped. 'No fair.' Her face was flushed and hot. Tendrils of her red hair escaped from her braided crown and stuck to her cheeks and the back of her neck. She rolled over onto her stomach, her arms straight down at her sides, tight to her waist, so he couldn't tickle her more, her forehead on the carpet. She knew the dusty smell of that carpet so well. It was like the ashes of Father's black and gold cigarettes.

Sonya and her brother Bruno were in the playroom, the vast cavern with the tiny windows on the fourth floor. Each floor of the palace had ceilings lower than the one beneath, and in this wide, low-ceilinged room just below the attic servant quarters, it was easy to imagine the fields of Moscow stretching out in all their snowy anonymity or the flat green plains of France. Old pictures of long-dead relatives and out-of-favor furniture were stacked haphazardly around the walls. There were piles of leather-bound books, papers in old trunks with broken latches. In one such trunk Sonya had found the illegible diaries and papers of her father's grandfather, who had actually fought Napoleon. In another were her mother's baby clothes and her own. For a long time her favorite souvenir had been the baptismal certificate of her mother's sister Sofia, who had died at the age of ten, of pneumonia. Time compressed. The calendar disintegrated. No wonder she and Bruno could create whatever battle they liked so easily.

She rolled over onto her side and stared at him. Their faces were so alike, and even now, when he was fourteen, and his features were thickening and his mustache coming (how could it be brown when the hair on his head was as red as hers?), even now they were unmistakably alike. Sonya smiled at the thought. Four years older than she, he was her mentor and guide. This year, when he had left for school, she had thought her heart would break. It was so hard, just seeing him on his vacations. She was used to her eldest brothers being away. Vladimir had been with his regiment in the Urals now for over a year. Vassily had graduated the corps last year with the highest honors. He had been picked as one of the Kammerpages, that elite group who guarded the royal family. He was hardly ever at home. Besides Bruno, only Anton was at home with any regularity. She hated Anton, and had been delighted when he had left for the corps two years earlier. It wasn't fair. It just wasn't fair. Even dolts like Anton could go to the corps and become officers, and she never could. She was braver than Anton by a thousand million times and if they sent her away at all, which they probably would, it would be to the Smolney, where she would be educated, true, but only as a woman. She might be a doctor if she wanted, but she could never be a general, so what was the use? Meanwhile she had to suffer through the series of monsieurs who came to teach her piano and singing and German and English, and worst of all had to put up with that ninny of a governess, Helene. Silly woman, always raising her hands in horror, squealing like a mouse, and mincing about. Helene was a coward, a spy, a traitor, forever telling on Sonya to her mother. Sonya would have liked to send her to the guillotine.

'What is it?' Bruno asked her. 'Why are you frowning?'

'It isn't fair. I want to go to the corps.'

'Certainly,' her brother Anton answered in his condescending manner. He was throwing darts by the window. 'That's an old story. But you won't.'

'Leave her alone, Anton,' Bruno said sharply. The sides were drawn again, as they had been since the first Christmas Sonya ignored the dolls with their painted china faces and taffeta dresses and gleefully discovered her brother's uniformed toy soldiers. Even now at sixteen, when he should have known better, Anton still teased her.

'Look at you, Sonya, lying on the floor. I thought Helene was calling you for a piano lesson. You shall never find a husband.'

'Anton, leave her alone.'

'I don't want a husband.'

'Well, that's a blessing for mankind.' Anton rubbed the

end of the dart across his thumb. Sonya prayed he would stick himself with it. 'I suppose you might be a spinster schoolteacher, except that no one can seem to teach you anything.'

'I won't be a teacher.'

'Sonya, pay no attention to him.'

'And you won't be a soldier. What will you be, I wonder.'

She hated his voice. 'I would be a better soldier than you.'

'Ha.' Anton threw the dart. It came within two inches of the bull's eye.

'I am smarter than you.' She shouted at Anton. 'Smarter than you. Smarter than Napoleon.' Anton sneered at her and continued to throw his darts.

'Oh, Sonya,' Bruno said softly. Anton laughed.

'I would have known not to march in winter.'

'Smarter than Napoleon?' Anton sniffed. 'You?'

'Yes. Yes. I can show you.' She jumped up. Anton turned his back on her deliberately and concentrated on his darts.

'Show me,' Bruno said, rolling over on his stomach to watch her.

'Kutuzov was lucky, that's all. Look.' She ran to the end of the room and pulled out three of the wooden chairs that were stacked in the far corner, busying herself arranging for battle. She would show Anton. To hell with him anyway, she thought, smiling at herself that she could curse like a man. Anton would never be any kind of a soldier. He was too petty and too vain, always curling his new beard and peering in the mirror to make sure his skin was unblemished and his hair waving the right way. He was handsome, but he was as empty as the yellow and green sack the magician had used at Easter, when he had made the pigeons disappear.

'Have you set it up?' Bruno asked.

Well, Bruno appreciated her, she thought as she piled two of the chairs on the embroidered red sofa that had been in her mother's room until she had it redecorated in the new English style. 'Here,' she said, 'watch. This is Borodino.' She heard Anton snicker from across the room.

Angrily she ran to the sofa and jumped across it, throwing the chairs on the floor. 'He should have waited,' she screamed in Anton's direction. 'Sometimes you can't attack. Sometimes you have to wait.'

'Sonya, what is going on here?' It was her mother standing in the doorway, out of breath from the four flights of stairs. In back of her was a triumphant Helene, her aunt Elizabeta, and her cousins, Lev and Irina. Obviously her mother had just come back from her calls. She was still wearing her feathered black hat and carrying her silk and jet-embroidered umbrella. 'I didn't even have a chance to undress. Helene told me there was such a commotion up here. She couldn't get you to come down for your lesson. You must listen to her, Sonya. Can't you spend any time off the furniture?' She leaned her umbrella against the wall and crossed over to where Sonya still stood on the sofa, offering her a gloved hand to get down.

Sonya ignored her and jumped off the sofa, landing on her knees and then sitting down on the floor.

'It's time for your piano lesson.'

'I will never play the piano, Mother.'

'Monsieur Maryeux thinks otherwise. He says you would have a nice touch if you would only practice more thoroughly.'

'He says that because you pay him.'

'Why are you so angry, Sonyasha? Get up. Get up. Come, lessons.' Her mother put her hand in the middle of Sonya's back as if to soothe her, but Sonya pulled away.

'I will never play the piano, Mother.'

'And you will never lead your troops into Moscow, either.'

'I should like to be a general.'

'Fish would like to fly.'

'There are flying fish, Mama.'

'And you will command your household, as I do.' Sonya was still curled on the floor, and her mother leaned down and touched the back of her neck softly. 'Look what you have done, you are so overheated you will catch your death of cold, and your hair is all over your face, like a rag doll's.'

Sonya pulled away. 'I should like to ride a huge white

horse and wear boots and pants and have a helmet with white and black feathers. I should like to be Joan of Arc.' She closed her eyes and put her hands over her face. She heard her cousins, who were sitting in the window seat watching Anton play darts, giggle. She heard Anton snort derisively, and she heard her aunt and her mother laughing. Then she heard the rustle of their petticoats as they walked toward the door. Men had such a different sound. They did not slip into a room like a slight wind in the leaves, they burst in like storms.

'Did you hear the news?' She had heard her father's oldest friend, Protopopov, asking him just that morning, while he slapped his arms and stamped his boots.

'What news?' Her father had embraced him.

'Kalzopin has shot both his wife and his dog.'

'His wife I could understand, but the dog was a fine hunter!' There was a pause while the two men looked at each other, their eyes alive with their common understanding, their mouths hard put to contain their laughter. Then it burst out of them, loud, chesty laughter, like a galloping cough. How peculiar, Sonya had thought, listening. The two of them have the same laugh, two Russian men as alike as twins. Tears slid out of the corners of their eyes. They were as together in their laughter as children, these two grown men, soldiers, fathers, ministers of state, so assured of the rightness of their lives, so secure in their maleness, their sameness. They made such a full sound. Women made no sound like it.

Sonya lifted her head. 'I could be a fine general,' she said evenly to her mother's back.

'Like your father?' her mother asked, turning toward her.

'Poor Papa, he never goes to war.'

'And thank God for that. I remember what it was like when I was a young bride. War is ghastly, Sonya, even for the men. Imagine what it would be like for you. Thank God we have no war.'

'God has nothing to do with it. It is not God who makes war, Mama, it is man. Don't thank Him for it.'

Immediately she heard her mother gasp and saw her bright face pale as she crossed herself. 'I shall speak to your father, Sonya. You shall be punished for such blasphemy!'

Anton's dart hit the target. 'Bull's eye,' he said maliciously, just as her mother closed the door.

'You had better go down for your lesson, Sonya. You mustn't irritate her so,' Bruno said.

'Let them punish me. I don't care. When you leave for the corps tomorrow, it makes no difference to me where I spend my time. Two days in my room will be just the same as two days roaming around this empty house with Helene always after me!'

Again, her cousins giggled at her. She paid no attention to them. 'I won't be like them, Bruno, I won't! You'll see. You'll see. I will be myself.' She started to the door. 'I will do something important!'

'Such as?' Anton asked.

'Ridding the world of people like you!' She charged out of the room, turned, and with all her strength, slammed the door in Anton's grinning face.

*　　*　　*

Sonya   September 14, 1891

Hello there notebook. Hello there journal of Sonya Leonovna Vera Irina Poliakovna. Today I am ten years, six months, and thirteen days old, an auspicious age to begin a diary. My brother Bruno gave me this before he left yesterday, once again, for the corps. He said it would help me not to be so lonely. Well, I shall keep this journal for him and for me. I shall try and write something every day. Here is a thought I would share: Dreaming is not the devil's work, as my old nurse insists. It is like a cup of tea in the morning, or the evening meal. Without it I would die.

3

The winter of 1894 had been so long, so dreadful, so empty, that even her thirteenth birthday could not console Sonya. It was colder in Petersburg than anyone could ever remember, more like a Moscow winter, actually. The sun hardly ever appeared, and the sharp bite of the wind made it almost impossible to stay outside for more than a moment, curtailing the riding of the ice chutes on the Neva, or even just an outing in the troika. The house seemed frozen, the marble floors like ice ponds, and the crystal chandeliers no different from the cold icy branches in Petrovsky Park.

Russian winters. Grownups made a virtue of them. Her parents, her tutors, Helene, even Marushka constantly extolled them, recounting again and again how it was winter that had defeated the French, winter that made Russians stronger than other people, winter that made their land so beautiful and unusual. Still, Sonya found it unbearable.

They were such long terrible months of darkness, contrasted by the whiteness of all the horizon. Rivers, buildings, streets, countryside, nothing but white. Even the tree bark shone white in the brief sunshine. And then the blackness of night, cold, cold. Peasants slept on their stoves. In the palaces on the Neva the lights were lit early. Gas flames everywhere. Her mother liked it bright, affecting a daylight for herself through hundreds of gas jets that blazed around the enormous house. It took one of the servants fully forty-five minutes to light the lamps. She started as the sun began to set, but the blackness arrived before she was finished. Another servant lit the fires. The whole nation struggled to be warm. How could this make a nation strong? Sonya wondered. She dreamed of summer. She would summon up the smell of summer and then, in a rush, it would come to her, the greenness of the Ukraine, the silver of the birch groves, the cool darkness of the piny woods.

'What are you dreaming of this time, little one?' Marushka was in the corner chair, knitting another of her endless scarves.

Sonya sighed. 'Summer,' she answered. 'Always summer. Always the sun.' She walked about the room, not knowing what to do with herself. How could the heroines in Tolstoy always be so occupied, busy even when they were waiting? Today, even reading was unsatisfactory. 'Oh, I wish it were summer!'

'By summer, Vladimir will be married.' Marushka smiled at Sonya.

'Maybe then Mama will have more time for me. If she isn't busy with the wedding, she is working for her committees. I never see her. Between Papa's book and Mama's starving orphans, I never see anyone in this house!' Sonya scowled. She kicked the potted fig tree, then shook its trunk to see how many dead leaves would fall. There were three. 'At least next year I will be at Smolney. Why are there so many interruptions in life?'

'A woman without patience rides in an empty carriage. Why don't you crochet?'

'How can Vladimir love that girl? She is such a ninny. He's worth ten of her. He's not the best of my brothers, but he's not the worst of them either. He deserves someone better.'

'Olga Morontov is a fine lady. They will make a fine couple. Here, hold my wool.' Sonya walked to the old woman and put her two hands up. Marushka put the skein of wool around them and started winding a ball. 'The Morontovs own vast forests in the south, I hear.'

'Maybe that explains why she is so wooden, more wooden than her father's trees, I wager.'

'They will make a fine couple.'

'She will bore him to death.'

'Then they will have many children.'

Sonya narrowed her eyes. 'Marushka, I can hardly talk to you anymore.'

The old woman smiled. 'He who speaks with the devil's mouth will soon be his visitor. Watch out for my wool.'

'You made that up!' Sonya cried, stamping her foot,

watching the old woman wind her wool left to right, left to right.

'There,' Marushka said, smiling at her as always, 'the wool is done.' She bounced the fat ball in her hands. 'Complaints slow the clock and deafen the neighbors.'

Sonya laughed. 'Will nothing make you still, old woman?'

'Nothing but death, my angel. May its journey to my door be a thousand years.' She crossed herself twice and spit over her left shoulder.

Two weeks after Vladimir's wedding, it was time to leave for the Ukraine. The packing lasted for at least a week, all the servants busy washing and ironing and sewing, getting on the dust covers, storing the china and silver, covering the paintings and rolling up the carpets. The general so hated that last week of May that he took his sons and went to stay with his brother Vladimir, whose house was across the Moika on Ligovsky Prospect.

Sonya worried about the cellar cats and whether Pyotr Ivanovitch would feed them if no one was there to remind him. She hoped her grandfather's dog would remember her from the year before and wondered if the peach pip she had planted last summer had taken root. She feared someone might go into her room and find the secret treasures that she had hidden in her bottom drawer. The night before they actually were to begin their journey, she could hardly sleep at all.

At first morning bells she got out of bed and dressed quickly. She wore her navy traveling suit with the sailor collar, a large, wide-brimmed straw hat, and high button shoes. She carried a blue linen cape.

'Everyone up! Everyone, get up!' she cried as she ran through the hall and down the stairs, happy to be able to yell out loud in the morning, knowing that this day was special, that even her mother would rise early on this day.

In the first carriage that pulled away from the palace were her mother, Helene, and her mother's maid, Eugenia. In the second was Sonya herself, Bruno, Anton, and Marushka. Behind them was a carriage just for the baggage and the rest of the servants, and behind that was

Papa and his valet.

"Stop pushing me, Anton.'

'I haven't touched you.'

'Keep your knee there!' she said, pointing to the other side of the line she had made with the belt from her jacket. The carriage was as bumpy as ever, and the constant sway, the ruts and bumps and the grumbling of the wheels, were combining to make her feel sick. She snuggled into the corner and shut her eyes, forcing herself to think of their destination, the most exquisite place in the world, Dosiaya!

The first stop would be the yearly three-day visit with her father's brother Feodor, at Malaya Vishera. That was always so boring. He was a bachelor and hated children, taking delight in pinching Sonya's cheek each year as hard as he could. He never asked any of the children about themselves. At Uncle Feodor's, Sonya slept in a large upstairs room with Marushka, her mother's maid, and her uncle's secretary. Every year the couch was hard, and this year it would be too short. She was growing like a weed. She must have grown two full inches that winter alone. So much for Marushka saying that idle minds leave the body dwarfed.

'Ah, Sonya.' Her uncle patted her head and pinched her cheek, twisting it between his thumb and forefinger. He looked nothing like her father. It was hard to believe they were brothers.

'You remember my secretary?' her uncle asked, gesturing to the tall blond lady on his left. Sonya nodded. She remembered her from the year before, only now there was something so changed about her. She wore her golden hair swept up on the back of her head with two dips in front softly outlining her broad cheekbones. Her skin was white and milky and her oval blue eyes were warmer and more lively than Sonya remembered them. She blushed as Sonya took her hand and curtsied to her.

Uncle Feodor introduced his secretary to Bruno and Anton and even to the servants. Something was so different in his tone. The woman was to be called Tatiana Grigorovna and not Mademoiselle, as they had previously called her.

Sonya noticed her mother and father lock eyes for a moment as they walked behind her uncle and Tatiana Grigorovna to the reception room, and it suddenly dawned on her. Her stomach turned hard and she caught her breath. This was her uncle's wife, even though they were not married. This woman lived with her uncle as his wife.

Her mother and Marushka had told her about husbands and wives, love and marriage, but Sonya knew about this other thing, too. She had read *Madame Bovary* and *Anna Karenina* and other such books that were in her father's downstairs study. She knew there were women as driven by passions as the lustful men who roamed the countryside ravaging maidens and wives. They were no better than prostitutes. They were without morals, without any sense of duty or honor. They were fascinating! She would have to watch Tatiana Grigorovna carefully.

There were to be twenty for dinner. The Yupokovs came with their child and her father's first tutor, as well as the old doctor Kovalinov and his wife. Outside on the verandah, the servants had spread a Persian carpet and moved the oak dining table to its center. They had strung Japanese lanterns around the low-hanging branches of the trees and lit torches to keep away the insects. They had always eaten outside on the verandah that way when they visited with her uncle, but this was the first time Sonya understood why, the first time she truly appreciated the countryside that sloped from the crest of the hill down and away as far as the eye could see. It was here that the sun set, behind the pink and white flowering fruit trees and the birches and elms whose leaves were so new and brightly green. Watching it, Sonya was so overwhelmed by the light and the beauty that her eyes filled with tears.

'Look at Sonya,' Tatiana called gaily to everyone from the other end of the long table. 'Look everyone, look at her face.' When Sonya turned back to the table they were all staring at her. A loon called in the distance. 'Your face, Sonya, it was so poetic and sad, like a painting,' Tatiana said softly. Sonya saw Marushka cross herself. Sonya, blushing, lost all taste of food, although the *pelmeni* and *kulebiaka* were her favorites.

That night, of course, Tatiana did not share the room

and Sonya slept in a real bed. 'Why did you cross yourself when Tatiana Grigorovna spoke to me?' Sonya asked the old woman as they lay in their beds just before sleep. Helene and Eugenia were still walking about in the garden.

'Shhhh,' came the reply.

'Will I be as beautiful as Tatiana Grigorovna?'

Marushka crossed herself again. 'Children should stay children.'

'She is the most beautiful woman I have ever seen. More beautiful than even Mama.'

'What is the matter with you tonight, my little one? You never care about beauty, you hardly let me comb your hair, and tonight it is all you think about. What is it? Go to sleep. I am tired.'

'She lives with him as his wife, am I right?' There was no answer. 'Marushka, I don't understand it. Is that all beauty is good for, to please a man like sour Uncle Feodor? Good heavens!'

'Good night. You talk too much.'

'She seems so nice and, well, so honest. Why should she waste herself?'

'Shut your eyes.'

'I will never do that,' Sonya murmured. 'I will never waste myself. Never never never.' She was still murmuring as she fell asleep.

They left Malaya Vishera early the following morning and traveled south to Kostroma, where her father's youngest brother, Alexander, had his estate. He and her aunt Nina had eight children, all boys, and they tumbled everywhere like clowns, yelling, punching, laughing. With eight subordinates, Sonya's battles were grander than ever, and again this year, by the time she left two days later, she had no voice at all from the shouting of her commands. Her cousins stood in the courtyard to say good-by and the littlest, Nico, screamed and carried on to see her go. But Sonya was not sorry to leave, as that evening they would be in Moscow for her father to oversee the printing of his book on Nicholas I that his friend, Protopopov, had arranged for publication by a first-class house, and only three days later, they would be on the train to Kiev and then, at last, they would be at Dosiaya.

Her father had booked three first-class sleeping compartments on the Moscow-Kiev train. The servants stayed in the third class with the baggage. In Moscow her aunt and uncle had supplied them with baskets filled with breads and chickens, cheeses and cold meats, sweet cakes and fruits. It seemed to Sonya that all Marushka and Helene did was urge her to eat. Sonya much preferred the soups and cakes the old babushkas sold in the stations along the way, but Helene insisted such slop would make her sick. Helene was such a ninny, suspicious of everything. Everyone knew that the best blinis came from the station babushkas. As the train charged through the countryside, everybody's excitement turned to irritability. Her mother never slept properly and ceaselessly complained about the noise and the dirt. Marushka grumbled that trains should not have been invented, they were like dragons, only more dangerous. Anton was worse than ever and even Bruno was not himself. The nearer they got to Kiev, the worse, it seemed, everyone behaved. There was no peace anywhere. It was so hot in the compartment, but standing by the window in the corridor didn't seem to be much better. How could there be so much activity? People were constantly walking by and jostling her.

'Up and down. Up and down,' her mother said as Sonya sat down again next to her. 'Can't you stay more than ten seconds in one place?'

'It's hot, Mama.'

'Are Bruno and Anton still sleeping?' Sonya nodded. 'It is hot in here but it is not any cooler out there, Sonya. Now sit still for a while.' Her mother sighed. 'Did you see your father?'

'I think he is still in the next car, with that fellow he met.'

'Lieutenant Morozov?'

'You would think that he was Papa's oldest and dearest friend the way Papa fell on him.'

'Your father doesn't like trains, Sonya. He can't read; he can't work. The man served under him years ago. I'm glad he is occupied for the present. He has too much energy for such a trip. Didn't anyone tell you to brush your hair this morning?'

'I have too much energy, too.'

'I told Helene to bring the embroidery you were working on. Doesn't she have it?'

'I strangled her with it!' Sonya kicked the empty seat across from her.

'Sonya, I have meant to talk to you about Helene.'

'Please, Mama.' She reached over and took the dog from her mother's lap.

'Poor Pushkin. Look how frightened he is, not at all like his namesake. I should have chosen another breed when old Pushkin died.' Her mother frowned. 'I should have known my angel could never be replaced. Look how this one shivers all the time.' Her mother rubbed her temples, hoping to rid herself of the headache that had just begun. 'What time is it, Sonya?'

'I don't know.' Sonya put the dog back on her mother's lap. 'I'll go and ask.'

'No, no. Sit down, Sonya.' Her mother's voice was tight. 'I have a headache. Sit down!' There was a sudden lurch, and Sonya fell on top of both the dog and her mother. 'Sonya!' her mother screamed. The train lurched again. There was a sharp braking noise, then a whistle. The dog whined and panted furiously, its little pink tongue half outside its mouth. Sonya managed to scramble to the seat across from her mother, who had held the small golden animal to her face and was covering it with kisses. 'Poor baby,' she was saying, 'poor baby.'

'Look, Mama. There are soldiers.' They had surrounded the train as soon as it stopped. Hundreds of them, on horseback and on foot, had come from the woods. 'Look how many there are, Mama!'

'Where is your father?'

'I'll get him.' She slid open the compartment door but was stopped by a soldier in uniform, his hand on his gun.

'Everyone is to stay in the compartment, please,' he said in Russian. 'There is no reason to be frightened. Everyone is to stay in the compartment.'

Sonya closed the door and backed into the seat next to her mother. 'Mama,' she asked, 'what is it?'

'Well, I'm sure I don't know. Perhaps they're hunting someone. They're always hunting people in Kiev.'

'Bandits?'

'Anarchists, more likely. I wish your father were here. Why would he want to stay so long with that silly lieutenant?' Her mother took her lace handkerchief from her sleeve and dabbed at the beads of perspiration that had formed on her upper lip. 'Where is he?'

The door opened and a squat soldier stood in the entrance. 'You are traveling alone?' he asked intensely, looking from the princess to Sonya. The dog started to bark, a high squeal. Its beady black eyes fairly popped out of its head. 'Are you alone?' the soldier repeated, keeping his eyes on the dog.

'I am Princess Poliakov. My husband, General Leon Poliakov, is in the next car chatting with a friend. My sons and my servants are in the adjoining two compartments. Can you tell me what has happened?' Sonya looked at her mother in amazement. Her tone was so forceful and controlled. 'Quiet, little one,' her mother said to the dog.

The soldier recognized the authority in that tone at once and his attitude changed. 'We have some information that an enemy of the state is aboard this train. We are searching for him.'

'Surely not in first class,' said the princess, arching her eyebrows.

'We are looking everywhere, Princess, but we will try to disturb you as little as possible. If you will excuse me, I must search your compartment.'

'Go right ahead. We have nothing to hide.' The princess did not move. The soldier stared at her. Obviously he had expected they would stand by the door, but when they did not, he was too intimidated to ask them to do so. He crossed to the closet and, opening the door, peered in. He closed the door quickly. Then he bent over and looked under the seats. The dog barked at him furiously. 'Are you looking for a person under there?' her mother asked. 'I hardly think anyone would fit.'

The soldier didn't answer. He smiled at them, nodded, bowed, and backed out of the compartment. The moment he had gone, her mother's hands started trembling violently. 'What is it, Mama?'

The door had opened again and her father entered, his

face white. 'Mariyenka, Sonya, are you all right?'

'Leon, thank God.' Her mother jumped from the seat and threw herself into her husband's arms. 'I was so frightened. They searched the compartment. What is happening? Are the boys all right?'

'The boys are fine, my love.' The general patted the back of her head as if she were a small child. 'Once they took me to the captain, he let me come through. I checked on the boys. They're fine.'

'What, who are they looking for?' The general whispered something in his wife's ear. 'No, Leon. Oh, my God!'

'What is it, Papa?' Sonya cried. She had not moved while she watched them. Why couldn't her mother still be brave? Why was she strong only with servants and children, or anyone she considered beneath her? She was murmuring, 'No, no,' and fanning herself with her hat. 'What is it?' Sonya repeated to her father. 'I am old enough to know.'

'They found a bomb in the third-class compartment. It was set to explode in less than an hour, just as we reached the station in Kiev.' Sonya heard her mother clicking her tongue. 'Someone tipped off the authorities, thank the Lord.'

Sonya went to the window and leaned against it, trying to see down to third class.

'Sonya! Get back away from there!'

'It's all right, my dear,' the general said, sitting next to his wife and taking her hand. 'The bomb has been found. They are looking for two men.'

'Murderers here on the train!' her mother went limp in her seat. 'They might kill us all, innocents. They might kill us.'

'Papa, help me to open the window, please.' The general reached over and helped Sonya lower the window more than the two inches that her mother allowed. 'Perhaps I can see them.' She leaned out and looked down toward third class. 'There is quite a commotion, Papa.' Men were running up and down the side of the tracks. Other soldiers stood, guns in hand, facing the train. They all seemed so stern. Would they really be able to kill a man if he ran from the train? It seemed impossible. Even with their caps and stern looks, she could see their light eyes and handsome broad faces. There, one had a beard so that he looked like her brother Vassily. She was about to tell her mother and then thought better of it. 'Look, Papa. Look, they are dragging someone from the train. Papa, I can see the top of his shaved head above the caps of the soldiers. They are dragging him over into the woods, Papa. What will happen to him? What will happen?'

Her father cleared his throat. 'I'm sure he will have a fair trial. Russian justice will see to that, although he probably doesn't deserve one.'

'Do you want to see, Papa?'

'No, Sonya, I have seen it many times before. The enemies of the czar are always captured and obliterated!'

The door opened again and a captain stood at the doorway. 'General Poliakov?'

'Yes, what is it?'

'If you don't mind, sir.' He motioned to a guard who roughly pushed a man forward. 'This gentleman says we have a mistaken identity, sir. He swears he is a close friend of yours, that he was in fact, just speaking with you. He says you can vouch for him, sir. He has been accused in this bombing business.'

Her father stood up and walked toward the man. 'This is Lieutenant Morozov. I hardly know him.'

'His papers show his name as Vladiavok.'

'Nonsense, he is Mikhail Morozov. Other than his name, I have nothing to say for him.' Sonya watched the man as her father spoke. There was nothing in his face, no hope, no anger, nothing. How had he had the gall to ask to have her father vouch for him? There was still nothing in his eyes as he was led away. Sonya wondered if he was going to die.

'Oh, Leon,' the princess said, 'I am just shaking, shaking.'

'It's all right, my dear. It's over.'

'They keep coming closer, those terrible people. And a lieutenant! He was in your regiment you said? How could he? The man must be mad.'

In a few minutes the soldiers were off the train and the boys came into the compartment. 'Was that your friend they arrested, sir?' Anton asked.

'Hardly a friend, my dear boy. Hardly even an acquaintance. I knew him from the guards. One can trust no one in this day and age, more's the pity.'

'You were just talking with him.'

'My point exactly.'

'He wanted Papa to save him,' Sonya added, 'but Papa wouldn't.'

'Really?' Bruno asked. 'Do you think he will die now?'

'I should hope so,' answered the general. 'If it were up to me he would. Siberia is too good for all of them, I've said that for years.'

'So you killed him, Papa,' Bruno went on.

'Bruno, really!' chided the princess.

'No, sorry. I mean he caught a criminal.'

'Bravo, sir.' Anton was smiling.

'Leon,' the princess interrupted, 'where is Marushka? I'd forgotten all about her. You must go and find her. She's probably fainted, poor old woman. And no wonder, at the sight of all those soldiers. Boys, go with your father and find Helene also. Make sure they are all right. Sonya, close the window, the train is moving. There is far too much soot in the air.' The princess kissed her husband on the cheek and watched as he left with the boys. Then she settled herself in her seat. 'Look, Sonya,' she suddenly called out, a smile on her lips. 'Pushkin has fallen asleep. All this commotion and my little one fell asleep. He is not such a coward after all. I wish my nerves were like his.' Her mother reached over, picked up the sleeping dog, and moved him onto her lap. 'Sonya,' she said with a sigh, 'I said to close the window. Pushkin will catch cold with that air on him. Will we never get to Kiev?' She stroked the dog's silky hair and cooed to him. 'There, there,' she said, 'everything is all right now.' Sonya could tell, just from watching her mother, that the incident was forgotten.

4

It was, of course, another eternity before they were settled into Grandpapa's carriages. Sonya sat on the edge of her seat, her nose pressed to the window, which Marushka insisted she keep closed. This was the longest part of the trip. The horses were never fast enough, and it took forever to get out of the crowded, dusty streets of Kiev and into the countryside, where, on both sides of the road, the fields that fed half of Russia were neatly plowed and stripped with crops. Such black earth, Sonya thought, remembering the old proverb. How lucky she was to be there, to see it all. Her eyes filled with tears as they had that night at Uncle Feodor's house. How peculiar, she thought. What is happening to me?

When they had passed the village and crossed the bridge, her grandfather's land began. Dosiaya! This was the family seat, her grandpapa's largest estate. Besides Dosiaya, there was his palace in Petersburg, the flat in Moscow, the villa in Yalta, and the other villa in Monte Carlo, overlooking the Mediterranean. Sonya had seen them all, although she could hardly remember the one in France, except for the purple flowers that climbed to the second floor and sand so hot it burned her feet.

Her grandfather demanded that all his residences be in a state of constant readiness should he or his family arrive unexpectedly. There were staffs of servants, flowers, and food at each one. Even the beds were turned down every night. Her grandmother had given the edict originally, but the old man remembered it as his own, and although he had not left Dosiaya in the five years since his wife had died (he was writing his memoirs, consumed with the subject of the Decembrist uprising, and her mother swore he would live in 1825 until the day he died), his houses were ready for him.

It had been her grandfather's grandfather who had won Dosiaya and its five thousand fertile acres in a thirty-six-

44

hour game of whist with Prince Boris Troubetsoy. Marushka had told Sonya all about it. Her mother insisted that the palace had been a grant from Catherine the Great in return for her great-great-grandfather's valiant service to the state, but Sonya preferred the old nurse's version, that Captain Eryenkov had been the handsomest and most daring of the empress's guards, and he was sent from Petersburg to Kiev in disgrace because of a scandal with one of the empress's ladies in waiting. (The empress had wanted him to herself!) In the country, however, he continued to embellish his reputation as a gambler and ladies' man, and because of that, he had been challenged to the whist game by Prince Boris, whose daughter had fallen wildly in love with him and wished to marry him. After that fatal card game, Prince Boris had ridden down to the red granite cliffs over the river and jumped to his death. Here Marushka swore on her life, kissing her hands and holding them both up to heaven, but holy God was so angry at him, he was not spared, and he lived three days, long enough to see his daughter marry his enemy.

'Fairy tales,' Bruno said, sliding back into his seat and crossing his arms. 'We are brought up on fairy tales. Why do you keep on with all those witches and ghosts?'

'Your grandfather's grandfather was almost seven feet tall, like Peter the Great. His fingers were the legs of a large spider. That is why he won at cards.' Marushka paid no attention to Bruno. 'He had the eyes of a cat and could read a man's thoughts.'

'Nonsense.' Bruno scowled. Marushka crossed herself. Bruno shook his head and turned away. 'Hands like a spider's and eyes like a cat's!'

'Why don't you like to hear her stories?' Sonya whispered to him a bit later while the nurse dozed, her round chin bobbing up and down on her enormous bosom.

'The peasants are children. They are full of romantic balderdash. You mustn't listen to them, Sonyasha. You are too smart to have your head turned so.'

'I know. Of course. I'm sorry, Bruno.' She blushed and looked toward the window. How many times had he told her to ignore the old tales? Yet they intrigued her. Why couldn't there be spirits or miracles? Anything could happen if you belived in magic. 'Magic is fun,' she said to Bruno. 'It can't hurt.'

'It can hurt,' Bruno said sharply. 'Wishing and waiting for magic prevents action. It's not wishing and waiting that makes me a marksman. It is work. Your *nyanya* is full of fairy tales.'

'You are so serious, Bruno.'

'We must grow up in this world. I am seventeen.'

Sonya thought for a moment and then looked up at him. 'But what if they are true, Bruno? What if it is not a fairy tale about the captain and Prince Boris?'

'It doesn't matter.' Seeing her baffled expression, he nodded his head emphatically. 'You are still young, Sonya. You will see. You will see.'

'Stop kicking me, Sonya!' Anton grumbled in his sleep, pushing her knees so hard she fell against Marushka.

'Children fight, the devil's right, children play, and God is gay,' the old woman said without opening her eyes.

Sonya felt uncomfortable. What did Bruno mean about the truth? How could it not matter?

Everything was upside down in her head. She looked out the window and there it was, the massive iron gate with its great crowned *E* surrounded with the scrolled letter *D*, the formal entrance to Dosiaya.

'I see it! I see it!' Sonya screamed. 'We're here! I see the gate!'

Some people said Dosiaya had been designed by Rastrelli. Sonya thought it even more beautiful than Czarskoe Selo, the summer palace Rastrelli had also designed for Catherine the Great. The main house was set some five miles back from the Dnieper. First came three miles of pine forest. Marushka said that on the birth of his children, the old captain had had each of his serfs plant a pine sapling in the baby's honor, and now, over one hundred years later, the forest was so dense that even at midday it seemed dark as night. Then the carriage came from blackness into bright sunlight. A broad avenue of linden trees flanked the road that stretched through the vast fields of orchards where her grandfather had had each tree pruned to the shape of a V in memory of his wife, Vera Vasilovna. Just where the linden trees appeared to converge, a mile farther up a slight rise, the formal gardens began. Sonya enjoyed looking at the gardeners as much as the garden. They came from San Remo, Italy, this community of short, dark-skinned men who sang constantly and always smiled at her. They were sent to Grandpapa's villa in France each fall after the roses had been put to bed for the winter.

The gardens ran to a low stone wall that marked the beginning of the courtyard, and just beyond, through another, smaller gate, lay the colonnaded front of the house with its two vast wings stretching out on either side.

Traditionally, after they arrived and tumbled out of the carriage, now full of energy, as the dogs barked their greetings, they would be carted quickly upstairs to the nursery for a bath and a nap. Even Bruno and Anton were sent there, and how Anton hated that! There they would wait the hours for the rest of the family to arrive. Each summer, her aunt Adele came with Maya, her aunt Elizabeta with Lev and Irina, and her aunt Gesia with her four sour daughters. Sometimes, her uncle Nicholas and his three boys came, but this year he had been appointed special representative for the czar in Japan and had taken his family there with him.

Their grandfather did not receive the children until after dinner on the night of the second day. They would gather in the huge mirrored and gold reception room and their grandfather's major-domo, Dupont, would lead them into the smaller receiving room, one at a time. There her grandfather, in full dress uniform, his helmet by his side, sat on the gold regency sofa like an emperor. Dupont called out their names as if their grandfather had never met them before, and each child would go up to him and curtsy or bow. Then they sat in the fragile ballroom chairs while this frail, translucent man with enormously long white mustaches and sideburns lectured to them on the divinity of the czar and questioned them on their history and mathematics.

After that, he never paid them the slightest attention. He never complained about their noise or scolded them on their pranks. If Sonya met him in the halls, he would just nod his head and smile and then ask her the date of a battle or the years of a czar. Such simple questions he asked. Sonya had answered the same questions since she was five.

As their arrival was the same, each summer of her life had been the same, idyllic days of games and warm sun interrupted only by meals or sleep or the rumble of the thunderclouds that came often in late June and early July, turning the lush greenness into a vast and windy gray place where the raindrops were the size of her tiny cousin Elena's thumbs. But this summer, this summer would be different, because when Mama left in the middle of July for the south of France, she would take Anton, who was finally old enough to be included as a grownup. Sonya could not wait for Anton to leave.

What a prig he looked that day, traveling in his dress uniform. As she watched the carriage disappear past the topiary, past the roses, and onto the roadway between the lindens, she felt herself released. Now Bruno and she could be alone again as they had not been since that time when Anton had left for the corps. Only Helene and Marushka were left to look after them. Marushka, who never cared what they did, and Helene, who was too exhausted from the heat of mid-July to do anything but lie stretched out on the white wicker chaise in her room and sigh.

Escaping the others in the early morning, Sonya and Bruno set out on horseback. Soon after they left the stable, but far enough away so that she would not be seen, Sonya would rein up, jump down from her tall brown mare, and dart behind a clump of elderberry bushes, emerging seconds later in boy's clothes, her hair stuck up under a cap. She rode well. Bruno had taught her long before, and she felt strong speeding past the trees or jumping the low fences surrounding the cow pastures.

Sometimes they would stop in the open meadow beyond the pine forest where the dip of the countryside and the surrounding wall of evergreens muffled every sound. It was there that Bruno first taught Sonya to shoot, both a pistol and a rifle. He set up a target for her on the edge of a wall just in front of the trees and had her progress from thirty paces to two hundred yards. Her arm was steady and her eye was good. This year, he wanted her to kill game.

'But Bruno, the target is enough for me.

'I think it's romance, Sonyasha. I think your nurse has spoiled you with all her fairy stories about talking rabbits and singing cows.'

'No, no, she hasn't.' There were so many wild animals on the estate. Deer and foxes and rabbits, pheasant and ducks. Because of Marushka's stories, she always thought them friends, but she would not admit that to Bruno. He was right, they were only animals; still she insisted, stubbornly, 'The target is enough for me.'

'I think you can't kill, Sonya.'

Like a weakling woman, she thought, that's what he means. He had one of Anton's condescending expressions on his face. 'I can,' she said emphatically. 'Of course, I can!'

'I don't think so.'

'But I say I can.'

'We can wait until tomorrow.'

'No,' she said slowly and deliberately, 'what about all your talk of action? Now! I will do it now. It will be just the same as diving into a cold lake, a momentary shock and nothing more.'

'Suit yourself.'

'We can go to the pond. There are always birds there.'

'If we wait a minute, you can get a rabbit. Which would you prefer?'

'It doesn't matter,' she answered, pretending lack of interest. She did not want to kill a rabbit.

'Get the rifle, then. Load it. We can just wait here behind this bush. It shouldn't be long.'

Sonya kneeled behind the bush facing the open meadow. What a day it was, the air so clear, the light so intense! It was almost noon and the sun was directly above them. There was hardly a shadow anywhere.

The rabbit came into the clearing hesitantly, making its way toward the bushes on the far side of the field. 'There he is, Sonya,' Bruno whispered urgently.

She watched the animal stop some fifty yards ahead of

her. It stood still, twitching its ears, then hopped a few feet to the right. She would have no trouble getting it. 'Go ahead. Shoot,' Bruno said.

'Where should I hit it?'

'In the back of the head. The way he sits now, it's the easiest.'

'Ah.' She had thought it would be the heart. She picked up the rifle and sighted it, moving it slightly as the rabbit hopped again to the right. The animal turned its head. 'He's looking at me,' she whispered.

'Perfect. Get him between the eyes.'

The noise of the shot was loud as a cannon. Sonya dropped her head on her chest, her eyes squeezed closed.

'Brava!' Bruno shouted. He was running across the field. 'Good shot, Sonyasha. Good shot. See how easy it is?' He was standing beside her again, and as she opened her eyes, she saw that he was carrying the rabbit, holding it by its ears. She had missed. The bullet had not gone through the creature's eyes. It had gone through its throat, blood leaking down its body. Its eyes were perfect as they always had been, staring at her, as if it were still alive. 'You see,' Bruno said to her, 'killing is easy if you make how you shoot the main goal, not what you shoot. The perfection of the means justifies the end. That is why soldiers can kill so easily in war. Never think of what you are killing, Sonyasha, just think of the rightness of the shot.'

The rabbit stared at her. 'Yes,' she answered Bruno. 'I see.' He was proud of her. She could kill. She had felt nothing. The rabbit had been alive, and now it was dead and staring at her. How many other girls her age could kill? Nothing else mattered after all. Bruno was proud of her. 'Well,' she said finally, 'so that is killing. Shall I do it again?'

'Are you crying, Sonyasha?'

'No, of course not,' she answered, shaking her head. 'Let's go to the pond. I should like to try ducks or geese.' She walked quickly toward the horses.

'Shall I bring this for the kitchen help?' asked Bruno. He was still holding the rabbit.

'As you like,' Sonya said.

*   *   *

50

'You see,' Bruno said to her several weeks later. They were resting among the pines. She had killed many things for him by then. She watched him as he brushed away the top layer of pine needles and revealed the black dirt, the fat brown worms. 'You see, the beauty of the new earth is that it is made out of rot, excrement, and decay, all of it hidden by the pine needles. Worms produce this rich clean earth. Richness comes of decay. Here,' he said leaning over toward her, 'put this on your temples, this black earth of Mother Russia. Let the coolness and the smell of it alway remind you of the strength and determination of worms. There are other worms in Russia, fighting undercover to make a new beauty also. When they succeed, the richness of this land will be for everyone.'

A sudden wind swept through the tall tops of the trees. They heard rumbling. In the pine grove there was suddenly no animal noises. The sound of the wind above became stronger.

'Come,' Bruno said. 'We must get to the hut before the lightning.' They mounted their horses and rode quickly out of the forest to the abandoned shack they had found some years before on the edge of the deep woods. The storm followed them as they rode. The wind was heavy. The sun had vanished, and fat gray clouds loomed above them. 'Come.' Bruno called her again as they rode the few miles through the fields to the cabin. The rain broke just as they entered, heavy drops that seemed to fill every space behind them. Bruno had brought his knapsack. Now he walked to the splintered wooden table in the center of the room. There was no other furniture, and the table seemed the place to be, since the thatched roof leaked all along its edges.

'Here,' Bruno said to her, opening his knapsack and taking out three worn books and laying them on the table.

'What are these?' Sonya asked, picking up the books and glancing at the names of the authors. Dubrolyubov, Chernyshevsky, Nechaev.

'I want you to read them all carefully. And I want you to read these, too.' He pulled two pamphlets from the bottom of the knapsack. 'Look here, on the second page.'

He turned the cover over and handed her a photograph of a woman with a round face and an enormously high forehead. The cheeks were full, like an infant's, and the lower lip was fat and wide, stretching across the whole of the lower part of her face. It was only the head in the photograph, but Sonya could see that her neck was short.

'She looks like Irina Fedorovna's sister, the one who is your age, Bruno. The one you tease all the time.'

'Who else does she look like?'

'I don't know.'

'What about the old doctor's daughter, Elizabeta?'

'Some, not much.' Sonya held the picture out to the light and squinted at it.

'What about Petya's daughter?'

'Petya? The footman in Petersburg?'

'Yes, he brought her last Christmas. When Mama had them all come for their gifts. Remember? She was the one who stood under the icon and hardly curtsied.'

'I do remember,' Sonya answered, vaguely recalling a sullen girl who had showed no enthusiasm for anything, not even the gift she was given. Sonya had thought her backward. 'She looks more like Iruska's sister. Why does it make any difference who she looks like? Why is it so important?' Sonya flipped back to the cover page. *The Strength of Women* was the title on the pamphlet.

'She might be any Russian woman, right? The face could be the face of any Russian woman. Exactly. And yet she is Sofia Perovskaya, and she was responsible for the murder of a czar.'

'My czar?' Sonya asked. She had taken to thinking of Alexander II as somehow part of her.

'Exactly.' He nodded. 'Exactly.'

Sonya picked up the pamphlets and ruffled the pages. 'Where did you get these, Bruno? They're illegal, aren't they? Aren't these the kind of journals Papa is always going on against?'

'They are very important.'

'But we could be arrested for having them, yes?'

'No one will find them. No one knows anything about their existence but the two of us. We will hide them here and you can read them here.'

She looked at Bruno. She was frightened. She wanted him to smile.

'Now you are a woman, Sonya,' he said. 'I heard the old nurse talking. Your time has come.' Sonya blushed a bright red; Marushka was worse than a telegraph. Damn her. She hated the old woman, that stupid old woman. It had been only last week that she had begun to bleed and they had stuffed her with rags. How awful that Bruno knew such a thing! They had told her that the first time would be light, but she had bled like a pig, all the time hoping Bruno wouldn't find out, but the old woman had told him. How could she be like him now? He would think less of her. She stared down at the bare floor boards. Pine needles filled a large crack in the floor across the room and a tiny ivy vine grew there, a miniature of those that covered the cabin. Sonya glanced up and saw the hole in the thatched ceiling that had let in enough sun and water to keep the plant alive. How hard it must work, she thought, to live. It does not care that its brothers outside are bigger and stronger. It does not care that it will never flower in here. It lives. Why can't I be like that?

'Sonya,' Bruno was talking. 'It means that we can be closer now. We are both grownups. We can work to make the world right. That's why I brought you these books, because you are a woman now. You will read all of these and then you will know who I really am, what I stand for. And you will help me. You are strong, Sonyasha, and brave. Women and men are the same in my new world. You will be a fine general in this world, as good as any man. I will teach you. I will show you what it is we must change. We will start the day after tomorrow, at the fair at Tvor. There you will see how the poor peasants in Russia must live. Your education is under way, Sonya.'

5

The fair was by the river between two small villages some three hours' ride from Dosiaya. She hardly had patience to stop and rest the horses, and she was tired of Bruno telling her to keep her cap on tight and to button the top buttons of her jacket or her breasts, which pushed against the white linen of her blouse, would give the lie to her careful disguise.

Outside the fairgrounds, they tied their horses with the others and started toward the throngs of people already there. It was a sizable fair but nothing at all like the one at Nizhny-Novgorod, with its fixed ambars and its acres of markets and its worldly atmosphere. Here there were just a few hundred wooden stalls and one marketplace, where peasants and peddlers sold their wares from baskets or high wooden trays on stilts. Gypsies walked around in a group of their own, their cheap trinkets too golden and their smiles as false as Helene's, calling to everyone to come have their fortunes told. A little bear on a chain wandered ahead of its owner, and children, wide-eyed and screaming, scrambled for protection beneath their mothers' skirts. Food vendors shouted at them to buy fruit and cheese, pies and nuts and cakes. She never tasted such watermelon, so pink and sweet she nearly ate a whole one. Not even the fetid, rank odor of the piles of scruffy furs the Tatar was selling interfered with her appetite.

Sonya stopped at a stall near the center of the market. It was better than the playroom in Petersburg, for here on a long makeshift table were the histories and oddments of a hundred families. Stacked and jumbled on one another were baskets, paintings, books, crockery, crystal glasses, footstools, frames, guns, and bottles. Sonya picked up a book.

'I have some with pictures, little fellow,' the merchant said.

'My brother can read,' Bruno proudly answered for her,

clapping her so hard he nearly knocked her over.

'Then buy the young fellow a book. This isn't a schoolroom. Four kopecks and it's his.'

'I say one.' Bruno pushed up the visor on his cap.

'For such a grand book? Three!'

'One.' Sonya was shaking her head at Bruno. The book was in Arabic and its pages were crumbling with age. He paid no attention to her.

'Two kopecks. Two! It is a rare book.'

'One!'

'Sold!'

Now it was hers.

'But I didn't want it!'

'It was a game,' he said, walking on. 'I wanted to see how well I could bargain. Put it in your pocket.'

They passed stalls of old clothing that women picked over, holding up a blouse or a shirt, putting it back and picking up another, then doing the same again. Their children pulled at their dresses and kicked at one another. A large, brightly painted stall had beautiful new silks and cottons from Moscow, but there was only one buyer, a tall, bearded man with a long black coat.

'A Jew,' Bruno whispered as they walked past. Sonya stared at him. She had never seen a Jew so close. All around them, talking and selling to each other, were men and women squatting on the ground amid their baskets and wheelbarrows of produce or wool or thread.

'Look, Bruno!' Sonya pointed to a man dressed in a long silk robe that covered his entire body from neck to feet. The robe was fastened around him with a sort of cloth cummerbund, and there was a dagger at his waist. Across his shoulders was a carved and decorated leather belt from which hung a curved and elaborate sword in a bronze holder. 'Isn't he splendid!'

Bruno quickened his step and she had to run after him. 'He's a falconer. He's going to give a demonstration. Come, let's get close to him.'

Many people shoved and elbowed in toward the falconer, whose voice was soft, yet his words and phrasing were so dramatic – he paused to smile or wipe a tear from his eye – that all who listened to him were enthralled by his story. His father was falconer to the emir, and since he had married against his father's wishes, he was unable to enter into the service that his father and his father's father so dutifully performed. He was disgraced by his love. This bird – he held his wrist aloft – this bird was given to him before his marriage, and it was the source of all his pride and all his livelihood. The bird sat on its leather perch at the man's wrist, its intelligent eyes staring at Sonya and Bruno. Now, the man said, the bird would show them all how well it performed. He cast the bird away from him, and the bird flew straight up in one seemingly unbroken motion, rising and rising until it was higher than any game that would be its prey.

The falcon was out over the plain in front of the fairground, and everyone, even the smallest children, watched its glistening black body, stationary on the air. Suddenly it swooped down upon its victim. It was another bird. The crowd roared and applauded as the falcon grabbed the bird in its enormous talons and brought it to earth. It was too far away from the crowd for any of them to see the kill, but somehow they sensed it, and there was absolute quiet for a moment and then whooping and yelling as the bird, calm and proud, came back to its perch on its master's wrist and listened to his words of sweet praise. Bruno tossed a handful of coins toward the falconer, and he turned in Bruno's direction, touching the top of his round fur-skinned hat with his fingers. More coins were thrown, and some children set out into the field to find the bird that had been killed as the falconer called for more tribute to be paid to his magnificent bird.

'Oh, Bruno, that was wonderful. Poor fellow! He seems so intelligent and educated, and yet he has to do this sort of thing at fairs just to live.'

Bruno laughed at her. He put his arm around her and hugged her. 'Sonyasha, you are incorrigible. He is just an actor. I doubt if he is even from Bokara. But the bird was fascinating. Did you see how he waited, how he hovered unnoticed in the sky until the exact right moment, the moment when he knew there was no escape from his prey? How effortless it was.'

'Bruno, he was dressed like an Easterner and he spoke

like one. How can you say he was an actor?'

'Well, little brother, dress does not mean everything!' Bruno slipped the top button of her jacket open and she blushed furiously. 'Come, let's shoot at the target. I'll make a wager on you. Time to show these country folk a real marksman, eh? Don't say anything, now. I'll do enough swaggering and boasting for both of us.' Bruno didn't take long to set his little brother up against a fellow from the village, ten kopecks to one that the little brother could put the first three shots in the center of the target. The older boy, grinning and spitting, loaded the gun amid both calls of encouragement and accusations of taking *kulebiaka* from a baby. Poised, cocksure, the older boy fired his three shots in succession, hardly taking a second longer than he had to. Two shots came within inches of the center of the target. The third, a bit wild, hit the second ring. Sonya tried hard not to look at the faces around her. Bets were mounting. The size of the small crowd grew until the boys and men stood four and five deep around her. She fired less quickly but steadily, the butt knocking her each time in the shoulder with enormous force. The stunned silence gave her the courage to look up at what she had done. All three shots were in the dead center, only millimeters from one another.

'Like eggs in a nest!' an old man said, clapping her on the back.

'Too bad David already killed Goliath,' another called.

'Any others want to have a go?' Bruno yelled. 'Twenty to one!' There was so much laughter, so many pats on the back. 'You could give the falconer a run for his money,' Bruno whispered, pushing her out of the crowd. Not one of the hundred men who grinned at her had taken the second bet. Matching her step to Bruno's, she walked away.

'That fellow would probably shoot his brains out if he knew a girl took him!'

'I could change my clothes and go back and make another wager. I'll bet no one would know.' She was so full of her victory, she almost took the cap off her head right there. Bruno held her hand back.

'Sonya, if you outshot him as a girl, he'd probably kill

both of us and about a thousand others.'

'Really, Bruno? Why?'

'Why? How can you ask that, Sonya! Why? Men are men, that's why.'

'Look Bruno, halvah! And the best raisins I've ever seen!' Sonya ran past three stalls of tea, their pungent, acried aroma searing her nostrils. The halvah was piled up in huge mounds, overflowing the counter. 'Bruno, please buy me halvah and pistachios! Or raisins. No, pistachios!' In the stall next to them were all sorts of bells, and customers were ringing them one after the other, making a terrible ear-splitting sound, and the man in the iron shop next door was screaming, complaining that his pans and barrows and nails were suffering as well as his customers.

'Sonyasha, you'll have a bellyache.'

'Bruno, please!'

'All right, Sonyasha, but then we must go. It is a long ride to Dosiaya.'

She squeezed his hand with both of hers as he handed her money. 'It was the best day of my life, Bruno.' She snuck an extra handful of pistachios and nibbled them, the salt stinging her dry tongue.

When they went for their horses, a man with a dirty yellow beard offered to buy Sonya's mare for twenty-five roubles. 'A hundred!' Bruno said, giving Sonya a boost up.

'For a hundred roubles, I could buy the czar's horse. And probably his wife, too!' the old men shouted at them as they rode away, kicking up dust and dry grass.

When they stopped five miles later to water the horses, Bruno looked up at the sky. 'I can see him still, Sonya. How intelligent that falcon is, how willful and stubborn.'

'So are dogs,' Sonya groaned, making a face of pain at the jab in her side, cursing the watermelon, the blinis, the meat pies, the raisins, halvah, and nuts.

'Dogs aren't patient. What a fantastic bird! So cautious and yet so deadly. Those in the revolution must take a lesson from the falcon.'

Sonya dropped from her horse. It was bad enough Bruno knew about her coming of age; now he would see her get sick. She walked away from the river's edge and vomited onto the rich, black earth of Mother Russia.

*   *   *

Sonya   August 11, 1894

I have read the books that Bruno gave me, and now I am rereading them. I am a new person. Bruno has made my dreams come true. What treasures, what treasures. I am so excited I can hardly keep my head straight. I knew that women members of the People's Will had ben executed for their part in the murder of my czar, but I never knew who they really were. Sofia Perovskaya – see how I am even named as she is – shall be my model. Why, their ideas are as modern as if they lived today, and yet it all happened over fifteen years ago. Such lives they led! They made bombs. They wrote pamphlets. They faced the police unashamed and lied to them blatantly. They pretended other identities, and when they were caught they took their sentences as bravely as men. I could be one of them. I could.

Bruno swears there are people with like beliefs everywhere, such as the lieutenant on the train. He has made contacts at the corps, even his professor, Kremsky, is one of them. Now, that is really exciting. I wonder if anyone at the Smolney thinks like this. I can't imagine anyone in my grade might; they are all such ninnies.

I must admit in all honesty that it frightens me to read that the revolutionary is a doomed man, without love, friendship, or joy, only revolutionary passion. Does Bruno truly feel this way? Yet he says he loves me. I must become more like him; then our love can become a revolutionary love. Bruno says we must restructure our whole way of thinking. The revolutionary has no morality outside of his service to the cause. Everything for the revolution is moral. Anything against the revolution is immoral.

Of women Nechaev writes: 'One group, the empty-headed, the senseless, the heartless must be exploited and made the slaves of men. A second group of women who were eager, devoted, capable, but not fully committed to the revolution mut be induced to reveal their sympathies, whereupon most would perish, while the rest would become true revolutionaries. Finally there was a third group of women who are truly ours, and must be considered our most valuable jewel, whose help is absolutely indispensable.'

Which one am I? Which one am I?

* * *

That October, Czar Alexander III died unexpectedly of a kidney infection. His successor, Czar Nicholas II, took the oath of allegiance, waited six weeks to marry his fiancée, Princess Alix of Hesse, and solemnly prepared for the transition. The coronation would wait a year through the official period of mourning.

To celebrate Anton's commission in the Guards, Princess Mariyenka gave a tea party for him and his friends at the palace in June. Because the nation was still in mourning, even Easter festivities had been curtailed that year, and she had limited the guest list to fifty of Anton's closest friends.

Sonya had watched them from her window before she had gone down to be introduced, handsome young men in their early twenties, their eyes wide with the wonder of life ahead of them, and the lovely young girls, with the long necks and the trailing silks, aglow with a rosy blush that made them all seem perfect, animated by the dazzling light of the sun and the lush colors of the spring flowers. The day had blessed them. They spilled out of the drawing room and onto the terrace, into the garden. From her room two floors above, it seemed an unreal world, the bodies and voices drifting like water lilies across the greenness of the spring lawn. How long had it been since the days had been so perfect this early in June? What wondrous thing had happened?

That night, just as she was on the verge of sleep, Bruno shook her. 'You are the only one I am telling, Sonya.' He was sitting on the far end of her bed, slowly twisting the tassels of her bedspread. She could scarcely make out the features of his face. He had turned up the light but it was behind him, making his eyes and mouth seem like black holes.

'I love them, Sonya, you know that. I love you.' Sonya

nodded her head. 'But I am possessed with something bigger than personal love. I am possessed, you might say obsessed, with Russia. I love Russia, Sonya, more than Mother, more than Father, more than family.' He paused. More than me, she wanted to say, but didn't. 'I am leaving. They will tell you I am dead. I have arranged for my own death. It will seem I am dead. I might as well be. I shall never come back here. I will lead a new life.' He stopped again. The black holes that were his eyes were even blacker. They sucked her breath into them.

'I have sworn to my new comrades that I will tell nobody, but I cannot. I suppose that makes me too weak from the beginning. I suppose they would be better off without me, a boy who cannot bear to leave his little sister thinking that he is dead. You will never tell anyone. I know, simply because I ask you, you will never tell anyone.' He stopped. His face was like Napoleon's, like the painting by Sermeyev in the Hermitage. They had gone there together many times to look at it. He had always said he looked like the portrait, and now, in the same half-flickering light, like the candle in the painting that had illuminated Napoleon's profile in a moment of reverie as he sat on the end of an army cot, now she saw her brother as a man who could also meet defeat.

'It is terrible now,' he continued. 'Everyone is nervous now that the czar has died. Nicholas will be even more repressive than his father, you will see. Romanovs forever, one worse than the other. As much encouragement as Kremsky has given me, now even he is afraid. He has a family. It is too late for him, perhaps, but not for me. I have spared you nothing, Sonya. You know the tyranny of our czar, our God on this earth. Conditions worsen every day. Kremsky has heard from a friend, a letter from Siberia. It is inhuman. There is no freedom anywhere in Russia. There is tyranny, only tyranny.'

Sonya's eyes were wide with awe.

'You remember old Petya, our footman? You remember Boris, his boy, whose clothes you wore when we rode out into the country?'

'Yes,' she answered, nodding her head eagerly, anxious to hear everything.

'I have been in contact with him. He has joined a group. In the countryside the peasants are finding weapons and banding together.'

'At Dosiaya?' She sat up.

'Yes. Yes. As slaves they starved and as free men they starve. What good does it do them to be free if they still starve?'

'I know, Bruno. I think about it constantly. Today, looking at the beauty on the lawn, the beauty of Anton and his friends, I knew it could not last. I know those silks and jewels, the linens and the flowers, we have them only through the sweat of others. I know. I know.'

'Exactly. Well, Boris and his comrades are no longer willing to see their children starve for our luxuries.' Bruno paused, his eyes looking deep into hers. 'I am going to join the army.'

'Our army?' she asked. It was against anything he believed in.

'No, Sonya, no, of course not.' A smile lit up his face; even in the darkness she could see his pride. 'I am going to join the revolutionary army. Those who are in hiding everywhere, readying for the destruction of old Russia.'

'Oh, my God, Bruno.' In spite of herself she said, 'Poor Mama.'

'No sympathy for them, Sonya, no sympathy. They are your parents, and mine, but they blacken the spirit of freedom in this land. I will be dead for them. No matter, they have three others that are exactly what they would wish me to be. They will soon forget me. But you, Sonya, must remember me, know I am alive, think of me, and always love me. This revolution will topple our parents. They could never understand it. They have outlived their days.'

'You are a true anarchist, then, Bruno? A true revolutionary?'

'That is what I am, Sonya. That is what I now will be.'

She grabbed him and held him close to her, taking his lapel in her hands. 'How proud I am, Bruno! How proud. It is thrilling. I am shaking from excitement. Will I wake up tomorrow and find this is just a dream?'

'This is real, Sonya, as real as my love. Remember that I

love you, Sonya. Remember, always, there is a dead man alive who loves you.'

She clung to him, her head now buried in his neck. Suddenly all that mattered was that he would be gone, that she would never see him, never talk to him, never run her hands through his wild red hair.

'Oh, why,' she cried to him, 'why must you go? Wait for me!'

'I must go to free Russia, Sonya,' he answered simply. He lay her back down on her pillows and leaned over to kiss her. 'Sleep, my sister, pretend it was all a dream. Remember, I shall always love you, and tell no one.'

His voice had become soft. She put the reality of his words away from her and listened only to the soothing sound of his voice, which seemed to sing her an extraordinarily sweet lullaby: 'Free Russia. Free Russia. Free Russia.'

Three days later they received the news that Peter Bruno Poliakov had burned to death in a small inn while traveling to the university in Moscow. The body was charred beyond recognition. It was interred in the Volkov Cemetery in Petersburg. Watching the red-rimmed eyes of her mother and father, Sonya felt pride that her brother was so clever. He is alive, she wanted to tell them. He is alive! But she turned away from their sorrowful faces and kept that solace to herself. And even so, she wept for him.

6

It was only a word, but it caused intoxication in everyone who uttered it or heard it. Coronation. Coronation! Czar Nicholas was to be crowned in May in Moscow. By the end of February 1896, people seemed to care more about the event itself than the young man who was to become czar. Even the arrival of spring took second place to the topic. Each night, Sonya would wake up to Marushka's mumblings as she knelt in front of the icon or paced about the room. The old woman whispered of crowns of jewels and thrones of gold, spoke to God, and warned the devils that were floating about the world to stay away from the new Little Father. Each day, Sonya's mother and her consoling friends sat in the salon bubbling like the silver samovar as they went over their wardrobes or their plans for the journey to Moscow and compared their lists of invitations to balls, musicales, lunches.

'I cannot wait! Not another moment! What a dreadful period this year has been. All this mourning. First the czar. Then poor Bruno. The season this year has been absolutely abysmal.' Sonya's aunt, her mother's sister Elizabeta, her mouth stuffed with strawberries and complaints, sat on the satin chair across from Sonya's mother.

'I wonder if the German woman is feeling up to it.' Tatiana Fedorovna, her mother's closest friend, sighed. Her light eyes were bright with her amusement. 'I think our new empress is capable of spoiling the whole thing. She's colder than the moon.'

'Come, come, Tatiana,' Sonya's mother said, smiling, 'the poor woman is just shy. The general says once she is used to our ways, there will be more balls than ever. One must give her a chance.'

'Well, I hope the general is right,' Tatiana murmured. 'I should be annoyed if the exhausting trip to Moscow isn't worth the bother.'

'I must say you are fortunate, Mariyenka,' Countess

Nina Borisovna said. 'Having a sister with one of the grandest houses in Moscow is lucky. We must stay at the Kalenkovs', and their house is more than fourteen miles from the Kremlin.'

'Adele was offered over five hundred thousand roubles for her house by the Germans,' Mariyenka announced proudly.

'That's impressive for Germans,' Tatiana retorted. 'They hold on to their money until it burns their palms.'

'Of course, my sister wouldn't hear of it,' Mariyenka continued. 'But she has already let four of her carriages out for the coronation festivities, and she tells me the English are paying her extravagantly for each one. The world seems to be coming to Moscow.'

'I heard they were painting the entire city, even the domes of the cathedrals.' Elizabeta yawned. Having finished the strawberries appeared to exhaust her.

'No matter what they do to Moscow, it won't be Petersburg. I find it so dreary.' Tatiana sighed. 'So backward somehow.'

'Hardly backward,' Nina answered.

'Then very slow,' Tatiana shot back. 'I know it is supposed to be the center of Russia, but really, it is the centre of everything that's wrong with Russia as far as I'm concerned. So disorganized and cluttered.'

'Mariyenka, I hear your sister's husband, Sergei, has resigned his commission and has gone into business.' Nina licked a bit of cream filling from the corner of her red mouth.

Mariyenka, a bit flustered, put down her teacup. 'I can't account for Sergei Mikhailovitch's behavior,' she said solemnly. 'Business is one thing, but to leave one's rank behind one . . .' Her voice trailed off.

'My brother has done the same,' Tatiana whispered. The other women were shocked. Alexander Leonovitch was in the Ministry of the Interior in a high position. 'Yes, yes, I know it will be a scandal, but my brother says we are in the middle of an industrial revolution and already Russia leads the world. He assures me rank will mean nothing soon and roubles, as always, everything.' Tatiana was crimson, even with her defense. 'Well, look at the wealth of the merchants in Moscow! Are we to give over all our industry to the English? And what good is it to be a prince or even a minister without a great inheritance?'

The other women cared nothing for serious talk. Without so much as a nod in Tatiana's direction, they went blithely on with more talk of Moscow and the coronation. Elizabeta took Sonya's hand. 'What a shame, my beauty, that you are too young to attend the balls. You should win the heart of every handsome officer.'

'At least she will see the procession,' Mariyenka said, smiling at her magnificent daughter and wishing she would pay a bit more attention to her hair. 'My husband has arranged for a balcony on the Tverskaya, and the entire procession will pass directly beneath us.'

'You see' – Elizabeta turned to Tatiana – 'there is still something to be said for rank.'

Listening to her mother's friends, Sonya tried to convince herself that such excess and foolishness filled her with disgust. Yet, when the day came for the family departure for Moscow, Sonya, sitting in the first carriage with her parents, was as excited as they had been.

Her brothers were already in Moscow and would ride with their regiments in the procession. Sonya had persuaded her parents to leave her governess, Helene, in Petersburg. Now that Sonya spent most of the year at Smolney, Helene had gotten, if possible, even worse. When Sonya was at home, Helene was forever at her. Only that morning they had had a furious fight.

'You insolent child,' Helene had shrieked at her, 'you have no regard for your happy position!'

'People around me starve, Helene. How can I take comfort in the fact that I am fortunate?'

'God is the manager of how the world is, not you!'

'Then God is a sorry manager!'

Helene had crossed herself with great violence. 'Blasphemer! Your list of sins grows with every word you speak!'

As the carriage rolled forward, Sonya saw Helene at the doorway, her envious eyes narrowed and her mouth in a tight little pout. Such a silly, wasteful woman, Sonya thought. When Bruno's revolution began, people like

Helene would be the first to go.

Settled at last in the red velvet-upholstered railroad car, Sonya pushed back the lacy white curtain at the window and stared out as the train moved slowly through the city. Everywhere ice and snow were melting in sunshine; the last vestiges of winter were disappearing in front of her eyes. Although the countryside that rolled past the train was flat, muddy, and uninteresting, she felt such excitement just in looking at it. This land was her mother, not the infernal woman near her chatting to her husband about the lack of time she had to accomplish fittings for her dresses or the repairing of the clasps on her bracelets and necklaces. She thought of Bruno and wondered if he would be in Moscow. She tried to tell herself that this coronation didn't mean a thing to her. Still, she was so excited. It must be the trip. The coming of spring. It could not be the spectacle of the coronation process. Liar, liar, liar, the train wheel chanted. Coronation, coronation, coronation. That is what makes you shudder with excitement. You are worse than Helene. You are worse than your mother. You are unforgivable because you know better. Hour after hour, she looked out the window. Coronation, coronation, coronation.

In Adele's moss-green palace on Kalinin Avenue, the tall, arched windows garlanded with marble flowers seemed to beckon the spring sunshine. Even in her cousin Maya Sergeievna's quarters at the back, where Sonya and Marushka had settled, light washed every corner. A large-boned girl of nineteen, Maya had a flat, uninteresting Mongolian face and poor skin, but she was possessed of an enthusiastic manner that always endeared her to Sonya. She was studying to be a doctor and had only just finished that year's examinations. Unmarried, and with no immediate prospects, she was not looking forward to the festivities surrounding the coronation and was delighted to be chaperoning her younger cousin about Moscow. It was only the second day of Sonya's visit, and already Maya had planned what appeared to be a month's worth of sightseeing. She was fiddling with her gloves, waiting for Sonya to finish dressing. Sonya was having trouble with

Marushka, who insisted she make another arrangement of her hair.

'It is a bird's nest, I tell you, and all the birds of Moscow will swoop to it.'

Sonya tried to push Marushka away but could not move her. Embarrassed that her older cousin thought her a child, yet seeing that there was nothing to be done but to repin her hair, she yielded to Marushka's command. 'I will leave you behind,' she said. 'You are a meddling crone.'

'If you leave your old one behind, my fine lady, your horses will go lame.' Marushka put on her coat and stood by the door.

'How lovely you look,' Maya Sergeievna said, staring at Sonya. 'How well green suits you.'

'What does it matter how one looks?' Sonya answered, trying to pay Maya no heed. 'It matters less than a hound's whimper. What matters, Maya Sergeievna, is what is inside a person.'

'It is very easy to say such a thing when one is as beautiful as you are, little cousin.'

'Beauty doesn't matter. It cannot help one accomplish anything important.' Sonya tied on her hat and pulled her cape around her shoulders, resisting the urge to glance at herself in the mirror.

'Oh, how wrong you are, Sonyasha! I assure you I would advance more quickly in medicine if I were beautiful.'

'It cannot make you a better doctor.' Sonya took her arm and started from the room.

'It can help one do whatever one wants,' Maya said, kissing her cousin's cheek. 'You will see!' They walked to the curving stairway, arm in arm, and started down, using one another for balance. Ivy tangled with itself up and down the struts and turns of the stair railing. The air was perfumed by pots of jasmine, which their skirts nearly knocked over on the landing.

That day Maya had planned to show Sonya the shops and the markets. The carriage passed through streets filled with people. From one corner to the next, the crowd seemed to swell. The soldiers in the colors of their regiments, the hundreds of peasant women with many-colored kerchiefs, men with bright turbans and pantaloons, children in gaily embroidered traditional dress, made a great undulating rainbow of humanity. Kuznetskay Most, the street with the best shops in Moscow, was so jammed, the carriage had to wait a long period of time just to pass through. People went in and out of the shops, peddlers shouted for attention, drivers cursed as they crossed themselves in front of churches. Flags whipped in the breeze and bells rang out. The initials N and A entwined on banners at every corner. It was like Easter, only richer, more vibrant.

Sonya begged Maya to take her to see the university.

'But it is closed, Sonyasha,' Maya said.

'I just want to see it. Besides, I cannot look at food.'

'Well, come along and I'll show it to you. It is like a graveyard; absolutely no one is there. A good thing, too. There are so many student agitators these days. My classmates think nothing but politics. There are arrests every week. And some troublemakers come from very good families. I wonder how they can be so stupid as to think the world can change overnight by changing those in power.'

'And you think it cannot change?' Sonya asked.

'My dear little cousin, why should it change! Russia is the envy of the world already. Our women are better educated than all the rest, and our men are the best-looking and the smartest. Even the lowliest serf has more than enough to eat and can rise to become whatever he wishes if he has enough pluck and brains. Look at Schuchin.'

'Schuchin was an exception. Geniuses are exceptions.'

'There are geniuses born every day,' Maya replied. 'And most of them are born in Russia!'

The carriage stopped in front of the university. Sonya looked at the deserted buildings. After the Smolney, she would go there and at last become an active partner in Bruno's revolution. It looked so plain. She had expected something grander. She frowned, catching herself again thinking like an aristocrat. How hard she would have to work to overcome her background. Once she got away from home, once she was at the university, it would be so much easier.

Maya tapped on the glass and the carriage went forward again. They were going toward the Kremlin, with its huge walls and towers, above which shone golden domes. As the carriage went under one of the archways, Sonya saw St Basil's ahead of her, topsy-turvy in the morning light. It was truly a fantasy, so haphazard, its bulbs and swirls and colors appearing to be so many spinning tops. Sonya asked that the carriage be stopped so she might go inside. She motioned Marushka down from her seat beside the driver, and together they walked toward the cathedral, Sonya resisting the urge to run to the walls to see if they were made of spun sugar and Marushka crossing herself with each step. Inside, Sonya waited as Marushka put a candle down among a thousand others and then knelt to kiss the icon of her favorite saint. There was no face beneath Marushka's lips. How could she tell which icon was which when most of them were worn away with the mindless adoration of pilgrims, peasants, and nobility? What fools they all were, Sonya thought, pretending equality before God.

The smell of incense followed them out of the cathedral onto the square where Maya was waving wildly from the carriage, half out of the window. 'Hurry, Sonya! We must be home early. Mama is having open house today. The French ambassador is coming!'

The rest of that day and the next and the week after went by as if Sonya had dreamed them all in one night. Watching her parents leave the palace on the ninth consecutive night for yet another gala, Sonya wondered how they could manage to stand. Maya and she were already in bedclothes, perched on the brightly patterned window seat in Maya's bedroom. Maya laughed as she closed the window. 'To think we cannot go with them because there will be prostitutes and Gypsies at the restaurant after the theater. I have seen things that would make my mother faint dead away, yet she thinks I'd be corrupted by the sight of a prostitute.'

'I have read of such women,' Sonya said.

'Ha! I have seen them,' Maya replied with great authority. 'They come to the clinic. Half of them are diseased and half are pregnant or both. It's just as well most of their children don't survive.'

'Every life is sacred, Maya.' Sonya frowned at her cousin, who was brushing her hair.

'Not so, my dear. The people who come to our clinic are animals. Science is very strict, you know. Genes are passed from one generation to the next. Good becomes better and bad becomes worse.'

'That is a social disease, Maya Sergeievna!'

Maya put down her brush and wagged a finger at Sonya. 'I shall report you, naughty child! You sound like a radical!' Maya burst into gales of laughter.

'Perhaps I am one.'

'Now, Sonyasha, be serious. How can everyone in the world be equal? Who would clean the streets? Who would cook? Who would work in the factories? Can you imagine your Marushka a professor and my Olga a doctor? They have hardly enough sense to get out of bed in the morning. Come, let's have some sleep. I for one am delighted at such a good night's rest. Tomorrow is the procession, and we must leave the palace before eight in the morning.'

Sonya followed her cousin to the corner where the icon was, crossed herself, and went into her room. She had wanted to answer Maya, but she had not spoken again. She remembered Bruno's warning: 'Be careful who you trust, my sister. Trust is survival.'

Sonya got under the covers of the bed and was silent. She wished Bruno had been there, for he could have changed Maya's thinking in an instant with his facts and his experience. Well, Sonya thought, closing her eyes, soon I shall have facts and the experience. For now, perhaps I have planted a tiny seed in Maya's mind. Marushka was already asleep, no doubt dreaming of her Little Father. Sonya thought she would never sleep, but sleep came as quickly as Cossacks and swept her away.

The next day was magnificent, clear and warm and bright with sun. After a hasty breakfast, they were all off to the Tverskaya and ensconced on the balcony in time for the procession. Thousands upon thousands filled the stands below them to watch the thousands upon thousands who came in the street. Helmets and swords and epaulets

71

flashed gold as the Imperial Guard rode by. In the distance one already heard the court orchestra playing. A bit after three in the afternoon, it seemed as if all the armies of Russia and all its nobles had ridden by. With so many men on horseback, Sonya had not imagined that so many were still left to stand and watch. Finally, there on his white horse, passing just beneath her, was Nicholas, more grand in his simple army tunic than the costumed soldiers that surrounded him. Sonya shivered with unexpected awe at his obvious majesty. Czar. King. Emperor. She turned away from the sight to meet Maya's wide, staring eyes behind her. She turned back. No wonder Maya could not blink. In front of them now was the gold carriage that had belonged to Catherine the Great, pulled by eight white horses, and inside was Dowager Empress Marie. A collective gasp came from everyone around them. There was hardly time to see the first carriage before there was a second golden carriage, which carried Alexandra Fedorovna. Even the horses seemed aware of the glory of their passenger, so carefully did they put one foot in front of the other.

'She is wearing her diamonds,' Adele whispered. 'Have you ever seen anything more beautiful!' The sun seemed to steal new brilliance from the stones around the empress's neck as she leaned toward the crowd, nodding and waving.

It was so dazzling Sonya could not think. Was there ever such magnificence? It was not possible. She had read of Greece and Rome. Surely what she saw before her was greater, more glorious. What power there was, what glory there would be! She closed her eyes. It was a holy moment. Nevertheless, she chose that instant to swear her allegiance to her cause. 'Bless the revolution,' she said silently. When she opened her eyes again, the carriages had passed and the czar on his white mount had disappeared from her sight.

The next morning, Sonya turned in bed just before noon, yawned, stretched, and decided against rising. It was nearly inconceivable to her that her parents and her aunt and uncle were already at the Oupensky Cathedral for the coronation ceremony. They would have to stand for hours.

Where had they gotten such stamina when she could not even move? Sleep descended again, and she dreamed of cathedrals, huge, soaring iconostases with jeweled icons winking at her. She heard the most heavenly choir sing to her and saw the czar on a diamond throne with the czarina on the ivory throne, and then there were shouts and the sound of explosions and blood was everywhere. She awoke screaming in Marushka's arms.

'Now, now, my dove! Sh, sh!'

'The czar! What has happened to the czar?'

'Nothing. He is crowned,' Marushka said with reverence.

'Are you certain? Oh, Marushka, I had the most terrible dream – beautiful and then terrible.'

'Dreams are dreams, my flower. You are awake now. Soon your parents will be home to tell us of the ceremony. How blessed they are to see such a thing.'

Sonya pushed out of Marushka's embrace and covered her eyes with her arms. 'They are only two among thousands,' Sonya said.

'Did I tell you that the footman Vladimir is there also? His wife's family are descendants of Ivan Susanin, the peasant who saved the life of Michael Romanov. Such a beautiful country this Russia is, for she never forgets the sacrifice of her sons and daughters. Always when a czar is crowned, Susanin's descendants are among the most honored guests. They sit with kings, with grand dukes. Bless the czar.' Marushka crossed herself.

'They sit in a room by themselves,' Sonya said.

'What difference where they sit! They are there, honored guests.'

'It would be better if you could be there, if anyone who wished to go might go.'

'I? Who am I?'

'My Matushka Marushka, the most important person in the world.'

Marushka messed Sonya's hair. 'You are such a silly child,' she said. 'Ah, ah, what a day, such a day. The sun shines and and I am filled with love. Come, lazy one, it is time to put on your dressing gown. Your poor cousin has been up for hours trying on her mother's gown. Poor thing, she looks lost in it. Your aunt and uncle will have to work fast to get her married or she will have no chance at all, even with her fortune.'

'Who cares for marriage? It is enslavement.'

'I will sew up your tongue! Get up, get up. It is nearly evening, and you must eat something or you won't have the strength to see your mother dressed or to hear what happened at the ceremony.'

Sonya felt no interest. Without Marushka's endless pleadings, she would have stayed in bed. The sight of her mother and Adele rushing about the palace like wild children, checking and rechecking each other's dresses for hidden flaws, readying things that had been ready for weeks only exhausted her. Although their dresses had come from Worth in Paris, dressmakers had come daily to fit and refit them. Sonya had never seen her mother so particular. First the thread had been wrong, then the color of the stones. Next the catches at the back of the dress, next the hem. It was a beautiful dress, an extraordinary robin's-egg-blue satin, shockingly low on the shoulders. Bands of gold and silver and stones of deep blue and green gently traced out delicate patterns on the fine French lace appliquéd on the satin skirt, and even finer lace and smaller stones traced the pattern along the bosom. By six in the evening, Marushka had helped Olga dress the princess. At six forty-five, the hairdresser had come and worked the shining hair into an elaborate coiffure held by hundreds of tiny hairpins. Around the rosettes of hair he had put in circles of pearls, and at last he had placed the diamond tiara over it all. Sonya's mother had looked at herself in the glass, sighed with appreciation, pressed the tiara down a bit farther, and then with a simple nod and a quick smile dismissed the man, who gathered his bottles of lacquer and his curling irons into a box, bowed to the princess, and left without a word. The manicurist finished her chore, admired the princess's hands and her sapphire and diamond ring, and followed the hairdresser.

Sonya, curled on her mother's bed like a cat, watched. Again, the princess looked at herself in the glass. She put on her sapphire and diamond earrings, which exactly matched her ring, and smiled at her reflection once again. Such indulgence, such self-involvement, such waste,

Sonya thought.

'Come, Sonya, kiss Mama good-by.' The princess stood up, smoothed out her dress, and held her arms open. Sonya kissed her mother's glowing cheeks and let herself be embraced. 'I will wake you when I come home. I want to tell you all about it. It is history, this day. Your great-grandchildren will read of it.'

The earrings swung at her mother's ears, the diamonds sparkled in the tiara. Perhaps tonight the earth would open up and swallow her mother and all of Russia's oppressors. Sonya trembled at the darkness of her thoughts.

'You are beautiful, Mama.'

'Am I? I am so happy you think so. At times I wonder what you are thinking, Sonyasha. Your little brow is often so furrowed. I fear it will leave tracks.' Her mother put a long scented finger at the center of Sonya's forehead.

'I always think you are beautiful, Mama.' Sonya pulled away from her mother's touch.

Adele ran into the room and took her sister's arm. 'We are all waiting, Mariyenka. Hurry! How do I look? I couldn't decide if I should wear my rubies or not. I have decided on the pearls. Do you think they are too plain? Perhaps I should run back for the rubies.' The two women left the room and Sonya could hear them all the way down the length of the blue-carpeted hallway. Pearls. Diamonds. Rubies. Sapphires. Waste, waste, waste. Sonya heard a little sob behind her and turned to see Marushka.

'Oh, how wonderful!' the old woman cried. 'Is she not the most beautiful woman in Moscow? I held her in my arms as I held you, and soon you, too, will be grown and off to a ball. Oh, life is so precious. God is so good.'

7

Later that night Marushka wept when Princess Mariyenka
woke the two of them. Marushka had fallen asleep on the
small sofa in Sonya's room and, half asleep, she had burst
into tears when the princess had started her descriptions
of the czar and his young bride.

'He is so handsome! So young!'

'And she, Princess?'

'Very regal, very icy, very German. You know.'

'Did you see them close? Were you near them? Tell us,
Princess! Please!'

'It took us an endless while to get into the Kremlin,' her
mother had said, leaning against the tiny desk near
Sonya's bed. 'There were carriages everywhere, and all the
coachmen seemed bent upon destruction, cutting in and
out. It's a wonder we were able to get there at all. The
carriages were backed up to Lemorov Square. And then,
on top of the waiting, we managed finally to arrive, only to
find we had gone to the wrong gate!'

'No!' Marushka gasped, fascinated.

'Luckily, the general spotted a captain we knew, and we
were taken through a roundabout way. Oh, so much
confusion. But it was well worth it. It was so beautiful,
Marushka, Sonya! There were millions of oil lamps across
all the pillars and the façades of the buildings, but the
Kremlin was lit with electric lights, can you imagine? It
was like daylight, exactly like daylight inside the walls. I've
never seen anything like it. The gowns and the jewels. It
was incredible. Or course, your father insisted that I was
the most beautiful woman in the place.' She smiled. 'Well,
I must say I was complimented at least twenty times on
my gown. Even my own sister commented on how well I
looked. Sonya? Are you listening? I said even Elizabeta
thought I looked well.'

'Yes. Yes,' Sonya answered, smiling, but she had not
been listening. She had been watching the diamonds

dancing at her mother's ears as she tossed her head. A rosy flush on her face had changed her face, the face Sonya knew so well, into one of a young girl. Was this her mother? This young, silly, beautiful woman?

'I danced with Prince Vassily and Bornokoff, and Count Tolchin, and of course your father, who said the champagne was not as good as the champagne at our wedding. Imagine! Princess Anna told me that tomorrow at the French ambassador's ball there will be fifty thousand roses from the south of France in bloom. I'm glad I saved the pink dress for tomorrow, since it will blend beautifully with the roses.'

'Tell me more about our Little Father,' Marushka interrupted.

'Oh, he is very handsome, so young. He reminds me a little bit of your great-uncle, Prince Anton, Sonya. And she, well, I have never seen as many diamonds as she wore around her waist. In his collar the stones were as big as walnuts.'

'You saw them close?' Marushka asked.

'Oh, yes, of course. The czar made a point of coming over and speaking with your father, Sonya. Think of that! You should have seen the face on our Princess Tatiana. She nearly burst with jealousy. Really, I have never seen such crowds. There were thousands, thousands. We went to the wrong entrance. Oh, but I told you that.' Her mother went on.

Sonya had lost interest. She wished she knew what her father's report would be of the evening. What he thought of this new czar, and what Protopopov thought, whether the German woman would be a hindrance to Russia, and whether Nicholas himself was a man equal to the task of governing Russia. Her father would have known what was important.

'I cannot wait to go to the meadow,' Marushka said excitedly.

'Are you sure, Marushka? There will be so many people there. It will be chaotic. You're sure you are up to it?'

'I am sure, I am sure. I have been to every coronation celebration at the Kholodny Meadow since I was a child. My mother took me when I was just a babe. I still have all the little cups that we received from each czar. It will be my first introduction to this Little Father. That he bothers at all with us, that he allows us to be part of his celebration, that he gives us, his people, little presents . . . oh, I could never miss that, Princess! Don't you remember, I went when our late Father was crowned. Don't you remember? You let me leave the baby Sonya and go to the meadow for that joyous time? Remember?'

'Yes. Yes, I do, but that was fifteen years ago. Even then there was such a crush of people. I will worry, Marushka.'

'I must see our Little Father greet us on Friday, Princess. I must have another one of those little enameled cups.'

Sonya fell back into her bed and closed her eyes. She thought of Bruno, and of the revolution, and the fight that lay ahead. Perhaps now it would finally start. Perhaps she would see Bruno again.

She heard the news Friday morning. Protopopov had come to tell her father of the disaster. Sonya and her father were together in her uncle's library when Protopopov yelled for him. Her father had gone to meet him.

'How many do they think were killed?' were the first words she heard her father say as the two men walked back into the room.

'There is no way to know yet. It was terrible. Hundreds of them just trampled over each other. The troops could do nothing to keep order.'

'But why, why did it start?'

'Rumors, rumors. They spread like wildfire – that there would not be enough cups, that there would not be enough beer. They went mad.'

'Oh, my God. I can't understand it.'

'You know the field, it is deeply trenched all over. They fell into the trenches, smothered, crushed!'

'But the soldiers?'

'They could do nothing. There were thousands of people. Thousands.'

'Had the czar arrived yet?'

'I don't think so. I don't know. There are no details. It was early, so he probably had not arrived. They are still bringing the dead and wounded into the hospitals. Every hospital in Moscow is crowded.'

'I don't understand how it could have happened.'

'Well, you know them, how they get. Some blessing, eh?'

'Are you sure about Sonya's old nurse? She was, poor woman, also my wife's nurse. Very loyal.'

'Yes. I am sure of practically nothing, but I am sure of that. My footman, Ilya Stephanovitch, was with her at the field when she was killed.'

'It is a bad way to start a reign.'

'Indeed, I hope they forgive him.'

Sonya had not heard the last words, only the part about Marushka. Marushka, her nurse, her friend, her second mother, dead! It was as if she herself had been struck down. Dead! Her wonderful, sweet-smelling Marushka who had gone only with love to see her czar. Dead. It was past understanding that these simple people, innocents all, united only in their love for their Little Father, should have been led to such a tragedy. The scream that had been building up in her unleashed itself, and she dashed out into the hallway and blindly ran up the marble stairs toward her room.

Her father excused himself from Protopopov and went after his daughter, calling to LeFaux to fetch the princess. He caught Sonya in his arms just at the doorway to her room. 'My dear child! How dreadful that you had to hear such terrible news with so little preparation.'

'Oh, Papa.' She clung to him, her cheeks hot against his. 'How could anyone be prepared for such a thing!'

'Darling child, life is so often cruel. One comes to accept it the older one is.' Her father carried her inside toward her bed.

Tears ran down Sonya's face onto her father's shirt and coat. 'How good she was! How good and pure she was! What will I do without her?' She felt him hold her more tightly and then kiss the top of her head.

Her mother burst into the room. 'Whatever is it, Leon Ivanovitch?' The princess was next to them, her eyes full of dread. 'What has happened?' He told her quickly, stumbling over the details. She gasped when he had finished. 'No! It cannot be! Perhaps Vassily Petrovitch was wrong, it was not our Marushka. Perhaps—'

'He was quite certain. His footman saw her plainly. There is no doubt.'

The princess uttered a prayer and embraced them both. 'How awful such a thing must have sounded to such young ears. My poor Sonyasha.'

'Oh, Mama!' Sonya wept, turning to her mother and putting her head on her bosom.

'It is a horrible thing, little one. But it is only temporary.' Her father took her hand. 'When I was very young my favorite pony was put down. I remember it so clearly. I could not sleep for more than a week. But soon there was another, a fine mount. Magyar. Yes. As strong and loyal as ever a horse could be. Time heals.'

'Sonyasha.' Her mother's hands brushed her hair gently from her face. 'It is God's way. We must lose things we love to make us strong.'

Sonya pushed away from them and stood unsteadily, swaying slightly. 'But she was not a horse, Papa. She was not a thing, Mama. She was a human being. I loved her! You loved her!'

'Of course, of course,' her father said, making odd signals with his eyes to her mother, who seemed to understand what they meant. 'But God is merciful, she will find her place in heaven.'

'I will call to someone to bring some tea and cakes, and then you will rest,' her mother said, her face moist with Sonya's tears. 'Yes, you will rest. It is such a shock for us all. Such a horrible thing. Come, my sweet child, let me help you with your clothes.'

Bewildered, Sonya let her mother take off her dress and shoes. Like a baby, she let herself be tucked under the covers. When the tray of tea and cakes came, she ate with unexpected appetite. Her mother and father stayed with her until finally she drifted off into a black and dreamless sleep. When she woke, the gas jets were already lit in the hall. She still felt exhausted, her legs and arms nearly numb, and she got out of the bed slowly, afraid she might fall into a heap. She would find her parents. The pain would lessen by their united grief as it had before she slept. O Matushka Marushka, she thought, there cannot be a God in heaven if you are dead. She ran to her parents' room. It was eight o'clock when she pushed open the door. She stared at her father, not believing her eyes. He stood in front of her in his full dress uniform, his gold buttons shining. Tonight! They were going to a coronation ball on this day of such tragedy, tragedy even in their own house.

'What are you doing? Where are you going?'

Her father looked pale as he turned to her. His eyes avoided hers as he answered. 'You forget, Sonya, tonight is the ball at the French ambassador's.'

'No,' she cried. 'No.'

'Count Tolchin will be here in a moment. He has been kind enough to offer to take us in his carriage.'

'But why wasn't it canceled? Surely the czar and the czarina are not going to a ball tonight when thousands were massacred this afternoon in their name?'

'The ball is not canceled, Sonya.'

'It has to be canceled.' He did not answer her. 'And even if it is not, how can you go? Marushka is dead. Doesn't her death mean anything to you?'

'Sonya, we mean no disrespect for her. I'm sure she would have wanted us to go.'

'Of course she would have. Of course. Just as I'm sure she would have been happy to die waiting to see the czar. That's no justification!' She was screaming. 'Is Mama wearing all her jewels? She must wear all of them, one for every year of Marushka's life. Yes, yes, she would like that, wouldn't she, Papa?'

'Hush, Sonya. You do not know what you are saying. You do not understand. You are still too young to understand either the ways of man or the will of God.'

'I can't believe the czar will go.'

'The ball is not canceled.' Her father emphasized each word.

'No, the roses would die. God forbid the roses should die, even though thousands of people have. Which is more important?'

'Sonya,' her father said sharply, 'it is not the czar's fault that those people were hurt at the meadow. You know that.'

'He is an evil man.'

'Sonya!'

'He will never be forgiven for this.'

'Sonya, that is enough. Enough!' Her father glared at her.

It was then that Count Tolchin was announced.

'I should like you to go downstairs now, Sonya, and meet Count Tolchin.'

'I would rather not, Father.'

'I did not ask you. I told you. You will go down, Sonya. Arrange yourself.' She looked into his eyes and was frightened. She was still too young to challenge him. In spite of herself, she quickly changed into fresh clothing and went downstairs.

'Sonya, come. This is our great friend, Gregory Andrei-vitch.' It was her mother, not holding her, not comforting her in this maddening moment, but introducing her, as if nothing had happened, to Count Tolchin. Sonya looked at him. He was a young, handsome man, with steely eyes, dressed in his uniform, like her father. His skin seemed very white, and he looked very strong. She had heard of Count Tolchin, but couldn't remember where. In some newspaper, she thought, or perhaps her father had spoken of him before. It wouldn't come to her. She knew he was important, though. Somehow. She didn't care.

'How do you do, Count. I have heard of you.'

He smiled at her. 'How serious your daughter is, Princess.'

'Oh, I've given up on my daughter. She has no social graces. Count. You must excuse her.'

'I have no time for social graces, Mama, only social causes.'

The Count was still smiling at her. 'Do I detect a malcontent, madame, here in your house? Your own daughter?'

'You may laugh at me, Count. No, I am not a revolutionary. I have no guns. I have no dynamite. I have only my heart, which seems rare enough these days in Russia. I know right from wrong.'

Count Tolchin stopped smiling. 'How old are you?'

'Fifteen.'

He came close to her, took her hand, and bowed, whispering so that only she could hear: 'You had best be careful.' As he came up from his bow he turned to her mother, as if it were all so natural, and asked if they were ready to proceed to the ball. 'You had best be careful.' The words rang in her ears as soon as he said them. She felt cold.

'Will you excuse me, dear Count? It has been such a terrible day at our house, a terrible day. I will see if my husband is ready. I am sure he is, and I will just make sure of the arrangements that have been made for Sonya. I will be back in a moment. I keep forgetting. It has been such a dreadful day.'

Sonya watched her mother leave the room. Was that all? Those words? She felt as if she would scream again, and she realized she had been staring at Count Tolchin.

'Why do you look at me like that, Sonya Leonovna?'

'I wish it would end.' She swept her arm around the room, and clearly indicated the rest of the world. He said nothing. 'The end of our dear Little Father, the end of this Russia, the end of stupidity and tyranny and people like you.'

'You are hysterical. Be quiet, Sonya Leonovna.'

'I will not.' She crossed her arms over her breasts and stood to her full height, feet apart, ready for battle. She thrust her lip forward defiantly.

He walked close to her. 'Listen to me, Sonya. I am going to talk to you as if you were a woman and not a child.' As he approached her, she looked into his eyes and felt herself startlingly weak. 'Be quiet about your revolution. About tyranny. Keep that enchanting mouth sealed, my little Sonya. Someone might hear you. Start listening instead. There is history everywhere, everywhere. I am history. You are history. Even your mother and father. Tonight is history. Know it. Learn it.'

She heard her father's footsteps coming toward them. Tolchin walked to the fireplace and leaned against it, hanging his foot on the rail. His eyes were filled with strange lights. No one should see a man's eyes like this, she thought. My God, it is as if he is naked!

'Papa,' she cried, 'thank goodness.' She ran toward him.

'So, my angel child, you have forgiven me?'

Forgiven him? For what? My God, she had forgotten. She, too, like her mother, had forgotten Marushka. How could she? Count Tolchin had done it to her. She turned to look at him. He was still leaning back against the fireplace.

It was just at this moment that Maya Sergeievna rushed into the room, almost colliding simultaneously with a lamp and a footstool. Blushing furiously, she looked at Count Tolchin. 'Count Tolchin, I came to bring you greetings from my parents and welcome you to our house. They hated having to go to the musicale at the German Embassy. They hope to see you at Conte de Montebello's ball.' She was at a loss to what to do with her hands and decided finally to clasp them together at her wrist. Count Tolchin quickly crossed to her, reached for her hand, and bowed over it, effortlessly rescuing her from her obvious gracelessness.

'And will you not offer greetings from yourself, Maya Sergeievna?' his eyes were on hers, his manner courteous and attentive.

'Yes, yes, of course. I—'

'It has been much too long since I have seen you or your dear parents. How lovely you look this evening . . . but I expected to see you later at the ball.'

'I . . . I am not up to it,' she said, stammering and still blushing. 'I only lately finished my examinations and there wasn't time to prepare . . .' Each time she looked at his face, she lost her voice.

'Oh, yes,' he said, so easily familiar with her. 'You are to be a doctor. I am sorry that your studies have deprived me of a dance this evening, but for so noble a profession, I am willing to make the sacrifice.'

'It is so good of you to take my aunt and uncle with you this evening, dear Count. You are ever so thoughtful.'

'It is my pleasure, dear Maya Sergeievna, a pleasure lessened because we must take our leave now. We are late as it is, and the traffic is fierce. I hope you are well until we meet again.' He bowed once more, soundlessly bringing his heels together, and crossed the room following Sonya's father out the door. Did Sonya imagine it or did he smile at her as he passed her, his face turned away from her cousin?

'Oh, I think I shall die!' Maya Sergeievna collasped on the chair nearest Sonya, holding her heart with both hands. 'Oh, I shall surely die.'

'Whatever is wrong with you, Mashyenka?' Alarmed, Sonya knelt by her, frightened by her stricken face, by her shallow breathing. She rubbed Maya's hands in hers.

'When I heard he was here, here in this house! Oh, I ran, how I ran from my mother's room. I must have seemed so foolish, but then what woman is not foolish in his presence? Did you hear what he said? Did you hear him say he would feel deprived by not having a dance with me? I should have gone to the ball. Oh, how I wish I were as beautiful as you, Sonya Leonovna!' Her voice was anguished and breathless at once.

'Do you mean you find him attractive, Maya Sergeievna? That arrogant fellow so full of himself?'

'How naïve you are!' Maya snapped, pushing Sonya away from her. 'He is one of the most respected men in all of Russia. He was an aide to Noriskayev in the Ministry of the Interior and now, at twenty-five, it is said he runs the Okhrana, the secret police. My father says that without Tolchin present, Coustoff would be a crying girl. If he is arrogant, he has every right to it.'

'But he is so insincere, his words are sticky with the phoniness of the court. I am sorry, I do not see his charm.'

'Well, then, you can count yourself the first. There isn't a woman in all Moscow, indeed, all Russia, who would not leave her family in the dead of night for a rendezvous with such a man! His lineage is impeccable. His father, Count André, is directly descended from one of Russia's oldest families, and his mother was a cousin of Viktor Vasnetsov, the architect. They lost their money during the land reforms, but I don't care if he hasn't a sou. Did you see the scar above his left eye? They say he fought a man last year for the honor of Princess Dasha Groveyenko, and they say one of the Youssapovs has offered him millions for an alliance.'

Sonya got to her feet and looked down at her cousin. 'I am surprised at you, Maya Sergeievna. That is all gossip. Surely you and your friends have better things to do than gossip about such a man. Whenever I walk through rooms where my mother and her friends sit, I am amazed that all they seem to concern themselves with is men and their exploits or men and their business. Surely women have failures and triumphs as well. Especially women who will be doctors.'

Maya Sergeievna laughed, her dark eyes full of merriment. 'Whatever are they teaching you at Smolney, little Sonya?'

'What is so funny?' Sonya put her hands at her hips and leaned toward her cousin, her face tight with annoyance.

'What is so funny?' Maya rocked with laughter. 'You are! Men are men and women are women. How can you expect a woman's triumphs to be great ones? When was the last time a woman was minister of justice? No, my dear cousin, we women must live through our men. It is well and good for me to become a doctor, but unless I am married to a man of substance, I will be nothing.' Maya stopped laughing. 'I will tell you a secret. If ever a man like Count Tolchin wanted me, even for my money, I would give up my profession, I would give up anything. Like that!' She snapped her fingers. 'Now what do you think of that, my fiery little cousin?'

'I think it is sad,' Sonya answered. 'I would have thought better of you.'

'We shall see what happens to you when you are of age, Empress Catherine!'

'Age has nothing to do with what I said or with what I believe. I will not change my mind, but I hope to change yours.' Sonya stomped out of the room, her hands in tight fists. Maya Sergeievna was backward. Too much Lermontov. Too many fairy tales. Count Tolchin was no more than a pompous clown who affected poses all over a room and took delight in turning the head of a cow like Maya Sergeievna. Then why, as Sonya climbed the stairs to her bedroom, did the thought of his smile make her stumble? Once on the landing, she ran to her room, suddenly at a loss.

*   *   *

Sonya   January 9, 1897

Tonight we went to the Kassalov Theatre to see *Boris Godunov*. It is not one of my favorite plays. Pushkin is not Shakespeare, and no amount of trying to turn the cat around by the tail will make him into that greater man. Tonight was especially bad. The actors seemed not to know what to make of their lines, and the fellow who played Boris whose name I hope never to hear again, ranted and carried on in such a way as to make his part seem asinine and effeminate. Bad actors are as much a curse as bad soldiers. May I never fail in any pursuit as this fellow failed tonight. The audience took sides during the first part, some applauding and some hissing and booing, but by the second half they all had turned entirely against him, and he could barely speak his lines without some sort of answer from the gallery. One old man was finally ejected, poor fellow, when right was on his side. No one should ever be forced to tolerate inadequacy.

Of course, in the first tier no one was the least interested in Boris. As usual, the business of the city was being conducted in the boxes. Princess Maria Groubetska, whose husband was so cruelly attacked just last week in the newspaper by none other than his eminence the minister of the interior, arrived with her daughter Maria Stephanova, looking as sour as turned cream. Everyone cut them.

I am glad that they fight among themselves, these elitists. The more they bite and claw, the easier will be the work of those of us who wish to destroy them. The money and power that sat in that theater tonight! If it alone were spread throughout Petersburg, we could all live in harmony forever with one another.

I must say I hate this new fashion that everyone seems to have adopted. No one moves easily in it yet, nor are they able to sit down quite properly. Elizabeta Antonova nearly fell on her face as she was seated. I could hardly keep from laughing.

Is it terrible? I love all the pageantry of the stage, and it is as if the lives of all those terrible creatures in the audience are part of the pageant. How terrible and how exciting to be alive in these days of intrigue and destruction. I await my chance.

I saw Count Tolchin again tonight. He did not see me. What a poseur he is. It is he that should 'best be careful.' He and men like him will be destroyed by the new order.

*   *   *

In April of the following year, Sonya met Count Tolchin again in the grand foyer at the theater during the second intermission of *King Lear*. Sonya hated the tragedies in Russian. Even Constantin Kazmanov couldn't stop himself from declaiming like a town crier. She loved to read the plays in English and only wished Shakespeare had written a play about Saint Joan.

'Sonya,' her mother said, 'you remember Count Tolchin.'

She curtsied politely. 'Of course. How good to see you again, Count.'

He was only inches taller than she, not so tall as Sonya remembered him. And he was too muscular, straining the fabric of his clothes. In fact, he would have seemed thick were it not for the length of his neck and the shape of his face. The color of his hair was as dark as his boots, his mustache and short beard somewhat lighter. Except for his eyes, which she remembered vividly, his features were no more nor less distinguished than those of many men around him. Count Tolchin's eyes were startling and distracting, not so much for the color, which was blue, nor the size, which was substantial. What gave his eyes their unique power seemed to be the fact that the center of the eye filled the clear white from top to bottom and the thick lashes along the fold of his lid both obscured and revealed his gaze, depending, obviously, on his whim.

'It is a great pleasure to see you, Sonya Leonovna. You are more charming than ever. How is she behaving, Princess?' Although he addressed her mother, Sonya was certain he had not taken his eyes from her face. 'The last time I spoke with her she had the voice of a radical. Indeed, I thought of Saint Joan.'

Sonya's eyes widened. Did he read minds? She heard her mother answer in her musical voice, little trills and melodies. Schubert. 'Ah, Count, I have such trouble with my Sonya. She tells me I am just a silly woman and accuses me of dealing only with the superficial. Can you believe, Count Tolchin, she will not have a debut?'

'Really?' His eyes were still on Sonya as a barely perceptible smile formed on his mouth.

'Yes. Help me, Count. Convince her that she must not break with tradition. Our country would shrivel up and die without its traditions.'

Tolchin turned his head to look at the princess. What had she said that interested him?

'Yes, Princess,' Tolchin was saying, 'I agree. Tradition has made this country whatever it is.'

Her father had joined them, and now his head was nodding vigorously in agreement. 'Exactly, Count. Exactly. Tradition is everything, and yet Russia is frightened of everything Russian. We believe the stigma that the West has put on us, that we are basically a nation of uneducated peasants with a culture that keeps us in the mud. And yet, at the same time, we are afraid of too much westernization, that we will lose everything Slavic. A pretty picture, eh? The insecurity of the Russian people will destroy them.'

'You are, as always, correct, General.'

Sonya had all she could do to restrain herself. Tolchin was watching her. No, she wanted to shout, to shout and yell at all of them. It is only tradition that has kept my country backward, muddy, barbaric. Tradition that no one may question the czar, that what was for our grandparents is for us and for our grandchildren. Her father was talking on. Tolchin was listening, but his eyes were fastened on hers. Reading her thoughts again?

The lights in the grand hall flickered and the roar of the chatter took a new turn as the audience made its way back to its seats. Sonya walked behind her mother up the long staircase toward their box. Tolchin had followed, stopping long enough to make his good-bys.

'Perhaps, Princess, your daughter will come back to the fold. She is so young, certainly. If only for her mother, she will at least change her mind and have a debut.'

'Never!' Sonya had almost shouted.

'Do you think so, Count?' her mother asked, frowning.

'Never, Mama. I have told you a hundred times, never.'

Tolchin smiled at her. 'In fact,' he added, 'I am sure of it. *Bon soir.*' Sonya turned her back. How he irritated her!

'I think' - Sonya could contain herself no longer - 'Count Gregory Tolchin is a fop and a fool.'

'Sonya Leonovna!' Her mother's expression was that of horror as she turned quickly to her right and then her left to see if anyone might have overheard her daughter.

'No one heard me, Mama, and if anyone had, what crime would there have been?' Her mother hurried her into the box and stood in its small anteroom, her shoulders besieged by little tremors that shook the ribbons and lace at her sleeves. With effort, she looked at her husband, who stood beside Sonya.

'Do you hear her? What am I to do? Her outbursts are intolerable!' Her mother then turned and entered the even smaller coat room to the left, dropping its curtain with great force.

Sonya continued down into the box and sat, her chin jutting forward, her eyes blank.

'Sonyasha, you must restrain yourself. Your mother is easily upset.' Her father sat beside her, fingering the program nervously.

'How happy she would be if I were Natasha Borissovna or Anastasia Pavlova, all simpers and smiles. How it would please her if all I ever did was to roll my eyes at every fellow who happened by.'

'You are quite wrong. She wants you exactly as you are. Perhaps just a bit more, shall we say, soft?' He smiled at his daughter. 'Now go, go and apologize to her.'

'But I have nothing to apologize for! Count Tolchin is just a dressed-up puppet!'

'Sonya Leonovna! You will do what I tell you!'

'Papa, am I forever to be treated as a child? We both know Mama is just in that room looking in the mirror and attending to her face! I only gave her an excuse to do what she wanted to do!'

Now the general's eyes were fierce and his voice was a low roll of thunder. 'You will apologize to her this instant. I will deal with you later. I will not abide your insolence!'

She stood up, her skin burning. Oh, if they only knew

what she really thought, these backward people who were her parents! She walked up the stairs, shaking with fury. 'Tradition, form,' she mumbled. 'I will blow those things to hell. Next year at the university, I will have my chance. Then the devil will take them all! Everyone in the theater will be blown to bits. Their fancy dresses and evening wear will be burning shrouds!'

'Mama?' She stood outside the cloakroom, trying to steady her tremulous voice. Her unexpected frustration had produced a wash of tears. 'Mama, I'm sorry. Please forgive me.'

The red curtain was flung aside and her mother stood in front of her, stern as a guard. 'I forgive you, Sonya Leonovna. I can only hope such an outburst will not occur again.' She leaned forward for Sonya's kiss. She had repinned her hair and brightened her color. Sonya kissed the offered cheek.

8

Often Sonya arose early in the morning, long before anyone but the servants were awake. Since Marushka's death, she had not known the meaning of that expression 'sweet dreams.' Hers were sour, melodramatic nightmares from which she usually awoke breathless and perspiring. That morning she did not wait to rid herself of the residue of her terrible dream. She decided to walk along the river. She dressed quickly and slipped out of the house.

Even in the darkness of that winter day, even as her breath ripped out of her in the furious cold, the river seemed to calm her. She walked slowly, surprised when thick flakes of snow seemed to come from nowhere. She usually knew the precise moment when a storm would come, but this one had come suddenly, and in no time her great fur coat and hat, her shawl and her face, even her eyelashes were covered in snow. Immediately, she turned to make her way back to her house before she would not be able to see her hand in front of her face. She noticed a man in a gray cape leaning against the embankment watching her, but she took no notice until he left his place and began to walk toward her. She began to run. It was too early in the morning to cry out. No one would hear her, no one was on the street.

'Sonya Leonovna Poliakova.' She heard him calling her. 'Sonya Leonovna.'

She stopped where she was and waited for him to approach her. He came closer, his great fur cape covering him completely. He was a mass of white fur. A man as tall as a walking bear with soft blue eyes peering out from his heavily wrapped and protected face.

His hand darted out from beneath the great cape, and for a moment she thought it held a knife. Instead, it was a letter he thrust into the creases of her folded arms. And then he ran away, moving quickly out of sight in the swirling, thickly falling snow.

She went home immediately and read it in the outer hall.

My Darling Sonya,

Has it been three years since I left you? I still fight for our cause. I am hunted. I work here and abroad. I am with the man known as Chernov. We shall win, my Sonya. One by one the villains will fall.

Are you still with us? Do you still believe in a free Russia, great and whole and at last belonging to her people? Do you still yearn for freedom? For the end of tyranny?

Someday you shall ride that great horse down the free streets of Moscow. Women and children will sing and throw flowers for you. Men will take off their hats to you. You will be their equal.

Help us, Sonya! I must ask you to do a difficult task for us. Please, Sonya, marry Count Gregory Tolchin. We have heard that he has expressed interest in you. We need help in observing and controlling this despicable man. With one step like that we can save the lives of our comrades and gain ten steps toward revolution. Please, my darling red flower. I ask so much of you, I know. Forgive me.

Your loving brother,
Bruno

For a moment after reading the letter everything was a blank. She was not faint. It was, instead, as if all her systems paused in surprise. Her mind and body stopped working. It lasted only a moment. When she again felt the blood pumping through her heart and into her head, it was with great speed and power. Her systems were energized. Her mind active. Tolchin, Tolchin, Tolchin. My God. They were after him, and she would help them get him. How wonderful! She knew immediately what she would do. Taking the stairs two at a time, racing down the halls to her mother's room, she knocked impatiently and opened the door without even waiting for her mother's reply.

'Mama,' she cried, 'I am going to make the most sensational debut in Petersburg.'

*   *   *

Her gown was the palest off-white. The satin clung to her, hugging her waist and accentuating her bosom. When she walked, the weight of the fabric slowed her, made her feel luxurious, as if she were wading through heavy cream. Her auburn hair was swept up into a crown made of lace, embroidered with seed pearls, which held fresh lilies of the valley. There were more lilies embroidered in the lace at the wrists and around her chest and throat. As Sonya stared at herself in the full-length mirror on the front of the cherry armoire, the slant of the sun's last rays hit the wood with a pinky color so that she was framed in a glowing auburn that matched her hair. The lilies in her hair and the pearls at her neck and the rich sheen of the fabric accentuated her golden skin. Her body was long, feminine, but undeniably strong. She looked older than her eighteen years. There was a presence about her. Sonya looked at herself, exploring her reflection. I am beautiful, she thought. How nice to be exactly the way one wants oneself to be.

'What are you smiling at?' Her mother was sitting across the room at her dressing table and had seen her in the mirror.

Sonya spun around. 'At myself,' she said to her mother's back.

Her mother twisted around and leaned into her chair, looking over at Sonya. 'I worry about you, my Sonyenka,' she said.

Sonya stared at her. Their lines of communication were nonexistent. In just a simple conversation Sonya had always felt her mother advance and retreat, advance and retreat, so that there was never any real commitment. Now, for a second, she had felt her mother advance on her in a great swoop. For a moment she felt vulnerable under the scrutiny of those hazel eyes. But then came the retreat, as she knew it would. Nothing. They had nothing to say to one another. I will never have children, she thought. Sonya shook her head. 'You shouldn't worry about me, Mama. Really, you shouldn't.'

Her mother sighed, and the powder puff she had held slipped out from her fingers and fluttered to the floor.

'I'll get it,' Sonya said, kneeling down and handing her mother the bunch of powdered feathers. She felt her mother's hands on her cheeks, lifting her face to see it better.

'I don't understand you, Sonya. First you say you will not come out, and then we must have the most expensive, the grandest party of the season. For years you run around without a thought of how you look, and now you think of nothing else.'

'Mama, we have been over this a hundred times. I have changed. I grew up.' Sonya shrugged.

'No. No. There's something else. Tell me, Sonya. Tell me what it is.' She was staring down at her, still holding her face. Suddenly she gasped. 'Sonya.' Her voice was high, surprised. 'What are you doing? You can't wear those pearls. Pearls are for married women. You know that. Now take them off. What is the matter with you?'

Sonya stood up and walked away from her. 'No,' she said simply. 'I won't.' She smiled calmly at her mother. 'If anyone should ask, you can tell them that I am wearing them in memory of Great-Grandmama. She left them to me.'

Her mother shook her head sharply and started to say something. Then she changed her mind and frowned. She was tapping on the dressing table with her nails. 'I won't bother to fight with you, Sonya. It's your father's fault. He allowed you too much freedom. I warned him. You're stubborn. You've always been stubborn.' Her mother turned back to the mirror.

'Mama, you mustn't worry about me.'

'I worry only that you will frighten away all the eligible young men.' Again her mother's smile broke through her serious expression. 'But then, how could you? You are too beautiful. They won't care as much as I do how stubborn you are.'

She saw him as soon as he entered, even before he was announced. He handed his card to Petya with a certain touch of disdain, and his air of condescension continued during the announcement. He did not hurry over to the receiving line, as many of them did. Rather, he sauntered over calmly, nodding and chatting with friends and acquaintances, immediately graciousness incarnate. I must remember, Sonya thought, that he seems to be an actor.

Now he was at the beginning of the receiving line with old Uncle Yuri, and he was laughing. He had become aware that Sonya was staring at him. He was aware that between each greeting, after each handshake, she would turn slightly to look for him, and each time she did, their eyes met. As she jerked her head away, she wondered if he noticed her sharp intake of breath or the slight tremble of her head. She did not look back at him immediately this time, but greeted the next guest with an intensity that was out of all proportion to what she had been doing before. When she looked back at Count Tolchin, he was speaking to Prince Orlovsky and still watching her at the same time.

'Yes, yes,' Orlovsky answered in his high-pitched whine, 'the weather has been unique this year.' Orlovsky began his litany, re-calling in tedious detail the great winters of Petersburg. Tolchin watched Sonya as the old man rambled on. She smiled at him instead of at the woman now offering her congratulations. He continued to stare at her even as the woman moved on.

The man behind him requested he continue down the line, and she saw him kiss her mother's hand and speak a bit with her father. He seemed to feel no hurry to speak with her.

'Sonya, darling. Of course you know Gregory Andrei-vitch?'

'Congratulations, my dear Sonya Leonovna,' he said to her softly, so that to hear him she had to place all her concentration on him.

'Thank you, Count. You see, *enfin*, I am a member of your society, even I.'

'Time, my dear Sonya, makes cowards of us all.'

'I thought, Count, it was conscience.'

'What?'

'Conscience,' she said, and spoke the lines in English. '"Thus resolution is sicklied o'er with the pale cast of thought, and conscience doth make cowards of us all."'

'Ah, Sonya, you have caught me. Of course you are right.' He said nothing for a moment. 'Which dance shall be mine?' he asked her at last, indicating the little card attached to her wrist.

'The first,' she answered, her eyes never swaying from his face.

'Shall I write it on your card?'

'I have written it there already,' she answered, her eyes still on his.

From the first dance, it was a scandal. She danced with no one but Count Tolchin. By the second mazurka, everyone was staring at them.

'Do you remember, Count, the first time we met?' They were walking on the balcony off the ballroom.

'Yes, of course I do.' He paused and leaned against the stone balustrade, his eyes on her face. 'Lilacs,' he said, looking at her eyes, her nose, her mouth, her chin. 'I love the scent of lilacs.'

She stepped toward him. Now, in the shadows, she could see his eyes caressing her face. 'Lilies of the valley,' she said, smiling slightly, 'are my favorite.'

'You are very beautiful tonight, Sonya Leonovna.'

She lowered her eyes, then opened them slowly, looking up at him. 'I had hoped you would think so.'

'Careful,' he said, gently reaching around to the side of her head, 'you are losing one of your lilies.' He slowly worked the flower out of the crown. With his eyes on her face he kissed it and put it in his pocket. 'Come,' he said. 'We must go back. I will call on you this week and the next and the week after that. Then I will ask your father for your hand. We will marry on your name day. The months between will be an agony, but' – and he put his arm through hers and started walking back through the great French doors – 'I will manage to survive, knowing I will have you. I will have you, Sonya.' There was a strange little smile on his lips as he said it the second time.

Sonya lowered her eyes. She had been victorious. She had captured her enemy.

*   *   *

Sonya   March 28, 1900
Last night was my wedding. I cannot write about it.

97

Perhaps another time . . .

April 19, 1906

On the night of our wedding I had no knowledge of what was expected of me. After I had been prepared for the night, and my maid closed my outer door, I was left alone with only the echo of her laughter and my hatred of Tolchin. I can see the room vividly. Very elegant, with cut-gold cloth on the walls, an enormous four-poster bed crowded with feather quilts and pillows. There was a gilt armchair and a footstool, an enormous inlaid armoire, and paintings of the Italian type with cupids and shepherdesses, and half-men, half-goats piping through fields. The ceiling was ornate, molded and frescoed. My mother had decorated it for love, but love was as foreign to me as the thought of my being married.

Tolchin entered through the side door within minutes. He had on a red velvet dressing gown and slippers with tassels, which struck me as very funny. Between nerves and anger and the tassels, I started to cry.

'It is not a human sacrifice you are making, Sonya,' he said. The words went through me like a chill. I felt sick. My face flushed immediately. My purpose was so strong, and yet I doubted. I doubted!

When he took me, my body played tricks on me. I was convinced of a sickness, a madness, a delirium possessing me to an extent beyond any that had been up to that moment imaginable. I left that gilded room and felt my body respond as if I were another person, a wanton. Imagine my shame. Even now I feel myself blush. How awful it was. That I should respond to him like a woman, like any woman. I, who was a soldier on the field of combat. I have never lived down that failure, that sickness, that uncontrolled passion. I am weeping now, even as I write of it, that night over six years ago, when I lost my youth, my ideals, and myself forever.

*　　*　　*

'So what do you feel, Sonya, what do you think? Or won't you answer me?' The voice was gentle. She knew he was smiling at her.

Sonya blushed and rolled away from him, over to the far corner of the bed. The smell of their act was everywhere. It shamed her. Her body was sticky and hot, and she wished she could wash herself. She pushed herself up on one elbow and felt her arm trembling with weakness. Off balance in the softness of all the feathers, she looked for her robe. A piece of the pale silk was crushed between the mattress and the bedpost at the foot of the bed, and she started to reach for it but stopped suddenly when she realized that her naked back would be exposed to Tolchin. Quickly she covered herself and fell back into the down mattress.

'I shall leave you to arrange yourself,' he said. 'Call the maid, if you wish, and when you have finished, come to my room.' He leaned over and kissed her gently on the forehead and then stepped naked out of the bed. He lit the lamp on the bed table and walked to the chair where he had thrown his robe. Sonya watched him. His body was strong and hard and thick, his muscles clearly defined. She could see them working as he walked across the room.

He picked up his robe and slipped it on, turning to face her. The robe was open in the front and she saw that part of a man she had never seen before. Quickly she looked up into Tolchin's eyes. He was still smiling.

'Have you ever seen a naked man?'

'No,' she answered.

'What do you think? Is it so bad?'

'No,' she said, forcing herself to stare into his eyes, to keep her head up and not bury herself under the feather pillows.

Tolchin laughed as Sonya blushed. 'Be quick, Sonya,' he said, and walked to his adjoining room, closing the door after him.

Sonya jumped up the moment the door closed, as if she could run somewhere to hide, but stopped, frozen, by the side of the bed. There was nowhere for her, she thought, nowhere. From the corner of her eye she noticed the spots of blood on the sheets and looked down at her body. There were streaks of blood on her, and she realized then that she felt no pain, as they had told her she would. No, she had felt only pleasure, delirium. She shook her head at that thought, back and forth and back and forth as if she could knock it out of herself. Her head pounded, and for a moment she wished only for a revolver, a shot through those banging temples. No, why? What did it matter what she felt? She had done what she was supposed to do. She had done her job exactly as she had been told. Tolchin would think she adored him.

She walked to the washstand. She would not ring for the maid. She would wash herself and then go to her husband and continue this confusing charade.

He was sitting at his desk, his hands folded in his lap, staring at the smoke that curled up from the cigar in front of him. He was still wearing his robe, but as he rose to greet her, she noticed it was wrapped tightly about him and tied in the front.

'Come, sit down,' he said, throwing an arm about her and leading her over to a settee. He pulled up a chair and sat down facing her, resting his arms across his knees, leaning toward her. 'So how do you feel, Countess Tolchinova, or won't you answer me?'

'I feel fine, Count.' She smiled at him demurely, almost flirtatiously. But her stomach tensed, and as she remembered, her head pounded again.

'Why are you frowning, Sonya?'

'Am I? I don't know.' His face was close to hers. Again, she made herself look into his eyes. 'I am not unhappy, certainly.' He cupped her face in his hands and stared back at her. She felt tears flood her eyes and trail down her cheeks. 'No, Count,' she added in a whisper, 'I am very happy.' She reached up and lay one of her hands upon his, smiling up at him, hoping, even feeling, that she looked lit up with love. His mouth came down hard upon hers and she felt his tongue in it.

He pulled away from her, getting up and walking across the room to stand in front of the fireplace, his foot on the railing, as she had seen him years before.

'This is how it is, Sonya Leonovna, Countess Tolchinova. I shall tell you simply, and then you may question me. It is a long story, and I must confuse you. I am sure I will confuse you.' He paused and walked over to his desk.

Sonya, frightened, watched him light his cigar again, slowly, puffing on it until it caught. He sat on the edge of the desk and stared at her for a moment. She looked back at him, waiting. Still staring at her, his eyes not wavering, not blinking, he spoke. 'I knew your brother Bruno in Kiev, years ago, after his supposed accident. I met him there.'

Sonya gasped and sat up straight in her chair. She started to speak, but Tolchin interrupted her, letting her say nothing. 'I did, Sonya. I knew him then. He was working with a group headquartered at the university. Later they were known as the Union of Struggle. Many of them were arrested and exiled about four or five years ago, perhaps you remember? Victor Chernov – do you know him?' Sonya shook her head no. 'It doesn't matter. He suggested I contact Bruno for my organization. He worked with me for a few months, but he was impatient. My work sometimes seems to be waiting more than anything else. He left to join a group in Moscow. I heard later he was in Geneva.

'He spoke of you, Sonya. He loved you with extraordinary tenderness. He spoke of you as if you were not a child but a woman, already grown, committed to be one of us, destined to be a heroine. He showed me a portrait of you he had taken with him. A young face stared out at me with much seriousness, and beauty, and innocence. You were twelve or thirteen in the picture. But there was no way for me to know, when I met you, more lovely than ever, there was no way to know if you were merely playing at being one of us.' He paused for a moment and took a breath as he tapped ash from the cigar into its ashtray.

'So many years have gone by since you have sworn your youthful allegiance to Bruno, you see. I didn't know if I could trust you. There was nothing I could do except what I did do. I wrote you the letter from Bruno, Sonya. I tested you in the vilest possible way by making you marry me, a man you were convinced was a traitor to everything you believed in. Forgive me, Sonya. There was no other way I could be sure of you.' His speech had slowed. He was speaking almost haltingly.

Sonya stared at him, unable to move.

'So you see, I am not what I seem. I find the despicable Count Tolchin as loathsome as you do, but I am using him to work for greater goals. I, too, want to see the end of the Romanov dynasty. You can help me when the time comes. I will be proud to have you work with us.' He paused. 'There is no need for you to be my wife in the biblical sense. Unless, of course, you wish to be. I know it will be difficult for you to understand that I am not your enemy, but your comrade. I am your comrade, Sonya. Perhaps now we may begin to know one another.'

Tolchin was staring at the stub of his cigar dying in the ashtray. Sonya watched it too as it flared up and died down, little pieces of ash breaking off and disintegrating.

'I am weak,' she said, rising unsteadily. 'I cannot think. I shall try to sort out my thoughts. I am too confused to say anything.'

'Of course,' he said. 'I quite understand. I am sorry, Sonya, that it had to happen this way. Whatever you want will be what I want. Whatever. Just tell me.'

'Where is my brother now?' She stopped and looked toward Tolchin.

'I don't know. He used many names after. I lost track.'

'Is he alive? Is Bruno still alive?' She felt that if Bruno were alive, perhaps everything would be clear.

'I don't know,' he said again.

'Ah, you don't know.' She nodded her head. 'I am so confused. If only I could see Bruno again.'

'The revolution asks people to do what must be done, no matter what it is.'

'Of course,' she said quickly. 'Of course.'

'I am proud of you, Sonya Leonovna. I must say' – his voice had become lower, and he paused, clearing his throat – 'I could be your husband if you wish it. I leave it to you. You are remarkable, even more remarkable than I thought. I hold you in the highest esteem.' He walked over to where she sat and kissed her gently on the mouth. His hands slid down her dressing gown, pulling it open and cupping her breasts. He stared at her naked chest. 'You have such beautiful breasts,' he said, slipping his arm around her and taking her back to her room.

Sonya   April 22, 1900

I am helplessly confused. My marriage was to be a revolutionary act. Now that my enemy has revealed himself my comrade, what is it? I don't know what he expects of me. I never hoped to be a new bride, and yet that is how I feel, as tremulous, sometimes as giddy. I wait for him to declare himself, not as a husand but as a worker in a cause, yet he chooses to be neither husband nor co-conspirator. Who am I living with, then? How long will I have to wait? And what of him? Did he act out of dedication or passion that terrible night? I shall never forgive myself for my abandon – with my enemy, with my enemy! Can I ever make it up to myself?

October 19, 1900

Still he hardly speaks to me, and I am afraid to mention the subject – the reason for this marriage. Tonight again we went to the Bolshoi with the Oblonskys. Either we are in the company of others at theaters and restaurants or he works in his study. The only time I have been able to find him alone is at breakfast, so I rise early and greet him. I try so hard for communication. Yesterday I spoke of the article on Jewish emigration that had been in the newspaper, I tried to discuss the new Chekhov play we saw last week, and I reported my mother's gossip. He seemed not to hear me. He complimented me on the color of my dressing gown, as he did last week, and told me again he liked my hair loose. He is so polite. He always stands and folds his newspaper and smiles when I enter the room. He treats me like a stranger. And I . . . God help me, I fall asleep every night dreaming of his body, his naked body.

9

The house her parents had bought for them from the Cheremeyev estate was directly on the Moika Canal. Princess Mariyenka had furnished the twenty well-proportioned rooms the same way she had furnished her own house, with taste and detail and no eye to her purse. As spring came and the ice and frost receded, the ceaseless slap and slither of the water against the banks of the canal and the strange atmosphere within made Sonya feel as if she were Ulysses, forced forever to ride this ship to some unknown destination.

'How charming you look when you hold your head like that,' Gregory said to her. He had been standing behind her at the samovar, getting another cup of tea. 'What are you looking at?'

'Mama had the heavy drapery removed yesterday, hadn't you noticed? I was looking at the reflection of the water that the sun makes on the ceiling. See there?'

'Every year when they break up the ice on the Neva, I feel it as an assault on my spirit. For me, spring is an overactive, whimsical child one must watch too carefully.' He walked back to the table.

She buttered her roll nervously as she attempted a rebuttal. 'I have never known anyone, Gregory Andreivitch, who did not feel so much more lively at its arrival.'

'Well, now you do.'

She put down her roll and busied herself with choosing another from beneath the napkin-covered dish in front of her. She could not understand him at all. In the spring everything was lighter, especially the air. Even revolutionaries should be able to appreciate it. As distracted as she was, she managed to enjoy the little springlike additions her mother was making to the house: gaily flowered pillows for the divans, pots of flowering plants for the hallways, and happy paintings of the countryside to replace the stiff ancestral portraits in the salon.

'I do not mean, Sonya Leonovna, that I am not captivated by the season.' He was smiling at her. 'It is only that spring takes my mind away from other things.'

'Oh yes, of course.' She smiled back at him, so eager for him to continue.

'I have been meaning to compliment you on your additions to the decor. The newest paintings are quite charming. It appears your mother and you have been busy.'

'My mother, really. She would like me to do more, of course. She is very happy with bolts of fabric in her hands and upholsterers hanging about.'

'And you are not?' He had pushed his chair away from the table and crossed his legs.

'I think much of it is a waste,' she answered, trying to disassociate herself from such trivia, hoping he would speak to her about what really mattered.

Unexpectedly, he did not excuse himself from the table as he usually did once he had finished his third cup of tea. Instead, he began to speak to her about his own childhood home on the family estate near Kazan, of its long winters and the simplicity of the life there, a life he sorely missed at times. He spoke not as he usually did, in French, but in Russian, and he seemed freed by that language, his voice more vibrant, more musical.

His descriptions were filled with loving detail; he even told her of the old torn Caucasian carpet under the unsteady mahogany dining table, of the dogs that dived onto it at the beginning of each meal, threatening to overturn the table with their exuberance and their ceaseless begging.

'To my childish mind, I related the activity under the table to the activity above the table. So much so, in fact, that on my first visit to relatives in the city, I was completely amazed to find that one could actually eat and talk without dogs between one's legs or their noses against the rim of one's plate.'

Sonya, radiant and relieved at this first personal conversation, begged him for more, to describe his parents, his *nyanya*, anything, anyone. She told him a little about Marushka, and he said she sounded like a

Pushkin invention. He said he had had no such luck with his nanny. 'Until I was three, she had so pinched me for my disobedience that I resembled a spotted cow. I would go to sleep at night and dream of beating her within an inch of her life. Unfortunately, she left long before I had the strength to accomplish that.' It was such a relief to be smiling and laughing at his stories. At last he had chosen to extend himself toward her.

At dinner, he even spoke of his difficulty with a subordinate in his office and prompted her for suggestions for that person's censure. He then asked her for her opinion of several articles in that day's paper and was in general agreement with them, nodding his head in approval. Her appetite immediately increased. She was hungry for her food, pushing it into her mouth, washing it down with wine, mouthful after mouthful. Whatever it was that had happened, she was grateful for it. They were becoming friends.

Early in May, while speaking about his education, he told her about the influences on him of Mikhail Sergozin, one of his professors at the University of Kazan. They had already finished breakfast. The window was opened and the freshness of the air was exhilarating, the noise from the street raucous and gay.

'Sergozin was the first man to point out to me that any country whose leaders did not speak the language of the people was a country led by fools.'

'My brother Bruno said the same thing to me when I was thirteen.'

'Until I was at university, I was convinced that what I knew of the world was all that existed. So simple a revelation acted on my mind with such force, I was nearly thrown backward out of my chair.'

'Was he the man who brought you to the movement? Who revealed everything? Bruno had such a teacher. How well I remember his name . . .'

'Whatever are you talking about, Sonya Leonovna?' The tone of his voice was totally changed. She stiffened in her seat.

'I . . . you . . . you indicated that this man, this Sergozin, revealed—'

'He revealed nothing. He was, in fact, entirely mindless. The revelation was mine, not his.'

'Then I did not understand . . .'

'To understand, first you must listen.'

'I was listening, Gregory Andreivitch.'

'Then you were listening to someone else.' He stood up and threw his napkin into his plate, kicking his chair away and then striding from the room.

Sonya was dumbfounded. Had she misunderstood him? And even if she had, was it reason enough for such immediate and terrible anger? She heard the front door smash like a cannon, exploding any hope for their new relationship.

All that day she found herself trembling. Her mother could not help noticing the flushes that came and went from Sonya's cheeks and the swatch of bright fabric in her hand that shook like a leaf in the wind. Just at her departure, Princess Mariyenka turned from the doorway and embraced her daughter. 'Sonyasha, darling, you must not be so upset. The first months of marriage are the most difficult.' Her mother pushed her gently away and put a cupped hand at Sonya's chin and looked at her. 'Men are so full of . . . well, one might say . . . demands. Really, it is the same for any woman. Soon it will be pleasurable, my dearest. Gregory Andreivitch seems a sensitive man. He will learn to please you.'

'He is very . . . sensitive.' Sonya's voice was as fluttery as her heart. What could she tell her mother?

'There is some price to be paid for being the envy of every woman in Petersburg, Sonyasha.' The gloved hand was still at her chin. 'Gregory Andreivitch broke many hearts when he married my little girl. Your cousin Maya is devastated.' Her mother's eyes were twinkling as she offered Sonya what she felt was full compensation for her wounds with an endless list of tormented, heartsick women.

'Oh, Mama, I wish he had married another!' Sonya cried.

At that exact moment, the front door opened and Gregory Andreivitch Tolchin, in his shirtsleeves, stood in the frame, appearing to blot out the world behind him.

107

Sonya's mother rushed by him, making excuses for her hasty departure. Sonya backed away from him until she could go no farther.

'No, I do not mean to frighten you. Please, Sonyasha, you have no need to be frightened.' His voice was very quiet, even tender, but still she stood rigidly in the corner of the foyer. 'I came here to apologize to you. My behavior this morning was without excuse. I have done nothing all day but think of what might have caused me to behave so badly, but I cannot think of a reason. Please forgive me.'

She looked quickly down at the floor, fixing her eyes to the rose marble flower in the center. The door was still open, and she could feel the breeze on her arms and at her ankles.

'I am glad to hear you say that,' she said.

There was a moment of silence and then she heard the door close. She looked up. He was gone.

That evening, he knocked on her door. 'I would like to speak with you, Sonya, before we leave for the ballet. When you are ready, could you come to my room?'

'Of course, Gregory,' she answered. His tone had been expressionless. She prepared herself for anything he might say. As she knocked on his door, she tried not to think of the last time she had been in his room. He opened the door and she followed him inside.

'By the way, Sonya, I'd appreciate another couch in here. I'm fond of this one because it belonged to my father, but it's far too short.' He sat down on the couch and looked at it, his left hand exploring it casually for some seconds. 'And it's lumpy.' When he looked up, he was surprised to see her still standing and made an effort to get to his feet.

'I would like to stand,' she said, motioning him to stay where he was. 'I'm a bit breathless. About the couch, what would you like me to do with it after the new one arrives?'

'Do with it?'

'You just said it was your father's couch, that you had a fondness—'

'Dispose of it. It has no value.' He stood up. 'Please, sit down. Here, take my place. The couch still has some little comfort in it.' She sat where he had been seated and felt his warmth on the cushion. Did he see her tremble as she sat? She looked up. His back was to her. He lifted a chair at the side of his desk and then carried it opposite her and put it down. He toyed with it, pushing it a few inches backward and then a few forward. Finally, he sat and crossed his legs. His right leg hammered a steady rhythm against his left, the heel of his boot leaving a patch of dirt on his trousers.

She was nearly hypnotized by the sight of him, by the swing of his leg when he snapped it forward, putting both feet on the carpet. She uttered a small cry and her hand flew up to the base of her neck.

'Did I startle you?'

'It is the way you move, Gregory Andreivitch. It is so sudden.'

He frowned for a second. He passed his hands over his face, his two middle fingers pressing at the skin of either side of his nose. 'I think I did too much hunting as a boy. There were all those hours of waiting, endless waiting, and then the enormous relief at finding the prey, at last being able to act. The relief at being able to act was far greater than the pleasure of the kill.' He paused a little and brushed his hair back with both hands. 'Sonya, I need your active participation in my work now.'

She did not restrain herself, but jumped to her feet. 'Finally! At last! What am I to do?'

He looked up at her. 'I shall disappoint you. It will not seem that what I ask is important. But I assure you it is most important.'

'Anything! I will do anything!'

'You must begin entertaining here at home. You must manage in a very short time to be the best hostess in Petersburg.'

'And?'

'That is all.'

'What!' She moved back, away from him, devastated. Her mind fought her rush of emotion. She remembered Nechaev's words, a list of instructions in one of the pamphlets she still kept. 'A revolutionary is merely a tool.' 'The end justifies the means.' 'One must always act for the greater good of the mass.' 'There is purpose to be found in every action asked.'

'I told you it would seem unimportant. But you see, for my work, for our work, everyone in Petersburg must want to come to this house. It is far easier to gather the information I am after in my own home than to have to track it from one end of the city to the other.'

'Will the people who come be revolutionaries?'

He suppressed a smile. 'They will not carry handbooks and pistols, if that's what you mean. Many different people will come.'

'Who are the ones who are with us?'

'I cannot tell you. You must believe that I consider you to be my ally, my confidante, and my friend. What I ask of you is most important.'

'If all you want is for me to be the best hostess in Petersburg, that is what I shall be.'

'That is not so easily accomplished, my little princess. You will need your mother's help.'

'Gregory Andreivitch, please, I beg you . . . don't speak to me as if I were a child.'

'That is unlikely, Sonyasha. I do not think of you as anything but a woman.' His eyes roamed her face, her bosom, her hips. The fingers of his left hand unloosened his collar button. 'What is it? Have you a question?'

'No, no. I was merely thinking of the time we might begin . . . entertaining. If I hurried a bit, perhaps we might manage a dinner by the end of the month. I could hurry things up and—'

He stood up slowly. 'That will be a perfect time to begin.'

'Good, I'm glad. If you'll pardon me . . .' She nearly curtsied to him but instead drew herself up to her full height and offered her hand. He took it and bowed over it, and she felt his lips graze her knuckle. She had all she could do not to break into a run.

*   *   *

Sonya   February 12, 1901
   I am preparing for our first party, and for the only time

110

in my life, I am grateful to have my mother's help. She seems to know everything – from where I can obtain the freshest flowers and caviar to which servant should pass the champagne and which the veal. The subtleties hidden under so frivolous a thing as party-giving quite surprise me. She has been overseeing the kitchen staff for days now, making them go through their paces again and again. No general has better command of his forces than my mother has of her staff and mine. She adores Gregory Andreivitch and asks his advice about everything – the time, the seating arrangements, the menu. She takes what he says to her quite seriously.

I rearrange the tabletops again and again, fly about checking and rechecking the silver and the serving plates, and I think of Marushka. How happy it would make her to see me so much like Mama. How thrilled she would be to see my mother and me like schoolchildren at Easter.

How I hate that it is all a lie, a lie from top to bottom. My husband does not touch me; my mother believes a fantasy. Still, who knows, if this party is a success, if I can show Gregory Andreivitch that whatever he asks of me, I can do, who knows what life holds for me? He is testing me again, and I must not fail any part of the examination.

*　　*　　*

Sonya's nervousness about the evening had finally lessened. The dinner was over. Everyone, including Maya Sergeievna, still green with her envy, could not have been more gracious in their compliments. The choice of food was sublime! The wine was superb! The order of the courses was perfection, the dinner conversation stimulating, the mix of guests inspired! As she watched her guests settle in the large salon for talk, Sonya allowed herself a sip of champagne. The blue-jacketed servants passed more champagne, brandy, and ten different varieties of vodka. Sonya watched her husband sit with a group of men at the far end of the room. Earlier, he had spoken mainly to women, notably to Vera Anatolyevna, who, she had been told more than once in the course of the evening, had been his mistress only moments before the wedding. Sonya wished that flirtation was not considered a great social sport, for Gregory Andreivitch excelled at it. At least now he was with men, sitting on a large couch between her father and Vashev, who was an adviser to the czar. Pretending indirection, she drifted toward him. She stopped to gossip with Princess Goncharov and compliment Count Voronstov on his new appointment to the Ministry of Education. By the time she stood behind Gregory, the discussion was at a boiling point. Vashev was waving his pipe in Gregory's direction, yelling at the top of his voice.

'How can you, of all men, make such a statement, Grisha? What other punishment can an enlightened nation give its dissidents save exile? We are not barbarians like the French with their guillotine or the English with their hangman's knot!'

'Calm yourself, Mitya,' Gregory said, spinning the brandy around in its goblet, first one way and then the other, as he puffed thoughtfully on his cigar. 'I am merely questioning the institution of exile. A sentence to Siberia is tantamount to a diploma in revolution. And why not? The harshness of the climate, the isolation and discomfort, serve to bind our prisoners together in a great brotherhood. There, they can write to whom they please, have their manifestoes published, read what they wish, and rail against the authorities to their hearts' content. I believe our government is entirely too relaxed in its attitude toward political prisoners. Surely there is something between our playground and the guillotine?'

Sergei Danielovich Youssapov, one of the assistant ministers of the interior, downed his glass of vodka quickly. 'You shock me, Gregory Andreivitch. Do you suppose we are a bunch of blind piss-ants? Don't you think our agency knows what they're up to? I say it's a stroke of genius to have our malcontents all in one place so they can be easily watched. And watched they are, believe me!'

'If only they stayed in one place, Serezha, we would have no problem.' Gregory did not remove his cigar as he spoke but held it firmly between his teeth. 'Revolutionaries are so many maggots, first one, then thousands. First one place, then a thousand places.'

'That is true, Gregory Andreivitch, but it is neither the state of exile nor the prison that spawns our revolutionaries. It is the university.' The general had joined the conversation. 'The very idea that education is to be primarily of benefit to the individual and not the state is an abomination! Blast the English for that infernal idea anyhow. Too many Western ideas pervert us! I am not one for going backward, but I see already that the cult of individualism can cause the destruction of the state!'

'I think the general has a point,' Vashev said.

'I mean no disrespect, esteemed father-in-law, but those in our universities constitute a threat to the system. They are nowhere near a majority. I think the great problem facing us is the rate at which we are industrializing.'

'Come, come, Tolchin, that is our salvation.' Youssapov took a glass of champagne. 'We already are ahead of the world in developing our industry. I see no problem with it.'

'Would you agree that our peasantry continues to be tied to the land, Serezha? Would you agree that most of those who are working in industry still return home for the harvest?' Tolchin's voice was pleasant. He smiled at Youssapov.

'Yes, but—'

'And you know as well as I the Russian peasant believes that he and God are joint owners of the land. Well, sooner or later he will extend that belief to include all that is on the land. Unless, of course, we give him something else to believe.'

'Such as?' Vashev put down his pipe and sat with his fat pink hands clasped under his belly.

'Such as a reason to abandon the land altogether. Better pay, better working conditions, certain bargaining rights.'

'The conditions at the cotton mills at Ramensk are a great deal better than those in the slums of Paris, Grisha.' Vashev intoned his words, trying for weight.

'Our best is certainly better than Europe's worst, but our worst is in competition with hell.' Gregory relit his cigar. 'We are already a nation of differing peoples, the Georgians are different from the Circassians, the Circassians from the Bessarabians, and so on, up and down the

113

map of Russia. In a sense, it suits us. There is little chance for these differing peoples to join together to upset the balance of things. However, every day there are more workers. Soon our workers will constitute a large majority, and their discontent will make them fearsome. The workers will quickly be a new class and, by its number, the most powerful one in the country. And they have much to unify them.'

'Come, come, Grisha, you are beginning to sound just like Count Witte. The czar makes us one people. We are already united by his office and his majesty.' The general pushed forward in his place. 'You can tell a unified nation by its army. Look at ours! Is there a finer example of unity existing? We are many peoples, yes, but our army is only one people, a living, breathing example of the power of the czar.'

'That is the most excellent point, General,' Vashev said, smiling.

'And what does my wife think of all this?' Gregory put his hand behind him and found Sonya's hand immediately.

'I think, Gregory Andreivitch, it is time for this band of isolationists to declare a moratorium on politics and join the ladies for more champagne,' she answered. Her father walked around the couch to embrace her.

'You have outdone even your dear mother as a hostess this evening, my daughter,' he said.

'Why, Papa, you know she prompts me every second.'

'The prompter does not make the performance, Sonyasha.'

Sonya turned back toward Gregory, but he was gone. It upset her that he had not had some small compliment for her all evening. She saw him less than ten feet in front of her, perched on the arm of Vera Anatolyevna's chair, in the exact center of a group of women. Old Prince Nicholai was the only other man seated there, and he was as adoring as the rest.

'Does something disturb you, Sonyasha?' her father asked.

'Nothing at all, Papa. I was just remembering that the English ambassador wanted to have a word with you, and he is just there, between those two Germans at the far door. You must rescue him immediately.' She pushed her father gently. When he had left her, Sonya took a breath and deliberately turned her back on Gregory. Calmly, she ordered more champagne to be opened, complained to her mother about the drunken behavior of the young Frenchman Nina Fedorovna had brought with her, and then chatted unhurriedly with Maya Sergeievna, who had given up her schooling to marry an uninspired, though handsome, architect from the provinces. No doubt her parents would arrange a commission for him at court. Slowly, and with great restraint, did Sonya make her way to where her husband was, sitting down directly across from Vera Anatolyevna on the loveseat.

'As I was saying' – Gregory looked at her for an instant – 'it is the women in a man's life that are his best teachers. My great-aunt, Anna Stephanova, who had blue hair, a wrinkle under her nose when she smiled, and even at sixty, many young, active lovers, was the best of my professors.'

'And what did she teach you, Count?' Princess Katerina batted her eyelashes about as if trying to dislodge dead insects.

'That it was unwise to become a Skoptsy.'

'A Skoptsy, Grisha? Pray, what is that?' Prince Nicholai's usually rheumy eyes were bright with mischief.

'A sect of holy men who believe that women are the root of all evil temptation and so, to avoid sin, castrate themselves.' There was a moment of silence before the laughter. The women fanned themselves wildly and pretended great interest in their jewelry.

'But surely you will tell us another of your old auntie's invaluable lessons?' Irina Nicholaievna, her cheeks still spotted with circles of embarrassment, touched Gregory Andreivitch's thigh with the tip of her fan.

Thoughtfully he lit a fresh cigar and slid it in and out of his mouth with slow deliberation. 'One can find truth only in the course of action.'

'But the Bible teaches us that the meek shall inherit the earth. Surely there is some little truth to be had in passivity?' Vera Anatolyevna thrust her body slightly foward and arched her neck so that her chin was only inches from his and her great dark eyes stared up at him.

'Alas, that has not been my experience, Verushka.'

'But you are very busy, Grisha. Do you find truth in all your actions?'

'I have found many truths, dear friend.'

'Many? Then surely you must be nearly at the point of exhaustion much of the time.'

'Indeed, my lady.' He fixed his eyes to her breasts. 'I find myself constantly searching for a comfortable pillow on which to rest.'

'You are a rake, dear fellow. No doubt about it!' The old prince choked on his wine, sending a foamy red spray out into the room and onto the carpet. 'And going on so in front of your bride, you should be horsewhipped! Comfortable pillow!' He was bent double with laughter.

Princess Katerina waited for the laughter to subside before she turned lazily toward Sonya and took her hand. 'Your Grisha was only amusing us, dear child.' Her eyes were full of mock consolation. 'But you must know it is only play.'

Sonya felt a great pit opening in front of her and fought madly for firm footing. She would be the butt of no one's joke, especially his. Unhurriedly she smiled at the princess.

'My husband plays as well as any man, Princess. In fact, I often think it is his . . . playfulness . . . not his search for truth that so exhausts him.'

'Brava, Countess!' Prince Nicholai called out, clapping his hands together. 'You see, Verushka, it is, after all, the perfect match. She is not only lovely but so quick-witted! A toast to the happy couple. May they "play" for years!'

At last, triumphant, Sonya had the courage to look directly at her husband. He looked back at her, his eyes expressionless, and went on puffing his cigar.

At four in the morning, streaks of light ruffled the blackness of the night. Sonya was shaking so violently she could hardly manage to knock at his door.

When she stepped into the room, she searched his face for a hint of his surprise as he got up from the chair at his desk and walked toward her.

'I have been expecting you,' he said, putting his hands on her shoulders and kissing her sweetly on her cheeks.

'Expecting me!' She was outraged and humiliated at

once.

'It was your decision, was it not, Sonyasha?' He looked at her, his eyes moving across her slowly. He held her so slightly, yet she could feel the strength in his hands. 'I am glad you are here.' He leaned down and kissed her mouth, his lips soft against hers. He picked her up and carried her toward his bedroom, yet when he approached the bed, he stopped and only held her. He kissed her cheeks again and then her eyes, the tip of her nose and her mouth. Overwhelmed with shame, she thrust her face against his shoulder and tried to bury it in his neck. He kneeled on the bed to put her down, but she clung to him so tightly she would not be released. He turned slightly and sat on the edge of the bed, holding her in his lap, and while one hand supported her back, he reached around and took her chin and carefully turned her face around to look up at him. 'It is unbecoming, Sonyasha, for such a beautiful woman to deny her womanliness. You are a woman now, not a child.'

Still, she kept her eyes closed.

'Open your eyes and look at me,' he whispered. She opened her eyes. He dropped his hand from her chin and moved it quickly to her bosom, where he undid the clasps of her dressing gown. The velvet gown slid off her shoulders, revealing a thin white silk sleeping garment that hardly covered her. She tried once again to hide from his stare, but his hand caught her chin and held it. With only the pressure of his hand at her chin, he kept her in place until she stopped her struggle.

'Say you want me, Sonya Leonovna.'

Why was he talking? With her eyes she begged him just to take her as he had done that first night. This was torment, a kind of violence.

'Say it.'

She shook her head, her cheeks burning. His hand slid down across her and then it was under her gown. She jerked about but the hand remained, stroking her so tenderly that she said it, cried it out, 'I want you!' She threw her arms around him, wanting him closer, on her, in her, surrounding her. Very slowly he stood up and turned to the bed, and this time she let go of him and seemed to drift onto the bed. She was face down in the pillows, but when she tried to turn toward him she felt his hand flat against her back.

'No!' she yelped like an animal. 'Gregory, please . . .'

'Not so quickly, Sonya Leonovna. Not so quickly this time. Just stay where you are.' His voice was so strange, present and distant all at once. She felt the pressure of his hand lessen, and then he moved and she felt her gown lift slowly and his lips on the back of her calves, his breath on her thighs, and then his hands were under her belly, lifting her slightly, and his tongue and his breath seemed to be inside her and her mouth opened in wonder. His hands, his breath, his tongue were so insistent, dominating her body so that there was nothing left but to let go of herself.

Finally he rolled her onto her back and she felt the taste of herself in her mouth as he kissed her. 'You are a wanton, my Sonyasha,' he whispered. It was then she noticed that her gown was bunched up around her neck and she was spread out naked before him. Desperately she pulled at her gown, trying to cover herself. He took her hands in his and kissed them. 'I want you to take it off, not pull it over yourself.'

'But . . . I . . .' She was astonished at his request, for hadn't she already pleased him? Hadn't she allowed his invasion?

'Because my wife is satisfied does not mean that her husband has had satisfaction. Take off the gown and then undress me.' He kissed her roughly and put her hand at the front of his pants as he straddled her. 'Undress me, Sonyasha.' He was kissing her again. Her hands were so clumsy and her body was burning again. He had called her wanton! And he was right; even now she wanted more of him, even after what had already happened. She yanked at his clothes, pulled his pants down across his hips, tore at his underclothes until she felt his nakedness on hers. Then she was tearing at the gown around her neck, tearing it off her. What was happening to her? What had he done to her? She was crying out again, in ecstasy, in relief – in triumph!

'And you say you have always wanted to be a man,' he whispered, the rhythm of him in her deliberate and steady. 'Are you at least grateful to be a woman at last?'

'Oh, God, yes. Yes,' she moaned. 'Oh, God, Gregory.'

'My wanton,' he said, kissing her shoulders, kissing her ears and her neck, 'how perfect you are!'

*   *   *

Sonya   March 15, 1901

Since my marriage to Gregory Andreivitch, many people have spoken to me about his father. According to all of them, Count André Alexandreivitch Tolchin died peacefully in his sleep at the age of sixty-three and is buried on what was the family estate in Kazan province. Yet this morning Grisha told me his father was executed by the czar. It was the very first time I have seen him weep, and weep he did as he told me of his father, that he was the embodiment of grace and goodness and had spent his entire life in the service of others, for which he was arrested and executed by the czar's police without explanation. Grisha's body racked with sobbing, his lips trembling, as he said that whatever violence there was in him was fathered by the violence of the czar against his father, that he would not rest until that office was wiped from the face of the earth.

I don't know what to believe about him, and I would swear that he delights in my confusion.

The same is true in our lovemaking. I feel he is serious yet I feel he plays with me . . . At least he honors my wish that there be no children. It doesn't matter, none of it matters. Why do I even try to understand it?

10

At first she was too frightened to move. A hand had shaken her from sleep and then had gone over her mouth so she could hardly breathe, could only thrash about under its force.

'Shh, quiet. It's me.'

'Grisha?' Her unbelieving voice came out like a growl between his fingers, and her eyes fought blackness to see his face. Earlier that evening they had made love, and when he had left, she had immediately fallen into a deep, untroubled sleep. He replaced his hand with his lips, and her fears lessened. Did he want her again so soon?

'Sonya, get up as quietly as possible and dress in the clothes I have put on the chair by your dressing table. Do not light your lamp. You must be certain no one sees you. Then come to my room. Please be quick. We must make our destination before we are stopped by patrols. For the next half-hour most of the patrols are in the center of the city.'

In less time than it took her to wake up fully, he had gone from the room. On the chair she found a loose gray dress, a filthy apron, plain shoes and heavy stockings, and a shapeless black summer jacket. She dressed as quickly as she could, overcoming her distaste for the smell and filth of the clothes. Then she hurried to his room. He was dressed as a footman out of livery or a peddler. He wore a felt cap, a dirty white smock over tight trousers that were worn through at the knee, and dusty boots whose toes turned up to show badly scarred soles.

He walked to her, holding something in his hand. 'Here,' he said, tying a large cotton scarf around her head. He reached down to his boot and rubbed it, lifting his dirtied hand to her and smearing dirt across her forehead and up one cheek and down the other. Then he pulled the kerchief down low on her forehead so that none of her hair showed. 'Come,' he said, 'we are already late.'

'Where are we—'

'Just follow me and don't speak,' he interrupted. He went down the empty hallway and through a door, down the servants' stairs and into the cellar. At the end of the cellar, near the piles of ice stored there, he kicked at a stone in the wall and it came out. He lit a match and held it out. 'This will lead under the street, and across to a hidden passage in the Vrontovs' cellar. From there we will come out on the street. Go ahead of me.'

She crawled into the damp darkness and waited for him. Moments later he was beside her and the stone had been replaced. Lighting another match, he motioned her to crawl ahead of him. She felt wet stones and the damp earth beneath her fingers. She shivered at the thought of rats and waterbugs. Her head hit something and she uttered a small cry. She felt him slap her. An animal scurried past them. She heard footsteps above her, growing louder and louder, then the sound grew faint again. They had reached a stone wall. His hand passed her and pushed another large stone, which swung back to reveal a passageway. He motioned for her to continue and they traveled down a long, narrow tunnel with stone walls and a dirt floor. At the end was a door.

'Open it,' he whispered. 'Get out.' She was outside, next to the steps leading to a street. She got to her feet quickly and waited for him. Now he was beside her, and together they climbed the stairs and then walked down the unfamiliar street. Out of the blackness, a wagon appeared and stopped in front of them.

He lifted her up over the side of the wagon and then jumped on top of the wheel and rolled in beside her. The wagon moved quickly toward the other side of the Nevsky. He took a deep breath, sat quietly for a moment or two, then reached under his shirt and brought out a packet of papers. 'Here, take these. If anyone at the meeting asks your name, it is the one written under your picture. If they ask for your papers, give them over. We are on our way to a meeting in the workers' section of the city. If we are stopped by a patrol, say nothing and let me speak. Is that clear?'

The wagon hit every rut in the street, and she bounced

121

from side to side, smacking into tied bundles and narrow pieces of pipe that rolled with her in the hay. She opened her new passport and tried to hold it steady so she could read it. Under her picture she made out the name Olga Yakovna Zentzov. Olga. Olga. It suited her. Her heart pounded so hard that she heard it in the carriage with them. At last he trusted her, at last.

When the wagon stopped, he swung out over the side and held his arms out toward her. Once on the street, he yanked her into the shadows of the gray building in front of them. The smell of decay was everywhere. Out of the dark ahead of them a street cleaner appeared, and she nearly screamed, but she felt one hand clap tight over her mouth as the other pushed her forward.

'Good evening, children. You and the moon are the only ones out tonight.' The street cleaner spoke to them, showing his rotted teeth.

'There are cats in the alleyways,' Gregory answered him, taking his hand from Sonya's mouth.

'Then the dogs are sleeping,' the man answered.

'The streets must be clean, grandfather.'

'I do my best.' The street cleaner bowed slightly and began to sweep. Sonya followed Gregory into the court-yard of the building. How strange – but of course, the old man must be a sentry.

'Does he guard the door?' she asked. Tolchin did not answer her. He had made his way to the farthest door and entered the hallway. She followed him in and up two flights of steps. Now he moved along the narrow hall, stopping at the second floor. Tolchin listened for a moment and then tapped twice. The door opened a crack, and then wide. She followed Tolchin and the man who had opened the door through a sparsely furnished room down a hallway to the back of the apartment. The stranger opened a door for them and they came into a dim hole of a room. The dark shades were drawn, and the only illumination came from a small lamp on the pine table. Even the lamp's shade was painted black. Despite the darkness, Sonya could make out seven others, five men and two women. For a moment, after their interruption, there was no sound. Then the man closed the door and a woman spoke, the one sitting by the table. The tone of her voice was like ringing crystal, sharp and clear. 'You are very late, Comrade Melinkov.'

'The error was on the side of discretion, Comrade Leader Tasha,' Gregory answered.

'For the sake of a woman or the sake of the cause?' asked a man Sonya could not see.

'That will do, Zubov.'

'A small joke, Comrade Tasha.'

'We are not here for jokes, Zubov. If Comrade Melinkov and his companion will be seated, Goremykin can continue with his report.'

Sonya followed Gregory, her hand at his back. He nodded her toward the only empty chair and, when she was seated, stood near her, leaning against the wall. The man sitting next to the leader began speaking.

'The proportion of women and children in industry rise quickly because of the recent crop failures. They are coming into the cities like floodtides. As they come, the men will no longer keep their ties to the villages and the old ways. Now that entire families work in the city, the children born to these families behind the cardboard partitions in the *kamorki* are a new class of proletariat, the very class we have been waiting for. I am here to report that Comrade Achevsky at the foundry has signed up seven families for the cause, the children to deliver pamphlets, the parents to work at politicizing others. That makes over seventeen families at the foundry. Comrade Petrov has enlisted eight families and three independents at the cotton mill, making the number of party members there, including Petrov, eighty-three. Comrade Pugachov at the shoe factory was arrested last week, and I was unable to contact his second or obtain any information. Otherwise, the news is good. Another hard famine and things will go even more quickly. There is some reason to believe that the educational reforms will go through. The government itself will provide us with the enlightened worker we need. Then we will show our fine czar how our "senseless dreams" are far from senseless.' The man nodded and sat down.

'That is so easily said, Goremykin.' The woman who

rose was obviously agitated, her head shaking and her voice tense.

'The Law of June second, 1897, clearly states—' Goremykin began.

'Law!' the woman interrupted. 'And since when does Russian law mean a thing? For a kopeck to the right man, the law is avoided. You are an imbecile, Goremykin. One bomb does more than getting a thousand signatures in your little book!'

'Our comrade Riga thinks of nothing but bombs. I wonder, do you sleep with one between your legs?' Goremykin glanced around the room to see if his remark had been appreciated. No one was smiling.

The woman, Riga, stamped her foot. 'Sexual insults again, comrades – now do you see what I mean about him?'

'Riga! Goremykin! This is not a playground. Sit down!' The woman leader's voice was firm. 'Let us get back to the matters at hand. Goremykin, according to your investigations, is the law being applied or not?'

'I can answer that,' Riga shouted, sitting forward on the edge of her chair. 'Yes, the government tells the factory owner he must provide time for the workers' children to obtain a certificate of primary education, but it does not order him to build schools. So where, then, does the child get his education? Where? From Goremykin and investigations?'

'Perhaps if the factory owners were made aware that a literate worker is more ambitious . . .' It was yet another voice, raspy and guttural.

'Ah, Shestov, please, please!' Riga mimicked his voice. 'Oh, yes, we must speak to the owners. They will be pleased to listen to us! When will you learn?' She slumped back in exasperation.

Now, from the corner of the room most deeply in shadow, another man stepped toward Sonya and Tolchin.

'I have a question for Comrade Melinkov. It is more important than all this slop about education.' The man was big and ugly as a boar. His hair was unclean and his mustache an unkempt gray weed that hung into his mouth. Sonya, frightened, pushed her chair backward, away from his side. 'Perhaps, Comrade Melinkov, you can tell us why all our literature is confiscated so quickly. Perhaps you know how the police seem to find our presses and our printers in a matter of days, often hours?'

Sonya felt cold, even in the hot airless room. As the rest did, she looked at Gregory. Only his eyes moved. 'Because, Zubov, the police are more vigilant than we are.'

Zubov moved toward Gregory slowly, his eyes bright and vicious. 'I say it is because we are infiltrated with police informers. Perhaps, even now, an informer stands among us. Who is this woman you so gallantly escort here? Why is it you are always later than the rest of us?'

'I will vouch for the woman myself,' the leader replied.

'And will you vouch for our Melinkov also? It seems to me that he comes and goes when it suits him. He does not work in the factories like the rest of us, he does not—'

'Zubov, we are not hunting witches. No one in this room is a spy.'

'But Comrade Tasha—'

'Zubov, we shall have no more of this!'

The big man seemed to crumble. 'I ask your pardon, Comrade Tasha. My brother, may the czar burn for eternity . . . my brother was taken today by the police and no one has word of him, no one.'

'I have word of him.' Gregory's voice was barely above a whisper. 'As far as I know, Zubov, he is unharmed. He is under secret arrest.'

'Forgive me, Melinkov, for . . .' He waved his hand about.

'You were within your rights to accuse me, Zubov. No harm has been done.'

'Since our Melinkov sleeps with the Okhrana, let him tell us how many of our people they have arrested already this year.' It was another man's voice and it came from in front of the heavily curtained window.

'Comrade Melinkov, will you answer that?'

'Nearly eight hundred of our people have been charged with political crimes since the first of the year. There are countless others, like Zubov's brother, under secret arrest. We can expect another thousand arrests before the year's end. By next year, you can nearly double that number, and

125

you can expect to do the same for the following year.'

'I say we rid ourselves of our fine czar or, at the least, Pobedonestsev.' The man sitting next to the woman leader raised his fist. 'I say enough talk. Action. Comrade Riga is right, action is what's needed. We cannot be treated like animals. We will not be treated like animals!'

'Comrade Panov, we are here for reports, nothing more. You know the policy of the Executive Committee.' The woman leader shifted her position on the couch, and as she did, her shawl dropped from her head and Sonya saw her handsome face, her huge dark eyes, her elegant nose, and her full lips. It was Vera Anatolyevna. Sonya's mouth dropped open and she tasted the dryness of amazement. Vera Anatolyevna turned to the man on her right. 'Tomsky has just returned from an investigation of the conditions in the Urals.'

Tomsky stood up and stretched and then carefully took off his spectacles, wiped them on his shirt, and replaced them. The brackish light in the room reflected on the wire. 'There is nothing new in the Urals. The average worker there works fourteen hours a day for less than four roubles a month. He is the lowest wage earner in Russia. While I was there, we tried short-term work stoppages to improve conditions, but we made no progress.'

'Who cares about the Urals? The place to strike is here in the city, here and in Moscow and Novgorod. We waste our time and our men in the Urals!' Goremykin hit the wall behind him with the flat of his hand.

'We should have a general strike!' A new voice thundered above the rest.

'Comrades!' Vera Anatolyevna shouted at them, but the chorus continued.

'We have enough workers already!'

'General strike!'

'Comrades! The time for such measures will be determined by the Executive Committee. You must lower your voices!'

Riga stood up again, her small eyes mad with feeling. 'Either we are all leaders or we are all led! Whom do you wait for, Comrade Tasha? Do you expect Goremykin to sign up Alexandra herself so we can all celebrate with a picnic in Khodynka Field?'

'Riga is right,' Shestov said. 'We must arrange for a national strike now.'

'May I remind you once again, comrades, our job is to organize the workers, not to make policy. First preparation, then action.' Vera Anatolyevna held tightly to the sheaf of papers in her arms. 'We are making progress. Not enough, but some. Our reports this evening show progress in organizing the industrial workers in Petersburg and Moscow despite some resistance, that the education of the workers' children is not being accomplished quickly enough, and that the police are active. You are all well placed, and if you are careful to avoid detection, great strides can be taken this summer. I can assure you that when the time is right, the Central Committee will see that bombs are thrown and strikes occur. Goremykin, you will meet with the man who has replaced Comrade Pugachov at the shoe factory and make that report directly to me. Until the next meeting, I bid you good night.'

Vera Anatolyevna tightened the shawl around her and stood up, moving to the door, opening it, and disappearing from Sonya's sight. The others quickly filed out behind her. By the time Tolchin and Sonya had reached the street, they were alone. They walked for a few minutes in a seemingly aimless fashion, but rounding a corner, Sonya saw the same wagon that had brought them. Again, he lifted her up and jumped in beside her. Again, the wagon clattered and banged its way through the streets, faster than before, as if racing the brightening sky.

Tolchin lay back on the straw, his head on a sack, his feet against the side of the wagon. His cap had fallen down and the visor rested on his nose. 'And so, my little red flower, what do you think of your first meeting with your comrades?'

'It is exactly what I thought it would be! It was exactly as it was described in the pamphlet my brother gave me when I was young. The woman Riga even looked like Sofia Perovskaya! Oh, Gregory Andreivitch, my head is spinning. So much happened!'

'Nothing happened.'

'But the reports! The plans for the general strike—'

'Nothing happened. I do more in one hour at the ministry to effect change than I will do in twenty years with my comrades.'

'At least your work in the ministry gives you important information. You knew about Zubov's brother.'

'Zubov has no brother.'

'But you said—'

'What you heard was merely an exercise, a warning to one in particular that I am quite indispensable. One of them was about to cause me some difficulty. Zubov and I took care of the matter with our charade.'

'Gregory Andreivitch, I do not understand! You say nothing happens, yet you go to the meetings! Zubov has no brother, yet you speak as if he did! Does everyone pretend? Is it all a charade? Is nothing true?'

'Sonyasha, do not trust the obvious so. The truth is elusive. Things are not what they appear.'

'People are not either. There are too many Gregory Andreivitches. Which one am I to believe? I look at you with the dirt caking your brows, with that filthy hat and your patched trousers and shirt! You even smell bad! I would pass you on the street for a peddler, and yet you are the same man who sits across from me at breakfast, who shares my bed, who works at the ministry.'

He pushed his cap off his face and looked at her, his eyes moving slowly across her face. 'There is only one Gregory Andreivitch, Sonyasha. And he is beside you now.' He smiled at her, his head cocked to one side. 'Come, lie beside me. We have a way to go before we are home. It's time to be quiet.'

She looked down at him. His eyes were dreamy and his expression sweet.

'Grisha . . .'

'Hmmm?'

'Were you and Vera Anatolyevna lovers?'

He looked up, directly back at her. 'I would never have passed you on the street for a peddler, Sonyasha.'

'Were you lovers, Grisha?'

Suddenly he reached up and pulled her down on top of him, kissing her. The wagon had found smoother stones, and they were nearly flying. She tried to wrestle out of his arms but he held her, kissing her with such passion she could not think or breathe. He did not release her until the wagon stopped. Then he immediately jumped down to the street and raised his arms toward her to help her down. In the eerie light of dawn, he looked like a devil, or one of the men on her ceiling. She had not thought of them in years.

They were nearly a mile from the secret door in the Vrontovs' cellar, but he seemed in no particular hurry. Together they walked through the still-dark and quiet streets arm in arm. It was as if nothing out of the ordinary had ever happened.

*   *   *

Sonya   June 8, 1901
   He continues to take me to meetings with him, but I still do nothing but listen and watch. When we leave, he is agitated, saying again and again that nothing happens. Save for these nights and the discussions we have afterward, I forget I am a dedicated revolutionary. Most days I am merely a grand lady making plans to entertain the best, most powerful people in Russia. And dare I say it? I enjoy it all! I am caught up in the planning of the menus, in the details of the clothes I wear, in the supervision of the household.

   Yet I want him to ask me to make an action. I need to prove to him and to myself that I can be more than a hostess, a wanton, and a wife. I am ready now to do something of importance, and I think he knows it. I must make an action! If I do not become what I must be, soon I will have no thoughts but thoughts of him and I will be a pitiful creature. *Sans lui, je n'existerai pas.*

*   *   *

Gregory Tolchin rolled over to one side of the bed. He clasped his hands behind his neck and stared at the ceiling. Sonya said nothing. She lay on her back, her face turned toward him, silent, exhausted, satisfied. He had been distant, and still he had been enough for her.

   Slowly he turned on his side to face her. The slightest

hint of a smile formed on his mouth, and she smiled back at him, radiant. He reached over and stroked her hair, then pushed it back off her face, sitting up on his elbow and leaning forward, his one hand holding her hair back, his other touching her cheeks, her neck, under her chin, pressing her, feeling her as if he were a blind man. He let go of her hair and knelt next to her, his hands now running down her body to her thighs, her calves, ankles, and toes. Still he pressed at her, as if he were molding her of clay, shaping her to his wishes. Sonya had not expected him to want her again so quickly. His hands were on her breasts now, outlining, tracing, shaping the nipples into tiny points. She turned toward him but felt the pressure of his hands holding her back, wanting her to lie still. She let herself give in to herself, and to him. Welcome darkness, she thought, welcome love.

'I want you to become Vashev's mistress.'

She could not have heard it. He could not be saying it. He said it again. 'I want you to become Vashev's mistress.'

She froze. Her breath came in short gasps. She opened her eyes. There was his face, the bones of his jaw working, his teeth grinding together.

'It is necessary,' he said. 'He is making too many decisions for Nicholas.'

'No!' she screamed, grabbing the sheet and jumping out of bed. 'No. No. No.' She ran around the room like a madwoman, wrapping the sheet around her, frantic, trapped in a maze of sheet. 'No.' She tripped and fell, frustrated, trapped, crying, unable to understand. 'No. Traitor. Traitor. Betrayer.' She freed a hand and punched herself in the belly.

'Stop it, Sonya. There is no place for self-indulgence in revolutions. This has nothing to do with the feelings we have for each other. I would have assumed you understood that by now. What kind of woman are you?'

What kind of woman was she? What kind of revolutionary? Hers was the reaction of an expendable woman. 'You must do it,' Tolchin went on. 'Vashev is dangerous. It will be easy. Sonya. I will leave for Geneva. You will meet him at the party for Prince Kartov. I am sure he will be honored to sleep with my wife. This is no different from your conquest of your great enemy, Count Gregory Tolchin. You did very well at that charade. You will do very well at this one.' He left the bed and walked over to the chair to put on his robe and slippers. Sonya watched him, the dim light making his naked body seem like marble. She unwound the sheet and got up from the floor, wrapping the rose silk around her shoulders. She went over to the chair where he had just picked up his robe, and she sat down. He ignored her and walked toward the door.

'This is different,' she said, her voice stronger than she would have thought. She felt lifeless, the blood drained out of her, her breath gone.

'It is no different.' He had opened the door, but now he slammed it shut and turned back to her. 'You were told to marry Count Tolchin, whom you hated, and you did it brilliantly. What is the difference?'

'Is this to be it, then, my contribution to history, my body? Will I roll bandages, too?'

'Don't be an idiot, Sonya.'

'Will I wipe the brows of the wounded? Will I let the world "*me fait merde*"?'

'We all do whatever is asked of us. This is what is asked of you. It is time to grow up, Sonya, and move on. Maturity is never what we imagined it to be. We all have to accept responsibilities we don't enjoy.'

'Am I one of yours, Gregory?'

The expression on his face changed. For a second she thought he was going to reject her totally, throw her out of the house, hurt her. She felt very frightened. But then his face softened. He shook his head. 'Oh, Sonya, how do you think I work for our cause? Do you see me running around streets with a gun in my hand? When I tell the minister how brilliant his plans are, or when I go shooting with Prince Ostrov and let him take the bird, do you think it is easy for me? Do you think I enjoy making them love me?'

'You don't have to do it with your body. It would be easier to do it with the mind.'

'Nonsense. I am betraying myself as much as you are, but it is not important. A man would never hesitate to use

131

his body, am I correct?'

'Yes. Probably.'

'Probably?'

'Yes. Yes.'

'Then what shall it be? You have always told me you were strong like a man. You will do it then, like a man, I am sure. You will have Vashev, yes?'

'Of course,' she answered. 'Of course.'

Tolchin did not mention the plan to her again. The next morning he went on about his business as if nothing unusual had happened. He kissed her good morning and smiled at her as if it were any ordinary day. He asked her to brush his jacket down, admire his suit, make plans for the evening, kiss him good-by, and then away he went, out into the ordinary world.

The world was anything but ordinary for Sonya. She hoped that he might change his mind, but she knew better. The day before he left for Geneva he said, in a voice as indifferent as if he were asking her if there were to be chicken for dinner, 'You will be sure to take care of that business with Vashev, when you go to the Kartovs' ball.'

11

Sonya became Vashev's mistress one year and six months after her marriage. It all went as Tolchin had planned. He had left for Geneva, and Sonya met Vashev at the Kartovs'. It was common knowledge that his wife lived mostly in the country, so society was not surprised that he paid attention to the charming countess.

Tolchin returned for a few weeks and then again was called away on business. Vashev met her at the theater. He sent her his card, some flowers, some chocolates. Could he take her for a drive out in the country? Of course. He sent her a bracelet of gold inlaid with pearls. Might he see her again some afternoon? Perhaps they might drive out to his mother's estate for tea? Of course. It was all so simple, so easy. His mother had been called away to her sister's. Only the servants were down below in the kitchen. Would she be his? Could he dare to hope? He had brought her a small brooch of diamonds and lapis and enamel. Of course. Of course.

The affair lasted eight months. Vashev, indeed, had been involved with the minister of justice in a secret scheme to wipe out subversives in the department. Sonya told Tolchin where the information was stored, what the information was, and what it was all leading to. Within a week there was a robbery that shocked all of Petersburg.

Vashev, his wife, who had been visiting him, and two of the servants were murdered. The house had been ransacked, the family jewels stolen. No one talked of anything else.

'Here,' Tolchin said, tossing the velvet box in front of her onto the dressing table. 'A memento for you.'

She picked up the box and opened it. The rubies and sapphires were so brilliant they seemed to burst out of it. She stared at them; then, after a moment, she looked at him.

'What is this?' she asked. 'A tip?'

'Rubies, Sonya. They are to remind you that there is

'blood on your hands.'

'Hardly,' she answered, dropping the bracelet on the table in front of her and holding her arms out to him. 'My hands have nothing on them but the foul scent of a man in the act of sex.' She left her arms stretched out to him as if she expected him to smell them. Finally her mouth turned down at the corners and she dropped her hands and turned away from him. 'I should rather be one of your butchers than one of your whores.'

He smiled at her, watching her. At twenty-one, Sonya was more beautiful than ever. Her hair hung wildly about her shoulders. Her high broad cheekbones were emphasized now that her face had lost its adolescent roundness, and her eyes seemed larger, greener. Her skin was unblemished, and even this new habit she had of turning down her mouth at the corners like a spindly old maid had not yet left its imprint. There was hardly a line on her.

'Why are you staring at me?'

'Do you know, Sonya, how beautiful you are?'

'A flea on a dog's back has no mirror. Why do you always talk about beauty when I talk about killing?'

'I don't know, though,' he went on, 'that I like the color of the rubies next to your hair.' He paused, still smiling at her. 'The fact is, you could never kill.'

'You lie. I could.' Her words attacked him.

'No. Too much emotion, Sonya. Your passions whip you around. An assassin can have no passions, no hate. It must be only a job.'

'I know how weak you think I am,' she said. 'You're wrong, Grisha. I will prove it to you one day.'

'Did you ever kill anything?'

'You have seen me shoot.'

'Yes, of course, at targets. I asked you if you ever killed anything.'

'I killed game in Dosiaya, when I was with Bruno.' The memory of it forced her to look away.

Tolchin laughed. 'Look at you, Sonya, even now you lose your color just telling me about it. Was it so dreadful?'

She looked back at him. 'I could shoot anyone if I knew he was a traitor. I could shoot the czar if you told me to, or the grand duke.'

'Could you shoot me?'

'What?'

'Could you shoot me? If someone else told you to? If I were a traitor? If I were a spy? A police informer? Could you shoot me? Could you?' He had moved close to her and knelt down so that his face was directly in front of hers.

'Yes,' she answered and took hold of his lapels, pulling him toward her. 'Yes. I could. I could. I would.'

She tried to hold on to him, but he burst out laughing and pulled away from her.

'Sonya, I say it again. You were never more beautiful than you are now. Don't you know your own worth? You are invaluable. Vashev would have destroyed us. It went further than any of us could have imagined. I always knew you could do this, do what no one else could ever do. There is no one in our organization comparable to you. Do you understand that?' He paused, but she said nothing. 'Remember that. Nobody is your equal. Why do you think I brought you these rubies? The rest of the princess's jewels have already been disposed of in Switzerland. It is sheer stupidity for me to give you this, but it is a tribute. You must understand that I meant what I said before. There is blood on your hands. Let the rubies remind you of it. Here.' He crossed over to her and knelt down again. 'Let me put them on your wrist.' She watched him as he lifted the fiery bracelet. 'There, Sonya, real Romanov blood. I am proud of you.'

He leaned over to her and kissed her hard on her mouth, until his teeth scraped against hers. For a moment she fought him, and then she gave in.

*　　*　　*

Sonya   May 25, 1902

I wonder how I can live, I am so torn by conflict. I live from one moment to the next. The sun shining in the morning. Sweet rolls on the table. The kitten climbing up my leg. My world has become only the momentary world of the senses. I am drinking too much. I have taught myself to play Beethoven's 'Moonlight Sonata' on the piano. I play it over and over. I will never get it right . . . Tonight at the Pleneminkovs' musicale I nearly screamed out. What a dumb joke. Could Grisha be right? If I had killed Vashev with a knife the consequences would be the same.

The worst terror of selling one's soul, the most indescribable foulness of ignoring one's deepest beliefs and contradicting the purest instincts of one's own heart, is simply, that it all can be forgotten. Self-betrayal can be forgotten. Principles can be forgotten. Then what can matter at all? If I betray myself, and then forget that I have done so, what is left? What is holy?

* * *

It took her longer to seduce General Krepov, whose wife was far less tolerant and whose position was more demanding. His information was also far more difficult to obtain, and it was almost a year before his riding accident. He was found on April 19, 1904, with his neck cleanly broken at the edge of a trail on his Kazan estate, his horse grazing peacefully in the field nearby. Hardly anyone paid attention to his grieving widow when she insisted that a general of the czar's cavalry who had spent his entire life on horseback would never have been thrown by such a gentle horse, on such a simple jump.

* * *

Sonya   May 12, 1904
Last night Grisha and I went with Prince and Princess Schertsky and the Golkonskys to see the new production of Maxim Gorky's *The Lower Depths*. It was wonderful, but our little group did not receive the play well at all. It must be too depressing for these dilettantes. No wonder the censors give the theater such trouble. This play might even be construed as revolutionary. Konstantin Stanislavsky was too effete as the gambler. He should have made a better baron. I might have been an actress, in spite of its being such a silly, unrewarding occupation. I think I could have played a better prostitute tonight than even the

extraordinary Olga Knipper - but then, of course, I shouldn't have had to act.

* * *

'Grisha, don't you think it crazy, don't you think it odd, don't you think that anybody will notice that everyone whom Sonya has an affair with, who goes near Sonya Leonovna, Countess Tolchinova, dies in some mysterious way immediately thereafter?' It was late at night.

'You are drinking too much, Sonya.'

'Only at home, my dear heart, only at home. The world still sees the innocent countess. I am a marvelous actor - nearly as good as you. You don't appreciate me enough, Grisha.'

'You are wrong. I appreciate you more than you could imagine.'

'Really, though, I can hear them whispering, "Don't go near the countess if you know what's good for you. Beware, beware."' She put her finger over her mouth and gestured grandly for him to be silent. 'Shh. Shh.'

'I hate it when you drink.'

'Good!' she answered quickly, straightening up. 'I do it so you hate it.'

'Will you ever make peace with me, Sonya?'

'Only after I make peace with myself, and that would seem impossible. I gave myself to some man and he is killed. You know what I am like? What is the name of that spider? The one that eats its mate? That is what I am like.'

'You will be of no use to anybody if you keep drinking.'

'It makes life a little easier, that is all. I certainly don't need it.'

The next morning she woke up with a terrible headache. She dressed quickly and went down to the study to find the bottle of vodka she had hidden there. As she walked she could feel it already in her body, warming her, the fire of it caressing her throat and chest, scorching away the knots in her stomach, bringing her peace. She almost flew to the cabinet.

'My poor Sonya feels so sorry for herself.'

'What!' She snapped her head around and saw him

137

silhouetted against the window. She had been miles away. His intrusion made her shake.

'Your lips give you away. They twitch. Twitch, twitch, like a little mouse.'

'I thought you would be gone.'

'Of course you did. But I have stayed to have breakfast with you. Come.' He walked toward her, his arm extended. He led her into the dining room. The table was set for a light meal and the samovar was going. 'Sit down. Would you like a roll?' He arranged a plate for her from the sideboard and brought it to her. 'Tea or coffee?'

'Tea, please,' she answered, her hands quivering.

'A rat, perhaps,' he said, giving her the tea and sitting across from her.

'What?'

'The twitching, Sonya. Like a rat.' He leaned over and picked up the newspaper lying on a tray at his elbow. Sonya watched him read.

'Listen to me a moment,' she said finally.

'I always listen, Sonya.'

'Put the newspaper down.'

'I can listen to you without looking at you. How many times must I tell you that?' He dipped his roll into his coffee. She watched the sugar slowly dissolve and drip down into his cup. He took a bite.

'You disparage me too much, Gregory.'

He swallowed and cleared his throat. 'That is a lie, Sonya.'

'You have put me in a terrible position.'

'Sonya, I think this morning the newspaper is much more to the point than you are.'

'This is not how I imagined my life.'

'I can tell you, Sonya,' he said, folding the paper with force and smacking it down on the table, 'that it is not how I imagined mine, either. I shall come to the point. I have thrown away your liquor. I have thrown away every bottle of liquor in this house. Anyone who calls will be turned away. I will be with you, Sonya, night and day, for the next week until that lovely mouth of yours stops its twitching and those lips are no longer dry and your hands stop trembling. We have important work for you, Sonya

Leonovna, and I will not let you destroy yourself or me. I need you. It never occurred to me that you would carry all this drama so far. I need you now, and I need you as sober and strong as you can be.'

Sonya leaned back in her chair and closed her eyes. She felt the life drain out of her. He had taken so much from her. Now he was taking the only solace she had. 'Who will it be now?' she asked.

'I don't think you have that much of a problem. In a week or so you will be fine. There will be no drinking. None. So think about what the two of us shall do together for a week. After I finish my paper, I will be at your disposal. Anything your heart desires.'

The first day, that day, it was awkward. They walked in the garden. She was hesitant, a child wanting to please. She was angry, a woman reduced to this childishness. He orchestrated the hours; topics one after another were introduced and examined. He entertained her, he provoked her. As always, he was present and elusive. The next day it was less awkward. They spoke of where they might one day go on vacation. He told her about his first time in Paris when he was a boy, about the hunting he had done in the Crimea with his father. She talked of the summers with Bruno, of the man with the falcon. He might have been a suitor again. He was relaxed and attentive, a concerned husband caring for his invalid wife. They went for a ride in the carriage. The day was brisk. She felt as if she might be climbing mountains, her head was so light. He pulled the carriage blanket over them and pulled her toward him, resting his lips against her temple. The rocking of the carriage and the warmth of his breath were aphrodisiacs. She was his, his, the confident and attractive Sonya Leonovna. She was rediscovering herself, and he was her guide. He could make her do anything, even love herself. That night he made love to her and she was shameless, hurling herself at ecstasy and connecting with it. The rest of the week was so easy, so beautiful, a long dream in which she was young, young and loved.

It was the last day of that week and she lay lazily in her bed stretching her body, rolling this way and that way in the sheets full of them both, rolling and brushing her red hair from her face and finally holding up the pillow he had slept on like a picture above her. She smiled at it.

'You look happy, Sonya. Lovely.'

She put the pillow down on her stomach and looked up to see him standing at the foot of the bed. 'How is it I never hear you, Grisha, but you are always there?'

'Symbolic, I would say. Remember what you said, it is true. You may not hear me but I am always there.' He looked serious. She stiffened slightly. It was all nonsense. Nonsense. He obviously was going to tell her who her next lover would be. He walked to the side of the bed and sat down.

'I love you, Gregory.' She whispered it. She had not known she was going to say it. Had he heard her?

'I am leaving tomorrow, Sonya.'

'I must be better. Eyes brighter, tail high.' She looked down at the pillow. There was no joke she could make to lessen the anxiety. 'Will you be gone for long?'

'Yes. I must go underground, take another identity. I may not even be able to contact you.' He looked down at her hands and then to her face. 'Actually, people will say I am dead. It is necessary for everyone to think I am dead. For all intents and purposes, you shall be a widow, Sonya.' She kept her face clear of emotion and she wondered if she were twitching again, a rat twitching.

She stared at the tiny white flowers in the embroidery of the cushion on her dressing chair. Someone had made petals and stems and leaves with such exquisite and caring detail. How very patient she must have been to stitch day after day. Or slow-witted.

'Sonya? Are you listening to me?'

She looked at him for a moment and nodded. Her eyes snapped shut as if he had slapped her. Did he ever care what pain she might suffer at his words? He was leaving her. She sat more stiffly and opened her eyes to look at him. The morning sun played with his dark hair. Here and there were strands as red as any of hers or Bruno's, she thought. My God, it is like Bruno. Am I to lose everyone I have ever loved?

'The day after tomorrow you are to go directly to

Lopuhin's office at Police Headquarters and petition to see only him. It will not be easy; you must be insistent. Once you get to see him, tell him he must investigate my disappearance, that he must find me, that I am no ordinary bureaucrat. You will be inconsolable! You know in your heart I am alive! You will offer anything in your power if he will find me. It must be the performance of your life.' He paused. 'Do you know Lopuhin?'

'Only by reputation.' She shuddered.

'It will be very difficult. He is a brilliant man. He must be convinced that you are quite innocent, my Sonyasha, merely a grieving widow who will not accept the fact that her husband is dead. He will have received information confirming my death; nonetheless he will suspect you, even your grief. He suspects everything, everyone. You will win him over. We must know all we can about Monsieur Lopuhin.'

'And after I convince him I am grief-stricken? What then, Grisha? What am I to do then? Have him at his desk?' She looked at him, her eyes already full of mourning. He leaned over to her on the bed and took both her hands in his. His face was flushed and he seemed so young. There was such urgency in his body and his voice.

'You have begged to be part of this cause in an important way. I promise that if you do what I tell you now you will be! Your work and mine can lead to events that will startle the world. It is the most important thing we will ever do, you and I.'

'Oh, Grisha, can I believe you?' She clutched his hands.

'Believe this,' he said, his eyes direct and guileless. 'Lopuhin is one of the most dangerous men in Russia and we must have someone near him. Someone who can report to my men whom he sees, what he appears to be doing, what concerns him. I must go underground. I must rely on you.'

'How can you be so certain, Grisha, that he will choose me? What if he dismisses me? He may know about my relations with Vashev and Krepov.'

He smiled so sweetly at her that she was at once soothed by his affection. 'That would only fascinate him. Besides, he will not dismiss the most beautiful woman in all of

Russia.' Tolchin stood up and held out a hand to her. 'Come, you must get dressed and come downstairs. We must go over this again and again. There can be no mistakes. Not one. There are many details, many names to familiarize yourself with. Come!'

She grabbed for his hand and then dropped it.

'What is it?' he asked.

'When did you say you were leaving?'

'Tomorrow. I must leave tomorrow.'

'For how long?'

'However long it takes. Just trust me. Even when I am not here, you must continue. You are as important to our cause as I, from this night on. Do not question anything I tell you, do not question anything Lopuhin asks of you. We are only instruments, and instruments have no minds. Come now, hurry. We have a great deal to do. It is all beginning now, and we will make it happen.'

That last night their lovemaking had such tenderness. He stayed with her afterward, not leaving her bed. He held her for hours and finally fell asleep, his head on her chest. She drifted to sleep in a haze, awaking only when his head moved and his body began to thrash against her. She held him tight and began to tremble, her mind churning. The shadows on the ceiling returned, black and elongated and terrifying. She heard Marushka's words as clearly as if they were being spoken for the first time: 'As you get older, as you mature, as your body tells you it is time to be a woman, you will forget about the shadows on the ceiling and being a man. You will be a beautiful woman, like your mama. And life will be as beautiful as you are.'

Sonya touched Tolchin's hair, kissed it, burying her face in it, and then she picked up her head and covered her eyes to keep her tears from touching that hair. You have all betrayed me, she thought, all of you.

12

The next morning, July 16, 1904, V. K. Plehve was blown to bits when a bomb placed by the Combat Section of the Social Revolutionaries exploded in his carriage. Plehve, a rabid, anti-Semitic reactionary, had been one of the most hated and feared men in Russia, and there were few who did not feel relief at the news that the minister of the interior had met his end. What most of society questioned, wondered about, gossiped about, was the disappearance that same day of Count Gregory Andreivitch Nicholai Tolchin. After Plehve's death, the subject of the controversial count was introduced everywhere and the subject of his magnificent young wife, Sonya Leonovna, poor think. They had been such a luminous couple.

Sonya Leonovna Tolchin was seen daily at Police Headquarters after her husband's disappearance. She swore to all that she would speak only to Chief Lopuhin. Those who told her that it would be impossible, that he was too busy, were greeted with a face of stone and a will of iron. She must see Lopuhin. No amount of persuasion could change her mind. At first she was treated as a joke, then as an annoyance. Had she been a man, it would have stopped there. But she was a woman and therefore a child. Like all beautiful childen, she was, in the last, indulged.

Her appointment with Lopuhin was arranged for the late afternoon. Sonya arrived promptly. Although the weather was warm, she wore a dark blue bombazine dress with a small ruffle at the high collar, the only adornment an ivory and gold pendant. He stood up to greet her. 'Madame,' he said, bowing slightly, 'what can I do for you? I am so sorry not to have been able to see you sooner. This Plehve business is difficult.'

Lopuhin was a large man, even in a country of large men. He seemed covered with an extra layer of flesh that belied his strength and the extraordinary conditioning of his body. His face was round and his head covered with reddish-brown ringlets. His hands were thick and covered with hair. He resembled a boorish peasant except for his eyes, which were deep-set, oval. When one looked into his eyes, it was as if his girth were some sort of disguise that he could dispose of at will.

She did not wait to thank him for seeing her. She stood in front of his mahogany desk, swaying slightly but speaking with such a ferocity that he could not sit himself nor take his eyes from hers.

'Please help me, your honor! My husband is missing and I know he is in danger, yet no one investigates, no one searches for him! And now there are such terrible rumors – that he was killed by the people who killed the minister! Oh, you must help me to find him! He is not dead! I know he is not dead!' Overcome with emotion, she pressed her handkerchief to her mouth and then to her eyes, which filled again and again with tears, soaking her small lace handkerchief.

'My dear lady, let me help you!' Lopuhin walked quickly to her side and guided her to the armchair facing his desk. 'I know how you must feel! Indeed I do.'

'Is there any news of my husband?'

'But I was assured that you had been told!'

'I have been told nothing!'

'Oh.' He hesitated a moment. 'We . . . we have reason to believe our dear Gregory Andreivitch has been killed by those same anarchists who killed Plehve.' He watched her face. 'Of course, he may have escaped. Yes . . . but it is unlikely. Still, he is a clever man. We are doing all we can to run those criminals down. All we can. No punishment would be severe enough!'

Sonya put her head back against the top of the chair and watched Lopuhin. Agitated, he spoke more quickly. 'How dreadful. You were hoping for other news. I wish I had something more hopeful to tell you. I thought they had told you. I loved him myself. It was he - perhaps he told you - who gave me the information that led me to this exalted position.' He waved nervously at his desk. 'Actually, it is you I should thank for it. Your information about Vashev and Krepov . . . I am forever in your debt. Gregory told me the lengths you had to go to obtain it. I

144

salute you, madame, I salute you!' Sonya's eyes widened in disbelief, but Lopuhin went on, perspiring greatly, seeming to bow to her between sentences. 'I see, dear Countess, you did not know how great was your contribution! But if it were not for you - and for Gregory, of course - how could I have known Vashev and Krepov were enemies of the czar?' Sonya felt the pounding of her pulse in her temples. Now he was moving excitedly back around the desk. He grabbed a folder and shook it up and down. 'It's all here, all of it! At first I was surprised that a member of the nobility would encourage his wife to use herself in such a way. The revolutionaries do that sort of thing as a matter of course, but never, never the nobility! Madame, you should be honored, and if it were not necessary for all this secrecy, well, certainly you *would* be honored!'

Sonya could not answer him. She was shaking, unable to stop herself.

'Oh, but I have upset you! Dear Countess, lovely lady, I do not mean to give offense!' He dropped the file on his desk and turned back to her. 'Grisha did not tell you I knew, that is plain on your face. Forgive me.' His voice was anguished. He hit at his forehead again and again with a doubled fist. 'Dolt! I am a dolt!'

'No, no,' she said weakly. 'No, it is nothing.'

'But madame, it is everything. I cannot risk offending you. You have became vital to our work, I assure you. Vital! If I might hope you would continue to help us . . . even if only to honor your husband's memory.'

'Help you?' A great wave of nausea came up from her core, and she took deep breaths to keep from heaving vomit at him. Seeing her white face, he ran from her and charged to his door.

'Bring me a cold cloth and some ice, quickly, man!' he called to someone in the anteroom; then, even more agitated than before, he was beside her again. 'If I may suggest, dear lady . . . your head, if you'll just put your head down below your knees . . .' He pressed against her neck gently and she lowered her head. I must not faint, she thought. Slowly, the feeling of nausea receded. There was a cold cloth at her neck wrapped around bits of ice. 'There, there. Is it better?' He was peering down at her, so concerned that he looked peaked and pale. She nodded weakly. 'Stay for a minute and then slowly, carefully, sit up. I will get a pillow for your head.'

She was invalided in Lopuhin's office, now propped up on a pillow, the cloth with the ice on her forehead making little drips of water down her face, into her eyes. Finally, she was able to sit up. He took the cloth from her, his hand trembling. This man, she thought, he cannot be the head of the police.

'I am well enough now,' she said, trying to square her shoulders, wiping at her wet forehead with her handkerchief.

'The trouble with life, dear Countess, is that it is never what we expect, eh? Of course, that is also its blessing.'

'Blessing?'

'You should have been what you were raised to be, a great hostess, a happy wife, a mother. And I should have remained what I was, a person of little rank. But these are odd times we live in, and we find ourselves in positions we never dreamed of. Obviously Grisha knew what he was doing by involving you, but . . .' He sighed and shook his head.

'You mentioned that I . . . I might be of help?'

'But you are in no condition, madame!' he protested. 'I cannot think of taking advantage of your grief! How shameful that would be. No, I couldn't . . .'

'But you must, your honor. I have lived the last year in the service of my country. If my husband is dead, I must go on serving his ideals or I too will die.' Her large eyes moistened with new tears, but she blinked them back. 'Ask me for anything, your honor.'

'It is a delicate matter, Countess. There was only one Gregory Andreivitch . . .'

She shivered slightly but her eyes did not leave Lopuhin's face. 'Anything,' she whispered, afraid.

'Your husband was a major source of information, and now that he is gone . . .' He shook his head again, sadly. 'We must continue to know what happens in the great and very royal circles in the city, what is being spoken of, what concerns our noble populace, and I . . . I have no access to such a world. If you, dear Countess, if you could tell me what is happening, see that I continued to be informed of all the juicy bits of gossip and carryings-on . . . I would escort you to the theater or some affair of state and you, if you would, you could tell me. With your help, perhaps, I shall find myself welcomed by your friends.'

'If my husband is dead, your honor, I cannot leave my house. I must be in mourning.'

'I am afraid that will be impossible.' Had his tone changed? His gaze flickered across her face. 'What I meant . . . it is not necessary for anyone but you and I to know Gregory Andreivitch is dead. Officially he will be missing and . . . you might tell your family that I have promised to help you, that I am your only hope. Everyone will understand your sacrifice is necessary. They will applaud your gallantry. In fact, your open alliance with me will make you quite popular.' The smile vanished as quickly as it had come. Lopuhin leaned down toward her. 'People imbue me with great power. True, the office is a great one, but as you see for yourself, Countess, I am a simple man.' He straightened up again. 'Oh, Countess, if you were but a few hours in my position you would have a high regard for gossip and rumor. They contain a spark of truth that, when caught, can prevent momentous con-flagration.' He folded his hands across his chest and leaned against the desk, his thighs pressing into the edge of the wood like Christmas hams. 'May I count on you?'

'Of course,' she murmured.

'Good! We shall go out together this evening. There is a gala at the Maryinsky tonight. You enjoy the ballet, I am told.' She nodded at him. 'I shall send a carriage for you at seven. I am partial to the color blue. It suits you.' He smiled as he offered his hand to her and led her to the door. 'I suspect any color but red would suit you. So, until this evening.' Surprisingly, he leaned over and kissed her hand with some grace.

That first night, after the ballet, Anton Lopuhin took Sonya to a small house within sight of the golden spire of the Admiralty, there to make her his mistress. Far from an accomplished lover, he was at least considerate to her and, afterward, admiring and grateful. He lay back on the small bed in one of the three bedrooms on the second floor of the house and made an attempt to arrange himself. Sonya stared at the terrible painting of a pack of dogs ripping into a buck that hung above his head. The room, unlike the others she had glimpsed, was moderately well furnished. There was a pleasant table next to the bed on which were files and a book by Tolstoy, *Childhood, Boyhood, and Youth*. There was an undistinguished but colorful rug from the Caucasus on the floor and a French side table against the wall underneath several bookshelves filled with books.

'Turn your back to me, Sonya Leonovna. I will help you with those buttons.' He reached to her, his fingers more nimble than she expected. He wrapped his arms about her and pulled her gently backward and kissed her neck, a fleeting kiss. She shuddered involuntarily and pulled herself up to a sitting position, her back still to him. 'I fear I have taken advantage of you, dearest Sonya.' With effort, he raised himself up and she felt his breath on the side of her face. 'You needn't say anything, but I know I have taken advantage of your grief. You believe that your husband is alive and I will find him for you, and so you are ready to do anything—'

'I am confused, your honor,' she said, her voice seeming to come from a very great distance. 'If he is dead, I have dishonored his memory. If he is alive, I have dishonored his love.'

'How it pains me to hear you say that. I wish a woman might care for me as you cared for him. I . . . I am such an ordinary fellow, I know, compared to him. How he infiltrated the highest echelons of the revolutionary party, no one knows. Very courageous. Brilliant. No other like him in the department.' Sonya still felt his breath as he leaned toward her. 'I know I am not his match, dear one, but I assure you I acted from passion, not without regard for you or your honor. Or his. Men are passion's slaves.'

How could Lopuhin know of Grisha's revolutionary activity? she wondered. Unless, of course, it was true that he was no more a revolutionary than Lopuhin himself. Unless Grisha was exactly what Lopuhin said and what she had originally thought him when she married him. She began to tremble uncontrollably.

'My dear, I was cruel! Oh, please, dear Countess, I could not help it. It was an act of love. I desired you from the moment I saw you!'

'I am nothing but a common—'

'No!' Lopuhin stood up, his eyes full of horror. 'I beg you not to think such a thing. It will never happen again, if you wish.' He buttoned his shirt quickly. 'I will get some brandy.'

'Thank you,' she whispered. She watched him walk to the sideboard and pour brandy into two crystal glasses. Everything he did surprised her – most of all, his concern for her.

'Here, here, drink this quickly. You will feel better.' Sonya choked back the brandy.

'Is it terrible stuff, this brandy? That is the curse of the middleclass palate, dear Countess. We who cannot afford the best like the taste of what we have. Unlike most Russians, God knows, I don't overindulge in spirits. This does me fine, just as, when I smoke, I am quite pleased with the rougher stuff. But I apologize to you. You are used to better. It is one of the few faults that I find with society the way it is. We of little rank cannot learn from our betters; they are as unreachable as the moon.'

'But surely there is no one in all of Petersburg whose company is denied you?' Sonya watched him drink. The brackish liquid caught no light from the lamp.

'That is true. But finally, I know as they do, that I am not really one of them. It is awkward. Even my son, who is better educated than I, patronizes me a bit. He is uncomfortable in our house . . . the little business of things, it is so hard to put one's finger on them, the way my wife and I handle objects or spoon sugar into our tea, those sorts of things offend my son. Rough edges catch fine silk.'

'It must upset you,' she said. 'Perhaps if you spoke to him . . .'

'No, I don't think so. What should I say?' He shrugged a bit. 'I am myself quite content. My wife and I are far removed from our beginnings, and so he shall be removed

149

from his. It is a natural progression. We are a democratic society, in essence. Of course, there is still the nobility, and into that one must be born - one such as yourself - but we of mean birth advance. In our way, that is. I have this house at my disposal, I have a carriage and a small dacha in the country and an apartment for my family. It is more than I require. Man is after all only a creature of habit. His habit is his love. Would you like more brandy?'

'Yes, please. It is . . . helpful.'

Lopuhin went to the sideboard again and brought the decanter back, filling his glass and then hers. 'I believe I have injured the very thing I so desired and respected,' he said, looking at her sadly. 'I had hoped we might become friends.'

'Your honor, I . . .' Sonya fell silent, turning her eyes from his, looking once more at the dreadful painting, wondering if the look on her face was that of the dying buck, surprise and pain.

'Please call me Anton Antonovitch.'

'Anton Antonovitch,' she repeated listlessly.

'How it pleases me!' He was smiling, his eyes beaming happily. 'I must not be the cause of any offense to you. I do not have the finesse to convince you, but I must convince you! If the small things I do and say . . . if anything I am offends you, you must tell me. Even when I am nothing to you but an escort, I must not shame you. I wish to be a comfort to you, not a burden. I am your servant, madame, believe me.'

He went on speaking, pouring her more brandy, telling her a story or two of his early life, rubbing her cold and bloodless hands. Finally he ushered her outside, carefully putting her cape around her, adjusting its collar. Walking outside, he hailed a carriage for her, paid the driver, and instructed him to take her home.

*   *   *

Sonya   July 30, 1904

It rained all day today. I am so tired. My head throbs so. The more I try to follow things to their logical conclusion, the more illogical it all becomes. What does he mean,

Lopuhin, this vulgar bear, what does he mean when he speaks of Gregory as his agent? How is he at once so innocent and so all-knowing? Was he prepared for me? Can anyone in his position truly be as common as he? I don't know anything for sure. I cannot write, my head aches so, I shall just do as I was told.

* * *

'Brava, Countess Tolchinova!' Lopuhin sat on the edge of the day bed, his great bulk overpowering it. He applauded her. He was so huge he made everything around him seem fragile. 'You see,' he went on, stopping his applause and smiling at her, 'I told you luncheons and teas were not a waste of time. Women can give you as much as men. More. More. They know more. What a waste for you to conquer merely one man when you can conquer twenty women in the same amount of time. My dear Countess, you deserve an honor of some sort. Go on, Go on.'

'Princess Nina Antonovna.' Sonya sat up straight in her chair across from him, affecting an air of wounded innocence, batting her eyes and pursing her lips.

'Oh, that's good, very good! What an actress you should have been. Go on!' He was laughing.

She curled her upper lip and stuck her teeth over her lower one. 'My husband,' she lisped, 'turned down twenty women waiting for me. He told me he vas frozen hard. That ven he looked out of the vindows of the train, all the trees in Perm reminded him of his vant of me.'

Lopuhin stopped laughing. 'I thought Prince Yuri had been in Paris.'

Sonya relaxed and leaned back into her chair. She picked up her glass and toasted him with it. 'Ah, well,' she said, 'there you are.' He smiled at her. 'By the way, Anton Antonovitch, I must compliment you on your new choice of brandy. Even the czar could have none better.'

'I am so glad, my dear Countess, that you noticed. I had the Baroff boy choose it for me. His mother was a Vronsky. I assumed he would know the best. I was right?'

'Of course,' she said. 'As always.'

'I drink to your mimicry, Countess. Do you have any

151

more?'

'You will forgive me, my head is beginning to ache. I can only tell you that Countess Brajanoski is available again on Wednesdays. You know she is the mistress of Baron Von Reimer. It seems the baron is busy at some sort of meeting an hour or two outside the city each Wednesday and has changed their trysts till Thursday so that he might have the whole day with her.'

'What kind of meeting?'

'Secretive. He will tell her nothing.'

'But of course he has told her enough. Men are such fools. They imagine the conversations they have in bed are holy. I doubt the prince or the baron would have told me any of that under the severest form of torture. Yet show them a woman, fill them with drink, sate them with kisses and they talk about everything. What else?'

'Only sexual secrets.'

'Ha, my dear Countess, those are far less interesting. Far. Far.' He paused for a moment and frowned. 'Why do you suppose women will talk so freely with one another? Why is it all just fodder for their gossip, for their friends?' He leaned toward Sonya. 'What do you think, my dear?'

Sonya laughed and rubbed her temples, then lifted her glass and drained it. 'I don't know, Anton Antonovitch. If nothing mattered, I might be like them. So many of them have nothing important in their lives; they give everything the same weight. Their husbands and their lovers are the same to them as a new gown or a night out. I suppose, too,' she said, 'that cementing their bonds with their women friends is more important than their relationships with their men. We offer our men as little gifts to one another. Once their masculine place in our lives has become assured, we have very little use for them.'

'I don't follow you, my dear, nor do I hope to. Whatever it is, it has been a godsend to me. As have you, my dear Countess, as have you.' He looked at her with such pleasure and amazement in his eyes that she could have almost believed he loved her. No, no, that was not it. She remembered the look exactly now. It had been on her father's face the first time that his new dog, the retriever Napoleon, had brought him home a bird.

Sonya   September 15, 1904

Today at my mother's a kitchen maid spoke to me. She is one of Gregory's agents. Last week there was a man, a blini seller, on the Nevsky as I went to the jeweler. As with all the others, I asked her this morning for some word of Gregory, begged her, and she, too, gave me nothing. They give me information to report to Lopuhin, and they listen to my report, prompting me again and again for details of whom I might have seen him speak with, who is working in his outer office, who drives his carriage. Things of such small significance seem so meaningful. When I ask them of Gregory's whereabouts, they look at me as if I am mad.

I am pursued by my suspicions. This man about whom I have always heard such brutal references, this monster, Lopuhin, so universally despised, is nice to me! He is chagrined at my slightest frown and attentive to all I say and do. When I correct his manner of speech, he is grateful! He takes such pleasure in telling me of Gregory's handiwork for the department, sticking it in among his conversation with such ease. Who is the Grisha that Lopuhin speaks about with such familiarity, this police spy, this police official?

My hands shake so that I can hardly hold this pen. At night I must have a glass of brandy merely to close my eyes and often another to endure my dreams. If only I might have some word of Gregory. How does he expect me to continue this awful and deadly performance unless I hear from him!

*   *   *

As Lopuhin had told her she would be, Sonya was constantly in demand, asked everywhere, consoled and admired. At least each month Lopuhin himself would escort her somewhere, always to a public event – the ballet, the theater, the opera. She was the scandal of all Petersburg, the widow who would not wear widow's weeds, and yet she was esteemed for the persistence and admired for her hope and her powerful liaison. She could hear whispers about her as she passed hallways, foyers, dining rooms, salons. Little by little, even friends asked her to intercede with Lopuhin for some small favor on their behalf. She was petitioned by Prince Bornov, by Protopopov, even by her brother Vassily. Never had she been so talked of and so welcomed. Was this power? Was this how Gregory felt striding through rooms, all eyes on him, all hearts beating a bit faster, all minds working to please him? Even tonight, as she and Lopuhin walked to their box at the theater, everyone stared at her, admiring her beauty, yes, but also her power.

Now Maya Sergeievna and her husband were bowing in their direction. As they passed through the corridor to the boxes, Prince Youssapov hurried to Lopuhin and whispered something to him and then kissed Sonya's hand and complimented her on her gown.

'I am so pleased you are enjoying yourself, Sonya Leonovna.' Lopuhin beamed at her.

'Anton Antonovitch, you know as well as I that I am here only as a duty.'

'Oh, yes, of course. But you must admit there are benefits to such a duty.' Prince Bornov bowed to them. Two ministers smiled and nodded. Sonya smiled back at them. How Gregory would have appreciated her. Did he even know? She had had no word of him for three months now.

'Do you know that handsome woman we just passed?'

'Vera Anatolyevna? She is a social friend.'

'How long have you known her?'

'She was a friend of my husband's,' Sonya said, regretting it instantly.

'Ah.' Lopuhin stopped for a second, looking after Vera Anatolyevna. 'Amazing man, Grisha, absolutely amazing. He had such an instinct . . .'

'Surely Verushka is not suspected of—'

'No, not suspected of anything.' He smiled widely. 'She is lovely, but no one is lovelier than you, dear Sonya. I never would have dreamed that life could be so pleasant, so entertaining.'

Sonya leaned toward Lopuhin as they walked up the

staircase. 'You must bow to the Princess Katerina, the large lady to your left, the one in the rose taffeta dress. You need not pause, but you must bow as you pass her and acknowledge the older Prince Nicholai with a nod of your head.'

He did as she told him and looked for her approval. She gave him a quick smile. 'What an instructress you are, my dear. Already I feel so much more at home among the nobility. Oh, I do enjoy it all. The lights are dimming, we must hurry. May I take you to dinner after the theater?'

'I am afraid not, Anton Antonovitch. I am very tired. My social duties require more sleep than I have managed these last months.'

He did not protest but graciously saw her to a carriage, making much of his good-by. The note she had received that morning from the man who delivered flowers had said simply that she was to leave the theater alone and order the carriage driver to start up the Nevsky toward Decembrist Square.

The carriage had hardly started when a door opened and a man sat down beside her. He smelled bad.

'What news have you?' he asked. 'What news have you, Countess?'

She looked at him. He had contacted her before. How many people did he contact each day that he found no time to bathe? She began to smile and then to giggle a bit, hiding her face in her handkerchief.

'I asked you what news?' His voice was harsh. Now she was laughing uncontrollably, her chest heaving with snorts.

'Excuse me,' she sputtered. 'Please, please, it has been a while . . . It struck me as a child's game, this business. My brothers and I would play . . .' The laughter died as quickly as an extinguished match, and no pleasure remained.

'Are you in control of yourself?' the man asked, looking away from her.

'Yes. It is only . . . I . . .'

'What news, then?'

'He suspects Vera Anatolyevna. There is more, of course. I cannot think . . .' The carriage was thumping on and on. 'He has men watching a house on the Nevsky near here – just there.' She pointed. 'He slows his carriage there each time we go out together. Since I told him about Von Reimer, he has an interest in something that occurs each Thursday, but he gives me no hint of what it is, only that he cannot see me Thursday evenings. I found a paper with an address in London, Scott Street, number seventeen. He will soon demote two of his clerks for incompetence. He complained of them to me.'

'Their names?'

'He did not say. Only that one is extraordinarily near-sighted and wears thick glasses, and the other has a mother he lives with who is dying.'

'Good. Anything else?'

'Gregory must contact me. I cannot continue if he does not.' Her voice was faint from exhaustion.

'Anything more?' the man repeated. It was oil. He smelled of oil. Sonya opened the window. Heavy mist seeped into the carriage and into every pore of her body.

'You must tell me where my husband is,' she said weakly, looking straight ahead of her. 'He must contact me. Send me word.'

When the carriage left the open square and entered the darkness of the side street, it slowed again. The door on the man's side was open and he was gone.

*   *   *

Sonya   May 30, 1905

Every day for months and months I have set out on my little rounds - this luncheon, this ball, that entertainment. And every few weeks there is another evening with Lopuhin. I am not censured because I have some power, and yet I feel my friends and my family looking at me with such suspicion. 'If only there had been a child,' I heard my aunt Adele whisper only yesterday to Maya, who is at least ten months pregnant, judging by how she appears, more like a beast of burden than a woman. And my brother Anton's wife does nothing but run on about her twin children, exasperating brats though they are. 'And how are things with our dear Sonya?' they ask, that awful pitying look in their nasty eyes. Well, I shall tell you, dear journal, how I am. I fare so badly when I am alone that lately I have found myself desiring this Lopuhin, this flea, this gnat, this poison. He is the only purpose of my life and my liaisons with him the only substance in a loathsome world. Surely Gregory is dead. If he is not, then he is a monster for not contacting me and I wish him dead.

July 28, 1905
I lit a candle today for Vera Anatolyevna. She killed herself after being sentenced to twenty years at hard labor. I told Gregory's agent she was suspected, yet nothing was done for her. It has been a year now that he has been gone, but no one brings me word of him. I was certain he would contact me after that terrible, that 'Bloody Sunday,' when so many workers were shot by the troops and police. I kept hoping that was the beginning and end of everything somehow, that this country would not let one hundred and thirty men, women and children be shot down in the snow and not rise in wrathful indignation. But so little has happened, some concessions here and there. The war with Japan has been disastrous and the government pays no attention to the people at home.

Oh, God in heaven, blessed saints, I am bored beyond redemption by my wanting of Grisha and worse, by my suspicions of him. Why will he not send me word!

13

It was almost two in the afternoon when her maid opened the curtains, and even the poor light of October caused Sonya to wince painfully. The bottle of brandy on her night table was nearly finished, and the breakfast tea on its server had long since gone cold. She could hardly sit. She heard some commotion in the hallway, and then her mother appeared in the doorway.

Sonya tried desperately to hide the brandy bottle, but it fell from her hands and rolled toward her mother's advancing feet.

Her mother ignored it, stepping around it, and continued walking directly to Sonya. 'I will not be turned away, Sonya Leonovna. You cannot be ill each day and then dance away each evening.'

'Mama, it is only that I am so often depressed I fear it will upset you.'

'My child, I must speak with you. It is not for selfish reasons that I do so. I have lived my life; rumor does not affect me so much any longer. But you, Sonyasha, you have barely become a woman. You can easily be destroyed by ugly words and ugly behavior. You haven't the liberty of a man to drink himself into oblivion and gamble away his chances. A man always has more, even at his lowest. Not a woman. Not you.' Her mother was still standing by the bed. Sonya's eyes had closed. 'I would not invade your privacy were it not that you have no one else to speak with, no one to lean upon.' Her mother sat down on the edge of the bed and turned Sonya's face towards hers. 'You must stop seeing that man. You must stop . . . well . . . that.' She indicated the brandy bottle. 'I know how much you loved Grisha, as who of us did not! But life must go on. You must forget.' Her mother took out a small handkerchief and wiped her eyes. 'Sonya, we must assume he is dead. Your husband is dead.'

'No, I tell you. He is alive.'

'Darling child, your father has done everything he can. He has used all his influence and he has been told that your husband was killed the very day Plehve was assassinated.'

'Then bring me his body, Mama. Bring it to me! I will accept his death then.' She began to cry, terrible weeping with no sound at all.

'I propose that after the first of the year, sometime afterward, on your name day perhaps, we shall have a grand party and you shall be reintroduced to society. A new life will begin. In the meantime, you must work to put aside your sorrows. You must sever your relationship with that crude policeman.' Her mother sighed. 'Oh, I cannot bear to see him touch your arm. How above himself he is.'

'He is a kind man, Mama.'

'Sonya! He is a policeman. A common man. Peddlers and fishwives are kind also, but they do not take my daughter out in public!'

'You are good to care about me,' Sonya said, the tears now stopped. 'But it is my life, Mama. I must do what I think right for me.'

'No, Sonya. Your father is at his wits' end. You must do what is right for everyone, for your father and for your brothers and their wives and children. We are a family, and we are disgraced by your disgrace. You must make up your mind to it. You must accept that Gregory Andreivitch Tolchin is dead. And you must bury your sorrow and begin again. You will do it for your father.' Her mother stood up, straightened her dress, folded her handkerchief, and walked away from her. 'Tomorrow evening I shall expect you for dinner. We will spend a nice evening at home together. I will expect you, Sonya, and if you are not there promptly at nine, I shall send your father for you.'

Sonya twisted and turned in her seat like a four-year-old, finding no comfort in any position. She had no appetite for the food or the conversation. Her father had started pacing around the dining room, leaving his dinner cooling at his place.

'Blast Witte! The czar would do better to listen to the devil himself. To provide these people with a forum and

159

with representatives and free elections will not satisfy them. History whas proved it a thousand times: give undeserving men power, and they will immediately think they are entitled to sit on the throne!'

'Leon, it has no teeth, that business of the Duma. It is only a small concession. The czar retains all power. It is nothing.' Protopopov chewed his food and reached for more. 'The war with Japan was a mistake, but we are recovering. As soon as the economy is at full throttle—'

'Ivan, there are strikes everywhere in the country. The workers already think they own the world.'

'Things are calming down, Leon. Sit and eat your dinner. It is a most sumptuous meal.'

'The next thing I know, my footman will sit down across from me. I have no appetite. We are in dire straits, I tell you. Dire!'

'Leon, please!' The princess's voice was firm. 'We are having dinner.'

'Perhaps, Papa,' Sonya intervened, 'it is not such a bad idea to make concessions.'

'Are you believing the drivel in the papers, then, my daughter?' He sat down again at the table but did not bother with his food. 'You have no concept of history. I have no quarrel with a slow progressiveness - education, literacy. But such rapid transition!' He shook his head.

'Rapid, Papa? Surely you cannot mean that! The inequities in our society are the inequities of centuries.'

'Don't speak to me of inequities, Sonya Leonovna! You of all people. Have you ever dealt with any of these wonderful masses? Of course not. Well, I have! Constantly. As a boy on my father's estate, as a soldier, as a politician. You have no idea what these people are like, how little they are capable of!'

'It is a good thing your husband isn't here to listen to you, Sonya Leonovna,' Protopopov added. 'He would be shocked by your attitude.'

'If he were here' - her voice wavered - 'perhaps he might agree—'

'Sonyasha, leave the politics to the men,' the princess said firmly. 'Let us talk about something more festive. Your party. Have I told you, Leon, I am planning a gala in

Sonya's honor? I thought sometime—'

'There will be no party,' Sonya interrupted, her jaw clenched. 'I told you that.'

'You forget the circumstances under which we discussed it, my dear.' Her mother stared at her, a slight smile on her mouth. 'I must insist.'

'Circumstances? What circumstances?' The general looked at them both.

'Nothing, Leon.'

'You are both red in the face; how is it nothing? Well? What circumstances?'

'Sonya was not feeling well when we spoke of it.' Her mother spoke softly, and her attention was directed to Sonya.

'Not feeling well?' The general raised his eyebrows. The princess glanced at him for a moment and then turned back to Sonya.

'It was nothing serious. Was it, Sonya?' There was a pause. Sonya stared into her mother's eyes. Would she really tell her father about the drinking? And why should it matter to Sonya if she did? The silence was so long that even Ivan Protopopov became aware of it, put down his fork, and looked from one face to another for a clue to what might have just happened.

'Perhaps, Mama, you are right. After the end of the year, perhaps we might have a party . . .' Her voice lost force. She pushed at her food with her fork, avoiding her mother's eyes.

'Women and their communication! Why is it I never quite understand what they are talking about?' The general had pushed his chair away. 'Unclear. It is always so unclear.'

'Leon.' Protopopov was smiling, relaxed enough to start an attack on the meat dumplings still steaming under their cover in the tureen. 'For a sophisticated fellow, you still don't understand that women have another language. Innuendo. Gestures. We don't speak it. Have a dumpling, dear friend. No innuendo here.' He plunged the silver server into the blue and white Staffordshire tureen. 'Ah, Princess, your table is always fit for the czar!'

*   *   *

Sonya   January 29, 1906

What is happening to Russia? My country is in as great a turmoil as I myself am. We found out yesterday that the peasants there have burned Dosiaya to the ground. Grandpapa was not hurt, but at his age the shock was so great that he is confined to his bed at Aunt Elizabeta's. All over, in Petersburg, Moscow, Kiev, the workers are striking, yet there is no organization, only chaos everywhere. I am as far from the people I desire to help as the earth is from the sun.

I am even farther from my own sort. Lately even Lopuhin's awful blundering love begins to satisfy me. I hardly know what I am doing or saying any longer. Last week I fell on my knees to one of Gregory's agents and pleaded with him for information concerning Gregory, but he walked away from me as if I were nothing more than an alley cat. I am only twenty-five and already I am besotted with drink, so much so that it takes me nearly an hour to make myself ready for my maids to dress me.

*   *   *

Lopuhin stretched his arms out, great slabs of meat. He grunted and dropped against the pillows. Sonya sat on the edge of the bed looking at him.

'Your mother has been to see you many times this month,' Lopuhin said. 'Does something concern her?'

'I concern her. She does not approve of my life. I am losing my position now. It has gone on too long. I have not been asked to Princess Maria Petrovna's ball and I was not asked to Louisa Ivanova's luncheon. My mother says it is because of my relationship with you. She says I must accept Gregory's death; there is no hope now. She says I must remarry before it is too late for me. She wants to give me a formal party on my name day. She says that I must be reborn.'

'Perhaps she is right. The fact is that if your society is closed to you, what good can you do me?' He made a moue of disappointment, eyes downcast, lips pursed. 'It will be a shame to lose you. But I cannot be selfish. A woman in your society with no position . . .' He shook his head sadly. 'It is worse than a man without rank or money.'

'I had thought, your honor, that you were above such things as position.' She fixed her eyes to his face. A slow smile spread across it like ink on a blotter.

'Dear Sonya,' he said quietly, 'I was born a peasant. To a peasant, there is nothing more important than position.'

*　　*　　*

Sonya   March 13, 1906

I have thought of killing myself. Chekhov's bourgeois are always killing themselves. It is a class solution. I would never do it.

Could I run to the sea and bathe my wounds? Would it heal me? The sun would burn my scars, my black and ugly scars. Count Gregory Andreivitch Tolchin, informer or hero, you are dead. The police chief has dismissed his whore. The party is tomorrow.

If someone will still have me, I will be somebody's wife and mother after all. What else is left me?

*　　*　　*

There were perhaps three hundred people that night in the ballroom. The musicians were the best in Petersburg. The princess had to fight to get them, they were so popular. She had hired eighty extras to round out her own regular staff. Never had she spent so lavishly, not even at Sonya's wedding, but never had it seemed as important. It had been the answer to her prayers. Twenty-six years ago the princess Mariyenka had asked God for a daughter, a solace, a friend and companion. He had given her the child then, and now He had given her again. This would be Sonya's resurrection.

From the first arrivals, the first strains of the violins in the ballroom, Sonya had been extraordinarily animated. Never had she looked more beautiful. She had chosen a pale ice-green satin gown edged with lace that crisscrossed the bodice and was worked in panels down the skirt. The lime lace accentuated the fire of her hair, which was piled in curls high on her head, supporting her simple tiara, with more long curls falling down the back of her neck. Other than the tiara, she wore no jewels except her grandmother's exquisite pearls, the ones she had worn the night of her debut.

She greeted everyone with an enthusiasm her mother had not seen in years – if, indeed, she had ever seen it. The princess had invited the most eligible men in society, and the ballroom seemed ablaze with their youth and good spirits. Sonya's brothers were there with many of their comrades from the service. There were uniforms everywhere, and laughter, the loudest of all being Sonya's.

Yes, she thought, I shall enjoy myself. Why not? Look how handsome all these people are. Everyone, as handsome as can be. So many uniforms. So many soldiers. So many shiny brass buttons. She had sworn to herself not to think about who these people were. She would dance with everyone. Love everyone. She would have a wonderful time.

She asked her brothers to dance with her, and the men of the Guards and anyone she found attractive, filling her card as she wished. She would not sit down, she would not rest until one after another they all swirled her around the floor, faster and faster. It must be faster! She wanted to dance into exhaustion and forgetfulness.

'Do you remember when we were little, Anton? How we played at soldier? I always had a gun in my hand. Bang.' They were dancing. She pointed her forefinger into his chest and pretended to shoot him.

'It was Bruno, I think, who played with you most of all,' he answered her, squirming, obviously ill at ease with her enthusiasms and with her finger in his ribs.

Pompous fool, Sonya thought. Anton was more stupid now than ever.

'What rank do you suppose Bruno would be today if he were alive?' Sonya asked with malice.

'I suppose a lieutenant,' answered Anton, who himself had just been made a captain.

'A general!' Sonya laughed and saw the frown on Anton's face. She was laughing too loudly.

'A general,' she said again, laughing even louder, sticking her finger again into his ribs. 'Bang!' She laughed. 'Bang. Bang. Bang.'

'The polka is over. I think I must return to my wife.'

We have the same blood, Sonya thought. Bang. Bang.

When she fell, she nearly managed to carry it off with a certain amount of grace. It was too much drink, too much of everything, and she had fallen while she was dancing with Michail Trevorivich, who was the handsomest one there, who looked, with too much drink, like Grisha. At the moment she had fallen, she was thinking that perhaps she would stop all of this madness and just be Sonya Leonovna Poliakov and fall in love again with someone like Michail Trevorivich who looked like Gregory Andrei-vitch. She had fallen and the music had stopped, but still she had managed to get up and wave for the musicians to continue.

'Excuse me,' she had said to Michail Trevorivich, 'I shall be back in a moment. Dance, everyone! Please! You must!' Her mother had rushed up to her, taken her arm, and held it for dear life, her face in anguish.

'Are you hurt? Sonya, what happened?'

'I am fine, Mother.' She tried to steady herself.

'You are perspiring, my dear. Come upstairs.' The anxiety on her mother's face was not for what might be Sonya's pain but her perspiration!

'Leave me alone!' The scream was violent, loud, piercing. No one in the room could have escaped hearing it. Her mother backed away from her, dropping her arm.

Sonya smiled at the faces that had turned to stare at her. Her ankle throbbed. Still smiling, she walked upstairs.

The party went on. She did not care. She lay in the bedroom where she had lain as a child. Tonight there were no shadows anywhere. She fell asleep finally, her ankle throbbing in time to the music, to the thump, thump, of the music.

It was very late when the door to the room opened and her father and mother stood there, the light from the hallway making them seem diminutive.

'I am fine,' she said, sleepily lifting herself up on one elbow.

'We are not so fine,' her father said, walking ahead of her mother. 'No, you have seen to that.'

'Please, Leon, not now, please. It is her name day.'

'There is never a proper time for you, Mariyenka.' He turned on the light next to the bed. 'You continue to disgrace us. You are my daughter and I love you, but your mother and I have lived through a most torturous year. Rumors. Nothing but rumors. Our friends can hardly look us in the face. You have always been headstrong, but to show yourself this way to all of society, to fan the flames of gossip about you by such scandalous behavior! I had thought Count Tolchin might have tamed you, Sonya, but alas, it is too late for that. He is dead and gone, and you remain as headstrong as ever.'

Her mother had picked up a small doll that was perched on the bookcase and covered her face with it. She was weeping into the doll's body.

'All of Petersburg knew how painful his death was to you, Sonya. Everyone, everyone sympathized. The whole of the court sympathized with you. It is a tragic thing for a young woman to lose her husband, but there are boundaries over which even grief cannot make one pass. I can no longer explain your actions even to myself. Certainly not your actions this evening in my house.'

Her ankle had begun to hurt again as she moved to a sitting position, dazed with drink and with sleep.

'Your behavior is outrageous. Your relationship with Lopuhin! Your behavior, Sonya! It is scandalous! Your mother is nearly in a state of collapse. She had hoped to smooth everything over this evening, to make a new beginning for us all, but you have ruined even that.'

Her mother ran across the room and pulled at her father's arm. He had been chopping the air just in front of Sonya's face. 'Oh, Leon, you must stop. I implore you, stop. The poor child's heart is broken.'

Her father put his arm down as if he had been stunned. 'There is nothing more to say. Nothing.'

'What would you have me do, Papa? I will do anything you ask.'

She heard him sigh, a long, long release of breath. She looked up to see his face, the eyes so like hers looking back at her full of defeat.

'Mother?'

Her mother still held the doll, the fragile bisqué face now pressed up against her bosom. Silently, she shook her head.

'Sonyasha, we love you, but you see . . .' Her father's voice was hesitant, reedy, and so distant that she strained to hear it. 'Perhaps if you went away for a bit . . . perhaps people . . . a little trip . . . things would be forgotten.'

A cold, heavy sadness enveloped her like a winter blizzard. She was a child in her child's room on her child's bed in her parents' house. She found herself weeping at their faces. She must do something, take action. Anything. She would not be powerless! She stood up, full of ambiguous resolve, and as she did her mother dropped the doll and cracked open its head.

The gun was in the library, in the secret compartment in the right-hand drawer of her father's desk. Sonya had seen him take it out and clean it once a long time ago, when he had thought her asleep at his feet. She knew her father. It would be oiled and clean and ready. Slowly she pushed the panel that sprung the drawer. There it was. And bullets, too. She almost laughed out loud. She had not thought about bullets. Perhaps she did have a simple woman's mind.

All through the ride in the carriage she clutched at the gun in her sable muff. She would show the world at last. She would do something important at last. This was no pheasant, no weak bird she was about to kill. This was Lopuhin, the chief of police. He was the embodiment of all the evil that she had pledged to eradicate. How could she have forgotten that? A woman would kill the chief of police. There would be headlines everywhere. They could find her, kill her, crucify her, it wouldn't matter. At last she would be a soldier.

Because she had telephoned him, Lopuhin was waiting to greet her in the entry hall. As he came forward, she pulled the gun out of her muff and pointed it at him. She saw his quizzical expression, the first rush of fear. He was looking directly into her eyes. He was saying something, but she couldn't hear him. He took a step forward, and then another, and then another. She had to pull the trigger, but it was stuck. She stared at the eyes coming toward her. What was stuck? Not the trigger. Her finger. She couldn't do it. She couldn't kill him. She still saw his eyes as he rushed her at the last moment, grabbing the gun and trying to pull it out of her hand. He couldn't possibly do that. It was stuck to her, frozen to her. He was twisting her wrist, hurting her, and then there was the noise, the loud, horrendous noise of the gun going off.

'What have you done!' He yelled it at her. The gun dropped on the floor and Lopuhin reeled away from her, stumbling, tripping over his enormous body. He was larger than he had ever been. A bear, a giant. There was blood all over him, blood everywhere, on the carpet, running down the sides of his jacket. He had managed to pull the shirt away from his body. Sonya stood frozen, horrified, beyond herself. No, no, no. It could not be. It was impossible. No.

'Finish me, Sonya,' he whispered.

'No,' she said softly, staring at him, staring at the blood, feeling fear.

'Finish me!' It was a hoarse cry.

'No!' She heard her own voice. 'No, no, no.'

'Dammit it, woman. Coward! Liar, whore! Finish it.'

The gun lay at her foot, but she could not touch it. She never wanted to touch anything again that could do this to anyone. 'No.' She repeated it over and over. She felt wet between her legs. Was her own blood pouring out of her? Her body was so disconnected from her mind that she would not have been surprised to find herself dying as well. There was a puddle of urine at her feet. She could not look at Lopuhin again. No one would find him until tomorrow, perhaps even the day after. She could be on a train out of Petersburg and miles away before they might remember or suspect her.

'Finish me, in the name of heaven!' She heard him, his voice a gasp.

She kicked the gun toward him and closed the door behind her.

14

Sonya   March 15, 1906

It was not really my mother's tears, my father's outrage or pain, nothing so grand as that. It was the doll she had picked up. The way she held it, the doll she had given me when I was young that I never wanted or played with, the doll that was to her dreams as brass buttons were to mine. Oh, the mind plays such tricks. The smallest things ignite us. When my mother dropped the doll and the bisque head shattered on the floor, it broke my heart. My whole life changed course in a split second because of a doll I had never cared about.

I am leaving Petersburg at once. I have the identity papers that Gregory arranged for use in emergency only. It was a long time ago. I hope the people I was supposed to contact are still there, are still working with us, but I have no alternative. I know there is a route, an underground. They will save me. I have sewn all my jewels into my hand case and gathered all my money. I must get out.

Oh, my sweet journals, my diaries, my true self. I must leave you here. I shall hide you down in the cellar, in the passageway that Gregory and I used to escape those nights years ago when I still thought everything was simple. My God, it is like leaving my children. I have you all here in front of me, and I remember the time, as if it were this morning, when Bruno gave me my first notebook so that I would not be lonely. Sweet heaven, how lonely I will be without you now. How lonely, and how frightened. I must leave. *Au revoir.*

*   *   *

As the coach pulled away from her home, as the horses fled from the coachman's whip across the Moika Canal, terror came, constricting her, squeezing all warmth from her. She remembered the many times she and Grisha had gone in disguise to the workers' section, but it did not comfort her. It had been child's play. Now she was alone. No one could guarantee her her life. Suddenly she realized her error in having taken her own carriage, and she banged on the window with her fists. Mitya, the coachman, like a machine, pulled the carriage to the curbing. She did not wait to tell him anything. She jumped down and began to run away, the hand case banging into her hip. She ran through the streets, the cold, curious eyes of the passers-by burrowing into her. Even in her simplest clothes, she was unlike any of them. She ran faster and faster, gasping in the icy air. When she reached her destination, she entered the front door of the building and walked to the back, knocking twice on the second door on the ground floor. The door opened slowly, and the man known as Josip B. stared at her with steely black eyes. He was smoking a pipe, and the foul-smelling smoke blasted her in the face, causing her to cough violently.

'Who sent you?' he asked, keeping the door only slightly ajar.

'Valentin,' she answered breathlessly, still coughing.

'Who are you?'

'Olga Zentzov. I must leave Petersburg immediately. Here are my papers.' She held them out toward him, but he merely stared at them as they shook in her hand. 'I am alone,' she said.

Slowly, he opened the door, glancing quickly about the hallway. 'Come in,' he said, turning away. 'Sit down.' She walked to one of the chairs in the sparsely furnished room. It was such an ordinary room, she thought, a sofa, a few tables, some lamps, a rug, family photographs on the walls, children and grown ups, all unsmiling. There was a picture of the coronation of Nicholas I over the sofa. A strong smell of cabbage came from the floor below. Suddenly a door opened behind the man and a tiny woman appeared, her brown hair in a bun. Without speaking, the woman went to a closet, opened the door, and started pulling things out. When she turned, her arms were full of clothes and she was hardly visible behind them. She dumped them on the sofa and then walked to Sonya. She wore thick glasses that had slid down her small nose and looked as if they would fall off her face.

'It will cost you ten roubles,' she said in a monotone. 'In advance,' she added. Sonya took out some money, counted out the right amount, and then began to add a few more roubles.

'Pay only what we ask,' the man said. 'Generosity is frowned upon.' Sonya handed the woman the ten roubles.

'I will start with your hair,' the woman said. 'Take off your coat.'

Sonya's hair and eyebrows were blackened. Her nails were cut and then her hands and face and boots were dirtied. She was ordered to change into the clothes on the sofa. She could keep her own or not, as she chose. She kept them, stuffing them into her case.

'You should leave the case,' the man said. 'It is too fine.'

'No,' Sonya said.

'Then keep it covered with a shawl. Always keep it covered.'

Sonya asked to look in a mirror. The woman pointed to the back of the closet door. Sonya walked to it and stared at her reflection. 'You are very clever,' she said to the woman. 'I do not know myself.' The woman said nothing. The man offered her some tea and cake.

'I will take you to the station soon. You are to take the train to Moscow and from there you go to Smolensk. You must not stop moving until you get to Kovosky Prospect number twenty in Smolensk. There you will ask for two students, Pierre Garenov and Lev Rubinsky, and they will arrange everything for you. If you fail to contact them in three days, go to Miriamne Yakovna Zubovsky. She is in the same building. She is a Jew who works for money.'

'And if she is not there, what then?'

'Then you are lost,' the man said without expression. 'At any rate, I will do my part and take you to the station. Already it is time to go.'

He drove her to the station in a cart, and after tying up his horse, he put her into the women's section, a second-class carriage, of the waiting train. Before she could thank him, he was gone. She kept her eyes on the policemen who walked up and down beside the train until it began to move. Then, slowly, she turned her attention to the occupants of her compartment. For all her commitment to the lower classes, she had never been alone in the company of strangers until that moment. Spread out among their meager belongings was an old grandmother, her daughter, and her daughter's daughter. After a few moments, the reason for their journey was apparent.

The old lady, her white hair yellowing along her crown, took out a large sausage in her bent, brown-spotted hands. She waved it up and down in front of her granddaughter, cackling like a hen. 'It looks like this,' she said, 'but it fills something besides a stomach.'

'I don't know if her Tolya knows where to put it,' the mother of the girl said. 'He is a gentle sort for a soldier.'

'He'll soon learn,' the grandmother said wickedly. 'They all learn. In and out.' She pushed the sausage up to the girl's chin. Then she looked at Sonya and grinned. 'You know, too, eh? We all know. In and out.' The old lady took a bite from the sausage, licking her greasy lips and then using the back of her sleeve for a napkin. 'I say get your rest today, my fine young thing, because after the wedding tomorrow you won't sleep again for a week. In and out, in and out.'

'And take a last look at your slim waist, my daughter.' The mother giggled. 'That will be gone soon enough. Your father got his fill and left you planted in my belly after the first night.' The mother patted the girl's flaming cheek. 'The only thing you can pray for now is that he takes off his boots first!'

'Your grandfather, may he rest with the angels forever, used me like a horse used a mare,' the old woman said, grabbing herself around her middle and spitting with laughter. 'Thank God he was in the army for so many years or I would be dead from that great thing of his battering away in me. Well, those days are over now.' She sat up and took a breath. 'Now I can rest, fart, and spread my legs in peace!'

'How my daughter blushes! She can thank me and the grace of the Virgin for keeping her father off her. Her sisters were not so lucky. What a howling there was those nights. You'd think the worst of the demons had come to sleep with them.'

'Your husband, may the most holy forgive me, is not much better than the Baba Yaga.' The grandmother crossed herself.

'It is the drink,' the mother said. 'May it rot his insides.' She, too, crossed herself. 'At least your Tolya has no taste for vodka. Kiss his feet for it.'

They went on like that for the remainder of the journey to Moscow. Their mannerisms, their accents, and their crudeness were so foreign to Sonya that she might have been watching a play, something of the sort Stanislavsky would mount at his theater in Moscow. These people were no more capable of understanding their place in history than they would be of attending a court ball. They had no notion of their ignorance or their deprivation, and Sonya was relieved when they left the train. They were nothing as she had imagined them.

Soon she was on another train, this time for Smolensk. As it jerked out of the station, terror advanced on Sonya. She thought of the lieutenant who had been arrested on the train when she was a child. Anton had told her that the soldiers and the police had no patience with traitors and no doubt had torn him apart with their bare hands. Did soldiers wait for her in some field? Her heart thumped in her chest, maddened by her panic. No, she thought, panic was her enemy now. There was no use in it. She must face the fact that she was on a moving train and there was no escape for her. She took a deep breath and then, with some deliberation, she lifted her case to her knees and removed a large sweater from inside. After closing it, she propped the case up next to her, folded the sweater, and put it onto the case, and then, after pulling her cape up and over her head, she rested her head down on the pillowed sweater and closed her eyes. It would make no difference if she slept.

In Smolensk, she bought the Petersburg and Moscow papers and looked through them for a mention of her or her crime. There was nothing. How could there be nothing? Perhaps they had not yet found Lopuhin. She hired a carriage and went to Kovosky Prospect. She inquired for the students, but no one knew of them. She

173

took a furnished room in the building for a week. She was afraid to leave, although she nearly was starved. Not meaning to, she fell asleep again. When she woke, it was already the next morning. Taking her belongings with her, she went out to buy some food. No one gave her so much as a glance. Again, she bought papers. Still, there was no mention of her or Lopuhin. Walking back to the building from the market, she passed two or three policemen. They did not so much as look at her.

For another night and half the following day, she waited. Finally, there was a knock on her door and she opened it quickly. The boys who stood there introduced themselves. They looked behind themselves as they entered her room and then walked immediately to the window and looked down into the street. The younger of the two, a blond boy with a full beard, spoke to her. 'We cannot help you now,' he said. 'The police are looking for you everywhere. Your identity has been found out and your description has been telegraphed to all the border stations. No one knows your crime, but it is serious.'

'Who informed on me?' she asked, thinking of Josip B. and the woman who lived with him. Perhaps, she thought, trembling, it was Mitya, her carriage driver.

'What difference can it make?' the elder boy said. 'You are known. We must take you to Miriamne Yakovna. She will get you out of Russia if anyone can.'

They hurried her out of the room to a room three flights above and handed her over to a stern, dark-haired girl. The girl, too, was young, hardly twenty, twenty-one at most. Her hair was tied back from her face with string. Her skin was olive and shiny and her black eyes were forbidding. In a firm, authoritative voice, she named her price and demanded half the money at that moment. Sonya gave it over, and the girl immediately put on her coat, hat, and a pair of heavy boots and pushed Sonya outside the door, locked it, and told Sonya to follow. 'We are taking a train to Kovno and from there to Suvalki,' she said. 'There is no time to waste.'

At the railway station, Miriamne Yakovna bought tickets for the third-class section. In less than an hour from the time they left Kovosky Prospect, they were on their way to Kovno.

Third class was crowded with Jews, the men with their little hats and long curled locks, the worn-out women with their huge families, all of them rattling on in Yiddish. The stench of onions and garlic and fish was overpowering.

'I can tell you have never been among such people,' Miriamne said, watching her. 'You must get used to the smells and the sounds. This is what life is really about.'

'What are they eating?' Sonya asked.

'Dried fish. For half a kopeck, I can buy you some to try.' Sonya handed her the money and Miriamne bought the fish. When she handed it to Sonya, the smell was so repulsive, Sonya quickly covered it with a piece of cloth and pushed it away. 'You are not hungry enough,' Miriamne said, 'but you will be.'

They huddled against one another, but still the cold in the car pervaded them. 'Why do you do this?' Sonya finally asked.

'I do it for the money.'

'But you must alway be so frightened!'

'Always,' she answered. 'But challenge keeps me alive. I have never been able to refuse a dare. Life, you know, is one continuous gamble anyhow, so why not? I pride myself on my work. I have smuggled out over a hundred people.'

Sonya suddenly got up and ran to the slop bucket, but once there, she could not even retch. She tasted only bile. She walked back to Mariamne.

'If you eat the fish, you will be better,' she said.

'But it will make me feel sicker,' Sonya protested.

'No. It will keep your stomach busy. Try.'

Nearly gagging with each mouthful, Sonya ate the fish. Miriamne was right. As offensive as it was, it was better than nothing, and her feeling of sickness left her.

At Suvalki, she followed Miriamne down the platform to a long, high wagon. Five or six slats had been put across the back to serve as seats. Some of the Jews had already scrambled up the spokes of the wheels into the wagon. Sonya and the others took the last seats as the half-starved horses pulled the wagon forward.

There must have been eighteen of them in the back, and

the driver, a young Jew in a long black coat, beat the horses mercilessly. No matter his zeal, they still moved slowly on the packed snow and ice.

Snow covered the fields dotted with spindly trees. Occasionally, they passed through a wretched town of thatched-roof shanties, black smoke from their stoves the only color on the endless white landscape. People appeared, poor, haggard, and motionless, staring at them as they passed. It was so cold, breath was like the stab of a knife.

The wagon stopped at every roadside inn. Bundles were thrown down, people got off, but always others took their places. At the fourth or fifth stop, Miriamne urged Sonya to get down, and they went into an inn and ate some soup and drank strong tea. By nightfall, after traveling ten hours, they stopped at yet another inn.

'You will sleep here,' Miriamne said. She took Sonya's case and went ahead of her, speaking in Yiddish to a round, short man with a sour expression. His tone was belligerent and he kept shaking his head negatively, but finally Miriamne motioned for Sonya to come toward them. 'Go with him,' she said in Russian, handing her back her case. 'I will be back in the morning.'

The inn was poor. Behind a door, mercifully closed, she heard men's voices laughing, singing, cursing. The inn-keeper quickly pulled her into a tiny filthy room with space only for a bed and a bench. 'Get into the bed,' he said, 'and pull the bed curtains. Russian border soldiers come and go.' He spoke in broken Russian, lapsing into Yiddish. Sonya wrapped herself in the spotted feather quilt and pulled down the ragged curtains.

The nightmare began immediately. Soldiers came into her room, whispered together, and left. Drunken women sang plaintive Russian folk songs; drunken men fought with one another. Men and women made love in the hallway. Even exhausted and shaking with fear, Sonya was relieved to see the morning light.

The dreadful man came for her right away. 'Get up,' he said, as if she might have been asleep. 'Follow me.' Outside, the sun was extraordinarily bright, almost blinding. He handed Sonya some bread. She ate it as they walked. After five minutes, her eyes adjusting to the brightness, she saw the familiar figure of Miriamne ahead of her. 'Don't speak,' the man said. After a mile, Miriamne stopped by a sentry box at a bridge. Sonya held her breath. The man grabbed at her upper arm, restraining her. 'Stay here,' he snapped. The two of them watched Miriamne speaking to the sentry. After a few minutes, she took out a large red handkerchief and mopped her face. 'Red is good,' the man said. 'White is no.'

Together they watched Miriamne cross over the bridge and disappear down the road on the other side. Sonya looked at her boots. They were soaked through and the ice had formed across them like a skin. The sun was so strong as it hit the snow-covered ground that it made her eyes water.

'We can go now,' the man said, moving ahead. Sonya's legs and her arms and her fingers were numb, but she forced herself to walk beside him toward the sentry box. Slowly, slowly, they approached, and then they were passing the sentry. Sonya glanced inside. The guard had his back to them. He was reading a paper. As they crossed the bridge, Sonya's heart nearly fluttered to a stop. After all the last terror-filled days, it had seemed too simple, and she had never even glimpsed the face of the man who allowed her to escape.

There were no sentries on the German side, and they walked until they saw Miriamne ahead of them. The man spoke with her for a moment and then turned back toward the bridge. Miriamne walked to Sonya. 'Here are some papers and some francs. A coach will be here soon. It will take you to Konigsberg, where you will make connections for Paris. Put on your better clothes. You are now a Frenchwoman, Lydia Mousset. You were a governess in Russia. Speak only French, and I would advise you to travel through to Paris. Don't stop in Berlin. The Russian secret police are everywhere in Germany. In Paris, they are not so organized. Keep away from the Russian section anyway. I have been told of a Café Bellenoir. You should find someone there. Do you understand all I have said?' Sonya nodded. 'I would like the other half of my money.' Sonya gave it to her, and she took it quickly from Sonya's stiff fingers, expertly counting it. 'Destroy those papers once you are in Paris. You will be all right.'

'Thank you,' Sonya said. 'You are a very brave woman.'

The girl looked at Sonya a moment, shrugged, and turned away. Before she was halfway back to the bridge, the coach came and stopped about fifty feet ahead of Sonya. It is over, she thought as she walked toward it. My life in Russia is over.

Book II

1

Sonya   April 12, 1906

I am disguised as a whore in Paris. How life's journey snakes to eternity. Well, here at least the profession allows me to live without question. I tell my fellow *femmes de la trattoire* here on the Madeleine that I am sick and will not work until I am better. It is understood.

Even though Tolchin told me never to take initiative, I am so sure that what I have done was right. I have tried to find comrades here, but I must be very careful. I found the Café Bellenoir, but I am frightened to spend too much time there. Who knows which eyes are seeing me? I cannot remember the names I should. Still, I must make contact with someone. I must. I sold a small pin that my mother had given me when I was ten years old. It was green enamel with pearls in a heart at the center. How sad it made me. How frightened I am!

*   *   *

It was, of course, his hair that she saw first. Carrot red, shining in the sun. He wore a cap like a French stevedore, but the red hair curled tightly all around it. It had to be him. He was sitting in front of the café, with a newspaper and bottle of wine in front of him. A newspaper! She had imagined him so many ways, running, wounded, dead, tortured. She had never imagined him sitting calmly at the table, reading a newspaper and drinking wine. He was heavier, much heavier, and he looked even older than his years. He wore glasses. He had never worn glasses. It couldn't be him, but it was. Bruno sat in a restaurant in Paris reading a newspaper and sipping wine. She thought it so funny she laughed out loud. She was still laughing as she approached him.

'My God, it is you, it is you!'

He stood up quickly. 'Get away from me, whore.'

'But Bruno, it's Sonya. I am Sonya.'

'You whores are the scum of this earth. Waiter! Get this woman away from me. What kind of place is this?'

The waiter had taken her arm and was pulling her away. 'Bruno!' She looked back into his eyes and saw nothing. Roughly the waiter pushed her out into the street away from the curb. '*Va t'en, vache,*' he growled at her. Sonya, completely dazed, walked away. But the waiter had pressed a piece of paper into her hand as he sent her reeling down the street. Bruno had known her! How could she have thought otherwise? Tears formed in her eyes. My God, she thought, I had given up hope of ever seeing him again. My brother. My teacher. Relief flooded her body so that she found herself shaking. She looked down at the piece of paper the waiter had given her. On it was written an address, a flat number, and a time. The time three A.M., was underlined. She was safe. She went to her room and slept, waking at midnight and waiting until two to cross the city to the appointed place, thinking only of Bruno's embrace. All she could hear was Bruno's clear admiring tone as he said, 'Brava. Good shot, Sonyasha.' Gone was the sickness she had felt, the terror that had been her companion for so many days. She tasted nothing but triumph as she went toward the building, then into the courtyard and up the three flights of stairs to the *deuxième étage.* She knocked on the correct door, and as it opened, she was startled to see all of those who were gathered there, so like all the others that had gathered in rooms exactly like it in Petersburg.

'Come in and sit down, Sonya Tolchin.' The voice that greeted her was not Bruno's. She looked for him, and when she saw him, his eyes were as hollow as those of the man who had just addressed her.

'I said sit down!' The man spoke roughly and with great annoyance. 'You have caused us enough delay, comrade!' Sonya sat on the wooden stool he pointed to. He had a face like a thousand others, and he spoke in Russian. 'You are accused of disobeying orders, of deliberately taking matters into your own hands, and for reasons having nothing to do with your assigned position, trying to kill the police chief Lopuhin.'

'He was an enemy of the revolution, Comrade Leader,' Sonya said forcefully. 'I did my duty for the cause and only for the cause.'

'Did your immediate superior order the shooting of Lopuhin?'

'No, but—'

'Silence! No one connected with the party ordered his shooting. You acted solely on your own behalf, and your action has had vast and unfortunate repercussions, Sonya Tolchin. It was finally nothing short of miraculous that we have managed to survive. Had Lopuhin died, we might have failed completely to put our plans into operation.'

'He is not dead?' Sonya was shocked. 'Lopuhin is not dead?' She turned in her seat toward her brother. 'Is he telling me the truth, Bruno?' Her brother, his face full of disgust, nodded his head.

'Why wasn't this woman thrown to the Okhrana? She has brought half of them with her. There are so many hungry dogs running through the streets of Paris. I say give them what they want so they will stop sniffing into everybody's else's droppings!' The man who spoke was tall and thin as a pole. Sonya had seen him before.

'Her freedom is an accommodation to Comrade Vontov.' The man nodded toward Bruno.

'Since when do we make accommodations, Comrade Leader?' asked a rotund man who smoked a cigarette. 'We have no word in our vocabulary for accommodation.'

'Comrade Vontov has petitioned the Central Committee. The committee has assured me that before her obvious emotional collapse, she served us with loyalty and valor. Nevertheless, a trial has been ordered.'

'Valor?' Sonya's voice echoed the word.

'Will you get her out of here so we can continue our business? The sight of her makes me ill. I have it on very good authority that she alone was responsible for the arrest of Vera Anatolyevna, a most important member of the Petersburg party.' This voice belonged to a woman, and Sonya looked to her right trying to see her accuser.

'I assure you I had nothing to do with the death of Vera—'

'You are not on trial tonight. Keep your mouth shut!'

Sonya began to cry, and her tears poured down her cheeks and into her mouth, making her choke on them.

'Will you take her!' the man said. 'We must get on with our work.'

She felt hands at her upper arms, fingers digging into her flesh as she was lifted from her seat. 'Comrades . . . Gregory Andreivitch Tolchin!' She was choking still, coughing up his name. 'Is he alive? Does he live? Please—'

'We have no such information. Get her away.'

She was half carried, half pushed, out the door. In the darkness of the hallway, she looked up into Bruno's face. Except for telling her to follow him quietly back to her room, he said nothing else to her until, an hour later, they were there.

Suddenly, he embraced her. 'God help me, it was I who did this to you! I who believed in you!' He held her against him. 'Oh, God forgive me,' he whispered. 'Sonya!' Then, savagely his fingers dug into her flesh again, and he shook her back and forth until she thought her chattering teeth would come lose in her mouth and spill onto his chest. 'Why couldn't you do what you were told? Have you any idea what the consequences have been?' The room spun, the floor knocking against the ceiling, the walls smashing into one another. When he let her go, she stood lifeless as a rag doll.

'I was not a whore. I could not degrade myself. He took my life from me. If Gregory were not dead, I would kill him, Bruno.'

'What has he to do with anything? It was your job to keep us informed about Lopuhin. He was a major source of information, and now we have lost that source and damned near lost every one of our police agents.'

'You do not understand, Bruno! Gregory left me powerless. You do not understand!'

'It is you who do not understand.' His voice was pinched and ugly. 'You are a fool, Sonya, and there is nothing to be done about it except to get you away from here so there will be no more trouble. You are to be made an example; that is the only reason they allowed you to reach Paris. I must get you out tonight. I have arranged with someone to take you to Marseilles and get you on a ship to America.'

'America? I do not want to go to America!'

'You have no say. It is decided. Besides the police, most of your comrades would like to see you killed. At any rate, your passage has been arranged. Once on the boat, you are to attach yourself to some man. At least you can still do that, I hope. They do not let single women into America easily. They do not want prostitutes.'

'Let them kill me. It would be much easier.'

'Sonya, Sonya,' he pleaded with her. 'You understand none of it, do you?'

'Do you hate me so much, Bruno?' she asked softly. 'You are my brother. You were so much of my life.'

'I love you, Sonya, yet I hate anyone who betrays my cause. You see how difficult it is for me.' He paused, frowning, his eyes on her face. 'Tomorrow morning someone will come to take you to Marseilles. He is a short man, he is lame.'

She began to laugh. 'Is he blind, too? I do hope he is blind, too.'

'You are my sister, Sonya,' he said, his voice tense and thin, 'but I did not teach you your lessons well enough. It is my fault you are here, my mistake. If you were not my sister I would turn you over in a second. I must betray all my better instincts for you. Oh, Sonya, I want you far away. I never want to have to do this again. As I said, tomorrow morning, early, someone will come.' Bruno walked by her and out the door without another word. She stared at the door and at her feet. I could not do as I was told because I am a woman, she thought. That was it, of course. Men could replace their feelings with commitment. Men needed nothing, not approval, not love. Love. There was no sustenance in love. It had betrayed her. She was a woman, silly and mindless. Let Bruno save her. Let him do anything he wanted. She was useless.

How many stations were there? How many stops? How many strange faces were there to meet her, how many strange arms to lift her into carts, to hand her to other strangers' arms? How many people told her where to go, whom to look for, what time to leave, what train to take, giving her food or drink? How was it possible that so many

185

people were kind?

She became an obedient child, passed from hand to hand, absolutely trusting. All the fight had been ripped out of her, even the fear. Huddled in a corner of a wagon or sleeping on the straw in someone's barn, she lived from instant to instant. Her shame was too great to allow thought. She had no strength, no will to draw upon. Perhaps one day she would be herself again, be able to stand up and fight back, do for herself. Perhaps not.

In Marseilles, someone gave her an exit card and a ticket for her passage to America. She was told to join the band of people who lived on the docks, some who had been there for weeks waiting for passage. She lived with them for days, sleeping under boats hauled aground for repair, eating broth and fish cooked over open fires, washing in the oily water of the port. At first there were only twenty, then forty, and then eighty, a hundred. They spoke in Yiddish, in Russian, German, Polish, Romansh, trying in some way to communicate with one another. Some had been on a train with her somewhere, or a wagon; others came on foot or by carriage. Young ones full of life, old ones half dead, some with religious books and scarfs, bowing and swaying to their God, others running from the police or the army or the toughs on the dock. At any rate, Sonya was one of them, moving with them, hardly speaking, a frightened Jew.

At night she dozed fitfully, straddled across her carrying case, her heavy cape wrapped tight about her body. Nightmares came, haunting her with old or new ghosts. Now there was a man with a pick in his hand, laughing at her, a giant, like the falconer at the fair near Dosiaya; then yes, it was the falconer and his bird, but the bird had its beak in her back and was pecking at her, pecking harder and harder.

'Don't move. There is a knife in your back. If you move I will shove it inside you.' It was a woman's voice. A hand slammed over her mouth. 'I want your ticket. I won't hurt you if you give me your ticket.' The voice was high and childish, the hand small.

Sonya nodded her head up and down, coughing and spitting on the hand. Her nerves were on fire. Every pulse point in her body pounded. She tried to sit, but the knife pressed into her back.

'Your ticket!' The voice spat in her ear.

Sonya pointed to the bag under her and nodded her head again. The hand came away and Sonya gasped for air, breathing deeply, feeling air cut through her like lightning. 'The knife is still in your back,' the small voice warned.

With all her strength, Sonya raised herself and turned, slamming the woman with her elbow. She heard a grunt and felt a sharp stinging pain in her arm. She could see nothing in the blackness. She pulled her knee up and kicked out blindly. She heard another grunt and heard the woman fall, grunting again.

She heard the sharp metallic sound of a knife hitting the stones. She kicked again and again, first at air, then at a form. She heard more groans and whimpering. She was sweating furiously. On her knees, she crawled along, feeling for the knife.

'Aiyee!' Sonya screamed, chills going through her body. She had touched the clammy hand of the woman. She pulled back and swung out and then she heard the woman's sounds now farther away. She was gone.

Sonya's breath was loud in her nose and her ears. She was trembling and wringing wet with a cold damp sweat. She drew her few bundles close around her and felt for her cape, covering herself and her possessions with it. Then she stared into the blackness of the harbor, listening to the sounds of her own labored breathing. She tried to calm herself, lying absolutely still, not moving until light broke across the horizon ahead of her.

The knife was near her. As she leaned over to pick it up, she saw the gash on her arm, the blood already congealed, the scab forming. She picked up the knife and put it into her carrying bag. There was no question about it. They were all animals, and the strongest would survive. She would be sure she was one of the survivors.

The first day and night on the boat, Sonya stood by the railing, unwilling to take her place in the stinking hold. At eight A.M. she still stared straight out over the water. Perhaps hell waited over the horizon. Perhaps they would all fall off it, this flat sea. If so, she swore, she would be the last to go. Everything but her resolve was exhausted. Her body ached. Her joints ground against each other. Her head banged. Juices in her empty stomach gurgled wildly. Her lips were dry and parched; her skin was rough. Her own smell made her nauseated. The black dye was fading out of her matted and tangled hair, leaving it the color of pine bark. Now I know, she thought, what it is, what man really does to man. How low I am! What I have become.

Suddenly the morning sunlight was gone. Dark thunderclouds swept in off the horizon. The swells became higher and a wet wind blew in from the west. As the first drops fell, Sonya was grateful. Perhaps this would cleanse everything. The boat stank of garbage, urine, and sweat. At its stopover in Marseilles nothing had been done to clean it, and yet she had been lucky to get aboard. Sixty or seventy were left behind, all of them with tickets, clamoring to get on the ship.

She made her way inside, steeling herself against the sights and the smells. So many bodies in such a small dark space. She sat as close as possible to the door. She had been right. They were all animals. Humans in inhuman conditions.

She propped her carrying case behind her, ran her hand across herself and the ten hidden pockets in her clothing that held her money and papers, and then, leaning her head against the case, she slept for a while. She woke to an insistent buzz of voices near her and, not making out the words, looked across the aisle between the inner and outer wall of the cabin at a woman who retched violently into a pile of rags laid out on the floor. A pale young man sat near the woman and a child sat by her legs, holding on to the fabric of her dress. No one made any attempt to comfort her, including the man. Was he her husband? How could they all allow themselves to be so demeaned?

Sonya got to her feet, hoisting her bag on her shoulder, and went over to the woman. 'May I help?' she asked. Getting no response, she asked again.

'She is beyond help,' the pale young man answered. 'She is dying. Let her alone. They have sent for a doctor.' Neither the woman nor her husband was over twenty. 'Go away,' he said.

The cabin door opened and two sailors and a man in a blue jacket came in and, following the pointed fingers of the others, walked toward the ill woman. Sonya backed away. The blue-jacketed man bent over the woman, turned her, shook his head, stood, and nodded to the young sailors, who bent down, lifted the woman up, and began to carry her out. The child stood, too, wobbling on her small legs, still holding the dress.

'Someone take the child,' the blue-jacketed man said. No one moved, not even the husband. Animals, Sonya thought, beyond human feelings. She put down her bag and knelt by the little girl, prying the small fingers open and yanking the dress from them. Sonya watched the child's eyes as they carried her mother away from her. There seemed no emotion in that face; not a cry came from the little mouth, not a tear from the hazel eyes. She is as helpless as I was, Sonya thought. She lifted the girl up in her arms and reached back for her bag. The child was stiff as a board. Sonya carried her out to the deck, pulling her own cape around the small, cold body. The rain had almost stopped, but the deck, save for the three men and the form of the mother, was empty. Sonya made her way away from them toward the stern of the ship, hugging the wall until she found a corner protected by lifeboats stacked one upon the other. She sat down, the child in her arms, and dropped her bag.

'Do you speak Russian?' Sonya asked. The child stared at her, unblinking. 'I wonder if you speak at all. Poor thing. Here, I will give you an orange.' Sonya reached into the deep pocket of her skirt and took out one of the five small oranges there and held it up to the little girl, who stared at the orange and then back at Sonya. Sonya peeled it carefully, taking a section and holding it out. The child did not move. Sonya peeled another section, opened her mouth wide, and popped it in. The child's mouth opened in imitation and Sonya pressed the orange section inside. The child sucked it and then chewed it. Sonya pressed another section against her lips and the child ate that and then another and another until the orange was gone.

Sonya pulled the child against her body and draped the

shawl around them both, sitting there in the rain. How thin the child was, hardly enough flesh on her to cover her bones. She felt the child's small warm breath on her neck. Poor thing, she thought, what is your destiny? My own mother, holding me like this, would never have guessed mine. 'Well, what am I doing? You have a father. That is something,' she said aloud, standing again and going back toward the cabin. She opened the door and looked about for the child's father. Three or four people backed away from her as she carried the child by them. She walked around the cabin from one group of people to the next. They all turned away from her as if she were a pariah. They were afraid of the disease.

Finally she went around the far wall that partitioned off the racks of boards five tiers high, which served as beds. She saw him sitting on the second tier by himself, his legs swinging, his eyes looking down at her dully.

'I have your child,' she said.

'She is not mine,' he answered.

'Not yours?'

'The woman, the sick one, she paid me to take her along. She had no one else. She said the devil Russians had murdered her family. She paid me to bring her. I told her she would not live to see America. It was for the child she came. Well, maybe someone will take her.' He slid down from the bunk and landed in front of Sonya, standing almost on top of her, his breath foul in her nostrils. He was smaller than she was by two inches and looked up at her. 'If you pay me, I'll sell you the woman's card and take you through immigration.'

'Is she dead?'

'She will be soon. The doctor said so. I took her card before they came for her.' He held it up in front of Sonya. 'One hundred roubles and it's yours. You'll have a daughter and a husband. You can get through with no trouble.'

'I have a card. I can get through without trouble now.'

'A woman alone always has trouble.' He smiled at her. 'Especially you will – when I tell them you are a whore.'

'Filth.' She practically spat at him.

'It is the whores who are filthy,' he answered her, still

smiling, 'not respectable fathers, like me. So what do you say? A hundred roubles is all.'

'Don't be an ass. Where would I get money like that?'

'I watched you even before we got on board. You always had money. You always managed to have food. I'm not so stupid, am I? As a matter of fact, I know people rich or poor. You've got plenty. Is it hidden in your cape?' He made a move to pull her cape off her shoulders, and Sonya's hand went for her bag.

'I have a knife,' she said. 'I warn you.'

'You're not so tough,' he said, nonetheless backing a few inches away from her.

'I have killed before,' she said. He didn't answer. 'You are right,' she added, 'I have money. I will give you a hundred roubles when we get off the boat together with the child in America. If you try to take the money or to touch me, I will kill you.' She leaned over and whispered very softly. 'That is why I am going to America. I am already wanted for murder; another would mean nothing to me. So? What have you to say, my loving husband?'

'Don't patronize me. There are other single women on the boat.'

'But as you so rightly thought, none of them has a hundred roubles.' Fool, she thought, watching his eyes appraise her and the situation, one ounce of flattery and you are mine. She smiled at him. 'You are very smart,' she said, 'to have figured me out.' She slipped her arm around him. 'Come, loving husband, let us find a little corner that we and our child can call our own. We have at least ten days to enjoy our marriage.'

That first night, the two of them, the young man and the child, fell asleep immediately, looking as comfortable on the piles of clothes and bundles as if they were a featherbed. He is like a child himself, Sonya thought, looking at him. His arms were tossed above his head, hands relaxed and opened, his face was sweet, little musical snores coming from his parted lips. She covered him with her cape, taking his arms down to his sides, tucking them under. The baby was curled up in a little nest of Sonya's sweaters, her head propped up on Sonya's ankle. Sonya looked around her. Everyone was sleeping, twisted around each other. But Sonya could not sleep; she was still fearful that someone, even the young man, might steal her case. Hours later, he sat up and pushed his sleepy face up to hers in the dark.

'You must sleep, too,' he said.

She shook her head.

'Don't worry. Sleep. Go ahead.' He took her cape off himself and wrapped it around her. 'Our child sleeps, why shouldn't her mother? Look, put your head on my lap, and that way, if I move, you'll wake up. Even suspicious people must sleep.' He smiled at her shyly. She acquiesced, putting her head on his outstretched let, and fell asleep in seconds. seconds.

When she woke, it was morning and he was still next to her. The baby was playing with his fingers and chewing on a crust of bread.

'You're not bad with her,' Sonya said, sitting up. She was so cramped and knotted she could hardly move. She rubbed an arm and then a shoulder as he continued to play with the baby, now making little faces at her.

'I had many sisters and brothers. My mother and father were good Jews. They did not spill his seed upon the earth. I was the third son, the fifth child. There were eleven of us.' He took a stone from his pocket and handed it to the baby.

'Mind she does not put it in her mouth,' Sonya said anxiously.

He took the stone from the baby and threw it up and caught it several times. 'This is a stone from my village, from the street. I wanted to take something.'

'Why did you leave?'

'Because I didn't want to go into the czar's army and I didn't want a part of me broken off to avoid going.' He looked away from her as he spoke. 'My family stayed.'

'Are you hungry? I have some food.'

Sonya opened her case and took out some cheese and bread and then reached in her pocket for an orange.

'You are not a Jew,' he said, watching her. Sonya shrugged. 'What are you then, Orthodox?' Sonya shrugged again. 'Why are you running away? Did you really do murder?' Sonya handed him a slice of bread and he handed

192

it back to her. 'Cut it in half. We have many days to go, and if there is a delay, perhaps we will be here for two weeks.' Sonya took it and cut it in half, handing him the larger piece. 'You are a very generous wife,' he said.

Sonya peeled an orange and put the slices of orange on the peel, and the child took them one by one.

'So what is your name, husband?' Sonya broke off some cheese. It had gone a bit rancid but she ate it anyway, putting a slice of orange in her mouth afterward.

'Yasha. Jacob. And yours?'

'Elena.'

'And what shall we name our child? The mother never spoke her name.'

They both looked at the baby. Her dark hair was matted and dirty on her small head. Her eyes were almost white in the dark as she looked from one face to the other. She was a pretty baby, with large, even features and a nice shape to her face.

Sonya thought for a moment and shrugged. 'I don't know. Maria. Something simple.'

'That's a terrible name!'

'Oh, who cares, Yasha! I am in no mood for games.'

'All right, I'll name her. Rachel for my mother.' He paused. 'No. Chaya. Bah, it's a dog's name. I say we call her Gittel. That is a good name. There was a lovely girl in my village named Gittel.'

'If we give her a name, then it should be something grand, something important. The name of a goddess. Artemis. Athena. Persephone.'

'They sound like ships.'

'There was an oracle that all the gods consulted, more powerful than anyone. She lived in a place called Delphi in Greece.'

'What did they call her?' Yasha folded his arms.

'The Oracle.'

'That is hardly a name.'

'Delphi. We'll call her Delphi. It is a fierce name.'

'A greek name for a Russian baby. It is ridiculous. She should have a Russian name.'

'Has Russia been so kind to her?' Sonya glanced at the

baby. 'It doesn't make any difference anyway. She belongs to neither of us, only to herself.' Sonya felt a quick jab of pain in her belly. 'Oh, dear, I must visit the facilities,' she said, awkwardly holding her stomach and leaning over for her case. 'I don't know which will make me sicker, the visit or the lack of it!'

'Don't forget to hold your nose,' he called, lifting the baby in his arms. 'Hey, what about Rebecca?'

Sonya turned a little as she ran, and she was holding her nose.

'Must you always have your way, Elena?' he yelled. She nodded her head as she ducked inside the odious room ahead of her.

'So what do you think will happen to that man there with the prayer shawl?' Sonya asked the day afterward. 'The one in the corner who looks like a frightened bird.'

'He will marry a rich American and forget his family in Odessa. The pious ones usually do. They are too used to a life of ease. Their mothers always took care of them, and then their wives did the same. They can't work, so they take the easy way.'

Sonya was eating a potato. When she had finished, she licked her lips. 'I would never have guessed a cold potato could taste so good.'

'I found those potatoes along the road and I cooked them in the fire the night before we left, skin and all. There is no fat on them to spoil. But look' - he held up a carrot - 'these have gotten all spindly and withered. If you give me money, I can get fresh food.'

'How?'

'I have just found out. There are ways. Give me as much as you can spare.' She turned her back to him and reached again inside her blouse and took out some francs and then turned back to him and handed him the money. 'This should do,' he said standing.

He was gone for a long while. It was already dark and most of the others around her slept, one or two fidgeting or complaining, some around the other side of the wall, moaning or praying. The baby woke and Sonya rocked her, singing her a lullaby Marushka had sung to her, the story of an enchanted horse named Gelb. The baby fell asleep again. How unreal everything was.

The door of the hold opened and closed quickly, and in only seconds, Yasha was there beside her, a large sack in his hands.

'I have fresh fruit and some fresh vegetables, a bit of cheese and more bread,' he whispered. He sat quickly, putting a sweater over the sack. 'No one must see it. It was simpler than I thought. Bribery is always so much simpler than one expects. A few francs to the right fellow and the task is accomplished.'

'I would never know which one to ask.'

'It is an instinct, I suppose. I think any of the stewards in the first class might have cooperated, but I chose the oldest one I saw. He might be more experienced, you see, and more in need of money.' He rubbed his eyes, curling his fists and pressing them into his sockets. 'We should sleep now. It is nearly dawn.'

On the sixth and seventh and eight days, there was some sun, and the three of them joined others out on the deck. They managed to find a place next to an air shaft where they were protected from the insistent wind.

'Natasha. That is a good name,' Yasha said. 'What do you think?'

'Will you stop! We have named her.' He was throwing the baby up in the air and catching her in his arms. 'Carefully, she can fall against the air shaft.'

'I had an uncle Moishe who was the town butcher, and he loved to throw me up very high and catch me. I hated it because his hands were always bloody and his apron was brown with it and he smelled of it, and I thought each time I fell, he would slice me up with his knife.' He had caught the baby and now was turning and turning with her in his arms, making a tiny smile appear on her face. 'Look, she likes it!'

'You must not smell of blood,' Sonya called.

Suddenly he stopped swinging the child and sat down next to Sonya, looking away.

'I did not mean to upset you, Yasha. I meant it as a joke.'

'I am sick of this – this boat, this stink, this pretense.'

Yasha scowled, stamping down on the deck with one foot, unhappy that there was nothing to kick. He squinted around at the clumps of people sitting on the deck. 'Beggars, louts, thieves, murderers, is what we all are. So what kind of country can it be that welcomes us? Who would come to this America if he did not have to?' He looked down at her. The shadows caught in lines at his nose and eyes, elongating his face, and Sonya shuddered, thinking of her old ghosts. 'I am sick of my life already,' he said.

'There is the future,' Sonya said blandly. 'Perhaps—'

'What future can there be, my fine wife? For you or me? We are scabs, clots – nothing.' He leaned against the air shaft, now looking out over the water. 'If I knew for sure what the future held and it held as little as I suspect it will, I would leap in to the sea and get it over with.'

'I am glad not to know it,' Sonya said, no longer concerned with him. He was a boy with a boy's impatience, already shaking his fists at life.

'You are only a woman,' he sneered. 'Good or bad, the future holds no surprises for you.'

'And you are only a man, as self-righteous as all men. Why don't you just forget it all and jump into the sea? At least that would add a little drama to this boring day.'

Yasha got up, walked to the railing, and spat into the sea. He turned and leaned against the railing and looked at Sonya and Delphi, watching them for a long time. 'If I were older, I might keep her,' he said finally. 'I hear there is child labor in America worse than in Russia. The children work in factories fifteen hours a day with no food. It is the reason my mother would not let me bring my younger brother with me.' He sighed loudly. 'She is so little and sweet,' he murmured. They both looked at the baby, who had fallen asleep against Sonya.

'Don't worry, I will see she has a good family take her.'

'Elena, you are very romantic. It is just pot luck for her. The same for us.' His eyes were thoughtful and then sad, and he turned again, looking back toward the sea. Sonya lifted Delphi and stood up and walked to where he stood.

'You have the eyes of an old man,' she said.

'Leave it alone, will you,' he snapped. 'At least there are

only three more days on this lousy ship.' They stood silently by the railing for hours, watching the lizard-green sea.

That night Yasha brought good salted fish, some boiled onions, fresh tomatoes, and good cheese as well as a loaf of fresh bread. It was a feast. Soon after, there was a storm and they slept inside the hold, for just to get near the door was to risk being carried out on deck by a gale. Waking and sleeping, Sonya thought how much stronger she was each day, how little she feared what waited for her in the strange new land ahead. My God, I hardly notice what surrounds me, she thought. A year ago I would have been stunned at the sight here in front of my eyes, yet I am perfectly comfortable in this dark corner of this unspeakable ship.

'Elena?' Yasha tapped her on the shoulder. 'I could try to arrange a bath for you if you like.'

'A bath? Where?'

'Never mind. Would you like a bath?'

At first she was delighted with the idea, but then she frowned. She shook her head. 'It is kind of you. But I am like the others. I am one of them. I might as well smell like them.'

He seemed disappointed in her answer, but he lay back and closed his eyes. 'Did you go through trouble already to get me a bath?' she asked. 'Yasha?'

'It was no trouble. Forget it.' He turned on his side.

2

When Sonya awoke on the last day of the voyage, Yasha was not in his usual place, his back against hers. She sat up and rubbed her eyes. The child, too, was gone. Panicked, she looked for her case. It was still there, just at her head. Sonya stood up, yawning, and looked around the dim hold. A young girl who was watching her pointed toward the door. Sonya walked to it and shoved her weight against it. The wind was still so strong that it did not give easily.

Outside on the deck the world was gray and misty and howling, but the heavy rain had stopped. The waves were almost to the top of the deck, and the ship shuddered and banged as each one snapped against the hull. Sonya steadied herself by holding the rope that ran along the deck, and she walked slowly against the wind toward their favorite place by the air shaft. There the two of them sat, Delphi between Yasha's legs, her back against his chest. He had put Sonya's shawl as well as both his coat and his jacket around them. He did not see Sonya until she stood in front of him.

'We wanted to see the statue,' he said. 'We wanted to be the first ones.' His eyes were guileless and glistening with excitement. 'Come.' He swung an arm open and the coats, like a curtain attached, hung there in the wind.

Sonya sat down beside them and he closed his arm around her, the coats and shawl encompassing her. The wind was fierce and dark and swirled like the Baba Yaga's rage around the three of them.

As they came within sight of the Statue of Liberty, the entire boatload of people emptied out of the hold and stood on the deck, clutching one another like talismans, weeping and saluting that great gray-green statue in the harbor. She was the last border they had to cross, the final barrier. They were a motley crew. Most of them had come from Kishinev, the last remainders of wave after wave of

Cossack brutality. Did they exaggerate? Had fifty thousand been killed? She had asked them what they knew of the baby's parentage, but they knew nothing. Even Yasha knew nothing.

The ship docked where another, smaller ship was waiting to take them to the immigration depot. She followed Yasha. We are herded about like cattle, like goats and pigs, she thought, going with the others to the smaller boat. The building ahead of them had turrets, and for a moment, only a moment in the early morning sun, it looked like a castle. Their boat landed and they waited at the mooring. So many hundreds ahead of them already and it was not even ten o'clock in the morning. It would take hours, perhaps a day.

Let this child be well, prayed Sonya. She held on to the girl's hand. Still not one complaint from that lovely full mouth even as the hundreds of other children wept and clung to their parents or each other. They walked ashore on unsteady legs; four by four they shuffled up to the big door to wait again. Already the terror caused by the barriers and the cages upstairs had spread to those below, and there was an outbreak of weeping, like a plague, weeping, screaming, clutching. Sonya had heard of what was happening up above them in that great hall, the examinations, the questions, the chalk marks made on the seemingly unfit so they might be reexamined later. In my way I am your entry card, too, she thought, lifting up the child now. Your mother would never have passed the eyes that will be looking at us. She brushed the girl's hair with her fingers and smiled at her. She must not betray me now, Sonya thought.

The din was nearly unbearable, and Sonya wanted to scream out at them and tell them there was nothing to fear up there. You fools! This is at least a little freedom. No one will kill you here. Instead, she bit her lip and put the child down again to tighten the bandanna about her hair. I do not need anyone to notice that the color of my hair and the color of hers do not match at all.

At last they were on the top landing, and she was separated from Yasha by cages and fences. There, too, ahead, were the doctors. She knew they were doctors despite their militaristic dress. The first doctor's hazy blue eyes looked at both her and the child in one swift comprehending stare before they moved beyond him. At least we have passed the first test, Sonya thought, as she walked slowly ahead in the tearful tide, anonymous as they and still uncertain.

She heard screams and such terrible weeping that she shuddered. Then she pushed slightly ahead and stood up on her toes. They were looking into people's eyes, pushing the lid back like a dead piece of skin. She looked into the child's eyes. They seemed clean and clear. Dear God, let her sight be unblemished! The second doctor was waiting with his button hook to push the eyelid back. First the child. Not a murmur. Then Sonya. The stinging was terrible, momentarily blinding. No wonder everyone was in absolute fear. Sonya bit down on her lip, this time drawing blood. The child was braver. Amazing, Sonya thought, this skinny bit of a child, how had she learned such forbearance?

The men were undergoing still another inspection in a separate line. Venereal disease? Women, too, had venereal disease. What craziness there was in this place, this great hall in this massive building with its four towers gleaming like beacons in the morning sun. She had watched a man with chalk marks being led into one of the detaining cages. Even to untrained eyes he had tuberculosis. You will die soon anyway, she thought. What difference where, poor fellow? Any soil is soil to die on.

After hours of waiting, Yasha rejoined them and they stood in still another line. 'Will it never end?' she asked him. him.

'Cheer up,' he answered. 'It must end. America is full of people like us.'

When finally she stood in front of the inspectors with her husband and her child, she reminded herself not to use English or French or German. How would a shtetl Jew know these languages? She had picked up some Yiddish on the boat, so she could use that and Russian. She was from Kishinev? She nodded. The child was one and a half. Did they have any money? Yes, her husband answered. He read a paragraph in a Russian book and she read the same one.

They were literate. The name? They fumbled with the card she had pinned to her chest, Schernitsky. No, they said, writing something on another card, stamping something and handing it to them. Stern. The name was Stern now. They asked her husband what his profession was. Tailor. Everyone on the boat was a tailor. Very well, they said, go over there. How simple it was, how simple!

'Wait a minute. You, with the black scarf on your head, lady, wait a minute.'

Sonya clutched Yasha's arm. She pretended not to hear the voice and kept going, pulling Yasha along with her. What could they want? Now there was someone standing in front of her, pointing for her to go back.

'You with the scarf, just a minute, come back here.' The fellow had a cap with a badge on it and eyes like a ferret. 'Come over here. Give me that child.'

'What do they want?' she whispered quickly to Yasha. 'What do they want with the child?' There was no way to go except toward the inspector. Yasha was behind her, his arm around her shoulder. Sonya was holding the child, shielding her from the eyes of the inspector. Yasha guided her back.

'Give me that child.' The inspector said it again.

Sonya held Delphi tighter, panic rising in her like bile. What could he want? She was standing across the examining table from him now, still clutching Delphi. The man leaned over and tried to take her, but Sonya held on. 'Put her down here on the table. I can't budge her. Put her down.'

'Nothing is the matter.'

'Are you an idiot, too? Give me that child. She's too silent. I want to look at her.' He shook his head at Sonya. 'Do all you people only understand when you want to? Put the child down on the table!' he screamed.

Sonya looked at Yasha, who grimaced and shook his head. 'You must,' he said.

'Why?' she asked him, still clutching Delphi. 'What will they do?'

'Nothing is wrong.'

'Shut up, the two of you. I haven't all this time to waste.

201

Put the child down now. I shouldn't want to hurt her.' Yasha nodded at Sonya, patting her on the back.

'I think she is an imbecile,' the inspector said. 'Why doesn't she move or speak?'

'She speaks,' Sonya cried. 'Ask my husband, ask the others on the ship, where are they? Yasha, tell him, tell him she speaks!' Sonya grabbed Yasha with one hand, still holding Delphi with the other, and pushed Yasha forward as if his testimony might change everything. 'Please, please!' she screamed.

'Quiet, stop screaming. It's not all bad. Your husband can stay. Just you and the child will have to go back. Now let go of her, do you hear me? Put her down.'

Sonya looked at Delphi, still silent, her eyes glued to Sonya's face. 'Put her down?' she repeated, as if she did not understand the words. The man walked around the table, his face in a scowl, anger all over him. Sonya held Delphi tighter, not believing it as the man grabbed Delphi and pulled her out of her arms. 'No!' Sonya screamed with such force she thought that the whole building would be silent. The man walked back to his side of the wooden table. The child looked at Sonya, her eyes full of terror, but she made no sound.

Sonya watched in horror as the inspector picked up Delphi's chin in his hand and brought his face down to hers. 'No!' She screamed again. Whether it was Sonya's last agonizing cry or the eyes of the inspector, the child was suddenly frightened.

'Mama! Mama!' she cried, scrambling to her knees and clinging to Sonya. Sonya grabbed her and hugged her, relief flooding her body. 'You see,' she cried, almost in hysteria, 'she is a perfectly normal child.'

'Normal? I don't call any one of you normal,' the man answered, dismissing the three of them with a wave of his hand. 'Next.'

Sonya turned to Yasha, and the three of them walked quickly toward the gate, Delphi still clinging to her, sobbing, murmuring, 'Mama.'

'What would have happened?' she asked.

'As he said, you would have had to go back with the child. I could have stayed here, a man with a trade.'

202

'I was so frightened,' Sonya said.

'I think you have become very attached to her.'

'No, no, I was just frightened at the thought of her going back alone.'

'But you would have had to go with her, Elena, don't you get that?' Sonya shook her head. She had been so frightened that they were going to take the child away that she hadn't even heard what the inspector had said.

'I'll walk you through this one last gate,' Yasha said, 'and then we'll say good-by. There are a lot of thieves out there, and a lot of people pretending they can help, so be careful. Come, I'll take you.' She followed him to the gate, and as it swung open she felt such relief and triumph she nearly hooted. There were crowds of people, more than had been in the immigration center. 'Elena, I wanted to ask you something. It has bothered me.'

'What?' Sonya asked.

'Did you really murder someone? Was it really the reason you were coming to America?'

'Did you believe me?'

'Yes,' he said. 'I wasn't frightened, you know, but yes, I believed you.'

'I did, Yasha. I did.' The baby's arms were around her and Sonya pulled her away and held her out to Yasha. 'Take her. I'll get your money.' He held the baby, awkward as he waited for her to fish out his money. She held the hundred roubles out to him. He looked at it for a second and then, putting the baby back in her free arm, took it.

'So good.' His face tried to find a suitable expression for his farewell, at first a smile, then a look of some seriousness. 'So, my wife and child. Good-by. May the Lord bless you.' His cheeks flushed as he spoke. He nodded his head once abruptly and quickly turned and walked away.

Sonya watched him disappear into the crowd. Delphi slept on her shoulder and whimpered in her sleep. Yasha would become a memory like Marushka, her mother, Bruno, Gregory. The child, too, would have to be a memory. There was no room for her in a new life. Sonya looked around her. She had to find a representative of some agency or other.

Such chaos! A man and a woman pushed close to her, jostling the child. Sonya clutched her hand case to her and transferred Delphi, who managed to sleep through all the shouting, to her other shoulder. She noticed a man in a peaked hat inside a booth some hundred feet from her. A small crowd milled around him, each one obviously waiting to question him. There was a banner with a Jewish star painted on it, some writing that she could not read, and in smaller writing, in English, below, the words JEWISH EMERGENCY IMMIGRATION. She would start with him.

'Sonyasha.' The voice was not raised, but it was so deep and strong it bubbled up from the bottom of the raging tide around her to stop her where she stood. Her heart pounded with fear and disbelief. It could not be.

'Sonyasha,' he said again. It was. Gregory Tolchin stood four feet away from her, staring at her, his eyes fixed on her. He wore a white shirt, a dark sweater, a pair of simple wool trousers, and workman's dirty boots, but he appeared to her to be in full uniform, elegant and commanding.

'Oh, my blessed God,' she whispered. She could not have moved. People hurried past her, pushing, pulling. She could not keep her eyes from his. She felt terror in her throat as a wave of fear washed over her. He just stood motionless, staring at her. Was she losing her mind? Still, she could not move, not a muscle in her body worked, yet she must. She would be a queen even in this chaos, even in filthy clothes that smelled of dampness and vomit. She took a step toward him.

'Let me pass,' she commanded.

'I have come to take you home, Sonya,' he said, his voice hard and icy. He had not moved. The shape of a man passed between them.

'Where I am going or what I do does not concern you.' She turned to leave, but as she did he quickly moved in front of her, blocking her. She was aware that her whole body trembled. She clutched the baby with both hands, afraid if she loosened her grip, her soul would sail out of her body to him. It was madness and yet he still possessed her. She shook her head. No! She clung to Delphi as if the child were an icon whose power could protect her from the

204

devil, pressing the small body tighter. He was in front of her, not a foot away. If someone had told her there was a rope around her neck and that this second was her last on earth, she would not have been surprised. She could be no more frightened of death than of this man. His eyes, she had forgotten his eyes.

'Mama! Mama,' the baby cried out. It was no wonder, Sonya thought, I have been holding her so tight I have hurt her. She looked away from him to Delphi.

'And who have we here?' He reached out his hand to touch the baby, but Sonya pulled her away from him.

'It is none of your business,' she snapped at him. She would not be his flotsam, riding his tides. She had no need to answer him.

'None of my business? But we are still married, you and I. That makes it very much my business. Since I have heard no mention of a child, I am intrigued.'

'She does not concern you. You know very well that I never expected to see you again.' He was paying no attention to her but kept his eyes on Delphi, who was awake and now peeked at him, a smile on her small mouth.

'Whose is she, Sonya?'

'Mine.' The lie slipped out easily.

'You must not lie about this, my dear. I would certainly have heard of a child.'

'Not all secrets are yours,' she said, raising her chin defiantly. 'At any rate, as I said, neither my daughter nor I concern you. Stand away.'

'What is her name?'

'Delphi.'

'And her father's name,' he said, 'what is that?' He appeared so calm, yet the vein in his right temple beat hard against his skin. Could he think the child was his? That was beyond arrogance, but he must. His vein betrayed him. Good, Sonya thought, it is my game now!

'Her father was a revolutionary who went underground and disappeared without a word.' Sonya's voice became stronger with every word she uttered. 'Perhaps you knew him, the late Count Tolchin?' She watched him closely.

Without blinking, he took his eyes slowly off the child and focused on Sonya. 'I find that difficult to believe,' he said, staring at her, the vein throbbing even harder.

'Believe it or not. Will you stand away from us!'

He would not move but crossed his arms at his waist. 'Who is her father, Sonya? Answer me.' His voice was even icier. She had managed to unnerve him. Good. At least that!

'If you do not believe it, corroborate it with one of your dutiful comrades. Tell him to visit the Admiralty. I kept her there, because Lopuhin thought she was his and that was helpful.' Sonya managed a small laugh. 'Men are so arrogant, don't you think? They are all so willing to be fathers if they have no real responsibilities in that office.' She continued to smile at him. 'Does that satisfy you enough to let me pass?'

He did not appear to move a muscle, but suddenly Delphi was in his arms and he was holding her up in front of him, staring at her. Slowly, he pushed the baby's hair away from her face. Sonya's anger was quick and fierce and she leaped at him, shrieking. 'You are the devil come from hell! Give me my child!' Delphi burst into tears.

Tolchin put his forearm under the child and lifted her away from Sonya's hand, trying to calm her. 'Not so quickly, my dear, if, as you say, she is my child, too.' Sonya swung her bag at him with both her hands, but it only grazed his leg, making him smile at her fury. 'How amazing you are, Sonyasha! Even filthy and growling like a dog, you manage to be beautiful.' Sonya swung the bag again, but this time it fell out of her grasp to the pavement between them. Suddenly she remembered the knife inside. His blood would purify her, sanctify her. It would be justifiable murder.

'I will kill you!' She screamed it at him as she started forward to the bag. Somehow he managed to hold the crying baby firmly on his left arm while he grabbed her wrist with his right hand, twisting it until it burned with pain. 'My bag!' she cried. She felt his breath on her face and heard his voice. It was full of amusement.

'Stop making a spectacle of yourself, my dear sweet wife. Already you have managed to collect a crowd about us. Must I remind you that assassins and anarchists are not welcomed here? Now show your audience how happy you are to see your beloved husband. Kiss me, Sonyasha.'

She tried to pull her hand away, but he held it with no difficulty. Tears blinded her as she shook with rage. Out of the corner of her eye, she saw Delphi's uncomprehending stare. 'I said kiss me,' he repeated as he lowered his mouth to hers. With that she pulled him toward her and sank her teeth into his bottom lip until she tasted his blood. She felt him shift Delphi a little in his arms before she felt him grab a fistful of her hair and yank her backward. When she looked up at him, his tongue was pressed hard against his bleeding lip. He bent over and lifted her bag and turned his back on her, walking away. She did not care. He thought the child was his. How it would please her now to go with him. She had the strength to leave him as quickly as it suited her. She had won the day.

In the carriage, she sat as far away from him as possible, ignoring the man he had introduced as his friend and refusing to answer any of their questions. Gregory played with the child, examining her, turning her this way and that, looking at her joints, her muscles, her bones, like a butcher, she thought. How she would torture him! How he would pay! She nearly smiled as she stared out the window, looking at this new city. February, and there was no snow, just the gray of the cobblestones, the browns and reds of the façades of the houses and factories. Suddenly, a huge plaza thronged with people, stores, carriages, streetcars, and then, as suddenly, a wide street with hardly anyone anywhere, just rows of buildings and an arch like the one in Paris. New York seemed a grimy city, full of uninteresting architecture, and with all she had heard of it, it was not a place where she would wish to stay. Perhaps, in a few days, after she got her bearings, she would take the child and go to Boston – after she had finished with Gregory Tolchin! How wonderful that he should believe that a strange child was his own.

3

Inside the narrow rowhouse to which Tolchin brought her, the dark rooms were piled haphazardly like old hatboxes on a closet shelf. There were people everywhere. The sliding glass doors to the parlor were only partially closed, and she saw four, perhaps five people seated there. Other voices came from the room on her left. Two men stood arguing toward the end of the hallway. They nodded to Tolchin and stared at her as she followed him down the hall.

'First you will have some food, Sonya. The child must be hungry. Volya! Anna!' His voice rang out down the hallway. Somewhere a door opened and a voice answered his. 'The food!' he ordered. 'Bring it to the dining room!' He motioned Sonya into a small room where there was a round table and six shabby chairs. A young dark-haired woman was clearing the table and she nodded to them. Tolchin walked to the window and yanked the dark curtains apart, letting in a little light. 'I must say,' he said, ignoring the girl who went on clearing the table, 'that I can never get over those people as they come off the boat. How innocent they are! They think this is the promised land, the end of tyranny. So they will not be mowed down like stacks of wheat by the Cossacks. Instead they will fall under the weight of injustice.'

Sonya listened to him ramble. What was he talking about? Why was he going on? Would they never be alone?

'Of course, for the wealthy, those in first class, there is no Ellis Island.' He glanced up at the tall, thin girl who had come into the room carrying a large tray of sandwiches, bread, butter, and several wedges of cheese. The girl set the tray down in the center of the table. 'We will need a tin cup and a bottle of milk. Does she drink from a cup, Sonya?' Sonya did not answer. 'Is there no fruit, Mira? No cake?'

'Anna will get it.' She nodded to the other girl. 'I will

bring the milk.'

Tolchin slid Delphi off his shoulder and put her down on the edge of the table, handing her an end of bread. Again, he pushed her hair out of her face and stared down at her, searching her features. The two girls came back with the cake, the fruit, and the milk, and a young man brought in a large pot of tea and cups and saucers.

Finally, they all left, the man closing the sliding doors. Tolchin poured some milk into a tin cup and handed it to Delphi, who drank it greedily. 'Well,' he said, sitting in his chair and leaning back, staring at Delphi, his hands behind his head, 'I cannot think why I have never heard about this child.'

'Do you think that you must always hear of everything?' Sonya shouted, suddenly outraged by his continuing arrogance, her years of anger uncontrollable. 'Did you hear about the torture you put me through while you were out of Petersburg? Did you hear about Vera Anatolyevna? Damn you, damn you to hell, Gregory Tolchin, what kind of a game were you playing?'

'I think you should have left all your questions on the other side of the ocean, Sonya.'

'Who are you to say such a thing? How dare you? You cannot imagine what I suffered. You cannot imagine what you did to me! Now you want me to forget it?' She backed away from him to the farthest corner of the room, her body trembling from her anger.

'Calm down, Sonya, and lower your voice!' Again he was abrupt and icy. 'No one else here needs to know how hysterical you can become, and look at the child, you frighten her.' Exhausted, half asleep, the baby lay stretched out on the table, her head resting on her arm, her lower lip curled down at the corners and quivering. 'No, no, little one, you must not cry.' Tolchin took the empty cup she still held in her small hand and gently patted her on the back. 'Sit down, Sonya. Although you are entitled to none, I will give you as brief an explanation as is possible. Then I hope never to hear about it again.' Sonya crossed her arms and stood where she was. Tolchin went on speaking. 'It is not so complicated, actually. At the time I disappeared, Evno Azev - you knew him by his code name, Valentin -

he and I were in charge of terrorist activity in western Russia. We also worked as government agents. Azev worked for Plehve, and I worked for Lopuhin. It was, of course, a delicate business, and I could tell no one.'

'So it was true! You did work for Lopuhin!' Her face was full of disgust.

'Of course it was true. We needed to keep track of Lopuhin. I used him and gave him only what I had to. Unfortunately, Lopuhin got onto Azev's trail and I had to leave rather than expose him. It was Azev who arranged the killing of Plehve. A year later, he killed Grand Duke Sergei. I had to leave, Sonya, for him to accomplish that, and I could trust nobody. Nobody, not even my comrade Azev. As a matter of fact, after the murder of the grand duke he was forced to give my identity to Lopuhin. I would have done the same in his position. At any rate, I cannot return to Russia until Lopuhin is out of the way. It should be soon enough now.' He stopped, fished in his jacket pocket for a tin of cigarettes, lifted one out, and put it to his mouth. Sonya stared at him. How could she believe him? He flicked a match into flame with his thumbnail, lighting his cigarette and carefully blowing the smoke away from Delphi. Sonya frowned.

'You don't approve?' He gestured at her with the cigarette. 'Bad habits are easy to acquire, Sonyasha.'

'I do not trust you, Gregory Tolchin.' It was a pronouncement, and he looked at her in amazement, breaking into laughter, choking on the smoke of his cigarette. The child's tin cup fell to the floor and rolled to the corner of the room, stopping against the wall.

'You astound me,' he said, 'astound me!' He stopped coughing, smashed out the cigarette, and wiped at tears at the sides of his eyes. 'Trust? The word is a joke in your mouth! Did no one tell you that you nearly ruined our entire operation? That you left Lopuhin quite convinced that you were a revolutionary and he took reprisals everywhere? We lost men, Sonya. Men you know. Shall I tell you their names?'

'Please do, Gregory. I already know your victims. How could you give them Vera Anatolyevna? What kind of a man could do such a thing?'

'It is not King Arthur's court, Sonya. We are revolutionaries. Some of us die.'

'Revolutionaries! It is another name for traitors, cowards, and thieves. You are good for nothing but to take innocent children like Bruno and hypnotize them with your poetry, with your promises. Nothing will come of your revolution, Gregory Tolchin, but killing. You fool yourselves, but you will fool me no longer. I am sick of all of it, through with all of it, all the child's play, and the deceit and double-crossing. Oh!' She shook her fists in the air. 'Why do I even talk to you about it, you will—' She stopped short. 'Why are you grinning at me like a hyena?'

'I have tried to imagine it many times, Sonyasha, but I never could see the part where you pulled the trigger.'

'I shot Lopuhin and I have your child. I cannot help the short-comings of your imagination.' Why was she even talking to him? It was no use. Fool! She shook her head and walked to the table, poured herself a cup of tea, and drank some. It burned the tip of her tongue. 'Damn!' she said, setting down the cup, spilling some on the table.

'Always everything a little too quickly, Sonyasha.'

'How tiresome you are, Gregory! Please just be so kind as to show me and my child a room where we might rest. You and I have nothing further to say to one another.'

'There is only my room,' he said, standing up beside her. 'Of course, if you like, I will sleep elsewhere.' He stared at her breasts.

'Please sleep elsewhere,' she said, her eyes on his. 'I am sure it will not inconvenience you.' She waited as he picked up the sleeping child and then followed him up two flights of stairs into a large, comfortably furnished room. He put Delphi on the bed and began to undress her. It was so easy the way he slid her out of her clothes and under the down comforter.

'She is a very sweet child,' he said. 'There is a bath down the hall, there, to your left. Is there anything else you would like?' He was facing her, walking toward her. He stood in front of her and very slowly, he touched her face. His hand on her flesh was cool. Dear God, no! she thought.

'Try to rest,' he said. 'I must say, Sonyasha, motherhood becomes you.' He was gone, his legs cutting into the distance between her and the doorway in two easy steps. The door closed. She found herself facing the small mirror near the doorway. She walked toward it. Curse her vanity. But she looked at herself, she looked at her face and her skin and her eyes, and she saw her skin burning, burning. She was beautiful, young and beautiful enough to do whatever she pleased in her life. She touched herself, shivering. And then she turned away. No! She would not think of it.

After her bath she stretched out naked under the quilt on the bed next to the baby and fell asleep. She dreamed of her first meeting with Gregory Tolchin, and when she awoke, he was sitting on the bed beside her. He lifted her up toward him and his mouth found hers. There would never be anything as terrifying as this possession of her by him, as awful as her response to him. It was as if her body were a pine forest and he the fire to destroy it. Everything in her crumbled, snapped at the heat of him, pieces of her falling everywhere, as the tongues of his flames attacked her. There was nothing to save her, nothing to stop the last loud rumble that preceded her total disintegration. As ever, she lay in ruins, smoldering, in ashes.

Afterward, she lay beside him, silent, her skin still trembling under his fingers as he lazily traced circles on her belly. She listened to the baby's even breathing from the floor below, where Gregory had laid her after wrapping her in the heavy down quilt. She felt Gregory's breath at the side of her forehead, his lips against it. His breathing, too, was small and even.

'My family, Gregory,' she said finally. 'Do they . . . Did Lopuhin hurt my family?'

'No,' he answered, taking a deep breath. 'It was, however, as you can imagine, necessary for many reasons to make it seem as if you had done away with yourself.' He paused, but she said nothing, lying on her back and staring at the ceiling. 'I'm sorry, Sonya. I had to arrange the suicide for you or there would have been too many unanswerable questions. Your mother was especially hard hit, but I understand she is less so now that Anton's wife

212

and children are with her.'

'Maria Kosnova lives with her?' It all seemed so far away, and yet their lives went on without her. How strange.

'Sonya, oh, Sonya.' He sighed and his eyelids fluttered. 'I don't want to torture you. I never did. You are here to find a new life. Perhaps we can find one together. You are, after all, my wife. We do have some history together.' He rolled over to the side of the bed, switching on the light and reaching for a cigarette. 'I went to London last spring,' he said, lighting it, 'for the Revolutionary Congress. There was so much squabbling. Each man believed only his way was the right way. It was nearly comical. There is some truth in what you said before. They are all czars, finally. And if they are not czars, then they are dreamers or thieves. I am afraid men too easily lose sight of principle in the face of power. At least I have learned to be more selective in those I choose to help these days.'

'What do you do here? There are so many people . . .'

'We do many things. We have a press on the top floor. We print material for distribution abroad, to London and Russia. People come and go, some are in trouble. Even in America, police are fussy. We have meetings here. I raise money. Some for the press, some for the underground, some I send to our revolutionary friends, the dreamers. The czars and the thieves are getting strong now and have no need of it.'

'Where do you get such a great deal of money?'

'From anyone I can. Russians, Americans. There is one Jew, a fellow named Borach, who has been most helpful. His family were all killed in a pogrom. He has made an enormous fortune here and gives generously to anyone who wants to rid Russia of the czar. There is positive work to be done here, Sonya, more than spying and carrying on. I would not force you to stay, but you might consider it. It would please me.'

She did not answer him at first, not until, surprised, she felt the tears running down her cheeks. 'I will consider it,' she said, knowing immediately she would stay. She had been right from the moment she had seen him on the pier. He was her devil come from hell. Nothing had changed after all.

He was not beside her when she awoke the next morning. He had put Delphi back beside her on the bed. Now Sonya watched her sleep, her little mouth open, her little body curled into a ball. 'What will happen to you,' Sonya whispered, leaning over to touch the little body, 'and to me, now that you have made me a mother?'

How sweet she was, this Delphi, this dark little girl from nowhere, this gift of fate. Perhaps she would be Sonya's chance. A new day, a new country, a new child, a new life. Her passion for Gregory Tolchin was her curse, and she would have to live with it as if it were a wound. The loss of an eye, the loss of a limb, would not have stopped her from accomplishment. Why should he? Even though she herself was not free, she could free others. Indeed, her bondage would make her stronger, make her work harder to release others from womanish enslavement, by a man or a country.

'We will show him what women are,' she said aloud to Delphi, and then, more softly, 'Whatever I cannot be, you will be.' Delphi's eyes opened a moment and then fluttered closed. Sonya frowned. Already, she thought, shaking her head, already I disturb your dreams.

4

Sonya   May 4, 1907

Gregory is here so little and only for such short periods of time, and yet it is months before I can begin to forget his effect. The fullness of my body and my feelings come together in his arms and for so long afterward – this long! – my senses and my soul remember. It no longer matters if he deceives me, my life only shines when I am in his light. He is a giant spotlight, and even when it is turned off, I am left with his image in front of my eyes, so that I never see the real world without him in front of me.

Since Gregory has left me in charge, I have made several concrete achievements. The press is more than paying for itself, and it supports its workers. Last month we had an excess of $89.47. Within the year we may begin to publish bimonthly. I see that the house is organized and clean. Fewer vagrant socialists pass through now that everyone is expected to do his share of work. Besides Gregory, Delphi, and me, there are only three others now in residence. Mira and Samuel are quite at home up in the fourth-floor attic, and one of the spare rooms is taken by a student friend of theirs on his way to the West. In future, I believe the less the spare rooms are used, the better. Mira and Samuel are quite enough underfoot, but since they are the backbone of the press, they must stay.

Delphi speaks in sentences and enjoys looking at picture books. She writes both the Russian and the English alphabets, and everyone who comes comments on how smart and well behaved she is. We work together each day on her numbers and letters. She is healthy and cries little. She is a solid child.

Perhaps this is all I will find from life; at least I am doing something. Let it be reward enough. I am like a wild rose smothered by a vine. I manage one pale pink flower here and another there, but think of what I could do alone and in the sun!

June 15, 1908

It has been confirmed that Lopuhin has been stripped of his office. He has been sent to the provinces, back to his beginnings, as it were. It has allowed Gregory entrance into Petersburg. I have had one letter from him in the three months he has been gone. He has seen my family. They still think me dead. How peculiar! Will I ever go to Russia? I wonder. I miss it so!

Although Gregory writes that certain negotiations have taken much longer than he expected, I have been assured by his friend Boris Osmarkian that he is in hiding after arranging a munitions shipment to our friends in Kiev. The police there, Osmarkian says, are fierce and Gregory must watch himself for several weeks more. I am in the dark about what he does, even where he is. He has helped another twenty Jews out of the country and they will arrive within the month. His Mr Borach will give us enough money for them and some extra for the running of the house. All the rooms here are filled again – so much for my resolve.

I am cranky and crabby and unhappy today, behaving more like a three-year-old child than Delphi. I must stop such self-indulgence.

Tonight I am going to a meeting at the Women's Political Union. I have been following their work with interest. The suffragists in England are provoking vast attention with their acts of disrespect and violence. I think the Union will soon start such tactics here, and I am toying with the idea of joining them. The fight for women's rights is another revolution. Mrs Blatch is speaking tonight. I have seen pictures of her. I like her face. She seems determined, as I once was.

*   *   *

Delphi's earliest memory was a man's leering face, his big red eyes staring at her and her mother, his fat lips curled back on his stubbly chin and cheeks as he yelled at them, 'If yer man don't keep ya busy enough, lady, I'll show him how!' And then Delphi would see his hips jut out, his front

216

moving back and forth in their direction as if he were pumping. Then she would see her mother's face, grim and set until the tomato exploded all over it, looking like blood, and then Delphi would nearly scream as she had the day it happened. They had been marching in a huge crowd of other women and children. For hours they had walked in the slight rain, until Delphi had thought that her feet would disappear into the pavement under her, and that's when the man had yelled at Sonya and started pumping, and the other had thrown the tomato, screaming like a demon, 'You don't need votes. Get back in the kitchen where you belong!'

Right after the parade, she would dream of it, her small chest heaving and frightened tears stinging her eyes. 'The man,' she would cry out, 'the man!' Then Sonya would come to her bedroom, wipe her tears, and sit on her bed and pat her hands, and sometimes smooth back her hair. Delphi would try to crawl into her mother's arms, but somehow Sonya always managed to push her gently back into the pillows and tenderly reassure her that everything was all right again.

Finally the memory persisted, but it no longer made her wake in the night. Now it came in the morning, just as she was waking. Delphi would make it disappear by opening her eyes to the bar of morning light that came at her from the window. The light always surprised her somehow. She would lay in her bed and watch it fill up her room, making little boxed rainbows, or strips of color here and there on the bare white walls. The first light meant silence, wonderful silence that was only for her. Too soon it would be gone. She would hear the morning noises of the others in her house, and, hoping to stretch the soundless time, she would put on her robe, tie it around, and, careful not to trip on it, run down the two flights of narrow stairs to the kitchen. It was still noiseless there, and she would wait until she heard the first one coming down before she would take the bread from the tin breadbox and put it on the table, put up the kettle for tea, and open the icebox for the butter, milk, and jam. Then she would settle into a chair and watch them as they came, one by one, to sit around the table.

'Good morning, Delphi.'

'Good morning, Mira.'

'Did you sleep well?'

'Yes, thank you.'

'Do we have any coffee?'

'Yes, I think there is some.' Delphi got up and scampered into the pantry. She heard Samuel's footsteps coming down the stairs.

'Did you get them?' Mira asked. 'Give them to me.'

'Only for a kiss.' There was silence.

'Delphi.' Mira called. 'Come, we have a surprise.' Delphi came back with the coffee. 'Look,' Mira said, holding up a brown paper bag. 'Guess what it is.'

'Explosives!' It was Josip Kerenov. He was new. It was only his third day. Delphi wasn't sure she liked him. He had bushy black hair and eyebrows, and he was short and his eyes were too close together.

'No!' Mira laughed.

'A bomb for Nicholas. I myself will take it to Petersburg.'

'Sweet rolls?' Delphi asked in a very soft voice.

'Yes, Delphi, yes!' Mira smiled at her. 'Sweet rolls for a sweet child. I sent Samuel to get them just for you.' Delphi took the brown bag and opened it. There were six sweet rolls, enough for her to have one all to herself. She put them on a plate on the table, then sat down and took the largest one. 'You see,' Mira had continued, 'the child thinks of food, not dynamite. You must eat sometime, Josip.'

'I do well enough.' They all laughed.

'Would you like some coffee, Josip?' Mira asked. 'I can give it to you the way the Americans drink it, full of cream and sugar. It is more like a sweet than coffee.'

'Yes, yes, I would like to try. I haven't seen many real Americans yet; everywhere I go there are only Russians. Are they really wild, like the cowboys?'

'Some are,' answered Samuel. 'They are mostly full of fun.'

'They are like children.' Sonya had come into the room. 'They are children, or they are imperialist exploiters. The ones like children are sweet and amusing, like children.

218

The others are the worst sort. Good morning, everyone. Good morning, Delphi.'

'Good morning, Sonya.'

'Who gave you sweet rolls?'

'Mira and Samuel.'

'Mira and Samuel are too good to you. Is this week's magazine finished, done, out, and sold, that they can afford sweet rolls?'

'I must have them, Sonya,' Samuel said, 'or I could never finish it.'

Sonya did not smile. She turned to Josip. 'You must tell Mira and Samuel what you were telling me last night, Josip. Josip just was with Gregory last week, in Germany of all places.'

There were parts of the story that Delphi loved to hear, but they were not the political parts, and they were not the parts she heard often. She loved to hear about the green of the Crimea, and the palace where Sonya had spent her summers, and the black men who waited on the czars, and the fair by the cool river where Sonya had beaten the young man at the shooting contest, and the snow, the whiteness, and the birch trees. Sonya talked so much about the Romanovs. She wanted them dead. There was a boy, Alexis, just about Delphi's age; would Sonya want to kill him, too?

'Never, never, never.' Josip was already screaming at Samuel. Delphi sighed and sucked on her roll. 'There is no need for violence and agitation any longer. The Duma will carry us toward a socialist state. Finally the people will have a real voice. Everyone is in too much of a hurry, and Lenin is an egomaniacal monster, I tell you. He is worse than a monster.' Josip's fist hit the heavy table and it bounced, sending the sugar bowl on its side. Delphi picked it up and scooped the sugar back in.

'Josip, you are a true donkey's ass. Shall we now give the idiot peasants who call themselves Russians a store to open, then?'

'You miss my point. Lenin and his followers sit at their conferences in Europe talking, but doing nothing. What do they have to do with any realities? Now that we have gotten rid of Stolypin, we will see the dangers of the autocrats even more clearly. Who can wait for the theorists? They prattle on and Russia suffers.'

'What does Gregory feel?' Sonya asked. Delphi looked at her. She was so very beautiful, her pile of gleaming red hair pinned in a fat circle on her head, her wide eyes full of light. Delphi wished she looked more like her. Even now, listening to Josip, the two lines between her eyes exaggerated, tiny lines appearing around her pursed mouth, even now she was beautiful.

Delphi dipped the other end of her sweet roll into the milk. Since birth, it seemed, they had taught her revolution, and for as long, she hadn't cared. She had learned it all, could even spell all of it, had made up a little tune to sing it to, Bolsheviks, Mensheviks, Social Revolutionaries, Marx and Engel, Constitutional Democrats. Such a mouthful of names. How could grownups argue about truths all the time, each one the only one, from morning until night, the endless words, endless names? They were all so angry and passionate, and that, too, made no sense, all that noise, those words.

'And who is teaching Delphi her lessons for today?' Sonya would finally ask, just before the great diaspora from the kitchen. One or the other of the people would agree it was his or her turn. 'I don't know,' Sonya said, stretching her arms wide, throwing back her head, and staring at the ceiling, 'whether Delphi should be a lawyer or a doctor.'

'A lawyer is a capitalist tool, Sonya,' Mira said, rinsing her cup at the sink. 'Besides, Delphi is only seven years old.'

'Nevertheless, by the time she is ready, the revolution will be over in Russia. It will be time to start a revolution here, and it will be good for her to know the law so she can change it.'

'First let them get the vote, Sonya.' Josip was already sweeping the floor in the kitchen, bumping into everyone else.

'Well, I am doing my best to help women get the vote,' Sonya said, then sighed. 'But sometimes I don't think it will change anything. Women are often no smarter than the men they live with. In this country the revolution will not be by votes or by soldiers, it will be by manipulation. Smart people will know how to get power. That's what I wish for my daughter, power. As I am impotent, let her have power.'

'Sonya,' Samuel said, laughing, 'you have power. You run this house, run the press – you are the leader here.'

'When Gregory is away.'

'No, Sonya, even when he is here.'

'I have no power,' Sonya said. She jerked her head around suddenly. 'Was that the door?'

'Sonya, Sonya.' The man's voice came closer as they heard him running down the steps and into the kitchen. 'A letter from England. They want copies of our magazine.'

Sonya took the letter he thrust at her and read it aloud: '"To the Editors of *The New Star*. Dear Sirs,"' she read. 'You see,' she said, looking up at Delphi, 'sirs, always sirs. "We have received copies of your journal via friends, and have found it exceptional in its content and style. If you could arrange for fifty copies to be shipped here, we would be more than appreciative."'

'Where in England is he?' Mira interrupted.

'Manchester. Let me finish, listen. "Your trends for the future are on target. There is a revolution brewing. Sincerely, Jonathan Blakesly. Eighteen North Barclay. Manchester."'

'Congratulations, Sonya.'

'Well, it is good to know that our little magazine is appreciated.' She was folding the letter and putting it back in its envelope. 'You see, Delphi, what hard work can produce? Attention. It is rewarding to know that our words are being read even across the Atlantic. Now we must work harder and harder, and more and more people will hear us. Work, work, work. So, begin, Delphi get your workbook. Let me see what you did yesterday.'

Delphi went upstairs for her workbook. How she hated this part of the day, when Sonya would look at her work. Sonya expected Delphi to be bright. If someone else complimented Sonya on Delphi's ability to learn, Sonya would quickly say, 'Of course she is extremely intelligent, what did you expect?'. Then her mother would look at Delphi in a certain way that Delphi recognized as pride and came to believe was love. For that look, Delphi worked for hours each day.

Delphi came into the kitchen again with her workbook and handed it to her mother. Sonya pointed to the other book she held and asked to see it. 'No, no,' she said, shaking her head. 'I never liked this book, Mira. It is a ridiculous book.'

'It's what they use in the schools.'

'It is a silly, biased book, as bad as fairy tales. Pick up any good book and teach her from that. Let her use proper words. Delphi doesn't need games to learn. Learning is game enough. Isn't it, Delphi?' She turned to look at the child. 'Look at that frown! You musn't be angry with me, Delphi, for having so many hopes for you. Someday you will understand me. You will see. Someday you will thank me for trying to make you strong.' Sonya pushed Delphi's hair out of her face. 'Now go. Off with you. Go. Study.'

Delphi wished with all her heart that her father would come home. He never expected as much from her as Sonya. It was different with him. At night, before she went to sleep, she prayed to him. 'Come home, Papa, wherever you are. Please come home.'

*   *   *

Sonya   December 13, 1911

I am thinking about really putting my foot down at these radicals who pass through every twenty minutes. Gregory might as well let in every stray dog. A young man arrived yesterday with a letter from Gregory recommending that he stay here for a week or two, the same old story. I took him to a room on the third floor and he asked for a bath. 'Downstairs,' I said. 'Really?' he said, offended. I still cannot believe that I did not throw him out then and there. He had such a supercilious look on his face, and I was – an ass, I suppose, is the only word.

At dinner he complained about the food, couldn't get his story straight, and drank so much wine that Samuel had to get Paul from Eighteenth Street to help get him up the stairs and into bed! Finally, the light dawned on my wooden head. Tolchin's signature was forged. The fellow confessed this morning. A bunch of anarchist students from the university were making use of us! Imagine! And of course Gregory is not here to deal with any of this. Enough! We don't need all of them passing through. Then again, the minute I have quite made up my mind, I am reminded of my own journey across France and how much I needed those safe houses to stay in. I shall leave it to Gregory, but I cannot manage all these vagabonds alone. I have more important things to do.

Delphi asks again and again to have friends in to visit her or else if she might go out and play. There is a runny-eyed little blond child named Lois whom Delphi insists on calling her friend. Heaven forbid! I have tried to remove children, friends, toys, and pets from Delphi's life. Only today I told her that I have nothing against dogs per se, but the way one grows dependent on them is quite destructive. It is important to love your own self and your own company first, I said. I suppose that's a difficult concept for a seven-year-old, but she understood, I know she did.

Everything I do for her is to make her stronger than others, stronger than I myself am. I tell her again and again, dependence creates betrayal. If you are strong enough you will need nobody. If it hurts her, then scars will form a skin so thick she will never have to worry, will never *need* as I do.

We had a good time last night. I am letting her use my typewriter, and she wrote a funny story about the sun and a lion named Golden Eyes. She is happy. She is happy!

August 18, 1912
I thought in 1905 that the revolution had begun, but now there is nothing. Will it never begin again? Gregory has always accused me of impatience. He is right. What has happened to our revolution? Is all our work only to be a footnote to history? Will nothing ever change? Even Stolypin's death has not produced the results we thought it would. Gregory was in Petersburg when it happened. I wonder if he had any part in that conspiracy. He is still so secretive.

This time he has been gone for close to five months. Every time he leaves, it seems to be for longer. Now that his trips take him out of the country, I can't imagine that we will see him much at all. I miss him terribly. He writes so little, saying that anything worth writing is too secret. So what is the use? I would like to know what he is doing, at least where he is. Will I ever get used to being without him?

Delphi loves him, too, and why not, he spoils her so, buying her this and that, turning her head with his attention. How odd that he is so strict with me and so open to her, so full of sentiment. Do all fathers need their children to think them Saint Nicholas and the angel Gabriel? Perhaps it is best for Delphi that he is gone so much. Already she melts at the sight of him. I must make her able to resist him and, therefore, any man. Why should she not be free of this dreadful wanting? My hopes for her are limitless, and she shows such promise. I could not want more for her if she had come from my belly and my bones.

I am working so hard in American movements now with this campaigning for women's rights, equal pay, and to be able to vote. I'm working, too, for labor reforms. When I was younger I used to see men wandering all over Russia searching for God. My father told me they were called holy fools. I feel I am one of them, wandering about searching for the salvation of man. Tolstoy turned into a holy fool, dying in some godforsaken railway station on his journey to salvation, so at least I am in good company.

January 3, 1914
My dear husband,

I hope this reaches you. My last letter was returned from London. Do you have a new address there? I am sending this to the old place in Geneva. If you receive it, please telegraph me a proper address at once. It is over six weeks since I have heard from you. Surely you might find a few moments to write!

I am sorry that you will miss Friday; it is Delphi's birthday again, although the present that you sent her arrived. A fur dog! Really, Gregory, will you never change?

I can hardly bring myself to give it to her. The child would be spoiled to distraction if you were here more. I myself am giving Delphi a journal. I was about her age when I started my own.

I have been forced to send her to a public school, but I do not encourage her to bring home friends. She is so much brighter than other children her age, I am afraid they will spoil her. I have engaged a woman to teach her Russian and German in the afternoons. Her schedule is as follows:

7:00-7:45 A.M.   Wake up. Clean up. Jobs.
8:00-12:00   School
12:00-12:45 P.M.   Lunch at home
1:00-3:15   School
3:30-4:30   Russian
4:30-4:40   Milk and cookies
4:40-5:30   German
5:30-7:00   Dinner preparation and dinner
7:00-8:00   Oral reading. We are finishing *Oliver Twist*, will start Gorky.
8:15   Bedtime

I believe she is still too young for political theory per se, and I monitor the history she receives in her school. They are so sentimental in this country. However, I am quite persistent in pointing out the deficiencies of democracy.

I have been very busy with my work here. Besides *The New Star* three days a week, I am working for a small American magazine, *The Masses*, and have written a few articles for them, one of which, on the struggle of women, appeared in their last issue. I shall enclose a copy. They have made quite a little reputation for themselves, and it is to my advantage to be printed by them. They are on Nineteenth Street, and I walk there when I go. I cannot stand New York. In this country they even cheat you out of true cold! They call this weather winter, and the people believe it, as they believe everything else that they read in the presses. At least in Russia people knew they were ignorant. Here, everyone believes he is an expert.

Your friend Julius Borach has called for you many

times. I tell him the truth, that I don't know where you are or when you will be home. He mentioned something about the Jews and socialism and reform in Russia, that he thinks he might help you in some way. He seems to like you so much. What does he do? Isn't he the one that helped you to raise all that money when you went to Philadelphia? You had best contact him immediately upon your return.

I went to a meeting of the Communist League here, and they spent more time talking about Rasputin than anything else. As usual, when they talk goals and politics they do nothing but argue. I have no patience with Russia or Russians anymore, Gregory. How long can you put up with it? My marching sisters have quite convinced me that there are more oppressed women than there are Russians. Why does so much of the world need saving?

Mira and Samuel are no longer sharing the same bed, although they still live in the attic and run the presses. Everything runs more smoothly now that they are no longer lovers. I no longer have to mediate, which is a blessing; there is so much work to do, and never enough time as it is.

I hope you will be here for Easter. Spring makes me homesick. I would never admit it to another living soul, but then, you know my weaknesses.

Please try to find the time to send some word, even just a card. Delphi misses you. So, for that matter, does your wife,

Sonya

The celebration had been small, hardly a celebration at all. Sonya had made Delphi her favourite meal: peasant soup, Sonya called it, cabbage and tomatoes and beef bones, and raisins and sour cream, and they had eaten it with black bread and butter. Mira and Samuel had given her a petticoat. Josip Kerenov had given her a pen, and then her mother had gone to the pantry and brought her the enormous fur dog that her father had sent from Paris.

'It's so frivolous,' Sonya said to Mira, 'that I think Gregory must have meant it for a joke.'

'It is so soft! I can't believe it's so soft!' Delphi thrust her face into the fur. 'I love it. Sonya, Sonya! Look at its eyes! They are almost real.'

Sonya shook her head. 'It is the epitome of everything wrong with a bourgeois society. I'm sure I could feed a child for a year for what that cost.' She sighed so deeply that her whole body trembled. Delphi looked at her mother. Why should this present have made her so sad?

'I won't let it spoil me, Sonya, if that is what you are worried about.'

'See, Sonya, what a good child she is!' Samuel leaned over and patted the top of her head.

'Of course you won't,' Sonya said, her face lit up again with a smile. How her face could change from one second to the next! 'But,' she continued, 'I have something for you that I know will spoil you. Close your eyes.' Delphi did as she was told. What could it be? Her mother never did anything to spoil her. 'All right,' Sonya said, 'you can open them.'

It was a cake, a birthday cake from the store, frosted white with nine pink and green roses on it and a large red *D* in the center. Sonya had never bought a cake from the store before. They always made their own cakes, because Sonya said that it was a waste to spend extra money when they could do as well, but Delphi had always asked her for one.

'Oh, Sonya,' Delphi said, 'thank you.'

'Such a waste.' Sonya shook her head. 'It is the only time, Delphi Tolchin. I must be mad. Don't expect such indulgence again.' Samuel and Mira laughed.

'You are terrible, Sonya Tolchin. We shall report you to the Central Committee. Buying a child a cake! It's at least' – Mira looked toward Samuel – 'what do you think? Two years of hard labor?'

'Well, let us eat it quickly,' Sonya said. She had given Delphi the knife to cut it and was passing out plates.

'Yes,' Samuel added, 'that way at least we can destroy the evidence.'

Later, when the two of them were in the kitchen, wiping the last dish, Sonya opened one of the drawers and took out a package. 'Happy birthday,' she said, plunking the package down in the center of the table. 'Here is your real present, Delphi. I don't know why I even bought you that silly cake. Your father's extravagance must have tainted me. Forget that I ever did it. And it wasn't good, was it? I told you! It was far too sweet, am I right?'

Delphi nodded in agreement, even though she had thought the cake was delicious.

Sonya went on. 'I shall give what is left of it to Mrs Durkin next door and have her take it with her when she goes to visit her son in the hospital. Now sit down, Delphi, and open your present.'

Delphi knew from the tone in Sonya's voice that it was something important. The sugary taste of the cake in her mouth made her feel bad. Sonya was watching her, one hand folded into the other just at her chin. Something in Sonya's expression made her not want to open the package. Delphi pulled carefully at the wrapping, trying not to tear it, taking her time, and finally took out a large plain copying book, twice as thick as the ones she used for schoolwork. She stared at it. She knew Sonya was still watching her and tried to smile.

'It's a journal for you to write your thoughts and feelings in. Just like mine. You know when I sit at my writing desk scribbling away all the time? Well, this is what I am working on, my journal! Now you will have yours! You can write something every day.'

'Thank you so much,' Delphi said. Work, that's what it would be, more work.

'Do you remember a year or so ago when your father sent me those books from Russia and they made me so happy? Those were my journals, darling. They were so important to me that your father had them smuggled out of Russia, at great risk to many people, including himself. They are my deepest thoughts and feelings. My true friends. Now you shall have such good friends and you will always know yourself.'

Delphi still could not bring herself to look up at Sonya, her disappointment was so fierce. 'Promise me you'll write something every day, just a line, a word . . .'

'Every day!' Delphi couldn't help the vehemence in her voice. 'Sonya, there isn't time enough to have another assignment!'

'All right, Delphi, all right. Every week, that will do. Since I cannot look at what you write in your book, you must give me your word that you will write something. Believe me, darling, it is the best present you will ever get! Oh, how lucky you are to be so young and have so much ahead of you.' Sonya touched Delphi at the back of her shoulders for a moment and then leaned down and touched the top of her head. 'Happy birthday, Delphi. I know this doesn't make you very happy, but it will be of so much more value than that silly wasteful dog.'

'Hello! Hello! I am home! Surprise! Where is my birthday girl?' His voice rang through the entire house.

'Papa! Papa!' Delphi looked at Sonya. 'Papa is home.' She ran up the stairs and down the long hall to the entryway and threw herself into his arms. 'Papa! Papa! Papa!' she kept repeating. Now everything would be all right again. She knew it. 'Papa, Papa, Papa.'

'Gregory!' Sonya had followed Delphi up the stairs and was standing now watching the two of them, such a peculiar expression on her face that Delphi couldn't tell if she was happy. Her tight mouth expanded into a smile, and her eyes were moist as if she might cry. Tolchin looked at her.

'Surprise,' he said softly.

'Sonya, can we give Papa a piece of my special cake? Can we, please, before we give it away? Papa, Sonya bought me the most beautiful cake for my birthday. Please, Sonya.'

'Tomorrow, Delphi, tomorrow we'll give your father a piece of cake. Why don't you go upstairs and get ready for bed now, and I'll send your father up to say good night. It is very late.'

'Are you staying a long time, Papa? Please stay!'

'I am,' he said, kissing the top of her head.

'Go along, Delphi, your father will be right up.'

'I got your present, Papa. I love it.'

'Go ahead, Delphi.' Sonya's tone was stronger. Delphi started up the stairs and halfway up turned back to look at them. Sonya was standing with her arms crossed.

'I brought you something, too, Sonya,' Tolchin was saying. He handed her the large box that lay on the credenza.

'And to what do we owe your presence?' She ignored the box and stood where she was.

'Aren't you going to take it? Open it?'

'Perhaps later. You didn't answer me, Gregory. What has brought you home? I didn't expect you for weeks.' He put the box back down. Now he was taking off his gloves and scarf and laying them on top of Sonya's present.

'I need to raise a lot of money, more than usual. Is this my mail?' he asked, picking up a stack of unopened envelopes. 'Money, money, money. Unfortunately, all the revolutionary fervor in the world is useless without it. I came over with Julius Borach. He's agreed to have a party for us next Saturday to help raise some. I'm sure the guest list will include the wealthiest Jews in New York. They are very charitable. I think you'll enjoy it, Sonyasha. It will be like old times.' He tore open a large yellow envelope. 'Why didn't you open this? It might have been important.'

'Next Saturday is out of the question. There is a conference in Washington, and I have made arrangements to leave here Friday night for the weekend. It is all arranged.' Tolchin put his mail down and turned to her.

'Ah, so you'll cancel.'

'I will not cancel.'

'This is very important,' he answered, still sorting the

mail and frowning.

'You have not been here five minutes and already you order me about! Do you think you can come and go as you please without a word for months and then rule the roost when you come home? You must be mad.' Tolchin's voice, when he spoke, was sharply condescending.

'I do not choose to leave you, Sonya Tolchin. I go where I must. I thought that was understood. Now, if you will excuse me, I will put my things away, and after I have eaten something we will continue this discussion. Thank you for this joyous homecoming.' He walked past her toward the steps, noticing Delphi. 'Get to sleep,' he said to her, already irritated.

'There is nothing to discuss.' Sonya called to him. 'I have my work, you have yours. You want to raise money for your bunch of fanatics, raise money. I am leaving for Washington next Friday. I am sick of your Russia. At least here there is a chance of accomplishing something. Delphi, you heard your father, go to sleep.' Her voice was high. 'Run along.'

'You won't forget to kiss me good night, will you, Papa?' They always had such terrible arguments when he first came home. 'Please?' she asked as she walked up to her room. Her father hadn't come home for her birthday after all. He would probably even forget to kiss her good night. She had hardly reached her room before she heard their voices from the hall below. As usual, her mother's voice was getting higher and higher.

*   *   *

Sonya   February 8, 1914

It is hopeless, hopeless. In spite of all my resolve, I have fallen apart. My body is still my ruler, and I belong to him. His gift to me was a dress to wear at Julius Borach's party next week. Borach has been long active in Russian Jewish emigration and will support any cause that attempts to overthrow the anti-Semitic Romanov regime. The family he left in the Ukraine was exterminated at Kishinev. Tolchin has always made good use of his sentiments and his dollars. He says he needs my help at Borach's party, that I will be an invaluable asset, that my telling of the tale of my escape will be irresistible. Again, the seductress! Even though I have sworn I will not go, we both know that I will. Besides him, everything in my life is unimportant. What will Delphi think as she sees me become everything I tell her women must never be? These are impressionable years. I do not want her to think she must be as her mother is. I must show her how my needs destroy my work, and my soul. Oh, my soul!

He says he loves me. Could it be? The dress he bought me is the most extraordinary shade of green. What am I thinking? He never gives me anything without making me pay.

* * *

The dress Gregory had bought her was so beautifully made, so extravagant. It clasped her lovingly at her bosom, encased her hips with smooth assurance, then spilled to the floor, where it was caught in jet rings placed at intervals around the hem. There, the gleaming fabric, studded with more jet and sprinklings of paillettes, was held captive just above her slim ankles. Only the best French seamstresses and the most clever lovers truly understood a woman's body, Sonya thought, appreciating herself in the mirror one last time before she went down the stairs to the hallway where Gregory waited.

As she came toward him, he turned. Although his cape was unclasped, it stayed at his neck over the loosely knotted, heavily fringed satin evening scarf. He managed to look as natural in formal dress in public as he did entirely naked in private. As natural, she thought as he took her hand, and as elegant. She smiled at him, remembering the first time she had seen him, the fit of his uniform, its jacket pulling slightly across his chest and shoulders.

Sonya thought she would have to play at the evening, for she was still annoyed at herself for agreeing to go to Borach's party. However, once inside Borach's handsome carriage, she was so comfortable, the carriage itself so appealing, she quite forgot her self-betrayal. She pulled the silver fox lap robe over her and settled back in the seat.

The smoky breath of the horses changed shape above their heads in the cold night air. She listened to the even clip of their hooves on the pavement, heard the snap of the driver's whip, and felt the sway of the seat moving gently on its heavy frame. The glow of the coach lamps outlined Tolchin's profile, accentuating his high cheekbones and the curve of his mouth. The light caught the sparkle in his eyes as he looked at her. What a handsome man, she thought. How exciting it was to be beside him.

It was only moments, it seemed, to the front of Borach's massive stone mansion just off Central Park at East Sixty-fifth Street. Inside the ornately scrolled doors, a liveried servant took her coat and immediately Julius Borach, a dear, enthusiastic man barely higher than her shoulder, was kissing her hand and urging her forward to the drawing room to meet the other guests. There was a large curving stairway on the right, an enormous chandelier hanging from the center of the vaulted ceiling above them, and thick carpets, one after the other, bisected occasionally by shining wooden floors. Gardens of potted flowers surrounded large palm trees at either side of the archway that opened to the drawing room. The perfume of the flowers mingled with the scents of the perfumed men and women who came forward to greet her. How familiar it all was!

The drawing room was paneled in mahogany and its walls were lined with tapestries. The gold damask furniture was heavily carved but still inviting. A string quartet played Vivaldi in the far left corner by the windows, and white-jacketed men passed fluted crystal glasses of champagne on oval silver trays. Julius Borach fussed over her, insisting on making elaborate introductions to each and every guest.

How immediately she felt at home answering their questions, asking questions of them. Soon she was quite surrounded by these friendly, inquisitive people who were now prompting her for stories of her life in Russia. What pleasure there was in such court! How witty and charming she was again under tender prompting. How she had missed such evenings! Why, then, was she looking for Gregory as she spoke? To catch and hold his admiration?

She was speaking about the Russian theater, and five people were listening intently, yet she was searching for Gregory between their faces, across their shoulders. When she saw him, he was quite oblivious to her conquest, himself circled with admirers, a woman at each side, another directly in front of him. How much the same it remained, Sonya thought, continuing her story without a pause. She had hardly found her full stride when dinner was announced.

Julius insisted she grace the head of his table and proudly led her into the dining room, its bay heavily curtained with velvet. She noted the gold flatwear, the fine imported china, the enormous crystal water goblets, the tight baby roses that appeared to be growing up the stems of the four high gold candelabra. There were exquisite Italian paintings on the walls and bottles of perfect French vintage wine on the English sideboard.

As she sat in the armchair, her eyes met Tolchin's. He bowed his head slightly. She had seen that same odd smile on his face a hundred times before as he had watched her night after night in the ballrooms and dining halls of the palaces of St Petersburg and Moscow. She had seen it over and over again at her own divertissements in their house on the Moika. He was pleased with her. He was proud of her. How simple to want it all again, she thought. How delightful the elegance, the comfort, and ambiance of privilege. How shocking that she should find herself attracted to it all. Would there ever be a moment of such ease and certainty in the life she had chosen for herself?

She nodded at Tolchin, her eyes on his. I am still to be reckoned with, Gregory Tolchin, she thought, lifting her chin just a bit. I am still enchanted. Before the evening's end there will be no doubt that I am any woman's match and every man's dream. She turned her head slowly away from Gregory and gazed at the gentleman now seated on her right. She fixed him with a smile so dazzling he nearly fell into his service plate.

6

Delphi heard them come up the stairs, laughing like children, and then the light went on and she saw them. They were so beautiful, she thought sleepily, lifting her head from between the two sets of pillows on their bed where she had fallen asleep under their soft rose-dotted down quilt.

'Look who we have in our bed, Grisha.' Sonya was standing by the bed, holding a tray with a dish of cold chicken and a bottle of wine. She was smiling at Delphi. She put the tray down on the table and sat on the edge of the bed. 'I know she wants to hear about the party.' Sonya took Delphi's hands and squeezed them. 'I had a cousin named Maya who would always wait in her parents' bed for tales of the evening.'

'Didn't you, Sonya?'

'Never. I was too busy planning strategy on how to defeat Napoleon.' Sonya laughed. 'Maya was in love with your father. Every woman in Russia was in love with your father. He was so mysterious and his uniforms were always a bit too tight.' Sonya smoothed back Delphi's hair. 'So, then, would you like to join our picnic? I am famished. Dinner at eight, can you imagine? Americans don't know what to eat or what time to eat it! Delphi you should have seen what they served. Lumpy white food.' Sonya picked up a piece of chicken and took a big bite and closed her eyes. 'Oh, Delphi, this is wonderful! What a cook you have become! Here, here, have some. Grisha?'

'Lisel helped me. I didn't know how much paprika to put.' Delphi pushed back the covers and got out of bed and yawned.

'You have put the right amount. Grisha, have some.' Sonya was licking her fingers.

Delphi walked over to her father and put her arms around him and leaned against him, still yawning. He was taking the studs out of his shirt and putting them on the

235

bureau. He lifted her up in one arm and handed her the checks and notes he had taken out of the breast pocket of his jacket. 'Here. See if you can add these in your head,' he said, setting her on top of the bureau. He took off his jacket and threw it over a chair.

'Four thousand five hundred dollars, Papa,' she said, handing the checks back to him, watching as he put them in his shirt pocket.

'Very good, Delphi. Do you know why we have so much? Your mother is brilliant, brilliant! We should put her on the Chautauqua circuit, Delphi, she has the voice of an angel.' Delphi didn't understand, but her mother laughed. 'If she can do this for Russia, imagine what she could do for positive thinking and Christ.' He walked to the plate of chicken and took two legs and brought one back to Delphi.

Sonya had been examining her face in the mirror. Now she walked toward the bed. 'I was so disappointed in that house, Grisha. Those dreadful fawn-colored Chinese rugs and all that ornate Renaissance furniture. And no man should have all those paintings to himself. Rooms and rooms of treasures for just one man. Czars, as you have always said, they are all czars. Still, he is a charming fellow. Can you believe that story about Julius and Henry Frick? There will be nothing left for the rest of the world.' She poured two glasses of wine, walked to Tolchin and handed him one, then turned her back to him. With his free hand he started to undo the tiny jet buttons on Sonya's dress.

'Ah, that feels so good,' Sonya said, stretching her arms up. 'Those poor deformed women still wearing their corsets. How do they breathe?' Tolchin had finished undoing the buttons and slid his hand in around Sonya under the fabric of her dress.

'They are not so blessed as you. Not only are you brilliant, you still have magnificent breasts.'

'Gregory Tolchin!' Her mother squealed like a tiny child. 'Whatever are you doing?' She was red from the top of her head all the way down to the split in her dress. She walked toward her closet, opened the door, and Delphi could see she was changing. When she closed the closet door, she was wearing a long white ruffly dressing gown that fluttered around her as she walked toward them.

'Well, Julius Borach seemed to think they were magnificent. He couldn't take his eyes off them.' Tolchin was smiling.

'Gregory!' Her mother glanced in Delphi's direction.

'I think the child should know when people appreciate you. You have always wanted to be appreciated. I have never seen Julius speechless before. You have made a great conquest.'

'Are you jealous? Is that why I have never met him before? Have you been keeping us apart, Gregory?' Sonya laughed.

'Be careful. I hear he is a great lover.'

'Oh, Grisha, don't be silly. He has a sweet face, but homely. And so short. Most Jews are short, I think.'

'Not Raymond Mannheimer. He is quite over six feet.'

'Do you know what he said to me, Mannheimer, or was it Mr Frankfurt . . . well, one of them? He had the nerve to tell me that perhaps the reason Russia produced such great artists and writers was censorship and repression. Can you imagine!' She took another piece of cold chicken. 'Then one of the others – I forget who was who, they all looked the same – he said that Russians always assassinated their best men. I reminded him that Americans assassinate their presidents, and he managed to change the subject. And oh, that dreadful woman, that Mrs Steiner, how can the poor man bear her?' Sonya spoke in a high, nasal voice: '"Oh, your necklace, Countess, I have never seen anything like it. Those magnificent sapphires and rubies. It is so, so . . . Russian!" I could have shot her! As if anything could be more vulgar than America.' Sonya leaned her head back and laughed. 'You should have seen her face when I told her they were paste. The real ones, I said, I had to sell long ago, but I do not regret it. So many people have lost so much, I can do without my jewels.' Sonya looked sadly down at her bare chest but could not contain herself and burst out laughing again.

Delphi was smiling at her mother. How wonderful it was to see her so happy, giddy, like a little girl. It only happened when her father was home, and then not very often; most of the time they were fighting. But now that it had happened, Delphi wanted it never to end. 'What else, Sonya, tell me some more.'

Sonya stuffed a pillow into the top of her dressing gown and then looked over at them. 'Are you ready?' She imitated Mrs Steiner again, this time making her hands bump into her bosom when she talked. Now Tolchin was laughing, too. Sonya got up and took the pillow out of her bosom and put it inside her gown around her stomach. 'Mr Liebman,' she said, adjusting her face, her mouth going down as she stuck her stomach out. '"Countess,"' she said, in a low, gravelly voice, '"perhaps you know my good friend in Russia, Prince Barinov. I'm told all you in the aristocracy know one another."' Sonya took out the pillow, sat down on the chair, and preened a bit, doing an imitation of herself. '"No, Mr Liebman, I'm sorry to say I don't. But you must know there are more princes in Russia than there are sturgeon. My mother had a footman who was a prince. Perhaps he was your Prince Barinov?"' Sonya doubled over with laughter. 'Oh,' she said, laughing, 'he was so devastated.'

'You devastated him, darling,' Tolchin said, sitting on the bed. 'His check was for two thousand dollars.' He reached for Delphi and pulled her toward him. 'Your mother gave the most beautiful speech tonight. I'd never heard the part about the wonderful Miriamne who let you out of Russia. Was that true?'

'Yes.'

Tolchin lay back on the bed and put his arm around Delphi. 'Papa, I'll get chicken on your shirt!' Her father took another sip of wine.

'Would you like to try some?' He smiled at her.

'Grisha! She's too young!'

'Nonsense. I had wine after mother's milk.' Delphi sat next to her father and took the wineglass and drank some. It was tingly and sour. She had another sip.

'Whoa, there,' her father said, taking the glass.

'But I liked it, Papa!'

Sonya walked to the bed and sat down opposite them, her back against the footboard, her feet under her. 'I had my first glass of wine when I was eight. My brother

Vassily gave it to me just before Christmas dinner, and I did a dance for everyone and then fell right into the carpet.' Sonya giggled and threw her head back and her hair tumbled down all across it. 'Poor, poor Vassily. My mother was so furious she sent him off to bed without dinner.' Sonya looked so young. She stopped laughing and pushed her hair out of her face. 'Grisha,' she said, her head to one side, 'if you are very good to me, I'll fill your coffers for you. I'll make thousands and thousands of dollars for you.'

'He is good to you, Sonya,' Delphi said, feeling giddy and happy. 'Aren't you, Papa? My papa is good to everyone.'

He looked down at her next to him and tickled her with one finger. 'Into the rug already. Like mother, like daughter.'

'Papa!' Delphi was turning and twisting and helpless with laughter.

'Grisha,' Sonya said, putting a foot out and pushing it into Tolchin's leg, 'did you hear me?'

'I heard you.' He stopped tickling Delphi and grabbed Sonya's foot.

'I know exactly how to raise money for you. It's really quite simple.' Sonya was serious. 'Just give me all the money in those checks.'

Tolchin sat quietly on the bed, holding Sonya's foot in one hand and looking at her in that odd way he had where his eyelids were over his eyes halfway, like a shade.

'What's the matter?' she said. 'I thought you were a gambler.' Sonya leaned forward a little and brushed her hair up and let it fall.

Tolchin's expression did not change. Without taking his eyes from her, he reached into his shirt pocket with his free hand and took out all the checks. He looked at them for a moment and then, just like that, tossed them all into Sonya's lap.

The next day, Sonya started. A tiny Italian man named Carlo arrived in the afternoon, and he and Sonya walked through every room in the house, jotting down ideas for the new decor. Delphi had never seen anybody walk the

239

way Carlo did, and he talked in such a high, squealing voice that Delphi could hear them arguing all the way downstairs in the kitchen.

'Twelve weeks?' It was Sonya. 'No, never.'

'I swear on my mother, it would take that long. How can I have such furniture built in three weeks? The fabric alone takes a month.' Sonya's voice was lower now, and then there was a high-pitched noise, like a cat at night. There was more screaming, and more of Sonya's low-pitched words, but she had obviously convinced him. When the door slammed and Sonya came downstairs for dinner, she told Delphi that they would have their first fund-raising dinner four weeks from that Saturday.

At nine the next morning, a huge moving van arrived and six sullen men started emptying the first floor of all its furniture.

'Not that table!' Mira screamed at Sonya. 'I have worked at that library table for eight years.'

'Can you fit it in the attic?' Sonya asked.

'Of course not.' Mira was scowling.

'Then kiss it good-by.'

'You are ruining everything, Sonya. What capitalist nonsense is this? We have an efficient organization here. It is not necessary to fancy everything up. Stop,' she shouted, seeing one of the moving men load her books into a large crate. 'My books go upstairs. Sonya, without warning you do this?'

'This will not interfere with your presses, Mira. It will pay for them,' Sonya snapped at her. 'The rich may enjoy thinking about poverty, but they will be offended by the actual trappings of it. Think of how much easier it would be to write out a check in a comfortable chair. We are just going to color the truth a little, make poverty more palatable. We will stress giving to the poor, but never mention taking from the rich.' She stopped herself, her hand flying to her forehead. 'Yes, yes. That is the essence of it. And Mira,' she added, 'get rid of your sour expression, please. I would never give you a penny.'

For the next two weeks there were plasterers and painters. Wallpaper was hung. Floors were shined and waxed. Marble mantels and gold-framed mirrors replaced the old wooden ones. Chair rails and molding were added to the plain walls; a carved cupid frieze was hung around the living room ceiling. In the dining room the electricians installed eight gold sconces with crystal pendants, two on each wall, and an enormous electrified crystal chandelier hung proudly from the center of the ceiling, dwarfing the entire room.

'Well,' Sonya said with a sigh, eyeing the chandelier skeptically, 'it may have been a mistake, but if it was, it was the only one. I shall just tell everyone that I found it at auction, that it reminded me of the chandelier in the dining room of the Alexander Palace, where Alexandra herself entertained my mother, and that I bought it as a constant reminder of the sins of mankind. That will do.'

'It makes no sense,' Tolchin answered her.

'Nonetheless,' Sonya said with finality, 'it will do.'

The following week the furniture arrived. In the front parlor an enormous overstuffed down couch with rolled arms done in an exquisite floral chintz of rose and green was set across from the fireplace, two matching chairs on either side, in the far corner by the window a green velvet tasseled loveseat and two Louis XVI chairs. In the back parlor was an Oriental fantasy: tigerskin rugs, chairs inlaid with ivory, tables covered with Turkish kilim carpets, swirled drapes of Indian fabrics spiced with gold. Potted palms were everywhere, mixed in among the many inlaid tables that were crowded with brass candlesticks and squeezed next to the enormous wooden fanback chairs.

'But you can't move in here!' Tolchin said to her. 'There's only room for midgets, my darling.'

'Very funny!' she answered him coldly. 'We shall never entertain more than ten at a time. With the two of us, that makes twelve. It is all we can fit in the dining room, at any rate. You will see, Gregory Tolchin. With room for only ten, by the time word spreads, we will have a year's waiting list. What is that?' she screamed as Mira came into the room. Mira was wearing a red velvet dress, cut low in the front and tight at the waist. With her large frame and tiny breasts, she looked like a man. 'No, no, no!' Sonya shook her head. 'Take it back.'

241

'Take it back? But you said a costume.' Mira was devastated.

'All black. Tailored. Like a schoolteacher in Chekhov. Like Masha in *Three Sisters*. Can you smoke a cigar, Mira? Well, you have ten days to learn.'

A Mrs Faber from the next block made the vest for Delphi's costume. It was a tight green thing with embroidered pink flowers. Sonya made the skirt, a fat skirt that went almost to the floor and made her look stupid. It was the red felt boots that made Delphi cry.

'They're so silly!' she wailed at Sonya. 'I won't wear them!'

'Stop complaining, my head is splitting open! Now, I won't hear another word from you. I'm wearing a costume. Everyone is wearing a costume.'

'Not Papa!' Delphi yelled. 'How come Papa doesn't have to be silly and I do?'

'I will hit you, Delphi Tolchin, do you hear me? Not another word!'

The final week there were rehearsals and rehearsals of what food was to be served and when, what wine and what vodka, what candles and what music. Balalaikas had taken over half of the downstairs and the air reverberated with their sound. The smells of cabbage and meat pies and spice filled the house.

When Sonya appeared in her costume the night of the party, even Samuel, who seldom showed any emotion, gasped. She was wearing a richly embroidered peasant blouse cut low enough to show the beauty spots on her breasts, and her waist looked only three inches around, tucked into the full green and white gypsy skirt. She wore red leather boots with a gun stuck in at the top, and across her shoulders and tied behind her was a shawl with a lot of fringe hanging and dancing around. Tolchin started to laugh.

'Gregory Tolchin, don't you dare!' she said. 'I am right and I will prove it. It will work wonders.'

'You would never have worn those boots in the Crimea,' he said still laughing.

'I tell you, the more Russian the evening, the bigger the check. If Julius sends the people I told him to, we will make more money tonight than you can imagine.' Tolchin stopped laughing, but his eyes were full of his amusement. 'You know what gave me the idea?'

'I can't imagine,' he said, walking closer to her.

'That night at Julius's, someone mentioned Leon Bakst, and all I thought about was what Bakst would have done if he were putting a piece of Russia on the stage. Well, we have it. Mother Russia down to the last raisin. A little taste for foreigners.' Sonya put her hands on her hips. 'We will have a fantasy of Russia before my little speech this evening. After all, it is theater. Well, isn't it?' She smiled at him. 'You know it is. Stop smirking.'

'Papa, I hate my costume!' Delphi said.

'Wear what your mother tells you,' he answered, pinching her cheek.

'And you, Gregory? Must you wear a dinner jacket? That embroidered blouse I showed you would be marvelous. You would look like Nijinsky.'

'I will wear the dinner jacket, Sonya.'

'What time is it?' Sonya suddenly got white. 'I've forgotten to ice the champagne!'

Just then, the doorbell rang. Tolchin took Delphi's hand and walked to the front door. 'Serve the vodka first, Gypsy woman, and they won't notice if the champagne is cold or hot.'

All Delphi remembered of the evening was the banging in her head. She remembered Sonya kept saying that her necklace was only paste and she remembered how loud the music became, but that was all. She never heard Sonya's speech. When Sonya told everyone at breakfast the next morning that the following Saturday there would be an even bigger party, everybody moaned.

'It was fine,' Sonya said, 'but next week must be better. Mira, hire some students and dress them up in white tunics and red belts, and Samuel, get more musicians.'

'Where will we put them, Sonya,' he yawned, 'in the closet?'

'On the ceiling if we must. I want more. And Delphi, you will learn a poem. And there will be *sterlets* and *kulebiaka* next week. We will have Easter here.'

243

'I won't learn a poem!' Delphi yowled. 'I won't!' Sonya looked at Delphi with astonishment.

'You will learn it. Pushkin. It is a perfect poem about independence. It will be wonderful. You want to help Papa, don't you? Well, don't you?' Delphi nodded her head.

All week long Sonya rehearsed Delphi, making her stand in the middle of the room and say the poem over and over. When Saturday night came, Delphi had memorized it. It was to be a surprise for her father. This time, the carriages and the cars came earlier, and by ten in the evening, all the people in the house were laughing and talking and even singing. Delphi had no appetite. Even her favorite babas and the sweet *pashka* did not tempt her. Sonya kept saying over and over again to all the women that her necklace was only paste, and all the men kept looking down her dress. That night, Sonya looked just like a princess, and her fiery red hair was piled high on her head and her neck looked just like a swan's. Delphi felt a fool in her stupid costume with its tight little vest.

Sonya got up just after the dessert and announced to everyone that her daughter, Delphi, would recite a poem about the true revolutionary spirit. Everything was so still so quickly. Delphi felt herself on fire as Sonya lifted her up on her chair. Delphi's mouth got dry and her lips stuck together, but she began her poem, trying to find her father's face in the candlelit room. She had hardly begun it, was only up to the line 'I want to live my way, serve no one but myself and please no other, not bend my mind, my honor or my knee to any power of livery,' when she just started shaking all over and her eyes filled with tears. She had no voice at all. She heard Sonya's voice prompting her with the next line of the poem, but her own voice couldn't work. Julius Borach was standing up and lifting her down from the chair over Sonya's protests and then he was carrying her out of the room. She felt so awkward in his arms, her legs nearly touching the floor. There was the sound of balalaika music again and Sonya was yelling for champagne. The door closed and Delphi began to cry, her head pressed into Julius Borach's neck. 'It's all right my dear, it's all right. Come, come, you need not cry. Please, dear child.'

The door opened again and Delphi saw her father behind Julius Borach. His face was white with rage as he pulled her out of Julius Borach's arms and carried her upstairs to her bedroom, ripped off her vest, and tore it into shreds. Just as he lay her down on her bed, the door opened and Sonya, furious, came in like a wind.

'Gregory Tolchin, what was the meaning of that?'

'I was about to ask you the same,' he said quietly, pulling off the dreadful red felt boots and then unbuttoning the skirt. His eyes were as angry as hers. 'Get under the cover, Delphi. It's very late.'

'Whatever I have to say, she can hear it!' Sonya said. 'Whatever you care to say to me, say it now.'

'I won't have my daughter a performing bear in front of fools!'

'We have given our lives to the cause; why should she be exempt? And since when are they fools who give to you? They weren't fools last week when they gave you five thousand dollars. Will they be fools tonight when they give you more?'

'All right, Sonya, you have made your point. I shall make mine.' He was staring out through the windows of the room, not even looking at Delphi or her mother. His voice was very quiet. It was the voice that always frightened Delphi. 'I will do whatever you ask me to do. You were right about your parties, Sonya, and I admire you.' He ran one hand across his forehead and down one side of his head. 'In fact, I am grateful to you. You are remarkable, as always.' He was quite still for what seemed an eternity so that when he moved, both Delphi and Sonya gasped, Delphi pulling the bedcovers up to her eyes. She could hear Sonya's breathing coming in great gulps.

'I thought . . .' Sonya began in a whisper.

'You thought what?'

'I don't know. That you were going to . . .'

'Strike you?' He looked at Sonya and then put both his hands behind his waist and rubbed his back. 'Hardly, Sonyasha,' he said. 'Have I ever done that?'

'No, of course not.'

'I want Delphi left out of this game of ours. I won't see

her humiliated by it. You asked me why she should be exempt? Because so far it isn't her choice to be involved.'

'It is not my choice, either.'

'Oh, yes it is. If you think about it, Sonya, you will see that it is.' He started for the door but stopped. 'This is the end of it for Delphi. Is that clear?' Sonya did not answer him. She stood still and watched him walk down the hall and listened to the sound of his footsteps as he went down the stairs.

Overcome with shame, Delphi turned her face into the pillow to cry. 'I'm sorry, Sonya,' she whimpered. 'I'm so sorry. I should have done better. I should have done it right!'

She felt the pressure of Sonya's palm at her shoulders.

'It's all right,' Sonya said very softly. 'Perhaps another time.'

7

There have been so many parties that my mind is
muddled with them. I am a revolutionary woman, or a
princess, a Gypsy or a peasant. Always I make my speech
about repression and the czar, Jews and the czar,
inequality and the czar. There are always more people,
and, God help us, more balalaikas. Always I tell everybody
my magnificent necklace is only paste. Poor Delphi, she
will grow up remembering me with tears flowing down my
cheeks, saying, 'The real one I was forced to sell long ago,
but my people have suffered so much, what sacrifice is it
to sell one's jewels?' I caught her looking at me the other
night as I said it. Such a strange expression in her eyes.
Gregory is probably right. She shouldn't see me behave
this way. How can I teach her about dedication and
strength with these performances? Still, it is necessary.
Money is necessary. I hate being a circus clown, doing my
tricks for those who come for enlightenment and blini.

May 3, 1914

The parties have been such a great success and take up
so much of my time that I find myself losing sight of my
other goals. My friends in the movement can no longer
rely on me. I have not marched or gone to a meeting in
months.

The war in Europe would seem to be coming closer and
closer, almost unavoidable. I cannot understand it. Could
I have really believed in violence? Ever since Grandpapa
died soon after that pointless attack on Dosiaya, I have
been unable to fathom the necessity for it. I understand
that man is capable of brutal destruction, alas, but for
what point, toward what end – to kill innocents?

Gregory is gone for a few days. He is in Boston,
organizing some meeting there. It is so quiet in the house.
I think it is the first weekend in months that we have not

entertained. The sun was so lovely today that Delphi and I walked all the way up to Central Park to go for a row on the lake. Fifth Avenue is quite elegant, nothing like the Nevsky, of course, but quite lovely, especially above the shopping district. It was a pleasant day. Just the two of us were together. I tried not to talk about anything more than the weather, the trees, the buildings, games – childish things. I think she enjoyed me. Sometimes I am so bad with her.

I heard that Anton Lopuhin was executed. Imagine! He was found guilty of revolutionary activities!

June 5, 1914

Again a scene with Gregory. I am so disgusted. Dinners and parties and smiles. He wants to entertain three times next week! He doesn't realize what effort it costs me. And he will be in Boston again Monday and Tuesday. I am sick of it all. The more money comes in, the more goes out. I can't keep track.

I want to work with the women again. I don't always have to be so bloody charming when I work with the women.

June 13, 1914

What has gotten into me? At tonight's dinner I flirted outrageously with Julius. I was so angry at Gregory. Of course, he pays me no mind at all, but I fear Julius is turning into a dribbling fool. It is cruel of me to use him. I must stop.

*   *   *

There were days that summer of 1914 that Delphi cherished, a few long, hot, iridescent days and nights when she was alone with her mother and father. The three of them took the Iron Boats at the end of Manhattan and went to Coney Island, where they would sit on the beach. Sonya would read the newspaper. Tolchin would stare out at the sea, and Delphi would play in the sand.

'Women in jeopardy indeed!' Sonya shook sand out of her newspaper. 'How the world loves to see a woman

248

whose only hope is a man! Half the nation is spending its time at the movies watching this Pauline person always about to be run down by trains. I don't know why women are not picketing the theaters.'

'Oh, Sonya, it is just fun,' Delphi said. 'It doesn't mean anything. I like it when the train comes to run over her - it's scary and—'

'Delphi Tolchin, I am surprised at you!'

'Your mother doesn't believe in fun,' her father said, smiling at Sonya.

Delphi took off her stockings and shoes and waded out into the water, carefully holding up her skirts so she wouldn't get entirely wet. She envied some of the boys who just ran into the waves to let the salty water crash over them. Tolchin and Sonya sat in beach chairs under an umbrella, eating food from the picnic basket. They both wore white, Sonya in a linen dress with a wide blue sash and a tiny lacy bib and Tolchin in a linen suit. They both wore straw hats with a striped ribbon around the crown, only Sonya's ribbon was longer and went down her back and blew back and forth like a flag in the slight breezes from the sea. When Delphi came back and sat in the sand near them, Tolchin started to bury her feet.

'That's enough sun,' Sonya said, squinting at Delphi from under the brim of her hat. 'It makes the skin like a piece of bark.' Sonya's eyes were so green, they shone like a serpent's eyes. Tolchin's eyes were blue and looked bluer in the little pockets of pinky-white flesh. She wished she had green or blue eyes instead of yellow eyes like a cat.

The sand between her toes was warm, and when she lifted her feet out from under the piles, it felt like water as it slid from her ankles and toes. She tasted salt on her lips, and she leaned back on her arms and looked up at the sun, blinking her eyes and seeing rainbows inside her lips.

'Sonya?'

'Hmm?'

'What is making love?'

Sonya narrowed her eyes and squinted at Delphi a moment before she answered. 'There's no such thing as making love,' she said.

Delphi turned her head to look at her mother, a puzzled

expression on her face. 'When a person goes to bed with another person, what are they doing, then?'

'Relieving tension,' Sonya said quickly. Tolchin turned his head to look at Sonya, but his face was all in shadow.

'Is that sex?' Delphi asked.

'Yes.'

'Do people always have tension to relieve?'

Sonya didn't answer. Delphi put her hands around her knees and turned to face her mother.

'Answer her. I'm interested in your answer.' Her father's voice was hardly above a whisper. Sonya shifted in her chair and then looked at him, her eyebrows up on her high forehead.

'There are times when one of them is just being helpful to the other,' she snapped, her eyes narrowing once more as her mouth tightened.

'I watched Mira and Sasha last night,' Delphi said.

'What!' Sonya pushed herself forward in the chair and her hat fell off behind her.

'They were very busy with it.'

'What did you watch? What were they busy at?' Sonya's hands clutched her breasts.

'Now, what do you suppose they were busy at?' Tolchin had turned in his chair. 'Relieving tension in every conceivable position, like everyone else in that house. The place is a rabbit warren by midnight.'

'Be quiet!' Sonya demanded.

'She is old enough to know the facts of life, my dear. She has just seen them with her own eyes. Make some sense to her. Either tell her all of it or tell her none of it.'

'Sonya, everyone but you says that they were making love.'

Sonya was as red as beets, and now her hands were pulling at the beads around her neck. Slowly she began an explanation that was interrupted only by explosions of laughter from Tolchin. When she had finished, Delphi was pale, less with understanding than revulsion.

'Congratulations, Sonya. You've succeeded in making the child contemplate a life of celibacy.'

'All for the better. What would you have said, comrade?' Sonya was clearly annoyed, still red as beets.

'A little about the joy, perhaps a bit about the occasional humor. Perhaps a feeling for ecstasy. Your clinical approach leaves much to be desired.'

'Then you tell her.'

'I think it is best I do.' He stood up and put his hand down toward Delphi. 'Let's go for a walk and I'll tell you a few of the advantages to lovemaking. That is, besides the relief of tensions.'

Delphi stared at his hand. How could he make a joke of it? She sprang up and started running away from both of them. 'I don't want to hear any more. It's ugly and terrible and I don't care!'

'Delphi Tolchin!' She heard Sonya's voice behind her. 'You come back here!' She ran as fast as she could over the hot sand that burned the bottoms of her feet. Ahead of her were the towers and domes of the amusement park, and she started running toward it and the crowds of people there. When she couldn't run any longer, she stopped. She was coughing and crying. The music from the park sounded above the yells and screams of children, and she looked up, seeing the huge Ferris wheel to her right. The sun glinted on the swinging boxes and the girders as it turned. She would like to be on it, going higher and higher, away from all the people who pushed against her. It was true that she had seen Mira and Sasha on the couch, moving all over each other, but she hadn't seen what Sonya told her, nothing like that. Did all these other people, the fat ones and the thin ones and the old ones, did they do that? She shivered in the sunlight.

'Well, what do you say to a ride on the Ferris wheel?' Her father was by her side. Without looking at him, she bobbed her head up and down. They got into one of the little wooden houses with windows on four sides, and the man shut the door after them. Slowly they rose higher and higher, the wooden house bobbing back and forth. At first Delphi was afraid it would fly right off its steel hinges and sail out into the ocean, but soon she was used to it, and she just stood quietly at one window and then the next, looking out. Up and up they went, and the swing of the box they stood in was easier. Everything below her looked so tiny and all of it shone, the domes and the turrets, especially the sea, which stretched out forever. There was no sound up there. The waves were breaking noiselessly on the sand, making puffy, silent foam. If only she could be up above the world forever, she thought, if only it could always be like this, silent and lovely.

'It looks a bit like Moscow,' her father said.

'Moscow?' she asked, turning to face him. 'How does it look like Moscow?'

'The shapes, the domes, even the colors. At least it is how Moscow looked to me when I was about your age. We always spent Easter in Moscow with one of my aunts. It was the most festive of all the religious celebrations, better than Christmas. The city was always dressed up, like an illustration in a children's book.'

Suddenly the wheel stopped turning, right at the moment their wooden house was at the very top, and it swung out hard for a second and then hung there in the sky. 'The world is quite different up here,' he said. 'The people look like so many busy ants and the towers are so many toys. Imagine what it must be like at night, with all the lights shining all over it.'

Delphi looked again at the ocean. Now it was flatter, like a pond, and the waves seemed to be only ripples one might make by throwing a stone into the water.

'Delphi, I have something I want to say to you.'

'I don't want to—'

'I have never lied to you, Delphi. Never. It is very important for you to know that what your mother said was not all there was to say about sex. Those were the physiological details, and they are secondary. Whatever else sex is, it is primarily a celebration. When a man and a woman make love to one another, they are really celebrating their bodies and their senses, the power and beauty of them.' The wheel turned and jerked still again, throwing Delphi against her father. She scrambled away from him.

'I saw them,' she said, looking at him. 'I saw what they were doing, and it was ugly.'

'Oh, it is ugly to look at, but it is not for looking at. It is not for putting on a stage. Sex is a private thing, and it is a natural and beautiful thing.' He touched her lightly on the

252

arm. 'You are very young, Delphi, but you must try to understand me.'

'I want to go home,' she said, shaking his hand off her arm. Her skin was tight, and now her cheeks were burning again. The ground was getting closer and closer. She could see the tops of things, the worn rooftops and the peeling paint. The wheel bucked and turned. Delphi heard the people below them squealing, and then she saw the lines and lines of people on the ground waiting for rides as the wheel came down faster and faster. The fact of them, their hair, their noses, and their sound, made her dizzy. She wanted to be at the top of the wheel again where she couldn't see anybody, only the world.

In the Iron Boat, going home, everyone jammed into everyone else, thighs touching thighs and elbows cracking into ribs and wrists touching breasts and backs. Delphi was mortified all over again. These people, she thought, made love!

The following morning, on her way down to the kitchen, Sonya called out to her from the front parlor. 'Come, Delphi, sit with us. What a glorious morning.' Sonya was lying on the chaise. She looked like a young girl; her head was thrown back and her long red hair was tossed about her. Tolchin sat in the embroidered armchair near her feet. Sonya pointed to the coffee table in front of her. 'Come, darling, we have tea and rolls, and your father' – she paused and smiled at him so lovingly that her cheeks were radiant with color and her eyes bottomless with contentment – 'he has brought us piles of apricots and peaches. Piles and piles.' She looked at Tolchin. 'Sometimes he is so good to us.'

Delphi sat on the thick Persian carpet and took some breakfast. She listened as they spoke to each other. It was such an easy, clear conversation. The defection of someone named Ulanova, the publishing of a paper in Geneva, some talk of the Borachs, some talk of art. It was expansive, as if there were enough time suddenly, as if they were all related to one another now and forever. Plans, trips. They touched one another, their eyes met, and tiny sparks flew out, and Sonya's expression was wholly changed, her eyes alive with light dancing. Was this what her father had meant when he spoke of a celebration? Did she imagine he was staring at her, watching her reaction? Had this just been a demonstration for her? Delphi could not eat.

'I must cut your hair. It hangs in your face, and who can see your eyes?' Sonya leaned over and pushed Delphi's hair back behind her ears. 'See how much better it is for seeing? Eat, Delphi, for heaven's sake. Your wrists are like chicken legs and you are pale as the moon.' Chirp, chirp. Delphi felt her stomach knotting. Tolchin poured her tea, and she watched it turn dark in her cup, light to dark.

'Oh, I wish you didn't have to go,' Sonya said, lifting her neck and swinging her hair from side to side, her eyes partially closed. 'Tolchin must go to Chicago and organize a lecture. How we shall miss him.'

'I won't be gone for long,' he said. 'When I come back we shall go to the beach. Delphi will take me on the water slide. She wasn't afraid on the Ferris wheel. I, on the other hand, was terrified.'

'You were not!' Delphi said. 'He wasn't at all, Sonya.'

'You will hurry home,' Sonya said, rising and going toward him, slipping her hands around him and pressing herself against him. 'I met your organizational leader from Chicago, and she is far too young and beautiful. I think you should replace her.'

'I keep her only because she makes you so jealous, my angel.' He kissed Sonya three times quickly on her mouth, barely grazing her lips, and then he leaned over to Delphi and kissed her on the top of her head.

The sound of the doobell interrupted them. 'Be a dear and answer the door, Delphi,' Sonya said.

Delphi ran to the front door and opened it. She didn't recognize the man standing there. He had dark hair and eyes and a worried expression.

'Is Gregory Tolchin here?' he asked her.

'Yes. Who shall I say wishes to see him?' The man pushed by her and into the front hall.

'Gregory!' he shouted.

Tolchin came out of the parlor. 'Boris. What is it? What's the matter?'

'Gregory! I have been trying to reach you! Your damned phone is out. Russia has invaded Germany. We are at war!'

'Stupid fools!' Tolchin's face had turned white. 'Damn! Damn!'

'You must come immediately, Gregory. We have arranged a meeting at St Mark's Place. A conciliatory meeting with all the Russian socialist groups, to discuss only – and I mean only – what effect the war will have on the revolutionary movement.'

'Disastrous,' Tolchin said. 'Nicholas is a madman!'

'Come with me now, Gregory. The others will arrive by noon.'

Sonya had come out of the parlor and was watching them. 'Russia has invaded Germany?' she asked.

'I shall be back later this evening,' Tolchin said. 'Do you want to come?'

'What for?' Sonya asked. 'To hear you all shout about what is out of your control? Women, at least, have learned to accept impotency over the years. I told you, I am sick of that lot of blathering fools.'

She and Delphi watched the two men run down the steps and across the street. Sonya caught a glimpse of herself in the mirror over the credenza and turned to look at herself. Delphi came up behind her.

'Are we at war?' she asked.

'Russia is at war.' Sonya's mouth twitched slightly. 'Not America.' Sonya ran her fingers through her hair and spread it out over her shoulders. 'You needn't worry. It is far away.' She sighed. Delphi inched closer and looked up at her.

'Will Papa have to go?'

'No. This is a Russian war.' Sonya elongated her neck and turned her face from side to side, stroking her throat and watching herself in the mirror.

'Sonya, when Papa goes away, you miss him, don't you?'

'No.' She said it too quickly. She turned and looked down at Delphi. 'Well, I miss his noise. I miss . . .' She looked at herself in the mirror again, catching Delphi's eyes. 'I want to talk to you, Delphi, like a grownup.' She turned away from the mirror.

'I am not a child, Sonya.'

'Perhaps not, but neither are you an adult. I think you must wonder about your father and me. Do you? I know I am so changed when he is home. Your father is a weakness, Delphi. Never . . . you must never need anyone as I need him. Have enough in yourself. Don't let your father seduce you as he does me.' Sonya dropped her arms to her sides, her hands clenched into fists. 'Don't hate me for making you strong. Don't hate me for the hopes I hold for you!'

Oh, God, Delphi thought, watching her mother in the mirror. It is another performance. It sounds just like when she talks about how her jewels are only paste.

8

Delphi   October 14, 1914

My father is in Chicago again. He left last night. He and
Sonya had a big fight. First it was about the woman in
Chicago and then it was about Tolchin's taking me to
Julius Borach's in the country. We are going to go next
weekend. Papa has sworn he won't change his mind.
Sonya yelled at him that the luxury would spoil me, and
then he yelled at her not to manage him but to manage the
women's revolution. Sonya swears that she will not go
even though Julius Borach called her especially so she
would change her mind. Good, I am glad she will not go.

First there will be the train and then there will be Mr
Borach's lodge. Sonya says it will be decadent, but she is
wrong. I like Mr Borach, and I don't think he could be
anything so bad as decadent.

I am wide awake. I shall never fall asleep.

Lois has a puppy and it is so sweet. It lies on its back and
likes it when I scratch its belly. I would like to hug it, but I
don't. Sonya says all dogs are dirty. I wonder if there will
be dogs in the country.

*   *   *

Delphi watched her father's face as he sat across from her
in the train compartment, staring out the window at the
rolling landscape. She had often seen him sit alone in the
downstairs room lately with the same expression on his
face, a look so sad that it altered his strong features
almost as much as if a shadow had come across them. She
shivered slightly and turned to the window to see what he
could be watching. The light of the afternoon was bright
on the land outside, making lines and valleys across it. She
had never seen so many different shades of greens and
yellows and tried to count them all. Before she knew it,
she was asleep.

Tolchin woke her only as the train approached their stop, and she hardly had time to get her coat and mittens on before they were slowing down and she saw Julius Borach outside on the platform, waiting for them.

She pulled her father to the steps, and there was Borach, rushing toward them, below them now, his jowly face seeming to make more than one smile.

'Well, here at last! And Delphi' – he took her hands and helped her down – 'how tall you've gotten, and lovelier, lovelier.'

'How is life, Julius? You look fit.'

'Challenging. Yes. Come, come, you must be hungry and tired. Let me help you, Delphi.' His carriage smelled of new leather and pine. The driver put their bags into the back and strapped them down and then jumped up on the box and snapped a thin whip over the heads of the chestnut horses, and the carriage moved quickly away from the station, up the quiet street to the town and along a narrow road right in a forest.

Delphi stared into the deep shade of the pine groves, seeing avenues of darkness pierced by the fading light. It was all so new to her she hardly listened to the men talking. Besides, like everyone else, they were talking about the war in Europe.

'It's good for the economy at least,' Borach said, shifting in his seat to face Tolchin. 'But I don't see that it will be of long duration. Surely no one would allow it to go beyond Christmas.'

'I'm afraid I don't agree.'

'Come, Gregory, Russia is solidly behind the czar, there's no lack of patriotism. And Germany has her hands full. How can it be but a matter of months, even weeks?'

'Patriotism is cheap in Russia, but it won't win a war. Our generals are as inept as they were when the Japanese made fools of us ten years ago. Nicholas, if anything, is worse.' Tolchin sighed and rubbed his face. 'As a matter of fact, I'm thinking of going home, Julius. It's one of the reasons I've come here – to give myself a few quiet days to think it out.'

'Papa!' Delphi had heard him and she looked at him, her face full of alarm. 'You are thinking of going to Russia?'

258

He pulled her against him and patted her shoulder, but said nothing.

'Really, Gregory?' Borach look at Tolchin in amazement. 'But what are you saying? I don't understand. You're not going back to fight for Nicholas?'

Tolchin leaned his head back against the carriage seat. 'Ah, Julius.' He sighed.

'But my God, man, how can you?' Tolchin rubbed his eyes with the palm of his hand. 'Really,' Julius Borach said again, 'how can you?'

'I am not going back to fight for Nicholas. I am going back to fight for Russia.' He smiled. 'I am a Russian. I love Russia, Julius. I love its customs, its landscape, its art, its people, its literature. I am the supreme chauvinist, and my fight has always been that everyone might have the joy in our great country that I have. My quarrel with Nicholas and his dynasty is that they choke the true Russian life out of the Russian people. Germany and Austria, though, Julius, they would be even worse. And the Jews will be the first to suffer if the war keeps going so badly. Russians, like others, always must have their scapegoats. No, this war must be won by the Russians, Romanovs or no.'

Delphi looked at the two men. Her father stared out the window, that same peculiar expression on his face. Julius Borach watched him. Finally he spoke. 'Nonetheless, Gregory,' he said, 'you are fighting for a czar.'

Tolchin laughed. 'I am fighting only for Russia, Julius, I swear it. The revolution will have to wait until the war is over.'

'I won't let you go, Papa.' Delphi pushed herself away from her father and looked him in the eye. 'You are too old to be a soldier. Sonya said so.'

'She did, did she?' he said. 'And what do you think?'

Delphi examined him carefully. 'You have gray hairs in your beard here, and there are more right at your ears. Right here.' She touched the curling hair at his temples. He tweaked her nose betweeen his thumb and forefinger. 'You won't go, will you?' she said. 'Promise me. You must promise, Papa, or I'll tell Sonya.'

'Sonya,' Borach said. 'What a pleasant thought. I am sorry that you could not persuade her to come, Gregory.

How is she?' He slapped at an insect.

'Stubborn like the sun, Julius. She lights everyone's way and burns herself up while doing it.'

'There is no one like her,' Borach said, touching Delphi's hair. 'This one looks like both of you, I would say. Except not today, for today you look like an old Russian, Gregory. Weary with passion.'

Tolchin laughed. Delphi smiled and snuggled up against him. He could be so melancholy one moment and so full of laughter the next. She was certain now that he would not go away.

The house, when they came to it, tried to hide its enormity with fir trees and vines, but it was so vast it took Delphi's breath. It was both on a little hill by the side of a great lake and also down on the shore of the lake, a great many rustic wooden cabins with porches, all connected. Inside the main house, all the couches and chairs, even some of the tables, seemed to be made of pieces of trees and their twigs. When Borach took her to her room, she was so excited she couldn't stand still. Sonya had been right. Delphi had never seen such lavishness. And the bathroom – the bathroom was as big as the bedroom, with thick towels and all kinds of soaps and china dishes.

'Use the netting at night, Delphi. The bugs are ferocious around here. It has been a hot, wet summer and there has yet to be a heavy frost.'

'I suspect they have acquired a taste for rich blood,' Tolchin said, carrying Delphi's small bag to the wood stand in front of the huge bed.

'Oh, I doubt that, Gregory,' Borach laughed. 'They just like to torment Jews like everyone else.'

'Even in America,' Tolchin said, laughing too.

'Oh, may I take a bath now?' Delphi asked, standing still at the doorway of the bathroom.

'Of course. You must do whatever you like. We will see you at dinner. Your father and I have a great deal to talk about. We are old friends who do not see each other often enough.' Borach clapped Tolchin on his back.

As soon as they left, Delphi ran the water in the tub. There was so much hot water from the tap! She poured perfume from the bottle on the corner of the tub right into the water, and the sweet smell of flowers burned her nostrils. There were other bottles full of crystals and colored liquid, and she poured some of each into the water. Then there were bubbles and colors and more smells. She lowered herself into the tub, nearly faint from the pure sensuality of the moment, from the warmth, the scent, and the absolute stillness around her.

After the bath, she sat on the edge of the tub, the huge white towel wrapped around her. It did not rub her skin like sandpaper the way the towels at home did. It enveloped her like a cloud. She finally lay down on the bed. It was the biggest bed she had ever seen, and it was both soft and hard, and before she could even think, she was asleep. asleep.

At dinner, Delphi met Mrs Borach. She was a smallish woman with very light hair and an almost handsome face, were it not for her eyes, which seemed to have no sight. Not even Tolchin could get her attention. Delphi had never seen a woman avoid Tolchin's piercing gaze, but Mrs Borach seemed not to see him. She spoke of the weather and the trouble with getting good food; she picked at her plate like a sick bird.

'How is your son?' Tolchin asked her. 'Still a genius?'

'My son?' She looked down at her plate. Her voice sounded like an echo.

'Studying?'

'Looking. He insists he is learning, but I fear he is only looking.'

Mrs Borach abruptly excused herself from the table and left the room.

'It is still the same?' Tolchin asked quietly.

'For her, yes. Worse than ever.' Borach put down his knife and fork. 'She never recovered and she blames the boy. Of course, his birth had nothing to do with it. She was not well from the beginning. But you know . . . Please excuse me.' Julius Borach left the table.

Tolchin looked at Delphi. 'You can continue eating. The atmosphere may not be conducive, but the food is good.'

'What is the matter, Tolchin?'

'It is too complicated to explain. Pass the vegetables please.'

'Whenever I ask you about anything between grownups, you say the same thing.'

'The best things between grownups need no explanation. The worst things are beyond explanation. It is a waste of time to try. Pass the vegetables.'

She held the platter of vegetables in front of her, looking down at the tiny orange carrots and the tiny green peas, the perfect thin green beans, and the slivers of tomatoes arranged like flowers. Finally, she passed it to Tolchin.

'I do not understand people, how they can always manage to be miserable.'

'Most people are fools, Delphi. They throw so much life away, always thinking there will be enough of it left when they want it.' He ate the vegetables.

'Will they come back to dinner?' she asked.

'I think not. Now, eat your food. Never mind the atmosphere, always eat when you can. Especially if it's good.'

The Borachs did not come back to dinner. Delphi and Tolchin ate alone and then went into the living room and played chess. She was certain that she had him beat when he took her bishop.

'Once I will beat you, you'll see!' She frowned.

'Never.'

'How can you be sure?'

'Because I am the best chess player in America.'

'Papa, Sonya is right. You are arrogant.'

'There is nothing arrogant about knowing you are the best when it is a fact. Now, get to bed. Tomorrow we are getting up at dawn to hunt, and you must go to sleep soon.'

'To hunt?'

'Yes.'

'For what?'

'Deer.'

'Why?'

'I think you will see something important. For me, the hunt reveals the truth of nature more than anything I have experienced. You will understand tomorrow.'

Before dawn the next morning, Delphi woke, her face still tingling from the cold. The room was like an ice cake. On the windowpanes frost had etched tiny flowers and trees. She blew long lines of steamy breath up toward the rough plaster ceiling. From the far-away kitchen came the smell of bread. It must be paradise, she thought. After Tolchin knocked on her door, she raced to the bathroom and back to the bed, putting on her clothes under the comforters and quilts.

At the breakfast table there were other men. They all looked alike; their clothes were similar, the set of their expressions was similar, and they were all excited. When breakfast was over, they all filed out the door, and she followed. Each man put on a heavy jacket and picked up a gun. The smell was of earth and oil and leather; she was dizzy with delight.

'This will be mild for you, Gregory. Deer are easy game compared with boar.'

'Did you hunt a great deal in Russia, Count?' one of the men asked with great interest.

'Some. Please call me Gregory.' Tolchin asked Delphi if she was warm enough, and wrapped the scarf around her neck.

Outside, the colors of the leaves staggered Delphi. Dying with such vibrance, they floated to the ground on early breezes.

They moved carefully through the forest, their footsteps making only slight sounds on the beds of leaves. She could feel the roots of the trees under her, feel the color of autumn seep into her. The sun was rising, and here and there it dipped down through pine and birch and elm to catch the edge of a curled red leaf, the spine of a yellow one.

When she saw the deer, she stopped where she was. How perfectly this creature was part of this place, its tawny browns and muted grays an extension of the trunks of the trees, the colors of the earth itself. In its presence was a complete knowledge of nature, its demand for order, its radiant choices. All her senses were heightened. This was what Tolchin meant. It was then that the crack of the rifle sounded; the bullet crashed into the sweet and tender creature to spin it around where it stood. It was as if the bullet had entered her heart instead, and she felt herself spin, too, felt her blood leak out of her. Delphi fainted.

When she regained consciousness, Tolchin was frowning down at her. Her head was propped up on the ball of his jacket. Just in front of her she saw the deer, blood cutting across its still form, and she turned swiftly and vomited on the ground. Out of the corner of her tear-stained eyes she saw the faces of the other men.

'I will take you back,' Tolchin said.

She wiped her mouth with the scarf and, looking at some distant shadow, got unsteadily to her feet. She would not humiliate him.

'No,' she said. 'I will be fine.'

She followed them again, this time looking only at the ground, and each time a shot blasted the still morning, she stared at her feet, for she could not see such a thing again and live. She could not watch such magnificence so senselessly destroyed.

When she returned, Delphi ran to her room and into the bathroom. Sick and exhausted, she put her head under the faucet of the sink. How many had they killed? Ten, fifteen? How much beauty was cut out of the world to lay on the golden ground of autumn?

She felt a hand on her and stood up, water cascading across her face and body. Her father stood next to her.

'How could you, Papa?'

'They would all have died in the winter. There are too many of them to survive it.'

'It is an excuse to kill,' she whispered.

'I have no need of excuses.'

'I will never kill anything, never.' She began to weep, to shake with sobbing. 'I want to go home. Please, Tolchin, take me home.'

'Tomorrow, Delphi.'

'No!'

'Tomorrow. Mr Borach's son has just arrived, and it would be impolite to leave.' His voice was firm. 'You must understand that your pain is of consequence only to you.'

'I won't listen to you.'

*   *   *

He gently lifted her face toward his. 'I am not telling you to reject your feelings. I am telling you to keep them to yourself. Understand them and be still. Only those who do not understand themselves inconvenience others with unnecessary displays of emotion. Now, get dressed and come to dinner.' Tolchin left her abruptly; she stood shaking with frustration and rage. He was a man without morals preaching morality. Sonya was right.

Delphi did as he told her and dressed for dinner. There was a younger man in the main room when she arrived. 'So, you're the little girl who doesn't like our ritual slaughter,' he said, a funny smile on his long face. He had deep black eyes and brown hair that was flat and straight. 'I'm Carl Borach, and it may make you feel better to know that I don't like the slaughter either. It used to make me sick when I was younger.' He was holding a large rectangular frame in his short thin hands. 'You look just like the woman in this painting.' He flipped the front of it toward her. She walked closer to it. She did look like the woman. Her face had Delphi's shape, and the eyes and nose were the same.

'Do you like it?' he asked. 'It's a gift for my father.' He watched her look at it, bending her face closer to it. Finally she straightened.

'It's very beautiful, but why did you get that for your father?'

'Why?' He shrugged. 'Because it's very beautiful.'

'But it is Christ and his mother, and your father is a Jew.'

'Ah.' He nodded. 'Well, that shouldn't be too difficult to explain.' He looked at the painting. 'Quite simply, in art, unlike anything else in the world, beauty is all that matters. A great painting could be of anything, have any subject, and still be beautiful.'

'Any subject?'

'Any subject. Even death.'

'Death is not beautiful,' she said, shivering, remembering the day. 'Not death.'

'Oh, but you are wrong.'

'I am not wrong.' Her hands were fists at her sides and she banged them against her. 'Death is brutal and ugly.

265

You said it made you sick.'

'The senselessness of the killing made me sick, not death.'

'Death is death,' she said. 'It is terrible.'

'Does it frighten you?'

'Yes!' she said with passion.

'I will show you something that will make you feel better. I will show you that it is nothing to fear at all. Will you come with me?'

She nodded. She wondered how old he was. She was nearly as tall as he was already.

'First I want to hide this picture. It is to be a surprise. Tell me, where shall I put it?'

'Right there, under the couch.' She pointed across the room.

'Good,' he said. He walked to the couch and slid the painting underneath. 'If it is what I think it is, then it should pay in part for the misfortune of my birth.'

'Was there something wrong with you?' she asked, following him toward the coat rack in the hallway. He looked amused by her question.

'No, my birth was not my misfortune. I am quite happy to be alive. But sometimes a child does not make his parents happy with his presence.'

'I know,' she said, thinking of Sonya, how she looked at Delphi, always with a little crease of worry etched in her fine white skin. They put on their coats and mufflers.

'How old are you?' he asked.

'Almost ten,' she answered.

'Only ten?' He looked surprised. 'You are very grown-up for ten.'

They stood in the outside air for a moment before he started off down the drive. 'I haven't been here in years,' he said. 'Years and years.' Tonight, even wrapped in the heavy coat, the cold air was sharp and bit into her skin and made pains in her chest with each breath. He walked very slowly. She did not have to hurry to keep up with him. 'Did they go this way?' he asked.

I think so,' she said, her voice shaky.

'They usually do, if I remember. The first kill is always around here.' She stopped walking and just stood there,

266

her head down. 'Come on, I promise you I'll show you something that is almost magic, and it will take away the fear. It helped me when I was young.' He made no effort to retrieve her, only stood in the path ahead, looking back at her. She continued walking, and when she reached him, they walked together. 'See, there where the maples lean over our heads and touch together,' he said, pointing up. 'I used to pretend this was my home and I was prince of the forest.' The huge trees on either side of them reached across the sky and locked branches. 'It goes on for miles like this.'

The first deer was there on the ground, not twenty feet from where they were standing. He took her hand gently and kept walking. 'You mustn't be afraid,' he said.

Her heart thudded in her chest and her head was light again. 'No . . .' she said. He held on to her hand and pulled her forward toward the deer. When they were only a few feet away, he stopped.

'Don't you see how beautiful it is?' he said. 'There is beauty when he is alive, and there is a beauty now, too.' He took out a pad and pencil from the pocket of his coat. 'Watch me.' He made some marks on the paper, his hand moving quickly, the pencil bobbing up and down, back and forth. 'Look how delicate he is, how strong and yet how delicate. And look, too, at how everything around him blends together, the trees and the ground and the deer. How different it becomes with him lying there. It becomes a holy place, a cathedral.' He was still drawing, and she could not take her eyes from the paper. 'If I could draw better, perhaps you could see that there is another life here on the paper.' He ripped it off his pad and gave it to her. It was magical, what he had done. She saw the curve of the deer's neck better after he had drawn it, noticed the frailty of the legs. He was right, it was a kind of beauty. The terror she had felt that morning was gone. Unbelievably, it had evaporated into the small lines and smudges on Carl Borach's paper. 'There is another kind of life, a life that continues into infinity.'

'I would not kill anything just to make it live on paper.'

'Neither would I. But I just wanted to show you a different way of looking. It is seeing things that makes life worthwhile. The more you see, the more life is made bearable.' The blood had dried on the deer's forehead and it was a deep brown, like the earth, like the color of Carl Borach's hair. 'Well, we had better get back to the house. There will be dinner soon.'

She was still looking at the deer, the white patches of fur shadowed with twilight. How strange it was to see so much of life in death.

'Delphi?'

'What?'

'We had better go back now.'

'May I keep this?' she asked, holding up his sketch.

'Of course. It is very poor.'

'I think it is wonderful.' She followed him back to the house, holding the sketch he had made against her chest.

When the two of them walked into the big room, Tolchin and Julius Borach were sitting at the chess table. 'Aha,' Tolchin said, getting up so quickly the chair he sat in went backward, 'the young prodigal returns.' He grabbed Carl by the shoulders and embraced him. Carl shrank away but smiled at Tolchin. 'Your father tells me you are still after the truth of beauty?'

'Is there anything else worth pursuing?' Carl asked.

'Anything else? I would say so.'

'Come there, Gregory, don't tell me that your Marxists have convinced you that beauty is only a bourgeois conceit.' Carl poured himself a glass of wine from the sideboard and sipped it. Tolchin joined him and poured himself a glass of vodka, then drank it all in one tilt of the glass.

'Art is important, of course,' Tolchin said, his eyes showing no effects from the vodka. 'Who would deny it? Life, however, is more important.'

'Your people are so self-righteous, convinced that their way is the only way.'

'Aren't you convinced of the same?' Tolchin stroked his beard thoughtfully. 'Fanatics are fanatics, whether it be guns or words or brushes or beauty. Best to be one and keep on a narrow path. Too many temptations otherwise.' Tolchin poured another glass of vodka and drank it.

'Carl, your mother has been waiting to see you.' Julius

268

Borach's tone had more than a touch of impatience.

'Tell her she was right, Father dear. It was a mistake for me to come home. I certainly don't have to hear her say it again.'

'But you must go upstairs.'

'No. Absolutely not.'

Tolchin walked across the room and picked up the chair he had knocked over and sat in it, almost primly. 'Parents and children, what misunderstandings come between parents and children. My daughter – there, gentlemen, sitting on the other side of the room as far away from me as possible – she will not speak to me now because I shot a starving deer. Carl will not speak to his mother for God knows what reason. What are we to do, Julius and I, with these ingrates? Although I admit it's difficult to be a child. I remember how it was when I was young.' He leaned into the twig chair and Delphi thought it would snap in half. 'The truth is, it is a wonder all children are not insane. Parents are always at cross-purposes. When I was a very young officer in the Guards, I gambled away my entire wardrobe, and my watch, in one night. Now, mind, it was a mark of a gentleman to gamble – to gamble and dance the mazurka well. I did both with some degree of proficiency. At any rate, I came to my parents' home that night entirely naked under my cape. My mother wept with shame, but my father swelled with pride.' Tolchin closed his eyes a moment and shook his head, a slow smile appearing on his face. 'Well, to right matters, the very next night I played cards again with the same fellow and I won his ring, his watch, his boots, his uniforms, and his horse. When I arrived home, my father was upset at my lack of compassion and my mother was extremely pleased at my victory. You see how life is?'

Carl Borach was laughing, and his father was wiping tears of laughter from his eyes with the back of his wrist. Tolchin looked at Delphi. 'I forgave my parents for my confusion. Will you forgive me for causing yours? I thought to show you life and I made you sick.' He got up from his chair and took a step forward. He looked out from under his thick eyebrows at her. 'I even' – he paused for a moment – 'I even thought to show myself I was capable of changing, but I find I am not.' His eyes looked as if a hot white light were shining on them, making them pale and misty. 'Good Christ, child, I'm waiting! The holy father himself would not take this long to absolve me of *all* my sins!' He strode to her, his arms open, and scooped her up against him.

'Tolchin,' she said the next morning, standing in the doorway of his bedroom, 'why are you packing? I want to stay.' All his clothes were neatly folded and stacked in his bag. 'Papa?' He didn't seem to hear her. 'Papa?' She walked into his room. It smelled of tobacco. By his night table were two empty bottles of vodka and a glass on its side filled with ashes. He was lying in his bed, his back to her. She could not hear his breathing or see him move as she approached. Slowly, on her tiptoes, she walked around the bed to stand in front of him. 'Papa?'

Only his eyes moved in his face, opening wide as he looked at her. 'I have made arrangements to take the train this morning. We will leave soon. You had best pack.'

'But I'm not afraid of the hunting. I wanted to tell you. I like it here now.'

'I know. I know. It is too soon to leave, but . . .' He took a deep breath and straightened his shoulders. 'Another time. There will be another time.'

Her face fell. 'You're going to Russia, aren't you?' She knew she was going to cry no matter how she sucked in her breath and held it. He sat up in the bed and motioned her toward him. She crawled up onto the bed, tears as silent as air falling down her cheeks.

He cupped her face in his hand, his thumb running up and down the length of her nose. 'It is too late for me. I'm sorry, my little angel.'

'Why, Papa? Why is it too late?'

His eyes had a blank look in them and she knew he wasn't seeing her. Suddenly, he pulled her up against him and just held her, his chin resting on the top of her head. She could hear the beating of his heart. It sounded like an alarm.

Back in the city, Delphi rushed to Sonya to tell her

everything. There was so much to tell. She could hardly get it all out. 'I had a bed as big as a barn, made out of a tree, and Sonya, the bathtub was as big as three together, and the trees were such beautiful colors. The train was long, Sonya, and I fell asleep.'

Sonya hugged her and took off her coat while she was talking, walking to the closet to hang it up with Delphi at her heels, still chattering. 'The lake was so big. We went in a rowboat but not for long because we had to get back for lunch. Lunch was like a banquet, Sonya. It was all wonderful. The only part I didn't like was the killing.'

Sonya stopped moving and her free hand went out to hold the closet door. 'What killing? What are you saying?'

'The deer. They killed so many. Twenty at least. And then they took off some of the heads. In the beginning, I fainted.'

'Dear God . . .' Sonya's breath came in short little gasps. Delphi could see her lungs laboring.

'Sonya, are you all right?'

'I'm all right,' Sonya said, her eyes closed.

'Uri was here?' Tolchin stood in the doorway of the living room, a paper in his hand.

'He was here and he left.'

'And when will he be back?'

'Why don't you stay a few days and find out?'

'Answer me, Sonya. This is very important.'

'If it is so important, Gregory Andreivitch, why do you blow about like the autumn wind, first here, then there?'

'There will be no games, Sonya. You will answer me.'

'You are not the only one, my deer hunter, who chooses what game will be played.' She put her hands on her hips, the expression on her face a mask of implacability. 'You are going to show Delphi the truth of nature, are you? And what does she see? Senseless killing, the province of the idle.'

Tolchin walked very slowly toward her, but she did not move, staring at him defiantly. Delphi lifted up her satchel and walked up the stairs to her room. She unpacked her belongings, lifting up her sweater to her nose to see if she could smell the pine. On the bottom of the satchel was Carl Borach's sketch of the deer. She picked it up and looked at it. Only a few lines, a few smudges, and it was a deer there on the paper. It was magical.

'What does that mean? You are going to Russia?' She heard Sonya wailing, her voice high and tremulous. 'What for? Oh, God, are we never to have a life? Will you get yourself killed defending Nicholas? Grisha, it makes no sense! Listen to what you are saying! Oh, my God!'

Delphi closed the door and slipped off her clothes, changing into her nightdress. She went to the table next to the bed and pulled up the rocking chair. She found a blunted pencil and a few pieces of writing paper and carefully put the sketch of the deer in front of her, up above the blank paper. She tried to copy it, a line here and there, a cross, a curve. No. Another piece of paper and then the last piece of paper. It was not so easy. She turned the paper over and began again, and finally, finally there was something. Not very much, just something like a deer. She looked at the lamp on the table. At least that was in the room with her. She would draw that. She saw things about the lamp she had never seen before, dents in the tin, lines actually carved into the tin for decoration. The lamp was not round at all; it was smaller at the bottom, growing fatter and fatter, spinning where it sat. She made it too large; the paper could not contain it. She made it too small and wrong, wrong. She erased and began again. Soon all the papers were erased and torn. She went to the bureau and got more paper. The tip of the pencil was worn down, so she pulled off pieces of its wood with her teeth to make more lead appear. Finally, the lamp was there on her paper. She felt so elated, triumphant. It was then that she heard Sonya's crying in the hallway.

How long had she sat there at the table, cramped and bent over her drawing? Her stomach was wrinkled with hunger. It must have been hours. How ridiculous that the hours had merely disappeared and all the pain she felt at her father's leaving had disappeared, too. Now it returned. The door of her room opened and knocked hard against the wall. Sonya stood there, her face wild with anguish.

'Your father is leaving us,' she said, bolting toward Delphi and clutching her where she sat. 'Delphi, he is leaving us!' Delphi put her arms around Sonya. Her mother's body pounded against hers, her hands grabbed the

the fabric of the nightgown, and she wept against Delphi's chest.

9

Sonya   December 1, 1914

So he is gone. I have been in such a state these last days, these last weeks, this whole year when he has been home, that I hardly know who I am. It seems I can do nothing without throwing my whole soul into it, even something I am loath to do. Well, there shall be no more parties. The Socialist cause would seem to be at a standstill until this war is over. It will be soon, I know. At least now I can continue with other work. He is not here to put me at cross-purposes. I feel like a new woman. This very afternoon I shall go up to the Women's Suffrage Party on Twenty-second Street and see if I can once again make myself of use to them.

January 16, 1915

Increasingly, it is clear that, had I no need for love, I would have functioned so much better. Delphi will see, sufficiency is poisoned by love. She misses him so – she has even taken to chewing on the inside of her cheek when his name is mentioned.

How strange that this child I did not want, this child who was to be only my passport to freedom, has enslaved me, that I love her so. But I will not encourage more affection – I will not! Instead I turn my attention to my work, trying to make an example. Besides my suffrage work, I have had some success working for Russian war relief. The news from the front is awful. How can people suffer so? Julius Borach remains the largest contributor, but of course the Jews suffer the worse when times are bad. Yesterday he brought his son, Carl, to visit. Such an effete young boy full of intellectual pretensions. He is advising some of his father's friends on the purchases of art. He has no interest in humanity. Delphi is already worth ten of him.

February 28, 1915

Still nothing from Gregory. I begin to believe it is just his aversion to the written word!

New arrivals at St Mark's Place bring terrible tales of Mother Russia. The emperor is at the front, inept, useless. The German bitch and the mad monk run the empire. No melodrama could be more improbable. The army is ready to desert. The peasants are hungry. The Socialists are scattered. Lenin pouts while the Germans line his pockets. Trotsky is here, an arrogant schoolboy, waiting for his master's voice. I cannot abide it all anymore.

My schedule is exhausting. I am sleeping less and less. Last night I closed my book at two and woke at six. Well, we shall see what happens this fall with the referendum in New York. Democracy shall be truly tested. All the women at the Union are working as hard as I. It is inspiring to be with them. Finally my gifts of language are being put to good use. On the Lower East Side today, I spoke in Russian, German, even some Yiddish. My Italian is limited. So many of these people would vote for the ratification if they could. I know it. Conditions in that dreadful ghetto are hardly better than they used to be. I spoke with a Jewish woman today with eight children, whom she can barely manage to feed and clothe. Her husband is dead and she has a business. She is terribly treated, she says, not by her own, but by the so-called Americans she must deal with, not, she says, because she is Jewish, but because she is a woman! Two of the children were sick today, crying in the back of her small store as I talked to her, and yet she is managing without having her oldest boy work. She insists he get his education. I was so moved I nearly wept for her.

I think that I must have talked seriously with twenty women. Perhaps four will work for the organization. Perhaps two believe that they can persuade their husbands to vote for suffrage. October 19 is a long way away, and yet I fear the time will be too short. We must abolish the inequities of the system.

The lady from England is here, Mrs Pankhurst, preaching violence and agitation. Twenty years ago I should have been working for her, instead of fighting for dear

Catherine Catt, and the democratic way. Well, we will see. It is only six months away.

Delphi does excellently in school. She is certainly smarter than most of her teachers.

October 18, 1915

Has it been a week since I have written anything? How unlikely, and yet all life is now unlikely. This week has rushed by. The vote is tomorrow and I am frightened. Gregory always said I should not be angry at things out of my control, and yet I am so involved with suffrage, and it seems so unreasonable that it should be out of our reach, that I am choked with fury. We will see tomorrow. We will see.

I must have made eighty phone calls today to our precinct leaders to rally their support for tomorrow. I spent the morning organizing the rally that is due for Washington Square this evening. I myself shall not go. I shall stay on the phone. Helen and her squad have been ceaseless in handing out the literature. I had it printed in six languages, and did them all myself. If only Mademoiselle were here to see me!

I don't know what to do about Julius. I can't have him hanging about like a sick puppy, and yet without his little attentions, I should hardly be able to manage. I am selling little bits of jewelry. I should probably get more if I sold it all outright, but then I should be tempted to spend all the money on a new printing machine. I have never had to worry about money before, and I don't like it. I suppose worry of that sort is the price of liberation.

Two short letters from Gregory. They say nothing. Impossible man! I shall never understand him. I hope he is well.

Please let it not rain tomorrow.

October 20, 1915

We have lost. We have lost! My anger is uncontrollable. Fools. Fools. Democracy fails when fools are the majority. I am sick about it.

Delphi   January 14, 1916

I am too big all over. My legs keep growling like stilts,

white and skinny wood. I am the tallest person in my class except for John Beecher, who is a giant. His hands are so big he can hardly hold a pencil when he writes.

Julius Borach came to dinner with a man named Guggenheim who has such a funny old crinkled face but still looks like a boy. I never saw anyone eat so much in my life. Sonya told the same old stories about Russia and her nurse, Marushka. She put on that voice she always uses when there is company. I left before she came to the part about going to the fair. Julius Borach just beams at her. Doesn't he know?

I made a good cake, three layers high with butter cream roses in different colors all over it. That Mr Guggenheim didn't believe that I made it until I showed him how I made the roses using the butter on the table. The easiest things seem the hardest for people to believe.

Sonya   February 14, 1916

I had a terrible scene with Julius last night. He proposed to make me his mistress! I still can't believe it. He spoke so sharply and with such vehemence, so unlike himself, that I was truly speechless. I suppose the fact that I said nothing encouraged him, and he went on and on until he was practically shouting at me, saying that I had taken advantage of his friendship all these years, that I had given him nothing in return, that he was a laughingstock among his friends, that I had made a fool of him. It was awful, awful.

When I finally recovered my wits, I managed to discover that he had been put up to it by his lawyer, Mr Jonathan Loeb, and his close friend, Jimmy Guggenheim. They had convinced him that I was the worst kind of opportunist and that he must, for his own sense of worth, have it out with me. They had spent some weeks and the better part of yesterday afternoon convincing him. I think they must have fed him too much wine! How it changed him. I have never before seen Julius yell at a soul. We were dining at Lüchow's when this occurred, and even our regular waiter was quite concerned for poor Julius. He got so red in the face. I can't imagine how he brought himself to believe those terrible fellows. Can people be influenced so easily?

Afterward, of course, he was quite abject, apologizing over and over as polite and as sweet as could be. This morning he sent me an enormous bunch of flowers. Poor man, I am embarrassed for him.

November 9, 1916
Despite all our efforts to defeat him. Wilson was elected again. We certainly did all we could, stringing banners everywhere and marching and calling, but all the protest did no good at all. Even the Women's Party is being forced to reorganize. I am quite admiring of Alice Paul, her efficiency and lack of emotionalism. She sees nothing but to continue the fight for women's suffrage and is determined to see it accomplished. As are we all. I cannot help but wonder how so many of us can be so ignominiously ignored. Perhaps it is only the war. Slowly but surely, it is all that anyone speaks of.

Gregory writes that Nicholas is entirely in Alexandra's power, and so Rasputin does, in fact, rule - a comic opera. He hints at plans to 'alter' the situation. He has seen my parents. My mother is caring for Vassily's children while his wife nurses him. He was badly wounded during the Austrian offensive. Vassily - he was the kindest of us, certainly. How I wish I could have know him better. Could it all have been different? I am of another place in another life, but there are times, even now when I would give all I had to see Petersburg - I cannot call it Petrograd! To see the faces of my family, to hover about like a spirit in the mist of summer, part of the white nights making days into infinity.

Delphi   January 6, 1917
Sonya is gone for a week to Washington again. I wish she would go more often and longer. I like it when nobody asks me what I did today. It makes the day mine. Today in Washington Park the trees looked like dancers, naked, all trunks and arms but when I try and draw them I can't get it right. I like to walk around and look at things and connect them up, or separate them. I can see them better, taking them all apart, making lines from one place to another and then putting them all together in new ways. I

drew Mira's nose on Samuel's face. When I was finished I knew their faces better.

I made a lot of sketches of Sonya from my head. They look like her! They do! She would be surprised.

I like writing in this journal sometimes. The house is very quiet and it is very cold. We heard from Josip. He is going to Europe to fight.

Washington, DC
January 6, 1917
My dear daughter,

This is just a short note to remind you once again to get *all* the New York City papers the day of next week's march. There are hundreds and hundreds of us here already to organize. I think we shall have an even better turnout than we did four years ago. I hope the weather is on our side, or some of our weaker sisters will use it as an excuse not to turn out. I shall come to Washington every Inauguration Day if I must, for as long as I must, until we achieve what we must. We are all prepared for anything, and if there are riots and hateful men filled with anger, as there were last time, we will continue, undaunted. Remember, get *all* the papers. Perhaps you will find a picture of

your loving mother,
Sonya

Sonya   March 13, 1917

I have word from Gregory, at last! Not through the mails, of course, the censorship is impossible. No one outside of Russia realizes the extent of what is happening there. The news here is nothing compared to what Gregory describes, but wait, I go too fast. The letter was delivered by an American friend of Boris Smernaev's, who was in France, and before that in Petersburg, Petrograd. Gregory is well, thank God. Here is his letter.

My dearest Sonyasha,

If this letter never reaches you it will not be for lack of trying. I am well. Thinner, older, but well. Since I have no

279

word of you for seven months or so, I pray you are well there in our house, busy, running about changing the world. How is my sweet Delphi? Such important years these are for her.

It would be impossible to describe adequately to you the conditions that exist here. Since the abdication, this great country just drifts. The situation in the army is terrible. Anarchy is too sweet a word. In the city there are lines everywhere for everything, but mainly for bread. Strikes, disorder, anger, all for bread. Politically, Kerensky is making an earnest attempt, but he will soon be gone. Lenin like a stalking wolf is everywhere with his Bolshevism and his tyranny. I have always known he was a despot. The Bolsheviks will grab at what the others only politely ask for. They lie where the others smile and say nothing, and in the end, he will win.

For the past months I have been working at the American Embassy, supervising a vast food relief effort. God knows what will happen to me after this mess. Trotsky told me he saw you in New York. How beautiful she is, he said. I hope I don't offend you if I tell you he never mentioned your politics or your press. Poor Sonya!

In spite of the chaos here, life goes on in some fashion. I have a wonderful landlady. I told you, I think, that I have a flat on Zhukovsky Street, just a few doors down from where Boris Savinkov and Doris Brilliant stayed just before they murdered Plehve. My landlady insists that I, too, am a spy and inquires into all my business. She wishes to impress her friend, the landlady who let those rooms to our comrades all those years ago. She prepares me the most wonderful meals, and I am almost sorry I cannot please her.

I am glad that you are not here to see the city, still the most beautiful in the world, as it is slowly being ravaged. Of course, nothing deters the rich. Countess Klein Michael is indomitable. There are balls and parties and gossip from one end of the Prospect to the other. What blindness, what obstinacy! It is crumbling, cracking, decaying around them. The worst of the vermin are coming from their holes to destroy them, and they toast each other with French champagne. Their stupidity, their arrogance! But they do not leave.

I thought it would amuse you to know that the Bolsheviks have their headquarters in Smolney, where you and your schoolmates in your white dresses learned your lessons of Russian history.

Stay well, all of you, until I rejoin you.

GT

April 7, 1917

I cannot believe that America has entered the war in Europe. It is just as Gregory predicted.

Will men always be little boys? Even I gave up my desire to be a general. It is useless to die for one's beliefs. One must live for them!

August 23, 1917

Delphi upsets me, distracts me. She does well in school, but all she seems interested in is drawing, drawing, drawing. I am so irritated by it I try to ignore it. Perhaps she will forget about it if I don't make an issue of it. Her sketches are quite nice, actually. She did one of the group on St Mark's Place that caught the spirit of the meeting, and she has been sketching in the hospitals for the wounded soldiers. The boys are thrilled by her doodling. I can only hope it is a phase of her adolescence. She is getting quite pretty in an odd way. Very long she is. He eyes are very good, and her bones are fine. She has a certain grace when she moves, rather like a young dancer. She looks remarkably unique, not stamped out like a curly-headed blue-eyed child in the Pickford mold. She doesn't show the slightest interest in boys her age, thank the saints. She is so bright, so very bright, she could do anything, absolutely anything. How many times will I write it! She doesn't have my spirit, but she may change. I am too dissatisfied with her. I must be patient. I have so many important things in my life, I wish I could stop forever thinking of her, yet I do constantly. Could my mother have cared so about me?

Why do I sigh so much?

Delphi   October 1917

Sonya said that I must begin to make money for our expenses. She says that she counts my contribution to the household as important, but that we need more money because things are expensive and there is no income. She is selling things. Last week she sold the silver and gold frame that held the picture of her family at Dosiaya. It made her very unhappy. I made her a frame out of some pieces of wood I glued together and sandpapered and then painted with yellow paint, but she said I had better things to do with my time. I do not think my mother loves me at all.

Sonya   November 2, 1917

Jail! I have been in jail, arrested twice for picketing the White House! Am I insane that I look upon those days as the most fulfilling, the most uplifting, the most spiritually satisfying of my life? Three days in that filthy hole! I wish the world could have seen me – not only me, the others, too – as we fought like men in the horrid place that could only have been created by men! The world is the same everywhere. The horror stories of Siberian prisons are no worse than what we women suffered at the hands of our tormentors. Rats and vermin. Inedible food. Filth everywhere. Even the crossing with the Jews was more bearable than this. I was so proud of us, so proud!

Oh, to have done this, in these days, work like this, when at the same time the Romanovs have fallen in my motherland. What sweet revenge! At last! At last!

Delphi   December 7, 1917

I did some charcoal sketches from the pictures of the battlefields in the newspaper. They were so gloomy. Bodies are difficult to draw. I have gotten much better at hands. There was a feeling of death in the drawings I did.

Sonya is teaching ladies to shoot guns to defend themselves in case the Huns come. She goes to Governor's Island twice a week and she wears an absurd uniform with knickers and boots and a hat with a leather strap under her chin. She has told me that we can't have meat on Tuesdays anymore. We must do what Mr Hoover tells us and have fasting days. She says in Russia when she was growing up they were always fasting, and I will soon get used to it. One of her groups met here again yesterday. All they talked about was the shame of women working so hard in a country that will not even give them the vote. Sonya's article in *The Women Citizen* on the liberated Russian revolutionaries of the seventies has been well received. The editors have asked her for another. Mira got a job in a factory in Brooklyn and wears overalls.

Last night I tried a sketch of Tolchin and failed miserably. I feel awful that I cannot remember his face. I wonder if he remembers mine, but I have changed so in the three years he has been away. He probably would not know me if he saw me on the street.

Sonya   January 23, 1918

Tomorrow the House will vote. How I wish I could be in Washington with my friends! It is, however, impossible. Delphi still has the flu that started at Christmastime. There are strings to being a mother, no question. Her fever has been high for the last few days. I will stay here. She is so good, even when she is sick. She amuses herself with her drawing.

Delphi   April 23, 1918

Tonight at dinner Sonya attacked poor Julius about how he was getting rich from the war, profiting from bloody sacrifice, but Julius stands up to her now, and he just said he had no intention of apologizing for his success in business in either war or peace, and that making money was not a crime and its proper use was a boon. That got her quiet. Then they had a conversation about men, and she kept saying that she had no use for them, that women are only hampered and limited by them, that no woman can be both courtesan and conqueror. All the time she was saying it she was flirting with Julius. Doesn't he see?

She is insisting I go with her tomorrow to Governor's Island to see her teach all those old women how to use bayonets to protect themselves from the Huns. I am not afraid of anything. Sonya would never use a bayonet. She would probably start flirting.

Sonya   August 7, 1918

It has been confirmed. They are all dead - Nicholas, Alexandra, Alexi, the girls. All gunned down. How happy that would have made me once. No more. His power was all we needed. He could have been spared his life.

Delphi   August 7, 1918

She is such a liar. She does not care about Russia at all, and all my life it is all I ever heard of. The Romanovs are all dead, the revolution is really there, and it is all the same to her. It makes me laugh to see her carry on about women being equal to men; she is so weak. I shall be strong.

Sonya   *October 8, 1918*

The war will end soon, I am sure. I will miss teaching my classes in self-defense on Governor's Island. How they have laughed at us. Well, let them. My little band of women is prepared to fight not only the Huns, but all enemies! I am frightened now by very little. No wonder men have always kept us in aprons.

I went to an interesting meeting on Monday evening. Even in Mexico, it seems, revolutionary fervor is brewing. There are groups of terrorists fighting through the countryside there. Their leader, a man named Villa, would seem to be a popular figure, one of those men who springs to power in times of great crisis. I wish I could be fighting there to end injustice, or anywhere. I am nearly forty, and my ideals are the same as when I was fifteen. Good! I shall stay young and strong.

I don't know what to do about Julius. I rely on him more and more while trying to make it clear to both him and Delphi that I needn't rely on him at all! It confuses everyone. I must say, though, that it is nice to go to the theater or the opera. Men are still attracted to me, and I am vain enough to be grateful for it, even if it is useless. The friend of Julius's from Chicago was very handsome. Bright, too, but all of that is out of the question. The thought of Gregory Tolchin is all I need to sustain me. If he were dead I should never marry again.

Delphi   *November 30, 1918*

Now that the war is over Sonya keeps talking about Tolchin coming home. That is a funny thought. I do not remember him very well. I used to have a picture of him in my desk drawer, but it got ripped up when the drawer stuck, or I lost it, I don't remember. I think I was very sad when he went away, but I don't remember that anymore either.

January 5, 1919

Today is my fourteenth birthday. I am five feet seven

inches tall. My hair is long, but I want to cut it short. I am very thin. I have big bones in my shoulders that I hate. My neck is too long. I look better when I draw myself than I look in real life. That is not because I make myself prettier, it is just that I am a better painter than I am a person. I have one friend, Lucy, a girl next door whom my mother can't stand. Lucy will be my friend forever.

I wonder what my mother will give me for my birthday. My father once sent me a fur dog from Paris with green eyes.

I bet Julius Borach will give me a present.

Sonya March 18, 1919

Word has arrived that Gregory is in prison, accused of counter-revolutionary deeds during the war. He is in the Fortress of Schusselburg, overlooking Lake Lagoda. That is bad news indeed. I shudder to think of his life, but I suppose he is lucky to be alive at all. They are killing and killing and killing. My stomach knots if I think of it. Gregory will survive. It will not end like this for him. Or for me.

Delphi March 22, 1919

I now have three students to tutor. Besides Gloria on Monday and Thursday, and Peter Grant on Tuesday (he is not so dumb as I first thought) I have Angelina Bianco on Wednesday and Friday. She at least lives right nearby. Last week her mother showed me how to make a dish with sausages and peppers and potatoes and onions that was so good and spicy. I am earning nearly five dollars a week! Sonya is very proud of me now that I am buying so much of the food in the house.

May 25, 1919

I like Pietro Bianco, Angelina's father. Once he was going to be a priest, but he became a stonemason. He said maybe he could serve God better with his hands than with his prayers. He built churches with his hands and repaired the insides of them and he always felt close to God. My Italian is getting quite good, probably better than poor

Angelina's Latin. I am afraid she was never meant to be a student.

June 19, 1919

I won a special Latin prize in the assembly this morning, and they gave me a book of English poems. I had to go up on the stage. I like winning prizes, but I don't like going up to get them.

July 28, 1919

I used to want to live with the Biancos, they are so warm and good with one another, but now I don't. Leno Bianco is going to be a stonemason like his father, and I just found out that poor Angelina is practically engaged to someone who still lives in Palermo, Italy. There is another sister who is already married and has a baby, and she is only three years older than I. I told Sonya and she just shook her head; then she said it could happen if I didn't watch out, and how old was Leno Bianco and to stay away from him. I told her he was only twelve and half my size. Angelina said that she was trying to learn Latin so that she could be an excellent student, like me. She said she wished she could have Sonya for a mother. I told her if Sonya were her mother she'd have to work and clean and get the highest grades and be practically a slave or Sonya would throw her out in the street. She said that was better than having a *fidanzato* who is twenty-eight years old and lives in Palermo, Italy.

September 21, 1919

Angelina Bianco left school. Her father said she couldn't come anymore. I told Sonya and she went over to speak with Mrs Bianco, but they wouldn't even let her inside the door. Sonya says ignorance causes more human suffering than war. I told her the Biancos were kind, and she said kind ignorance was no better than cruel ignorance; in fact, it could be worse.

There are only two people living here: Mira, who is going to law school and working in a clothes factory at the same time, and Samuel, who came back from the war and went to work for the magazine *The Nation*. I think he used to be Mira's lover and now he isn't. She doesn't seem to care at all. She is too busy, I think.

October 14, 1919

It is terrible in the house. Sonya is all puffed up as if there were a big swelling under her skin. She talks to herself and then she cries. Her family was killed. She worries about Tolchin. She runs into her room and then she comes out swollen and red and walks about the house with no purpose and then runs back into her room. I have never seen her so sad. Usually she is angry, and that is easy to ignore, but this past week she is so sad. I have called Julius Borach and he is coming this evening to see if he can calm her. Why do I feel as if it is my fault?

How does she still think of Tolchin? He has been dead for me for so long. I used to feel myself an oddity, with no father, but now, with so many men lost in the war, I am just like everyone else.

November 20, 1919

I seem not to have written about the hospital in the Bronx where I go to write letters or to read to the wounded soldiers who came back in pieces from the war. Sometimes they let me draw their faces. One of them, Harry Johnson, killed himself. He had lost an eye, but he told me he didn't mind because he had seen enough with it. He was very cheerful even though he had a fever, and I read him stories because he didn't want to write letters to anyone. He liked me to tell him about my life. He laughed when I told him about Sonya's old parties and how she dressed up in so many costumes I hardly knew who she was. He was one of the patients who wouldn't go home. He didn't want to be sent home like a package. Once I even thought about asking Sonya to let him come here.

Today when I went to see Harry they told me he had killed himself by drinking some poison. I feel so terrible inside, sick and hot and strange. Sonya talked to me for a long time. She said inside pain is as awful as outside pain, and sometimes a person just doesn't want to live because it can hurt so much. She said once she wanted to die, but then she decided not to and she had never regretted it. I wonder if that was when Tolchin left. If she had died long ago, I never would have been born. Everything is an accident.

I am never going to the hospital again.

February 17, 1920

Two men came and took away the press equipment from upstairs and then packed away the type. Socialism and Socialists are very unpopular since the end of the war. There have been many arrests; even Emma Goldman was arrested.

I don't even know which side these two men were on, whether they were acting for the government to destroy the press, or acting for the Socialists to hide it. It doesn't matter to me. It is all talk, talk, talk, as usual. Words mean nothing. All of them here are so swollen with words they are like cucumbers caught in a fence, blown up and bursting. How excellent it is to be a painter. I will never have to use words.

February 20, 1920

I am working for Michel Beauronde on the weekends, decorating cakes. I have learned to make everything from boats to cats on the top of a cake, but the colors are only pink, white, and blue. I use lard and sugar and vanilla and food coloring. Michel is a funny old Frenchman whose glasses are forever getting steamed up so he can't see half the time, and he curses like a sailor. He has lived here for thirty years and he still speaks only French. How do I find such wonderful jobs? He says he was once chef to the queen of Rumania or somebody and his cakes taste like plaster of Paris. Still, it is better than working many other places. He does not mind at all when I give up my lunch hour to draw him and the other bakers or the customers. He thinks I am very talented, but I know that is only because he thinks I am French.

March 3, 1920

Sonya has had word from Tolchin. He is coming home! I

am afraid. What will it be like to have a father now that I am grown up?

April 4, 1920

Tolchin is in detention on Ellis Island. They are giving him a terrible time about coming into the country, even though he has a British passport.

He is not here and already there is such madness in the house. Sonya is impossible. She stands in front of the mirror, shaking her head. She cries. She is hysterical, nervous. The house shines. She says everything is decayed and falling apart. My God, she is like a little bird, flittering and fluttering. How unbecoming.

April 9, 1920

He is here, a stranger. I try to be polite. I feel nothing. It is peculiar, nonetheless, to have another person in the house. How Sonya dances to his tune! Good. She has less time to devote to me.

There is something wrong with the way he looks at people, as if he's going to laugh at them or say something mean. He doesn't, but he looks like he is going to. He told me I draw very well. How does he know anything about it? Obviously he is one of those people who think they know everything about everything. He is going to have a job with Julius Borach on Wall Street.

Can they really be making love? They are both so old.

Sonya   March 8, 1921

Gregory has been home now for nearly a year. They have been long bad days. His time in prison has deeply wounded him, but he refuses to talk to me about it. Last night he burst out at me for asking him about it. Whatever it was, he is so changed.

Of course it is easy to disapprove of socialism these days. The news from Russia is ugly, and Gregory is proved right, Lenin is worse than Nicholas ever was, but now Gregory has no interest in it at all! He has no heart for idealism of any sort.

He gets the most peculiar look in his eyes whenever I talk about Russia, or freedom, or equality. It is as if he is laughing at me. Still, he is tender with me most of the time. Sometimes he withdraws. I wish I knew what it was.

Now that the women's movement has been so successful and our fight is won, I find myself with too much time on my hands. Perhaps that is it. I must find something to do with this old head of mine besides sit and worry about my husband.

Delphi   December 22, 1922
We are having a very grand Christmas this year. Tolchin wants an old-fashioned Russian Christmas. He doesn't care what it costs, he is making so much money. It is driving Sonya crazy. Why does money make her so nervous? She is not a Communist anymore, either. I think she must be having her changes. She is so crazed all the time.

I have made my decision to go to Hunter College next fall. There is a fine art teacher there, and at least my parents will not scream at me if I am in school, learning, learning, learning.

I will be eighteen next month. I am already an adult.

January 13, 1923
Thank God for my painting. My feeling translates through my eyes and becomes clear only through my hand. Sonya has always hated my interest in art. She still tries to ignore it. Good, I ignore her. I have my own world. I don't need either of them. I am going to be a great painter. I need only paper or canvas.

Sonya   February 25, 1923
I am to be forty-two soon, and already the slow disintegration of my body begins! Some days I am shot through with heat for minutes at a time. I feel my organs dry up, even my mind. I shrink inside and soften outside like decaying vegetables in an autumn garden. What woman can believe in God or nature or justice? As we wither, men flourish. I torture myself with the notion that Gregory has mistresses now. Why does it matter to me now when it never mattered before? It is because he is capable of doing as he pleases, of fathering children if he

290

pleases! and I am quite stopped in my tracks. Not one organization wishes my services these days. Socialists are entirely out of favor. I am punished for my youthful ideals although I am a fine organizer, a tireless worker. Worse, I am punished by Delphi, my own child. How she infuriates me! She makes no pretense at any interest but art. Is it a joke? Am I failed at everything? I keep telling myself it will pass, that she cannot be content with so feeble a desire. I must find myself work. It is ridiculous to be so at the mercy of one's weaknesses! It seems all I do is cry these days.

10

Julius Borach had come unexpectedly during dinner to discuss business with Tolchin. The two of them had been closeted away for an hour or so, but now they were all having dessert and coffee. Delphi brought it up from the kitchen to the salon. Sonya was lying on the chaise, holding her wineglass. She had been drinking all evening. 'Sometimes I see the future in my mind as clearly as the past,' she said. 'Well, they are both dreams. I could have lived either.'

'My wife should have been a fortuneteller, Julius.' Tolchin leaned over the back of the chaise and kissed her forehead.

'Oh, you are upside-down, Gregory.' Sonya laughed, spilling a little of her wine onto the carpet as she propped herself up on her elbow. 'I don't know what is the matter with me tonight. I am at sixes and sevens.'

'It's the wine, my love.' Tolchin took her glass from her.

'It's not the wine.' She leaned back into the couch and looked from Tolchin to Borach. 'Have you finally finished your "business"?' She said the word with disapproval.

Julius Borach smiled. 'He is quite a man for making money, this husband of yours. The entire banking community of Europe would seem to have fallen under his spell.'

'I'm sure,' Sonya said.

'I shall have to take him away from you more and more, Sonya.' Borach crossed his leg at the knee and shifted his weight in the plush pillow under him. He looked tiny in the fantastical ebony and ivory inlaid chair that held him.

'Money,' Sonya's lips curled distastefully around the word. 'For what, I wonder?'

'Come, come, Sonya, it's good to have.' Julius smiled at her. 'Even Communists must be warm in the winter. Convictions are not corrupted by comforts and fine food.'

'Food is food. The cook makes it fine or not.' Sonya was

scowling.

'My wife likes to subsist only, Julius. Anything more than necessities are to her as a spike in the breast.'

'Hypocrisy, my dear husband, is the only spike in my breast.'

'I've heard from my son,' Julius Borach interjected, self-consciously trying to change the subject. 'He says things in Europe are nearly back to normal. So quickly, eh?' No one answered. 'It amazes me how quickly we recover from war.'

'How is your son, Mr Borach?' Delphi tried to help him in his discomfort. How rude Sonya and Tolchin could be.

'Oh, he is well, Delphi.'

'But, alas, he is making money, poor man,' Tolchin said lazily, walking to the sideboard and pouring himself a brandy. Sonya glared at him.

'Sonya,' Julius said to her brightly, 'you must see the new hall. The orchestra is first rate. Absolutely first rate.'

'It costs money to go to a concert.' Tolchin's eyes filled with amusement. 'Besides, my wife is too busy with her good works to bother about Mr Carnegie's new hall. Tell us, Sonyasha, how is the real world doing?'

Sonya frowned a bit and then turned her eyes to her husband's face, her gaze steady. 'Since you seem so interested, Gregory Tolchin, I will tell you. I don't know. I am a woman without a cause at the moment. I am not trusted by the anti-Socialists because of my Socialist connections, and I am not trusted by the Socialists because of my husband's money.'

'My poor darling, I had no idea. Our old friends betray you?'

'A Socialist with financial holdings is hardly above their suspicion. You and Julius will soon own America.' Sonya stood up and strode to the sideboard to pour herself more wine. Tolchin played with the brandy in his glass, twirling it first one way and then another.

'You should have known Sonya in Russia, Julius. You should have seen her, Delphi. She was quite different. She was so fragile. She could crochet.'

'Never! I could never crochet!'

'So you say now, but I know differently. Your parents

told me. You could crochet and do needlepoint and play Mozart nicely on the piano.'

'Never! I grew up as a man. I was trained like my brothers.'

'Sonyasha, you are shouting.' Tolchin walked to the fireplace.

'I beg your pardon, Julius. I am a bit turned around this evening. My head is banging so.'

Again, Julius Borach tried to change the subject. 'Sonya, my dear, I know you don't approve of collectors, but I have just managed to purchase a very fine Della Francesca, thanks to my son, of course, and you must see it. It is so very magnificent that it gives comfort to the viewer, a sort of reassurance that there is a God in heaven.'

Sonya's laugh was short and sarcastic. 'Dear Julius, I am glad that you believe in God! Since his presence in this world or the next has never given me the slightest comfort, I don't need reassurance of his existence.'

'I would like to see the Della Francesca, Mr Borach,' Delphi said.

'How can Carl still indulge himself questing after beauty while the world remains in such turmoil, Julius? How can he manage such a preoccupation?' Sonya shook her head. 'I still can't understand it!'

'He manages because his father has money,' Tolchin whispered to her exaggeratedly, putting his glass down.

'It would appear that my daughter's father also has money. Does he propose to support her as she dabbles her way through life?' She paused, expecting Delphi to defend herself, but Delphi said nothing. Sonya sighed. 'I don't know what has happened to us in these last years. We did have ideals. We did have priorities.'

'I lost mine in prison,' Tolchin said. 'I can't speak for you, Julius. Do you still have yours?'

Sonya glared at him. 'I have been in prison, too,' she said. 'There are people whose ideals are reinforced there. Do you suppose ideals are so many lost-and-found items, nothing more?'

Julius Borach shook his head. 'I don't like to think that I have lost my ideals or that my son has none. Ideals aren't only a matter of politics. I don't rule out the importance of his present contribution.'

'Contribution, Julius? Sitting in his villa in Italy and studying paintings so he can tell rich men like his father which is worth more. What have ideals to do with that?' Borach didn't answer. He sipped his coffee and looked over at Tolchin, who had just sat down on the enormous wicker fan chair by the fireplace.

Tolchin stretched out his legs, crossing them at the ankles. Taking out a long gold cylinder from his inside pocket, he carefully opened the attached top and took out a cigar. From another pocket, he took out a silver cigar cutter and sliced off the end of his cigar. Then lifting it to his ear, he rolled it gently back and forth between his fingers.

'Gregory, please, I would prefer that you didn't.' Sonya's voice smarted with her disapproval. 'My head.'

'Of course,' he said. He reinserted the cigar and looked at the case, turning it, letting it catch the light. 'Did I tell you, Sonyasha, that I saw Princess Anna Pavlova and her daughter in Paris last month? The girl, what the devil is her name?'

'Lydia.' Sonya's voice was tight.

'Ah, yes, Lydia.'

'You told me yesterday that you thought she was beautiful.'

'Did I?' Tolchin smiled at Sonya. 'At any rate, there she was with her mother at the Paris opera. They were both as bejeweled and bedecked with furs and splendors as they would have been at the high season in Petersburg. They put me in touch with a dealer in Paris who is now specializing in *les objets russes*. I bought this case from him. You see here, Julius, it's solid gold and lapis, and look at the fine workmanship in the initialing. You see the *N* and the *P* in pearls and diamonds? I am becoming quite sentimental about things Russian these days. This case belonged to old Prince Nicholai. There's even a small music box inside the lid.' He flicked it open and pressed a tiny button, and a tune played, hardly audible even in the silence.

Sonya sat listening to the tune while it played. When it stopped, she rose from the chaise and walked shakily over to face her husband.

'What have you become, Grisha?' she asked him tensely, her face full of disbelief. 'How is it that you carry such a thing, you who thought such things and such people as Prince Nicholai were the cause of so much misery? You carried on so about him, making such terrible jokes at his expense, cursing him for his disregard of the real world. Now you are no better. Your fine English tailors, your splendid French shirtmakers, your royal friends! *Les objets russes!* You and Julius should build a museum for your treasures so the world might enjoy your unspeakable extravagance! You are middle-aged gluttons. I hate your obsession with money. I hate you for it.' Sonya left the room without another word. Delphi stood up, shaking her head.

'I don't believe it. I don't believe it,' she said, looking after Sonya.

'What?' Tolchin wet the end of a cigar as he stared at her.

'Sonya. All the drama and the performance. That's the way she is now. Lectures and grievances day and night. No one can even talk to her. Just because she never accomplished anything, she just carries on and attacks everybody all the time!'

'Sit down, young lady.'

She stood staring at him, her hands at her hips.

'You heard me. Sit down.'

The flat sound of his voice had so much force, Delphi would rather he screamed at her as Sonya did. She sat and looked right at him, the same look she had learned from him, direct, unblinking, harsh. 'Now, my dear daughter, let me make something quite clear. You are never to use that tone of voice when you speak of your mother, you who have risked nothing in your safe young life. Unlike most of us, she is passionately dedicated to her principles, her conscience as inflexible as the North Star. Without her and people like her there would be little of value accomplished in this thin and godless world. One day, when you are older, you may be privileged to know her accomplishments. If and when you risk anything, you may make a judgment on others.'

Delphi looked down into her lap, hoping Julius Borach wasn't looking at her. It was too degrading that her father should treat her so like a child just for speaking her mind. When she had the courage to look up at him, he had struck a match, and a long, flat tongue of flame shot up nearly to his eyebrows. She hoped he would burn himself. Slowly, he puffed at his cigar, now looking at the case in his hand. 'Your mother will, no doubt, shoot me for having this,' he said, holding it out to them. Delphi looked at the onyx and gold match case. Outlined on its side in sapphires and rubies were the imperial eagles.

*　　*　　*

Delphi   March 29, 1923
I have worked very hard on a painting this last month. The model was bad and dull, and yet I found a way of exciting myself through color. The model became un-important in the final composition, so my accomplishment sprang out of some feeling I had for her. I can't write what I mean. It is enough to say that I set myself a challenge, and after endless work I accomplished it. Mr Van Vries was very pleased with it, although I think it took him somewhat by surprise. He talked about echoes of the Armory. I was delighted he knew about that. I always thought him so rigid, yet here I am, wrong. He attacked some of the execution, even after I explained the reasons behind it and the emotional interpretation. He was quite sweet, actually, hemming and hawing about it. I know he is very pleased. The finished painting is the best thing I ever did.

*　　*　　*

The trouble with snow in the city was that it made everything filthy and wet instead of smooth and clean. Still, Delphi was too excited to care really that her feet were soaked and cold, her coat dirty. She pushed open the front door and put the heavily wrapped package against the inside wall of the hall as she stamped her muddy boots on the mat. 'Sonya!'

There was no answer.

'Sonya!'

'I am in the kitchen.'

Delphi kicked off her boots, took off her coat and scarf, and hung them on an empty hook next to the small coat closet. Carrying the package, she ran to the kitchen.

Sonya was standing at the counter, cutting a piece of black bread from a loaf. 'You are very excited. What is it?'

Delphi ripped the paper off her painting and put it on the table directly across from where Sonya stood. She tilted it back and forth until she was satisfied that it caught all of the kitchen's feeble light on its surface and held it for Sonya to see. Sonya put the slice of bread in the toaster behind her and then turned to look at the painting. She stared at it and then she stared at Delphi. She folded her arms firmly under her breasts and looked at the painting again.

'Sonya, the toast is burning.'

Sonya reached over to the plug and pulled it out of the socket. She made no attempt to retrieve the burning toast. She looked at the painting again.'It's the best thing I've ever done, Sonya. My teacher chose it for the student exhibition. Obviously I can do much better. If I worked a bit more, I could make the definition of the features clearer, but my professor thinks it is fine, really fine. He thinks I am very talented, Sonya. He thinks I could become a good artist.'

Like an attacking animal, Sonya picked up the bread knife and slashed the painting with three successive strokes, cutting it irreparably. When she looked at Delphi now her eyes were wild and frightening. Delphi screamed and dropped the stretcher of the painting; it clattered against the kitchen table and fell to the floor. Sonya threw the knife into the sink. 'Not in this house. No! It is useless and unimportant!' Sonya's voice tore from her chest. 'I will not have it! You will be better than that! You must be better!' She pulled at the neckline of her dress. 'Don't you see! My God! My God! What is happening!' Her hands erased Delphi and the painting, flat palms moving in the air as she stumbled by her out of the room.

Delphi stood alone, accompanied only by the sound of her own sharp breathing. The place was suddenly foreign, a dark, alien place filled with the smell of burning toast. She looked at the toaster. Red and black ash smoked. She looked at the painting. It was gutted, only flaps of color on the floor. I will hate her until I die, she thought. I will hate her always. She picked up the carcass of her work, opened the kitchen door, and hurled it against the alley wall.

When Sonya went to Delphi's room that evening, she took a tray of cold food. Delphi watched her set the tray on the bureau, for the first time noticing the slight heaviness in her jowl and the wrinkling of her knuckles.

'I am very sorry for what has happened.'

Delphi wanted to yell at her that Sonya would be sorrier, that she was going to be an artist no matter how many paintings Sonya destroyed. She picked up one of her bed pillows and held it tightly against herself. She said nothing.

'I have my dreams, Delphi, as you have yours.'

Delphi would not answer.

'I would like you to promise me that you won't tell your father, Delphi. Please.'

Delphi stared at her mother. How pathetic she looked, how frightened, still afraid of Tolchin, afraid of losing him.

'Please, Delphi, please promise.'

'I won't tell him,' Delphi said without emotion. 'I promise.' None of it made any difference to her any longer.

'Thank you.' Sonya stared at her, but there was nothing to say. 'I'll leave the tray here' was all she could manage.

'I'm not hungry.'

Sonya looked at her sadly. 'Well, perhaps in a bit you'll be hungry. I'll just leave it.'

Delphi gripped the pillow even tighter and pulled both her legs under her and looked away from her mother's face. Sonya's skirt rustled against her petticoat as she left the room.

Delphi had never thought of her father that way, behind a desk in an oak-paneled office. When he came forward to kiss her, she was oddly repelled by him in his dark business suit, which of course she had seen before but never in a place like this one, where other men looked exacly like him. She noticed the lacquer and gold traveling clock on his desk, the brass and crystal inkstand, the precise way his pen and pencils were put, like so many regiments of soldiers lined up for duty, on the maroon and gold-stenciled leather top.

'Have you come to see my desk?' he said, watching her stare at it.

'Of couse not,' she said. 'No.' She put her book bag down on a chair behind her and then turned to face him. 'It is strange to see you here.'

'We all become strange out of context. You are no less strange to me here.' He lit a cigarette. 'So, what is it that brings you? Sit down and tell me.' He sat in a tufted leather wing chair and pulled the table next to it closer to him, turning the ashtray so that its lip faced him.

She noticed the bigness of her feet as they sunk into the thick carpeting. She picked up the book bag and opened it, fumbling around for the paper she had put there. Finding it, she took it out, unfolded it, and handed it to him. It had taken her a week to think of everything and what it cost, and now the items and the numbers were neatly written, ledger style, on the paper in his hand.

'I came to ask you for money. It isn't very much, just enough for the rent of the studio - I found a perfect one just five blocks down from the house. It's big enough for a bed, and there's room for a small ice box and a hot plate. I won't need very much. I've looked for two months now, and it seems the best place by far. I can't just go on living to please her. I can't go on being just a child who is supposed to learn everything but isn't allowed to speak her mind or do what she wants to do.'

The telephone rang but he made no move toward it. He folded the paper and then folded it again, holding the cigarette in his mouth. Smoke danced around his face. The telephone kept ringing.

'And what do you propose to do in this studio?' He continued folding the paper until it was hardly larger than his thumbnail.

'What do you mean, Tolchin? I'm a painter, an artist. You know it's all I care about. If you give me the money for this studio, I'll keep going to college until I finish, although it's a bloody waste of time.'

'And if I don't?'

'I'll leave school and get a job.'

'I see.'

'Papa, I am eighteen years old and I'm not a foolish person. I know what the others are like, and I'm not one of them. You and Sonya have seen to that. I know what I want to do with my life. I know it like you knew it.'

'That's fortunate.' He put out the cigarette, smacking the lit end into the ashtray. The smoke died at once. 'I don't see any problem, then. If you want something, just who is stopping you from getting it?'

'Only money stops me, or rather the lack of it. If I had my own money, I could do as I wished and go where I wished and be my own person instead of a nice obedient child who is not allowed to be what she wants.'

He began opening the piece of paper a little at a time. 'You are right about money. It's a decided advantage. You will have to get some, I suspect, if you are serious about your choice. However, I will not give you any.'

'Why?' She nearly screamed with outrage. 'It's not like you!'

'But Delphi, it is exactly like me. Your mother and I agree on that point. You must work for what you want. I don't finance anyone's dreams but my own. I am quite firm on that point.'

'But don't you see, you are only making me lose time. If I have to find another way, it will just take me longer!'

'Then it will have to take you longer. If you want something, Delphi, get it. Don't ask me to get it for you.' He handed her the paper, but she flung it back at him. It fluttered between them like a big dead leaf and fell to the carpet.

She stood up, furious at herself and at him. 'You'll be sorry, because I will get it. I will!'

'I won't be sorry at all. I shall applaud you, respect you, and continue to love you.' There was a long, low buzz and it sounded three times. He picked up the telephone on the table next to him. Without a change in tone, he began to speak German to a Mr Freundlich from Zurich. Cupping the receiver between his neck and shoulder, he picked up a pad and pencil and began to write numbers on it. Briefly he looked up at her red, unhappy face before he again focused his attention on the pad. She grabbed her book bag and stamped out.

Julius Borach's office was larger than her father's, with huge windows that looked out over Lower Manhattan and the sea. As he stood up from his honey-colored desk, he seemed smaller than usual. She walked to him, clutching the folder under her arm, and leaned over for his embrace. He kissed her lightly and smiled. 'You were very serious on the phone, Delphi Tolchin. You are still serious. It must be very important.'

'It is very important.' She paused. She had thought over exactly what she would say to him. She took a deep breath and smiled. 'First, I have work to show you. I hope to be an artist. You know about art. I want your opinion.' She quickly undid the strings around the pieces of cardboard that held her work and took out her sketches and drawings.

'I'm hardly an expert, certainly not a judge,' he answered, watching her.

'Oh, I think you're an expert. I'd like it if you looked at these. There isn't much. I have a few larger ones that I couldn't carry, and my best work, well, I don't have my best work, but there's enough here for you to get an idea.' She put everything on his desk, and he walked around behind it and picked up the charcoal sketch on the top.

'Sonya,' he said, smiling.

'Yes,' Delphi answered.

'You've certainly caught her.' Bobbing his head slightly, his smile faded. Delphi didn't want to watch him. She turned and walked to the window, looking out at the busy harbor, the mouth of the river, and beyond, the Statue of Liberty and the open sea. There were so many boats, all full of people with other lives. Could things be as important to them? She heard Julius sigh and make a little crooning noise. Which could he be looking at now? The pencil drawing of him and Tolchin having brandy and cigars? She turned to look at him. He was still standing, bent over the desk. He had put on his glasses. Suddenly he glanced over and their eyes met. He didn't smile, didn't even acknowledge her. His attention went back to the drawings, and he sat on the edge of the deep leather chair.

Delphi took another breath and looked around the room. In the far corner the ticker-tape machine spilled its endless coils of paper onto the floor. Delphi watched it, listening to its irregular rhythm, almost like her own. For a moment the machine was silent and she became aware of the tapping of her own foot. She looked down, startled that her own feet should now seem so unfamiliar. Her eyes followed the pattern of the parquet floor around the Oriental rug. In the outer office a telephone rang and then stopped. How long would he take?

'Well, they are good,' he said finally, settling back into his chair, 'very very good. Especially the ones of the soldiers. Moving, I would say. Very good.' He nodded at her as he took off his glasses, then he frowned, cocking his head to one side and clasping his hands under his chin. Delphi watched his thumbs play with one another. 'Why have you brought them to me?'

'I really didn't want to involve you in this, Uncle Julius. I would have preferred not to.'

'Involve me? Well, tell me in what, Delphi, in what?'

'It's really between me and my mother.'

'Yes? Well, then, I suppose I am a little involved already. Sonya mentioned to me that you and she had had a fight of some sort. You know, with your father away so much, she confides in me.'

'A fight? Was that what she said?' Delphi was incensed. 'It was more?'

'You won't want to believe this, Uncle Julius, because I know that you love her. I mean, you are so fond of them both, but she is not the woman that she seems to you. She is mean and ugly.' Delphi said it without emotion. Julius had not even blinked when she said he loved Sonya. She had to be careful not to upset him.

'Delphi, now Delphi, mothers and daughters—'

'This is not just mothers and daughters. This cannot be dismissed as mothers and daughters. I am embarrassed for

303

her, Uncle Julius, embarrassed to tell you what she did. I would not, except that then you would never understand my desperation.' She stopped and studied Julius's face. He seemed to be interested.

'Well,' he said finally, his deep brown eyes fixed on her face, 'what did she do?'

Delphi took a breath. It really was difficult to tell him. How awful for Sonya, how awful. 'She took the best painting that I ever did.' Delphi began. 'I did it in school. I had worked so hard, Uncle Julius. My professor thought it was excellent, and I came like a good daughter to share my excitement with her, my pleasure. I came to share joy with her, and she cut my painting to ribbons. Slashed it with a bread knife. Again and again.' Delphi stopped and swallowed, forcing down an uninvited swell of renewed anger and hurt. Julius's eyes had not left her face. 'Do you understand now?' she asked him.

'I'm sure, my dear Delphi, that there were explanations—'

'No! No! Only that I dared love something that she did not love. Only that I dared to be a person that she hadn't molded and couldn't control. I cannot help if it I am not in love with all her causes!'

'It's hard for mothers, my dear. Sometimes—'

'You don't understand. If it had been some petition I had circulated, if I had spent the night in jail, she would have been so proud of me. She hates who I am.'

'Delphi,' Julius interrupted, 'that will all pass. She doesn't—'

'No, it won't, Uncle Julius! Sonya will never change. Has she changed since you knew her? I have to get away from her, and besides it will be better for her, too. She won't be reminded all the time of her failure.'

She could not see the expression on Julius Borach's face. He was looking down at his desk, his head bent over, the jowls and cheeks spilling forward, almost hiding his mouth. His body was suddenly heavy, defeated. 'What is it, Uncle Julius?' Delphi asked, alarmed.

'Nothing, nothing, Delphi. I was suddenly just overwhelmed with the similarities within families so dissimilar.'

'I'm so sorry, Uncle Julius.' She had forgotten his wife, that haunted face at the lodge all those years ago. 'I'm so sorry.'

'It's all right, my dear,' he said, straightening up, pulling down on the edge of his vest. 'Well, well. What about your father? Why did you come to me? Won't he help you?'

'My father won't give me any money. He plays with me like a cat with a mouse.'

Julius laughed. 'Oh, I don't think so.' He had clasped his hands again under his chin, and his thumbs were tapping hard against one another.

'Can you get me a job, Uncle Julius? Help me get some kind of decent-paying job? Then I could move out, get by.'

'And your schooling?'

'If my father wanted me to finish school, he would get me a studio. I told him that already. He won't. I don't care about school. Certainly it will never help me be an artist.'

Julius Borach chewed on his lower lip, frowning. 'When do your classes end this year?'

'June.'

'Do you have any secretarial skills?' he asked, still frowning.

'I can type and take some dictation. Sonya saw to that.'

'There's one thing I might do. That is, until things can cool off a bit, you know? Perhaps I can arrange for a summer job with my son. Sometimes it is better to be apart. Three months should calm everyone down. What do you think?'

'With your son? In Italy?' He nodded his head.

'Oh,' she said, sinking back into the chair across from his desk. Her head was muddled with her excitement, and her lips and her tongue were dry in her mouth. 'But I have no money for passage and no passport.'

'If you can manage the passport, I can manage the money.'

She looked at him in amazement. 'Then you think I am talented? You like my work?'

'Yes. Yes, God help me, I do.' He shook his head slightly. 'How perverse life is that Gregory and I, so entirely different, should lose our children to the muse of art. And Sonya . . .' He closed his eyes and was silent for a moment. 'Still, I don't know. Siena is a long way from West Fourth Street, Delphi, and you are very young.'

'You would not say that to me if I were a boy.'

'How like your mother you are,' he said, smiling at her. 'And of course, you must have her permission to go. You must tell your parents, for I could not go against either of their wishes. Although there shouldn't be a problem. Three months is a short time.' He assembled the drawings into a pile and touched them lightly with his hand. 'So, you think it is a good idea?' She nodded quickly. 'And one more thing. If we can arrange this job, you must promise not to tell Carl you wish to be an artist. He thinks everything worth doing has already been done and the only great artists are those who are long dead.'

'He is wrong.'

Julius Borach laughed. 'How fine it is to be so young and so certain!'

'Certain enough to know that someday I shall repay you. I shall think of you as my patron.'

Such a kind man. What a burden he carried. She had never even thought about it before, never thought about him except to say hello and exchange a few words when he came to the house. She smiled back at him, watching the crinkles near his eyes deepen and then retreat. On the way home, she thought, she would drop off the drawing of him and her father at the framer on MacDougal Street. He could hang it right next to the Caravaggio.

11

It was almost Easter before Julius Borach called and told her that Carl had agreed to take her on as his scretary for the summer months, provided she obtained both Sonya's and her father's approval. Delphi was convinced that there would be no problem. Sonya certainly could not object, and why should her father?

Sonya had made her usual fuss about Easter. She had kept the housekeeper busy baking and cooking all week, and Saturday she had shut herself up in the dining room to do the decorations. Delphi had thought it would be different this year, seeing as there would only be the three of·them. What with Julius away on business, her parents had decided not to have the usual crowd. Too bad, Delphi had thought, she and Sonya were hardly speaking to one another, except to keep up a pretense in front of her father. It would have been easier with more people.

'Turkey and ham!' Tolchin was saying. 'My God, Sonya, there is enough food for an army.' He filled his plate at the sideboard, which fairly overflowed with the food, including the traditional Russian breads, the thick round *kulichi*, little ones stacked upon larger ones, the initials *X B* written in red and white frosting, and next to them, the creamy white *pashka*.

'Ah, like the old days,' Tolchin said as he took his heaping plate and sat down. He dipped his hard-boiled egg into the *pashka* and followed it with a swig of vodka. 'We have become so sentimental, Sonya.'

'I enjoy the traditions, not their meanings.'

'One cannot escape the other,' he answered, breaking off another piece of bread.

'I can appreciate the form without honoring the content, Gregory.'

Were they about to argue? 'I love your centerpiece, Sonya,' Delphi remarked, changing the subject. 'Clearly, this year's is your best.' Sonya had colored all the eggs red

307

and white and decorated them with bits of ribbon, colored glass, and stones. She had written Easter sayings on them and stacked them like a conifer on a silver tray in the center of the table. Ribbons made of sugar and chocolate topped the thin end of the cone. 'It must have taken you forever.'

'If I had been smart, I would have bought all the Fabergé in Petersburg. The government finally confiscated it. Do you know what that stuff will be worth in ten or twenty years?'

'You keep forgetting, Gregory Tolchin,' Sonya said, dipping her spoon first in the caviar and then into the soured cream, 'that we had other priorities. We were revolutionaries. You keep forgetting.'

Delphi looked at them. Revolutionaries? It was becoming harder and harder to visualize them running through the streets of Petersburg dressed as workers. She looked at Sonya, trying to remember her as she was only a few years before, when there had been agitators staying at the house and the press had been going, but she couldn't remember it clearly. Even now, just for the three of them at Easter, Sonya looked as if Poiret were responsible for her simple green sheath with the copper threads at the neckline and the edge of the sleeve. It was so cleverly cut it masked the slight rounding of her body. She has gained weight, Delphi thought, looking at how the skin on her neck puffed around the three creases that Delphi never remembered seeing.

'I wonder what became of my mother's collection of eggs. Remember them, Gregory? She took them out at Carnival and left them on display past Easter week. One had a little chick inside with diamond eyes. I don't think it was Fabergé, but it was certainly similar.'

Again, Delphi thought, they will talk about money. She listened to them throughout the rest of the meal, interrupting only when she thought their bickering might turn to anger. It occurred to her that this would be the best time to tell them about her summer, but her stomach kept turning over. After the blini, she thought, with dessert, tea, and brandy; then I must tell them.

When she did, Tolchin continued to sip wine, filling and refilling his glass. Sonya merely sat at the table, drumming endless rhythms of annoyance on the tabletop. When Delphi stopped talking, Sonya pushed herself away from the table and stood up. 'You will be wasting your time,' she said. 'With your mind, Delphi, how can you consider a subject like art to be enough for you? Really, it is such an elitist business and so limited.'

'But I have explained all that, Sonya. Simply, for me, it is all that matters. I don't have a choice. It consumes me.'

'Consumes you? How does it consume you?' Sonya started walking back and forth in front of the sideboard. 'Only passion consumes, and you don't have any. Don't be silly. The world doesn't need another aspiring artist.' She laughed. 'At any rate, I won't hear of it.'

'Sonya, I am not going to paint now. I am just going to be Carl Borach's secretary.'

'Nonsense. You are too young to travel around the world by yourself. What do you know about anything? Why waste yourself as a secretary?' She stood at the head of the table. 'I have worked all my life for you, to see that you get the best education possible, and you intend to throw it all away, all that learning, all that exposure? Well, I will not let you do that. Not while I have the strength.' She shook her head violently. 'Carl Borach, of all people!'

'Sonya, you said you were married at my age.'

'Yes! And look what it cost me. I could have—' She had stopped for a moment and stared at Delphi. 'You will not throw away your life in this manner. How dare Julius interfere?'

'Sonya, it is only for the summer. You of all people—' Delphi tried to interrupt her.

'I am not all people!'

'Sonyasha, listen to yourself. You are making no sense whatsoever.' Tolchin's voice was very soft in direct counterpoint to Sonya's.

'I don't have to make any sense. The topic is closed. Do you both understand me? I did not spend all these years bringing up someone who is going to run off to some Bohemian life under the pretext of the need to be an artist. I have never in my life heard of such ridiculousness.'

'I think, Sonya, you will have very little to say in this matter.' Again Tolchin.

'Are you so selfish?' Sonya came to the table, put her hands down flat onto the surface, and then leaned over them and stared into Delphi's face.

'Delphi is a grown woman now, my dear. She will do what she says with or without your permission. You are only behaving like any mother who feels rejected. Besides, it's only for three months. She'll be back before you know it. Let her go.' Tolchin's voice was weary, barely a rasp. 'No house is big enough for two women. You would be at each other's throats no matter what she did.'

'And since when did you become an expert on mothers and daughters?'

'You are off the subject. Just get her the landing card and tomorrow she can begin arrangements for the passport. It is time, Sonya. Not your time but her time. Just let her go.'

Sonya put her hands on her hips and took a long breath. 'I lost the landing card. If she must go, she will have to go without a landing card. But then I'm sure you can make the arrangements, get the papers, bribe the officials as you always have.'

Delphi looked up, finally. There was no air left in the room. 'I'll manage,' she said. 'I'm sure I can go to the immigration and tell them it was lost. I always forget I wasn't born here, right here, practically at this table.'

Tolchin had resumed sitting. He was pulling at his eyebrows, pulling at the long twisting strands of hair. 'So you have lost the landing card.'

'Yes. It was so many years ago, after all. Who knows what happened to it.'

'What a terrible liar you are, Sonyasha. You will do anything to make it harder for her.' Tolchin now was looking at the ceiling.

'How dare you call me a liar!' Sonya's anger was false. There had been an imperceptible shift in Sonya's attention. Delphi watched Sonya's hands come down from her waist. Her fingers pulled at the fabric of her skirt.

'Because you are a liar, my dear.' He scratched at his forehead. His eyes shifted from left to right as if he were watching a game played out in front of him.

'Who knows what happens to things like landing cards

after so many years? Why are you making such an issue about this? You know how I am about those things. Who knows better than you?'

'That's right. Who knows better than I?' He now covered his eyes with his palm, pressing the upper part of the palm at the ridge of his nose as if there was a pain there.

How quickly it all went wrong, Delphi thought. How quickly the subject of her leaving had been bridged by something else. Tolchin's hand was now massaging his right shoulder slowly and his head was back, his eyes fixed again on the ceiling. The two of them were just locked coils always too tightly sprung. One could pull them apart for a few feet and attempt to attach them to something else, but they snapped together again.

'Stop making innuendoes, Gregory Andreivitch. I'm sick of your innuendoes. I lost the card. I just lost it.'

'You?' He sounded surprised. He turned his head and then looked at her. His voice was almost sweet in tone. 'My little ferret? You, who save everything? The very model of efficiency and organization who can put her hand on any appropriate quotation, on any list, on any justice or injustice done her by man or beast? You say you have lost your landing card? Well, perhaps I can assist you in finding it.' He got up, his eyes never leaving her face, his lips white.

'I don't need your help. I'll look for it when I have the time.'

'You just said you had lost it.'

'Maybe I can find it. It isn't so important that we have to do it now.'

'It will only take a moment, dear Sonya Leonovna. Don't trouble yourself.'

She flew at him, grabbing at his shirt. 'I'm sick of you! Do you hear me, sick of you!' He carefully retrieved his shirt from her fingers and left the room with her running after him, and Delphi heard the slam of doors and the opening of doors, and then they were back again, Tolchin first, Sonya behind him. He held a small steel strongbox in his hands, put it on the table, and opened it, flicking it open with thumb and forefinger. In a matter of seconds he had found the card. He glanced down at it and then pushed it away from him. Unhurriedly he poured himself more wine and drank the entire glass. 'So it wasn't lost at all. Do you have any explanation you feel might be appropriate?' He did not even turn his head toward her. He seemed as easy as a snake in the sun. Even his eyes had closed.

'I need no explanation,' Sonya answered.

'Perhaps a small one. For instance, the name you chose? Why wasn't the name given you in France good enough for you?'

'This is the name they gave me at immigration.'

'Then why the lie about having lost the card?'

'I don't know. Because I felt like it. I am not on trial! Because you make me crazy!'

'Ah.' He shook his head up and down.

'I don't know why I said I lost it!'

It wasn't human the way he swung around and out of the chair. It was too sudden and explosive. But suddenly he was standing and the chair was halfway across the kitchen floor. His hand had reached back and cracked Sonya on the face, the sound so strong it made Delphi avert her own face. Sonya was hurled in an arc against the wall of the kitchen.

'Is she my child or is she not?' He took a step toward Sonya and with his arm grabbed the front of her dress. Sonya's face had turned to his and her eyes were black and her mouth was so contorted she was unrecognizable. Her voice was a strangled growl.

'No! She belongs to neither of us, you swine! She belongs only to herself! I found her! Yes, yes I found her. A woman died on the ship and I just took her child and her exit card. What a joke, eh? It wasn't even the name of the landing card. The name was some long Jewish name, but the man at immigration just wrote "Stern" on the card.' Very slowly the realization of what she was saying must have dawned on Sonya, because for a second she stopped speaking. She might have become aware of Delphi, for when she started to speak again, her tone had changed to a more reasonable one. The words were uttered more slowly. She stood up straight as if her posture could restrain her hurt and anger, as if her physical dignity could restrain his. 'But what difference can it make? She might as well be our child. She is certainly as much our child as if we ourselves had conceived her.'

'Damn you!' He had dropped his hands from her clothes. 'You have made my life a mockery.'

'Was your seed so important? I knew it! I have always known you loved only yourself. You are like all men. And that is why I never told you, that is the reason, that alone! She is your child, but you will make it a lie because of some insignificant physical fact, and you will deny that you cared at all. I should have destroyed that card. So your sperm did not make her! So what! Can you really deny her?'

He swept her away from in front of him as if she were nothing more than a curtain of dust, but she caught herself before she fell and ran after him. 'Go! Destroy yourself and me because of your vanity! She is ours! Why are you doing this to me! Gregory Tolchin, if you leave now I will curse you to your grave and beyond it. I hate you. You are vile, despicable . . . Do you hear me?'

The outside door had opened and then banged closed, but it had let in a blast of air that shot through the room. The candles that had burned on the table were snuffed out.

Delphi watched Sonya. Slowly, she had turned from the door to face Delphi. The green eyes were bloodshot and teary. Her tongue licked again and again at her swollen lips. 'Delphi, you must listen to me. I always meant to tell you. I always—'

'You found me? You found me on a ship?'

'You were a baby, an infant. You were mine from the moment I held you in my arms.' She reached across for Delphi's hands, but Delphi pulled away from her. 'I didn't tell you because it wasn't important. He loved you immediately as I loved you. You were a baby, Delphi, you were mine, you were his . . . For the love of God, don't look at me so!'

'Who was my mother? Who was my father?'

'I promise you – may God strike me dead – I only know your mother was a young Jewish girl who died the first day out on the ship. I asked everyone where she came from, who she was, but no one knew. I had never wanted a child, didn't want a child, but the moment . . . I . . .' Sonya began to weep uncontrollably, her head in her arms. 'I thought they would take you away at immigration . . . I—'

'I am Jewish?' Delphi looked down at herself as if she might have changed somehow, then she looked back at Sonya, whose weeping had subsided. She sat now at the table, sobbing more quietly, her head on her arms. Delphi walked close to her. 'Why did you do this, Sonya? Why did you? Why did you choose to tell us now? Why, Sonya? You could have never told. Why was it? To hurt him, wasn't it? You don't care about anything as long as you make him suffer. You don't care about me at all. This has nothing to do with me. It never has.'

Sonya did not answer. She had her head still on her arms, her hair spread out on the table, her breath coming in short gasps in between her sobs.

'I hate you, Sonya Tolchin,' Delphi said to her in an almost even tone. 'I hate you, and I hate him. It is all lies, as I should have known. You are all lies. He is all lies. My life is all lies.'

Sonya looked up at her for a moment and then pushed herself up from her chair and ran to Delphi, pulling at her clothes, trying to shake her. 'No! You are mine! You are his! There is no lie. None! None!'

'Let go of me!' Delphi cried. Sonya was holding her with all her strength. Delphi beat at her, against the back and against the head, pulling, twisting away from her, but Sonya held on. 'You used me to keep him! You used me like a club! I'm nobody's child but my own! Let me go! Liar! You liar! Let go of me!'

Sonya held on even as Delphi's fists smashed into her breasts. 'There is no truth! There are no lies! There is only life! Delphi, you and he are my life!' Delphi lunged at her, her nails ripping down across Sonya's face, leaving a raw and bloody trail. Sonya screamed and dropped her hands, and they fell lifeless at her sides. She stood still for a long time, looking at Delphi, then walked slowly to the table and picked up the landing card. 'Here. Run. Go. Take it. It is what you have wanted.' She reached for Delphi's hand and put the card in her palm and closed her fingers over it. 'Go. I cannot stop you now, Delphi Tolchin.'

12

For the first time Delphi could remember, there was silence in the house. Tolchin had not returned but sent a man to pick up his bags the following afternoon, and, alone in the house, Delphi and Sonya, like defensive chessmen, fell into the halting rhythm of avoidance. Mostly Delphi managed to avoid Sonya, slipping in and out like a boarder behind in her rent, spending her time in her room, darting down to the kitchen only after she was sure that Sonya was not there, listening for Sonya's sound as if it were her enemy. If, as she did at times, Sonya gave her some pedestrian household instruction, Delphi answered only in monosyllables. When Delphi cut off all her long hair in the latest fashion, Sonya, standing half hidden in the dim light at the end of the hallway, her eyes dark wells of disappointment and guilt, said nothing. In her room, Delphi made a calendar and marked off the days.

The week before she was to leave, Tolchin returned, and the familiar sound of fighting drifted into Delphi's room like the cold. He did not come to see Delphi the next day, and when Sonya begged Delphi to go to him and make some kind of peace, Delphi did not answer her. The arrogance of him, Delphi thought. I will never go to him. Let the three of us live in silence.

The morning she was to leave, Delphi woke at sunrise, stripped her bed, and cleared her room of any vestige of herself. By eight o'clock she was ready. She picked up her suitcase and handbag and opened the door to the hall, wondering if they were listening for her, hoping they would not come to say good-by. She heard nothing as she tiptoed past their room and quietly went down the stairs, but there was Sonya, waiting for her, sitting in the chair at the side of the credenza, fully dressed.

'I am going with you to the ship,' she announced, standing up and squarely facing Delphi. 'Here, let me carry something.'

'There is really no reason to. I don't need any help.'

'Not to help. Just to see that everything is all right.'

'I'm sure Julius will leave nothing to chance.' Delphi's face was expressionless.

Sonya cleared her throat. 'You must be careful on the ship, you know. A young girl, traveling alone, one can never tell what kind of men there are on board.'

'Really, Sonya!'

'Well, it's true. Keep away from men on a ship. and in Italy, too.'

Delphi's eyes narrowed. 'Don't you think it's a little late for this conversation?'

'Someday, Delphi, you will forgive me. You cannot hate me forever.' Delphi didn't answer her. 'If you are unhappy with Carl Borach, you can come right back, you know. And I want you to put down your suitcase and go upstairs and say a decent good-by to your father.'

Delphi bristled. 'I shall say nothing to him, Sonya. He is unforgivable, so puffed up and full of himself. God forbid he should ask me to forgive him. God forbid he should say anything to me.'

'You misunderstand him, Delphi. He is so embarrassed, so hurt by his own behavior, that he cannot ask you, but he does love you, he wants you to come to him. It's not so much.'

'I will not go to him, Sonya. He is insufferable.'

'I can understand your anger at me. Delphi, but your father, why must you feel this way about him? After all, he did nothing to hurt you, it was I—'

Delphi slammed down her suitcase and crossed her arms. 'Will you stop saying that! Nothing to hurt me? What about walking out on me for over a month because, as you yourself said, his seed was more important than my feelings? What about that, Sonya, can you just explain it away?'

'It was his anger at me, Delphi, I promise you. His feeling for you had nothing to do with it.'

'There are no feelings for me in this house. Whatever is between the two of you, it is obviously more important than anything that I might be. Neither of you even knew that I was in the room with you that day. You actually forgot that I existed. I was invisible. What do you think? Am I wrong?'

Sonya looked at the floor. Delphi moved toward her. 'You could have gone on with the lie, but you sacrificed me to wound him, and he just followed your lead. I was your club and his sword more than I was anyone's child. It is because I understand that that I am free to go.' Sonya started to say something, but Delphi interrupted her. 'Please, Sonya, I do not enjoy all this ranting and carrying on.' She stopped and raised her hands in protest at Sonya. 'And stop sighing, for heaven's sake, you have done nothing but sigh since Easter.'

Sonya's mouth twitched. Her lips were down at the corners. 'I have never been fond of Carl Borach,' she said; 'he is so unlike Julius.'

'Please!'

When she spoke next, Sonya's voice was soft and pleading like a child's. 'I do love you, Delphi, even though I have never said it and even though it is against everything I would have had you believe. It is my weakness, that love. Don't look at me with such hatred, please. I am not perfect, but I have done my best.'

Delphi stared at her. In spite of herself, she knew Sonya was telling the truth. Am I mad? she thought. Will I leave here feeling sorry for her? She took a deep breath, picked up her suitcase, and turned away. 'If you are coming with me, Sonya,' she said, 'it is time to leave.' Sonya picked up some parcels on the credenza and followed her out the door into the bright sunshine, and they walked east toward Sixth Avenue to find a cab.

'You have your tickets and your passport?' Sonya asked, squinting at her, the sun making diamonds in the green irises.

'Yes.'

'Did Julius give you a phone number for Carl? He told me he was having trouble locating it.'

'I have it, Sonya.' Delphi walked more quickly.

'What a day it is! At least you shouldn't have any trouble with storms this time of year, but if you do, you must remember to keep eating. I brought you this bag of fruit and cheese. I was never sick traveling in the middle of winter because I never let my stomach get empty. Do you hear?'

'Yes.' Delphi hailed a cab and it slowed as it came toward them.

'How much money do you have?' Sonya asked, climbing in after Delphi. The driver made a wide U-turn and headed west. 'Did Julius give you any?'

'A little.'

Sonya leaned back into her seat and opened her purse, clearing her throat and pushing back a stray strand of hair. 'Delphi, I saved part of the money that you contributed to the house. I have always thought of that money as yours, and even though I would certainly not contribute personally to your folly, I think you are entitled to that money.' She handed Delphi a well-creased envelope. 'It comes to almost one hundred dollars. Use it for any emergency.' Delphi stared at the white and gold envelope. 'It is your money, Delphi,' Sonya said, seeing her expression. 'I know you would take nothing of mine. It is, I swear, your money.'

Delphi could not decide what to do. She looked up at Sonya, but Sonya had turned her back to her and was staring determinedly out the window. Delphi slipped the envelope into her pocket. Frowning, she moved slightly away from Sonya and looked out her window. They spent the rest of the ride in silence.

The pier was crowded with people, but Sonya made her way resolutely, and Delphi followed her, letting Sonya get the passes and show the papers, comforting herself with the thought that this would be the last time.

Julius Borach had been fair, but not extravagant. Delphi shared the small second-class cabin with three school-teachers from the Middle West who were on a pilgrimage to the Holy Land. Sonya could barely disguise her horror at their stark appearances and religious fervor.

'Would you mind awfully,' she said to the one with the long pinched nose and jet black cross, if I asked you to move to the upper berth? My daughter, unfortunately, has a long history of asthma and night spells.' She looked at Delphi, shaking her head ruefully. 'I think it would be easier for everyone if, when she woke in the middle of the night, she had easier access to the exit.' If the woman was going to protest. Sonya never gave her the chance. 'I knew it would be all right,' she went on, moving the woman's bag and parcels to the upper bed and replacing them with Delphi's. 'Darling,' she said then, looking at Delphi with something akin to pity, 'why don't you get some air for a moment while I chat with these nice ladies. I'll meet you by the stairs on B deck, you know, where we came down?' Delphi looked at her wide-eyed, silently signaling for her to stop, but Sonya paid no attention. As she closed the door, Delphi heard Sonya begin what was obviously to be some tale of woe. She was using her 'these are only paste' voice. Delphi was mortified. She ran up the stairs and waited where Sonya had told her, trying to forget Sonya entirely, forcing her attention to the throngs of people below her, waving and smiling or hurrying still to get on board. A stout fellow in a bowler hat was weeping and embracing a frail old woman. A governess held a screaming child, pointing up to the deck above Delphi, trying to get the boy's attention there. A tall, pretty woman squeezed in next to Delphi and searched the crowd, finally spotting whomever it was she was looking for and frantically signaling to him, leaning far out over the railing and waving her long silk scarf. The iridescent green fabric caught the sun and shone at Delphi. It was a familiar color, the same as Sonya's eyes. Delphi turned just in time to see Sonya coming toward her, an expression of triumph in those eyes.

'What did you tell them?' Delphi asked as Sonya pushed in between her and the tall, pretty woman. 'Sonya, what did you do?'

'Don't be silly, Delphi, those terrible women with their crosses and prayer books - I just wanted to be sure they didn't convert you.'

'What did you tell them, Sonya?' Sonya looked down at the pier. 'Sonya!' Delphi's voice was so loud that the pretty woman turned to look at her. Delphi blushed as Sonya whooped with laughter and leaned over to half-whisper in Delphi's ear. 'I told them you had been seduced by a mad priest and would only burst into tears if they talked to you of God. They swore not to. I had them close to tears.' Delphi's cry was blocked out by the noise of the smokestack. A young boy in a brown and gold braided uniform walked by them calling 'All ashore' into the orange mouthpiece of his brass megaphone. Delphi turned to Sonya. She knew her expression. It was her brave soldier face. As they stared at each other, the smokestack blasted again, tearing the silence between them.

'Good luck, Delphi,' Sonya said at last.

'Thank you, Sonya.' People were pushing past them. Sea gulls swooped above their heads, barking.

'I shall miss you.' Sonya cleared her throat and swallowed. 'But it will be good for you to get away for the summer. You have been, perhaps, too much with us.' Delphi watched the pretty woman in back of Sonya start to cry, the tears rushing down her face and spilling onto the green scarf that she had draped about her neck.

'Yes,' Delphi answered, wishing desperately that this moment were over. A man and a woman were kissing at the top of the gangplank.

'I took the liberty of addressing some envelopes. I put them in the bag with the apples. I hope you will write us frequently.'

'Of course,' Delphi answered, knowing she would not. The couple had broken apart and the woman had walked quickly down. Perhaps the man might find the pretty woman next to her, Delphi thought. They could comfort each other.

'Well,' Sonya sighed, then looked quickly at Delphi and smiled. Delphi stared at her. 'Well, then, what else is there to say?'

'Just good-by,' Delphi answered. The crowd in back of them had grown larger, all of the visitors now heading for the gangplank.

'Yes. Good-by, Delphi.'

'Good-by, Sonya.' Delphi made no move to embrace her, and Sonya at last turned and joined the others leaving the ship. Delphi watched her make her way along the deck and then down the gangplank itself, holding on to the rope and carefully placing one foot in front of the other like an old woman. Delphi did not wait for her to reach the bottom before she turned away. The smokestack let out another belch of steam, and the gulls shrieked again, laughing at Sonya.

Delphi was free.

Book III

1

The ship docked in Genoa early Monday morning. Delphi stood on the deck, watching the sailors throw over the ropes and the officials board the ship, waving back to the men on the dock who were shouting, smiling, trying to sell hats, flags, postcards, souvenirs, even from that distance. Everybody was handsome, dark from the bright sun that sat over this city built into the hills above the sea; before her stretched strata upon strata of buildings, one on top of the other, white and stucco, with rosy pink-orange roofs unlike any she had ever seen.

During her two weeks on the boat, the schoolteachers had pampered her as if she were wounded. The more she demurred, the more they coddled, until she decided to enjoy them, enjoy life, leave all her anger and betrayal on West Fourth Street with Sonya, which was, after all, exactly where it belonged. She looked forward so to freedom, to work. It was all she could think about as she stood on the deck that bright morning.

She was one of the first to collect her luggage and was at the front of the line through customs inspection. The old taxi drove quickly through the town, bumping down the crowded cobblestone streets, dispersing men, women, children, and animals as it went. She saw in a jumble the narrow buildings, one close on another, the people half hidden in doorways, staring at the old car. Fountains stood everywhere, small and large, the water running through the streets. Women in their black dresses filled buckets or stood idly by, staring.

'*Aranciata? Signorina, aranciata?*' A boy of eight or nine with a wide smile and bright white teeth squinted at her, his face covered with dust as he held up a glass of juice.

'No, no,' she said, pushing his hand away from the window as the taxi started up again. The boy waved to her as she left.

Once at the station, she found her train had been delayed more than three hours. When finally she was safely on it and on her way, they were stopped again because of an accident. Her connection in Florence left without her, and it was not until 11:30 PM, some five hours later than planned, that she arrived at last in Siena. There was no one to meet her. The station was empty except for the stationmaster, one porter, an old man selling oranges from a tray that hung on a leather strap around his neck, and a few obvious foreigners looking as bedraggled as she.

Delphi approached the stationmaster. She had thought her Italian impeccable, but he seemed unable to understand a word she said. Finally, the old man with the oranges interceded.

'The phone is broken. You buy an orange? Very good orange. Very Cheap. I'll give you a special price.'

'No thank you. Are there any taxis?'

'You English? These are better than English oranges.'

'No, please. Is there another phone?'

The old man stepped back and looked at her. 'No phone. I said no phone.'

The foreigners on the bench to her left all glanced at her. Delphi noticed that each held an orange. 'Please,' she said again. 'Is there another phone? Somewhere? Anywhere?'

'You try the bar,' one of the foreigners said in a heavy German accent. 'A bar across the street.' He pointed with his forefinger. Delphi thanked him and made her way to the door, clutching her suitcase. There was something eerie about the station. There was no electricity, and the oil lamps made unnatural shadows. She walked quickly to the street. The bar across the street also had very little light, just the few candles and the small oil lantern she could see through the window. She stopped, looked up and down the empty street, and sighed. Then, squaring her shoulders, she crossed the street and went inside.

The man behind the marble counter was short and olive-skinned. The half-light made him appear sinister. He did not smile at Delphi. He just stared.

'Excuse me,' she said, 'I must use the phone. My train

was late.' He did not answer her. 'May I use the phone, please?' she said more loudly. He walked away from her and turned on the water in the sink behind him. She turned toward the other man in the bar, who was seated at a table to her right, staring out into space. 'Please,' she said, trying to keep her frustration and impatience from her voice, 'where is there a phone?'

'Who are you calling?' The bartender had spoken, his voice higher than she would have thought.

'Carl Borach. Please. I am going to Signore Borach's house. I must call. My train was late.'

'The phone is broken. The lights are broken. In Siena, in all the town, it is out.' He was shouting at her, enunciating very clearly, moving his lips in an exaggerated way as if she were deaf.

'Then I must get a taxi. A car.' The bartender shook his head. She looked back at the man to her right. Now he was smiling at her. He was very old, very yellow in the half-light, like a gnome.

'Can you help? You know Carl Borach?'

'I don't know, signorina.'

'But he lives here in Siena.' The old man shrugged. Delphi closed her eyes a moment to clear her head. Everyone had told her how friendly the Italians were. She had not found it so at all, not the entire day. She walked back outside to the empty street.

'Signorina?' The man startled her so that she almost jumped. She looked down at him. He was so small she might have mistaken him for a child. He, too, had olive skin, and there was an odd expression about his mouth. No, the mouth was scarred, little ribs of flesh upon other ribs of flesh. A burn, perhaps.

'I know Carl Borach. I will take you. My father, well, he is superstitious.'

'What do you mean?'

'Signore Borach is, how do you say, ah . . . he makes discomfort for people. All his wandering, you understand, all around cellars of monasteries and they say cemeteries . . . the objects he brings back . . .' He, too, shrugged. There were obviously no words for Carl Borach that could be spoken. 'But I take you. Come. Sometimes I do work in

325

the garden at Villa Santa Rosa. I do not mind going. Not me. Some people . . .' With yet another shrug he picked up her suitcase and led her down a side street to a small horse and carriage. Delphi got up onto the seat beside him. The horse was old and the carriage swung uncertainly on its frame. It was almost half an hour to the house, which was beyond the town. Mario, her rescuer, talked endlessly about himself. She was glad she had no need to smile at him or even to look at him to encourage his aria. How peculiar it was, riding through this ancient Italian town, so unreal in the silver light, the man's voice droning on and on like a lullaby, the cool night air filled with its special perfume. How tired she was, now hardly able to keep herself upright on the wooden seat.

'There. Just there.' Mario pointed to a house far ahead of them on top of a gentle hill above a series of rising terraces, the moon above its right shoulder like a spotlight, illuminating the carefully tended grass, terraces, and the pots of sun-swollen geraniums and daisies lining the path that went up from the cobbled street to the door. Vines sprawled across the outer wall, dripping and looping color.

Delphi paid the man and watched him turn the carriage around and head back toward the town. Her suitcase felt unbearably heavy as she walked through the outer gates and slowly up the pathway to the front door, a block of wood set into the stucco wall. The only thing less than simple was the ornate bell that hung above her head to the left. She hesitated and then pulled the rope, causing a raw clang in the steel-blue silence. She waited, listening for footsteps. Then she rang again. Finally she heard them, soft and light on the other side of the door. The door swung open soundlessly. She smiled at Carl Borach, an uncertain little smile. 'I'm sorry to have come so late but the train was delayed . . .'

He looked the same. Narrow and dark and very straight. He did not smile at her, merely studied her face for a moment. 'You still look like a Lippi Madonna,' he said.

She did not know what he expected her to say, so she said nothing.

'If compliments have such an effect, I must make

certain never to compliment you again.' His sliver of a mouth hardened.

'I'm sorry,' she offered. 'I am very tired. I have been traveling so long.'

'I know, I know.' He backed away from the doorway and let her pass by him, making no offer to help her with her bag. She entered a small courtyard to the smell of the jasmine and bougainvillea that surrounded a tiled fountain. She stumbled across the stones to the open door and waited for him as he walked toward her in a slow measured step.

'Come, you'll go to your room.' He picked up two candlesticks from the twelve or so lighting the entrance and walked up the stairway ahead of her, his footsteps soundless on the red-brown tiles. 'Here is your room,' he said, putting one of the candles down on a small stand by the door. 'I will see you tomorrow. The electricity will be fixed by then. Rest. I hope you are comfortable.' He was so formal, rigid as a fence post, not at all as she remembered him. Perhaps it was the sight of her, dirty and exhausted. He had turned and walked by her, leaving her at the entrance of the room. She took a step forward and her mouth fell open. There was gold everywhere. The table, the chest, the candlestand, the frame of the mirror were golden. The chair was golden, and even the large bed had a carved, gilded headboard. Yet for all the gilt, the room was stark. The walls and bed coverings were plain, the floor wooden. And the silence - simple golden silence. For this moment alone it had been worth the trip halfway around the world.

There was a gold and white envelope on her pillow. Delphi recognized it at once. Still, even in this place, Sonya would follow her. She picked it up and sat down on the edge of the bed, slowly opening it and taking out the familiar stationery.

'Delphi,' she read, 'I hope this letter reaches you on your arrival. I mailed it before you left. Perhaps the journey, and the vantage point of such a faraway place will make you look at things here in America with clearer eyes.

'I cannot apologize for who I am. I can only apologize for what I did. It is not easy, middle age, and I have fallen into the trap of it, allowing myself to dwell only on my problems and my decay. I have resolved to change all that, as it only leads to irrational action, as I have proved. It is not too late, Delphi, for us to grow to know one another, or rather, for me to grow to know you, as I am afraid you already know me too well.

'Again, I ask your forgiveness, your indulgence. It is never too late to wipe the slate clean. Am I right? Please answer. Sonya.'

Delphi crumpled the letter and tossed it on the bed table. She took off her cape and shoes and climbed up onto the feather mattress. It was so comfortable and she was so tired she could not even sit straight. She blew out the candle, leaned to the side, fell across the bed, and closed her eyes. No, Sonya, she thought, no, you cannot reach me here.

She woke startled to find herself in a strange place. Her small room at home had been as familiar to her as her face in the mirror. It was exhilarating to see nothing she recognized. She stretched out and the coolness of the sheets sent a chill up and down her body. Suddenly she gasped and sat up straight. She was naked, stark naked, and she remembered falling asleep in her clothes. She looked about the room and saw her case open, her clothes gone, just her toilet articles and papers stacked on top of the chest. Someone had come and undressed her in the night and taken her things. Could it have been Borach? She blushed. Why would he have done such a thing?

There was a kimono lying on the end of the bed, bright scarlet satin heavily embroidered with ivory, ebony, and magenta peonies. On the gold Bombay chest was a simple blue and white vase filled with giant peonies whose white edges were lacy and streaked with the scarlet and magenta of the kimono. For the first time she noticed beside them, on the wall to the right of the chest, a painting of peonies, gigantic, bursting, jagged, as if they had been torn from clouds, and nearly a reflection of those in the vase. She was sure that the flowers on the chest had not been there the night before. Certainly she would have remembered their perfume. What care there had been to make such an arrangement, to mingle the lifelike and the real to such a degree that it was impossible for the eye to see one without the other, to be certain that they were, indeed, separate.

She went to the bathroom and when she came out, she stretched again and put on the kimono. It was so cool and soft against her bare skin. She was ready now for Carl Borach, whoever he was. He would have to explain what had happened to her things. She went out into the hallway, down its length, and carefully down the stairs.

The room below was completely white except for the deep rosy-pink tiles on the floor, each tile fit against the next so tightly they appeared natural as earth.

In the center of the room was a long refectory table of smooth polished wood. Another wooden table, lower and round, separated a large sofa from two chairs in the far right corner. Everything was white save for the wooden furniture. The only color came from the rainbows of refracted light streaming through the windows. The only ornament was a marble statue of a man, naked and bruised by time, its features blunted, its hands chipped, and its feet no longer encased in its sandals.

'So, you are finally up.' Borach was just below her. He wore a loose caftan, its wide skirt stopping just at his ankles.

'Yes, I'm sorry if I slept too long. What time is it? My watch—'

'I suppose you are starving?'

'Yes.'

'Come down.' He watched her moving down the stairs, his eyes fixed on her so avidly she nearly stumbled and had to grasp the railing. As she stepped down next to him, he turned abruptly. 'Follow me.' He crossed the large white room to another arched doorway hidden in a corner. 'I have no maids in residence,' he said, walking down the small hallway, Delphie following close behind. 'A woman comes in every morning, does my shopping, fixes lunch, comes back at seven, and fixes dinner. She has already left. At this hour there is no one.' His caftan rustled on the floor. Then perhaps it was the maid who undressed me, Delphi thought. 'The kitchen is here, of course. I rarely come in here. You will have to find things yourself. Can you cook?'

'Some,' she answered, walking into the kitchen. Here, too, there was so much light, light tumbling onto the counters of yellow tiles, some engraved with flowers or sprigs of herbs. Braided ropes of onions hung from pegs on the wooden beam that circled the room and dried bunches of herbs made the air pungent and sweet. Iron pots were carefully stacked on open shelves around the black stove, and piles of pottery dishes, blue and white and green, filled other shelves.

'The job does not require cooking, but it's good you can cook. Why did my father want to get you here so badly? Were you dallying with the wrong fellow?' She felt his eyes on her back.

'So to speak,' she said, turning to look at him. He backed away from her slightly. For some reason this little man didn't bother her, although she felt he was trying to unnerve her. His intensity, his pointedness, did not upset her; they made her want to laugh instead. How disappointing. This was not the man she remembered.

He pointed to a basket of fruit and vegetables. 'Help yourself.'

He intended to watch her. So he would watch her. She found a knife and picked through the basket for three perfectly ripe tomatoes and a cucumber, sliced the tomatoes lengthwise, making a circle of them on a pottery plate, and quickly peeled the cucumber and cubed it over the tomatoes. Then she took the dried basil and parsley and picking off a sprig of each, crushed them directly over the plate. She sprinkled the plate with oil and vinegar from the two large bottles at the sink and then took a piece of cheese and a corner of a baguette of bread and put them on another plate and sat at the worn table in the corner, facing him.

'Would you like some wine?' he asked, standing exactly where he had stood for the past five minutes. She shook her head. The food was delicious, and she ate with her fingers deliberately.

'Did you take my clothes?'

'I'm getting you new ones. I had the maid take your clothes so my tailors could make everything to your

330

measure. I want you to look a certain way. I can't be distracted by anything that doesn't appear the way I want it to appear, do you understand? My mind must always be clear, no stripes and tweeds and ginghams and checks and plaids.' He shuddered. 'No, nothing like that, and no reds and greens and yellows messing everything all up. You will be in browns and blacks, like a frame. At least my father did not lie about how you turned out, lean and long, angular. Less like a Lippi, really, more like a charcoal or Japanese ink. Please, no rouge or powder, just white. Your skin is white, good, like rice paper.'

'I have never worn rouge.'

'I don't know what you wear or what you don't. Sonya wears everything, kohl, that heavy perfume. Her eyes are like an owl's. She makes masks on that exquisite face so that one hardly knows what she looks like.'

'I am quite different from Sonya.'

She got up from the table with the empty dishes and washed her hands, reached for two enormous peaches, lines of red like smiling mouths across them, and put them on one of the clean dishes and went back to the table.

She smiled at him as she bit into the peach, the ooze of its sticky sweet juice dripping off her chin.

'Why did you bob your hair?'

'My hair?' She touched it. 'Because it's easier for me. It requires no attention.'

'I hope it's not a statement of some sort. Women seem to have gone quite overboard in their quest for freedom, smoking and short hair and wild parties . . .' He was still frowning at her. 'You don't smoke, do you?' She shook her head. 'I don't mind your hair. You have a good neck and classical features, and you have excellent eyes. Well, I will let you finish your meal. I shall wait for you in the other room. That kimono is very becoming to you. You may continue to wear it. Yes, I should like you to wear it, but not while I am working. Never when we are working. Red will never help me work. Red. Scarlet. Such a color.' He stood up, smiling. 'I shall wait in my library. It is to the left of the main rooms.' He stopped after he had taken one small step forward and turned. 'You see, everything in my life must be in harmony. I am making a study of beauty. It sounds quite simple, but I assure you it is most demanding. One must define what that greatness is, make its intangibility actual, trace its origins through all of time.'

'Like Pater? Berenson?' She put down her peach and looked directly at him.

He raised his eyebrows and tilted his head backward slightly, squinting at her with his head cocked to one side. 'You know of Pater and Berenson?'

'Some,' she answered.

'Good. My father promised me you were bright. Perhaps this time he won't be wrong.'

'I am just one of a procession, then?'

'An endless procession, my dear. My standards are difficult to achieve.' He smiled. 'Now, if you will excuse me, I will wait for you inside,' he said, and walked quickly out of the kitchen.

When she entered the library she found him sitting at a table that was cluttered with books, papers, and hundreds of file cards. The room was dark, the shutters closed on the tall, arched windows. Books lined the walls in sturdy cases. Other books, some opened, some closed, were on every other surface of the room – tables, chairs, sofas, and sills. The only light came from a round, dull brass lamp under a white-fringed shade. Everything was brown or gray; even the thick Persian carpet on the floor had no distinct pattern.

'Sit, sit. Push the books to the corner of the sofa, but be careful. They are all opened to the precise page I want. What do you know about art?'

'The history of it? The names of artists?'

'That is my question.'

'I know something.'

'Can you draw? My father said you had studied art. Surely you can make a floor plan, can you not? I mean with the proper measurements – to scale – you can do that?' She nodded. 'Good. For the next few weeks I want you to make a floor plan of each place we visit and include the exact placement of the objects about which I speak. I am focusing on the placement of art. Not enough attention has ever been paid to it. Some things become astounding simply because of their placement. Your job will be to go with me each day I go out and to record everything I say. Then you will come back here and copy out what I have said and put down a detailed floor plan, exact. You will then research and write down everything else ever written about that same place, that same art. You will find those writings in the books in this room. Tomorrow we will go to Verona. There is a monastery there I must explore. I have already made arrangements. Why do you smile?' He had stood up and walked toward her.

'The man who brought me here told me you were under the evil eye.'

'Perhaps I am. Stand up.' His eyes were blank, opaque brown smears, and his face was expressionless. She stood up. She was taller than he was by inches. He reached over and quickly pulled away the sash of her kimono. Her arms instinctively wrapped the silk around her again.

'Take it off.' He stood very still, holding the red sash in his hand. 'I said take it off.'

She could not move. She swayed slightly, clasping the gown. Carl Borach moved swiftly, ripping it away from her and embracing her with his sinewy arms. His mouth pressed at hers, bending her lips back, pressing against her teeth. His fists were knotted against her back so that she could not move away, could hardly breathe, and then his body was pressing her down backward against the couch. Books fells around them. He forced himself against her, harder and harder. It was so sudden she had neither breath nor strength. For a moment she felt herself being battered, her head against the back of the sofa, then her head was on the floor, on the carpet. There seemed to be a quick stab of pain and a numbness. Was this to be a joining, this brief struggle on the floor?

Fury overtook her. He was still on top of her, climbing her, when she hit him, smashed at his face and his head and his body, pushing herself up on one arm so that he spilled off her onto the floor. She beat him without mercy, again and again and again. It did not matter to her that his eyes were swollen red puffs and his lips were black with blood or that he was gasping from pain and surprise. He was on his knees, bent over, his arms covering his head, his face against the wooden floor, and still she hit him.

She stopped only from exhaustion. His head still covered with his arms, he waited for more blows. When they ceased to come, he looked up at her.

'Don't you ever touch me again! Never! Never! If you do that again, I will kill you.' Her face and neck were wet from perspiration and her breathing was so labored her shoulders and chest ached from her effort. 'I am going to stay here, do you hear me! I am going to stay and I will do everything you ask me to do. I will be the best secretary you ever had. But you will never touch me like that!'

He looked so small below her. I could have killed him, she thought. I could have killed him.

The next morning when she came downstairs, Carl Borach was at his desk. When he became aware that she stood in the room with him, he got up quickly.

She gasped at the sight of him, but he held up both his hands, their forefingers extended, and beat out the rhythm of his words. 'No. You mustn't mention it. It will heal quickly. We must postpone the trip I had planned, but I'm sure we can leave by the end of the week. There is so much to do. Always so much to do.' He sat down again and looked at the papers in front of him.

'I have no clothes,' she said. 'I do not want to wear this kimono.' Her voice was very slight, a scratchy record sound.

'No clothes?' For a moment he looked puzzled. 'Oh, yes. Yes, of course. I forgot. Well, they are here. They came this morning. Signora!' he called, clapping his hands. A maid came quickly.

'Si?'

'The clothes that came this morning. Bring them to the signorina. Bring them to her room.' He looked at Delphi. 'Yes, of course. The clothes. She will bring them right up to you. I think you will find them comfortable.' Again he looked down at his papers, dismissing her.

She went back to her room. The maid brought in three dresses and some boxes. The clothes were exactly as he had described them, simple, tailored, the colors muted, the line soft. The boxes held underwear, stockings, and shoes, everything black. Delphi dressed quickly, combed her hair, and again went downstairs to his study.

'Everything fits perfectly.'

'What?' He looked up at her distractedly.

'The clothes . . .'

'Good.' Now he was appraising her thoughtfully. She felt awkward standing there. She was certain that the sooner she showed him how capable she was, the sooner he would stop looking at her as an object. What could have provoked his attack on her the day before? Was it an attempt to humiliate her? To own her? She shuddered at the thought of his touch.

'I should like to start my work, if you don't mind.'

'Yes. Of course. There is more than enough to do. You can begin there, with that pile of notes on the desk. It must all be transcribed, typewritten very neatly. You can work there at the far table. If you have any trouble deciphering my scrawl, I will help you. There is paper in the drawer below. We will stop at one o'clock for lunch.'

She soon found out his habits. The days were long ones. They started work at eight, stopped at one, then worked again from three until seven. After dinner, Delphi went to her room, exhausted. Carl Borach rarely slept at all, so that when she returned to the library after breakfast there was always new work. By the third or fourth day he had relaxed somewhat. He was still not the boyish, eager man she remembered from their first meeting, but neither was he the caustic poseur who had first greeted her. Perhaps he appreciated her quickness and intelligence. Her anxiety began to disappear along with the black and blue swellings on his face. He was healed within a week, and in a sense, as hard as it was for her to believe, it was as if the incident had never happened.

2

Delphi   July 14, 1923

I am getting used to it here. Can one get used to anything, I wonder? There has been no 'second attempt,' as it were, nor do I think there will be. He is the most peculiar man I have ever met, and he reinforces that impression daily. Today the town policeman came to the door to straighten out some minor misunderstanding involving Carl's gardener and a wagon he used, which, quite by accident, had never been paid for. Carl became frantic, unable even to listen to the policeman's words. I don't think he can talk to real people. It took me only a minute to clear up the matter. Carl is nothing like his father. He is so tense. Besides the work, my greatest challenge will be to make him laugh.

I am working so hard that my hand cramps constantly. He likes the way I work, I know that. I must learn to anticipate him, to become indispensable so that I can stay here. I am never going back to West Fourth Street.

Last weekend I was able to do some sketches. Not bad. The color here is magnificent. I must get some pastels.

*   *   *

The first time they left the Villa Santa Rosa, it was to visit the monastery in Verona. There, Delphi followed Borach for five hours, up and down stairs, into cold, musty cellars, onto balconies, into naves, sacristies, catacombs, one after the other. Her pencils wore down as she drew approximations of the room shapes, noting their dimensions, indicating where the objects he cited were placed. Her hand cramped and ached, but there was no time for complaint. Carl Borach never faltered, never once stopped moving and talking.

'I think you did well today.' He was sitting up straight in

the car, his legs crossed at the knees.

'Thank you,' she said.

'Was I too fast for you?' He looked at her, arching his eyebrow. 'Actually, I went slower than I usually do. You will catch on. Was there anything you didn't understand?'

'I don't think so.' She frowned. 'I did want to ask you about the painting in the cellar, the large oil of Christ at the tomb, you remember?'

'What about it?'

'You hardly stopped at it. Wasn't it important?'

'There is no need to write about that one. I am going to own it.' He paused. 'You needn't look so surprised, it's not illegal, you know. A church buys and sells just like an art dealer. This church, in any event.' He turned away from her and rolled down the window of the car. 'It is not so damp today as yesterday, do you think?' He had started the day before speaking to her about the weather. Aside from art, it was the only thing he mentioned.

'Yes,' she answered. 'It is pleasant today.'

He recrossed his legs, holding on to the strap, shifting his weight over toward the window. 'No one conceives of how demanding scholarship can be. They call me a dilettante! Can you imagine? As if I spent my time lunching and dabbling. I could build an empire with less effort.' He shook his head and sighed. 'God knows, there is no time for rest.'

*   *   *

August 4, 1923
Delphi,

It is six weeks now, and still I have heard nothing from you. I know you have arrived and are well only because Julius tells me so. You must write me. Forgive me, and let that be an end to it. I care too much for you to punish me so.

How do you find Carl Borach? Can you abide him? I always found him so effete. The gardeners at my grandfather's house, at Dosiaya, came from San Remo. You must go there and let me know if the roses are really a foot in diameter!

It continually surprises me that you are not here, although it may be for the best. This city and this country seem to have run amok. People have lost all sight of human values. As usual, money is king. We have given women the vote only to find that they do not use it and behave more and more like blithering idiots every day. My worst fears are confirmed.

I came across one of your drawings. It is a pencil sketch that you did of your father. It is a very good drawing of him, and the person who did it was no stranger. Do you see what I mean?

Write me,
Sonya

*   *   *

She had finished reading Sonya's letter and was about to prepare for bed when she heard a knock on the door, and Carl's voice beyond the door asked her to come down to the study. After dinner? she thought. It was a marked breach of form.

When she went in, he was sitting at his desk. He peered at her over his glasses. 'I have had a letter from your mother,' he said.

'You, too? From Sonya?'

'She is your mother, is she not? She writes to say she has not heard from you, and that if she does not hear from you within the new few weeks, she suggests that I ship you home! She says . . .' He fumbled through some papers on his desk, finally locating Sonya's letter, the white stationery with the gold borders, the same as the pile that lay unanswered on Delphi's golden bureau. 'Here,' he read, '"Tell her that what happened between us is forgotten, that recriminations are the province only of villains and fools, that anger cannot support truth, morality, or,"—the "or" is underlined - "beauty, and that she is my daughter and had best write me." Sonya had always had a penchant for melodrama. What can have happened that is so world-shaking?'

'You are right,' Delphi answered. 'It is only melodrama, not worth exploring.'

'I would write her, Delphi. Sonya is not one to let things alone.'

'I am not either,' she replied, looking him in the eye.

'I would just rather she didn't get my father involved. I have enough trouble, and I can only assume that it would be Sonya's next step.'

Delphi cleared her throat. She was staring at Borach, still looking into his eyes, which seemed larger now, the glasses under them accentuating their slight protrusion.

'What is it, Delphi?'

'I must stay here after this summer is up. I have no intention of going back to New York.' She watched him for a hint of his reaction. There was none.

'Yes?' he asked finally.

'I can make peace with Sonya only if I know I do not have to go back to her. I will make peace if you tell me I can stay. You know I am a good and capable worker.' His face was still expressionless and he said nothing, just staring at her. It occurred to her for the first time that he really might not let her stay. 'There is, after all, a certain afternoon that I remember, one that your father, I am sure, would not wish to know of.'

He stood up sharply and she froze.

'Are you trying to blackmail me? Sometimes, Miss Delphi Tolchin, you give your age away. I am not quite so easily manipulated as you would think, and I do not like being used or being thought of as a fool. You will answer Sonya's letter because if you do not, I will send you home now, instead of whenever it is that I decide in the future to send you home, do you understand that? Anything that you might tell my father would probably only reinforce his deepest convictions about me; that is to say, you may hurt him as much as you like, it doesn't matter to me. You will stay here only because of your ability to do what has to be done. At the moment you serve me perfectly, and you may stay until you stop serving me, but you must write to Sonya.' He looked at her angrily for a moment and then slowly sat down. 'Well?'

What a fool she was; she had angered him. 'I will write to her.'

'Good.'

'There is one other thing,' she said.

'Yes?'

'I would like you to call me Delphi Stern. It is the name on my passport. It is the name I had when I entered America, and it is the name I choose to use now.'

'Ah, the final break with parental authority. The final blow. Another name, eh? I will call you Delphi Stern. I will call you anything you like. Stern,' he repeated, making a face. 'Are you sure?'

'Why not?'

'It is so German,' he answered, smiling.

* * *

August 23, 1923
Dear Sonya,

I am sorry for not answering you sooner, but there has been so much to do. Carl works at such a furious pace I have everything I can do just to keep up with him. I know you do not appreciate his work, but I think you would appreciate his dedication. I believe you would admire any man who gives up an easy life to pursue difficult goals. Certainly I am learning a great deal more from Carl Borach than I ever did at college.

How is the weather? It rains here very little. It is good that I like the heat, for it certainly is hot every single day. The sun even is brighter.

I am sorry I cannot write more now. I must work.

Delphi Stern

Delphi   September 2, 1923
We have cut short our trip to Asolo for the study of the Palladian Villas. The longer we stayed there, the more agitated Carl bécame; the intensity of the experience was obviously too much for him. By the end of the first week he was in such a state of tension that I was almost frightened for him. He could barely sit still; he ran about, flapped his arms at his sides, and, for the first time, lost his concentration. Evidently he has these fits from time to time, periods when beauty overwhelms him and he rushes home to his room to stay there like a monk in his cell,

fasting. The housekeeper told me not to worry, that in three or four days it will be as if nothing had happened.

How amazing that the intensity of beauty should affect him so. Yet he is right. There are men like Palladio who come into the world and change it so irrevocably because of their minds, their eyes. Their language is greater than the written word, for it bridges generations, nations, centuries. Oh, I wish I could see like that.

Carl is so oversensitive. At one point he was showing me a room that he said enveloped him, like a womb, a core, and his excitement was so great because he had never seen it that way before, and he kept going round and round in the core until he made himself dizzy, but with joy, with laughter. Great art does not make me as happy as it does him, because I am always jealous that I did not do it.

September 28, 1923
Dear Delphi,

As you supposed, I am not at all pleased with your decision to remain in Siena, but I shall respect your request not to try to convince you otherwise.

Your father has begun to speak of our moving from this house, but I refuse. We must all remember our beginnings. I have suggested to him that he find himself a flat at a fancy address and use it without me. Aside from Julius, the people we see nowadays are the worst sort, full of ostentation with a smattering of knowledge and enormous social and intellectual pretensions. *Haute bourgeoisie!* I rarely go out with him. The two of us have very little in common besides our history. We shall see how long that can keep us together.

Please take care of yourself, and please continue to write, even if, as has been the case up to this point, it is only to recount dispassionately the events of your life.

Also, do you think you might send a letter to your father?

Sonya

Delphi February 8, 1924

It is damp and cold today again. Carl is still coughing. It is a week today he has been in bed. I am so alone.

341

Strangely enough, I think of Sonya. This morning I remembered vividly a time we walked all the way to the zoo and she bought me ice cream, and then we went and looked at the mansions of Fifth Avenue. How beautiful she was; no wonder he loved her so.

Pain is more difficult to remember than pleasure.

I have done some excellent sketches this week, notes for many paintings. I have enough ideas to keep me busy the rest of my life.

April 3, 1924

Carl has outdone himself today. He is absolutely brilliant. Venice has brought out the best (and worst!) in him. We lunched with a wealthy Jewish lady from Boston who collects modern art and wears her hair cropped like a man's and smokes cigars. Her palazzo on the Grand Canal is more beautiful than many of the finest homes on Fifth Avenue and filled with such treasures! Picasso everywhere, Cézanne, Matisse, even the Dadaists. And the most wonderful sculpture of a bird by a man named Brancusi. Another artist - Modigliani - draws people who look like me. Of course, I admired him. I had never seen his work before. Carl stuck his nose up at all of it and somehow convinced the poor lady that it is all a fad and, as all fads do, it will pass. He so intimidated her that she has agreed to redo her sitting rooms and bedroom with old masters that Carl will provide! I think Julius Borach would happily support Carl if he wanted it, but he insists on making his own money, providing his expertise for a fee. I don't understand why he does it since he cannot stand the people who buy from him. They are the sorts of people who use art to establish a social position. He claims he is above commerce. He is not.

There was a handsome American boy there, her nephew, and he would have paid me a great deal of attention were it not for Carl's behavior, which, although not rude, was undoubtedly possessive. I wonder if people think anything about us. He is so strange; how could they think I might be interested in him physically? Yet I notice them looking at us most peculiarly. I still shake when I think of that first day in Siena.

Tonight we are going to the opera with all the Americans. We met ten at lunch here. There is to be a gala afterward, and Carl has gotten me a dress to wear. It is chiffon, very Grecian. I like it very much. I told him I did not expect him to take me, but he says he must because I protect him. I think he likes to show me off, for he takes care of how I look and with such devotion. I don't mind. What would happen if I flirted with the American boy? Sonya would do that. I am very shy with all of these wealthy, artificial people. They are just the sorts that came to Sonya's parties. I have no friends at all, and I thank God I have no need for them.

July 27, 1924
Dear Sonya,

After spending so many months here in Siena finishing his book, Carl has decided to take his vacation this September in the south, at Paestum. Of course, it will be no vacation at all, but an investigation of the classical antiquities there. He says the south is very different, very lush, more as you must have imagined Italy.

In answer to your questions, I draw in my room only. I have not done any painting since I arrived. Julius was very clear that Carl would not stand for it, and I am sure he was right. I am frustrated, but I regard this as an apprenticeship. I am willing to wait. The rewards of Carl's mind are well worth it.

Yes, we see other people. Carl has a vast network of friends, mostly admirers. Wherever we go, we are entertained most royally, but the people are the sorts that you have always detested, very wealthy, but with no other outstanding characteristics. They are very nice to me, but I cannot be with them without seeing them through your eyes.

Do you think you might send me some money? Only a bit? I hate to ask, but I have some small personal needs and I cannot ask Carl for extra money. I have been sending my salary back to Julius to repay him, and I have used my money for personal needs. It has been, after all, over a year. One day I will repay you, I promise.

Delphi

343

September 11, 1924
Delphi,

Your father is heartbroken that you still won't write to him. Stop it now and do as he asks. Here is his new address: 2 East 54th Street, New York City. It is a hotel where he has taken a suite of rooms. Among his other pursuits, the Russian government has asked him to arrange purchases of food and machinery for them. I tell him he is a capitalist for the Communists now and we will have to rewrite all our manifestoes. He answers that he has done more for Russia as a capitalist than he ever did running about in a peasant's tunic with a gun in his boot. I am wearing silks in spite of myself. I am living too grandly. It makes no sense whatsoever.

It is hard to believe you have been away for such a long time. Where does the time go, I wonder?

I am exhausted. Everything is breaking down. This week it is the plumbing, last week it was the roof. Next week I suppose it will be me. It is so nasty this spring, teasing us with its coming and then turning into awful windy, wet days.

I have made a new friend, a charming, bright woman named Martha Wellons. Surprisingly enough, I met her at one of your father's dinners. She is much like I am. Her husband is a wealthy stockbroker and, like your father, spends a great deal of his time at pursuits that do not interest her. Today we had a delightful lunch. I am grateful to have met her. It is difficult to make new friends as one gets older, yet that is when one needs them. Martha lost a son in the war and is dedicated to world peace. I quite agree with her that there must be an end to war. We are starting a group to discuss the possibilities of world peace.

How little most people expect from life. The women in this country have less freedom today than my peers did in Russia twenty years ago, yet they think themselves quite free. Actually, it is a country of men only. Women are serfs. And it is beginning to sound as if you yourself are content in that role.

You must make peace with Tolchin. He is your father, Delphi. You must forgive him for his anger that night. He does not understand why you return his letters unopened.

Are you eating well? The last photograph you sent made you appear tubercular.

I am pleased you find some significance in your pursuits. Your enthusiasm, however, still does not persuade me they are valuable in any way. I am not Julius Borach. I will not finance anything I cannot believe in and I will make no exception for you.

Perhaps you might ask your father for money.

Sonya

*   *   *

It was on Delphi's own initiative that she undertook the exploration and attribution of the frescoes in the Campo Santo at Pisa. Now Borach was reading her work, glancing up at her from time to time as she sat across from him in his study, watching the thin cat drink some of the milk she had left in a saucer outside on the sill.

'Quite frankly, this is rot.' He put down the papers and sighed. 'Traini was second rate, a copyist. He wasn't the author of such magnificence.'

'Suit yourself. I went and I saw the work of a master, and that master, as far as I'm concerned, was Traini. If you disagree—'

Borach's face was blotched with sudden rage, splashes of white across his cheeks, red ridges at the sides of his nose. 'Defend yourself, then! If you think he is so brilliant and such a master, defend your perceptions!'

'All I have to say I have said in that paper.'

'It is dry. It cracks in my mind!'

'I'm not a writer, Carl. My words won't make my vision clearer to me. You have the metaphors and the music.'

'You know nothing!' He tore the papers in half and threw them onto the floor. Delphi watched the blue-black cat sip the milk, ignoring Borach's fury. He picked up a brass dish and threw it at the window. The glass breaking was an explosion, and Delphi held her ears.

'Already you put yourself into my category. Already you

have convinced yourself you know what I know. You know nothing! You are better suited to watching cats!' He stood up, frenzied. 'I am going for a walk to clear my head of such pretension. I expect you will find time to do your work on the dictations I gave you at Assisi!'

She had touched a nerve, had ventured an opinion that was good enough to threaten him. The closer she came to any original perception, the more furious he became. It was so senseless that a man who could be both elegant and brilliant carried on like a child. That Carl Borach was no more than a churlish, frightened boy was such a waste, such a disappointment.

Delphi climbed the table by the windows so she could see if the cat was injured. The glass had exploded out, and it glinted at her from the leaves of the vines and the yew bushes. She saw the cat lying on the stone path that led into the kitchen garden, and she ran out of the house to it and kneeled down to lift the creature carefully. Its heart was beating uncontrollably as if it might push itself out through the fur, rip itself loose, but the cat was unmoving. Delphi searched its body to find cuts, but there were none. Perhaps it was only stunned. She held it against her, hearing the motor of its purr begin and feeling its feet start to pad against her breast in a mime of nursing. She felt triumphant that Borach had not hurt it. It was time to get away from Carl Borach, time to paint. She had to get money.

3

The second week of March, Delphi accompanied Borach to Florence. 'This time I am going to buy,' he said to her, a glint of excitement in his eyes. 'A dealer says he has a Giorgione. I have dreamed of owning one.' His eyes hardened. 'But it won't be a Giorgione in all likelihood. It seldom is.'

'He made very few.'

'No one knows how many. It amounts to the same thing; they've either disappeared or been bought. There has been too much money in the art market for too long. This one, at least, has an impeccable provenance. It means little, but it is at least a clue. I shall be bringing a good friend of mine to see the painting. Luis Marra. His eye is certainly as good as mine. You've heard me speak of him, have you not?'

'You said we were to stay with him in Florence.'

'Actually, he lives a bit above Florence, out of the city.'

'I look forward to meeting him.'

'Yes. He is quite a fellow. Quite a knowledgeable fellow.'

Finally the car passed through a large rusted iron gate onto a dirt road. The day was mild for March. Chickens and geese roamed at will, pecking at the earth. Ahead of them was a simple farmhouse just on the crest of a sloping hill that, as they drove closer, suddenly gave way to a sharp incline and then to a flat, lovely valley. Around the house were groups of men and women working with rolls of canvas and pieces of wood or sketching the landscape.

'It's a school!' Delphi said, delighted, opening the window to put her head out.

'It is supposedly one of the finest art schools in the world,' Borach said. 'I don't believe one learns to be an artist at a school, and I don't believe Marra thinks so either. Still, there are always too many students here from everywhere on the globe. It seems to me they stay for years, waiting on the master like so many supplicants. Their feeling for him is nearly religious.'

As the car slowed and then stopped, a large man, surrounded by what seemed an army of dogs, walked toward them. Rigid, the dogs stood only two or three feet from the door of the car, their teeth bared. Delphi reached for the handle on her side, but Borach pulled her back. 'It would be a bad idea to get out until he comes forward. Just wait until he gets here. Bloody dreadful curs.'

The man walked steadily toward the car, and just before he approached, the dogs backed away. He brushed his long, dark hair away from his face and stared at them both with his agate eyes. It was a warrior's face, Delphi thought, pitted, irregular, and strong.

'So, Borach. Come. Lunch is ready. You are late.' He opened the door on Delphi's side and extended his hand to her. He pulled her forward with just enough force, his strong fingers lightly around hers. 'I am Luis Marra, and you are welcome.' He looked her over with unhurried appreciation. 'You are most beautiful, signorina.' She did not blush at his compliment, yet she took her hand from his quickly.

Borach climbed down from the car, yawned, made a small stretch with his hands in front of him. 'I must make amenities first, Luis. Some of us perform bodily functions, you know.' Borach's chauffeur, a cross-eyed, heavy Umbrian, handed him his traveling case and his jacket. 'I will be a little while yet. I should like to change my clothing.'

'Someday, Borach, you will wash the skin off your hands. You must have slept in shit when you were young.' Marra laughed as Borach's face tightened with annoyance, and he turned away from them to walk toward the house.

Marra smiled at Delphi. It was a smile at once playful and mischievous. His eyes made no attempt to hide his interest in her face and her body. She could not excuse his lack of manners and yet he did not offend her at all. Perhaps it was because he was not the least surreptitious. His was not a hot little glance; he was not a rooster crowing and beating his wings. He looked at her the way Carl Borach looked at paintings. 'Do you wish to change also, signorina? The food will wait for you as well.'

'My name' – she held out her hand to him – 'is Delphi Stern, and I am just hungry.'

He took her hand and bowed over it, his mane of hair covering his face for a second before he lifted his head up to smile at her once again.

'Well, Delphi, since we must wait for Borach, we can enjoy the springtime a moment. I think poor Borach never notices anything not on canvas or hewn into marble. Life eludes him. You speak very good Italian. Have you worked for Borach long?' His voice had a deep resonance that made it easily heard above all the other sounds around them. He continued to ask her questions as he ambled toward a group of his students. Although they all went on working without so much as a glance in his direction, Delphi could feel their apprehension and then, just as certainly, she felt their dismay as he passed them and their open sketch pads without comment. 'You were saying?' he looked at Delphi again, leading her toward the house.

'I've worked for him almost a year now.'

'Ah.' He moved with extraordinary grace for such a large man, she thought, watching him walk up the stone stairs ahead of her to the open door. As she approached, he suddenly turned and went back down the steps to the students. She watched them each look at him with rapt attention for the moment it took him to speak to them. 'You must excuse me,' he said, running back up the stairs to rejoin her. He smiled. 'It occurred to me that they were wasting their time. They were not quite ready for the assignment I gave them. So now, you see, I am too often rude.' He showed her into a sparsely furnished waiting room in the main building. 'Please sit,' he said, motioning her to a chair. She wondered how old he was. 'Would you care for an apéritif?' She shook her head. 'I like Americans. They make enthusiastic students. At times a bit sloppy, you know, effusive, running over themselves. But still, I like them. Are you rich?' Delphi shook her head. 'Not rich? But all Borach's secretaries have been rich. He tells me he doesn't pay them because he is giving them a free and great education.' He was staring at her.

'I lack for nothing.'

'Nothing?' His eyes made her uncomfortable.

'Only . . .' she looked down, avoiding him. 'Well, I should like to be an artist.'

'You will not learn to be an artist from Borach.' Marra laughed and put his hands behind his neck. 'Do you have talent?'

'It doesn't matter if I have talent. I will paint anyway.'

'You must have been a stubborn child,' he said, nodding at her. 'A little hellcat, yes?'

'No. I was very well mannered. Docile, even.'

'Then you must have been waiting.' Why had the tone in his voice changed so? Why was he still staring at her that way?

'I was waiting,' she answered.

Borach came into the room. He had changed his clothes, and Delphi could smell the faint odor of soap, even powder. 'What were you waiting for, Delphi?' he asked her.

'She was waiting for lunch,' Marra answered, getting up lazily, grinning at Borach. 'Now that your highness is ready to dine, we shall do so immediately. You are so elegant, my friend. This new jacket is from London?'

'My tailor is in London.'

'You will eat well in your splendid jacket. Come.' His hand fell across Borach's shoulder, and Delphi saw Carl wince at his touch. Taking a step forward, Marra's other arm scooped Delphi up so that the two of them flanked him as he walked into the dining room.

When they had finished dinner, Borach, obviously satisfied pushed himself slightly back from the table, touching his stomach contentedly. 'You live better than kings, Luis.'

'I take advantage of all of my students,' Marra answered, looking at the men and women who scurried like mice everywhere now, clearing the table, bringing the coffee.

'I have an appointment at five this afternoon with Conviglio, Luis. I trust you will come.'

'Of course.'

'In the meantime, Delphi and I have work at the Uffizi.'

'Go. Your driver is fed and watered. I will meet you at five.'

* * *

350

Near the Conviglio Gallery later that afternoon, Borach recognized Luis Marra instantly. Delphi did not. His hair, carefully combed back behind his ears, seemed finer, even lighter in color. His face was somehow more oval, its features narrowed and slighter. The elegant man in the dark blue pin-stripe suit who carried a cane with a gold and ivory handle in a gloved hand bore absolutely no resemblance to the man who had just dined with her at lunch.

'*Ciao, bellezza,*' he said, delighted at her surprise.

'Hurry, we are late.' Borach walked quickly across the street into the small gallery as Luis Marra followed.

'Signores.' A slight man from the corner of the room rushed forward to greet Carl and Luis. 'Welcome! We have not had the honor for months.'

'Please, the Giorgione.' Borach's voice became impatient. The man nodded and walked to the back. Two boys appeared at the door carrying a large canvas covered with dark cloth and, with effort, placed it on an easel in front of the men. The dealer pulled the cloth as if undressing a beautiful woman and then closed his eyes at the sight of the painting.

Nothing was said. Delphi watched Borach, then Marra. 'It is exquisite, Borach.'

'Truly magnificent?' Borach whispered.

'*Oui, c'est un objet du maître.*' Marra circled the painting slowly. '*Sans doute, un exemple par excellence.*'

'*Tu es sûr, mon ami?*'

'*Bien sûr.*' Marra touched the frame of the painting. The dealer held his breath.

'How much?' Borach had not stepped forward at all but had stayed where he was, four feet from the front door.

'Two hundred thousand pounds, Signore Borach.'

'I will have it.'

'Certainly. Would you care to remain for a while? I will be glad—'

'No. I will take it with me.'

The dealer's mouth fell open. 'Now?'

'Now.'

351

'But I—'

'You will have my check in the morning.'

'Sì, signore.'

Conviglio clapped and the two boys appeared. They placed the cloth reverentially around the painting. 'How shall I pack it?'

'For a journey, of course. I live, as you know, in Siena.' Conviglio and the boys left the room carrying the painting. Borach turned to Marra. 'How long will you need it, Luis?'

'A month or two should be enough.'

'Make certain that when it is returned, it is the same Giorgione I lent you.'

'How you flatter me, Borach. I am good but not that good.'

'You underestimate yourself at times. Happily, I seldom do. Don't make too many Giorgiones, eh, Luis? One will do.'

'I am wondering if I will outlive Matisse. I am enjoying his greatness. I would like to try his eye, too.'

'Don't be a fool.'

'Borach, I am a fool. To be counseled against it is a waste of your time and mine. But I am well aware that copying the work of living artists is suicide. I will stay with the dead.'

Marra looked at Delphi and paused in his speech. 'I see. I see.' He looked disapprovingly at Borach and then back at Delphi. 'I can tell from the expression on your face he has not told you of our little arrangement.'

'This is neither the time nor the place, Luis,' Borach snapped, walking away from them both and seating himself primly on a chair against the far wall.

'Then may I suggest you make a place and time, Borach. Miss Stern is upset by our conversation.' Marra put on his hat, touched his gloves to the brim, and bowed to Delphi. 'So, until this evening.' He opened the door and closed it gently behind him.

The two of them waited in silence until the painting was crated and put into the trunk of the car. Once inside the car, Borach turned wearily to Delphi and sighed loudly. 'Well, you might as well know it all. To put it as simply as possible, Marra is a forger and I sell his work. I have excellent contacts and Marra is a genius. Don't look so startled, Delphi, this sort of thing has been going on for centuries. Today, I bought a Giorgione. I lend it to Marra, he makes another Giorgione. The one he makes will not be remotely like the one I just purchased, of course, but it will be magnificent. When he has finished, and made the painting appear to have sufficient age, when I have established an impeccable provenance, I will sell Marra's forgery to a collector, or better still, to a curator. That way the original Giorgione will cost me nothing.' He wiped his mouth with a clean handkerchief and settled back in his seat. 'Don't look so appalled, my dear.'

'I cannot think why you would do such a thing! You have no need for money.'

'I do it because it gives me the greatest of pleasure when I watch some vulgarian or some so-called expert swoon over his exquisite fake. I loathe the fact that people with no education at all think they are entitled to advance their position in the art world or in society with another's greatness.'

'What you do is immoral, despicable!'

'I find it more despicable to advance merely because of money. I stop no one from knowing the difference between the real thing and a replica. I struggled long enough to attain that knowledge, God knows. I am fully armed and my cause is just. Since no one has my knowledge, why should they have what I have?' He sniffed a bit, touched the handkerchief once again to his lips, and dabbed at his mouth. 'I told you commerce did not interest me, Delphi. I told you that art was my religion. If anything, what I do is vengeance in my God's name against those who are not worthy of the divinity of art.'

'And Luis Marra, why does he do it?'

'He needs money to run his damn fool school.'

'You said he was a genius. I have never heard you call any living man a genius before. If he is so gifted, why doesn't he do his own work and sell that?'

'I haven't the least idea.'

'But if a man can fool the world with a Giorgione, surely he is a genius.'

'He can fool the world with a Lippi, a Giotto, a Memling. He even managed to fool me for years.'

'Then why?'

Borach inclined his head to his left and squinted at her. 'You seem quite interested in Luis Marra. Does he attract you?'

'I am only interested in why he does what he does.'

'I hope so, Delphi, because I will not be made a fool.' Carl Borach's soft eyes were vacant. 'No one will make a fool of me.'

'I think you are behaving most queerly,' she said, turning away from him.

'Perhaps,' he murmured. 'Perhaps you are right. At any rate, I think we shall return to Siena immediately after leaving the painting for Marra. Elation exhausts me.' Borach yawned and put his head back on the tufted leather seat. The evening air was heavy with the fragrance of cypress. 'Poor Delphi. However do you put up with me?'

*   *   *

Delphi   May 18, 1925

Carl Borach and Luis Marra sell forgeries as if they were grocers selling cherries, yet it is such a crime. I am frightened that it has prompted me to think that if I can make one simple good likeness of an even minor artist from the quattrocento, perhaps I could sell it and have money for myself. There is a dealer named Nervi that Marra and Borach do business with. I have found his correspondence to Carl. He has a gallery in Rome. I could go to him. I am afraid to try because I am certain I could do it easily and well.

June 14, 1925

I have finished them. The paper that I stole from the cellar at the Pitti palace has worked perfectly. I fear it is not difficult to be a thief. At least it is not difficult if one is desperate. Desperation has quite blinded any moral judgment, and it is almost as if Carl were my accomplice. He told me just this afternoon that we must be in Rome next week. I must prepare what I will say to Nervi. I think I will take the Zuccaro, not the Traini. The Zuccaro is truer, I think, as good as the one Carl has.

*   *   *

In Rome after nearly four hours in the Vatican Museum, Delphi pretended fatigue and told Borach she would meet him at the hotel. Hours in the museum would be moments to him, and she would have more than enough time to see Nervi. In spite of the heat, she walked quickly to the address she had copied from Borach's book. It was an elegant shop. A Bassanio oil hung in its window against a background of deep blue velvet drapery. The boy inside told her that Signore Nervi had not yet returned from lunch and showed her to a comfortable armchair in the back of the gallery. She sat in the chair, crossed her legs, and balanced her drawing in its folder on her knee. She was surprised to find that she was not in the least nervous. It was nearly twenty minutes before Nervi arrived, and when he did, Luis Marra was with him.

'Delphi! What an unexpected delight to find you!' Marra came toward her quickly, his hands extended, but then he stopped before he reached her and frowned, his large brows knotted. 'But how is it that I find you here?'

'I came to see Signore Nervi.' She met his displeasure with calmness.

'Borach sent you?' Marra looked at her intently now, waiting for her answer. She made none. He inclined his head toward the man who now was beside him. 'You didn't make her a proposition, did you, Nervi?' The man coughed violently into his fist. 'Come, Angelo, don't choke on the taste of your little crimes or you'll end up gagging to death.'

'I assure you I have never seen the young woman before in my life, Luis.'

'Ah.' Marra looked back at Delphi, who now held the folder against her breast. 'Tell me what is the matter, Delphi?'

'Nothing. Nothing at all.' She stared at him without expression.

'You stand in a thief's house waiting to do business and

355

tell me nothing is the matter?' He walked to her, lifted her up from the chair by her elbows, and looked at her again, shaking his head. 'Come, you'll talk to me. Perhaps I can help. Perhaps not. We shall speak to one another.'

'Luis, you will deliver on the sixteenth of next month?' Nervi stepped forward.

'Of course. In fifteen years, have I ever been late?'

'No, but—'

'Why should I be late now, Angelo? You think because I have my hand on a beautiful woman it will interfere with my promise?' Marra laughed at him, pushing Delphi gently ahead of him as he walked to the door.

'*Scusi*, Luis.' Nervi rushed to the door and held it open for the two of them. '*Arrivederci*.'

Marra took Delphi to a garden restaurant just at the next turning and hastily ordered wine for them both. Delphi looked at the cupids clinging to the wall, their blind eyes looking at the garlands of stone flowers running around them.

Marra nodded at the folder in her arms. 'Show me what you had for Nervi.' She passed the folder to him without a word and he quickly opened it, looked at the drawing, and closed the folder, passing it back to her. 'I thought for a moment you might have taken something from Borach.'

'Of course not.'

'Then you did that?' She nodded briefly, staring down at the folder. 'Why Zuccaro? He is an odd choice.'

'I thought he was little known enough for my attempt . . . I did not want much money.'

'If you commit a crime, you are desperate. If you are desperate, it should never be for merely a bit of money.' He tapped the table with the fingers of his left hand. 'Have you any idea what Nervi would have done? He would have given you over to the authorities immediately.'

'But why? You and Borach—'

'I have done business with Nervi for years and he makes a great deal of money from it. However, forgers he does not know he happily sends to the authorities, as all the dealers do. They must keep the police at bay. You would serve to perfume his air for a moment or two, nothing more.' Marra clapped his hand for the waiter. 'The wine,' he commanded. The waiter brought the glasses and the carafe and immediately put them down in the center of the table.

'The Zuccaro . . . was it very poor?'

Marra laughed and smacked the table. 'How like an artist! Even when she is confronted with a crime, she cares only for a compliment!' Delphi blushed furiously and looked into her lap. 'Your Zuccaro was not poor. It was not grand either. It was, shall we say, a talented attempt.'

'I must leave Carl Borach.' Marra nodded at her and poured himself a glass of wine. 'It doesn't surprise you?'

'Why should it? You told me you wanted to be an artist. Learning what is great art and making files about it doesn't teach you. Having a little money won't teach you either.'

'Could I learn from you? Would you teach me?' She looked at him as directly as she could. His eyes were always so unsettling.

'Why not?' He sipped his wine.

'I do not know if I am talented.'

'So we shall see.'

'Thank God!' she said. 'Thank God!'

When Delphi returned to the Excelsior, Borach was waiting for her in the lobby. 'You were so ill you crawled here? I have been waiting for an hour!' His arms were folded tightly across his chest.

'I need to talk to you.'

'I see no need to talk. An explanation of where you have been for over two hours will suffice.'

'Something has happened, you see. A coincidence . . .'

'What could have happened? You know no one in Rome. How could there have been a coincidence?' He glared at her.

'Carl, I ran into Luis Marra.'

'I see.' He turned abruptly and walked away from her toward the elevator.

'Carl!' she called, running after him. 'Please, you must listen. I tell you it was a coincidence. I hadn't planned to . . .' She touched his upper arm, but he ripped himself away from her.

'Luis Marra is what has happened, is it not? And you will try to make me believe that was a coincidence. Spare me, Delphi.' He stepped into the elevator, and she followed him. When the door opened at their floor, Carl walked quickly to their suite. She chased after him. What could she tell him if he did not believe the truth?

Once inside the room, he turned to her again and his eyes were huge with anger. 'I have devoted my life to you for a year. How dare you do this!'

'I have not done anything. Nothing!'

'Get out. Take what you have here and get out!' He began to pick up her things and fling them at her. 'If you are in so much of a hurry to lie to me, and to think I am so ridiculous as to believe in Marra and chance, then you must think me of less intelligence than a bug.' Her sweater, notebooks, shawl, and hat landed at her feet. 'You women are all alike, thieves, every last one of you! You take away years of a man's life!'

'How can you say that! I have treasured every hour of the last year. It is only that my life must proceed, don't you see that? It must—'

'You have a lover. Run to him! Get out, thief, and run to Marra!'

'He is not my lover!'

'Either he is your lover or you expect him to teach you to be an artist. And we both know that couldn't be the reason. That couldn't be the basis of your meeting, could it?' Seeing her stunned, he began to smile. 'But you could never be an artist, dear Delphi. It is much too late for that. Oh, surely you must know . . . or is it possible you don't? Look at you! Oh, it is too silly, too impossible!' He began to laugh at her. 'A year with me looking at the greatest art known to man and you imagine yourself capable of . . .' He was sputtering with laughter. 'Oh, how deluded you must be, how utterly deluded! Did Marra convince you he could teach you to be an artist?' He shook with laughter.

'Why are you laughing? Why?'

'Why? Because it is the funniest thing I have ever heard!'

4

Delphi   July 21, 1925

It is fine for me at Casamarra. I have just changed my room and am now on the second floor of the farmhouse. This room is lighter, bigger, even the bed is more comfortable. There is a pretty flowered wallpaper that is beginning to peel in one corner near the headboard. The window faces south, and I have a view of the woods and the valley below.

There are eight others living in the house. They are nice enough, but it is too crowded. I am reminded of my childhood when there was an endless wait for the bathroom and Sonya screamed constantly about her lack of privacy.

I might not actually have left Carl, were it not for the laughter. It was his laughter, his utter disdain for my hopes, for me, that forced me to leave. Ugly, brutal, filthy laughter! It denied me as surely as Tolchin's anger had that night on West Fourth Street. I have been propelled forward by rage and laughter. What will force me on now?

How good it felt to send off a letter to Sonya and tell her I am at last doing what I came to Italy to do, work at my craft. I am, after all, her daughter.

*   *   *

For the first months with Marra, Delphi worked with the others in the building called the factory, fitting stretchers with linen, aging canvases, shaping canvases, making frames, repairing brushes, making paint. Marra would give impromptu lectures there, explaining the need for them to know all their tools, insisting that they learn their alphabet, demanding perfection, prodding them to work harder, learn more quickly, absorb more. Restless as a nomad, he would prowl around the room, his movements as unpredictable as his words. Sometimes he would suddenly ask a question: 'What does an artist paint?'

The answers from his students came in relays or in chorus.

'His subject.'

'His feelings about his subject.'

'Shapes.'

'Form.'

'No!' Marra would yell. 'He paints masses of colored light. All artists paint colored light. We do not paint dogs or people or trees but light in color, which appears to be dogs or people or hills or stars. What are our materials? We are not God! Our materials are paint and brushes and canvas. That is why you are here in this factory and why you will remain here until you are as familiar and comfortable with all of this as I am. Then you can pretend to be God. Then you can try.'

After three months, Delphi was allowed to draw. She was permitted pencil, pen, and charcoal. The months of waiting were worthwhile. Her work exploded onto the paper. She could not keep herself from drawing.

No matter what she showed Marra, he was never satisfied. He refused to let her paint.

'It's not fair, I tell you. I have been here six months and he won't let me do a watercolor.' She and Joseph Nordheim were out in the field doing studies of the olive grove. 'I'm so sick of these black and white trees I could throw up!'

Nordheim smiled at her. Blond and confident, he was the oldest of all of them, had been with Marra the longest. 'Delphi, relax, it's his way. I was here at least a year before he let me do pastels.'

'Pastels? I had forgotten that. Will I never get to paint? What an arrogance, what an arrogance! Well, I will whisk through pastels and astound him with my watercolors.'

'Talk about arrogance.' Joseph laughed.

'What do I care about his approval? What do I care?'

'Unfortunately, we all care, Delphi.'

'There was life before Luis Marra, and there will be life after him.'

'Perhaps,' Nordheim answered. 'But there will be very

little life if you don't get back to those drawings.'

Damn him, she thought, damn them all.

*　　*　　*

Delphi   March 1, 1926
The longer I am here, the more frustrating it becomes.
More, more, Marra says! I have done that bloody olive
grove at least two hundred times, and each time he wants
it again. I am sick of it! I could sell the pen and ink I did
yesterday in any gallery, and he says it is not good enough.
Work, work, work, it is as bad as West Fourth Street, only
now it is Marra instead of Sonya. Marra, the master,
striding about with those ridiculous dogs at his heels.

*　　*　　*

It had rained unexpectedly, and their plan, to sit out in the
piazza and pass the evening watching the world go by, had
been ruined. Instead they were squeezed into the restaurant, a long, narrow space only twice the size of a hallway,
where they were forced to scream over the clatter of the
kitchen and the jabbering of the men of the town.

'One day, just one day, I would like to see these men
around here with a woman,' Barbara announced.

'Oh, I have seen them with a woman, Barbara, just
never with a wife.' Emil thought that was very funny.

'Please,' Delphi said, 'no more about men and women. I
would rather talk about Brueghel than men and women.'

'Oh, my God!' moaned Emil. 'No, no. Please not
Brueghel. I need more wine just hearing the sound of his
name. Centa, Centa.' He called to the waiter, motioning
for more wine. 'Brueghel or Marra, which one torments
more?'

'Marra has a gun.' It was Leda who spoke. They all
turned to look at her. 'He does. I have seen it.'

'Does he keep it in his bed, pretending it is his member?'
Nordheim asked innocently. They all laughed.

'You are impossible, Joseph.'

Joseph turned to Delphi. 'Do you think so?'

'What? That Marra has a gun in his bed, or that you are
awful? Both, I think both.' Again they laughed. The

waiter came and set a carafe of red wine on their table.

Delphi leaned over and whispered to them all conspiratorially, 'Why is it that all Italian waiters are so short?'

'Why?' Nordheim asked.

'I don't know.'

'Oh, I thought you had an answer. I thought it was a riddle.' More laughter.

'It is.' Still more.

'Where is Estella?' someone asked. 'I thought she was coming with us.'

'She was too mortified. Weren't you there when Marra tore her to pieces this afternoon?'

'She should know better than to take it personally. Just like a woman. He is only angry at our stupidity.'

'He doesn't understand women.'

'What is there to understand?'

'Oh, shut up, Emil.'

'How old do you think he is, really?'

'Forty.'

'Please, at least fifty.'

'Will he ever marry?'

'Why, Edith? Are you interested?' Nordheim blew smoke at her and rolled his eyes suggestively.

'What does he do in that house all alone?'

'Wouldn't you like to know!' Emil laughed, choking on his wine. 'Ask Leda.'

'Leda?' Delphi said, turning to look at her, as they all did.

'He called her down there. He said it was to paint her. What do you say, Leda?'

'I say you are all idiots. I sat for him, that's all.'

'There is always a favorite,' Barbara whined. 'Only it's never me.'

'Sat with him or on him?' Nordheim giggled. His laugh was loud, silly, like a child's. 'I say he can't get it up.'

'Tell us, Leda.' Emil's voice had risen.

'She won't say a word.'

'Years ago there was a woman, before I came.' Nordheim spoke with great assurance. 'She left because he wouldn't marry her. That was what Vivian told me. She probably left because he couldn't get it up.'

'Joseph, you're drinking too much.'

'Do you suppose he carries on the same in bed?' Nordheim got up from the table, leaned over Delphi, and in a loud voice mimicked Marra: 'Notice these tiny brushstrokes on your breasts. Notice the gossamer lights on your derrière.' With the swoop of his arm he gestured at Delphi and knocked right into a waiter. Coffee cups splattered to the floor.

'Joseph, stop it, everyone is looking at us.' Delphi's cheeks were red with embarrassment, but she was laughing. Her head was light with wine.

* * *

Delphi June 23, 1926

It is all we talk about and all we think about. We live and breathe Luis Marra. Well, I say enough. I am sick of him. Whatever I expected, this was not it! Nordheim is flirting with me. I like him. He makes me laugh. He is handsome, too, even if he is so pale. I hadn't known that he'd been here as long as seven years. My God, I hope I'm not expected to stay that long. Joseph is almost thirty-one, Marra should kick him out, except that Joseph does everything for him, accounts and bills and ordering. I suppose it's time for me to have a real lover. I can't go through life knowing only Borach's pitiful attempt. I might, after all, enjoy it. Hmmm! Would Sonya approve?

Joseph and Tim have promised to teach me to swim this summer. I will like that. Brava, Delphi! At last you may allow yourself to be your age.

* * *

'It is my turn, clod. There are no Olympic Rumanians.' Joseph pulled her out of Tim Jankelescu's arms. The water was cool on her skin, and she was as pliant as the current that ran through the spring-fed pond. 'You can't just lie like a log, Delphi. You must kick, you must pull the water with your arms.'

'I want to float, like a branch.' She stretched herself out, hands together above her head, face in the water, water in her ears and eyes, and dropped to the bottom like a stone.

'You see! I told you.' Joseph, Prussian annoyance making him flap around like a penguin, was next to her. 'Swimming is moving. Like a knife you have to go through the water, a knife with arms and legs. Like this.' As he bent down and showed her how to stroke, Delphi pushed his head down into the water while Barbara splashed at them both, laughing. Water babies, she thought, laughing too, loving this place, loving all of them. Jean Claude was swimming back and forth lazily across the pond, paying no attention to anything. Edith Cowles, her great breasts swelling out against the cloth of her suit, was a nymph. Delphi stretched flat again and began to kick and pull against the water and they yelled at her, bursts of Italian, sputters of Rumanian, English, French, and she was swimming, actually swimming.

Joseph was in love with her, Ruccio Scaramella was in love with her, even Tim Jankelescu, who spoke to no one else, found time for Delphi. Their days were full of work, their nights full of wine and laughter. Even she drank wine, spilling tales into the night wind, telling funny stories about West Fourth Street, funny now for the first time. She made feasts out of nothing, she made art, and at night she often made love to Joseph.

'There is no one like you,' he said, lying on his back.

'There is Barbara, there is Rose, Agnes, Edith. We are all the same in the dark. Even in the light.' Her eyes were closed.

'They have no mystery.'

'I have none either. I play at it.'

'You draw better than they do. You look better. You have longer legs.'

'I draw better than you, too,' she said.

'In a pig's eye you do.'

'I do. You never look at my work. Not really. Or rather you compare it only to that of the other women. Compare it to that of the other men, too. It is better.'

'You will marry me and you will have beautiful babies and I will be great enough for both of us.'

'Rot. I will never marry. You all dream about continuing traditions. I will make my own tradition.'

Joseph looked over at her. 'Was Titian a woman? Or Hals? Rembrandt? Michelangelo? Leonardo?'

'It was different. Things were different then. Now is now.'

'Jankelescu wants you, you know? Brooding Rumanian thief.'

'I think if I had his hands, I would sculpt. Great axes, his hands. He would need no chisel.'

'I said he wanted you. I don't care about his hands. He has no talent anyway.'

'Perhaps he will have me. Because I do care about his hands.' She turned toward Joseph and smiled. She touched his face lightly with her fingertips.

'Get away from me.'

'You're silly, but you have an interesting mouth.' She kissed him. He grabbed her and pulled her over him.

* * *

June 26, 1926
Dear Delphi,

I cannot come this summer after all. There is just not enough time to do everything, is there? I remember when my own mother said that to me when I was a child, I looked at her in amazement. There was all the time in the world then. Where ever has it gone?

I am just so busy. Martha and I have started a press! (Yes, I know you are thinking, 'Not again!') The house is the same as it was all the years you were growing up, except you are not here.

We are printing a pamphlet on the dangers of war and the arms race. The League of Nations was a body ahead of its time. My heart breaks for poor old Mr Wilson. How he was betrayed, but that's all the same old story. Money, money, money. Our pamphlet is quite clear. I have sent you a copy. Perhaps I can politicize you, what do you think?

I don't know if I like all this that you write me about the 'good time' you are having. I have never heard of anything productive coming of a 'good time.' I still believe excellence only comes from sweat, pain, and sacrifice.

Send me one of these drawings you are talking about, and keep away from charming Italian boys who study art. They can do you no good whatsoever. I spent some time last weekend with people who had just returned from a trip abroad and are quite knowledgeable in the art world. I asked them about your Luis Marra and his school. They had never heard of him.

Again I say it – write your father. Although he no longer expects it, one day you will regret it if you don't.

Sonya

*   *   *

Delphi was wearing a Grecian gown and standing on a platform of stone while Joseph and Edith drew her.

'Make piroshki for dinner, Delphi!' Jean Claude was kneeling at her feet. 'Make piroshki and you can have me.'

'And me.' Agnes was lying prone on the grass.

'But I don't want any of you.'

'Nordheim is not enough for you, piroshki queen. And he can't draw drapery worth shit.' Ruccio was standing over Joseph's shoulders. 'Left, here. It goes left, you idiot. You are making a great clump. You have no soul.'

'You have no talent, Ruccio. What do you know of soul?'

'We Italians are born with soul, Nordheim. Soul and the ability to make love.'

'Delphi, are you Greek somewhere?' Agnes asked. 'You look so authentic.'

'If a Greek Cossack came through the village, then perhaps I am.'

'Raping, pillaging, and looting – it must be a fine life!' Jean Claude had started a charcoal sketch. He was good.

'Everybody, pick up your pencils and pretend to work. Marra's coming up from the studio. I feel the silence of his wolf pack around me.' Nordheim's voice was raspy. Each one of them started drawing furiously. Marra said nothing as he passed them. He looked briefly at each one's pad, his face set, his eyes narrowed. When he passed Delphi, he stopped and turned back to her.

'You, the model, come with me.' She jumped off the

platform and ran after him. He continued ahead of her, walking into the main house and down the long hallway to the kitchen.

He stopped in front of the stove. 'Make me dinner.'

'But it is only four in the afternoon.'

'I am hungry.'

'But I was working . . . I was posing for Joseph and the rest. I . . . what would you . . . I was going to cook dinner, you know, later. But I could . . .'

'Are you a cook, Delphi Stern? Is that what you are? Or perhaps a lover, a playmate.' She felt stupid suddenly in the thin white garment. 'It has been over a year and you have cooked a hundred meals and you have made love to nearly everyone, yes?'

'Is it a prerequisite for the great Marra that one be celibate?'

'It is of no concern to me if you sleep with all of Europe. But I warn you, you are a woman, and soon you will have used up any opportunity you have to be more than an ornament or a cook.'

'And if I were a man?'

'You are not a man.'

'Is time different for them maestro? If men can play and be serious, so can I. I will not give up my life when I have only just found it. This is the first time I have ever been young.'

'Good.' He turned away and started out of the room.

'I can do everything! I will do everything!'

He stopped and turned toward her, staring.

'Say something!' Her bare feet felt the cold floor and she shivered. 'I have choices.'

'You have choices. You can choose to be everything or you can choose to be an artist. Don't you understand that to make a place for yourself in this world you will have to create it? And to create it you will have to make balls.'

'What of talent!'

'You are a woman. Talent, even genius, means nothing.'

'But my life! Are you telling me to give up my—'

'I see a nymph who cooks and plays and makes pretty pictures. If such a life appeals to you, keep it.' His anger made his eyes darken and his knife-straight hair quivered at his shoulders as the thick muscles of his neck pushed at the skin. He held up a series of her drawings, shaking them within inches of her face. 'These, these, what are these?'

'Where did you get those? I did them for my own pleasure. I did not mean for you to see them.'

'What are they?'

'They are drawings, damn good drawings, too! Is my privacy not to be respected? Those were in my sketchbook.'

'Privacy? I doubt you have a shred of privacy left. You loll around with the others in one great bunch. Is it your Russian heritage, this communal living? Or is it just that you find free love more interesting than good art?' She was stunned at his anger and she stared at him, astonished. 'I never want to see anything resembling these cow-eyed cows again. If love is responsible for such sentimental shit, become a nun. Do I make myself clear?' He threw the drawings on the kitchen table. She picked them up and looked at them. He was right.

'I am ashamed that I lost sight of my work. Nothing is so important.'

'As what? What is so important, Delphi Stern?'

'As painting. I want to paint. I want nothing else.'

'So now you want nothing else, eh? We will see. I have been watching you. Your hands have just begun their dance. We will see if they are mad. Do they tremble at the thought of even touching a brush? They must. We will see. I do not waste my time, I warn you. Soon you will paint.'

She was not the only one Marra chose to begin his painting classes. There were four others. Together they spent their days working, at first making little boxed color charts, each box containing a gradation of one color from light to dark in infinitesimal degrees. Boxes upon boxes running up and down page after page. There were hours of lectures and demonstrations on the application of paint to canvas, on the need for a carefully chosen and executed underpainting, on the methods of glazing, varnishing. Assignments were made and the result of them dismissed until further results were accomplished. At the end of seven weeks, each student was given a reproduction of a master and made to break down the painting into geometric shapes of light and dark; when that task was done to Marra's satisfaction, he allowed the student to copy the painting itself.

Delphi was given Vermeer's *Lady with Jug*, and she was completely certain when she finished the second version that she would please Marra with the result.

'No. Absolutely not.' He shook his head.

'When will you be satisfied?' she exclaimed.

'Paint it a thousand times,' he answered. 'Then, maybe.'

'But it is good. The likeness is good!'

'Again.'

'I cannot. I cannot!' She sat down dejectedly on her stool. 'You do not push the others so hard. You are satisfied with their first, their second attempt.'

'I remember your first pen-and-inks. Do you?' he said. 'If you care to be compared favorably to the others, then I shall use them as my criteria.'

'No, please . . .'

'You must battle against your satisfaction and risk yourself. You are too facile. To risk takes arrogance. You are not arrogant enough.'

'Ask the others, ask Nordheim if I am not arrogant enough!'

'You are speaking of a woman's arrogance, not a man's. Against whom do you match yourself?' He sighed loudly and squinted against the glaring sun.

'Man this, woman that – I am sick of it! Do you really think of me as a woman artist when you look at my work? Must I have a gender?'

'I am afraid you must.' He looked at her and then back at her work. She watched the linen of his shirt pull hard against his chest as he lifted his arm to wipe his forehead.

'I would like to watch you work,' she said. 'I have always learned more quickly by example.' She looked up at him. 'I would be very quiet . . . I could pose. After all, you do need models every now and again. I can hold a pose for a long while . . . I . . .'

'Yes. I can see no problem.' He scratched distractedly at

his shoulder and looked at her again. 'Come tomorrow, then. By eight, before the heat.' She nodded quickly. 'Good. Now return to your work. My advice would be to stop appreciating the artist and begin to appreciate the subject.'

Even at eight the next morning the sun was hot. How would it be by noon? Delphi remembered how impatient she had been at first, finding that everything Italian was suspended for three hours in the afternoon. The impatience lasted only until she had her first touch of July sun. Borach had laughed at her then. Now she took a deep breath and glanced down at the geraniums that lined the path to Marra's house. She was having a personal battle with the geraniums. They dared her to find their color, so bright that it hurt her eyes. Everywhere at Casamarra there were geraniums, and everywhere they challenged her. Would she ever have the skill to mix that orange? Were there colors in nature that she could never transfer? She would ask Marra, she thought, looking up and taking the path that veered from his house to his studio, which was only a large room at the back. She was curious to see where he worked, imagining it a special place, unlike any other. When she opened the door, she was disappointed, for Marra's studio was like any other, filled with canvas and frames and drawings tacked haphazardly to the walls, full of the mess and smell of art.

'Sit there, please.' Marra glanced up for a moment and motioned to a plain wooden chair near the window. She picked her way toward it, only to be called back. 'Perhaps you might like to see the problem I have.' She came around the clutter to the front of his easel. There was a portrait of the Virgin and Child, with scenes of the rural Florentine countryside seen through a window in the background. The arch of a woman's back, the detail of the hands and fingers at prayer, the folds of her heavy burgundy velvet garment, and the lightness, the delicacy, the grace of her lace cap were all breathtaking. Delphi looked at the face. The mouth was right, the narrowness of the lips and the suggestion of a smile were those of the fifteenth-century girls that Lippi used as his models.

'You see here, I am making it too like this Lippi.' He pointed to the wall across from him at the print that was hung there. 'You know that, yes? The one in the Uffizi?' He shrugged. 'I know it too well. I must go beyond it, but each time I do, I lose Lippi altogether. There is a problem here at the bridge of the nose, here at the eyes.''

'Borach told me I looked like a Lippi,' she said.

'Perhaps you will solve everything, then. Who, after all, knows better than Borach? Come, I'll get you arranged on the chair.'

From where she sat she could not see his face. 'Borach never mentions you these days. I saw him again yesterday. He has gotten himself a male secretary.' She smiled. How peculiar that Marra spoke while he worked. She herself never could.

Marra chuckled. 'I can't imagine he'll last long.' His face appeared around the corner of the easel. He was squinting at her. He smiled and disappeared again. She did not say anything. She watched his feet. They were small for a man his size, almost feminine. He kept tapping the right one. 'Look up, please.' He was there again, his face on the side of the canvas. Now he turned to the small table that held his tubes of color, and she could see his back and neck. 'This painting' – he spoke haltingly, gaps of concentration between his phrases – 'has given me' – his foot was tapping – 'more trouble than . . . all the rest.' Silence. Then just the brushes on the canvas, the squeak of the floorboard in one spot whenever he turned for more color, and through the thick stone walls, faraway noises, a dog barking, a horse. Now only her own breathing, and his. The morning passed away.

'Come, look, here.' She left the chair and went to stand by him. 'Still, it is not right. Better, but not right. The left eye is finer, more like yours, actually, the way the light glints from it as you sit there. Something peculiar, though, with your other eye. There's more yellow. Let me see.' He lifted her chin and peered into her eyes. 'Yes, the left one has more yellow.' He stood only inches from her. The noises were louder. A fly whizzed around the room. One of his dogs lay snoring in the corner. There was a rush of wind in the trees outside the studio. She wanted him to

371

kiss her. 'Yes,' he said again. 'Odd. I will have to ask you to come again tomorrow. You may go along now. But tomorrow at eight, yes?' He was frowning at the painting, moving up and back, frowning and squinting. She walked away from him, her step all at once unsteady.

*   *   *

Delphi August 2, 1926
There is such energy in him! Such a concentration! Such force! Beauty! And between the two of us, there is such a communion, an excitement. He makes love to me with his expectation of my accomplishment. He makes love to me with his gift of art. And now he makes love to me when he paints me. Posing for Marra is a sexual experience. It is the rarest sort of joining. He has used me as his model for four days. Joseph is so jealous. He is beginning to hate me. I taunt him with Marra. What makes me enjoy being so mean to him? I think it is because he thought he owned me. No one owns me.

*   *   *

On the fifth day, hardly an hour or so had elapsed when she heard him push the easel a bit and take a deep, full breath. 'So. It is finished.' His face was obscured by the center of the easel. All she could see were his hands. She sat where she was and looked at them. He was putting his brushes down. He lifted one back up, wiped it on a clean cloth, dipped the bristle into turpentine, rubbed it on the palm of his hand, and then wiped it again on the cloth. He lifted a second. She watched him, unable to get out of the chair.

'Come. Take a look.'

There was a small ache at the base of her neck, and she rubbed it as she stood. The smells of the studio made her dizzy as she walked to the easel. She stared at the painting. It was so rich with the thickness of life that she wanted to touch the hair, feel the smooth skin of the face, kiss the lips. She trembled. The rough cloth of Marra's smock grazed her bare arm. It was hot, yet her feet were icy. She felt bloodless. She turned to see him staring at her.

'Borach was wrong,' he whispered. His eyes were flat, dark circles moving across her face. 'You don't look like a Lippi at all. You look like the Bellini Madonna in Milan.'

Her eyes followed his eyes. The snap of his step on the floor surprised her. Suddenly she was in his arms and he was holding her with such force she thought her bones would splinter. His mouth on hers left no breath. She could taste paint, salt. He was lifting her off the floor, his hands cupping her buttocks, his mouth pressed fiercely on hers. She could not breathe, but she could not let him go.

He was kneeling over her on the floor, and it seemed only a moment before he was inside her. The swiftness of it made her cry out. Shameless, she pulled him down on her with all her strength, needing to feel his weight on her. He thrust himself into her again and again, and each time she cried out. He overwhelmed her, slapping himself against her, pushing her into the floor. The pressure and the pleasure were part of each other as she was part of him, and the sounds she heard were sounds of her own ecstasy as each nerve tangled with the next and she lost herself utterly. She clung to him until she was extinguished, until she was too exhausted to hold him.

When she opened her eyes, his face was in front of her and it blotted out the world. Maestro, she thought. My master.

*   *   *

August 19, 1926
Dear Delphi,

This Luis Marra sounds rather mythological from your description – half man, half beast, part God. How love dissembles! You say your feelings do not interfere with your work but instead give you more impetus toward it. Perhaps you have found a sort of perfection not given to mere mortals. I needn't give you my list of apprehensions; you know them all too well.

Apart from not seeing you, I feel quite peaceful, although I look a fright. Age does not settle on me with any grace, while it positively caresses your father.

I will ask you again to write your father. Your deliberate refusal to do so is by this time merely an act of regrettable stubbornness on your part. You disappoint me.

Thank you for the last book of sketches. I have taken the liberty of removing two of them for framing. So, you see, I admit your talent.

Sonya

*　*　*

She was on the chair behind him, her knees pulled up to her chin, watching him work. With a flick of his brush, a tiny ruby appeared on the subject's finger, and its light jumped and flickered like a flame.

'The fact is I will never understand it. You are so devoted to the genius of others that you forget your own.'

'Genius is a very special category,' he said, dulling the blue of the subject's jacket, moving back a step to assess his choice of color.

'What would you say if someone else were painting what you are painting?'

'I would say he was a trickster, a circus performer, nothing more.'

'Then all greatness is a trick.'

He put down his palette and brushes, wiped his hands on a rag, and took a breath, his back to her. She watched his back as the breath filled his lungs. She had been at him for days about his work. 'Delphi, what I do has nothing whatever to do with genius.' He turned to face her. 'Even to approximate these masters takes all the talent I possess. That is not greatness.'

'Then what is greatness, Luis Marra?'

'Let Borach find the definition. I can see it, I can smell it, and I can touch it, but I do not possess it. Do you think I chose this for my life? Idiot child, would someone choose this? It is my profession by default. No one sets out to become a critic or a painting instructor. Certainly, no one would want to be a forger. I spent years fighting for my greatness. In Paris I worked with Picasso, with Braque, drank my wine at Cirque Medrano, traded my stories with

Jacob, spent evenings with the Steins. And, I had great success.' He put his hands on his hips and shrugged, smiling at her surprise.

'Then I am not wrong,' Delphi said.

'Not yet. I said "success." I was successful because I was talented. Women took me to bed, men took me to dinner, both bought my work. It was romantic and nearly perfect until I realized I lacked the one essential thing I needed to continue producing art. Uniqueness, Delphi. Vision. I knew that no matter what I did or what success I had, I could never change the way men saw or felt or thought about form or color or subject. It is why I drive you all, to see if any of you can do that. If I have any uniqueness it is as a teacher, not a painter.'

Delphi stood up, facing him. 'You are always at me to have a man's arrogance. Well, you have just given me a good example of it. I want no part of that arrogance. How dare you pass judgment on yourself? It is nothing but a cowardly act!'

The muscles at his jawline jumped against the skin and his eyes went black with anger. 'Here.' He reached to the table next to him. 'Take this brush. Take it! Finish this painting!'

'What do you mean?'

'I mean what I said. Finish this.'

'But I don't know what you intend. How can I—'

'Do as I say. Finish it.' He slapped his brush into her open palm. Her hand was unsteady as she took the brush and turned toward the painting. Marra stood behind her. She felt the always palpable tension between them, and it pushed her closer to the palette. Her hand began to work.

It took her three days to finish the painting.

'So, is it great? Tell me, have you made a "great" painting?'

'I have only finished yours,' she said.

'You have finished it as well as I could with half the effort. My congratulations. You see before you your baccalaureate.'

His tone unnerved her and she looked at him, frowning. 'What do you mean?'

'You will have to leave me.'

She started to laugh but stopped when she saw he was serious, unsmiling.

'I have nothing left to give you. Nothing.' He looked suddenly tired. 'You have learned enough from me. Perhaps too much.' He looked again at the finished portrait. 'Without trying, even without thinking, you have finished the portrait exactly as I started it, with the exactness of its true master.'

She could not protest. He was right. She had created a perfect Duccio.

'There will be no more classes, no more lessons from Marra. No more Duccios and Vermeers, only Sterns.' He frowned and rubbed his temples, pressing at them with his thumbs.

'Does that please you, Luis?'

'It does. It does. I am happy for you, only a little, secretly, sad for myself. I am selfish.' He ran his hand through his hair and smiled at her again. 'Part of me wants you to need me forever. It is the curse of a teacher, or a parent.'

'Or a lover?'

He laughed. 'A lover, too. You're right.'

'I will need you forever, Luis Marra.'

'No, Delphi.'

'The others leave because they are not good enough to stay. I am good enough to do anything I want. I am good enough, Luis, and you know it.' She smiled at him and then rushed at him, putting her arms around his neck. 'We will eat Russian tonight and then make love like peasants. Come, come to the kitchen and watch me cook. I have created a Duccio and you have created a woman!'

'I have created an artist and she must leave me.'

'Don't say that, Luis. Please. How could I live? How could I paint? How would I ever know if I succeeded? Who would tell me if I had achieved anything if not you?'

'You would know.'

'How?'

'Because I will forge Stern. It will be a love letter. If you are good enough, I will send it.'

376

5

Delphi August 20, 1926

I finished a painting last night and it is good, I know it.
There is no one painting like it. Is that enough arrogance?
Well, I can defend my egotism with the painting. I put it
up on Marra's easel when I finished, and I knew, in a
moment, that it was a painting no one else could have
done. It is, indelibly, a Delphi Stern.

September 14, 1926

I am tired and my back aches. It has rained for a week
now, and still it rains. I had such an argument this
morning with Scandino (the butcher). He still refuses to
itemize the bills, and I am sure that Maria Luparro (a
housekeeper) is cheating us. Of course, they all cheat us. I
cannot ignore it, even though Luis says I should. The other
butcher, whose name I cannot remember now, my God,
his veal was always tough and stringy and the rabbits must
have been ancient. Oh, dear. I am so tired. It is late. Luis is
still in Paris. There is never enough money for him to run
this school as he wishes. I am lonely without him and
think of him too much.

I am seriously considering signing my works 'Stern'
instead of 'Delphi Stern.' Is that cowardly? Then I say, no,
I will not. I will shove my sex and my paintings down the
throats of all those bastards. I will show them all. I will.

*   *   *

The dogs were penned, but Delphi knew from the tone of
their barking that a stranger had arrived. Had she been
with Marra so long that she could even understand the
dogs? There had been so many interruptions in the last
days, and she had promised Marra she would finish the
background of this still life for him before he returned

from London. The barking was louder, the tone more antagonistic. Surely someone else could go and see what was causing such distress from the dogs. I am not, she thought angrily, the only one who lives here. She sighed, put down her brushes, and started for the door. Still the dogs were barking, howling, crying, carrying on. Sometimes the noise of them drove her mad.

When she opened the door she saw him at once. He was at the far end of the path that led to Marra's studio, walking toward her. The door in the main building was just closing. Someone else had, in fact, gone to check on the dogs. She stood still, her instincts at cross-purposes. She wanted to run to him. She wanted to slam the door and hide. The figure coming toward her was exactly the same as it had been . . . when? Was it only four years ago? She had thought him the handsomest man in the world.

'So you see, the mountain has come to Mohammed,' Tolchin said. She didn't answer, still at a loss for the appropriate behavior. 'Is this your house?'

'No,' she answered quickly, realizing that he should not see Marra's studio. 'Come. Come to the front.' She walked quickly around to the front of the house, Tolchin following her.

'You needn't run away.' His voice was as she remembered it, so assured and smooth.

'I'm not . . .' she said, finally having the nerve to look into his eyes. 'It is only the heat. The inside of the house is cooler.' His eyes were gentle.

'You understand that you made it mandatory that I come and see you.' He smiled. 'You look just the same.'

She brushed her hair from her face and held it back with her hand. 'It wasn't so long ago,' she said.

'Yes, it was. You were just eighteen. Let me look at you.' She was uncomfortable under his scrutiny. Had Sonya made him come?

'I'm sorry that you will not be able to meet Luis. He is away, in London.'

'I am sorry, too, but I did not come to meet him, just to see you. It is easy for you not to write me, but it is not so easy for you to ignore me here. Am I right?' She could barely look at him. 'Am I right?' he repeated. 'I was merely being selfish that last day. Hurt like a schoolboy. For a moment I felt that I had lost some thread of myself . . . when she told me you were not my daughter. But of course you are, so my reaction was ridiculous. As usual, I thought of no one but myself.' He put down his ebony and silver walking stick, carefully leaning it up against a chair, and looked at her, his head tilted a bit to the left. 'You cannot still be angry with me,' he said thoughtfully.

'Of course not,' she said. And then she repeated it.

'Then come, make an old Russian happy.' He held out his arms and she went to him more easily than she could have imagined and embraced him. She was surprised. It had been so simple to forgive him. She was freer than she had believed. Sonya's child, after all.

'So,' he said, 'you will show me your work, and tell me about yourself.'

'I will show you my work, but you will hate it.'

'Why so?'

'Because it is too revolutionary.' She laughed.

She made tea, and because she knew it would not do to serve him in the kitchen, she put the cups and the pot of steeping tea on a tray and carried it outside to the wicker table under the swooping larch tree. His eyes were full of sweetness as he sat in the wicker chair, watching her pour out the tea into his cup.

'You must tell me about Sonya,' she said, sitting down on the grass at his feet.

'She is magnificent, of course. Actually more beautiful now than ever. She would have come with me except she has finally found her true calling and has no time. Pacifism. Your mother is a dedicated pacifist. She would kill for it.'

'I know.' Delphi laughed. 'She writes me about it.'

'She is frustrated because it is difficult to get attention for peace through peaceful means.' He took out a white linen handkerchief and dabbed at his temples.

'She writes me that you live apart.'

'Apart and together. It is her decision, not mine. She claims I alienate her from her finer instincts with my base materialism. Actually, we have never been more compatible. She even wears the clothes I buy her. She refuses jewelry, of course, preferring her paste ones.'

'Her diamonds and rubies and sapphires!' Delphi began to laugh again. 'Oh, how I remember them. "Only paste! The real ones I sold long ago!"'

'That is a fair imitation,' he said, smiling down at her as he folded the handkerchief.

'If I have too much wine, I do better,' she said, shading her eyes.

He looked out at the valley. 'That grove there, does it produce?'

'No. But I have a garden that does produce. See it there?' she asked, pointing to the right. 'Your daughter has gone back to the soil. Tomatoes, lettuce, zucchini, cucumber, finochio, and basil. There has not been a better crop than this one. But it takes such time just to force the others to do their little part. They all think a drop of field sweat will stop their internal creativity. Oh, damn, Eric and Hadia were supposed to weed that. It is so annoying. They do nothing when Luis is gone. It reminds me I must stop in at the studio and see if Jessica or Benjamin has ordered the provisions for the week. And then' – she sighed, getting up – 'there is the new instructor. He has good credentials but he is not Luis. It will be only a few moments.'

Tolchin and she sat in the rear of the factory and listened to Raymond Gomez urge the trial of tempera despite its inherent failings. There ensued a heated conversation with Jessica, who, of course, had forgotten to order anything. Delphi checked the art supplies and spoke to Gomez before she took Tolchin to see her work.

'Revolutionary or no, your work is gifted,' he said, sipping the wine she gave him. 'Why is all of it unfinished? From your letters I assumed you did little else but paint. You have either been elevated or demoted.'

She drank a bit of her wine, but it tasted sour. She put it down. 'I think you do not quite appreciate the time it takes to run a school.'

'I thought Luis Marra ran the school. But, if you have chosen to be an earth mother, it is your decision.'

'I am not an earth mother!' She was horrified.

'Oh, then I misjudge what I see?'

380

'What, what do you see? You see only a few hours one day and you make it a life. It is not my life. It is only temporary at best. There has been some trouble, some changes . . .'

Tolchin lit a cigar, and she watched the smoke curl up over him, become a cloud above his head, and disperse. 'Let it go,' he said. 'I am wrong to mention any of it.' He put out his cigar in the brass dish in front of him. 'I am the last person on earth that should quarrel with you. It is idiotic. You are right, how can I know anything in a few hours? Besides, perhaps Sonya has been right that it is a man's prerogative to own himself, not a woman's.'

'No one stops me from owning myself! You know something, Tolchin . . . You know . . .' She had begun to cry, small bleak tears squeezing out of her eyes. 'You and Sonya, both of you, would deny me love! You would! What good is love that is tiny and insignificant? Love that is controllable? And yet when love that is huge comes, it overwhelms one, smashes out priorities. you would both say it is worthless. You would say it is destructive because one loses ownership of oneself. Well, I have used my own hands between my legs and I have demanded my own accomplishment in my work. Those have never been enough for me!'

'Why are you crying?' he asked, his voice hardly audible.

'Because you sound like Luis,' she answered, burying her head in her arms.

* * *

Delphi July 29, 1927

My father has left. I am glad he came. I feel I have changed completely, while he remains as arrogant and irresistible as ever. It is just as well Luis was not here. They are both too full of judgments. I do not accept what Tolchin said, as I do not accept what Luis has told me. They are both wrong about me, about women. We can do as much as men, more, I think. We are stronger, clearer. We are nurturers, born creators. I will show them both that it is possible to be many things. It is not difficult for me. Ideas do not disappear when I am in my garden, no amount of bother with beds and food or transportation gets in the way of my inspiration. I know I should have ten times the work I have, so I will. I will.

* * *

She felt his presence before she heard his step. She tried to keep working, but even a simple brushstroke was too difficult when he was close to her. She turned slowly and smiled at him. 'I am not like you. My concentration vanishes when you are near me.'

'It is quite good,' he said, looking at the large monochromatic wash of yellow on her easel.

'I am experimenting.' She put down her brushes and wiped her hands on her smock. 'I had an urge to use only color as form . . .'

'I am not here to speak about your work,' he said, pacing back and forth. 'No.' His boots made a slight sound on the earth floor. His head was down. His black hair was red in a shaft of sunlight. 'I am here to speak about the child. I have been waiting for you to tell me about it, but I cannot wait any longer.'

'You must be a magician,' she said with astonishment. 'It is only seven weeks. How could you know?'

'I knew before I left for London. How could I not know? I know your body.'

She grinned at him and shrugged a little. 'I was waiting to tell you. Our child. I have said those words to myself each hour of each day for so long. I wanted to tell you right away, but first I wanted to be certain it was not a fantasy.'

He was standing in front of the chestnut beam that stretched from the ground to the top of the peaked roof. It shadowed his expression and pointed a dark finger at her. 'You cannot have a child, *cara*. You must know that it is an impossible idea. You are only beginning your life. To hand it over to another now would be tragic. You will lose all your impetus, your power, your strength. We will go to Switzerland tomorrow and I will make arrangements. I will stay with you, and when it is over, we will come home.'

'Luis!' She shrieked his name.

'Delphi.' He came forward and took her gently in his arms. 'It is not given to everyone, this talent of yours. You know it yourself. One in ten thousand, one in a hundred thousand. But it is not enough, your talent. I told you that from the beginning. Already you spend your days distracted with the nonsense of this school. I can hardly forgive myself for allowing you to do that. How could I forgive myself if I let you have this child?'

'But it is *our* child, Luis. *Ours.*'

'No. It is yours. The child is not inside me, Delphi. It will not pain me in the least to have it cut out or to suffer its birth. If it is born, it will not feed at my breast and eat into my days with its hunger. For a man, a child is something outside of him. It is your child.'

'Luis, I can do it all. It is natural to be a mother. I promise you, Luis, I can do it all! I will put the child in a little bed right here in my studio and . . .'

'Delphi! Are you blind? Are you deaf? Stupid, stubborn girl!' He gripped her arms and shook her violently. 'You want to know the reason there is no great woman artist? Because all women are stubborn. Because they must triumph over their lives, not their art! Well, I will not let you have this child. If you have it now, it will take everything. You would have to kill it to paint again.'

'But you have let me help you with the school, have expected I run it when you were away. That has taken my concentration, my attention, and still I have worked. And I have done good work. Do you think there is—'

'Stop that!' he exploded, frightening her. 'Stop that! I have regretted every moment that has taken you away from your work, every hour when you were not able to paint. You should resent me for it!'

'But I didn't Luis. I didn't resent it. I did it because I loved you. I love you, Luis.'

'No. You will not give yourself up to being a sated wife and mother.'

'But Luis, I love you. I will love your child. I—'

'No!' His anger was enormous. 'You will not throw away your talent and your life.'

'Wait, what are you talking about?' She was screaming

at him now. 'What you mean is that I could take care of you and your school, your beloved school, I could do that, but you will not share me with a child! Is that it? Are you so selfish? You could destroy me for your own needs but not for a child?'

'There is no time for a child.'

'Then there is no time for you.'

'You will have to decide that. If you want to stay here, you must get rid of it.' He turned to leave her. 'That is final.'

'I don't believe it. I can't . . . I won't believe it.'

'As you like,' he said.

'I am going to have it, Luis!'

'Then you must leave here.' He had turned slightly to look at her.

She stared at him. 'You will never let me go. I do not believe you will let me go.' Suddenly there was an ugly little pain in her side and she uttered a cry as she nearly lost her balance. He started toward her but stopped as she caught herself.

'Is it all right?' he asked. 'Are you all right?' She nodded her head, her eyes closed. When the pain was gone, she opened them. The first thing she saw was her painting, just at the edge of his shoulder. It was as hot and burning as the pain in her side, as the concern she saw now in his eyes. He would never let her go.

In the days that passed, Luis became increasingly remote from her, making not the slightest gesture of intimacy. If he came to bed after he finished working, it was long after Delphi had fallen into a hot and exhausted sleep. If they were in a room together, he avoided any attempts at conversation with a dark glance. Still, that night Delphi resolved that they would talk to one another, make love to one another.

She had lain awake for hours listening to him walk back and forth in his studio, prowling like a night animal. Finally, she heard the snap of the door as he came into the house and then his certain step as he crossed the threshold of the bedroom. Soundlessly, she turned to look at him walk to the chair by the desk. She could barely see him in the dark of that corner, but she heard the scrape of his trousers as they moved down across the flesh of his thighs and the soft side of his shirt as he yanked it up over his head. He sat down in the chair, naked and unmoving. She pushed herself up a little in the bed, digging her elbows into the soft mattress.

'Make love to me,' she said, her voice gentle. 'Please.' She whispered it again, the words sticking in her throat and coming out too hesitantly. He did not answer, but sat still and stared into the darkness. In his silence she heard the doves hooting at the approaching day. She heard the sharp sound of the chair legs scratching against the pine as he stood up and walked toward the window in front of the bed. He leaned against the shutter bar and it shifted, washing him away in unexpected light. He knocked the bar up and disappeared, now into dark. Her eyes refocused. He took a breath and let it go quickly, as if it pained him. 'Is it to be my punishment that you will not touch me because I want your child?' she asked him.

He glanced up at her for a moment, his eyes enormous in the dark sockets of his sleeplessness. Slim bars of light from beneath the shutter slats held him fixed in a cage of light and shadow. 'Please love me?' she asked again, her voice feathery, her lips trembling.

He turned toward her, walking to the edge of the bed, his hands low on his hips, his breath just audible. She heard the scutter of mice in the eaves over her head, and she shivered.

'It is no use pretending everything is still the same, Delphi. It is not. I have made the arrangements and we will leave for Geneva at the end of this week. I am not a dreamer. There can be no child in my life. There should be none in yours.'

His tone was too dry and his words so final that she flinched as if they were stones thrown in her face. Still, she would not lose him. That would be impossible. She crawled toward him on the bed and flung herself at him, locking her arms behind his back and holding him against her face, pressing her cheek against his belly. 'I love you,' she said, holding him with all her strength. 'I love you so much.' Her crying made her words into sick, awkward sounds. She kissed his skin and held him until her arms were too tired. Leaning against him, she stayed weeping and motionless on her knees.

She felt his hands at either side of her face, felt his thumbs trace the path of her tears down her cheeks. Then he turned away from her. She put her hands over her eyes. She could not see him go. She put her hands over her ears. She could not stand the sound of his leaving her. Still she saw him and she heard him. If I do not die now, she thought, I will live a hundred years.

6

She had never liked the public rooms at the Palazzo
Rivizza in Siena. They were pretentious even for a first-
class hotel. Venetian chandeliers and yards of brocade
overwhelmed its lovely proportion. She sat in the one
simple piece of furniture, a green leather couch near the
writing table at the farthest end of the room. She glanced
at her watch. Carl Borach had not replied to her letter.
Because she had not heard from him, she was certain he
would come. As perverse as it was, it was what he would
do. She even expected him to be prompt.

He appeared exactly at one, more pinched and narrow
than she remembered him. The concierge brought him to
the couch where she was waiting. He immediately sat in
the large Florentine needlepoint chair to her right, higher
than she. 'My dear Delphi, you look quite well. A bit older
perhaps, but then, we are all older.' He looked down at
her. 'I was amused by your letter. So you come back a
supplicant, do you? I always knew you would. Marra's
mistresses always leave him after a few years or so. His
bag of tricks must be somewhat limited.' He smiled at her.
She expected abuse, innuendo, triumph. She would let him
go on. 'Marra has told me you are very talented. Is he
jealous of you, I wonder?' Borach's laugh was loud and
forced. 'Well, I hope you are satisfied with yourself.'

'I have always been sorry that I left you in that manner.'

'I do not wish to talk about it.'

'I did not come to talk about it.' She sighed a bit. 'I shall
be very honest. I have come to show you these drawings. I
have a Zuccaro and a Traini. I want to sell them. I cannot
leave Marra without money. We need talk of nothing else.'

'Let me see them.'

She handed the portfolio to him and he opened it,
looked at the two drawings carefully, and then stood up.
He walked over to the window, held them to the sunlight,

rubbed the paper between his hands, and then put on his glasses to examine them further. He looked at them again in the natural light and then turned on the table lamp at the writing desk and held each one of them above it, going over it carefully with a small magnifying glass he kept in his vest pocket. He studied them for a full twenty minutes. When he had finished, he put them back into the portfolio and handed it back to her. He sat back down on the needlepoint chair, took off his glasses, unhurriedly wiped each lens with a clean handkerchief before putting them back in their case, and then neatly folded the handkerchief and placed it in his breast pocket, looking down, arranging its corners so that they were symmetrical. When he finished, he patted the handkerchief and looked at Delphi thoughtfully, his eyes half closed, his face expressionless.

'Where did you get these drawings?' he asked finally.

'Marra gave them to me,' she lied.

'Love tokens?' He raised his eyebrow.

'He gave them to me.'

'As his or as originals?'

'He didn't say.'

'They are very, very good.'

'Yes?'

'But they are not originals. They are Marra's. I am surprised that he would cheat you so.' Borach paused, waiting for her to say something.

'You always said his were as good as originals.'

'Nearly as good.'

'I think I was quite straightforward in my letter, Carl. I need to get away from him. I am not fussy how I do it.'

'I certainly have you, don't I?' His eyes danced malevolently.

'I beg your pardon?'

'I won't buy your drawings, Delphi.'

She felt her stomach knot, but she did not take her eyes from his. 'I see,' she answered.

'I won't even help you sell them.' He was smiling at her. 'You must know you can't sell them yourself or you would not have come to me. Even forgeries must have a fine provenance.' He was still smiling. 'Marra surely told you that.'

'Yes, he did.'

'Poor Delphi.'

'If you will not help me, I will go elsewhere.'

'I did not say I would not help you. I said I would not sell your drawings for you. I am prepared to make you a proposition.' He shifted a bit, still smiling. She held her breath and watched him. 'If you come back to me, I will support you.' His cheek twitched slightly, escaping his control.

'I could never be your secretary again. I am a painter.'

'I am not asking you to be that. It may surprise you, but I have found that you are one of the few people I wish to talk to and one of the few who can talk back to me. I appreciate your intellect and your enthusiasm. I have, in fact, missed them. I am willing to make the stone house into a studio for you and to give you back your old room in the main house.'

'I do not understand, Carl. What would I have to do?' She thought of her first night under his roof. 'Certain arrangements are impossible,' she said tensely.

'What I expect would be dinner conversation, companionship. I am not traveling as much as I used to. Guests occasionally drop by. You might help me with them. I have just finished a book on the patronage of art called *The Medici Complex*, and I must spend the next months editing it. You could help me a bit if you had the time. You were an able critic of my work.'

'You want my companionship? I find that most peculiar.'

'I have always been peculiar, Delphi, we both know that. Indeed, the world knows it. In all events, that is my proposition. Does it suit you?' She thought for only a moment and answered him with a nod of her head. 'Good. I am glad you will be back where you belong. Part of me has always considered you mine. Make the arrangements quickly.' He got up from his chair and leaned over to kiss her briefly on the cheek. Walking away from her, he looked larger than he had when he first arrived.

*　　*　　*

Delphi   August 15, 1927

A week today, in Siena. Carl has gone out of his way to make me feel at ease, hovering about as if I am a trophy of some victory of his over Luis. How awful!

How can I bring myself to tell him about the child? I was so sure and now I am not so sure. I wake up choking on the thought that Luis let me go. I hate him, his selfishness, his insensitivity. How is it possible? And still I love him. Sonya will not like the idea of the child either.

I cannot paint in the morning, I am still so nauseated from the smell of the oils. I tire easily. Most of all I miss Luis and force myself not to think about him. I miss Florence. I am so young and feel so old.

I pray that the child is a girl.

*   *   *

The dinner party that night had gone extremely well. Delphi knew Carl had been pleased. She had, for the first time, overseen the minutest details, thinking all the while of Sonya, laughing to herself at this strange area of expertise, even going so far as proposing, at the table, a toast to the innate abilities of children to acquire their parents' knowledge. She had drunk too much champagne, that was sure.

Now it was well after midnight. The last guest had left and Carl had called her into his study to compliment her. Awkward in his enthusiasm, he could barely contain himself. He walked about, he whistled, he smiled, he waved his hands and shook his head like a sparrow at a party of crumbs. 'You looked wonderful this evening, Delphi, and the dessert! The cream was just so, however did you learn to do that? I thought the baroness would have an apoplectic fit over the hors d'oeuvres. Why did you never do this for me before, you silly girl, instead of just taking all that endless dictation! What a brilliant party! Am I not the best of hosts?'

'I'm going to have a baby, Carl.' It had come out of nowhere. Amazement, she thought, would be too gentle a word for his expression. 'I'm pregnant.'

'When? What do you mean?' His hand flew up and

covered his heart as if she had taken a slingshot and shot him there. Poor sparrow!

'It was terrible of me not to tell you before, deceptive as can be. Do you believe that I somehow thought you would never mind?' She felt like smiling, laughing out loud.

'What are you talking about, Delphi? A child? A mewling, puking infant smelling of old cheese, here?' – again he waved his arms – 'In my house?' She did smile at him. 'And besides . . .' He frowned. 'What will people say? Not that I care what people say, my dear, but nonetheless . . . why are you smiling, Delphi? This is some sort of a joke, isn't it?'

'No, Carl. It isn't.' She pursed her lips to stop smiling, biting on the inside of her cheek. 'I take it you have reservations.'

'Delphi, this is cruel if it isn't a joke. That Marra's baby should be born here – I assume it is Marra's baby?' Delphi nodded. This was exactly the opposite of how she imagined it. She had thought she would be in tears, and here she could barely bring herself to keep from laughing. Champagne was wonderful! 'I am certainly not comfortable with Luis Marra's baby in my house,' Carl continued. 'I can't imagine it – anybody's baby. It would be so . . . so disruptive, I imagine.'

'Tell me, Carl.' Delphi smiled at him again. 'Why did you let me come back here in the first place?'

'Why? Because you are a help to me, Delphi. I enjoy you, you are the brightest person I know.' He smiled back at her. 'Probably,' he added, 'because you were educated by me!'

'Well, you will certainly let me stay here until the birth, then. There will be no changes. I can still talk with you, work with you, fulfil my secretarial duties, entertain.'

'Really, Delphi, you can hardly entertain with your belly sticking out in front of you. It would make me quite uncomfortable to have people coming here see you in that condition, and we couldn't travel anywhere. I couldn't take you with me anywhere, heaven knows.'

'You hadn't told me you were planning to go anywhere.'

'I wasn't, but I might.'

The sight of him so completely ill at ease, so irritated,

such a perturbed little bird, made Delphi start to giggle. Could anyone have been more the opposite of Luis? She suddenly could not control herself any longer and she laughed, her laughter starting like a tiny silver bell and then getting louder and louder. He frowned at her for a moment and then, miraculously, a smile formed on his mouth. Suddenly, he was laughing as loudly as she, his surprised eyes nearly out of his head. 'Oh . . . oh . . .' She pointed at him and then rolled over onto her side, cackling and choking. 'I knew you would let me, I knew . . .'

'I have no idea at all . . .' He held his sides as his laughter got more and more shrill and tears came down his sallow cheeks. 'I have no idea why, why I am laughing!' This statement made her laugh even more forcefully so that now she was snorting laughter.

The two of them laughed and laughed. He attempted to recover himself at one point, but the demon of laughter still played at his lips, tormenting him into a great hail of sound. Now he was afraid to speak, so he sat hopelessly across from her, soundlessly pleading for her to stop her sputtering. She thought of the taste of a lemon and then of alum so she could stop.

Finally they were both quiet, staring at one another. 'I have just one request,' he said, looking away from her.

'Yes?' She could not imagine what he would ask her.

'You must spare me the details of it. I do not want to hear the details. At least you must spare me those.'

Early in the morning during her fourth month, she had caught a glimpse of herself in the mirror above her bureau and sensed, for the first time, her own strangeness. The reflection of her thickening body, more mysterious in the morning half-light, made her stop to stare. She pushed the bureau away from the mirror to see all of herself. Fascinated, she lifted her nightgown to look at her body swelling out in its reflection. Slowly she slipped off the light cotton gown and studied herself entirely naked. She was as golden as the room, as the spread of the sun on the polished wood floors behind her. Her skin shone with tautness. Her nipples were cinnamon and coarse, but they glistened with moisture. She thrust herself forward to look at her pubis. From between her legs she saw an enlarged ruby furrow. She sat down in a chair and turned to look at each part of herself, ankles, neck, hair, back. She was ripening like an August melon, changing every minute, and she had not been aware of it.

She walked quickly to pencils and pads at the side of the bed and then sat down in the chair again to sketch herself. She made one sketch after another. As her body grew she drew herself daily and, for the following five months, kept a visual diary of her pregnancy, its boldness and honesty influencing all her work, reducing her line, and simplifying her concept.

One afternoon she had made yet another ink of herself. When she finished she stared at it and thought of sending it to Luis. In this small drawing he could see her arrogance clearly enough, in the work and in the body itself.

There had been minute buzzes along her sides for days. Delphi looked down at her naked belly, the belly button sticking out of her like a tiny finger. It would be soon, she thought. The buzzes had become stronger.

In those last weeks, unable to sleep for long, she had begun to make corrections on Carl's *Medici* manuscript, suggesting over and over that he slow down his narrative and excise any overblown phrases. The book would have a broader appeal if its style were less intricate. He had listened to her, and now the book was clearer, finer. They were sitting in the library after dinner, going over her notes. He was pleased with her observations.

'You are really astute about my work,' he said. 'No one will ever understand my intentions as well. I think I work harder just to please you.'

'You know I think it's nonsense in the end.'

'You are my catalyst because you think so. You stir my intellect.'

'I think I stir your imagination.' Delphi pushed away her teacup. 'You and Lorenzo de' Medici are shining knights in some fairy tale, aggrandizing yourselves with art and riches.'

'How cruel you are.' His laugh was brusque, nearly a cackle. Delphi felt a twinge of a cramp in her left calf. She shifted awkwardly, trying to get at it.

'By the way' – Carl leaned back in his chair – 'why haven't you told your parents you were having a child? I had a letter from Sonya this morning. She talks about visiting, asks if she'll be welcomed should she come. See for yourself.' He handed Delphi the letter. 'Poor thing has no idea, does she?'

'No. It would not please her.'

'Are you still so afraid of her? Sonya, with all her crusades, all her "communal" thinking, certainly she wouldn't disapprove of an illegitimate child?'

'That wouldn't bother her. The child's legitimacy would mean nothing.'

'Then what is it?'

'She has other expectations for me.'

'Such as?'

'Accomplishment. Usefulness. Sonya spent a great deal of energy on me. I am marked by her. I thought I would spare her these few months of disappointment. I am not able to make a case for my choice until I do something with my life. I intend to.' Delphi took a breath and shifted her position. The cramp showed no signs of relenting. She rubbed at it with her other hand until that, too, was numb. Carl put a record on the massive cherrywood Victrola. The record immediately stuck in a groove and repeated its musical phrase.

'Damn that housekeeper. She must dust my records with a rake.' He lifted the needle, turned the record, and replaced it with delicacy. 'There. The Bach is pleasant at this time of night.' He sat down in the chair behind his desk, putting his chin into his upturned palms. Delphi watched a spider that dangled by its thread at the top shelf of the bookcases. It was slowly making its way up toward its web.

'I would prefer something more languid, less male, less German. Chopin.' Delphi put her head against the arm of the couch.

'Let it finish. I don't want to risk damaging it.' He ran his chair legs back across the carpet, setting her teeth on edge. 'I had to go to your studio today. That thief of a gardener, Luccio, said he mended a hole in your roof the size of a cabbage.'

'It was the size of a thumbnail.' The spider had managed its climb.

'All Italians exaggerate. I think it is to compensate for their lack of wit. At any rate, I had to see what he did. I saw the sketches you have been doing of yourself.' Delphi stiffened where she lay. 'I assure you I wasn't prying. They were all set out just there on the table. Luccio certainly must have spent time looking at them.' The pain in her calf intensified, aggravated by her tension. She pressed it with her fingers as hard as she could. Embarrassment crawled up from her chest to her cheeks. Her inks would have offended him, and she prepared herself for his abuse, pretending a lack of interest in any reaction he might have had.

'I thought them immensely beautiful.' He stood up and went to the Victrola, his narrow back to her, one shoulder higher than the other. He took up the needle from the record and slid the record into its cardboard sleeve without looking at her. 'Are you surprised?' He placed the record in his cabinet and chose another. He wound the Victrola and put Mendelssohn on the turntable. 'I found them all very moving in some sort of way. I should like to own one.'

'They are rather, well, intimate. I intended them as a sort of diary. You see, I—'

'Suit yourself,' he snapped, shoving his weight against the housing of the Victrola, scratching the record badly. 'Damn.'

'Carl, stop it. Of course you may have one. I am just a bit overcome with your compliment. It is the first you have ever paid my work.'

He sat down again, joining his fingers together and pressing his palms away from him until he had cracked them all at once. He was enjoying her bafflement. 'I am rather intrigued by the birth of this child of yours. I have come to feel somewhat like an expectant father.'

Delphi laughed sharply. 'I hardly think it is your role.' The music stopped. The needle stuck again.

'Certainly. We both know I am incapable of feeling.' He pulled the record off the machine and held it in his trembling hands. It was another moment before she realized how much she had hurt him. 'I am only a piece of wood, at best.'

'I did not mean . . .' A terrible pressure became fiery claws tearing at the muscles beneath her belly.

'What did you mean, then? Certainly you don't expect Luis Marra to come back at this late date, do you? I can assure you he has no intention of ever setting eyes on you or your child. I hear he has already taken another mistress. He is not long without one. As for children, he has them from the boot of Italy through the mountains of Switzerland.' He put the record down on his desk.

He would abuse her now. She had forgotten this streak in him; he had been so pleasant to her for so long. Why had she snapped at him? He began the little peacock strut that she remembered. She thought he should have a mustache, a narrow one like a stenciled line. It would suit him to be able to press at it with his little fingers. Why was she so bothered with him? Was it the pain in her belly? Would that make her lash out at anything? How stupid of her to have broken the boundaries of their life together. They had it so well charted these last months, even the choreography of their anger had been chàrted so that they avoided all the old scar tissue, doing each other no further injury, and here she had broken the rules.

Carl was lashing out now, at Marra's absence, at her chilling naïveté, his voice full of rage. She had hurt him and now he would hurt her, fair exchange. The band of pressure came again and wrapped itself around her lower body. It went quickly. How remarkable, she thought, that something so brutal can be unremembered in a moment. She pushed a pillow behind her and sat up straighter. Clearly it was the start of her labor. Still, she said nothing. She closed her eyes for a moment, trying to relax.

Carl continued ranting against Luis Marra. Delphi continued not to listen to him, the pain in her abdomen demanding all her attention and blotting out his words. The pains were stronger now, the time between them less lengthy. She heard Carl's voice: 'Luis Marra,' he screamed at her, the rest of the words dissolving in the wash of pain. A chill shook her body and she felt she was about to throw up. Suddenly she was frightened with the knowledge that the baby was really about to come.

How would she care for this body within hers? A baby was forever; there was no changing one's mind. Was hers the defiance of a child rather than a woman? Beads of sweat formed on her brow as she closed her eyes, and the pain took her breath away, making her dizzy. Damn you, Luis Marra, she thought, damn you, damn you! Your child is being born now. How could you let me go? Damn you, Luis.

She heard Carl's voice, far away now, echoing her.

7

The flat, thick face of the midwife did not alter its expression for the fifteen hours that Delphi labored. How long must a person sit beside such pain to ignore it so, so that not the least flicker of concern lit the eye? But it made no difference to Delphi. The eruptions that came with such force that they stopped her mind would not be lessened by meaningless ministrations. Delphi's body was no longer hers but belonged entirely to this invader inside her. Over and over, the force and then the surcease. Over and over the betrayal of the body, until finally she was blasted through and she could not still her cry. It pierced the silence, erupting as the child itself erupted from her. Everything was white, the world stretching thin and white and hot, like membranes. Only then did the woman move toward her, the signal clear. She pushed Delphi back onto the bed, for her pain had made her curl forward, another fetus. The practiced hands spread Delphi's legs, reaching for the emerging infant, the face still implacable and dull. As the woman took the infant's shoulders to turn it slightly, Delphi's hands reached down to push hers away. The woman fought with Delphi, pushing her back again and again. But Delphi had to touch it, had to feel its coming, and she pushed at the woman's chest with all her might until the woman was thrown off balance and fell backward. It was Delphi who lifted her son from between her thighs to pull him forward to her.

Delphi growled like an animal. She clutched her child and licked his birth blood. She rocked him from side to side across the slickness of her sweat and his mucus on her belly. When the midwife tried to touch him again, to take him, Delphi rolled across him, covering his tiny body and shielding him from those foreign hands. She tasted herself on him. Triumph! She had never known its truth before.

From the first, Carl Borach was as delighted with the child as Delphi. The two of them would spend hours discussing his miracles: his full head of hair, his sturdy body, his tiny fists – he even slept with them clutched – his maddening scowl, his sweet breath. Delphi was amazed at Carl's reaction, at first delighted, then even a tiny bit jealous, but his love was so protective, so petite, so caring, that in the end it simply touched her. He even overcame his distaste with her nursing, bringing her the baby now and afterward walking about, patting him until he burped for them. And what burps! No child had ever burped more loudly or with more distinction.

Morning after morning they spent out on the terrace waiting for David to wake up, then feeding him, and afterward simply watching him, entranced by his slightest performance. Delphi had not worked since the last sketch she had done of herself the afternoon before she had given birth, and the thought of painting, of oils or brushes or canvas, was as distant as the moon.

'There, little boy, see, see the moon, the full moon,' she crooned to him in the middle of one hot Italian night. 'It is your first full moon, little treasure.' Someday she would make a drawing of herself holding the baby with the moon, and the brightness of that night, the trees casting eerie shadows in the silver light. When David was older, and there was more time. Now there was just time to wonder at him. How could his hands be so small and perfect? And his nails, translucent opals that grew of their own accord, how could that be? This miracle.

Carl cut David's nails while he slept. Delphi could not look, but Signora Corelli had insisted they do it. He had scratched his little cheek again and again. Carl had used a tiny scissors and very slowly, very carefully, cut each little nail. David had not stirred. Victory! He was not hurt. Carl was so proud of himself. Every day there were new victories.

The day David first laughed, little spasms starting in his chest and gurgling up and out of him, they celebrated with champagne. When he first sat up and then fell over crying and confused, they both were there, watching him on the blanket they had spread out on the terrace. Even Signora

Corelli told Delphi that she had never seen a man more concerned and helpful than Signore Borach.

Delphi you know, you must tell Sonya. Your father will eventually come to visit. Even Sonya has said that she may. My father also. Certainly you cannot keep this child a secret forever.'

'I know.'

'Well, why won't you do it?'

'I will, I will. Carl, please.'

'Perhaps you should take a trip, go back and visit them. Just bring them David, a *fait accompli*. Hmm?'

'No, no. I could never do that. I would never have the strength to leave.'

'Delphi, this is nonsense, all this fear you have of them. My God, you carry Sonya around with you like some giant sack on your back. It's been, what, close to five years—'

'Five and a half,' Delphi interrupted.

'Five and a half. More to the point. Five and a half. It's nonsense, Delphi.'

'I am going to stop nursing David, Carl, then I can get back into my work. My concentration is gone.'

'My dear Delphi, you can lie to them. Tell them you are working. Tell them you have sold a million paintings. Just tell them that you have a son.'

'Hmm.'

'Delphi, do you hear me?'

'Next week I am going to stop nursing.'

The night before she did, she wept. How she would miss that little mouth nuzzling at her, the warmth of his head locked onto her chest, the tiny pangs that played her when he took her rosy nipple in his mouth, and afterward when he slept, his mouth still holding her in such an absolute perfection of peace. Oh, how she would miss it. She cried until finally she fell asleep.

It took three weeks until her breasts no longer engorged with milk at the sound of David's cry for food. Her only reward was that now she could start to sketch more, to work.

The spring leaned into summer, was caught in the summer heat, on the thickening air. Delphi took David out onto the terrace each day to draw him by the garden, to chart his growth by the flowers themselves.

One day – David was nearly eight months old – as Delphi sat by the garden in their daily ritual she saw that the face was emerging, the nose getting thinner, the lips less round, the eyes springing out of the flesh pocket around them. Time was racing Delphi's perception, and she shook her head at its audacity. No, she would own this day, too. She would see in her son's face everything that could be seen.

She opened the pad and took out the watercolors and the pen, a tiny drop of water from the jar spilling on the dewy grass, soon lost. Nothing would spill away from her eyes to be gobbled up by nature. What amazing order and strength there was before her. And on her paper, he was their perfection, his feet the roses, his mouth the lilies, his skin the peonies. She was feverish, joined to what she saw as she joined everything on her paper. Nasturtium trailed over and under clusters of gray-green Irish spume, a crawl of clematis adorned the face of the rock wall creeping toward the last fall of wisteria, tiny white blossoms clinging to a thin green tongue. This garden, this jumble of shape, it was the child's life and all life.

It was then the scream came, piercing and horrible. A windbird caught in hell. Delphi looked up at the sky. Nothing was falling. What was the sound? Not a child or an animal but the Italian housekeeper, running, screaming, across the yard toward something Delphi could not see. And the baby, where was the baby? Not in front of her on his blanket, nowhere in front of her. There was the blanket and nothing else. Delphi froze in the sunlight. Signora Corelli was over the hedge that ran the length of the crumbling parapet across the yard. Across the yard! The rear parapet was stone dust and decaying stones above a drop of a hundred yards.

The signora was on her knees, scrambling into the thicket through its spiny branches, her hair and clothes catching on thorns, becoming brown and blue strings on ugly branches. She was screaming and cooing, making a lullaby of terror. She was calling? To what? What was she calling? Delphi could not move backward or forward, could not drop the pen in her hand.

David's face and arms were streaming blood. His small forehead was only blood, running red rivers into his eyes and mouth, gashes spitting up blood. Dear God, all she could think was that the blood was the color of raspberries, dear God, the color of raspberries ripe and oozing. She had been standing there at the bottom of the parrapet. How had she gotten down? When? Signora Corelli was tight and white holding the silent baby to her, hot ember eyes expressionless as she stared at Delphi and then moved past Delphi, ignoring Delphi's arms as she whispered to the bleeding thing in her arms. 'Little one, you are safe now. I have you. My child, *senta*, I have you. My little one, my baby.'

Delphi did not know what to do with her arms. There was nothing to hold. It was unthinkable that her concentration could have been so intense that she could blot out the existence of this child – this precious and most magnificent thing. She watched David being carried away from her, bloody and still. Away from her and her outstretched arms! Dear heaven, I have murdered him.

On the way to the hospital, the car speeding through the streets, its horn blowing its alarm to the people, the cars, the animals, Delphi heard only David's breath. Small and shallow, it continued rhythmically. She cooed at him, gently rocking him with her upper body, 'Baby, baby, my baby . . .' she sang to him. 'Yes, yes . . . Mama's baby boy . . .' How perfect he was, she thought; even the rips in his flesh could not make him faulty. 'Baby . . . shush . . . shush . . .'

At the hospital, a doctor took David from her arms immediately, rushing his still form away on a shrouded steel cart. Another doctor told them to wait in the waiting section, and both Carl and she were led down a wide corridor toward two benches.

'Delphi, I want to call my doctor in Rome. Perhaps there is someone he can recommend to us . . . a specialist . . . someone . . .' Carl walked unsteadily away from her as she sat down to wait. She was of no use, she thought, watching the purposeful strides of the nuns in their starchy nurse aprons, their strict caps perched on their heads. Their hands were trained to soothe or heal, while hers lay useless in her lap. Their long skirts made silent breezes along the marble floors as they moved back and forth like gentle waves. Delphi nearly drifted away from herself watching these Sisters of Mercy and listening to the rubbing sound of those hems on the slick, scrubbed floor.

She saw Carl appear again at the end of the corridor, and he was diminishing as he walked toward her, his face turning to ashes. Then he was closer and the ashes were only fine hairs on his unshaven beard. He sat down next to her, gripping the bottom of the bench with his hands and staring out across the corridor. 'I . . . spoke to my doctor in Rome. He said that Dr Fratti . . . is as capable as anyone in all Italy. He is with David now . . . Dr Fratti.' Carl's voice was creased by his sorrow. 'Delphi . . . David is in . . . grave condition.' He ran his pink tongue across his bottom lip and then pressed his lips together. 'He—'

'I want my son,' she said, now as full of purpose as all the Sisters who glared at her as she ran toward the big desk at the front door to the woman who was seated there. 'I am his mother. David, the baby, my son . . .' She looked down at her dress and saw his blood there and pulled at the fabric with her fingers. 'My baby . . .' she screamed.

'You must be quiet, signora!' The woman was outraged. 'There are people here who are very ill, and you must not disturb them. May I suggest you speak to your husband. The boy's father has already spoken to your son's doctors.' She pointed a stiff arm toward the rear of the building. 'Please remember this is a hospital.'

Delphi spun around wildly. Was he there? The boy's father? Luis? She turned and turned, but she saw only the figure of Carl hunched over on the bench. Yes. Of course. He was. She walked back to the woman at the front desk. Why was the woman so annoyed with her? Perhaps she didn't understand. 'I want to see my baby,' she said, very quietly. 'I must see my son.'

'Patience, signora,' the woman said, nodding her head. 'You must wait now.'

'No.'

'His doctors are with him. You cannot see him now.'

'I am his mother,' Delphi said. Why would this woman not understand?

'Delphi.' Carl stood beside her again. 'They are trying to find out the extent of his injury. Please. Give them time.'

'I'll never take my eyes off him again,' she said. 'Please tell them I promise never to take my eyes from him. If God gives me my baby, I'll never . . . please . . .' She wept, her hands holding nothing but air as they reached out toward the nun at the desk. 'Please. I know it was my fault, but I'll never . . . please . . .' She stretched out her arms to the woman, pleading over and over again to be taken to her baby. The woman nodded at Carl and left the room.

'Is it because they know what I did?' She cried it out.

'You did nothing, Delphi. It was an accident. Children fall all the time. An accident.'

'No,' she said. 'I . . . let him . : .' She sat on a chair in front of the desk because she could not stand. She swallowed tears and air and now she swallowed her words.

'Delphi, Dr Fratti is the best surgeon in nearly the whole of Italy.'

'Surgeon?' She went cold. Her tears froze on her cheeks. 'What are you saying? What are you telling me?'

'There is hemorrhaging . . . internal bleeding . . . they are doing all they can do . . .'

'*Oh, God, no.*' She was standing again.

'Delphi, look at me. *Look at me!*' His hands were at her shoulders and his red eyes bulged. 'They are operating on David. You cannot go into the operating room!'

'No. Oh, God . . . no.' She felt the ground giving way under her, but she stood, gasping for breath.

'Delphi . . . I . . .' He could not offer her anything. He stood in front of her, as bereft as she, as anguished. He covered his face with his forearm and his breath came in snorts and shudders like bellows. How selfish she was even in her love. Her love had never understood his. She was weeping with him. They sat down again together on that bench in the corridor to wait.

The hospital was so familiar, the falseness of the hushed voices and the soundless grief, the smell of the lye and the alcohol, the noiseless doors opening and closing. She would be still for moments and then she would cry again, helpless. It might have been hours. It might have been minutes. The man wore glasses in round frames that did not quite fit onto his face. Carl stood up. The man shook his head. His glasses made his face look odd because they did not fit.

'I am sorry,' the man said. 'We did everything, but . . .' He shrugged and shook his head. His glasses slid down the bridge of his nose. 'Signora . . . I am so terribly sorry.'

Delphi stared up at him uncomprehendingly.

'Delphi, this is Dr Fratti.' Had he changed into a suit to tell them that David was dead? How long ago had he died? Why was Dr Fratti wearing a suit? Carl's voice cracked out a dry sob, and it sounded like a loose slat smashing against one that was fixed. Delphi looked up at Carl, but she saw nothing at all, just a spinning ball. She fell forward into a hard sea, and two huge dolphins came and carried her away.

8

Delphi did not understand the weight of her sorrow. She knew she could not sit up in the bed, but she did not understand why. Some cord of herself fixed her to the mattress like a captive. She turned her head on the pillow and saw Carl. He tried to smile at her, but he could not manage it. He leaned forward.

'You fainted,' he whispered. 'It is nothing unusual.'

'David . . . I dreamed . . .'

'He is dead, Delphi. That is all there is to it. Dead.' Carl shivered and then wiped his eyes with a wadded-up piece of cloth. 'It is just as well. He had hemorrhaging on the brain. It is at least a reason to be grateful that he did not live.'

She could take no comfort in any reason for his death. She could find no reason now for her life. Something came apart inside her and she cried again, so helplessly that Carl Borach had to wipe her tears away before she choked on them. How was it possible that she had ever loved anything so much and let it be destroyed? How was life possible for her now?

The next day she watched the little polished box that held her baby lowered into the earth. She had to fight to have him buried immediately. How could anyone want to prolong such grief, she wondered, watching the tiny stones on the rim of the opening roll down on top of the box? How could people sit for days and look at someone dead lying in his coffin in a bizarre masquerade of sleep? No, she had said, she must insist that he be buried. She could not pretend he was alive for another hour or moment. No.

When the coffin was gone from her sight, Delphi stepped forward toward it. Her weight made gashes in the earth at its rim and she felt herself going down into the ground, sand and rocks covering her feet. The gravediggers rushed forward to grab her, but she pushed them away and fell onto her knees, sticking her hands into the earth to touch the box.

'My God, Delphi, stop!' His tone was so full of pain. 'For the love of heaven, let it be over!' Carl screamed at her, his face white. 'Please. Please, Delphi.'

She stumbled to her feet and covered her face with her hands. There was dirt in her mouth. 'Oh, why?' she keened. 'Why?'

The room was the same as always. It was golden. It was beautiful. Carl had replaced Signora Corelli with a young, fat-cheeked girl from a farm a few miles away. Delphi could not remember her name. At times, the girl smiled at her. Other times, she saw the girl scowling at her in the doorway. She had heard that Delphi was a monster and now she would never smile at her again. Then why was she smiling? The days were very confused. She heard rain drilling on the roof at night, but the days were hot and clear and the pots of geraniums on her balcony were always too dry. It could not have rained.

She dreamed of her baby, saw him as an angel, saw him covered with his blood. She cried helplessly. To what end, she wondered, weeping, remembering how he smelled, the sweet skin and the sweet excrement all together every-where on her, on her fingertips, under her nails, in her nostrils. She would not sleep. The room was always golden, like a piece of sunshine. She wanted a tomb.

'Delphi, it has been nearly three weeks. You cannot go on like this. I cannot be responsible . . .' He tried to be imperious, but he understood her grief, and finally his voice dissolved until it vanished. Carl sat far away from the bed, looking out at the geraniums. He had grown a beard. It was getting darker. Night shadows? 'Delphi, listen to me. What is the point of this? We cannot grieve forever. We must . . .' Again his voice faded.

'Did he come?'

'Who?'

'Luis. Did he come to the hospital?'

Carl shook his head.

'Did you know that he once told me I would kill my own

child? He did.'

'It was my own fault as much as it was yours. It was Signora Corelli's fault. It was her job ...' He sighed. 'What is the use of it?'

'I am a monster. He knew I was a monster.'

'Stop it, Delphi. It is too tiresome.'

'Do you hate me?' Her voice was hollow again, and it kept repeating its words.

'Of course not. No.'

'I hate myself. I want to die.'

'It is too late for any more regret. We will live, you and I, and we will do our work.'

'No,' she said. 'No.'

'Yes. Yes. Yes. Get up. Get up!' He stood and walked to her bed. 'Get up!'

'I can't,' she said, weeping again. 'I can't.' She turned across her arm and buried her face in her pillow. 'Oh, God, Sonya,' she said, shuddering where she lay. 'Sonya, what am I to do now?'

At the news that Sonya was on her way to Siena, Delphi stared at Carl in absolute terror. She could not have heard him correctly. She sat up in her bed, her pale, thin arms holding the coverlet.

'I said she was coming. I wrote her that you wanted her, and she wrote back that she would come.'

'Wanted her!' Delphi felt her cheeks burn.

'Delphi, you have done nothing but mutter about her for weeks. You've begged her for help in your sleep, for heaven's sake. Two weeks ago you asked me outright what I might do to get her here. It was Sonya this and Sonya that, as if you were a small child with no mind of your own.' Carl pulled the curtains apart and hot light slapped her face, and she turned from it, shielding her face with her forearm, grimacing. 'I can't cope with you any longer, Delphi. I can't finish my work. I can't do anything. I need her as much as you do. Perhaps she can do something with you. Anything would be better than this ...' He motioned around the room with one arm, its palm open. 'I must finish my book.'

'Why?' She hadn't meant to say it. Not really. 'I'm

sorry. I shouldn't say that. Of course . . .'

'Do you expect me to nurse you like an invalid for the rest of my life? I loved him too, Delphi, but he is dead, after all.' He started to leave, then stopped and turned back to her. 'Had it ever occurred to you, Delphi, that he was the first love that either of us ever had? Perhaps he should be the last. I shall go back to my work, and you should go to yours. It is far better if Sonya comes. You are her daughter. She will know what's to be done. I do not.' He pulled down his jacket, passing his hands over the lapels, pressing them flat. 'I have begun my work again, and I must see to my schedule.'

She watched him leave the room in his measured gait, small step to small step on the balls of his feet. He was right to have sent for Sonya. I want her, Delphi thought, not moving, staring up at the ceiling, feeling the new tears hot on her eyes. I want my mother.

'My life has at least made me a competent traveler,' Sonya said, brushing Delphi's cheek with a kiss. 'Look at the rest of them laden down with their luggage like coolies.'

'I have a car,' Delphi said, motioning to the waiting Mercedes. It was the first time she had been out of the villa since they had buried David. The whole world was topsy-turvy; nothing was more surprising than anything else. Of course Sonya should be there.

'Let your driver take my case, such as it is. May we walk a bit? Italian trains must be the worst I have ever been on. The ground is swimming under me, and I need to feel it firm again. Tell him to wait.' Sonya handed her case to the driver and grabbed Delphi's arm, leading her out of the station and down the street, leaning on her to steady herself.

Sonya's hair was lighter with its gray and pulled back into an uncompromising bun on the top of her head. Whatever slackness might be in her skin was held tightly against the beautiful bones of her face by the grasp of pins that held the bun. She was dressed in a thin cotton suit, fashionably pleated at the front and side of the skirt and carefully tailored to her rounded hips. 'I tell you there is nothing graceful about getting from one point to another.

Your father insisted I have a suite aboard the ship. In its way, it was worse than steerage. There are so many demands to privilege. All that dressing and undressing and dressing again and having to bother with all those anxious little stewards. The food was good. I have turned quite plump in the last ten days. Now all I wish to do is lie down in a cool room and drink lemonade. Well, now my legs are strong but I have a terrible thirst. Come, let us get back to the car and to the house.'

They said little else to one another until they were in the guest room at Carl's. The shutters were closed against the day's heat and the air was sweet with the perfume of the garden just outside. Delphi had asked for lemonade, and the girl quickly delivered it to them in a generous pitcher full of lemons and ice.

Sonya poured herself a glass and added nearly the entire container of sugar and then drank it all. She took off her clothes quickly and put on her dressing gown and sat on the edge of the bed. Taking out the pins from her hair, she shook it out and then lay down on the bed, arranging the pillows under her head and closed her eyes.

'He said you were more beautiful now than ever,' Delphi said. 'He was right.'

'Who? Tolchin?' Sonya opened her eyes and made a face. 'I suppose it is a compliment.'

'Of course it is.'

'Perhaps. Beauty means something quite different when everything is cracking and sliding. Well, I did not come here to speak about it at any rate. Your father can't imagine why you didn't send for him. I told him that mothers occasionally have a place in the lives of their daughters.' She closed her eyes again. 'Well, tell me now. I cannot wait any longer. And tell me all of it.'

Delphi recounted the story – the details, the defiance, the pain. The sound of her own voice made her ill with her loathing for herself. It filled her head as it filled the silence, drumming against the inside of her skull. Sonya listened, fanning herself or sipping lemonade, stretching an arm, shaking a hand. It was interminable, this story, awful, Delphi thought. 'I cannot work. I can do nothing but sit and stare out into the trees. I have no life left,

Sonya, no reason to eat, to sustain myself. I do not even weep anymore. Nothing will make those moments of his fall disappear . . .' Sonya looked up quickly and then looked away again. 'I even prayed, Sonya. Does everyone pray when they are powerless, when everyone else is powerless? To whom was I praying, I wonder. Certainly not to a God who could let my son die . . . who could let me kill what I so loved.' Delphi began to retch where she sat, and then she ran toward the bathroom, her retching uncontrollable.

She felt Sonya's hands behind her, holding her, putting a cool hand at her forehead. 'Sit down here. Come, sit.' Sonya pushed Delphi onto the top of the toilet. 'Let me wipe the perspiration.' She ran the water in the basin and wet the end of a towel and wiped her head and her neck. 'There. You can go back and lie down. It is better for you to lie down.'

Delphi looked at her blankly, but she stood and walked into the bedroom and collapsed onto the bed. 'It is so like a stage play. I can't remember why I called for you, Sonya.'

Sonya sat at the dressing table, her face resting in her hands. She was rubbing at her face, washing it with her dry hands. She dropped her hands from her cheeks. They were red and puffy although she had not cried. She seemed to be in some interminable dialogue with herself, and her expression changed as her thought changed. She frowned, her lips turning down at the corners. She pursed her lips. A twitch began in one cheek and stopped when she shook it away. Her eyebrows arched and then were leveled. Jolted by her own silence, she shrugged. Suddenly embarrassed, she sighed and waved toward Delphi. 'You must pay me no mind. Go on.'

'There is very little to tell. At first I thought of suicide, but I am too much of a coward. It made me seem more despicable to myself. It was such a bad thought, as bad as not being able to bring back my son . . . my David . . . my angel.' Her scream surprised her but not Sonya, who stood up and walked to her, her hands resolutely at her sides. 'What can you do, Sonya? What can you do to make me forget his smile or the way he yawned?' Tears poured down her face. She seemed not to notice them. She lay where she was, staring up at her mother. 'Did you bring magic charms, Sonya? Have you enchanted words? How will you do it? How? There is nothing left of me.'

'I will manage,' Sonya said, sitting on the few inches of bed between Delphi and the end of the mattress.

'I don't think so, Sonya.' There was no emotion in Delphi's voice, neither hope nor sorrow. 'I will never care for my life, and you cannot change that.'

'I will not leave here until I do.' Sonya sighed and brushed back a lock of her hair. 'I did not come on any fool's errand.'

The second day Sonya was there, they had started walking, the first time a mile or so to an abandoned church down their road. Sonya had picked flowers in the field and Delphi had leaned against a crumbling old stone wall and watched her. They walked there every day that week, little bouquets of flowers sprouting on every table in the house. The following week they walked a little farther, to the small café on the road beyond the church, where Sonya had a cup of coffee and Delphi watched. By the third week they had walked into the town, a forty-minute trip. They walked there early in the morning and then came back and had lunch, or Sonya did, Delphi still just picking at her food, removed, a step away from real life. In the afternoons they set out again. They walked like old people, holding arms and leaning on each other, Sonya talking about whatever came into her head, a running stream of her history, Russia, Tolchin, the boat that had brought her to America, and the boy husband, whatever had happened to him? The parties when Delphi was a child – did Delphi remember? Had she forgotten the costumes and the noise?

Sometimes Delphi would lose all the sense of Sonya's words and even Sonya's voice was foreign to her, but then she would find the sense again as if it were loose thread, and she would pull it through the fabric of Sonya's words to mend the tale. In small observations and facts that were as indisputable as the earth beneath their feet, Sonya gave Delphi back her life. Gradually, as an injured person might relearn the use of wounded limbs, Delphi relearned her motivation. Little by little it was clear to her that her talent was as inexplicable and immutable as the shape of her leg or the length of her spine, that despite her insistence that it could no longer exist, it had emerged, too huge for her to deny it, as apparent as the sun.

'It is in your nature,' Sonya said. 'It is very simple. There was never any choice at all. It is a fact of you. Since you did not kill yourself, you must live. And for you to live, Delphi, you must pass through the doors you have insisted upon opening. You must try to be the artist you think yourself able to be.'

Sonya had been in Siena for nearly three months. Although there had been no potions used, no spells cast, and no incantations sung or whispered in the dark of night, she had made magic. Delphi had recovered herself. She could not sleep through one night without tormenting dreams or anguished thoughts, but she could confront her days. They had substance again, purpose. Sonya gave her enough money to go to Paris for at least five months. The rest would be up to her. She had to begin again.

BOOK IV

1

Delphi had already been his Rachel at the Well for six hours, and now he insisted she lay naked on the couch, innocently seductive, her shoulders back on the pillows to allow her stomach to jut upward. Her nipples stiffened in the cold air, and goose flesh crawled up her thighs.

'Part your knees just a bit,' he commanded. 'Ah, more. A touch more. Yes. He stared at her. 'Good. Yes. Good. Don't . . . move.' His eyes were the same eyes as those of the bureaucrat Chaumière, running and brown, like tobacco stains on a white cloth. Delphi looked at Delbay and thought of Chaumière, of his treble chins and nervous hands. The sound of Chaumière's voice had been scratchy.

'So? So?' he had said as his nervous hands scuttled around his desk and over his papers.

'I have come for my *carte de séjours*. My resident permit.' She had stood at his desk because there was no chair. 'Here is my application.'

He had grabbed it and put it on top of his other papers. 'And how long will France have the honor of your residency?'

'Five years,' she had answered him, hoping then it would be less.

She took out twenty francs and held it toward him. He looked at it with distaste. She added another thirty francs. He picked up her application in his left hand and indicated with his right hand that he wanted more money. She added another five francs, then another ten. He nodded and held out his hand for it. After he pocketed the money, he withdrew a small calling card from the same pocket. 'My cousin is at the Ministère du Travail. You will also need a work permit. He can arrange one with no delay.'

He held the card close to his chest so that Delphi had to lean over his desk to take it. As she did, his free hand darted like a mottled spider to her breast. Without even thinking, she had smashed a closed fist on his forearm and made him grunt loudly. 'Filthy pig!' she had yelled. 'Keep you pig hands to yourself!' She had flung his cousin's card at him. 'I curse you and your cousin and his cousin besides. Now sign my card or I will report your behavior to your superior if it costs me a thousand francs!'

'American,' he had growled as he signed the card. 'American,' he repeated to her back as she left his office. She had had some spirit even two months before, she thought. Now she was ground into the mud.

'Lift your breasts.' Delbay's voice was hoarse and strained. 'Higher. Yes. There. Good.'

Delphi thought of the first day she had modeled for Luis. How easy it had been to sit for him, to be connected to him in that heat and that light, to listen to him drumming his foot on the floor, to listen to the touch of his brush on his canvas. It was nearly beyond endurance to sit for Marc Delbay. If it had not been the only job she could find in all her time in Paris, she would tell him now what she thought of his cretinous smears, of his singularly abominable approach to art. If only she could relieve the frustration she felt at being a part of anything he did by telling him what she thought of him and his academy training! Again she watched him grapple with his colors and she felt her hatred choke her. Yet Delbay sold every painting he made, and there were as many commissions piled on his desk as there were bird droppings on the huge sill outside his north window. She could get no one even to look at her work. No one.

She watched his hands. He wore a gold ring on his middle finger.

Delbay did not do preliminary drawings at all. He drew directly on the canvas with his charcoal and immediately painted his picture, making no attempt at even a cursory underpainting. Luis would have been apoplectic after thirty seconds in this studio. Luis. Luis. She could not stop thinking of him in this place.

God, she thought, make me stop thinking of him.

'Stop crying!' Delbay slammed his palette down on the ordered table near him, upsetting tubes of paint that rolled, like her tears, across its surface.

'I am not . . . crying.'

'Stop. Stop! *Stop!*' He kicked at the leg of the table but with hardly enough force to knock over a china plate.

'You have cried continuously for three days in a row. Unless you have lost a parent, there is no reason for it!' He folded his arms and strode back and forth between his easel and the window. He was by turns waspish and then annoyed and finally furious when he was interrupted, not unlike most men. What made his fits of temperament unbearable to her was his insistence on being regarded as a genius whose concentration was worth considerably more than anyone else's. When Delphi addressed him at all, he insisted she call him *maître*, when just to say the word made her wince. She watched him now, rubbing at his temples with his hands. 'I have just reached the point when I was committed to the drawing. Then you cried. I can't work under these conditions!' He looked at her, a terrible, injured expression on his face. 'I have obligations, many, many obligations. As, may I remind you, do you. Are you listening?'

'Yes.' She wiped her eyes with her free arm. He waited, exasperated. '*Maître,*' she added.

'Unless you are willing to control your emotional outbursts, I will find another model. You were the best *pensée* I have ever had, and certainly you are a fine Rachel. But I am now painting a naked woman, my *maja*, and if your nudity causes you pain, I will find someone to whom it is no burden.'

She nodded at him and turned away, unable to find a word that would leave her anger unexpressed. She watched the early evening light slide toward the Tour Saint Jacques. He was waiting for her to say something. She could hardly bear the humiliation of answering him. 'I am sorry. I will certainly . . . that is . . . tomorrow . . . *maître*, I am sorry.' She made herself look back at him as she said it. *Maître. Maître.* Luis. Marra. Marra. Even now, almost two years since she had left Florence, she saw him everywhere, felt his presence, especially there in Delbay's studio. It was Marra's face that haunted her continually, even more than the baby's.

'All right, Delphi. It is quite enough for one day. Get out, out.' He pointed to the door. 'And when you come

419

back tomorrow, come back as my model or not at all. Go, go!'

Outside, waiting for the bus, she did not look up at the zinc and slate and tile rooftops, did not notice the color of the stones beneath her feet or the curve of the street. Already, she thought, I have become a Parisian. Soon I will be as paralytic as the fishermen who line the banks of the Seine each day, my face lined with regrets and disappointments, thinking only of the food I will eat that night, the wine I will drink. The night before, she had fought an old bum for possession of a man's opera-length cape that both had claimed from a garbage pail in the XVIième Arrondissement. Because the rich of that quarter had a need to cast off nearly as great as their need to acquire, the place crawled with bums and the poor by midnight, all hunting for treasure. Her arms still ached from the old man's punches, and she had only won the cape because she had given him the high hat and the ivory pipe she had found the hour before. At least she would have a coat to wear that night when her father came to pick her up and take her to dinner. She was anxious to see him and yet so ashamed. She had spoken to no one for four months except to offer a bribe or stop some unbearable humiliation. Still, she would not let her father know anything was wrong; she could not bear his feeling sorry for her in the slightest. Hunching into her seat on the bus, she planned what she would wear and how she would greet him later that evening.

As she passed the ancient, wall-eyed concierge of her building, she shuddered involuntarily at the crone's familiar greeting, delivered in the worst whiskey-sotted voice, as loud and as resonant as Notre Dame's bells.

'Et voilà! La grande artiste de la cinquième étage!' The dreadful woman looked exactly like her counterparts had looked during the French Revolution, gray, cruel, and bloodthirsty.

The old hen's cackle followed Delphi up the stairs. 'Rot in your wine,' Delphi yelled back, fleeing from her.

She had been careful with the apple-green silk dress. Luis had bought it for her in Rome three years before because, he said, the color made her eyes into topaz and her skin into gold. Why had she never noticed the rip under the arm? She found the needle but could find no thread. She had used it all long before. She tried to pin the rip but the pins would not hold the silk and only tore it further. It was, at least, minute. Her father would not see it. She wished for ropes of pearls about her neck to detract from the wear of the collar, but she settled for a man's white-fringed scarf she had found in November tied to the banister of the Métro in Montparnasse. It looked heavy and awful on the green silk. She stared at herself in the badly lit mirror. Her face had lost the fullness of the quattrocento and now looked as angular and severe as an African mask. She lifted her arms up to fluff out her hair, and the dress ripped another inch. The knock on the door made her fairly leap out of her skin. She had wanted to meet him downstairs! She opened the door to face an impeccably dressed Gregory Tolchin. Certainly, it was a mark of his savoir-faire that he did not look the least bit horrified at her appearance. 'Oh, Papa!' She threw herself into his arms and held on to him as hard as she could so he could not look at her. His appraiser's eyes searching for value would find only defect.

'Dushka, Dushka,' he murmured, holding her close to him, patting her like a child. 'Hush, now. Hush.'

'My dress has torn. My dress . . .' She could not speak but only cried, her body full of spasms, her hands still clasped around her father's neck. He closed the door behind him and continued to hold her. Was he just now staring at the sad straw mattress on the iron bed? Did he see the poor cache of food on the sill, the stale loaf of bread on the table where it had been since the night before, when she was too tired to try to cut into it?

Finally, he managed to hold her away from him. 'Stop now,' he said quietly. Her lips trembled convulsively and she twitched like a corpse. 'Look at me, Dushka.' She raised her eyes to his. He was looking at her with such sweetness in his face that she cried again. 'Ah, Delphi, is it so serious?' He held her again for a moment and then half carried her to her bed, sitting her down, looking at the man's cape that lay across the end of the bed with a slightly quizzical expression.

'I got that from a garbage can last night,' she spluttered. 'It is quite hopeless, Papa. I can't . . . I . . . The truth is I am too tired. My dress is torn. It is all like the last months here. Everything is torn.' She covered her face with her hands and cried, 'I have no money, and I can't ask Sonya for money again. I know what it must have cost her to finance my trip here. Her heart betrays her again and again, and for what? I failed her, I failed in the worst possible way. All she asked is that I be independent, and what have I done? I've been dependent on one man after another, exactly what she warned me against! The only job I've managed to find is as a nude model for the worst painter in all of Paris!' She blew her nose in the handkerchief he gave her and pressed it against her eyes. 'I don't even make enough money to feed myself properly, and yet I'm lucky . . . I'm lucky I didn't have to take to the streets and be dependent on every man in France! Oh, Papa, I never thought the price of eggs and oranges could matter to a person, and it's all I think about.' She wadded the handkerchief now and blew into it again, shivering and shaking and full of shame.

He took off his jacket and wrapped her in it. 'Perhaps I should make a fire. It's very cold in here.'

'The newspaper is too damp. The flue doesn't close and it rains into the chimney and . . . oh, Papa, the only thing that even got me this far was that I remembered what you used to say about the French – that in France a bureaucrat would rather take a two-dollar bribe than be a minister, a concierge would rather have a three-dollar bribe than own her own building, and a wine steward would rather get a four-dollar tip than inherit the best vineyard in Burgundy. You were right, but how right you were! It took me so long to know it. When I first arrived the gendarmes woke me every night for a month to ask for my *carte de séjours* and to stare at my breasts until I gave them a few francs to go away. I was pawed and pinched by every man in Montparnasse. My God, Papa, men are the most cruel, the most greedy human beings on earth!' Remembering those few months, she threw herself face down across the bed and wept again. 'Do you think Picasso had any such trouble finding his room at the Bateau Lavoir when he came from Barcelona? Do you think men pinched his ass purple and then asked him for money?'

'How did you manage to get your *carte de séjours?*' His question was so direct and his voice so matter-of-fact that she turned to look at him.

'I gave the man at the immigration five dollars, the man at the Bureau du Travail ten dollars for my work permit, and to get this room I gave the concierge three. It was only because I finally remembered what you used to say. I am as thick as the walls of the *quai*, so it took me a long time to think of giving them all a few dollars to leave me alone. The gendarmes still come once a month.'

He stroked his beard with the thumb of his left hand. 'You are a nude model? Is that what you said?'

'It is not for lack of trying to find other work, but there is nothing here. Nothing. I waited in line to work as a chambermaid for hours and had to pay a franc for the privilege of being told the job was filled. I cannot even find work as a chambermaid! I was even refused a job because I was too tall. Can you imagine such a thing? A man in the florist shop just there' – she pointed toward the street – 'he advertised for a flower arranger, but when I applied he just kept saying I was too tall!' For some reason, that made her weep again, and it was only his continued silence at her outburst that finally stopped her tears. She pushed herself to a sitting position and looked at him, pulling his jacket more tightly around her. 'I know what you're thinking, that I'm no better than the other American women all over Paris full of glorious intent and no talent.'

He said nothing and continued to look down into the street. After a few moments, he walked to her bed and sat down beside her, unhurriedly lighting a cigarette with a thin lighter that flashed like a sun in the dimness as its flame leapt from it.

'And what makes you think I see you as a talentless American woman?' He inhaled the smoke less deeply than she remembered, letting it out more slowly. His eyes never left hers.

'I took my paintings to every gallery in Paris, and no one would even look at my work. No one. The gallery owners are just like the pimps. They see all women as whores. There are more rotten paintings in the galleries of this city than warts on a frog, but no one would even bother to look at my work because I am a woman and a whore.' He put the cigarette out on the sole of his shoe and then flicked it into the fireplace. Then he folded his arms and crossed his legs, stretching his upper body a moment before relaxing again. It was obvious he was not alarmed by anything she said. She might just as well have been reciting Jabberwocky.

'Do you paint here?'

'What?' She frowned at him.

'Do you have time to paint?'

She got up, her hands still holding his jacket, and walked back and forth in front of him. 'How can I paint? I have been the twelve muses and the four seasons in just six weeks for that abomination Delbay. I haven't the time to sleep and I can hardly find the strength to eat.'

'But you will tonight.' He smiled at her. 'I am stiil taking you to dinner.' He stood up and yawned as he looked at her. 'Now change the dress and we'll be off.'

'I cannot go, Papa. I am like a great ox. Please don't make me.'

'I think we have had enough self-pity for one evening, Delphi. Wouldn't you agree?' He walked to the lamp and lit it. It hardly gave enough light to outline his figure. 'Get dressed.'

'I said I have nothing—'

'Then you shall wear what you have.'

'No.'

'Yes. It is to be yes, Delphi. I take it this is your coat?' He leaned down and picked the cape off the floor, shaking it slightly. He removed his jacket from her shoulders and put the cape around her.

'How can I? You are dining at the most expensive restaurant in all France!' Her tone pleaded with him. 'How do you expect me to walk in the door? Please, Papa!'

'If you walk in with enough assurance, my darling, you will convince everyone there you are dressed in the latest style. We must hurry. We are already late.'

* * *

Across Paris at Le Canard Bleu, every appointment was so splendidly subdued, so unobtusively apparent. The crystal sconces graced the velvet-covered walls like fine jewelry. Early French and Dutch flower paintings hung about the carefully placed tables, with their splendid silver and china settings. Even at the front door, Delphi's head went light and her stomach queasy at the wave after wave of glorious odors, butter and vanilla waltzed with garlic and cognac.

In the anteroom, Tolchin handed Delphi's cape to the captain with the suggestion that it might be cleaned. He took it as if it were sable and informed the count that his party was waiting for him in the private dining room at the head of the stairs.

'Your party!' Delphi's mouth dropped open. 'Oh, how could you bring me here when you knew there would be other people! Papa, I refuse to go there. I refuse.' She swallowed again and again as if something stuck in her throat. 'Why didn't you tell me there would be other people!'

'As much as I don't wish to share you, they are at least a nice enough bunch for business associates. Besides, we shall have a bit of time together after the dinner. Come now.' He held out his hand toward her.

'Business associates! I know less about business than politics. My dress is torn and I can't remember my Russian!'

'They are not all Russians, and we speak French at table.' He looked at her sternly. Would she always be afraid of him? God, she was going to cry again!

'Please . . .' she asked in a tinny voice.

She knew it was no use pleading there in the hallway. It was quite clear that he would drag her up the thickly carpeted stairs if she did not acquiesce, so she took a deep breath and stepped ahead of him toward the stairway and then walked up into the room at the top. It was filled with flowers and firelight, and around the table in its center, men stood to greet their host and his daughter. The women remained seated, smiling up at them.

Her father introduced Delphi to three Russians, one of whom was a man as thin as a stick named Kelbinov and two of whom, Rachinsky and Dubrov, were plump and as pink as piglets; a Swiss named Mann whose head was pointed under a shredding of orange hairs; a Frenchman named Gilbert Bachoux who looked displeased; his wife, Thérèse-Hélène, who was overdressed in a flounced white satin gown; two Italian women, one Barbara di Monti who was darkly beautiful and the other, Graziella Danielli, who was as young as Delphi and exquisitely blond. Delphi sat between Kelbinov and Rachinsky, feeling as tattered and unkempt as any street urchin. Her discomfort was not lessened by her first glass of wine, nor her second. The fish course, however, took her mind off herself.

Her belly was shrunk from lack of food, and she knew she should be less assertive with her fork, but she could not resist eating it all. She even used a piece of bread to scrape the remaining Nantua sauce from under the rim of the plate.

'Fish are the triumph of French cuisine,' the Swiss announced. No one paid the slightest attention to him. Boris Kelbinov started to rave to her about his new apartment on the Quai d'Orsay, which he had just let from a French baron and was, he said proudly, full of important French furniture, fine enough for the czar. Rachinsky, the eldest of the Russians and the fattest, ate his bread and Kelbinov's after buttering each of the rolls lavishly with his fish knife. With his mouth quite full, Rachinsky asked the French banker, Bachoux, about the rates of exchange between the Swiss and Russian banks. Bachoux, still eating his fish, suggested he ask Mann, the Swiss. The Italian blonde, Graziella, congratulated Tolchin on the advantageous deal he had made in Milan that past month, and the wife of the banker, Thérèse-Hélène, and Delphi turned their attention to their wine while Rachinsky finished the fish left on Barbara di Monti's plate almost as quickly as he had eaten his own.

When Dubrov started to talk to Delphi about how Sonya had looked each week among the crowds at the Maryinsky, her eyes exactly star sapphires, her mouth as ruby-colored as her hair, Delphi lost all sense of reality. She could only think it was her own isolation all those months that made everything going on around her appear to be comic. '. . . Your mother was of the most delicate beauty, so fine, so exquisite, like Lalique . . .' Dubrov droned on describing someone so unlike Sonya that Delphi could not even force herself to listen.

The lamb was served, pink under a filmy sauce of champagne and mustard; Barbara di Monti made a toast to Bachoux and French excess. The Swiss proposed that everyone purchase land in the south of France before the Germans bought it all. Rachinsky attacked Mann, accusing him of charging extremely high interest rates on the Russian loan, and Graziella Danielli screamed that she was sick of Russian grievances, at which moment everyone including the Russians banged fists on the tabletop, shouting in agreement.

Barbara di Monti told a story of how her grandfather tried to get an Italian musician to write a song as grand as the *Marseillaise*, and then she laughed, her laughter as light as a balloon sailing up and up toward the ceiling.

'Everyone wants a song like the *Marseillaise*. It is the best thing about France,' Dubrov intoned.

'He is right, Gilbert,' Thérèse-Hélène said to her husband. 'We French are despicable, and we' – she giggled helplessly – 'are French.'

'The only thing worse than the French are the Poles,' the Swiss said.

'Or the Swiss,' mumbled Rachinsky.

Delphi experienced a bit of *mal de mer*, but she continued to eat the lamb and drink her wine. They are all useless, she thought, they are all foolish. None of them will ever do anything that matters. They are exactly like the people who came to West Fourth Street to hear the crazy anarchists play Gypsy music. At least I have my work. At least I can make something that might be important.

Kelbinov began to cry and then to sob. 'What is the matter now, Boris?' Rachinsky asked, his mouth chewing his meat or someone else's.

'I have blood on my hands.'

'So do I. So what?'

Delphi looked at her plate. She did not know where else to look. Was she as drunk as they? Her hands were bloody too. Kelbinov stopped crying and poked her. '"So what," he tells me. "So what!" Did you hear him?' He hit Rachinsky in the upper arm. 'He does not have bad dreams. I am visited by evil spirits every night.'

'Oh, tell me what yours look like, Boris,' Graziella called to him. 'My evil spirits are always in the latest fashion and very handsome.'

'It is not a joke.' Kelbinov's face was white. 'It is terrible.'

'Boris Alexandreivitch.' Tolchin's lowered voice broke through the banging of utensils and the bits of conversation. Everyone looked at him as he raised his glass, revolving it slowly around the table, his eyes moving from one face to the next. 'There is no one who is not bloodied by his life. To live is bloody business. I drink to you all.' He downed the wine in his glass and then laughed. Delphi peered at him suspiciously. Was his toast for her? His face came and went behind her winy exhaustion. She felt cool air come in through the rent in her dress to tickle her underarm. Did anyone notice the dress was torn? Kelbinov had stopped sobbing and was now taking comfort from Thérèse-Hélène, whose neckline ruffles were nearly in Rachinsky's plate as she leaned across him. Was her father as silly as they all seemed to be? Delphi could never tell. His eyes were always masking his feelings. Salad was put in front of her and she ate some, tasting dill. How could there be dill in winter? Her mother had once told her that while the peasants starved, the Russian aristocracy ate fresh vegetables and herbs all year long because it was specially grown for them under glass. These people were as foolish as any Sonya had ever told her about. Her plate seemed at least two feet from her fork suddenly. Would she stab Kelbinov's arm instead? Now her father's eyes were as big as rabbit holes. Sonya always said he was a magician with his eyes. They seemed to be swallowing her up.

'Oh, look!' Barbara di Monti's voice was full of rapture. 'They are more beautiful than diamonds!' She was pointing to the desserts stacked on the wagon that rolled toward them slowly with the pomp of a coronation carriage. Delphi knew she was getting ill and jumped up from her place and ran toward the wagon, her hand clamped over her mouth. The waiter in his white, gold-braided jacket hissed the directions to the lady's room as she ran past him. Were women always sick at Le Canard Bleu? she wondered. Finally safe inside the room with the toilet, she pressed her head against the cool tile wall. At first she thought she might faint, but the roiling inside her had subsided and she felt better. Alone, she thought, I am fine alone. I am not good with other people. Life without anything in it is useless. It is better to have work that matters than anything else.

There was a quick knock at the door and then Barbara di Monti came in and, after closing the door, leaned against it to look at Delphi. 'Your father said he thought you would be sick.'

'I am not used to such rich food.'

'He said you were used to no food at all.'

Barbara di Monti took a breath and wrinkled her long, fine nose in disgust. 'My God, the French are filthy. What a terrible stink! Are you better?' She looked at the greenish water dripping from the tap into the basin. Delphi nodded. Barbara di Monti's eyebrows were darker than her hair, which she wore wrapped around her head like a turban. A huge hibiscus was dying behind her ear. Delphi wondered if her father slept with this woman. The question must have been plain on her face because Barbara di Monti answered it in her next breath. 'Your father and my husband do some business together. Your father sometimes stays with us at our villa in Maggiore in the summer. You must come with him this year. It is very restful at the lake.' She looked at herself in the mirror above the basin, opening her mouth, flicking her tongue across her teeth to clean them and then closing her mouth again. She touched a corner of one eye with the tip of her forefinger and then, lifting her eyebrows, leaned closer to the mirror to look deeply into her own eyes. 'Your father said you would be trying to escape through the window. He said to tell you if you wished to leave, his chauffeur will gladly see you home.' Barbara di Monti closed her eyes and opened them and looked at herself again. Obviously satisfied, she turned her attention back to Delphi. 'So?' she said, forcing a smile.

'My father means for me to go back upstairs and rejoin the dinner party.'

'No, no. I am sure not. He is very straightforward. He said you must do what suits you.' Delphi shook her head. 'Really, my dear, you are mistaken. I am certain he meant what he told me.'

Delphi stood up, surprised that her legs felt substantially stronger under her. She smoothed her skirt down where it had clutched at her knees and reached up to run her fingers through her hair.

'Oh, my dear, Delphi, you have ripped your dress!'

'Have I?' Delphi slowly discovered the tear under her arm. 'Oh, my.' Her father had been right. If there were enough assurance, no one would see the defects, the rips and tears.

'Here, here, you must have my shawl.' Barbara di Monti took off her dark green wool shawl and put it around Delphi's shoulders. 'I shall retrieve it later from your father. Yes, that is better.' She stepped back and looked Delphi over. 'You might put some color into your cheeks. You are very pale. Here, I have some rouge.' She opened her bag again and took out a hand-painted porcelain rouge pot. Delphi put a finger in it, took out a bit of color, and worked it into her cheeks, leaving a little more than was necessary.

When he rose from his place at the table, Delphi could see that her father was pleased by her return, and there was just the slightest arch in his eyebrows and smile on his face as he noticed her shawl. When the men were seated again, Tolchin proposed a toast to all the women at the table, his eyes full of private amusement.

In the car, she watched the city flash by them. It looked beautiful – its magnificent façades, its wide boulevards, its ribbon river tying it to itself. 'Would you have been terribly disappointed if I had left?'

He was settled comfortably into the seat, his profile flattened by the light of the city on one side and the dark on the other. 'You would have left if you were desperate enough.' He lit a cigarette, this time with a match, and opened the window a little. His smoke drifted outside into the cool, clean air. 'I watched you this evening. You are still too proud to be desperate.'

'I don't know, Papa. There are moments when I am confused. I believe, exactly like Carl, that art is the most important thing in life. But I wonder if my hands should be bloody when I serve no one but myself.'

'Who is to say that?' He smiled. 'Don't be so serious. At best, life is ridiculous. One moment does not proceed from the last. One day is quite unlike another. Life is accidental in the extreme.'

'Perhaps there are some safe lives.'

'None. Most people live in disorder and die for nothing. Those who are afraid of death fear God and believe in Him. Those who love life love God and don't need Him.' Tolchin yawned and put out his cigarette. 'It makes no sense for you to live in Paris if you don't paint. What do you propose to do?'

'To keep looking for a job that allows me time to paint. I told you, I look everywhere. *Il n'existe pas.* I am quite determined, so don't talk to me about going home.'

He put his hand in his inside pocket and took out a folded piece of paper. Holding it between his thumb and forefinger, he presented it to her. 'Gilot will give you work. Look him up.'

Pieces of the Left Bank flashed by her. Tiny squares, narrow streets, large buildings, flowerpots. The piece of paper fluttered down from her shoulder onto her lap. Delphi picked it up and opened it. It was too dark to make out the writing. The car turned into a narrow street, and its front tire caught the edge of the curb and she fell backward against her father. 'What does it say?' she asked, smiling up at him.

'It says Dumas et Fils. It is a bakery in the rue Moufretard and there is neither a Dumas nor a Fils but a Jacques Gilot there, and he will give you a job because he is my friend and you are my daughter. When you are very poor, it is good to work in a bakery. You can eat what you can steal.'

'What do you think Sonya would say to my working in a bakery again? Did you know I once made magnificent

roses in a bakery? They were the envy of Hudson Street.'
She stayed in his lap, looking up at him. The aftertaste of
the *soufflé citron* was sweet in her mouth, and the smell of
leather was sharp and pleasant. She put the folded paper
into her slip and felt it rub against her skin as the car
bounced on the stones. 'How is Sonya, Papa? Why doesn't
she come with you to Europe? She never comes.'

Another automobile passed them and its light swept
through the car, catching the corner of his face, the high
Tatar cheek, the jawline, his shoulder, before it crossed
over and was gone. 'Your mother is afraid that she will see
her brother Bruno in her hotel lobby. In fact, he is easy to
avoid, as he seldom leaves Moscow. Bruno is high up in
Stalin's government, and Sonya believes Stalin is worse
than the czar and has corrupted her brother. She hears
things.'

'She used to talk about him, about when they were
children together. She loved him so much. Do you ever see
him? Do you know him now?'

'Yes.'

'And has Stalin corrupted him?'

'Your uncle Bruno was corrupted long before he found
Stalin. He wanted a cause, but he settled for a leader. It
makes him a very dangerous man.'

'Poor Sonya.' The car turned again and then again.
Seeing only the tops of the buildings, she knew the Dome,
the Select, the Blonde Vache, the café where she ate her
fifteen-franc dinners. How quickly the geography of
Montparnasse had slid into her. It was becoming as
familiar to her as the olive groves at Casamarra. 'Oh, God,
Papa!' She sat up. 'What if your friend Gilot wants to
poke me or pinch my ass?'

He laughed softly for a moment, putting his head back
against the seat, looking up at the felt-covered roof of the
car. 'Let him. We had a saying in the corps that a
Frenchman without an index finger had a virgin for a wife.
I cannot tell you what we said about the English and the
Italians. You are my daughter, after all.'

How good it felt to laugh again! How marvelous it
would be to work. 'I can't wait to tell Marc Delbay what I
think of his atrocities and his technique. Imagine' – her

eyes narrowed – 'that despicable man made me call him *maître*.' She swiveled around to face him. 'Papa, thank you for tonight. Thank you. At last I can begin to do my work.' The car slowed, and he glanced out the window for a moment and then back at her. 'There is an odd expression on your face.' She leaned toward him, her eyes searching his. 'What is it?' The car stopped and there was suddenly no sound but their breathing. 'Papa?'

'It is really nothing,' he answered very quietly, 'only that your mother is quite right. You and I are very much alike.' He did not wait for the chauffeur to walk around the car but opened the door himself and stepped out to hold it open for Delphi. He seemed removed and strangely formal as he kissed her on each cheek and lightly dropped his hands from her sides. 'So, *bon soir, grande artiste de la cinquième étage*. Look after yourself,' he said, ducking quickly back into the car and closing the door.

The Daimler started again and slowly moved away from the curb to fill the street. In seconds it had rounded the corner and disappeared. At first she felt alone and then, suddenly, very cold. She had forgotten to give him Barbara di Monti's shawl. It didn't matter. She stood where he had left her, staring at the turn the car had taken. Her cape smelled of naphtha. The management of the restaurant had indeed cleaned it for the count's daughter. Was she like him? He had never once betrayed himself the way Sonya betrayed herself. He was exactly the same, even his unpredictability was the same. If I am enough like him, she thought, I will get past this and more. I will live a man's life. She smiled to herself as she walked toward the door of her building. Not even the ugly words of the concierge could upset her now. I will be what I want and what Sonya wants, she thought, throwing the cape around her like Napoleon. Tomorrow she would find Gilot and get her job, and then she would tell Marc Delbay exactly what she thought of his bathroom art. And then – she turned the bell with all her force so that it rang for a long time – then she would begin to paint again.

2

February 15, 1930
Dear Delphi,

Your father tells me he does not like the life you are living in Paris. He says you work too hard, you look awful, you have no friends, and your mind is on nothing but your work. I hope so. All your symptoms sound like the illness of dedication and accomplishment. Brava.

Your mother,
Sonya

April 9, 1930
Dear Sonya,

Gros Gilot, the owner of the bakery where Papa got me my job is a huge man, always chewing on pastry. He shakes his head at me and wonders aloud why Tolchin makes me work so hard, muttering that he has heard Papa is a rich man now. The other day he told me that Papa, when he was young, could 'piss out the fires of hell,' whatever that means. I thought it would make you laugh.

The work in the bakery is mindless enough to let me save my concentration for my painting, and my painting is good now, very good and fast. Paris is flowing over with women pretending they are artists, pretending they are poor, pretending they work. I do not pretend. I have exactly a man's life except if I were actually a man I might be obliged to have many mistresses and drink too much, so I have the best of a man's life.

Thank you for the raincoat, umbrella, galoshes, and the pamphlet on pantheism. Yes, I promise to read it and I promise your generosity will not be in vain.

You ask if I have any personal involvements. In truth, I have been a tree's lover for nearly two months now, a great elm tree in the Bois. I've already done two oils and six watercolors of it. I know your Sigmund Freud would probably have something to say about that choice and suggest that I choose church spires to paint next, but his words are just words to me, either obvious thoughts or piles of horsefeathers. Forgive me, Sonya, I don't believe that human behavior can be reduced to absolutes, and I still wonder why so many people gobble all that stuff up. I fear you are wrinkling your forehead and sighing loudly at my stupidity. Just tell yourself that I will come round someday. I'm dining with Carl Borach tonight. Between Carl and Papa, I have gotten to sample the best of France's cuisine. Don't tell either one of them – I prefer Italian food. What it lacks in artifice and serenity, it makes up in lustiness! (Would Freud call me sexually repressed? Of course!)

Carl agrees with me that it is not always a sign of success to sell one's work – witness the rotten paintings all over this city. However, both he and I know it is not a mark of success to remain unsold. I have not given up hope. I still try for a gallery.

The old drunk who was the concierge died last week, and this morning the landlord, Monsieur Breuil, a man who has small pebbles for eyes and the bank of France for a heart, offered me the concierge's apartment in exchange for night work plus the rent I pay for this forlorn little cubicle. That way I shall have two rooms and be able to sleep away from the stink of the turpentine and oil. Now I can do much bigger work, huge, as befits the tree that is my subject.

Tomorrow I will take my work around again. I fear I am no good at selling. I get too angry when the men look me over like a piece of meat. Spring is certainly here, but I still don't care for Paris any more than I do in winter. Again, thank you. You are very good to me.

Love,
Delphi

*   *   *

That night, she drew a section of the bakery – the stacked pans, the pastry bags and their intricate flutes, trays holding rows of madeleines, éclairs, erupting with pastry

435

cream. She heard the envelope slide under her door but she went on working, trying to finish what she was doing so she would not lose the thought. When she did stand up to stretch, she remembered the sound and looked down by the door. Luis Marra's bold writing was clearly visible even in the poor light at the end of the room. She could not breathe. How could he know where she was? She began to breathe again, now too rapidly. Was he there? Had he been there? She stared at the envelope. It was not an apparition. She bent to pick it up, but then, instead, she covered it with her foot, pressing down with all her weight to drive it through the floorboards. Her baby was dead, and any thought of his father must be dead, too, she thought, terrified now.

Hesitating at first, but then with sudden certainty, she picked up the envelope and tore it over and over again and threw the pieces into the small fire in the stove. Still, turned her back as the flames gobbled at the pieces. She could not watch. Why did he write to her when she had almost stopped thinking of him? Why did he write now, just as she was nearly able to get through the night without thoughts of the baby? His letter could have been nothing more than an invitation to hell. Nothing she could do could exorcise her thoughts of him. She walked to the cupboard and poured herself a tall glass of wine. Let them come, then, she thought, drinking down the wine. I cannot stop these thoughts of Marra tonight. And so they came, one after the other, until finally her exhaustion extinguished them.

The sound of the bell was an assault. Delphi looked quickly at her clock. It was two A.M. She had let in the fifth-floor Marriots at midnight and Monsieur Gilbert an hour before that. She hadn't thought there would be anyone else that evening.

The bell rang again and Delphi stumbled up, smoothing back her hair and grabbing the green woolen shawl that lay draped over her armchair. Tolchin had given her the Louis XIV chair so he would have a place to sit in comfort when he came, and its yellow and red damask splendor looked as awkward as a grand dowager in Montmartre.

Again the bell. She opened the door to her room, walked to the front and began struggling with the lock on the entrance door. Still, the landlord had not fixed it. 'But who is it?' she called, jiggling the lock.

'Monsieur Chasson.'

'Who?'

'Chasson. Chasson. Hurry.'

Good heavens, Chasson, of course! The landlord had told her that the rooms on the entire third floor had been let, and that he would be arriving, but at this hour? How could anyone expect to move in the middle of the night?

The impatient male voice was deep and imperious, used to giving orders. Delphi finally yanked open the door, the night air making her shiver despite the heat of her anger. She squinted up at him, focusing and refocusing her eyes in the hard glare from the naked bulb above their heads. He was too tall for a Frenchman, too beautiful to be a man. His face was exactly that of a Flemish angel, cheeks rosy as plums, the most sensual mouth bedded in a dimpled chin, a perfect nose, and eyes the color of the dark, clear winter sky. Perhaps she was still asleep.

'Are you the porter?' he asked. His evening cape whipped back into the blackness, showing a red satin lining.

'The concierge,' she replied.

'There is no man here?' He emphasized the word *man*.

'Why do you need one?'

'See there.' He pointed behind him at the car. 'I have all my stuff - my trunks, suitcases. My photographic equipment is very valuable. Who will carry it in?'

'You will,' she answered him, her annoyance having returned in full measure.

'But I need help. I need a man.'

'Then we will,' she said, walking toward the open car, the back of which was jammed with suitcases and trunks as well as boxes of cameras and lights and stacks of plates. 'What an absurd hour to arrive,' she muttered. 'You couldn't wait until morning?'

Just as they reached the car, a mound of fur in the front seat moved its two furry arms over the top of the seat, and a head inside a fur hood rested its chin in gloved hands.

437

'Hurry, darling, I'm freezing.' Large eyes heavily penciled and colored stared at Delphi. A red, almost lacquered mouth let out a pencil-thin stream of blue smoke, causing the fur around it to shudder. How ornamental she was Delphi thought, her nose hardly large enough to stuff an egg, her cigarette glowing like a welcoming beacon. Delphi shifted uncomfortably. She was annoyed at the girl's presence. She started to lift out the smaller leather cases on the top of the rear seat.

'The one with the straps is too heavy. Let me take it.' He reached across her and lifted the case with one hand. 'Take that one there, the green, and mind, be careful. It has plates in it.'

For over a full hour, he told her how and why she should take what and exactly where she should put it. Then he began barking orders at her as they carried the trunks from the street. He told her when to turn to her left and then when to turn right, when to straighten, when to lift, staring at her the entire time as if it were his prerogative.

At three-fifteen he suddenly stopped and studied her for a moment. 'You stay here,' he said, 'and hold the door for me. I'll manage the rest.' He continued looking at her, casually stretching himself like a tomcat.

'No one is the Colossus of Rhodes at this hour, not even you,' she snapped at him.

'You are in my way now. You are dropping your end so that the load is nearly mine anyway. You're very strong for a woman, but I'm afraid not as strong as a man. Excuse me now.' He walked toward the stairs and carried the last two suitcases up the three flights of steps by himself. She followed him, and he asked her for the key to the flat, locked the door, thanked her for her help, and left her at the top of the stairs while he ran down them to his car. He wasn't even going to stay the night in the room. He was only moving in his belongings in the middle of the night because it suited him to do that.

Delphi walked down the stairs slowly. Her legs had gone quite numb. Thank God for Sunday; she could sleep the next day. Damn him, he had left the front door wide open. She closed it quickly, but not quickly enough to miss the sight of his car pulling away down the street, the round fur head of the girl on his shoulder. He was too handsome, she thought. Worse, he was already so conceited and demanding for one so young. He was far too self-assured – like Luis, she thought. Oh, *merde*, would thoughts of that man never leave her? She walked back to her rooms. She had left her door open when she had answered Chasson's ring, and the cold air had filled up her flat so that now she was frozen. She wrapped a heavy wool blanket around her and curled up, her legs pressed tight against her for warmth. The fire had gone out, and she was too tired to light the stove. Perhaps Sonya's blanket would keep her warm enough after all.

The bell. No. Yes. She couldn't believe it. She had been on the tip of sleep. Who could it be?

'Chasson,' he answered when asked. She would kill him. She shook with anger as she opened the door. 'I owe you an apology, and I have brought it and some soup and bread. Come.' He handed her the large silver pot that had been at his feet and, picking up the rest of his packages, marched ahead of her down the hall, stopping by her door. 'This is your room, right? You smell of oils and it smells of oils. You are a painter and work at night answering the door. See? I know your whole history.' She frowned. 'I suppose you thought that no one could smell the oil, right? Well, I will tell you one thing, two things, about myself.' He shifted the things under his arms and rolled up onto the balls of his feet, then back down again, then up, like a yo-yo. Delphi watched him grow and shrink, his golden curls bobbing in front of her. When he smiled, he puffed up like a parakeet. He was smiling now.

'Two things,' he continued, 'about me. One, I am a great photographer. Two, I have a brilliant nose. Nothing fools my nose. Your face is wonderful, by the way. You move well, too. I must photograph you. Come, the soup will get cold.' He motioned her into her room as if it were his, marching ahead of her. 'Come, come, where is the lamp in here? I can't see a thing. Ah, here is one.' He turned the switch on the narrow-necked brass student's lamp that stood on the table next to the door. A dim light came on.

'My God, what jumble! There is no room to walk in here with that bed in the middle of everything. Ah, I see, the other room is only for painting, is that it?' Delphi nodded. 'But it is so cramped in here and so cold. How can you live?' Delphi shrugged.

The room had been small to begin with, already overpowered by its ancient cookstove, the large vat of a sink, a fussily carved armoire with doors sagging from years of dampness and overuse, and a heavy pannier daily pulling plaster from the wall, so that now it barely hung where it was. Still, Delphi had shoved the bed into that room also, to enable herself to hear the night bell more easily. Seeing immediately that there was no hope of harmony or comfort in such a space, she reasoned she could move in all the furniture from the other room and at least have an adequate studio. She had done just that, managing to pull out the huge marble-topped sideboard festooned with carvings of marsh grasses and dead birds, but she had been forced to abandon it just to the right of the studio door, where it remained to bisect what little space there was left. She had once attempted to soften the bed's bulk with a paisley shawl and a fur throw found at the flea market, but at the moment they were balled together at the foot of the bed, looking as ornamental as a wounded beast from a German fairy tale. But it was neither the disarray nor the absurd amount of furniture that made the room so preposterous. It was Tolchin's chair. There, in its ancient aristocratic aloofness by the front door, it was so sublimely elegant that its mere presence was severe censure to the disorder around it. Delphi felt the urge to laugh as she followed Chasson's gaze about the room to the chair.

'What a wonderful chair,' he said with a tone of reverence. 'What a magnificent chair.'

'You are right,' she intoned soberly, 'it is a wonderful chair.'

'I must photograph you immediately in this chair.'

'You must.' She sat primly down trying still to restrain her laughter, but it sputtered out to become a whoop of sound. She couldn't help herself. He amused her, this martinet with a rogue's smile on his angelic face.

'First we will make the photograph and then we will eat the soup. And drink the wine. I brought wine. Not bad either.' He removed the china globe from the lamp by the bed, lit it, and dragged it closer to her. He then took a camera from its leather case and fiddled with the front of it, making adjustments before he held it to his eye. He put it down once more, lit a candle quickly, and put the candle at her feet.

'But the soup is getting cold,' she said, watching him with fascination.

'Then sit still. The quicker I make this photograph, the sooner we will have the soup. I don't know . . .' He circled her, looking at her through the lens. 'Perhaps . . . well, we shall see.' Suddenly he stopped for a moment and looked straight at her. 'My name is Jules Chasson, by the way. And yours?'

'Delphi Stern.'

'Delphi Stern.' He looked through his lens as he repeated her name. 'You have a most extraordinary face. It will be fantastic, this picture.' He snapped the button and put the camera down.

'Only once?'

'Of course only once. My eye is right on the button.' He hurried to the sink and retrieved two bowls and spoons, wiping them efficiently with the clean towel she kept folded across the back of the nearest chair. Expertly, he poured out the soup, sniffing it with obvious pleasure. 'Excellent soup, excellent. From the Café Pinchot. Do you know it?' He handed her the bowl. 'Ah, I wish we had champagne, you and I.'

'But what have we to celebrate?'

'Your face, Delphi Stern. Yes. Your face and my camera. I think they are in love.'

3

Jules Chasson and the summer came into her life at once. She could not tell which one disturbed her more. She found the greenness of the full flowering trees that lined every boulevard as distracting as Jules and his omnipresent camera. The hot thunderclouds that swept in from the south each afternoon were no more threatening than Jules himself, demanding that she come with him to a restaurant or an exhibition, or pose for him immediately before the sun changed or a cloud moved or it started to rain. Like summer, Jules Chasson was full of demands, but she was sure, like summer, he would pass.

'For me, it was the camera right away. A friend had one and let me use it and da-dum! I found my métier. I could never study anyway since my mind drifts like a river. I cannot paint. I cannot sing. I cannot work. I could never arrive someplace each morning exactly at eight. I am too frightened to be an actor or a thief, so I found the camera! And I am so lucky. My Leica is a new tool; everything that I do is new. I am much more an inventor than your Picasso. You see, men have barely used cameras before, so I chart unexplored territory. I am the right man in the right time – how many people say that? The camera and I were born together. Can't you understand my excitement? I am perfect with a camera in my hands.' Jules danced around his apartment as he photographed her seated on an intricately carved and tufted velvet sofa that had belonged to his great-grandmother. He insisted he was descended from a long titled line. Delphi rubbed the soft fabric and stared past him out his window. How bright the sun was that day as it hit the green gables of the buildings across the way. 'Stop squinting, Delphi!'

'I still do not understand the art of the camera.' she said, yawning.

'But you admit it is an art!' His head came up quickly and he looked gleeful.

'A mischosen word,' she said.

'Come, Delphi, look at this. I have just finished it.' He picked up the top one of a stack of grainy black and white pictures that lay on the oak table by his side and handed it across to her. 'I dare you to say it is not art.' Delphi looked at it closely.

'But that's my tree! My elm. You know it's my tree. I have fourteen paintings and watercolors of it!'

'Exactly! But now, at last, you can see the perfection of it. See the light here and how it falls on the branches and the bench. It is exactly the feeling . . . exactly the strength . . . it is exactly it! I have even managed the rain.'

She looked at him in disgust. 'Perhaps you can manage it again. I hear things are quite dry in the country.' She paused. 'Stay away from my tree, Jules.'

'Your tree? Who would ever know which tree was yours? I spit on all your emotional interpretations. Such an ego! I would rather see God's objects than your emotions.'

'It is the artist who makes art!' she countered.

'It is God who makes the artist,' he answered.

She narrowed her eyes and a small smile formed on her lips. 'I had resisted friendship with everyone in Paris, Jules. It was a mistake not to resist it with you.'

'You could not help yourself.' He was staring at her, his eyes brazen, a great smile on his lips. 'Now bite the apple there. One more time.'

'Enough! I must work myself!' She stood up angrily. 'First you take my tree and then my time. I don't know which is worse.'

'Here, look, in the newspaper. Here.' He folded back the paper and handed it to her. It was a photograph of her in the red chair. 'It is the one I took the first night, remember?'

'You never told me I would be in the newspaper.'

'Indeed I did!' He looked at her in surprise. 'You don't remember? I told you the day you let me photograph you in your studio. You really don't remember?'

'No.'

'But I asked you then if you would agree to my selling pictures of you . . . you *must* remember! I even told you what I would pay you if I sold one. Surely you can't have forgotten that, you who think about nothing but money?'

'Well, I did forget it. Worse, much worse, I never heard you say it. That is why I simply can't have anyone watching me work. I don't know what I'm saying or doing.' She frowned and shook her head. 'I don't like it, but there's nothing to do about it.' She looked straight at him. 'How much did you tell me I would make?'

'Two hundred francs.'

'But that is as much as I make at the patisserie in a week.'

'And that is why I thought you would remember!'

'Are you joking?' She looked at him suspiciously.

'About the two hundred francs? No. I told you, Delphi Stern, that I am successful. Why didn't you believe me?'

'Will you sell more?'

'Probably.'

'Oh, my God. I am so excited!'

'I also told you you would be excited.' He lay himself on his back below her. 'Now, pick up the apple and bite it.' She picked up the green apple and bit it. The magnesium glowed, popping light. 'Accomplished!' he announced, sitting up.

'For two hundred francs I will eat as many apples as you like,' she said, 'as often as you like. I have a very strong stomach.' She turned her head to give him a more elegant profile, to show him the full length of her neck, the way her hair framed it like a dark border running onto her shoulders and across her breasts.

'Delphi Stern, you are a fox. I thought you had to work!'

She looked at him seriously for a moment. 'Maybe you will be lucky for me, Jules. Maybe that is why I like you so much.'

'Don't move, don't move, it's perfect. For this picture, I may even get more than two hundred francs.'

'Hurry.'

'You are all soft today, something very soft. I am discovering and I am exploring!' he called to her, setting his other camera at an even lower angle and kneeling on the floor.

'*Farceur!*' She could not help but smile at his immeasurable joy in his work, so different from her own dark moods.

'One day, Delphi Stern, you will take me seriously. I risk as much as you for my art.' Again he lay on his back below her. 'Pick up the apple and bite again.' She smiled and did as she was told.

In truth, Jules's work had reached her. Because of it, she began experimenting with a new style that excited her. She used her brush as he did his camera, editorially and nonobjectively. Familiar objects and scenes were at once new with such an eye. Suddenly they were as mysterious or hostile, as serene or horrible, as the unposed human face, and she searched for other essences in the things around her and began to find them.

She finished the painting that was her best work so far, a painting of the cesspool cleaners at night. In the background, the buildings were very tall and narrow, blackened, bereft, with no sign of life. Giant heavy horses were to the front, pulling the crazy cleaning machine with its tubes and smoke and brass hoses and knobs as if it were the weight of the world behind them. And so it was, she thought, or rather, the weight of a demiworld. The street light was a full moon, their only sun, fighting its battle against the darkness, too, as did the figures of the men in the foreground. When Delphi looked at it, she could smell the human excrement. It was her hell she had painted in that canvas.

When Jules sold more photographs of her, she gave up her job at the bakery and devoted herself entirely to her new perception. She worked quickly and intensely, making one canvas after another. She allowed herself to be interrupted only by Jules and his infernal camera. How she began to hate it!

In the Bois in November he photographed her surrounded by children. She wore her great black cape, a black suit, and a black wool cloche. She was monastic in her severity as the children played around her everywhere, clamoring, shoving, giggling, and singing.

'These will be wonderful shots.' He was putting away his equipment. She was chilled from sitting for so many hours. She stood up stiffly and stretched, watching him.

Even in late autumn, he was full of summer, his energy and enthusiasm as bountiful as ever. She crossed her arms and pressed them to her chest, trying to get warm, still looking at him. He must certainly be the handsomest man I have ever seen, she thought, looking at his profile as he stood stooped in deep concentration, staring at one of his cameras. His thick blond hair fell in layers like the ruff of a swan, and she watched as a raw wind blew it back and showed his neck. She wanted to kiss his neck at that second, exactly below the hairline, just under his collar.

Oh, my God, she thought, what is the matter with me? What am I thinking?

'What is it?' he asked. 'You look very thoughtful.'

She smiled at him quickly, trying to cover her discomfort. 'I was thinking how well you worked with children.'

He looked away from her and continued to fold his plates in cloth and put them into their felt-lined box. 'I like kids. I think they made you nervous.'

'They did not.' She turned away from him and walked around in a slow circle, toe, heel, toe, heel. 'It just took so much time to get them set up.'

'They are so open, you know, everything right there on their faces, little messengers with no need for words.' He stood up and looked at her seriously for a moment and then hoisted one of the large cases to his shoulder. 'You looked very beautiful today. Savage almost. It was interesting. Here, carry this. I'm taking you to Café Louise for lunch. I have such news for you. I want to tell you over a good stew.'

'Stop charting my life!'

'Why are you suddenly so angry at me?'

'Just tell me here, will you? Tell me and let me go back to work.'

'One moment.' He put down the case and took up his camera from another and focused it on her.

'Stop it, Jules. Stop it!'

'Someone is coming to see your work. Henri Ferrar who runs a gallery on rue Bayard is coming on Saturday.' Jules changed the lens, biting his lip with concentration. 'He is having a show of new painters, and if he likes your work, he will include you.' Her face froze as he told her. She was staring at him in amazement. He snapped her. She looked away and then back at him. He snapped her again. She took a breath and her body seemed to grow, energy coming from nowhere. Again, his camera. Then her smile as broad as that of a child. Then the smile collapsing, replaced by a frown. Hesitation, suspicion. Fear. Joy. Each had been a moment and he had photographed each. Delphi had not noticed him at all.

'Why?' she asked.

'Why? What do you mean, "why"?'

'Why would he come? Does he owe you a favor?'

'He is a friend. It's not a favor.'

'Of course it is. He may take the work because of you, not because he likes it.'

'I made it very clear that he is under no obligation to me. If there is a favor, it is only to come and look.'

'I wanted to do it myself, Jules.' She shook her head.

'Then tell Monsieur Ferrar to go to hell when he comes.' He grabbed his cases angrily, slipping the straps across his chest and over his shoulders, and started to walk away from her, out of the park.

'You're sure he won't take my work only because you asked him?' she yelled after him.

He stopped and walked back to her, his cases banging against one another, smashing against his legs and chest. 'And if he does, what does it matter? You are the most stubborn woman I have ever known. You must have everything your way or it is better to have nothing. This is business, Delphi Stern, and you had best understand how it works. If he likes your paintings and he thinks they can make him some money, he will take them. It's business now, understand? No time for doing it this way or that, only time for doing it any way you can. Understand?' He was so close to her she could feel his warm breath on her face. She nodded. 'Be an artist about the work, please, not about the way it gets sold.'

'Yes, yes,' she answered, wanting to get away from him as quickly as possible. 'Yes. Of course.' She slipped his tripod from under her arm and hurried out of the park.

*　　*　　*

What is the matter with me? Must there always be sex in a relationship with a man? If I sleep with Jules, he will possess me. I will behave like a woman. These thoughts I have had all day are as good as suicide. I am going to stop all this. The hell with my body. The hell with Jules Chasson. I will not prove Sonya right again!

Meanwhile, Saturday some stranger comes to judge my work. Sweet Jesus, I may never survive the week.

*   *   *

That Tuesday she went to the gallery on the rue Bayard to see what appealed to this Ferrar, returning home in a fit. The three oils in the window were dreadful, nearly as bad as Delbay's fulsome canvases. Inside, one or two of the landscapes made an attempt at a statement of some sort, but most were insincere, trifling works. Monsieur Ferrar had no eye. There was no way that he would ever appreciate her work. There was no reason for him to come.

She could barely work that week, worrying over it, but finally Saturday arrived.

'I can't do it, Jules. You go downstairs and be there with him. I can't watch . . . I can't.'

'Delphi Stern, how unlike you!'

'No. This is like me. I won't go down there. I can't look at him as he looks at my paintings.'

'You? You are so sure of your work.'

'I am. I am. But I am not sure of Monsieur Ferrar. I confess it, I am a nervous idiot, a fool, a child. I know, I have had other rejections, but those people never even bothered to look. I cannot bear the thought of rejection when someone actually sees the work. I can't do it, Jules. You go.'

He made her go with him, finally, and she stood dumbly in the corner, trying to see her work as the man who liked overblown still lifes did. No, it was impossible. Yet Ferrar agreed to take two and include them in his exhibition the following month.

'Look at you.' Jules shook his head and walked around

her. 'Ferrar took two of your paintings. He has a good gallery. Yet you are not the least delighted.'

'Why would a man who had such a bad eye agree to take my work?'

'How bad is his eye? He took the work!'

'He will misrepresent it. It will be a disaster.'

'Then it will hang with eighteen other paintings, and they will succeed or fail on their own. You will be judged by others one day whether you like it or not!'

'Who are they, these judges? How do they know where I have come from? How do they know what my intention is?' She kicked at the frame of the door. 'Damn Ferrar! Damn them all!'

'You are a stupid child, Delphi. I do not expect a kiss on the cheek, but I do not wish abuse either. Nothing is right for you. Nothing is as you want it. You are never satisfied.'.

'Because I hate needing money! I hate it!'

'Then marry a man with ideals and money in the bank. Like your father!'

'Go to hell, Jules.'

'Immediately. I will go there immediately. It is better than this heaven of yours.' He walked by her out of the room and slammed the door behind him.

*   *   *

Delphi   December 13, 1930

I think I have won the war in my battle with myself against Jules. I am well under control now. I have never been, after all, a creature of passions, and nothing proves it better than the way I have handled these extraordinary feelings for Jules. Now I can say, Brava, Delphi!

*   *   *

That month before the showing at Ferrar's gallery, she could not work at all. It was a month of brooding, a month of regret, and a month of ecstatic anticipation. Nothing, not even Jules, took her mind from the show. The day before the official opening, when she was certain Ferrar would be at lunch, she went into the gallery and stared at

449

her paintings. These had been part of her for one year, she thought, moving forward to look at them. She saw only the mistakes – the facility, the lack of unity – and she stilled an impulse to tear them off the wall and stomp on them. Slowly she backed away from them, hitting up against the opposite wall. She took a breath and dared to look at them again. She had been wrong. There it was after all. There was too much of the mind, yes, perhaps too much of that, and there was too much facility, but there was boldness and there was something compelling and unique in that work. It was her talent.

It was at that moment that she noticed the legend over them: LES PHOTOS. Ferrar had known what she was doing. Even a man who specialized in ornamental paintings recognized her intent. At least that.

In the next weeks she was at the gallery almost daily. I am shameless, she thought, watching the stream of people who paraded past her paintings, noticing their expressions, trying to overhear their every remark. She was not even embarrassed when Ferrar asked her not to stay for such long periods of time. She kept returning, but now it was for two or three shorter periods a day. Still, all her wishing didn't help; the paintings were unsold.

4

March 28, 1931
My dear daughter,

Thank you for your letter, although I daresay I could have gone happily on without this birthday being marked. A half-century! For one who always thought she would die at an early age, it is such a surprise! Of course, the true surprise is that I find myself exactly as I found myself at twenty, and here I am stuffed into the body of an old woman, but you shall only understand that when you have lived as long as I. The older I become, the more amazing the world. Circles of repetition, each generation the same as the last, only never realizing it. If I had it to do over, I think I should be a historian – only so that I might read the future. Thank you for thinking of me on this major event.

The depression has swept through this country like a plague. Your father is just beginning to recover. It is easier for him than poor Julius. I never saw a man more surprised at adversity, as if his fortune were truly his, and even though the two of them were not so badly affected as the rest. Do you remember Fred Hamburg? He was completely wiped out. I understand his wife had a nervous breakdown just at the thought of poverty. Imagine! It will be a great test to turn this country around, although your father says that if all goes well, business will be back to normal within two years. I hope that there is some lesson to be learned here, now that the exploiters have fallen as low as the exploited. If communism had flourished in Russia as it was supposed to, the moment would be now to bring it to America. But Stalin is no selling point. If and when we get through this, I think that America will just be America again. Or so history would tell us.

Enclosed is the picture of your face that appeared in *Vanity Fair*. The caption says that you are appearing everywhere, *Photographie, Le Style*, etc., etc., as well as in all the best Sunday supplements. Why doesn't it mention your work? Your father says he has never seen a picture of Picasso or Matisse without the caption making mention of their work. I told him he should support you and and save you from yourself. He understood that.

I am on my way to distribute food. Houston Street sees a different group of people these days, not only the new immigrants, but men of substance, once men of property. They are so ashamed to come, but they must eat, too. There is no work, none at all. So much for capitalism. I must hurry.

Write soon. Your loving mother,

Sonya

*　　*　　*

Delphi knew from the sound of his footsteps that he was upset, so it was no surprise when Jules burst into her room, his anger exploding at the sight of her. 'Have you been posing naked for that pig?' he screamed. She looked up at him. 'Have you? Have you, who are supposed to know art, posed for Delbay, a talentless fool? Well? Have you?'

'Jules, just let me explain and you won't be—'

'There can be no explanation that would be at all satisfactory!' Turning, he punched his fist into the door behind him and then walked by her and kicked one of the carved doors of the sideboard, splintering a duck's head.

'Stop it, do you hear me!' She screamed at him, her hands on her hips, her body leaning toward him with her fury. 'I couldn't find a job when I first came to Paris and so I posed for Delbay!'

'I knew it! I knew it! Whore! Liar!' He threw himself into the big chair to glower up at her. 'Whore.'

'What is so terrible? He paid me to be his model!'

'What is so terrible, eh? Who will want your face when your ass is everywhere?'

'He only did one oil of me naked. That hardly constitutes—'

'One? Did you say *one*? Is that what you thought? There are four naked paintings of you in his gallery this moment.

452

One is winter, one is spring, et cetera, et cetera. And they are awful. Awful!'

'Oh, quit it! I did it to live and I would do it again. In fact I should do it now. Now, I am at least well known enough to get a good sum. I will do it! If you want an exclusive contract, pay me more. I must find a way to stop being the night porter. I am too old to stay up all night and expect my work to be anything worthwhile. That is it. You will pay me more.'

'Pay you more? I gave you everything you have. I gave you the shirt off my back!' Suddenly he was quiet, studying her. 'Why are you so sour?'

'I do not like being yelled at by a lunatic.'

'That is not the reason. I yell at you all the time.' He sighed and closed his eyes. 'Never mind. I know. Ferrar sent back your paintings today; I am sorry, Delphi.'

'He said he will put me in the show again next year, that he likes my work.'

'So that is wonderful.' He smiled at her.

'You would settle for that, but I cannot wait for next year!' She strode to the window and slapped the shutter against its frame again and again. 'I must sell something now.' For a moment she thought the shutter would break. She stopped its movement with her hand.

'I am glad I am not your lover,' he said, sighing.

'What?' Her face flushed as she spun around.

'I said, I am glad I am not your lover.'

She started to laugh, great peals of laughter rolling in waves from her chest. She threw her head back and closed her eyes, crying with laughter.

'Why is that so funny?'

She could not speak but laughed again. What a relief to laugh about it! 'Because' – she paused for breath – 'because you might as well be my lover. God knows, you are as demanding and possessive as a lover, and as stingy.'

'Is that so?' His eyes were very blue in the center and lighter around the rim as he looked at her. A chilly silence filled the space between them.

'It was a joke,' she said, self-conscious, looking away from him.

'Do you have lovers?' He lit a cigarette and held it in

that strange way he had, rolling it back and forth between his second and third fingers. 'The answer, I think, is no. Isn't that right, Delphi Stern?' She flushed. 'Oh, we are friends, you and I. Nearly brother and sister. But we seldom talk intimately. You avoid intimacy. I even wonder if you are interested in me aside from where I fit into your little world.' He tapped his ash onto the floor with deliberation. 'Do you have affairs?' She looked back at him angrily. 'You know that when I am not with you, I am with other women, and that we are often making love to each other.' He stood up and walked to the fireplace. 'I know when I am not with you, you are alone. I think that you are always alone when I am not around. I think you need a man.'

She smiled at him for a moment. 'Every man thinks a woman needs a man.'

'Freud has proved—'

'Freud has proved he is a man, too.' She was still smiling as she sat on a crate and put her arms around her knees. 'Think of me as a priest,' she said, bowing her head. She hiccuped loudly. 'Oh, my God, I have the hiccups. Damn, I have the loudest and the longest hiccups!'

'It's a waste of time to talk to you seriously. Hold your breath and look at this. This will take your mind off your hiccups.' He put out his cigarette and took a magazine from his pocket. 'Page thirty-three, I think,' he said, handing it to her. He watched her open the magazine and shuffle the pages until she reached the page he had mentioned. 'A full page of *Elle*. You see why I was furious about Delbay.' He shook his fist under her nose. She hiccuped again.

'I thought' - she pushed the shutter open again to get more light - 'the editor at *Elle* had sworn never to print your photographs.'

'He never will again if he sees Delbay's paintings of you.'

Delphi began to read aloud from the paragraph at the bottom of the page. 'Her face and style are like no other. Daughter of a Russian princess and a German banker, Delphi Stern is the new American woman, the first generation. Bold, beautiful, brilliant, she is an artist, a woman of integrity, a woman of her time.' She fixed Jules with a hard look. 'Jules Chasson, what is this nonsense about the princess and the German banker? It is not true.'

'True, false, who cares? It's the picture that matters. See how brilliantly it reproduced? It is magnificent. The picture is magnificent. Because of this, dear Delphi, you will sell your paintings.' He slapped the magazine. 'I know the concept is difficult for you and your integrity, but nonetheless, it works. I had a phone call from Georges Marriac and he wants to meet my black angel. It is a first step. A giant step.' He smiled gleefully.

'Why? Who is he?'

'I suppose one could call him an arranger. If he is interested, he can arrange for anything to happen.'

'You mean for the daughter of a German banker and a princess? It is humiliating, Jules!'

'Go back to your bakery!' he screamed at her. 'What difference if they said you were the true Anastasia? What difference so long as it makes a moment? You must take advantage of the moment, you hear me! I am selling your photographs like wool in winter. Next week you are on the fashion pages of *L'Official*.'

'So now I am also fashionable!'

'You are my black angel! You are starting a trend. You will only wear black from now on.' His face was shining with anger. 'Don't you dare to refuse me. My camera will make the world see you and your work!'

'Your camera is the devil and it takes my soul!' She threw the magazine across the room and it slid out of sight, under the bed. Crossing her arms over her breasts, she walked angrily to the fireplace and stared at her own reflection.

'Take a good look at yourself, Delphi Stern, I know what is right . . .'

Her scream interrupted him, so long and loud that it kept him from saying anything more. When she finished she stared defiantly at his reflection in the mirror. He merely pursed his lips, shaking his head and clicking his tongue with mild disapproval.

'Are you finished?' he asked quietly.

'Yes.' She sighed. 'You are right, of course. I shall meet

with this arranger of yours, this Georges Marraux.'

'Marriac, M-a-r-r-i-a-c. I will call him right away. He has already invited us to dine. He mentioned the possibility of making a book of my photographs of you. He is close to Avignon, the publisher. A book would be good for both of us. It means money and exposure for both of us. Think of it, Delphi, a book of you in your studio with your work, with your paintings. Everyone will see your paintings and they will give you twenty shows, whatever you want.'

'Carl Borach had many such friends. Arrangers. Vultures is more accurate. They feed on celebrity and wealth.'

'I warn you, Delphi!' He pointed his finger at her. 'I warn you!'

'All right! Yes! Dammit, I won't care. Let us meet this Monsieur Marriac. Let us see what we can do with him!'

He put his hands in his pockets for a moment as if he were looking for something and then he withdrew them and stood, frowning at her. He pushed at the hair that fell across his forehead, brushing it back and letting it fall again through his fingers. Suddenly he walked back to the large chair and sat heavily, letting all his weight pull him down at once so that the chair rocked backward, creaking on its sturdy frame as it scratched across the floor. He was still frowning as he crossed his arms. Then he looked toward a spot midway between them, his eyes distant.

'We should be lovers,' he said finally.

'What!'

'Shut up.' His voice was almost a whisper. 'I am very tired of your pretending you don't care about me. I am exhausted by the notion. I should have rammed you that first night and we would have done with all this dancing around.'

His expression was ferocious with feeling, and she stopped trying to say anything. 'I know every expression that has ever passed your features by this time,' he said, staring at her. 'I also see every thought that crosses your mind, no matter how infinitesimal. It is my busine s, you know, to see. The only reason I haven't touched you is your fear of it. Yes, fear. Damn my eyes, I see the fear in yours.'

'You are exactly like every man in this world, an

egotistical—'

'Why did you give me a key to the front door of this building? You needn't bother to answer. I know the reason. So you won't have to see me with other women.' He sighed and put his head back against the chair and looked at her, eyes unblinking.

Delphi turned her back to him and walked to the bed, slowly sitting on the corner. 'You are wrong about the women, Jules,' she said, her voice a monotone. 'I pray there are other women. I sit in my bed to listen for the strike of their heels on the floor, for their laughter, for the clinking of their beads, for any sound of them. You see, if there are other women, then I can go back to sleep and stop thinking of you.' She turned to face him. 'It is very easy to want you, Jules Chasson. I spend moments of every day fighting my desire for you, fighting the urge to make you a special dinner, to draw you something that might make you smile, to buy you small things that will bind me to you. I fight and I win because I refuse to let anything happen between us. I refuse, do you hear me? Already my feelings take time from me, and I cannot let it continue. I must own myself and that is final.'

'Nothing is final.'

'No. It is final.' Her eyes were so dry in her head that her eyelids scraped across them and hurt her. 'If you know me, you know that I cannot allow it. It is not the pain of losing what I want that frightens me, Jules. What frightens me is my capacity for wanting. I am like a man, you see. Immoderate and cruel in wanting. And like a man, I want my success more than I want anything else. I will not have you, Jules. It would make me forget myself.'

'Nothing is final,' he repeated.

'No. It is. It is!'

He was up and out of the chair and across the room to her in seconds, and he lifted her up to him and kissed her. She felt the warmth of his mouth, of his breath, she felt her body warming against him. How she wanted him. He kissed her harder, his tongue now in her mouth. No! She would not! No! No! 'No! No! I will not. I will not!' Her fists beat against his chest as uncontrollably as she had beat against Carl Borach and before that against Sonya.

No! He would not take her freedom either! Her rage mounted and washed away any trace of her desire. 'I can't. I can't. I can't.' She said it over and over until he stepped back from her. Still, she beat at him, her fists making hammers in the air. 'I can't.'

He grabbed both wrists in his hands and held them up between the two of them. 'All right,' he said. 'All right. All right. Stop now. Stop, Delphi. It's all right now.'

She struggled against the pressure of his fingers but he continued to hold on to her until she was calmed. When she could see him clearly again, she saw his swift comprehension of her terror and his acquiescence to it as he slowly released her arms. 'So,' he said, 'at least your hiccups have stopped.'

5

Everywhere in the restaurant she saw herself in mirrors, reflections of herself and Jules and Georges Marriac and the boy he had brought with him. They were four and thousands of themselves. The more she drank, the more images of them she saw repeating and repeating. Georges Marriac was amazing. There was not a scandal in all of France that he did not instigate or feel free to describe in thick detail. Hemingway this, Fitzgerald that, the countess and the critic. Marriac was a grand vintner of gossip, and he distilled his information carefully, making it sparkle.

'And so I said to her, "My lady, a lover without proper credentials is like wine without age or writing without style - purposeless. What satisfaction is mere satisfaction? One's taste is above all things." I am happy to report that her lovers, as well as her wines and her reading, have vastly improved!' Marriac laughed, waving the dessert menu and peering at the others above his glasses. Delphi was uncomfortable there, trying to listen, distracted by the wine and the endless reflections of herself.

'. . . and then I told him to take his wares to that Greek, and the rest is history.'

'Are you always so right in your little marriages?' Delphi stared at him as she sipped her wine.

'I don't try to be right, Delphi. I try to be successful. Now, tell us what you've been up to lately.'

'Up to?' Delphi put down her glass.

'Oh, tell him, Delphi,' Chasson said, nudging her with his knee under the table.

'I just paint, Georges. It's all I'm ever up to.' There was a small silence.

'But how would you categorize yourself?'

'I wouldn't.' Delphi stared blankly into his narrow gray eyes. 'If you like labels, ask a critic, not an artist.'

'I see.' Georges Marriac kept looking at her. 'What

influences you, then?'

'Everything. Even you. Your eyes flit around this room like insects in a summer garden, seeing things I never would see, as I see things you never would.'

He continued to smile. 'I have heard you lived with Carl Borach.'

'Do you ever sleep, Georges?'

'I sleep quite well and every night. Can you say the same?' He turned from Delphi and patted the hands of the boy next to her. The boy smiled beautifully back at him. Delphi turned to the boy.

'So he is your lover?'

'Delphi!' Chasson choked on his food.

'Stop kicking me, Jules. It's a fair question. All questions that can be answered with a simple yes or no are fair.'

She turned back to Georges Marriac. 'I can tell you what I'm up to, Georges, and it is not talking about this woman and her lover and that writer and his Sylvia Beach or whether I lived with Carl Borach. I think it is all stupid and silly. I am here, Georges, because Jules says you can do something for me. Well, what is it you can do?' She stared at him and he stared back, smiling slightly.

'I can get Jules's book of you published, and then I can surely get you a show. I can do that because I do not think talk is silly or stupid, but valuable. If you want my help, I also think you must come out into the real world more often than you do. In fact, I must insist on it.' He did not take his eyes off of her.

'And why will you help me?'

'Now, for cachet, finally, for money.'

Delphi stood up. 'Fine. I will come out. Jules will take me out. I will drink more wine and learn more insults. Arrange whatever you like for me. When will I have my show?'

'Six to eight months.'

'A bargain, Georges Marriac. It's not such a long time to be a trained dog.' She did not thank him for dinner. She turned her back on the table and walked out of the restaurant. Jules followed her.

'You disgrace me,' he said, his hands deep in the pockets

of his blue velvet pants.

'Don't be an ass. He is a fairy who loves confrontations
and indiscretions. I told you, I have met men like Marriac
before. When people of real talent insult them, they take it
as a compliment.' She stopped and leaned up toward Jules.
'I will go out in the great big wonderful world. For me and
you. But I warn you, I will often be angry at the amount of
time it takes and wastes.'

There was so much perfection and total harmony in the
main salon of the Lassères' massive flat on the Île de la
Cité, nothing caught one's attention. The tapestry on the
walls, the gold silk upholstery with its pale orange stripes,
the Sèvres candelabra, the gleaming, carefully worked
parquet floors, even the muted rose and blue and gold of
the rugs blended together seamlessly. The people were as
at home in this perfection as the vases of regal lilies
perfuming the air. Jules, immediately surrounded by his
admirers, rattled endlessly about anything that appeared
to enter his mind. How he adored attention, Delphi
thought, walking away from him. She had not been alone
for months. Georges Marriac had swamped her with
obligations, climaxing with tonight's. Lassère was the
money behind the book. Probably Avignon's lover, Delphi
thought. She saw a chance to be alone and she took it,
walking to the windows in the corner of the room. Below
her, traffic surged in the twilight, making long white and
red arcs of continuous light. Thousands of small yellow
moons shone at the sides of the curving streets and
boulevards. The sky was momentarily caught at its
horizon on a cranberry ribbon. She drifted in her thoughts
until a woman, her face crimped at the edges, like a pie,
interrupted her.

Her very red lips had been drawn onto a fuller mouth
and she had tiny bat's teeth. 'I have a painting of you! Isn't
that a marvelous coincidence. Marc Delbay did it for me. I
needed something and Marc and I settled on you. You are
my spring.' How maddening that a likeness of her was
hanging in this woman's house, this pretentious woman
with her stenciled brows and patronizing tone. Delphi
walked away from her quickly, only to be joined by two

461

other women and a man. The women were both wearing bizarrely colored clothes and began to talk across her. The man, listening to neither of them, told Delphi how much she resembled a Roman statue he had seen in Bologna. Another man began talking to another group several feet away from her, and she found herself staring at his hand. They did not fly about like the hands of Frenchmen. She could not hear him at first; the fellow next to her was still speaking about her remarkable resemblance to the Madonna in the Church of the Assumption. She edged closer to the man with the quiet hands. He was a bit taller than she, with a broad, even-featured, ruddy face. His square jaw was matched by his full head of wavy gray hair. His eyes were not large, but they had a compelling expression in them. His French was badly accented, but it was fluent, and he was speaking with immense passion. Honest passion, she thought, made a unique sound.

'But of course I am certain. It will be an unmitigated disaster, I assure all of you. Beyond the Jewish question, and I am not speaking solely in their behalf, Adolf Hitler is a madman. If he becomes chancellor—'

'My dear Hasse, everyone has been trying to get rid of the Jews for years. If Adolf Hitler manages to rid Germany of them, I think we will all invite him to Paris!' Lassère was grinning as he lifted his glass in a toast.

'As I said, the question here is not of religion, it is of freedom.' The color had drained from Hasse's face. He looked from face to face before he began speaking again. Someone moved in front of him and cut him out of Delphi's line of vision. As she began to move toward him, Georges Marriac stood in front of her.

'Chasson said you were here, Delphi darling, but I haven't been able to find you. Listening to the Jew lover, were you?'

'Who is he?'

'Hasse Manufacturing, one of the largest companies in Germany. He's made millions in needles and buttonhooks and keys. The middle class couldn't exist without him. Except for his money, he's so tiresome, always going on about politics and the Jews and Hitler.'

'In less than five seconds, Georges, you have managed

to say the word *Jew* with less than appreciation in your voice.'

'But, my dear, I am an anti-Semite. There are few Frenchmen who keep that a secret. Remember Dreyfus.' Marriac smiled elaborately.

'I am a Jew, Georges.'

'You are a beautiful woman, which disqualifies you. Come, come. I want you to meet André Lassère. He has shown me the first proofs of the book. It is even better than I had thought.'

Despite herself, she followed him.

* * *

December 16, 1931
Dear Delphi,

If the devil is unknown, he is dangerous. Don't distress yourself. You know your devil and therefore he can do you no harm. There have always been such fellows as your Marriac. Perhaps they are a necessary evil for those of us who do not court commerce. You must live, you must eat bread. Let him find you your gallery.

Your father has been home nearly three weeks now with some small injury to his spine. The doctor says he must have complete bed rest or risk chronic recurrence. He is a marvelous patient. It is even festive to have the house filled with his admirers once again. Julius and a dashing Italian named Oscar Manfredi have just now come to cheer him, and it is obvious that it is working, for there is the grand sound of men's laughter from the next room. They laugh as if they had not a care in the world. It is the only thing men do that women do not quite manage.

Soon it will be Christmas and then the New Year. I find myself remembering the smells and sounds of those seasons, not the sights. I can hardly recall the rooms I lived in for the first eighteen years of my life, but I can smell the Christmas cakes baking, the incense in the church, the sounds of the runners of the sleighs on the icy snow, and the screams of delight as we children plunged down the ice slides.

I was told by your father that your friend Jules Chasson

is making a book with you. May I know about it?

Take love from your mother,

Sonya

*   *   *

A little before Christmas, Jules had surprised Delphi with his book, leaving it for her gaily wrapped in shiny green paper with a huge red satin bow on it. Respectfully she unfolded the wrapping and took the book out. Slowly and painfully she looked through it. Toward the middle of the book there was a succession of nine photographs of her in her studio. In all of the photographs, her paintings were clearly visible and, if anything, formidably richer with the addition of Jules's carefully placed lights. They were perfect compositions, she thought. Their only failing was that they were all part of Chasson's brilliance, not her own.

Jules came into the room carrying a large round gold tray that held a magnum of champagne and a large tin of caviar in a stockpot filled with ice. 'So?' He turned excitedly to her after putting the tray down on the pine table. 'So?'

'It is certainly interesting. I would be interested if I saw it in a bookshop. The photographs are really quite revelatory.' Her voice was too high, she thought, clearing her throat and starting again. 'Really, Jules, I think you have captured so much. I do wish the prose were a bit less flowery and I . . .' She put a hand over her eyes for a moment and then, taking it away, saw how disappointed he was. 'Oh, Jules, what would you have me say? I cannot be objective at all. It is so humiliating to see one's paintings become so many objects!'

'Maybe you will be lucky and the book will go unnoticed. I am so sorry to have cheapened you!' His voice was hoarse with hurt. 'I did think you might be pleased for me.'

'I want everything for you, you great cow! Your work is fine, very fine. You know I think that.'

'Good, then we can celebrate.' He took a towel from the back of the chair and wrapped it around the neck of the

464

bottle and began to pry at the cork.

'What are we celebrating now, *mon brave*? Does Picasso want me to model? Perhaps Chanel?'

'No.' He was most solemn, carefully uncorking the champagne and pouring it into the two fluted glasses he had also brought. How handsome he always was, she thought, God's messenger. He handed her a glass with a low bow. Champagne rolled down its sides like tears. 'You are to have a one-woman show at the Hercule in less than three months.' He held up his glass. 'I propose we drink to the devil.'

She felt her hands go numb and her mouth dry. Her lips became parchment and her heart beat in her ears.

'So now what, Delphi? Because you cannot abuse me, have you lost the gift of speech?' She shook her head and drank some champagne. It was smoothly explosive in her mouth. Jules went to the tray and pushed a big soup spoon into the caviar, filling it up. He carried it to her, and she opened her mouth wide for it.

'Yes, yes,' he whispered, slipping the spoon between her lips and watching her pleasure at the taste of the plump gray salty eggs popping in her mouth. 'Give a woman what she wants and see her shine like a star.'

'The Hercule, eh?' She said the name softly, repeating it. 'The Hercule.' She smiled at Jules, her eyes full of delight. Lazily, she held up her glass, pressing it against his. 'To the pimp Marriac. His whore has finally had satisfaction.'

6

Jules had photographed her all day as she supervised the hanging of her work in the gallery. Hercule had allowed her to do whatever she wished, so she would have no one to blame but herself. Still, she had complained all day, first about the lighting, then about the space. When she was finally finished, she sat on the floor of the gallery, chewing her lip. 'I am frightened,' she said to Jules, 'and so nervous I will be sick.'

'No. I am taking you to Fokine's. I want to see just how Russian you really are. I want to measure how much vodka it will take to make you weep with joy!' He yanked her to her feet. 'You have made me money this week. The book is selling all over France. Today in the paper, Michel Sourian called it "a hallmark in photography and the quintessential love letter to a woman." If he is right, how can I let my love be sick? Besides, I have already reserved the best table for us.' She did not refuse him.

He was utterly magnanimous with her, heaping her plate with caviar and blinis and filling her glass with vodka. With each new glass of vodka, her Russian, rusty with disuse, became more and more available until she was as fluent as her father, full of Russian curses and Russian toasts. Her appetite was marvelous and she was eating everything, even picking food off Jules's plate with her fingers.

She was not certain exactly what time the dancers from the Ballet Russe joined them, but suddenly the tables added to theirs filled the restaurant and they were surrounded with balalaika players, louder than those at West Fourth Street. By that time, Jules had ordered all the different vodkas in the cellar so that there might be a tasting. Delphi announced her empty bottle of Smirnoff raspberry vodka the best one, and the colors in the room flashed like lights in a harbor. One of the dancers swung her up to the tabletop and was dancing her easily around the room. Tables tipped under them, but none fell. Whoever held her had strong, smooth arms. She looked up into his face. It was a good Russian face with wide cheeks and a wide mouth. Traces of silver eyeshadow on his lids flashed as they turned so they seemed to be under a halo of diamonds.

Below them, faces became only features, and as they danced faster, noses flew off into the room and eyes were everywhere. She felt his groin against hers and she tightened her grip at his neck. Perhaps she had had too much vodka. She stared up at him as he slowly slid her up the length of his body to bury his tongue in her mouth. She heard other voices singing somewhere as Gypsy violins drowned out the balalaikas. He felt so good, full of salt and youth. She could take him home. It would cost her nothing to have a lover with such a beautiful body. It would be perfect. His tongue was silken.

When the young Russian lifted her down from the table, she saw Jules looking at her expressionlessly. Yes, she wanted to yell at him. I would rather it were you, Jules Chasson. A thousand times I would rather. But the Russian is the only choice. He will be gone in less than a week.

The day after the opening, the social critics in the early editions of the newspapers wrote about Chasson's 'black angel' and the throngs of *le haut monde* who had come to pay her court. Delphi waited for the evening papers and the more serious art criticisms. When there was nothing, she waited for the magazines. They had all been there, had all seen her work. Finally, in one, a critic called her work 'adequate' and in another, the critic called it 'somewhat impressive for a sideline.' The model had eclipsed the artist. The opening at Hercule had been merely another evening for the rich and the spoiled, a divertissement and nothing more. Those who had commented on her work had done nothing more than dismiss it. Delphi would not allow it. Arrogant, certain she was an artist worthy of greater attention, she refused to let her paintings hang in the gallery a day longer.

When she went to Hercule to tell him so, she was surprised to find that he had already sold five paintings.

'No. I will not sell those paintings,' she said, fists at her sides as she paced the gallery. 'Absolutely not.' She shook her head as she walked. 'My paintings may not be bought like trophies from a fashionable vendor.'

'Get hold of yourself, Miss Stern. These four paintings are sold, and they will remain sold along with the large gray and black canvas in the other room. I sold that this morning.'

Delphi ran to the other, smaller, room. Where the *Cesspool Cleaners* had been hanging there was nothing, only wall. 'Where is it?' she shrieked at Monsieur Hercule, who had been only kind to her. 'Where is my painting?'

To his credit, he merely looked amazed at her outrageous behavior, his mouth dropping open to reveal his very white teeth and pale pink tongue. 'I sold it,' he said.

The vacant space looked vast. Delphi doubted she would ever make anything like it again, and she was suddenly saddened and quieted at her loss. She looked at Hercule and whispered in a barely audible voice, 'Why is it gone?'

'I told you, Miss Stern, I sold it. The gentleman was on his way to Switzerland and insisted on taking it with him, as large as it is. Good God, it took us an hour to pack it! I know how unorthodox it is to sell something off the wall at a showing, but he offered me such a grand price I simply could not refuse.' Hercule, who had been watching Delphi closely and speaking very rapidly, chanced a small smile. It lingered nervously on his face. 'Come to my desk and I will show you. Come.' She watched him literally run toward his office, but she stayed, dumbly staring at the empty wall. 'Look, look!' Hercule brought a folder toward her with some ceremony. 'This is what the gentleman paid for your work, Miss Stern. It is more than even you could imagine. Have you ever seen anything like it? A Massanio. Perfection, sheer perfection. Mind your fingers, Miss Stern.'

It was Marra, of course. Marra had bought the best painting she had yet done with a drawing no bigger than a passport that had taken him only moments to make. And was perfect. He had been there that morning. When? Did he stand where she stood? Was he alone?

'I think he has overpaid, Monsieur Hercule. Certainly, my painting was not worth a Massanio.' She handed the folder back to Hercule and looked at the empty space again. Marra. In spite of herself, she wished she had seen him.

'Well . . . I had to include a few other things, you understand, but it was your painting that interested him the most. Without it, he would not strike the deal.'

'How curious.' Was he the same? Had he gotten older? Was he alone?

'What is even more curious, Miss Stern, is that he says he will buy more of your work but nothing else he has seen here. He has another drawing, even larger, that he is willing to part with.' Hercule held his breath a moment. 'He will let me have it, but I must get him another Stern of the same quality.'

'Quality?' She felt a terrible anger begin.

'It was his word, mademoiselle, certainly not mine!' Hercule, a thin band of sweat across his upper lip and his forehead, put his hand on his heart. 'I am so sure he did not mean offense, not such a fine gentleman, such a true connoisseur. I cannot tell you how well spoken and knowledgeable he was. In fact, it seemed to me that he was quite familiar with your work. He said to tell you he will not hesitate to buy, but he much prefers the earliest work of this period. He said, "Les Pictures"—'

'Les Photos,' she interrupted.

'Yes, of course, Les Photos . . . yes, well the later Photos were no match for the one he bought. He did not think you were mastering your subject as you had done.'

'Damn him.' She said it quietly.

'My dear woman, for the price we can get for a larger Massanio, you might put away your pride and give him what he wants.'

She turned and walked toward the door. 'Damn you, Luis!' she yelled to the street itself. 'Damn you! I need no more teaching! Let go of me!'

Was he watching her? Was he always watching her? Was he often in Paris? How many times? How she had loved him! There were still moments when she felt him nearby. Someone on a bus would move a certain way and she would think it was Marra. Once there had been such a feeling of his presence, she had run through the streets toward home to be safe. She was running now, pursued by thoughts of Marra, and behind them, as fast, came thoughts of Jules. Demon thoughts, they made a deep pain in her side, making her chest turn into bony fragments that tried to rupture her heart. She had run from these thoughts before, but today it was so difficult. Paris was ruthless in its beauty. It tumbled metaphors in the mind. The wash of sunshine blurred everything, melting the morning into its surroundings so that the streets and buildings and trees and flowers at the stalls blended into one another. There were symphonies of flowers, daisies ebullient as horns, and a percussion of anemones, tulips, and irises. And with the color came the thought of David's blood, the same color of the blood-red tulips. She saw it all but not the man coming around the corner. She landed on the sidewalk covered with the flowers he had been carrying. She ached with a dull pain and her head was full of the lemony smell of pollen. The man was on his knees, his creased and spotless pants now in the dirt. He smelled of cologne and starch. 'Mademoiselle! *Ach du Lieber!*'

She sat up, sneezing. She was looking into the face of the man from Lassère's party so many months before, the man Georges Marriac had called the Jew lover.

'Are you hurt? But I am a donkey! You must not move. You may have done injury to your spine.'

'I am fine.'

'No, please. You must be still. You may be in shock.'

'That is for a doctor to say,' she said, ignoring him and pushing him away from her with some force.

'But I *am* a doctor,' he answered. 'Yes, really. My name is Ernst Hasse. I have to insist you just lie quietly Miss . . . Miss . . . ?'

'Delphi Stern,' she said, standing. She put her hand down to him and he took it, surprised as she easily pulled him to his feet. 'Don't forget your case,' she said, brushing at herself. 'And don't worry. I am fine.'

'No,' he said vehemently.

'I beg your pardon.'

'No. I must keep you under observation for at least an hour. It was a nasty fall.' He reached out to hold her arm. 'Fauchon is just there. You must let me buy you lunch, Miss Stern. I could not forgive myself if I let you go now.'

'But I am not dressed for Fauchon,' she snapped, 'and you are not a doctor.'

'Yes. I mean I am a doctor. Really.'

'Look here, I saw you last year at André Lassère's, and Georges Marriac told me you were a manufacturer or something.'

'Everyone in Paris confuses me with my brother Rudolf. Of course, I have some interest in our family business, but it is Rudolf who is the industrialist.' He bent over and picked up his leather case and then, resolutely steering her toward Fauchon, he continued to talk to her. 'I get many invitations because people like this Marriac think I am so wealthy and powerful. Now you must watch the maître d' at Fauchon. He will give us a table right away because he is convinced I am my brother. If he knew I was just a doctor, we would wait for days.'

Indeed, the head waiter did motion them toward the front of the crowd, graciously accepting a few francs pressed into his hand as he greeted Ernst Hasse with some effusiveness. 'You see,' Ernst whispered to her, pushing her gently ahead of him, 'he is quite convinced I am Rudolf.' She was still tense and angry from the episode at the gallery and looked forward now to a drink of good wine. Just as she was nearly to her table, the way was suddenly blocked by a young dandy who stood up directly in front of her.

'Our black angel is here, fellows,' he said, grinning down at Delphi.

'Yes,' called a second man next to him. '*Bonjour, ange noire*. To what blissful heaven do you take our good Jules that he will not come out these days?'

'I am nobody's angel,' she said, backing away from him.

'Then you must be mine!' said the first man, opening his arms.

'No, mine!' said the last of the quartet as he blew her a kiss.

It was suddenly too much, and without thinking, Delphi

lifted a plate of *oeuf à la neige* from a passing pastry cart and flung it directly at the table of leering young men. 'I am nobody's angel,' she yelled at them, grabbing the mousse and flinging that too. 'I am not black or white or green or purple! I am an artist!' Now she took a huge bowl of whipped cream and dumped that at them. She felt like Sonya then, shrieking at her enemies. She had picked up a smaller bowl of raspberries, but two waiters had finally managed to pin her arms at her sides and take it from her.

'*Merde!*' the first man shouted at her as custard dripped from his handsome face onto his fine silk shirt. 'You have ruined my suit. *Merde alors et merde toujours!*' He raised his fist and might have launched an armada of invective at her were it not for the sudden laughter of his pals.

'She has shot you down with custard, Phillipe,' one snorted, pointing at him.

'And me with chocolate,' said another, holding his heart and falling over against the next man.

'She has killed me with meringue,' the very tallest said, standing and clapping a napkin to his head and falling over the table in a parody of death throes. Several of the other people nearby began to laugh as well, and despite herself, Delphi also burst into a great blast of laughter. When she turned, she was entirely surprised to see Ernst Hasse smiling at her. She had quite forgotten he was there.

'But what spirit! You are a true Valkyrie! Yes! It was wonderful! But why did it make you so angry to be called an angel? You must tell me.' He led her proudly to their waiting table. Little bursts of isolated applause came as he seated her. 'I have not laughed so much in a year,' he said. 'But you must tell me—'

'I will tell you a bit later,' she answered. 'I am too bored by it all now. And I am suddenly very hungry.'

'Then you must order whatever you like. Please.' He clapped for the waiter and was entirely delighted with her order of soup, trout, salad, potatoes, asparagus, and raspberry tart. He ordered the trout as well and asked that the wine be hurried to the table.

'So,' she said, drinking the first glass of wine quickly and watching as he poured another, 'you must tell me about Herr Doktor Hasse. Have you a specialty?'

'Yes. I am a surgeon. That is ... a plastic surgeon. Congenital malformation and accident cases, mostly. Occasionally some burns ... but this is not the proper tone for our conversation. No. I must ... well ... at least I can tell you as an authority ... you have wonderful bones.'

She could not help laughing. 'Only my bones?'

'Forgive me if such a compliment is too skimpy. I am quite out of practice. I should have managed a better one for you. I am not very imaginative. No. I am too German. But I will try to think of something more suitable.'

He reminded her of Julius Borach, and she was completely at ease. He was appealing in his way, not at all like the young boulevardiers around them or the café intellectuals across the river. He was quite sweet and rather innocent. Even now, as he held up his wineglass, his cheeks were tinged with his embarrassment. 'I drink to you,' he said almost shyly. 'And to myself for having the nerve to force you to dine with me.'

She smiled at him. How odd, she thought, that such an ordinary fellow should amuse her.

*   *   *

Delphi   April 17, 1933

Could it be that fate is at last kind to me? I quite like Ernst Hasse, the fellow I nearly ran down two days ago.

I have finally broken with Marriac. Jules has been livid with me all day. Such great carryings-on about it all. He doesn't care what I feel about it. The hell with him.

September 23, 1933

Ernst Hasse teaches a course at the medical school in the university. He comes three days each month and he tells me he will continue to teach here in Paris next year, if only as an excuse to see me. We have been with each other a few days in each of the last five months, and I still enjoy his company. He is interested in me, quite intelligent and undemanding. It is just right to have an admirer for a few days each month and keep the rest of the time for oneself.

October 10, 1933

Well, I introduced Ernst to Jules finally. It was unavoidable. Jules immediately sold Ernst two of his photographs, and they are great friends. This evening Jules has talked us into a tour of the secret Paris, promising to show us every seam in the city's underpinnings. Jules seems to go everywhere in safety. He knows every pimp in Paris personally.

Ernst is quite looking forward to Jules's tour, while I am trembling. What has Jules up his sleeve, I wonder? He has been much too gallant with me lately.

7

At the street fair on the place de la République, Delphi was disappointed when neither Jules nor Ernst would take her inside the tent that promised Tableaux Vivants showing Naked Libertines, Eve and Her Snake, and the true descendant of the Queen of Sheba. 'If you love acts of the flesh' – the old woman who was the announcer quickly found Ernst, and her eyes fixed on him – 'then, monsieur, you will love our tableaux. Be a good papa, bring your daughter and your son inside and let them see at first hand what delights there are to be had in this world!' Ernst turned the color of the red sign that flashed above their heads, and Jules, winking at Delphi, grabbed Ernst by his jacket and Delphi by her arm and pulled them inside a fortuneteller's stall. The Gypsy's crystal ball and its wooden stand were perched on an elaborate china cake plate in the middle of an ordinary round table that was covered with a ghastly lime-colored cloth.

'Well, my wise friend,' Jules said, smiling at the woman who sat there, 'how much for a fine fortune?' The middle-aged Gypsy had sallow skin and small eyes the color of burned wood. Crude black hair dye had left a dark band across the top of her blouse collar and the edge of her bandanna as it folded back across her forehead. Her cheap golden earrings had bits of colored glass stuck into them and hung from her wrinkled earlobes nearly to her shoulders. 'Eh, *voilà*,' she said, looking directly at Ernst, 'what fortune can I tell for this fellow except that he will live to be ninety and nine.' She shrugged and then grinned at Jules. 'But if you give me twenty-five francs, my stallion, I will tell you the name of the woman who will kill you in your sleep.'

Jules burst out laughing. 'It would take all the fun out of life, my Romany princess. No, you must keep that secret and instead tell this lady about her future.' He put his hands at Delphi's shoulders to push her toward the table. 'For ten francs,' he added.

'No!' Delphi said, pulling away from him. 'I don't want to know anything at all.'

The Gypsy squinted her eyes and nodded her head, 'It is a clever woman who runs from her future.'

'You're a wise old tart,' Jules said with some seriousness, throwing a few francs onto the table. 'I may even come back with my twenty-five francs after all.'

'You won't be disappointed,' she answered, not smiling. 'I assure you, you will not be disappointed.'

Jules was still smiling as he bargained for a cap for Ernst from one of the vendors. Getting it for less than half the amount asked, he plopped it on Ernst's head and pulled the brim down across his eyes. 'There. It's better. We must make you part of the population here. You look much too much like a banker.'

'But I think he looks exactly right,' Delphi said defensively.

'Not for the rue des Vertus.' Jules raised his eyebrow for a second as he noted Delphi's protectiveness. 'Unless, of course, you and Ernst would rather have an ordinary night's tour of Paris? Then, of course, he has no need for a cap.'

'No, no, I want to see the secret Paris you promised, Jules. I am glad to wear the hat.' Ernst tried for a sinister expression, making Jules laugh again.

'Jules Chasson, I am not at all certain I trust you,' Delphi said, still holding firmly to Ernst's forearm. 'The next thing you'll suggest is that Ernst dangle a cigarette from his lower lip like a hood.'

'But exactly,' Jules said. 'The dance hall I'm taking you to is very authentic. The Argentine gauchos in the band may be from Neuilly, but the customers are the low life of the world.' Jules hailed a taxi and gave the driver the name of an alleyway near the place d'Italie. 'This place is perfect, full of sailors and serving girls. Seduction is everywhere in Au Clair de Lune.' Jules rolled his eyes and lit a cigarette. 'Look here, Ernst, you wet the paper *comme ça* and put it on the lower lip and just let it hang there.'

'I cannot think why you are taking such delight in my

corruption,' Ernst said, licking his cigarette's paper, 'but I am certainly willing.' His cigarette rolled from his lip to fall into his lap, making all three of them burst out laughing again.

The dance hall they entered seemed much like the others they had already passed around the place d'Italie. Music blared out into the street from an opened door, huge mirrors inside reflected Venetian glass globes of light that were placed around the room, and a prismed ball spun in the middle of the ceiling, shooting colored light like confetti.

Once inside, Delphi was immediately aware that wherever she looked, especially on the dance floor, bodies were intertwined with one another. The young girls who weren't dancing wandered in search of men, their young breasts pushing against their tight satin blouses and suspenders. The innocence of their stylish pouts was given the lie by the spit curls pressed against their foreheads and cheeks and by their suggestive struts.

'Well,' Ernst whispered to Delphi as they watched, 'Jules was not wrong. Every man here is wearing a cap. And look, just as he said, the table *is* nailed to the floor!' Ernst demonstrated the fact by pulling at the table after he sat on the imitation leather banquette. 'Jules, you are a perfect guide to this secret Paris.'

At that second, the band music stopped all at once and some man at the front of the hall announced loudly that everyone had to pay up. There was a dreadful silence.

'Jules, what in the world are they doing?' Delphi asked as she watched every man on the dance floor, one hand pressed into the small of his partner's back, the other fumbling deep into a pocket of his trousers.

'They have to pay five sous for every dance. By the way, there's an unwritten law here, Delphi. You have to dance with any man who asks you. Just don't drink with him.'

'But why not, Jules? It would seem impolite to refuse a drink.' Ernst leaned over toward Jules, his hand over his mouth like a conspirator. 'I don't seem to understand such an arrangement.'

'It's an unwritten law, too. Drinking with a regular is making an agreement to sleep with him. So, my friends, dancing yes, drinking no.' Jules seemed pleased at Ernst's embarrassment and looked about the room carefully before signaling for one of the waiters. The waiters passed with enormous trays of glasses lightly balanced on one upturned palm, having, it appeared, absolutely no trouble whatsoever threading their way through the labyrinth of loving couples at the tables and on the dance floor. 'By the way, one is never served by the bottle here, always by the glass. Bottles are considered potentially dangerous weapons,' Jules told them as he ordered three glasses of absinthe. Just as he placed the order, a thick-bodied, heavily bearded hood, his cap low over his left eye, approached the table. 'Delphi,' Jules ordered, 'stand up and pretend I have already asked you for this dance. Quickly, I tell you. And take no notice of him.' Delphi stood up immediately, a shiver of fear going up her spine into her skull. 'Ernst,' Jules said, looking back over his shoulder as he pushed Delphi roughly ahead of him, 'unbutton your shirt and don't talk to anybody.'

The moment they reached the other dancers, Jules yanked Delphi's arm and spun her hard against him, holding her there. 'What do you think you're doing, Jules Chasson?' She tried to pull free of him as the music began its slow constant rhythm.

'Saving you from having to dance with a pimp,' he answered, his arms solidly around her.

'I think you are deliberately making fun of Ernst.'

'Nonsense. I like Ernst. I wouldn't make fun of him. Besides, he admires my work.' He rammed her leg back, the front of his thigh taking the weight of the front of hers as he dipped her, holding her still against him, his hand spread across her back and above her buttocks. 'You need practice,' he whispered. 'We should dance more often.'

'Bastard,' she said, unable to move, her legs awkwardly spread apart in the step.

'I just want to know what the hell you're doing with Ernst Hasse? He's a decent man, Delphi, not some Russian ballet dancer with a cheerful groin. It is very clear that he loves you. I think you will hurt him badly if you're not careful.'

'It is none of your concern,' she said sharply, her body

denying her fury as it unhesitatingly followed his. The smoke drifted in lacy blue clouds above her head as the beat of the tango became more insistent. His face was so close to hers, the taste of his sweat was on her lips. She felt the muscles of his stomach tense slightly as he pulled her across him to drop her over his thigh. His mouth grazing hers, he held her in a low embrace. She could feel the power in his hands and shoulders and the dark curious glance of other dancers as the crystal prism blinded her with dots of color. Then the music stopped and the same man who asked for the price of the other dance asked again, and Jules slowly lifted Delphi up and let his arm drop from hers as he reached for loose change in his pocket. Suddenly, panic flooding her, she broke away from him and ran back through the crowded room toward the table. 'Ernst,' she called out wildly, 'Ernst! Please! You must take me home. Please. I am suddenly dizzy from all the noise . . . the smoke . . .'

'Of course,' he said, rising immediately and taking her hand. 'Of course,' he repeated, frowning. 'Jules, would you please see to the bill? Delphi is not well for the moment. Perhaps some air will do her good. I would take her home myself, but I would be lost without your guidance. We will wait just outside.' Had he seen Jules's performance? Worse, had he seen hers? He walked her outside the dance hall past a carload of pimps and prostitutes, his face as implacable as ever and his arm as steady as if he were walking her into the dining room at the Ritz.

As the taxi retreated from the place d'Italie to make its way toward the center of Paris and Ernst's hotel, Jules was as subdued in voice as he was in manner. He did not betray the least surprise when Delphi got out of the taxi with Ernst, and Delphi felt Ernst's surprise instead. Still, she did not care. She wanted Jules to know once and for all there could never be anything between them. He had pushed her into Ernst Hasse's arms a good deal sooner than she had intended. Perhaps, she thought, he had pushed her far beyond her intention. Had she ever thought of sleeping with Ernst Hasse? No, she thought, she had not, but now she would. She would do it to spite Jules

Chasson. And to stop her thundering heart from its response to him. Knowing that Jules watched her, she took Ernst's arm possessively and led him away from the taxi to the front door of the hotel.

She lay flat on the bed, staring at the ceiling. It was so peaceful in his rooms. The satin sheets were newly pressed. The pale apricot walls were free of any burden but the delicacy of their moldings. There were no paintings. There were no photographs. No clippings. Nothing at all. She smiled as she looked at his suits hung neatly in the large closet across from the bed. They took up no more than a quarter of its space.

'Delphi? Are you asleep?'

'Me?' She turned lazily onto her side. 'No.'

'Oh.' He sounded disappointed. 'I hoped that perhaps you were.'

'Why?'

'Because I just proposed to you.' He smiled at her. 'I just asked you to marry me.'

'What?' She sat up, making no attempt at modesty.

'I want you to marry me. Will you?'

She was amazed at his question. 'But Ernst, I do not want to be married!'

'I am not a good lover,' he said softly. 'Is that it?' He waited for her answer a moment, and when it did not come, he shrugged and shook his head. 'I might lie and say I used to be, but I cannot lie to you. I was never good enough. My wife was tolerant, my mistresses always disappointed. I lack finesse.'

'You are fine for me,' she said. She kissed his cheek lightly and lay down her head next to his on his pillow. 'Fine,' she said again.

'I'm not a man who is too proud to take a bit of direction from a woman he cares for . . . so if you wish to guide me . . .' He turned slightly. 'Perhaps if I am a better lover, you will marry me.'

'But I never want to be married,' she said softly.

'I don't understand, Delphi.' He struggled onto his elbow. 'My intentions have been quite clear from the beginning. I know you have teased me for my conventions, but I am a product of those conventions. I was given to understand, that is, when you came home with me tonight . . .' He took a long breath and looked away from her and then sighed and took another breath. 'In my world, it is an unwritten law that if the woman sleeps with a man who loves her, she is rather aware of the seriousness of that act. Certainly, I have not presumed upon you in any way, have I?' He looked back at her face.

She shook her head quickly, refusing to look at him, looking instead at the bump of her knees under the satin sheet. Had she known this sexual act was a capitulation to his desire for marriage? She took a swift little breath and let it go to take another. Jules had certainly warned her on the dance floor just hours before. There was no excuse at all. Was this proposal what she wanted? She felt her panic begin again. Was she so afraid of Jules Chasson that she would marry a man she did not love at all? She shuddered, the satin shimmering around her.

'I must be an impossible man to elicit such a response from a proposal of marriage.' He tried to cover her shoulders with some of the top sheet, but it slid off them again and again.

'No, it is not you. It is me. I am surprised. I really thought you would never marry again. I mean, so quickly, after knowing me so short a time . . .' She sounded so desperate to herself. She stopped, too embarrassed to look at him. He touched her arm gently.

'But I am nearly fifty, Delphi. I haven't so many years left that I can afford to waste any. I am in a hurry to be happy. You make me happy. You make me feel young, and it's good to feel young. Marriage isn't so bad. You don't know because you've never been married.'

'I don't have to cut off my finger to know I would miss it!' Her voice was filled with such vehemence that he flinched at its sound. She retreated from her words at once, not wishing to hurt him. 'It is only that I am so selfish I never considered marriage. You see, it would never be fair to anyone I might marry.'

'I am not asking you to be fair. Just tell me what you want, and I shall arrange for you to have it. Tell me what you don't want, and you need never think of that.' He touched her cheek lightly with his hand. 'Even the most selfish woman must admit such an offer is agreeable.'

She looked at him, her eyes boldly on his face. It was a pleasant and undistinguished face, so full of concern. She was startled to find that she cared for him, that his concern mattered to her. She did not answer right away but stopped and started and stopped again until finally she understood she must say something. 'I would be terrible for you, Ernst. I just want to do my work and live my life and not be interfered with. I could not survive the demands of marriage and the demands of my work.'

He smiled at her sweetly and then pushed himself toward the edge of the bed and, placing his feet together on the floor, stood up, self-consciously keeping his back toward her as he reached across to the chair and put on his robe. He put his hands in the pockets of the robe and walked up and down beside the bed, finally stoping at its foot and looking over at her. 'You have not said you do not care for me. Am I wrong, then, to assume that you might?'

'But of course I care for you—'

'No, let me finish. I said I was prepared to give you anything you want, and I am, but not because I am so generous, Delphi. Rather, it is because I am quite as selfish as you. I am aware that you do not have the same measure of feelings for me as I have for you. However – please, let me finish – I think that one day you will. Is it terrible to say it? I know it will be true.' He cleared his throat and frowned, the creases in his forehead puckering. 'I have been looking for a wife since my wife died nine years ago. I have been with many women, but none was . . . suitable. You are the first suitable woman I have met. I am very old-fashioned, I admit, but I must marry someone I love.' He stopped speaking and smiled again, the creases in his forehead leaving and two broad dimples appearing on either side of his lips. 'If you like me here, Delphi, I promise you will like me even more in Berlin.' He sat at the end of the mattress facing her, holding the rounded brass knob on the side of the footboard. 'I think I am taking advantage of you, Delphi, but you see, I want you to be my wife.'

'You are very surprising, Ernst Hasse,' she said softly,

lying back against the pillows, looking up at the ceiling again. 'You must know I am a Jew. Surely, there is a woman somewhere who has no hesitancy about marriage and is properly Aryan for Germany. I read the papers, but I fear you don't.'

'Didn't you hear me, Delphi? I said I wanted you for my wife. I don't give a damn what's in the papers. Not all Germans are Nazis. If necessary I would claim that your religion was Russian Orthodox as is that of your parents. It is not a problem.'

'But I am a Jew. My name is Stern.'

'You are quite off the point.' She could not see his eyes now. His face was toward her, but his eyes were deep in shadow. 'Will you marry me or not? If you will not, there is no point to any discussion.' His voice was not in the least threatening. 'I will give you everything you wish. My house is vast. There is a whole wing you can convert to a studio if you wish.'

'Yes,' she said.

'What?' The mattress groaned as he shifted his position and turned to look at her more closely. 'Did you say yes?'

'Yes.'

'I see.' He was silent as he stood again and walked toward the window and then turned to walk back toward her.

'What is it?' she asked, startled by his reaction.

'There is one other matter,' he said very seriously. 'Are you sure you are talented and not just mad?'

She sat up and put her arms around her knees. Was it wrong to marry him? He was so trusting, so loyal. He would take care of her so easily, and she would not have to think of anything but her work. She had been honest with him, and still he wanted her.

'Well?' he asked, leaning toward her, squinting now.

'I am both,' she said finally.

'Good,' he answered, 'because I am neither.'

The woman who came to her door early on the following Tuesday morning stood on its threshold, shivering in a lynx coat. On her beige hat, quills of elaborate feathers issued from a pennant of ribbons and swept up and out, trembling in the cold air. Under the brim of her hat, her smile was irresistible as it stretched across her face, making ripples in her flesh. She held out her hand to grasp Delphi's and shook it with enthusiasm. 'You are Delphi Stern, of course. I am Nicole Clément from Galerie Clément. I was so glad to get your call. I am delighted to look at your work.' She walked past Delphi, put a cigarette in her mouth, and lit it, blowing smoke everywhere, coughing and spitting a piece of cigarette paper from her lip. 'That was a fantastic book, eh? Jules Chasson must love you. He makes most women look like the broadside of a mule.' She walked about the room, dodging the furniture and slowly letting out a steady stream of smoke as she carefully examined the paintings on Delphi's walls. 'I am so amazed at my preconceptions. I hate them in anyone else, but I have them all the time. From Jules's pictures, I thought you would live in understated luxury – low, functional chairs and that sort of thing, with perhaps one calla lily in a Lalique vase. I throw darts at pictures of those soulful ladies in their white Grés tunics mooning over their Lalique vases. Is this your studio? May I go in?' She put her cigarette out in a saucer on the sideboard and immediately lit another, not waiting for Delphi's permission to enter the studio.

How remarkable, Delphi thought; she has two distinctly separate faces. Her profile was not remotely related to her full face: one was gamine, the other the face of a much older woman. Her eyes were large and heavy-lidded, with tiny, delicate eyebrows penciled over them. Her wrists were so slim that it appeared it might take all her strength merely to hold the cigarette to her lips. She stayed inside Delphi's studio for five minutes while Delphi waited for her, sitting in Tolchin's chair and listening to her sounds.

'Can I offer you a drink? Cognac perhaps?' Delphi asked as Nicole came back into the room.

'Cognac,' she answered. 'It's cold.'

Delphi got the glass and poured out a good amount and gave it to Nicole. 'Thank you for coming,' she said, bowing her head slightly. Nicole lifted her glass up toward Delphi and drank some of the cognac.

'I will be frank. I came here for two reasons,' Nicole

said, managing to inhale her cigarette smoke as well as swallow her drink. 'I came first of all because I admire your work.' She waved her arm about, trying to diminish the amount of smoke she caused. Her gold bracelets clicked against one another like castanets. 'And' – she gulped the last of the brandy, putting the glass on the floor beside her – 'because your behavior confuses me. No doubt it confuses any serious dealer.' She put her cigarette out in the small rubber tree by the side of the bed behind her and lit another, sending great gusts of smoke toward the ceiling. 'I am confused by the fact that you allowed a fellow like Marriac to make you a trifle, a silly girl riding the back of a circus elephant, this season's darling. This is very disconcerting to me. Excuse me for saying so, but you have spit in your coffee.'

'I thought that some attention would not hurt me.'

'Hurt you!' Nicole laughed, her laughter at least an octave higher than her voice. 'It damned near ruined you! Are you stupid?'

'I was,' Delphi said, 'very stupid.'

'I hope you are no longer tied up with Marriac.' Delphi shook her head. 'Good. I like you. I would like to help you.' Nicole flipped off her coat. She was even slighter than Delphi had imagined her, hardly a hundred pounds.

'You represent an old friend of mine, Emile Norbet.'

'Emile? You are a friend of Emile's? He is so good. He sells so much and is so serious. The Americans have made quite a market for his work; now the French are warming up.'

'We studied together in Italy.'

'With Marra?' Nicole's eyebrows nearly flew off her face. 'You must tell me about him one day. He is the only teacher I have ever known of who produces artists the way a box factory produces boxes. It is quite fantastic, no? Four of his students – Nival, William Lawrence, Emile, of course, and you – are all so gifted.'

Delphi brought Nicole an empty plate and handed it to her. Nicole put her cigarette out in the plate. 'It is disgusting, this smoking. I know it. I burn half my clothes and nearly set my desk on fire daily. Disgusting.'

'My father smokes. I'm quite used to it.'

Nicole stood up and walked over to one of the paintings she saw and turned it toward her. 'Is this one you had at the Galerie Maight about three or four years ago? I am surprised nobody bought this painting. It is rare.'

'You remember it?' Delphi was startled.

'Yes, of course. I inquired about you at the time. I was prepared to take you on if you were interested. I am a woman, after all, and so I look out for women. There are few who are intelligent artists or gifted ones. I was going to call you when, *voilà*, Chasson's pictures are printed, and there is your face everywhere. Suddenly you are a model. It convinced me you were not serious.' Nicole put her hands on her hips and bit her bottom lip for a moment. 'What do you want? Tell me.'

'I want you to show my work. To represent me. I want to be taken seriously.'

'I will be frank with you. I saw the show at Hercule, and it was better than its reception. You are extremely gifted, but I will not show your work in my gallery until the public forgets your face. There is an old saying that a serious woman should be neither beautiful nor notorious. You are both.'

'Hardly,' Delphi said. 'My face was merely in fashion for the moment.'

'It must be forgotten. I will handle you only on the condition that your fashionable face is forgotten. It can best be forgotten if you are out of Paris. Even better, out of France. I will mount a showing of your work when the time is right and not before. It may take months or years. Think about it and let me know.' She picked up her coat and swung it around her like a matador.

'I have thought about it, Mademoiselle Clément,' Delphi said without pausing. 'If you take me on, you will have no problem. I am getting married soon and I will be living elsewhere.'

Nicole smiled and shot out her hand. Delphi took it, surprised at the strength of her grasp. 'It is time for a woman to be great. I hope it is you. I will have these paintings picked up at the end of this week, and then you will give me the address where I can reach you.'

'It is funny, but I always thought the Galerie Clément

was owned by a man,' Delphi said, letting Nicole's hand drop from hers.

'It was, but my father had no sons. *Au revoir*, Delphi Stern. Let me hear from you soon.' Nicole pivoted on her high-heeled shoes, pulled open the door, and was gone. Delphi phoned Ernst immediately to find out her address in Berlin.

'Is there anything more you want pushed and shoved anywhere else?'

Jules had finished moving all of her furniture, but she had hardly progressed at all in packing the last of her trunks. Now he sat down across from her on the closed trunk against the wall, his white linen trousers still rolled high on his muscled calves. She was aware of his eyes and his silence. She folded a black sweater and put it inside the opened trunk, hesitated a moment, and took it out again, holding it against her.

'Is that the sweater you wore when I took those pictures of you in the Bois with all those kids?' She nodded briefly, putting the sweater on her lap. 'On that day, I thought I might marry you.' He rolled the light blue shirtsleeves down the length of his arms and buttoned the cuffs.

'You won't get married until you're eighty. You just wanted to add me to your stable.' How odd the room looked without the usual mess, she thought. How empty and lifeless. Ernst had called only three days before with the news that her papers were in order. Why had she been so impatient to leave that almost all her packing had been accomplished so soon? The movers would be there that afternoon and Ernst would arrive that night, and the next morning she would be married and on her wedding trip through Alsace and then across the Alps. Ernst and she had never been alone for a full week. Delphi shivered slightly and put the sweater back into the trunk, then reached around into the armoire for the last of her clothes, her hands finding the green silk dress Luis had bought her. Marra? My God, she hadn't thought of him in months. Was it possible? She stared at the dress.

'Did you run from him, too?' Jules's voice was gentle. 'I think you run too much.' Delphi stood up, still holding the

487

dress.

'Let it go, Jules,' she said, tossing the dress away from her back into the armoire. It clung to a shelf there for a moment and then fell to the floor.

'It might cheer me some if you let me take a few pictures for old time's sake.'

'Never.'

'I might believe you were actually gone if I had a record of it.'

'Your pictures nearly took my life.'

'I think you have that wrong, Delphi,' he said, standing up angrily. 'The way I see it, they gave you your life. Nicole. Hasse. *Moi*. The good as well as the bad. Don't be a victim. It doesn't suit you.' He turned his back on her.

'I'm sorry, Jules. I'm behaving badly. It's never been easy for me to move from place to place even though I don't have many possessions. Come, let's have some lunch. Maybe I'm just hungry.'

When she sat down across from him at the table, she poured herself a large glass of wine and held it out toward him. '*Salud*, eh?' she said, drinking half of it quickly and then sipping the rest. The summer food made a still life of exceptional beauty. There was something so compelling about pure color, great arches and swirls of color, one illuminating the other, she thought, suddenly finding that she was staring at Jules. His hair was thick and his lashes were golden above the dark blue eyes that looked intently back at her. Oh, my God, his face, she thought. It was more beautiful than ever.

He reached for a wedge of tomato with one hand, a slice of pâté with the other, and clamped them together and offered them to her. 'I'm not hungry,' she said, staring at the length of his hands.

'Take it.' He continued to hold it toward her. When she took it, he made himself another, looking away from her face. 'Do you love Ernst Hasse?'

She pretended she was not watching him when he looked back at her.

'Not yet. But I may.'

'Perhaps you should love me instead. It's safer.'

'You?' She forced a laugh. 'Why would I love you? You

488

could never love anything so much as your camera.'

'And you will love nothing so much as your paints. Poor dear Ernst, will he ever understand that? We are so alike, Delphi. I'm the one who should take you away from here.'

'Oh, shut up, Jules,' she said, standing up from her place, smashing her fist on the table. 'Where will you take me? To the Twelfth Arrondissement? You love Paris almost as much as your camera.'

'Can Ernst guarantee your safety in Berlin?'

'His house is outside the city. There will be no one to bother us.'

'No one to bother you!' He laughed uproariously.

'Stop laughing! Jews have always been persecuted. Ernst believes that now Hitler has gained absolute power, the Nazis won't need to castigate the Jews any longer. They have already relaxed some restrictions. Besides, my papers say I am Russian Orthodox. Ernst is sure I am quite safe. He wouldn't let me go otherwise, you know that.' She sat down again.

'If hatred achieved Hitler his office, then hatred will keep it for him. And there is no doubt of the fact of hatred – I showed you my pictures of his glorious Gestapo leaders. I must say, though, the man has talent. He did turn that country around quickly. After all that chaos, I would never have thought he could manage it.' Jules was silent for a moment and then handed her a package. 'I have brought you a wedding present. Open it.'

In a delicate silver frame edged in smiling cupids was a portrait of Jules with such a soulful expression that even his curls looked forlorn. Delphi had never seen him look that way in life. 'Isn't it wonderful? I took it myself. I have all your photos, you see, to remember you by. I want to make sure you remember me. I want you to cry every time you look at my picture.'

'I will not cry, Jules Chasson. It would give you too much pleasure.' She leaned slightly forward. 'Will you cry when you look at mine?'

'Occasionally, but only because you are no longer here to make money for me.' He started to smile but stopped. His joke had fallen flat. They stared at one another across the summer food. Finally, Jules spoke. 'I hate any sort of good-bys,' he said. 'It is the beginning of history, and that merely means that some things have run their course.' He was staring at the green dress that lay on the floor in front of the armoire.

'Surely we will meet again,' she said, falsely cheerful. 'It could not be the end of our history.'

'In any event, we are fools.' He poured the last bit of wine into his glass and lifted it towards hers. 'You are a fool for going to Germany, and I am a fool for not stopping you. *Salud.*' He drank half of the wine and offered the rest to her, watching her, his eyes fixed on hers, as she finished it.

8

July 6, 1934
Dear Sonya,

So I am married! We had the most horrid, affected, typically minor French bureaucrat to perform the ceremony. Afterward he would not even have a glass of champagne with us but ran out of the room as if we were lepers. Well, German nationalism can't be worse than French chauvinism.

The trip here was uneventful, very beautiful. I am full of mountain air and sights, rested and ready for my new life. From what little I have seen, Germany is clean, well ordered, and full of soldiers and swastikas. There seems to be no poverty at all. Everyone we have come in contact with at the inns and the restaurants and on the streets is most cheerful, and all of them are delighted to meet an American. I have noticed a few anti-Semitic posters and signs, but there is no knife at any throat and I am comfortable here. In spite of my training at my mother's knee, politics goes in one ear and out the other, so I can't answer your questions. I have told Ernst that he must write and explain it all to you. Please don't make me live to regret it.

Our house is well outside Berlin behind stone walls and back from the main road. It is an enormous dark, drab cavern that could use your touch. When you come here to visit, I expect you to call in the painters and upholsterers, add a few windows, make magic, and give me some light!

I have a staff, Sonya! There are servants all about who nod and call me Frau Hasse all day long – whoever she is. I have taken exception to the head housekeeper, whose sternness even I may be unable to ignore, but the upstairs maids are delightful young girls, running about changing linen and ironing nightgowns, so that I expect to see the ghost of your mother come here to order them about as you told me she did in the palace on the Nevsky. Dear Sonya, will you forgive me for enjoying my luxury? I have never had it before.

It is soon to say so, but I know that this marriage – this move – was the right one. By the way, could you send me a copy of the wedding picture of you and Papa? The one that used to be on the dresser in your bedroom? I would very much like Ernst to see it.

Be well and write to your
Frau Hasse

*   *   *

There would be only one dinner party, Ernst swore. Solitary man that he was, he was still obligated to introduce his new wife to a few friends, his colleagues from the hospital, some relatives. Apologizing profusely, he had promised to make the evening as simple as possible for her, swearing that the preparations would in no way interfere with her work, that he and the staff would arrange everything – food, flowers, drink, extra help. Delphi was merely to spend her day as she wished and then bathe and dress and come downstairs, the honored guest.

Delphi stared at her reflection in the mirror of the dressing table. How odd she looked in the simple navy silk dress that she had picked out in Paris just four weeks before. This was no Delphi Stern, this was someone's wife. For the first time she regretted the dress and the diamond earrings that Ernst had given her for a wedding gift and that now dropped delicately from her ears and moved in the drafty room, catching more blue light from her dress.

'Are you nervous about tonight?' Ernst was behind her, looking at her reflection.

'I don't think the role of second wife suits me.'

'What about "wife"?' She jerked her head around to look at him. 'Are you sorry, Delphi?'

'I will tell you when I am, Ernst. I warned you, after all. But look here, look at me. I think I've done an excellent job. Have you ever seen anyone look more wifely?' He laughed and she smiled up at him. 'I've just had a letter from Sonya. She finds it remarkable that I arrive in Berlin just as Dorothy Thompson is being expelled.'

'But who is Dorothy Thompson?' Ernst frowned. 'I don't think I know her. Should I know her?'

'She's a frumpy old zealot who writes unkindly about Adolf Hitler. I don't imagine her articles have been published in Germany. No, of course not. I'll show you some of the articles if you like. Sonya sent them to me. Dorothy Thompson has every quality of which Sonya approves. How happy I would have made her being Dorothy Thompson. The older I get, the harder it is for me to be such a disappointment to Sonya.'

'I don't think you disappoint her.'

'Ernst, what shall I do with you? I suppose that to be any sort of doctor, one must be an eternal optimist and think one can cure or fix anything. But even you, Ernst Hasse, cannot cure or fix Sonya, and you cannot cure or fix me.' She smiled, and he laughed at her again. 'Well,' she continued, 'what do you think?' She stood and turned in front of him. 'Too skinny for Germany taste?'

'I think they will understand why I married you.' He walked to her and touched her hair, which she had piled on top of her head and fastened with two gold-edged combs. 'Thank you for going through this, my dear.'

'What time is it?' she asked, already eager for the whole affair to be over.

'Seven-fifteen. I asked Sylvia and Hans to come early, so you could chat with them first. They should be here any minute. My cousins, aunt, and colleagues will arrive promptly at seven-thirty. My son, he is unpredictable. He is moody, you see. Also, it depends on my brother. They will be driving together.' He paused and frowned, taking off his glasses and rubbing the bridge of his nose, as was his habit. 'If it is possible, Delphi, I would ask you to avoid politics. The subject may come up, but it is unnecessary for you to join in.' He put his glasses back on. 'My brother is in the party. My son, also. It was necessary for them to join for the factories to continue. They have very little to do with politics, actually. They make no decisions, have no power, it was all for the sake of the business, but nonetheless it would be better if—'

He was interrupted by the phone and went into the

sitting room to answer it. He was back quickly. 'It was my son, Johann. It seems he is not so happy with my marriage to a young American. He will not come tonight.' Ernst was obviously upset. He tried to smile. 'He had a German widow all picked out for me. A ghastly creature who weighed two hundred pounds but had impeccable lineage, back to the old *Volk*.' He stopped smiling and took off his glasses, shrugging his shoulders. 'He will come round. He is only nineteen, after all. Like most boys his age, he is headstrong and is infatuated with Hitler. He likes Hitler's uncompromising views. After his mother died, I was not much of a parent, and I think perhaps Johann needs discipline in his life just now. It will pass. It will pass.' He frowned as he waved his thoughts away. 'Let me go and tell Hilda that there will be one less for dinner. I'm afraid you'll have to sit next to my aunt Berthe. She means well but is not very stimulating.'

Delphi watched Ernst walk out to the hall. Could it really be that he would always make the best of everything? She heard the doorbell ring and she jumped a little. How silly of her. It was, after all, just a dinner party.

'Come, Delphi,' Ernst called to her from the bottom of the stairs, 'meet Sylvia, who is thrilled that I finally married. Now she can stop protecting me from the hordes who were after me. Also, you must meet her husband, my colleague and dear friend, Hans von Ribben.'

Delphi greeted them, smiling. They were a handsome couple, both tall and strong-featured with light hair and piercing blue eyes. They exuded good health and warmth. They looked, she thought, shaking their hands, like brother and sister.

'Sylvia is our true German, the only one of us in almost any room in the country who can really trace her ancestry back to the fourteenth century.'

'Will you stop teasing me about that, Ernst!' Sylvia reprimanded him gently and then stepped forward and took both Delphi's hands in hers. 'I'm sorry I couldn't get here before tonight. I have heard about you so much between Ernst's visits to Paris that I think I will like having you here in person far more than listening to

Ernst's endless and tiresome stories about you.' She smiled at Delphi. 'No one can be as wonderful as he has described you.'

'But she is, she is!' Ernst laughed at Sylvia's teasing. 'You will be the first to know it, Sylvia. Come and have a drink and get acquainted before the rest arrive. And Sylvia, be sweet to my cousin Eva and my aunt Berthe when they arrive. Please, no funny business.'

'I swear,' Sylvia said, wrapping one arm about Delphi's waist as they walked into the drawing room. 'His aunts and cousins are insufferable. I think someone should warn you about them.' Her sunny face changed suddenly; the dark expression came quickly and then vanished. Why, she reminds me of Sonya, Delphi thought; her moods are as easy to read as a primer. 'Is Rudolf coming, Delphi?' Delphi looked at her blankly. 'Rudolf, Ernst's brother?'

'Yes,' Delphi answered.

'Ah.' Again Sylvia's face changed. 'Well, then,' she said, defiance stamped across her features, 'let us go and have a good stiff drink and prepare ourselves.'

At dinner Delphi sat at the head of the table, Rudolf to her left, and Aunt Berthe, replacing Johann, to her right.

'Do you speak Russian?' Aunt Berthe inquired.

'Yes, although I am out of practice at the moment.'

'Your German is good.'

'It was important to my mother that whatever language I spoke, I spoke it well.' Delphi smiled at the old woman, and she nodded back. She had extremely fine skin covered with a layer of white hairs like frost. Her eyes were gluey, pale and colorless under her glasses. She had small breasts for a German woman, Delphi thought.

'Were there many Germans in New York City?' Berthe asked her.

'Yes. Quite a few.'

'I always admired the cowboys,' the old lady said, a sudden sparkle coming into those glazed eyes. 'What can you tell me about them? Did you ever meet a cowboy?' Through the first course Delphi regaled her with tales of the Old West. Aunt Berthe was charmed.

Delphi knew that it was time to turn her attention to Rudolf, but she kept avoiding him. Rudolf sat in his chair like a soldier, his body straight forward toward the table. When at last Delphi glanced over at him, he lifted one eyebrow with chilly precision as he turned his head toward her slightly, just enough for the monocle in his right eye to reflect her own image back at her. There was indeed a family resemblance to Ernst, but she would have never confused them. She quickly bent once more to her right and Aunt Berthe.

'I understand you paint,' Rudolf said as the soup plates were being cleared and Aunt Berthe had looked toward her son-in-law Erich to answer a question.

'I beg your pardon?'

'You paint.' He said it louder.

'Yes,' she answered.

'You are very young.' Was she supposed to answer that? She wondered. She simply smiled. 'Do you sell your paintings?'

'I have a gallery in Paris.' He turned in her direction a little more, showing the eye without the monocle. It was the palest blue, remarkably like the Meissen candelabra.

'Really? Perhaps we can arrange for an exhibition here in Berlin.' Delphi looked toward Ernst, but he was laughing at some joke of Sylvia's.

'I think not. My contract with Clément is an exclusive one.' Would the meat course never come?

'I know the Galerie Clément.' He rubbed his lips together as if smoothing them down. 'You look surprised. I am quite a connoisseur, actually. I have rather a notable collection. Wait a moment.' His body leaned toward her for the first time. 'Did you have a showing a few years ago? It was not at the Clément, but I seem to remember quite a stir in the papers. I was in Paris at the time. Was that you?'

'Yes.' She looked again at Ernst. Rudolf cracked a breadstick in half and then cracked each piece in half again.

'You used another name, I think.'

'Yes.'

'Stern, wasn't it?' She held her breath. 'But your father is Gregory Tolchin. I know him.'

'I beg your pardon?'

496

'Yes, I know him. I met him in Munich at a meeting of the International Gold Committee a few years ago. He was very charming. Is he a Communist or a capitalist? I can't quite decide. Ah . . .' he said, lifting his monocle from his eye and cleaning it with his napkin, looking entirely different without that silly piece of glass and its attendant black ribbon. 'Ah, here is our food. At last.'

The food was good enough. The service was efficient, and before too long, Delphi was looking down at dessert, a dry nut torte with a chocolate butter frosting.

Rudolf threw his napkin over his cake and pushed his chair back, crossing his leg at the knee. 'I never take sweets,' he announced.

'Rudolf was always our spartan,' Aunt Berthe said. 'Ernst was our angel, and my son, Thomas, our poet.'

'But I didn't know you had a son, Aunt Berthe.'

'He was killed by Russians,' Rudolf said, meeting Delphi's glance. 'The war,' he added.

'He was too romantic by half,' Aunt Berthe said. 'He thought war was something that showed the best of men.' Berthe had lost interest in her dessert and put down her fork across the edge of the silver-rimmed plate. 'Too many Germans think war is wonderful,' she said, looking up at Rudolf.

'It would be good for our factories,' he said dryly, 'and that is all I care about.'

Hans von Ribben stood and made a sweet toast to his host and hostess before Ernst stood to bid them all move across the hallway to the sitting room for brandy and coffee. Rudolf, without rising, interrupted Ernst. 'I would like to make a request of you all, please. The son of a business acquaintance of mine is a soloist with the Berlin Philharmonic this evening. I have taken the liberty of setting up the wireless, and I would like you all to listen. It begins now. He is the first on the program, and it should only take a short while.' Without waiting to be acknowledged in any way by his brother, Rudolf abruptly got up and switched on the wireless he had set up on the sideboard, standing stiffly next to it. After some minor announcement, the music played out into the room, sounding tinny and contained. Everyone sat respectfully listening to it until it concluded twenty minutes later.

Applauding loudly, Rudolf switched off the wireless. 'Very good, wouldn't you say?' he said with enthusiasm. 'It's his first performance with the Philharmonic, you know. His parents have paid a price, let me tell you. Yes, quite a price. Now they shall have ample reward. A brilliant technician. What do you think, Delphi?' He smiled at her. His monocle made his right eye opaque, and she could not see his left eye at all.

'He sounded fine to me. My ear is not highly trained, but I enjoyed his performance. The piece was by Mendelssohn, wasn't it?'

There was an immediate silence as each of them, their heads snapping in her direction in unison, turned to stare at her.

'It was Schubert,' Sylvia said, standing at her place. 'I often confuse the two.'

'Mendelssohn is not played anymore in Germany,' Rudolf said, looking at Sylvia. 'There is no need for your further confusion.'

Ernst stood quickly, clapping his hands. 'Come, come, our coffee will get cold waiting for us.'

As they walked toward the sitting room across the hall, Sylvia fell into step beside Delphi, linking her arm through Delphi's. 'How well you did, my dear,' she said in a hushed voice. 'I would rather try for conversation with a cobra than with Rudolf Hasse.' Just as they stepped over the threshold of the brightly lit, overfurnished room, Sylvia slid her arm from Delphi's and drifted toward her husband after patting Delphi's hand warmly. The enormous clock just outside in the hallway struck ten as Delphi walked toward Ernst and Marta von Hummel, the wife of the head surgeon. She could smile now, she thought, taking a generous glass of brandy from her servant's tray. This evening was nearly over.

'So what did you think of my world?' Ernst asked her. He was already in bed, his magazine spread out on the satin comforter as he watched Delphi brush out her hair.

'I like Sylvia so much.'

'Ha!' Ernst clapped his hands. 'I knew you would. Of

course you would. She is Jewish.'

'But you said she was the truest German in the room, that her family . . .'

'Yes, goes back to the fourteenth century. They happen to be a Jewish family. That is all. They made quite a fuss when she married outside her faith, let me tell you.'

'Well,' Delphi said, bending from the waist and brushing all her hair down over her head, feeling the hard bristles of the brush in her scalp, 'perhaps that is what so attracted me to her, an instinctive sense of my own kind.'

'Nonsense. She is charming, bright, and active, that is why you liked her.'

'There.' Delphi stood up straight, red-faced, her hair spreading wildly about her face and neck. 'Now I am myself again. Ernst, put down your magazine and look at me. Now I look the eccentric artist again.'

'Come to sleep, Delphi.' Ernst put his magazine on the bed table and turned off the light. 'It is already past my bedtime.'

Delphi sat on the edge of her side of the bed. 'Sylvia reminded me of my mother.'

'But I thought your mother was a redhead.'

'Not her hair, her manner.' Delphi reached over and switched off her light and lay back into the cool satin pillows.

'I am afraid to ask what you thought of Rudolf.'

'He was fearsome, very fearsome. Did you know that he has met my father?'

'No, but I'm not surprised to hear it.' Ernst put one arm behind him to prop the pillow under his neck. 'Rudolf and I seldom communicate. We were never very close and, except for the two weeks we spend together every summer in the Black Forest at the family house, there is seldom any reason to speak to one another. His offices are in Munich.'

'How could you be close with such a man anyway? You aren't the least alike.'

'Don't be so hard on poor Rudolf. He hasn't had such an easy time of it. It was hard being the eldest son. He was expected to go right into the family business. He had no choices, none at all. And he worked so hard all the time, especially when my father was ill, and then again, all through the financial crisis. In my family, I was the lucky one. Rudolf never had time for life. I think it is why he has never married. He is not a bad fellow.'

'I think you would find good in Genghis Khan.'

'But he is my brother . . .' Ernst was about to protest again, but she started giggling at him. 'Ah, but you are teasing.'

'Yes. But what I said is true. You're not in the least alike.'

'By the way, Sylvia has invited us for dinner in a week's time.' Ernst yawned. 'You don't have to go if you don't wish. She would understand.'

'But I do wish.' Delphi sat up and folded her legs under her. 'Am I contradictory? It's just that I've never had a close woman friend. Not ever. And there was something about Sylvia that I liked very much. But I don't know, I find it hard to communicate with her. It's difficult for me to be comfortable speaking to a woman. Maybe I will take her to lunch this week. Would she like that, Ernst?'

'She liked you, darling. That was very apparent.' He turned his face from hers and was silent. 'Delphi?' He kept his face averted and cleared his throat.

'Hmm?' she was watching him in the dark.

'I would like to ask you a question, but I want your honest answer. Do you promise to give me an honest answer?'

'I'll try. Although my father always warned me not to make promises I couldn't keep.' She yawned, stretching her legs out and pointing her toes. 'Well?'

'I was wondering . . . that is . . . are you at all sorry? After tonight especially. Are you?' His carefully modulated voice was tinged with such fear she almost laughed at him as his eyes met hers. 'Are you?' he repeated in a whisper.

'Well, Herr Doktor Hasse, the truth is . . . that is . . .' She sighed very loudly and then swallowed. 'The truth is that I am not sorry at all.'

9

December 10, 1934
Dear Delphi,

I am part of a group petitioning President Roosevelt to intervene and stop the spread of fascism in Europe. This is the first time since my young radical years that I have felt so vehemently about the world situation. I received Ernst's letter, and in spite of his rational, practical explanations of politics and finance in the Third Reich (of which I believe not one word), Germany is no place to be. It is not only your personal safety that worries me (even if your father has assured me Ernst is well connected enough to keep you safe), it is a question of your morality. How can a person of moral worth live in that society? There is an article in *The Nation* on the German corporate community, which has already benefited from the expropriation of Jewish businesses. Has Ernst Hasse? You say he has shares in a factory. Support can be active or passive, and men who allow the flourishing of fascism are, quite to the point, immoral. What will he do when they come to him and force him to join the party? That day cannot be far away. What decision will be make? More important, how can a woman artist live in a country that declares Cézanne, Picasso, etc., etc., morally objectionable? If it has not done so already, your work will suffer. Mark my words, your work will suffer.

You must understand that I am flattered that Ernst took the time to write me, but I do not accept his explanation, and I fear for my daughter.

Merry Christmas, my dear, to you and Ernst. I wish both of you were here to celebrate. I risk making you angry, but you know me well enough to know I must send this letter or I would not be your

loving mother, Sonya

January 3, 1935
Dear Jules,

Happy New Year! How I missed trailing you down to the Dome and toasting the cobblestones with champagne this year. Ernst and I had a staid and sensible dinner at home. He is so dear. He wanted to take me skiing – we have the use of a lodge in the mountains – but I am truly frightened about falling and breaking my bones.

How life plays tricks. You would laugh to see me. Not only do I paint, I have friends, I go to the theater, I go to the opera. I am not possessed any longer. I can leave a painting now and know that I will be able to finish it in the morning, no longer staying up all night worrying that my 'artistic muse' will desert me. Can you imagine creation without continual chaos? I find it astounding, revelatory. I suppose one might say that I have matured, and I suppose you would add that it is, after all, about time.

Ernst is so good for me, Jules. I grow fonder of him every day. He wants you to come and visit us, and so I ask you to, even though I think it might not be for the best. I have painted you out of me, Jules. I have painted everything out of me but my desire for my work and serenity. Can you understand?

And you, my friend?

I have met a wonderful woman, a wife of one of Ernst's associates. She is Jewish, full of life, very beautiful, and very smart. You would love her in an instant.

Have you been in touch with Nicole? She has sold three of my paintings! Three! She still doesn't think the time is right for a showing of my work, but she is building up a clientele and hopes that next year she will sell many Sterns. Soon they will be as ubiquitous as Chasson photographs. What do you think of that? Watch out, *mon brave*, I am closing in!

Love from Frau Hasse

March 5, 1935
Dear Sonya,

The major irritant is the insistence of Herr Boedecker, the head gardener, on keeping the trees around this house from growing taller than eight feet. I would think he would have been told long ago to do anything he could to hide this house's monstrosity. George Grosz would have painted it as a fat wealthy Frau in a bathing costume, swollen with heavy jewelry, all the more obese and unattractive for her lack of modesty. To add to the interior gloom, an ancient row of privet still grows around the first-floor windows like a girdle to choke out any light or air.

Thank you for the copies of the *New York Times*. The situation is not so drastic to one living in the middle of it. I assure you no one has showed the slightest interest in me. At the opera the other evening, I was introduced to William Archer (who is originally from Ohio). We invited him to dine with us this week, but evidently the German government has asked him to leave the country because his portraits for the London *Times* have been too unflattering. I assure you that is the most sinister news I have yet heard.

Please come to see us. Papa looked so well the last time he was here. I wanted you, too.

With love,
Delphi

* * *

Delphi had grown so used to the sight of stormtroopers in their brown uniforms and their red and white armbands with swastikas that she barely took note of them as she and Sylvia followed Sylvia's children through the Tiergarten and past the thousands of roses just coming into bloom. 'Those soldiers seem to be everywhere,' Sylvia said. 'Like locusts,' she added, shivering, her light brown silk suit patterned with tiny jade and orange butterflies rippling at her shoulders. 'I am convinced, Delphi, that every young man in Germany is a Nazi.'

'No,' Delphi said, putting her arm through Sylvia's, 'they are not all in the party. They are just soldiers.'

'You see them in a far more kindly light than I,' Sylvia said, stopping for a moment to admire a salmon-colored tea rose. At the sound of her children's shrieks, she looked up quickly, her face tight with apprehension and fear. Ahead of them Arabella and Hans Josef were just being lifted into the air and spun around by two soldiers. Sylvia quickened her step and clapped her hands. 'Arabella! Hans Josef!' she called in an unsteady voice.

Delphi held her back. 'But they are so happy, Sylvia. Let them be. Those boys won't hurt them.'

'There is rather too much gaiety these days, don't you think?' Sylvia said, watching her children as their blond heads blurred and their laughter came across the rows and rows of roses.

'I think it is just a very beautiful day and even German soldiers feel happy about summer.' Delphi smiled reassuringly at her friend.

'It is all so difficult. The newspapers say one thing and yet . . . oh, I don't know, most of the people behave in the same way toward me except . . . my maids. The young women who have worked for Hans and me for years now, and seemed so happy in my house, have left. The Nazis made it illegal for a Jew to employ domestic workers under the age of thirty-five, and they left us. How can I tell you, it so pains me! Both of them have lived in my house since the children were born, and yet . . . they became such enemies, so full of hate! They even called me names, such dreadful, such unkind names.' Sylvia lowered her head to hide her emotions. 'Excuse me for my outburst, Delphi. It was just so horrible for the children to hear. They are so innocent. They do not understand at all. Last week we had to take them out of their school. Because they are the children of a Jewish mother, they cannot join their schoolmates in the Hitler Youth. They were ostracized so constantly by the other children, even the teachers, we were forced to remove them. We tutor them at home now. Perhaps Hans is right. He is insisting that I take the children and leave Germany until this Nazi business is over.'

'But I have read nothing about any of this! My mother writes me that I am mad to stay, and all the while I have paid no attention to her letters.'

'It doesn't concern you, Delphi. No one knows you are a Jew but Ernst, Hans, and I. And there are no children.'

'Is it so serious that you would leave the country, Sylvia?'

'I don't know any longer, Delphi.' Sylvia trembled as she looked into Delphi's face, her large eyes shimmering with her feelings. 'It is confusing for me. I was raised to have great feeling for Germany. I have German pride in the very marrow of my bones. Now I find I am no longer considered German. What shall I do with my pride, I wonder?' Sylvia looked away from Delphi and then, adjusting the brim of her beige straw cloche, she began to walk forward again, her gait slower. 'My family has been here for five hundred years. How can I be the first to leave?'

Delphi watched the distant horses and their riders on the equestrian paths. Each rider was in full habit, and both they and their graceful mounts looked wholly unreal in the perfection of dappled light that filtered through the ring of ancient trees around them.

'Arabella! Hans Josef!' Sylvia's voice was very firm as she again called out their names. Hearing her, the two soldiers instantly put them down and, tousling their hair with gentle roughness, sent them off in Sylvia's direction. Then, with startling precision, each soldier removed his cap, clicked his heels together, and bowed courteously toward Delphi and Sylvia as Arabella and Hans Josef hurtled toward them their healthy, sweet faces sweaty and beaming and the sound of their voices nearly deafening.

'Mama! Mama! Can we ride the camel? Please! Auntie Delphi has never been for a ride on a camel! May we take her? Please!' Arabella turned big saucer eyes toward her mother, mutely pleading with her. When Sylvia did not soften, Arabella, with an eight-year-old's guile, turned her charm to Delphi.

'I should love to ride a camel,' Delphi said immediately, grabbing both their hands in hers. 'Will we have to go to Egypt for one?'

'No, no!' Arabella laughed. 'Berlin has the greatest zoo in all the world.'

'I will teach you to ride the camel, Auntie Delphi,' five-year-old Hans Josef chimed in. 'I have been many more times than my sister.'

'Just remember, we must hurry,' Sylvia said as she caught up to them all. 'You are to have an early lunch before your English tutor comes. Besides, Delphi and I must do our shopping before the stores are too crowded.'

'Are you going to buy me a birthday present, Auntie Delphi?' Hans Josef asked, his fat cheeks full of dimples.

'But how rude, Hans Josef!' Sylvia exclaimed.

'But it is why you are going shopping, is it not, Mama?' he asked his mother, surprised at her admonishing voice.

'It is always his birthday,' Arabella said, her lip drooping. 'It is never mine.'

'I shall buy you both a present,' Delphi said as they neared the zoological park, 'but only if you let me off the camel when I ask!'

In the car after the last camel ride, Delphi held Hans Josef's squirming little body on her lap. 'I feel as queasy as if I had been a week at sea, Sylvia. These children of yours have strong stomachs.' She patted Josef's stomach tenderly and then tickled him mercilessly. He turned and twisted delightedly in her arms.

As the chauffeur slowed the car at the Leipziger Platz and then stopped in front of Wertheim's department store, the children stopped grumbling about the English tutor and covered their mother's face with kisses before leaping onto Delphi to kiss her, too.

When the two women were finally out of the car, Arabella opened the rear window of the limousine, and as the car pulled out into traffic, both she and Hans Josef started waving frantically and blowing kisses. Passers-by were laughing and waving. It was as if they were on some glorious holiday, Delphi thought, watching them until they were out of sight.

'You are very good with my children, Delphi,' Sylvia said, smiling at her. 'Perhaps you should have one of your own.'

'No,' Delphi answered quickly. 'I am too devoted to my work.' David would be just Arabella's age, she thought as she walked quickly into the store. She could no longer remember his face.

At the toy department, Delphi bought Hans Josef a stuffed camel with an Arab rider, Arabella a stuffed goat with satin horns and a silky gray beard. Sylvia purchased a huge bear on wheels that Hans Josef could ride and a game that would teach him to tell time. 'His father will buy him everything else,' Sylvia said. 'He spoils the children so.'

Afterward, after lunching at one of the sidewalk cafés along the Kurfürstendamm, Delphi and Sylvia walked leisurely along Unter den Linden arm in arm to window shop. Delphi was aware of hundreds of smiling faces. The noontime crowd filled the sidewalk and spilled out into the street. So many of them were young couples full of flirtatious animation, the boys in their uniforms holding the girls with strong bronzed arms. Was it their sameness, Delphi thought, looking at the boys, that made her suddenly uncomfortable? Could Sylvia be right?

*   *   *

July 7, 1936
Delphi!

Your father is taking me to Russia! Even as I write this my hands tremble, my heart jumps in my chest. Can you imagine, my daughter, I am to go home again? Your father says if we are to go at all, it must be now, as there will soon be another war. I tell him he is becoming a cursed Cassandra. He says it has nothing to do with dark lights and crystal balls; it is an economic and political fact. His facts are no better than those in crystal balls as far as I'm concerned. We must be done with war. The world will not survive another.

He tells me he dined with you and Ernst Hasse again when he was in Berlin, and he says Hasse is still very pleasant and good to you. Fine, that is what a man should be. But you know my feelings.

Still I am preaching to you, and all the while I am giddy with anticipation, feeling like a bride! No wonder you lose patience with me. At any rate, after we leave Russia, I will visit you in Germany.

To Russia! My life, my life - it is so like a dream after all. I am going home!

Your loving mother,
Sonya

September 12, 1936
Dear Delphi,

I cannot come to Germany. It is just as well. I am not myself. The trip to Russia was a nightmare. I was prepared for the worst – but even so, I cannot believe what I have seen. There is no glory – only bleakness, a sadness, an indescribable melancholy.

Although I have tried to keep no illusions about Bruno, it was not possible. Because I knew all of my family was gone from my country, that not one, not the most distant of cousins or even Anton's children or his dragon wife, remained alive, I could not let go all my hope for Bruno. We met for only a portion of one afternoon. The irony was that it was our mother's name day, a fact he said he cared nothing about to the point of denying it. We still have such a great resemblance one to the other that it was noticed by everyone down to the least titled person in his grand official bureaucracy. I would like to think it was because he saw me as a reflection of his better self that he was so immediately put off by my presence. Of course, it was not so. He spoke to me of the necessity of Stalin's purges and his part in them. I asked him how he could justify a reign of such terror, terror that is burying thought, justice, poetry, art . . . killing all the flowers in the field. He said he had no need to justify anything that Joseph Stalin thought necessary. He and the god he serves, Joseph Stalin, are exactly the same monsters as your Aryan god, Adolf Hitler.

Your father takes a kinder view of Russia than I, which I find confusing in the extreme. He says I am an emotional refugee and that if I could allow myself to see beyond Bruno and his crimes, I might see the beginnings of my dream. For that, I will need new eyes, a new mind, a new heart. Freedom is elusive, but there is none in Russia. I think I must look closer at this adopted country of mine. Way down, at the bottom of the pot, I think freedom bubbles. Am I the only person who knows it?

Your father has left for Switzerland, but Julius watches over me. He comes with smiles and candy or flowers and fruit. Poor Julius, he is as completely sad as I am. He lives a dreadful life. His wife is now in a hospital. I hope she dies soon and lets him out of his misery. I told him to take a mistress the way Gregory does. He laughed at me. Does everyone think I am so stupid?

I have a confession. There are moments when I wish you were here. I wish I had grandchildren pouring through these rooms. I should have become a doctor, like Ernst.

Your mother,
Sonya

10

November 5, 1936
Dear Delphi,

I was too incoherent last evening on the telephone, I fear. But now, in the bright light of day, I am still able to send you my congratulations, and this time I won't have to hear my words echo back over the long-distance wire, interfering with all my thoughts.

It is a week since the opening, and the people are filling the gallery. The reviews are so far uniformly excellent. I am sending copies of all the reviews to you, under seperate cover, as I receive them.

Your good friend and teacher, Luis Marra, was here today. He is a charming man, much younger than I ever thought. (My preconceptions again.) He was offended by Emile's latest work and unfortunately told him so. I do not think Emile will recover quickly. Luis Marra is formidable!

Your work is in demand, Delphi. Paul Marks, an American dealer, thinks there will be a good market for you in New York. He is fair and well respected, and I recommend him to you. There is so much excitement about you here in Paris, and no one, thus far, has even mentioned your fashionable face! We were absolutely right in deciding you not attend this showing. Your work has finally received the attention it deserves. I am so happy for you. And so proud.

Nicole Clément

*　*　*

Ernst held the sheaf of Delphi's reviews in his hands and, smiling, he sat in the largest and most dreary of the library's chairs. He settled the papers on his lap and then, after adjusting his glasses, pulled the lamp on the table closer toward him. Delphi, across from him, pulled back into the worn velvet pillow behind her, swinging her feet up and around onto the couch. She crossed her arms over her breasts and stared down at the gold bracelet on her right wrist. 'So,' Ernst said, clearing his throat and touching the nosepiece of his gold wire glasses with his forefinger and pressing it upward, 'I think we will begin with the first one, Surmain. He's respected, I think. Let me see. Yes. Here. Look.' He held up the headline. Under NEW SHOWS was a large subhead: DELPHI STERN AT CLÉMENT.

'Please just read it,' Delphi answered, watching the rapid rise and fall of her own chest.

'But we know they are all good, so you must relax.' He smiled over at her.

'Please, Ernst, please.'

'All right, my darling. Here, I begin. "Although Delphi Stern's earlier work was accomplished, it in no way prepared us for the work currently at the Galerie Clément. These paintings are the work of a highly gifted artist. In a flood of color across a mysterious landscape, a strange and compelling language is being spoken as a unique vision is shared."' Ernst peered over at her. 'Well, that certainly is good, isn't it?' Delphi did not move. '"Stern's work is no longer womanish."' Delphi made a noise of exasperation, and Ernst read more quickly. '"These works are definite, bold, and powerful. Each of these paintings is worth exploration. Is the artist a social critic, one who warns against conformity as perversion? Whatever she is saying, no one can ignore Stern's walls of linen. They sear our eyes and question our complacency. They elevate and captivate. I believe that something extraordinary is happening at the Clément now, and I recommend that anyone concerned with the direction of art immediately see the brilliant showing there." So, that's good, is it not?'

'Oh God,' Delphi said, putting a pillow over her head as Ernst shuffled the papers to select another review. He tried to ignore her responses as he continued to read each of the twelve reviews, slowing down for the final one.

'"Delphi Stern has finally muted the hard edges of her vision to produce a show of startling power and clarity. Using color as form, she accomplishes a fine juxtaposition of emotionalism and intellectuality. It would appear that a major talent had declared herself."' Ernst looked up as

Delphi continued to lay on the couch with the pillow over her face. 'Well, I am very proud of my wife. Reviews like this must be very rare.'

Delphi threw the pillow down on the floor and sat up angrily. 'Rare . . . I don't know. The critics are always so full of themselves, more interested in their own prose than in the paintings they review. How can one use words to judge a nonverbal reality? I tell you what they should do. They should take a picture of the critic's face as he looks at the painting and print that. That would be accurate!'

'If you can't be happy with such reviews, I refuse to discuss them with you.'

Delphi was staring at the carpet. 'What do you suppose the critics will make of my new work? They have all become so damned enchanted with me, they'll probably spit at everything I'm doing now.' Delphi stood up and walked back and forth, taking carefully measured steps, her hands on her hips. 'If only . . . damn!' She made a face, pursing her lips and frowning. 'Marra is the only one who knows anything anyway. Damn him wherever he is.'

'You always say you don't care what anybody thinks.' Ernst arched his eyebrows. 'You have certainly never cared what I thought.'

'Marra's opinion is holy, in its way.' Holy. Marra's opinion and her art. She stopped moving and looked up at Ernst. 'I am completely unnatural, Ernst. Completely possessed with my own ego. How I stink of it!' Delphi's sigh was painful, and Ernst winced slightly, listening to it. 'How can I continue to exempt myself from the responsibilities of my life?'

'Because' – Ernst looked directly into Delphi's eyes above his glasses – 'I am here.'

*   *   *

February 18, 1937
Dear Daughter,

At last someone has heard of the artist Delphi Stern. Yesterday evening at a dinner Julius had for Carl and his fiancée, I overheard two guests speaking of you. They had seen your showing in Paris and were duly impressed. If

512

your father had not stopped me, I might have made them repeat the conversation ad infinitum. (Carl pretended he did not hear, but I saw his ears perk up at the mention of you.) Carl's intended bride is a lady from Philadelphia who is at least fifteen years his senior and fusses over him like a maiden aunt over her only nephew.

How good to have your father home again! You see him more than I since all he seems to do these days is to sell foreign currency, the whole time hoping the money will lose most of its value so that he can buy it back. I do not understand how he sells something he does not own. He says it is called selling short. No matter how he explains it, I cannot understand it. This causes him to chuck me under the chin and tell me my financial acumen was not allowed to flourish at Smolney and has since died of my fundamental uninterest. He is correct on both counts.

I am plagued by a terrible cough that won't go away. I've been to the doctor, but he seems unable to do anything for me. I am also terribly upset and cannot sleep at all. You remember Mira Slavaska, I am certain. She was with us from the first. She was killed by a truck crossing the street last week. She had become a lawyer, you know, and was quite successful. I cannot stop thinking of her death. What a cruel waste.

Enough of this morbidity. I think it is because I am so cold. Write soon to

your mother,
Sonya

*   *   *

The bar at the Adlon was as busy as ever, filled with every American journalist in Berlin. Delphi recognized the man at the far end as the reporter for the *New York Times* whose anti-Nazi articles Sonya insisted on sending her. How peculiarly American his face was, as were all their faces, combining an intense ingenuousness with a boozy ennui. We have seen everything, their expressions proclaimed, and nothing astonishes us.

Sylvia still was not there when the head waiter came to tell Delphi that the table was ready. Was it one o'clock

513

already? She had not seen Sylvia in three weeks, not since her trip down the Rhine with Ernst, and she was impatient to tell her about their stop to see brother Rudolf's art collection. Had Sylvia known all along that, far from being a token Nazi, brother Rudolf was very high up in the party? The golden eagle holding the swastika was not only to be found in Berlin. It was to be found over the breast pockets of half Rudolf's guests. Wait till Sylvia heard about the paintings, paintings that even the Hasse wealth, or Sylvia's own, could never buy.

Delphi took the menu that the captain handed her and put it down beside her service plate. How she wished Carl Borach might have seen Rudolf's paintings. He would have laughed with joy at the Titians, the Rubenses, and the Rembrandts, while she herself nearly wept for the Manets, the Corots, the Van Goghs and Gauguins. Rudolf's guests had included General Jodl and Field Marshal Keitel and even Goebbels himself, the man whose Reich chamber of culture had proclaimed Nazi art above all other, and yet no one seemed to be in the least put off by Rudolf's hobby. Delphi had recognized the Tintoretto as the one Carl had sold to the Mannheims of Stuttgart. She remembered vividly lunching with Josef Mannheim at the Hassler in Rome the day he decided to buy it. How had the Nazis forced him to part with it, she wondered, or had they just stolen it outright? And how many of Luis Marra's paintings were among the masterpieces?

Delphi waited twenty minutes longer for Sylvia before she telephoned her. The maid who answered told her that madame had left early with the children. She was taking them to their music lessons, then dropping them at a birthday party. She was sure madame would be there soon. It was unlike her to be late. Delphi's eyes scanned the crowd to see if she could spy her friend. There had been trouble recently over Sylvia's status in Berlin, some inquiries from the Dresden police. More and more Jews were leaving the city daily.

'Frau Hasse?' The maid's voice was still insistent on the other end of the line. 'Frau Hasse? Please answer me.'

'Yes? Yes, Gerta.'

'Frau von Ribben will be arriving at any moment, I am

sure.'

'Yes, thank you. Perhaps traffic is heavy at this time of day.'

'Yes, Frau Hasse. The city is full of activity.'

At one-forty, Delphi decided to order the trout and a salad. The noise level in the room had risen considerably since she had first sat down at her table. How could men drink so much during the afternoon and still manage to get through the day? She thought of Johann Hasse's face. They had finally met at Rudolf's house. He was a pale version of Ernst, grayed and dull. There was nothing vibrant in his eyes, nothing joyful in his smile. She had known that as soon as he could, he would take to wearing a monocle in imitation of his idol, Rudolf. There was not a moment when Johann's glance did not seek out that of his uncle for approval or encouragement. Even, Delphi thought, when he spoke to his father at some length before dinner, he was always looking up, searching for Rudolf. It was no use pretending to any appetite, she thought, dabbing at her mouth with her napkin and putting it down near her plate and signaling for the bill. She called home and was told to call Dr Hasse, who was with Herr Doktor von Ribben at his home. She did not call but went there immediately.

'Hurry, please!' she said to the familiar neck of Albert, the chauffeur, as he drove the broad streets.

'Yes, Frau Hasse,' he said respectfully, careful not to exceed the speed limit despite his mistress's frantic wish to the contrary.

She had prepared herself for the worst, but her apprehension grew as the von Ribbens' butler told her that both her husband and Dr von Ribben were in the library. Suddenly everything seemed dark and corrupt, even the faces of Hans's family who looked down at her from each side of the long corridor. When she opened the door of the library after a warning knock, Ernst was standing at the window, a brandy in his hands, while Hans was seated in the overstuffed chair in front of his own desk, his face ashen. Neither of them said anything as she closed the door behind her.

'What has happened?' she asked. 'Please, what has

happened?'

'The Gestapo have picked up both Sylvia and the children.'

'Why? What for? The children?'

Hans put his hand over his eyes and bowed his head. Ernst sighed. 'We don't know why, Delphi. The driver came to the hospital and told Hans that their car was surrounded as Sylvia stopped to leave the children off for their music lesson. They were taken to the police station, but they have already been moved from there. We can't find them at the moment, but we will.'

'Oh, my God, Ernst!'

'I have called Rudolf to see if he can help, and Hans has been in touch with the head of a Jewish organization to see if they can find them. The SS has been very bad this month – many Jews have been relocated, sent to labor camps.'

'No!' She felt foolish standing there, but she could think of nothing to do at the news.

'It seems to be all whim.'

'How could the police take her away?'

'They took her, that's all we know.'

'The police took the children? Why did they take the children?'

'Delphi, please, we have called everyone who might know anything, who might help us. We don't know why and we don't know where. Trust us. We have done all we can, and now we must wait.'

'Oh, God,' Delphi said again, barely audibly this time. God? What God?

The telephone rang. Ernst picked it up immediately and then put it down after a few moments. 'Who was it?' Delphi asked, looking at his blank expression.

'Johann. It was Johann.' Now his face was full of pain. 'He said if I lie down with dogs I will get up with fleas. He will do nothing, make no inquiries at all. He said whatever the party does has its own reasons and he would not lift a finger to help any Jew.' Ernst closed his eyes for an instant, pressing on the lids, and then he opened them. 'I will try Rudolf again later, although it is quite clear he has no intention of helping me. Johann merely follows Rudolf's lead. I am so sorry, my friend Hans. I have been so blind. And I saw it clearly this time in Munich because I saw it through Delphi's eyes. And still I turned away from the truth. They are both full of hate. My son and my brother are lost.'

Delphi looked down at the lunch tray that Hans had left untouched on the table next to him. The edges of the bread were curled, and the salad had discolored. She could think of nothing to say. Hans stared out the window, his hands holding the arms of his chair tightly. Ernst paced back and forth. Delphi, silent, looked at the telephone. When would it ring? It was unbearable not to know what was happening.

'My God!' Ernst could hardly find his voice. 'My God, Hans, it's Sylvia!' He looked at Delphi and Hans and then back through the open window. His mouth opened and his eyes grew larger and larger as if to make room for the image in front of him. Hans sprang out of his chair and ran to the window, and then he was out of the room, running like an Olympian toward the front door. Delphi stared at the vision of Sylvia walking up the front path, her head as erect as ever. How was it possible? Perhaps, Delphi thought wildly, Rudolf had done something after all. Delphi ran to Ernst, shaking. He put his arms around her and they stood together, waiting for Hans and Sylvia to come into the room. It took forever before Sylvia stood in front of them. 'The children are still with the police,' she said, answering their unasked question. 'The police released me on condition that I return within two hours. I have been asked to make a "donation" to the German government.' She looked straight at her husband. 'They want my jewels.'

'Sylvia! Oh, my dear!' Delphi ran toward her and embraced her with all her strength. Sylvia stood like a cold iron statue and let herself be embraced before she pulled away from Delphi. She stared down at the tips of the fingers of her left hand as she wound her handkerchief about them. 'They have given me two hours, but I must be quicker. I cannot bear the thought of my babies there alone.'

Hans had already walked to the paneled wall. He reached out and pulled the still life of fruit and cheese that hung at eye level by its carved wood frame. The

517

picture swung toward him on hinges hidden from sight, and Hans's surgeon's fingers expertly spun the tiny dial of the small safe that lay behind the painting.

'I have a collection of Renaissance jewels left me by my grandmother,' Sylvia explained. 'They are very well known and we have been warned to get them out of the country by many, but' – she shook her head – 'at any rate, the Nazis want them.'

'Give me your bag, Sylvia,' Hans said, motioning at her. 'Let me have your purse.'

'It is too small,' Sylvia said, looking across the room at the chair that held Delphi's large leather bag, the one she had carried for years.

Delphi walked to it. 'Of course you may have it. Please, take it,' she said, dumping its contents on the table next to the couch, keys and coins and handkerchief, cards and papers, pencils and pens and comb spilling out. As she held out the bag to Hans, she could not believe what she saw. Hans took handfuls of golden jewels, their precious stones shining like miniature searchlights, and laid them one upon the other in her bag. All of them watched silently.

'No, darling, not those,' Sylvia whispered to him. There were emeralds as big as Delphi's knuckles in his hands now as Hans stopped and looked up at Sylvia. 'Those were separate. I think they want only the Renaissance collection. Those were never photographed, only the gold. The old pieces are all set in gold.' Hans put the emeralds quickly back into the safe and closed it, spinning the dial and replacing the painting in an instant.

'They have asked me to come back alone,' Sylvia said, looking at Ernst and Delphi, who stood together now at the window. 'There is a car below, waiting for me. I hope I shall be right back.'

'Good luck,' Delphi said.

Hans took her outside to the black Mercedes limousine that idled across the street from the house. As the two of them approached the car, two men in raincoats stepped from behind the car, guarding either end. Hans spoke to them, but they shook their heads. Hans held the door open for his wife, closed it slowly, and watched her being driven away.

'I am an imbecile,' Hans said when he returned to the study. 'I knew it was unavoidable and yet I listened to my wife. "Don't worry," she said. "It will pass. It will pass."' He walked to his desk and sat there, lighting a cigarette.

'They will get out with no problem, won't they, Hans?' Delphi asked. 'After she gives them the jewels, they will surely let her go?' She barely recognized her own voice.

'The Nazis have a perverted sense of honor, my dear Delphi. In this kind of bargain, I would trust them to keep their word, the bastards.' Hans kicked at the bottom of the sofa and it banged into the paneling behind it. 'The sons of bitches.'

'What can we do for you, my friend?' Ernst asked. 'Can we be of any help?'

'Once I get them back safely, I must send my family out of the country.'

'But Hans, they will be safe now. She has given them what they want.'

'My sweet good friend,' Hans said, smiling at Ernst with great feeling, reaching his hands out to Ernst's and holding them as he looked up, 'you are as blind as ever. How long do you think it will be before the Gestapo want something more from my wife? The deed to her vineyard perhaps? The rest of her jewels? Our house? God knows.' He dropped Ernst's hands as he stood up. 'According to their corrupt minds, she has no business being married to me and therefore, as a Jewish woman who has lured the flower of German youth and used him to her purpose – I am quoting here from something I read in a recent edition of *Der Stürmer*, mind you – she has no business being alive. She is worse than a decadent and her children are lower than she. You know all that yes? I must get them all out of Germany while I can. Once this starts, they will bleed her dry, and when there is no more for her to give them, they will take her and the children away.' His voice broke and he crossed to a table and put out his cigarette in a dish there. 'I am so stupid! How could I have let Sylvia talk me out of it?' He banged a closed fist into the back of the leather chair again and again. 'I might have approached a man I knew who lives in Bremen. He could have helped me, but he was arrested early last week for aiding Jews. I am at a loss. I have heard Sylvia's parents are helping people, but we have not had any contact with the Goldmanns. They would be the ones to ask, but they will not speak to me. I know the Nazis will let them out of Germany probably, for the right price, but what country will let them in?'

'What do you mean, Hans? I don't understand you.'

'Other countries in Europe, even the United States, will not let the Jews in after they leave here. The price of freedom is very high if it is even to be had at all. There are people who know what to do . . .'

'Delphi and I will speak to Sylvia's parents, Hans. Yes. Immediately. Don't worry, my friend. They are still in Dresden? I will contact them. We will drive there as soon as possible, perhaps this weekend. We will ask them in person. It is better, I think, to avoid the telephone. Don't worry, Hans, we will let nothing happen to your wife or your children. Nothing, I promise.'

Hans's worried eyes tightened even more. 'Sylvia would not go before, you know. She would not. I begged her, over and over. Still she would not go.'

'She will go now,' Delphi said.

'I am sure.' Ernst nodded. 'She will go for the children.'

Delphi studied her husband's face. She had never seen such a look in his eyes before. What would happen when he began to question the safety of his own wife? It would be so easy for anyone to find out she was a Jew. Everyone had known it in Paris, and before that in Siena, with Carl, with Luis too. They would both have to start thinking about her safety as soon as this madness with Sylvia and the children was resolved.

11

Delphi and Ernst drove to Dresden that weekend along icy
roads, the countryside around them frozen and bleak. By
the time they reached their hotel, it was already after
lunchtime. They had been traveling nearly five hours.

Once in the hotel room, Ernst immediately placed a call
to Sylvia's father. It had only taken a moment, it seemed,
before he was hanging up the telephone, his hand still on
the receiver. Sitting on the bed wearing his coat and hat,
his wool scarf open and dangling at the sides of his lapels,
he looked to Delphi like someone's discarded teddy bear,
so old, so forlorn.

'What is it?' she asked anxiously.

'He said he once had a daughter named Sylvia but she
had died. Then he hung up the telephone.' Ernst shook his
head in disbelief. 'You will call the mother. After lunch,
you will call. We must eat something, I think. My head is
spinning.' He stood up slowly as if whatever youth he
possessed had just drained out of him.

The best the waiter could offer them was a warmed-over
lunch of sausage and cabbage, as the dining room was
closed until dinner. They ate without speaking to one
another, like strangers in a railroad café. Delphi finished
her coffee and then drank the ale Ernst had left in his
glass. She was parched from anxiety.

After they were in the room, Delphi quickly went to the
telephone to make her call.

'Yes?' The voice was male. 'Yes?' The man was annoyed
at having to answer his telephone.

'I am a new dressmaker and I have been recommended
to Mrs Goldmann.'

'A dressmaker? Hannah? Are you expecting a call from
a dressmaker?'

'Yes, hello?' Now the voice was a woman's voice, even
and resonant.

'Mrs Goldmann?'

'Yes?'

'My name is Delphi Hasse. Delphi' - she paused - 'Stern,' she said emphatically, 'Hasse.' She took a breath and continued. 'I am a friend of Sylvia's and she is in trouble.' There was a long silence on the other end of the wire. 'Mrs Goldmann, are you on the line?'

'But where did you get my name? Who has recommended you to me?'

'I am from Berlin, Mrs Goldmann. We are close friends, Sylvia and I, and there is some problem with her exit visa. May I see you, Mrs Goldmann?' Ernst sat facing her on the opposite bed; she did not take her eyes from his. Delphi listened to Mrs Goldmann speak to her husband.

'It's a dressmaker, darling. Stella Mannheim recommended her to me. She is just opening a shop here.' Delphi nodded her head slowly to Ernst and waited for Mrs Goldmann to speak to her again. 'Where is your shop, Miss Stern?'

'I am at Berlin Haus in the Altmarkt. Room' - she stopped as Ernst quickly held up the key so she could see its number clearly - 'room twenty-six.'

'Perhaps I will drive by this afternoon if I have a minute. Do you have some heavy satin, by any chance?'

'Yes. We will be here all afternoon. And if you are delayed, we will wait for you.' Her hand shaking, Delphi set down the receiver. 'You would think my own life were at stake for how nervous I am,' she said. 'My heavens, how inconvenient to have such a good friend! I have such a bad case of nerves. You would never think I was the daughter of a Russian bombthrower and a spy.' She crossed quickly to Ernst and put her arms around him. 'I pray she hurries. What if she doesn't come?'

They waited until after three and were about to ring for room service and some tea when there was a hard knock on the door. Delphi ran to it and let in a woman nearly as tall as she. She wore a seal coat and a hat with heavy veiling that covered her face. 'I am Sylvia's mother. I cannot stay long. Just tell me what has happened.'

She refused to sit down or unbutton her coat but stood without moving and listened to Delphi tell her what had happened to Sylvia and the children.

'But they are unharmed?'

'Yes,' Ernst said.

'My husband would like us all to consider her dead,' Mrs Goldmann said in a very quiet voice. 'Sylvia was my only daughter. Can you imagine what it has been like all these years to have a daughter who is living and consider her dead?' Mrs Goldmann did not move a muscle but stood absolutely still. Delphi did not move either, as if the other woman's emotions held her where she sat. 'Men have no soul when it comes to their children. Only a man could kill off a daughter like this or send a son to war.' In an action that was so surprising Delphi knew she would remember it all the days of her life, Mrs Goldmann pushed up her veil and spat on the floor at her feet. 'That is what I think of men,' she said. Then, as if nothing had taken place, she replaced her veil and opened her purse. 'Here, take this envelope. It contains the names of people you must contact in Berlin. They head a network that gets Hitler's enemies out of this country and sees them safely to London. They will charge a great deal of money but not more than Sylvia can afford. Get her out quickly.' She turned to leave before Delphi or Ernst had managed a word. Just as Delphi was about to wish her well, the woman turned back toward them. Her carriage was exactly like Sylvia's, Delphi thought.

'My grandchildren,' she said, looking at Delphi, 'what do they look like?'

'The girl looks very much like you, Mrs Goldmann. The boy looks more like his father. They are wonderful children, so full of life.'

'Thank you,' she said. 'Thank you both.' She turned again, and without another backward glance she left the room.

Ernst Hasse arranged the transfer of 50,000 reichsmarks to a certain Henrich Bollinger, and within three weeks from the date of the transaction, Sylvia, Hans Josef, and Arabella were in London. Hans promised to join them on the next holiday.

*   *   *

February 15, 1938
Dear Papa,

I am worried about my safety and that of Ernst. Something unspeakably sinister happened today. I was not sick enough to stay in bed but not well enough to work, so I roamed the house like a trapped cat. Suddenly, I heard unfamiliar voices in the kitchen, and I went in to find two strange men there questioning the housekeeper and cook about Ernst's habits. They wished to question me about my passport and visas and the income from my paintings, demanding to know where the paintings are shipped and if I made money from any sale, and if so, then where was my money on deposit. I was so frightened I told them that Ernst handled my affairs and I fled the kitchen, but not before those men indicated that Ernst and I were in some sort of trouble.

Papa, I need your help. Please let me know as soon as you can what I should do. I know you will not mention this to Sonya. I hope this letter reaches you. I am sending it out with an Italian doctor who is an associate of Ernst's.

Delphi

March 12, 1938
My dear,

I cannot get through to you by telephone again tonight and it seems useless to try any longer. So much for Nazi efficiency.

The news: the series of tree watercolors has been sold to the Rijksmuseum in Amsterdam! Congratulations!

Your latest work arrived Monday. I am enthralled. I could sell most of them with a few phone calls, but I am going to wait and show them, unsold, as a group in the spring. It will give us better prices. I am especially excited by No 2 *red*. Beside the color, the arrangement of figures is so powerful and dramatic. I may save that one for New York. Paul Marks and I plan to show you there next winter, and this spring's showing will give us great momentum. Paul has convinced me that marriage with a much younger man has its benefits – he is nearly twelve years younger than I. I have been so busy proving myself to my father's ghost all these years that I have not found time for the consideration of marriage. I may actually marry him. Don't shudder. I will keep the gallery here in Paris as well.

I was invited to be one of the delegates to Berlin regarding an exchange of German and French art. I wanted to accept the invitation on the chance of spending time with you, but I am far too busy at this time of year. I know, I know, the Nazis are making nothing but pornographic art these days to encourage the men and women to keep having children. (Does Hitler's Reich really reward mothers with more children? Do mothers with more sons really get greater rewards?) I promise I will try to keep all pornographic militaristic paintings from Germany out of France by petitioning my friends in the delegation.

One last thing. I have had several letters from a branch of the German government concerned with German artists. They want to know how much your paintings bring in the marketplace. I have managed to lose both letters. Do you wish them answered?

Nicole

August 3, 1938
Dear Delphi,

I think I am doomed to outlive everyone who has meant anything to me. Julius has died. His wife hangs on by a thread for years and he, hearty as a bear, falls over from a heart seizure. How I grieve for him! He was the one person in my life who found me entirely credible, and often that alone gave me the will to proceed when so much had failed me. I think he was the only man who truly loved me. If I did not have my meetings, I would be overwhelmed with a feeling of uselessness and loneliness. I tell you, Delphi, I cannot endure ever hearing anything has happened to you. Leave there now. Enough!

Nicole Clément came to lunch with me this afternoon. What a lovely woman! She cheered me considerably. We talked about you, and we talked about politics, of which she is extremely knowledgeable. I had a delightful time. After lunch we were joined by a James Sherwood, who is doing a biographical portrait of you for the catalogue. He

525

asked so many questions that what I couldn't remember I just made up, so if you find your life is not exactly as you remember it, you will at least know why.

In a more serious vein, Nicole brought me a book filled with clippings and a list of all the museums and private collections that now own your work. I am so proud of you. I promise you I have accepted art as a worthwhile vocation, especially now that the WPA shows how it can lift the intelligence of the workers and the illiterate. I should like to see a mural or two of yours in a terminal or public building here.

Delphi, when you were barely eighteen, you declared yourself a Jew. Be one of honor and leave that terrible country. Your position is impossible. Come home.

Your mother,
Sonya

*   *   *

Tolchin handed his coat to the butler and quickly lit a cigarette. 'After all the elaborate control at the Russian border, I am always amazed at how simple it is to get into Germany. Hitler is obviously very proud of his country. I think he hopes to spread the word of his great accomplishments through the tourists. The station was mobbed. I'm glad Ernst sent his car.' He kissed Delphi on both cheeks. 'I need a drink of brandy.'

Delphi returned his kisses. 'You stink of tobacco. I thought you were giving it up.'

'Yes, yes. I am a chimney and I am always giving it up.' He glanced around him as he followed Delphi along the hallway into the brighter drawing room. 'I continually forget what a dreary house this is. Appalling.'

'I have gotten used to it,' Delphi said, closing the heavily carved walnut doors and walking to the satinwood sideboard to pour her father his brandy. He looked well. His hair was cut closer to his scalp now, his beard shorter than she remembered. There was a slight thickening of flesh around his collar, and under the eyes a slight puffiness. Time had made such slight alterations, she thought, looking at him. He was ageless, this handsome man.

'What do you think?' he asked.

'Think?'

'About what you see? You are staring at me.'

'I think the devil has kept his part of the bargain. What must you have promised him to stay looking like this?'

Tolchin laughed. 'To the devil,' he toasted.

Delphi had poured herself a drink as well. 'And to you,' she said, lifting her glass.

'To Sonya, Ernst, you, and health. *Na Zdorovya.*'

'*Na Zdorovya,*' Delphi echoed, feeling the warm liquor spread inside her chest. She took his glass back to the sideboard, opened the etched-glass doors, and took out the brandy and refilled it. 'Now you are staring at me,' she said.

'I have a packet of good news for you.' He leaned down and opened his briefcase and, taking out a large manila envelope, handed it to her. 'Nicole sends her congratulations and these clippings. The show has been a tremendous success. On the top sheet is the list of everything that has been sold. You will notice my name is there. I bought the painting *Interior Portrait.* Is it Sonya, or you?'

'But I would have given you any painting you wanted!'

'I was proud to buy it. I gave it to your mother, and it has replaced the silver mirror in the dining room. Such a compliment to you, Delphi. She tells everyone that it is as good as art can get with no social message.' His smile was abrupt.

'Tell her there is a message. She just has to find it.' Delphi paused to look at him a moment. 'I am so pleased to see you here. What has brought you?'

He eyed her with displeasure. 'Did you forget that you sent me a frightened letter? Are you unaware that I have not answered it?'

Delphi stopped smiling. 'I'm afraid I put it out of my head. I have developed a facility for putting unpleasant things out of my head.'

'Have you?' He walked to the fireplace and put his hands on its mantel, leaning forward. 'And has your husband done the same?'

'He watches over me like an angel.'

'Indeed?' He stayed, bent slightly toward the flames, his back to her. 'Do you really think so? Really?' His voice was so musical, the tone rising and falling hypnotically. Still, she recognized signs of the icy inquisitor.

'Gregory!' Ernst came into the room with enthusiasm. Tolchin turned toward him but he did not move. Ernst, feeling his coolness, stopped where he was. 'Of course, there is something out of order,' he said. 'Please tell us immediately.'

Tolchin walked by him and closed the door. 'A letter Delphi wrote me some months ago finally caught up with me. Because of it, I looked into certain matters. It would not be so simple for me to do that, except that most of the world's secrets are in her banks. Also, I have a connection in the SS and he has been helpful.' Tolchin took a long, unmarked envelope from his inside pocket and handed it to Ernst. 'I cannot think what has taken them so long to question your activities, Herr Hasse. Had I been in charge of the department, I would have found you out long ago.'

Ernst looked as if Tolchin had slapped him in the face.
'I have a son and a brother in the Nazi high command. I thought that between the two men and my donations to the local commandant, I had no need to fear close scrutiny.'

'It is not the local commandant who is scrutinizing you.' Tolchin looked at Ernst, took a deep breath, and massaged the side of his head. As he played with a thought, his eyes moved from side to side. Finally, he closed his eyes and sighed. When he opened them again, all traces of expression were gone. 'My dear Ernst,' he began in an even tone, 'you know how inordinately fond I am of you. However, I must point out that in this underground business you are the sort of man I should avoid most, like the plague. Evil has no honor, it is merely evil, brothers, sons, or greedy commandants included. If you wish to blunder your way into suicide, that is your decision, but I will not let you take Delphi with you. Besides your activities, a Captain Johann Hasse has been making inquiries into her background. As coincidental as it may seem, I would say he is as close to Delphi's secret as the SS is to yours. Which means they have in all probability found you both out.'

'What secret? What is Ernst's secret? Do you see me in

this room? What are you talking about? Damn you both, why don't you speak to me?' Delphi's voice was fevered and furious.

'Your husband has been helping Jews leave Germany by providing refuge in buildings he owns in Munich and Frankfurt until he is able to buy them their papers and escape routes. He also provides them with money and the locations of safe houses in Italy.'

'And what is so terrible about that, Gregory Tolchin? You might do the same!'

'There is nothing terrible except that they are about to find him out!' Tolchin took out a cigarette and lit it with a match he scratched across the rough edge of the green tile above the fire screen. 'You know this business of the young Jew who murdered the Nazi third secretary in Paris?' Delphi nodded. There had been nothing else in the German papers or on the radio for the past two days. 'I am told,' Tolchin went on, 'that the Nazis are about to use it to start a campaign of terror against Jews. If that occurs, all timetables will be speeded up. There is no telling when they will reach the two of you. I have made arrangements for you to cross the border tomorrow night. In the morning, Ernst, you will get an emergency exit visa from your greedy commandant. Your wife's mother is sick in America – there is a letter from her – and the three of us will drive to the nearest exit point. There will be no problem crossing.' He snuffed his cigarette out in an ashtray on the desk. 'So,' he said, looking down at the bit of tobacco burning at the edge of the ashtray, 'you must pack tonight. Take enough so that it looks as if you are going for no more than a month, but make certain you bring everything you need. You are not coming back here.'

'My work, Papa. How will we take my work?'

'We will cut it off the stretchers and put it at the bottom of the valises.'

Ernst walked to the fireplace and removed the screen and threw the envelope Tolchin had given him into the flames. 'I will not continue to be a fool,' he said, 'but I cannot leave, Gregory. Delphi, of course, she must go. But I cannot leave.'

'You will be dead, Ernst, within a month, maybe less, if

you do not.' Tolchin's gaze was harsh.

'Ernst!' Delphi stared at him. 'You must!'

'No, I will stay and do what I feel is right.'

Tolchin's voice cracked across the room like a horsewhip. 'Damn you, Ernst Hasse. You will get the hell out of here! Do you think it will be as noble as all the books you have read? That they will lead you to a scaffold, blindfold you, and give you last rites? That music will play for you in the background and historians will lift their pens in poetic salutes? No! They will use you and torture you until you take down twenty others with you. Why don't you understand that? You will give them the names of the people in Stuttgart, the men and women in Italy. I promise you you will give them every last name. I'm sorry if I raise my voice, but it is hard to control my anger. I am so sick and tired of well-intentioned innocents. They do not even see evil as it happens, yet they think they can impede its progress! Now get ready, the two of you! I am sorry if I offend you. But you must leave it all to me, please. You are in the hands of an expert.'

At first Delphi thought the light that flashed from window to window in the studio was a hallucination, but then one large, flat circle of light fell in at the center window, joined by a second, to dance across her floor. The voice that called Ernst's name came through a bullhorn to echo in the hallways. Ernst looked up toward the sound, surprised by it. 'I think it is my son,' he said, squinting at the light as he stood up and brushed the dust from the knees of his pants. He walked slowly to the window, shading his eyes from the hot light as he peered into the yard below. 'I can hardly see. I will go out.'

'You should stay here.' Tolchin had come into the room as the brighter lights from outside continued to dance across them.

'No. It is only my son and his gang of thugs. I don't know why they're here.'

'Ernst. I think my father is right.'

'No, Delphi.' Ernst looked down into the courtyard again. 'They are not even wearing their uniforms. I'll go down and see to it.' He handed Delphi the large kitchen knife he had been using to cut the paintings off their stretchers. Tolchin had moved into the hallway and was hidden behind the brocade drapery at one window, also looking down into the courtyard. 'Don't go, Ernst. Listen to me. There must be more than a dozen of them.'

'But one of "them" is my own son. I will go down.'

'You are still a fool, Ernst.'

'I cannot believe as you do, Gregory, that evil leaves no room for good. If I believed that, I should have given up long ago.'

'No,' Tolchin contradicted him, 'you would know better how to fight it. And you would have fought sooner and with proper ammunition. I am telling you, Ernst, do not go down there.'

'I cannot be afraid of my own son.'

He walked down the mahogany staircase, Delphi and Tolchin following him down and then along the hallway to the front door. Only her father's restraining hand on her upper arm kept Delphi from following Ernst outside.

'What is it, Johann?' Ernst called out to him from inside the portico.

'You are accused of being a traitor, a Jew sympathizer, an enemy of this country.' Johann stood silhouetted by the headlights behind him, his shadow reaching forward toward his father.

'Have you nothing better to do with your gang of rowdies than to threaten me?' Ernst's shadow lengthened back over Delphi as he stepped out onto the top step. There could have been no preparation for what happened then. The shot that was fired sounded like a crack of a branch in a quiet forest. Ernst Hasse pitched forward and disappeared from Delphi's sight. Not even Tolchin's steel hand kept her from running out of the house. She stood above Ernst's body, staring at the crescent of blood across his chest. he looked so small below her, too small to be a man. She felt nothing, neither warmth nor cold. Slowly, like a marionette, she jerked forward and down the stairs and soundlessly dropped over him.

'Is he dead?' One voice.

'Of course.' Another. 'You at the top of the steps, if you value her life, stay where you are!'

'Shall we shoot her as well?'

'What about him?'

'The orders are to harm no foreigners.'

'But you said she was a Jew.'

'She is my father's Jew whore, but she is an American.' Delphi felt the boot and heard its thud as it landed on her thigh. 'Bitch whore,' the man said as he stood over her. 'It is all your doing. I should have known you were a Jew the moment I saw you. You corrupted my father with your filth. I should put a bullet through your brain and protect the world from your Jew rot.' The boot landed again. Ernst was so cold in her arms. She felt nothing but that cold as she looked up into Johann Hasse's pale face with its blank eyes.

'You have killed your father,' she said, her voice full of revulsion.

'You killed him, Jew!' He spat at her and she felt the spit on her forehead.

Behind her were the sounds of windows breaking, of rocks smashing against the stone façade of the house, then hitting ground. There was the sound of motors racing and tires skidding across the drive. Then there was only night and silence.

It was on that night, November 9, 1938, that all across Germany the Nazis retaliated against Jews for the shooting, by a Jew, of the Nazi third secretary at the German embassy in Paris. Tolchin's information had been correct. Hitler had secretly ordered the burning of all synagogues, the destruction of Jewish places of business, the arrest of thirty thousand Jewish men and their placement in concentration camps. Members of the SS and the SA carried out these orders in ordinary dress, as these incidents were to be perceived by the world as spontaneous demonstrations. Ernst Hasse was not the only sympathetic German killed that night.

On November 11, 1938, Delphi Stern and Gregory Tolchin left Germany, Delphi in a state of near shock. Her father arranged to send her to her mother in New York. She went without protest.

12

Sonya was standing there in full costume, a red jacket over her gray skirt, high black boots, a fur hat, and a black cape seemingly blown by interior winds. Her makeup was thick and took away any trace of natural color. What color there was was a stain across her cheeks and across her mouth. Great drifts of eyelash sailed up into her brow to nearly obscure her green eyes with their shadow. Had it been ten years?

'You have always been too thin.' Sonya spoke to Delphi in Russian, kissing her, holding her for a moment just a little too tight. They stood looking at each other, reassessing, readjusting. Both of them began to cry.

Sonya gently wiped Delphi's face with her gloved hand. 'Your father says that it was a nightmare for you. He instructs me to take very good care of you. Come, we will go home right away. Nicole has arranged for a car, and that man with the long face and the eyes of a spaniel will take us directly through customs.' She took hold of Delphi's arm and led her through a wall of people, her head high, her stride strong and purposeful. She kept up her chatter for the nearly twenty minutes it took for the car to arrive at West Fourth Street, fussing over Delphi as if she were a sickly child and it was only yesterday that they had been together. Delphi looked at the house, surprised to see how small it was. How could it have held so many incendiary people under its narrow roof?

Refusing to let Sonya help her with the valises, she followed her up the steps, her feet feeling the uneven wear on the stone beneath her shoes. At the sight of the battered wooden door and the two tall curtained windows at each side, she half-expected to hear or to see Mira, Samuel, Vladimir, Lena. Instead, the sound she heard was the sharp bark of a small dog. 'Don't say it,' Sonya cautioned, opening the door to scoop up a bundle of black and gray fur.

'I was wrong about animals.' She kissed the dog's tiny black snout. 'This' – she held him out, squirming in her arms – 'is Pashka, my little whatnot. And those are my cats.' Three or four cats came toward her to rub up against her ankles. 'What can I do? People abandon them every day in this dreadful city.' Sonya was looking at her and trembling. 'Oh, my dear,' she whispered, 'how grateful I am to see you alive. It is such a relief!'

Silent, Delphi watched Sonya walk to the bottom of the stairs. 'Come upstairs now. Nicole and I have a surprise for you. It is not finished, but it is at least begun.' Sonya was already halfway to the second floor. Delphi followed her, still clutching the handles of her valises. At the third floor, Sonya flung open the new door ahead of them and stepped aside. 'Look! What do you think?'

The entire ceiling had been removed so that Delphi walked into a two-story room. It was filled with plaster dust, and great loops of electrical wires lay about like pythons. 'It is a studio for you. Do you like it?'

I am a brain-damaged person, Delphi thought, standing there in the blue light of the winter afternoon. I am so relieved to have been provided for, so wholly pleased that all that will be required of me is to paint my little pictures. 'Thank you, Sonya,' she said, aware that it was the first time she had spoken since she had begun her journey a month before. 'I am very grateful.'

'Did you know I prayed? Did I tell you that? I prayed to every God and every devil invented by mankind.'

'I wonder,' Delphi said, trying to smile, 'which of them answered.'

* * *

Delphi   February 6, 1939

I cannot quite get to sleep but skim along its edge like a skater at the frozen edge of a still-running pond. Nicole says I am an artist, not a politician, and I must forgive myself and keep working. Although she says I will not ever want for buyers, I wonder if she is right. The work I am doing now is awful, like the claw marks of a terrible beast.

Sonya still possesses such remarkable energy, busy all

day with her animal shelters and her peace groups – peace groups even though war has begun in Europe. Tolchin writes that he will be in Europe until the war is over and has sent us a way to reach him in emergencies.

I am frightened all of a sudden. I do not feel well at all.

*   *   *

It was her body that betrayed Delphi. Since her arrival in New York it had hinted, but she had paid little attention. She had so seldom been ill. Save for an occasional headache or a runny nose, a fever that a few aspirin had quickly knocked out of her, she had enjoyed only health. She was curious now at her body's reaction. She was also frightened. The fatigue was growing daily. In the last five weeks, it seemed she was fighting her body for the minutes of her work, and fight as she would, the weight of the fatigue pressed her down. She began to ache. Every muscle felt tired, misused, grating against some other muscle. A simple walk along the street became impossible. A pain in her lower abdomen, which at first she thought she had imagined, became sharper, longer. And then the spotting started. Some mucus, some blood, for a week and then another week. Perhaps, she told herself, it was menopause. If it were, then it was wholly natural. It was her turn and once it was over, then it would be over. Yet she put off going to the doctor, terror and anger assaulting her with each new drop of blood, each new ache, each new stab of pain in the groin. She became too frightened to do anything.

She forced herself to sit in her studio, but the smell of the oils made her retch and the aches in her arms left her without enough energy to stretch a new canvas. Still, she stubbornly sat in the black wicker chair in the corner and tried to make some pen and ink drawings in her notebooks, to will concentration, but her sketches were forced, as if her rhythms were out of synchronization. Her body was breaking what spirit she had left.

At the first noise of Nicole's voice in the hallway, she felt relief. She got up slowly and tossed the notebook and the pen on the cluttered desk by the window. She might have tossed herself forward as well, for she lost her balance and fell, grabbing at the edge of the desk.

'Delphi!' Nicole shouted her name as she ran toward her. 'What is it? What is the matter?'

'I don't know,' Delphi answered.

'Then we shall find out. You are shaking like a leaf in the wind. Can you walk to the chair? Good. Walk to the chair. I will call the doctor. How long have you been so ill? You are as white as your walls. Sonya!' Nicole shouted as loudly as she could, 'Sonya!'

While the two women waited for her in the doctor's waiting room, Delphi was examined. Dr Holland was a tall, thin man with a pinched mouth and a nervous tic in his left eye. She had lain on his table in the examining room for what had seemed hours, and now her knees were forced up into stirrups and his hand was inside her, poking and pressing. 'Well, here it is,' he said. 'You are simply pregnant.'

She felt blood rushing to other places as she lifted her body to look at him. Pregnant. No. 'No!' she said aloud, the word escaping involuntarily. She closed her eyes. The word had no meaning. She thought of Marra and felt her heart pounding in her chest. The doctor's head appeared over the white mountain of sheet spread over her knees. Why had she expected him to be Luis?

Why? It was Ernst's baby she carried, she thought, now seeing Ernst's face smiling at her. She began to cry and she could not stop even after she had dressed and was sitting in front of Dr Holland. He didn't look up at her but held his pen in his left hand and continued to write whatever it was he had been writing.

'I don't have your age here,' he said, glancing at the paper.

'Thirty-four.' Or thirty-five. Delphi was not certain of the exact number. How strangely Dr Holland held the pen.

'Have you had any other children?' She did not answer. 'Miss Stern?'

'Yes.'

'How many?'

'One. Only one.' Had he written 'one' or 'only one'?

'Living?'

'No.'

536

'How did the child die?' His face registered nothing at all. He was used to his questions. How many dead children were noted on the pages of his files? 'Did the child die from natural causes? A childhood disease? Influenza, perhaps? Miss Stern?' His voice raised itself an octave and was much louder. 'Will you kindly help me here?'

Don't write anything, she wanted to say. Help *me* here.

'I am only trying to take down your history.'

'The child died in an accident. It was an accident.'

'Was it a normal delivery?'

'Yes.'

'And the child was normal?'

'What?'

'At birth, was the child normal?'

'Yes, of course. Normal.'

'And you?' His hand tightened around the pen and now he looked at her, exasperated. 'How were you during the delivery?'

'Fine.'

'Labor?'

'Fine.'

'Position?'

'What?'

'Was the baby in a normal position at the onset of labor?'

'It was in a fine position.' She had not thought about it in so long, not since she had gone to Paris. Now, suddenly, she felt those first warning pains as they had come to her, smelled the sun in the sheets as she had thrown her head into the pillows and bitten on the knuckle of her forefinger until the midwife had stuffed a wad of toweling into her mouth. She was back in that room, there were geraniums everywhere, and on the ceiling, the dappled reflection of the sun on the leaves. She could hear the maid's voice calling her . . .

'Miss Stern. Miss Stern. Are you all right?' The sharp smell of the ammonia brought her back to the doctor's office. Her eyes widened and she shook her head furiously. The smell was making her gag.

'Enough!' She screamed it.

'Lie down there,' he said, pointing to the couch.

'No!' She was pushing away his hand with the terrible

537

smell.

'How many times have you fainted?'

'No.'

'Do you faint frequently? Did you faint during your first pregnancy?'

'I'm wringing wet,' she whispered, reaching for a tissue at the side of the couch.

'Have you fainted during pregnancy?'

'No.'

'How old were you when your first child was born?'

'Twenty-three, twenty-four.'

The mouth pinched even tighter. 'You are not certain?'

'What difference does it make?'

'Please answer my question.'

'What did you ask me?'

'How old were you, Miss Stern, at the time of your first pregnancy?'

'Twenty-three.'

'And there have been no pregnancies since that time?'

'None.'

'None terminated?'

'No. *No!*'

'Please, Miss Stern, relax!' He grabbed her wrist and pressed his fingers into her flesh. He was taking her pulse. 'Do you practice any form of birth control?'

'No. I just knew I would never be pregnant again.'

'Well, you were wrong, weren't you?' He laughed, his hand still around her wrist. 'I would say you are about four months pregnant. When was your last period?' He resumed writing.

'I don't keep track of such things.'

'I should say a good four months. How do you feel in general?'

'I have been very tired.'

'Yes.' He was impatient again. 'Of course.' He stopped writing and put the top of the pen squarely in the center of his chin. His face changed expression. 'I must warn you, Miss Stern, that at your age there can be complications. There seems some softening around the cervix that may account for the bleeding, you see. It's not an ominous sign, but if you want this child you will have to try very hard to

538

have it.'

'I do not want this child.'

'What?' The hand holding the pen dropped to the desk.

'I do not want this child. There must be some way of getting rid of it.'

'Your husband . . . surely he . . .'

'My husband was killed.'

'Oh, yes.' He took a breath. 'Yes, I remember your mother saying something about that. Yes. Of course.' Dr Holland pursed his lips, scratched at this head, and touched his earlobe before he decided to stand. He picked up her medical chart and looked through it again. 'I am sorry to say it, Miss Stern, but at this point, nothing can be done about aborting this child. I might have suggested such an option were you not four months pregnant. It might be more. Nothing can be done. You will have to give birth to this child.'

Her scream was piercing. Sonya would tell her later how it had frightened both her and Nicole to see her running toward them from the doctor's office. 'I don't want it,' she had howled, 'please, please! Oh, God, Sonya, help me! It is the child of a dead man and a monster!'

Dr Holland had no conclusive reasons for her continuing sickness, which had by the last weeks of her pregnancy become so severe she had already lost nine pounds. She felt as if her gut were perpetually filled with curdled milk, and there were constant cramps in her belly. Worse, her spine or its attendant muscles had ceased to function properly so that when she stood, she risked collapse. It had been a long, unproductive time when she could not even sketch, could hardly read. She lay most of the time like some loathsome thickening piece of flesh, dreading each new day. It all seemed more horrible in light of Nicole's cheerfulness that day as she continued to insist that Delphi dress. The heat was already oppressive, and perspiration covered Delphi's skin, running into its hidden crevices. She smelled as foul as she felt.

'You are all stomach,' Nicole said, looking at her in the light flowered gown she wore. 'Does that mean it is a boy or a girl?'

Delphi pointed to Nicole. 'If you light that cigarette, I will kill myself.'

'I won't, but you are coming if I have to dress you myself.' Nicole chewed on the unlit cigarette as she settled a full white summer blouse over Delphi's head, lifting one of her arms through one sleeve and then the other. 'You will be ashamed to make me work so hard. I tell you now this is the happiest day of your life, and you look at me as if I had come to do you injury.'

'I have never felt so invaded. I have never . . .' Delphi put her forehead against Nicole's bony hip and wrapped her arms around her narrow waist, pressing her sweating face against the raw yellow linen of her skirt. 'I cannot want my life any longer,' she said, weeping. 'It frightens me.'

Nicole smelled of lemons as she held Delphi, her arms tight around her shoulders. 'You are very young still. There is time for everything. There will be time.'

Delphi pushed her quickly away and stood up, pulling the blouse down across her stomach, not bothering to wipe the tears from her face. 'I might have achieved something finally. I might have delivered out of my pain and darkness something powerful to startle the world. Instead I will deliver only another child. When will I work again, Nicole? Three years? Four? Will I throw myself or the child out of the window first? I have already killed one child.'

'There is Sonya, Delphi. She is anxious for this child. You have no need to worry about your time. You must stop this. It is unbecoming.'

Delphi pulled up the stiff poplin skirt, its band stretching across her bulging stomach. 'Sonya is more selfish than I. How the hell do you think I got this way?' She ran her fingers through her hair, but it clumped damply at her shoulders. 'Sonya had no use for me at all, and it will be unlikely she will have any for my child. I can't fool myself on that score.'

'So then I will take it. I am good with children. Even my stepchildren think so. Hurry now. It is very important what I am about to show you.'

In the cab, Delphi quickly lowered the window, but the hot wind that rushed in did not relieve the heat. She fanned herself with the newspaper and closed her eyes against the gritty air. Horns blew with urgent hostility at one another. Huge buses, their exhausts level with the windows, blew in gusts of gaseous clouds. There was a series of hot iron pains at her left side. She no longer cared if she were hot or cool. She put down the newspaper. When she opened her eyes again, the car had stopped in front of the Museum of Modern Art. Delphi got out and stood on the sidewalk, waiting for Nicole. There was a sudden vice across her stomach, but it went with the next breath.

Nicole walked quickly, and Delphi was suddenly even too exhausted to ask her to slow down. At least the inside of the building was cool.

She followed Nicole dutifully past the guard and down a corridor. Someone was lecturing a group of women on cubism in a voice full of affectation. Someone smelled of gesso and charcoal. Delphi watched her feet, uncertain that they could hold her.

'Hurry,' Nicole said, motioning her inside a room marked NEW ACQUISITIONS. 'So? Do you wish to leave your life now?' Nicole was smiling at her and pointing to a three-paneled painting done on wood, each panel at least three feet high by two feet wide. Delphi walked toward it. 'It's quite an honor, Delphi. You are so young. Of course I always knew you would be here, but so soon, and with such a work! Delphi? You cannot just stand there and say nothing.'

Delphi, speechless, stared at the painting, looking at one panel and then the next and the next. On the left was a sensual young girl, full of expectation and desire, and yet somehow stilted, pursued, the color behind her jarring, discordant, and unexpected. In the right panel was a Madonna and Child in typical Rennaissance pose, the child on the mother's knee, the mother with one breast exposed, serene, maternal, obliging, and yet this panel, too, had a feeling of terror, of madness and death – the feeling in *Cesspool Cleaners* transposed into maternity. In the larger center panel, dominating the others, was woman as worker, the body not Delphi's own but stronger, larger, the face a study in determination, one fist raised toward the sky in defiance. She looked for the name of the artist and found her own engraved on the brass plaque beneath. It read:

TRIPTYCH. Delphi Stern. Berlin. 1938.

'They told me they bought it from Arnold Cooper in Geneva. Why did I never know of it. Delphi? I was so hurt I did not know.'

Nicole's voice seemed a million miles away. 'I had to leave it behind, in Germany,' Delphi murmured. 'I was certain that it must have been destroyed.' She felt faint.

It was Marra, of course, and it was beyond irony that his love letter should have arrived at that moment, when she was racked with the pain in her body, the difficulty of her work, and the hopelessness of the world. It was Luis's paean to her life, his obeisance not only to her art, done in her best style – for she could see now, in a moment, what it was he so appreciated – but also his appreciation and understanding of her. The pain on the canvas was precisely her pain, but so was it her triumph, and it was for the triumph that he had sent it to her. She was an artist. The work was there. More work would come. 'Battle against satisfaction,' he had said to her, 'stride across definitions, smash preconceptions.' She closed her eyes and saw the red of the geraniums in the pots outside the window of his studio. She had done it. She had made her own arrogance, her balls. And now Marra had released her from any more doubts. Marra. Pain dimmed her sight as she held her sides tight against the raging fire within. Her labor had begun. In the midst of the pain and the heat, she could hear Marra's laugh.'

EPILOGUE

Delphi   August 6, 1939

Even though I am finally unburdened of my enormous stomach, the weight of that little life is still pressing in on me. What shall I tell myself about Ann Sonya Hasse – that I knew it was a grave error? Sonya says I am full of necessary defenses, but I think I am La Belle Dame Sans Merci. There is nothing in me that responds to this child, not the wish to hold her, not the wish to hear her, nothing. Sonya does everything. She even named her, saying that she was to have a very American name. When I protested, Sonya said that she had done well enough by me, or had I forgotten? All I know is that I thank God for Sonya.

Of course Papa did not come to see his granddaughter. Instead he sent a massive bouquet of flowers with a note saying to be sure and name his grandson after him. Perfect!

July 6, 1940

Ann is a year old today. Sonya baked her a chocolate cake and let her stick her fist into it. She never would have let me, but then she never devoted so much time to me. The baby is with her constantly. I don't know how she can do it, how she doesn't gag from boredom.

The new work is very hard. Nicole has sold enough of the old to stop any money worries for the next months. My father's fortune is inaccessible without him, and only God knows when he will return. Occasionally, as if by whim, a check arrives. There is no rhyme or reason for his behavior.

The baby – Ann – it is still hard for me to think of her by name – is a stranger, a little doll who calls me mama and kisses me good night on my cheek. I am forever surprised to hear her voice in the house.

January 29, 1941

Sonya remains enchanted by the baby. She has made a sling that fits across her shoulders and somehow holds Ann at her hip. Off they go each day, paying absolutely no heed to the weather. They come home in the early evening quite exhausted. I am quite alone, which is all that seems to matter to me.

I am irritated by everything today because the work has been going badly for two weeks. Why won't it come?

December 14, 1941

Now that I have finally finished the damned mural, I am full of distress over this newest work. I do not sleep at all, only worry, worry, worry myself into a dense thicket of nothingness. It was in this frame of mind that I went to bed with John Rothman. I was full of panic, and such dread. Clearly, it is impossible for me to have a lover.

Something awesome is inside of me.pushing at these new things, something very black indeed scratches at the core of me. Yeat's rough beast?

I almost forgot to mention it: we are at war.

May 11, 1942

The market strengthens for my work. One of my trees has been bought by the Mellon and another is now in the permanent collection of the Boston Museum of Fine Arts. Nicole is furious that we make no money from these sales. I tried to remind her how grateful we were when we sold them originally, but it didn't console her. It is so off-putting to see the earlier work. It is good enough, but I hardly remember it. There is a possibility of a large mural commission. Nicole is being very harsh about the terms, but they are still interested. I wonder if they chose me because all the men are going off to war?

Ann is a sweet child. I think there is nothing of me in her. Sometimes when I see her with her friends trudging through the door, I do not recognize her. Her extraordinary good cheer is her only distinction. (Ernst's extraordinary good cheer.) Next month, she is to begin at the Montessori school on University Place. Such a long day for a little girl hardly old enough to dress herself.

I think Sonya is up to something. There are weekly meetings in the afternoon, although the elegant people who arrive bear no resemblance to the poor bunch of anarchists and idealists from my youth. I fear the samovar may bubble again. Sonya should join the WAVES. At sixty-one, what energy! What would I have done without her? I am a frenzied woman. Sonya asked me today what it felt like when I painted. Was it, she wondered, like making love? No, I told her. It is an obsession that cancels out feeling and even pleasure. Why are people fascinated with obsession? It can be of interest only to the one who has it, and then, not even. I think it is a curse.

No word from Papa.

October 14, 1942
Each new day brings worse news. So many dead that there is no room for more grief. People walk about with purposeful strides and vacant eyes. I have done a poster of vacant eyes that will be auctioned off for war bonds. I finished it last night. I hate part of it. I may have another mural. This one would be smaller, and I would have to go to Los Angeles. I don't want to leave now. The poster has put me on a whole new track. I just want to work.

Ann sat in my studio for a long while this morning, content to watch me. I gave her some pastels and paper, but she showed not the slightest interest.

Sonya has named her group At Home Against War. She intends to make a contribution to the war effort while at the same time protesting war for all time. I do not dare ask her how she can do both! She has become a tiger again, eyes blazing, words sharp, claws cutting down the opposition. I listened to the beginning of her meeting last night. What a command of parliamentary procedure she has, although I think she manipulates it to her own benefit. It is an articulate, intelligent group, but from what I could surmise there are as many plans as people. They have not the least idea how to proceed.

. Still no word from my father.

August 18, 1943
Nicole brought me the magazine, even opened it to your picture, and I look at you now. There you are, your merry face smiling out from under the most enormous steel helmet, its wide chinstrap hanging down nearly to your shoulders. My fingers have traced the black border that runs around that page until they are stained with it. Sticky prose insists the great war photographer Jules Chasson has been killed. How is it possible, *mon brave*, that it can be so soon over for you? How could it have happened?

It is such a lie, this life. I was certain we would meet again, so sure! What would you have seen in my face, you who could see in that lens of yours my least softening, my smallest confusions? Nicole says that I am a necessary monster, that to triumph in this world one must forfeit one's heart. I think she must be right, for even now, I am unable to cry at your death. There is so much pain I have not felt. It is debris clogging my mind. Is life always to be so unfinished? How could you die, Jules Chasson, before we met again!

*   *   *

It was the stink that finally brought Delphi downstairs that hot September afternoon. Like the heat, the stink had risen to fill the studio so that she could hardly breathe the foul air. The doorbell had been ringing every few minutes for hours, its unpleasant buzz drilling into her head. Delphi had hardly reached the first floor before she was so assaulted by the sour smell of old shoes and dried sweat that she had to stop for an instant. She peered over the banister to see a barricade of cardboard cartons and brown paper bags against the left wall.

'Sonya?' Delphi fanned herself with a piece of newspaper she had carried from the studio. 'Have you any idea how it smells in here?'

Sonya glanced back at her from her position on the floor counting the number of boxes and bags. 'Your father used to say that no good deed went unpunished.' With some agility, Sonya stood up and continued to count the second layer of boxes. 'If you're interested in what it's all about, there's a pamphlet on the table below you. I would have told you myself, but you're always locked away.'

The doorbell rang again. Sonya opened the door to a rush of children, obviously from a private school, for they all wore little blue smocks with a gold insignia at the heart. As each one dumped the contents of his or her pillowcase of ancient clothes in a pile by the closet door, Sonya carried on with lavish praise, full of the poetry of self-sacrifice, until each child who left seemed assured that he was more important to the war effort than an entire battalion of armed men.

Delphi reached down over the railing to the table and picked up the glossy, expensively printed pamphlet on whose cover was AT HOME AGAINST WAR! Inside, on the second and third pages, its purpose was explained under a very well produced photograph of a child's tear-stained face. In strong and direct prose, it was stated that children were war's real victims, suffering the most and longest from its violence, and so it was incumbent on every man, woman, and child to donate what clothing or money they could to any depot of hope listed on the last page. The prominent names and addresses of those 'at home against war' were listed alphabetically. At the head of the list, in capital letters, was the name and address of the chairwoman, Countess Sonya Tolchin.

'So.' Sonya smiled at Delphi. 'Have I managed to find a case for pacifism?' Her smile broadened as she circled the odious piles of underwear and boots.

'And to think,' Delphi said, 'I worried that when Ann went to school you would not have enough to do.'

'Are you the only one in the house allowed to do anything of significance?' Sonya peered at her.

'You are truly indomitable. I'm glad to see that your Annushka is about to get a taste of the mother I had.'

Sonya sighed and wiped her neck and bosom with a lightly scented linen handkerchief she kept in her sleeve. 'Just a taste,' she said softly. 'I wonder how you will be when you are my age.'

'As I am now,' Delphi answered.

'Probably,' Sonya said. 'Why don't you help me with this for a moment, instead of watching?' Delphi nodded, and started wading through a pile of starched shirts.

As the days progressed, simple navigation through the first floor of the house became impossible. The deliveries far exceeded the pickups, and even with the men, women, and children who filled the house daily to do the sorting, the bundles and boxes full of shirts and sweaters, shoes and belts, socks and underwear, made a maze in every room. As the carters took the sorted clothing away, even more bequests were made. Delphi, risking Sonya's wrath, had ordered that nothing be brought above the second floor. 'Your lack of patriotism astounds me,' Sonya had said, her gaze absolutely withering.

'I warn you, Sonya Tolchin, I will leave here if one sock is found four feet beyond the second floor of this house.'

'If the newspapers knew that I lived with someone who

kept that attitude, I doubt they would write another word about our organization.'

'You learned to live with Papa, and you must learn to live with me. You are always saying we are alike anyway!'

No matter their arguments, orders, and counterorders, not only socks but every other article of clothing imaginable made its way onto the third floor. Sonya stopped short only at Delphi's studio. A series of articles about committee members and contributors appeared in the *Daily News* weekly until even more people visited the West Fourth Street brownstone to leave bags of old pants and starched collars. Finally, *Life* magazine dispatched a reporter and photographer to capture the story of the radical patrician with the soft green stare whose fellow Russians were now fighting gloriously beside America's boys at the front.

As soon as the story was published, Sonya was flooded with fan mail and calls. Groups and societies and committees everywhere pleaded with her for a public appearance. At Home Against War soon had chapters across the country, with Sonya constantly organizing, telephoning, recruiting, working, working, working. Yet she never accepted any of the offers for her appearance.

'Sonya, it's bad luck to keep saying you are in ill health and cannot lecture or attend meetings.'

'Oh?' Sonya's right eyebrow raised itself exquisitely as she wrote down the name of the caller and his request in her book of records. 'What a nice man,' she said. 'He asked me to speak at a bond rally at Madison Square Garden. Can you imagine?' She looked off into the middle distance, her eyes dreamy. 'He said his name was Mr Haggard. He had a voice so like my brother Bruno. What a beautiful boy Bruno was, Delphi. It is still hard for me to accept that such a boy could become Joseph Stalin's chief butcher. You see, he really was the one who gave me my life. Of course, Stalin finally had him killed. He killed all his old friends. Oh, Bruno . . . his voice was full of music.' There was a furrow of concern in her forehead as she stood. 'I must get Annushka into the bath. Time . . . how it runs away.'

She walked in short, quick steps through the narrow pathway leading around the piles of boxes. 'Anya Hasse! Where have you got to, devil child! It is time for your bath!' As she disappeared around the tower of bags, Delphi noticed that Sonya's sweater hung about her like a large feed bag at a horse's mouth. Her ill health was no frivolous and dramatic excuse she had made up to suit her convenience. 'Oh, God, Sonya,' Delphi whispered, standing and racing to the stairway. 'Sonya!' She found Sonya on her knees in the bathroom, filling the tub. Sonya turned toward Delphi and looked at her quizzically. The sleeves of her blouse had been rolled up on her frail and white arms.

'Then it is true, Sonya,' she said, her voice full of her anguish. 'How could you not tell me?'

'Tell you what? That I am ill? But you heard me tell others. Oh, I have managed to live at least thirty years longer than I thought I would. I think I might manage a few more.' She got to her feet and rolled down the sleeves of the blouse and fastened her cuff buttons. Catching a glimpse of herself in the mirror at the back of the door, she put both her hands to her face in alarm. 'My God, I look like my father's mother, that dreadful old witch.' She pushed Delphi to one side as she opened the door to call for Ann. 'I must put Annushka into her bath. It is too late to talk of it. In the meantime, you must not mention it to anybody. Is that clear?' Closing the bathroom door behind her, she began to call for her granddaughter. The steam covered the mirror with a layer of vapor. Delphi could not see herself.

*　　　*　　　*

Delphi   March 2, 1944

Now that I have managed to get Sonya to the doctor, I regret it. He scheduled the operation as soon as possible, and she must be hospitalized in five days, less than a week, for tests. Sonya spends these days going through everything, making piles and throwing away piles. She demands to die in order, she who has always lived in chaos.

She did not flinch when she heard the prognosis. It is devastating. I tell her doctors have been known to be wrong, but I cannot talk her out of her death no matter what I say. I have sent telegrams to everyone that might be able to reach my father. In the middle of a war, I expect him to be here. How I wish he were.

I cannot work at all. I have convinced Sonya that I can manage the house until she is better (better?), but I am not convinced. I can do nothing because the truth is I want to be with Sonya, to sit with her and talk to her. To be near her.

I am possessed of the most terrible despair.

I hear her calling. How anxious I am to go to her.

* * *

'I wanted to make certain I told you about the journals,' Sonya said, looking up at Delphi. 'I'm sorry to tear you away from your work, but I must make sure that I tell you everything, and I keep forgetting things. You see,' she went on in her official voice, which was rather more imperious than her normal one, 'I want them all published. I do. Yes. They are really history. It was life and events as they were lived and felt, not the dry and distant observations of historians. I think these journals have value or I would not ask you to oversee their publication. They are stacked and ordered now, and I am exhausted from them. Yes . . .' She smiled, her voice warming. 'I wish I could find the time to read them again.' She began sorting out the contents of her long, deep Russian ivory box. Now she folded back the corners of some photographs that were bent and yellow and allowed herself a moment or two of reverie, sometimes adding a date to the backs before she put them into yet another pile. Delphi watched as she looked at her odd mementos, an Arabic book, a dried lily of the valley. She was both wistful and happy as she held each one, turning it in her hands before putting it on the desk. Moskva, the largest of the houseful of cats, sat in her lap and stared at Delphi. The air of the room was filled with the separate and distinct fragrances of the burning apple wood and the clove-studded oranges piled in the cachepots on the mantel.

Sonya lifted strands of colored stones out of the box. They glittered like the cat's eyes. 'I have something else to tell you,' Sonya said, looking at the stones in her hands. 'My necklaces are not paste. I always said they were, I know. Well, they are not. They are quite real. This one' – she held it out – 'is sapphires and rubies. This' – she held the other forward – 'is a fortune in pearls. The rest are diamonds and emeralds.'

Delphi's mouth dropped open as she sat forward on the couch facing Sonya's desk.

'Don't you see, Delphi, I couldn't have worn them if they

were real. No, I could never have done that. So I pretended they were false. You see how contradictory I am.' She smiled. 'How shocked you look!'

'I am.'

'I could not part with my jewels because your father had given them to me. And the pearls belonged to my great-grandmother. I'm only telling you this because I don't want you to toss them away thinking they had no value. I want my granddaughter to wear them one day.'

'I would not have tossed them away. I resent that.'

'Your sentiment is shaky. At times I fear it doesn't fill a thimble.' Sonya put the necklaces back into the ivory box one by one, closed the lid, and looked across the room. 'I think fireplaces will soon be a thing of the past. I believe everything graceful is doomed. There is no time in this world for grace.' She nuzzled the cat. 'War swallows it. No time. Time.' She smiled, rubbing her chin over Moskva's crown. 'Time . . . how I cursed it when I was young. How slowly it went! An elephant might sew the empress a new gown faster than it took one winter day to pass. Those frozen white months when we never got warm enough. And when we were nearly warm by our fires, it was over. One day there was the sight of an icicle dripping, and the next, quick as anything, it was summer. A hot summer that took forever.' Sonya leaned back in her chair contentedly.

'There were so many extremes in Russia – cold, hot, rich, poor.' Sonya sighed majestically. 'Russia's extremes were the reason for the Russian soul. Certainly, they were the reason for the unpredictablity of the Russian heart.'

'Ah, yes, Sonya. The great Russian soul! The traitorous Russian heart!' Delphi laughed as she intoned the words. 'Where would I be without them both?'

'I might have been better off without them.' Sonya was amused. 'I wonder what would have happened if I had never left Russia.'

'If you had stayed in Petersburg, I would have perished in the mid-Atlantic, thrown into the sea with the rest of the garbage.'

'Isn't it extraordinary that I never think of that.' Sonya sat forward, looking at Delphi seriously. 'I always think that you are exactly mine, that I would have had you no matter . . .' She got up and, still holding fast to the cat, walked to the chair nearest the fire. Delphi watched her progression in the large, round mirror that hung against the far wall on a heavy woven gold rope. The last of the daylight went in that instant, and the room was suddenly lit only by the firelight and its reflection in the mirror. 'Perhaps, Delphi, I should have divorced your father. Life would have been more straightforward. What do you think?' The cat jumped from Sonya's lap and landed with a thud on the carpet.

Sonya immediately patted her empty lap. 'Come, Pashka,' she commanded. The dog lifted his head wearily from the hearthstone before grunting his way to his feet and walking to Sonya, who lifted him up and sat him on her. 'Pashka, Pashka, your breath is poisonous. I should feed you parsley.' Sonya shifted in the chair and folded her legs under her like a small child. 'Why don't you have a lover, Delphi?'

'I have done with love, Sonya. Its loss is too painful and its presence too demanding.' Delphi twisted the long coil of her hair around and around in her hand. 'Love of one's self is all that matters. Wasn't it you who taught me that?'

'I suppose it was.' The telephone began to ring in another part of the house, its sound plaintive and insistent. Both of them listened, but neither woman made a move to answer its call. It rang a long while before it stopped. 'I remember Petersburg before there were telephones, before the world was inexorably linked with wire.' Sonya grimaced. 'You have no idea how much more exciting it was without telephones. Life had so much more expectancy. It was so rich, like an opera. One held one's breath all the time. We all knew one another's messengers, you see. That fellow with the dangling mustaches and thick legs belonged to the Cheremeyovs, and the other with the belly like a pudding and a head like an egg in a cozy belonged to the Rostopoviches. Oh, there were hundreds of them. All day long, everyone watched their progress as they crisscrossed the city, their little envelopes tucked into their pockets. How everyone waited and held his breath. Would one be invited? Accepted? Loved? Ah, it was wonderful!' Sonya put her head back against the paisley-covered chair. 'It made the senses so alive, Delphi. Now they are so neglected. Everything is too fast. There are no delicious secrets. Everybody knows everything. It is so . . . boring!' She threw up her hands, and Pashka squealed with alarm. 'Really,' Sonya asked, patting the dog, 'do you think I should have divorced your father? He might have been happier with another woman. I might have been happier with Julius.'

'My father has never been a man to take less than he wanted, Sonya.'

'What man does?' Sonya pursed her lips. 'Only women take less.'

'My life suits me.'

'It does, doesn't it?' Sonya nodded. 'I am so glad of that.'

'I think the only trouble with living in my own world is that I am no good in anyone else's.' Delphi's voice was lower than usual. She watched the gauzy inner curtains blow out along the rotting sills. 'I can't imagine another world for myself any longer, Sonya. Thank God I am successful in this one.'

'I think the best one can hope for is to be born into an exciting time. In that way, Delphi, we have both been lucky.' Sonya shivered and Delphi walked to the fire to add more wood. The weight of the new logs broke the ones beneath them, and they fell into the bed of ashes, sending up a spray of embers. Another cat skittered by to pounce on Moskva, who was asleep on the rug's center medallion. There was a hiss and a howl and silence. Delphi sat on the rug by Sonya's chair.

'What are you thinking, Delphi?' Sonya's voice was sweet.

'About the time I couldn't finish the Pushkin. I still wake up from time to time in a night sweat, the words on my lips. Isn't it strange that I still have that kind of nightmare?' Delphi put her head against the seat of the chair and looked up at Sonya. 'I don't understand it. I have enough from life. It allows me to pursue what is important to me.'

'Exactly what your father would say.' Sonya hit the arm of the chair with a delicate fist. 'I am always astonished at how alike you are.' Sonya turned her face toward the fire. 'When I die, you must make me a promise about Anya. I know it will be hard for you, Delphi, but you must not estrange her. It will be difficult when I am not here.' Sonya smiled wistfully. 'You must promise me you will take care of your daughter.' She paused.

'I will, Sonya.'

'You will get help, I know, good help, but you must give her some of yourself. Not too much, not so it interferes with the painting, just a little bit more.'

'Maybe, after all, when you are my age, when you have grandchildren, maybe you will feel other things, too. I have changed so. No one ever believes that he will change, and yet change is all that life is about.' Sonya blinked back her tears, her mouth pursed tight in a tiny smile. She sighed. 'It's like a good book, you see, life. I want to know the ending. I don't want to leave in the middle of the plot.'

'Sonya . . .'

'Do we have any wine? I might manage a bit. It may even give me an appetite.'

'We might.' Delphi stood and went to the rosewood cabinet and picked up the heavy decanter. As she poured the wine, she saw the richness of its color catch the gold of the firelight and felt an unimaginable longing for Tolchin.

Above her head, she watched Sonya's profile in the mirror. How beautiful she was, the slightly upturned nose, the full mouth, the curve of her high, round cheek, and the great length of her eye under its thick, arching brow. Delphi walked to her, carrying the glasses and the decanter on the brass tray. Sonya took a glass and held it up. 'To your father, wherever he is. May he live a thousand years and never want for a warm bed or a good breakfast.' Sonya's hand trembled as Delphi touched her glass to Sonya's glass. They both drank. Sonya stopped after one sip, pressing her tongue against the inside of her mouth before she slowly swallowed the wine. 'How I loved him,' she said.

Delphi filled the glasses again. 'If there is a God, may he bless us. If there is a devil, may he ignore us.'

Sonya grinned. 'You remember that, eh? Who used to use that one all the time? Was it Julius? Boris?'

'Not Julius. Julius always asked God to be good to the Jews. It was Boris. Oh, Sonya, do you remember Misinsky? He was forever toasting the czar. "To the czar! If it weren't for his evil, I would still be as valueless as dung and smell no better!"'

'Let us drink to Misinsky!' Sonya held up her glass and finished the wine. 'He had no neck, Misinsky.' Sonya held out her glass for more wine.

'And Sasha Vinover? Wasn't it he who used to bellow, "I toast all women who have the sense to want me. May God see them safely to my bed!"' Delphi lifted her glass and then drained it. 'I can close my eyes and hear all those toasts, see all those faces. "May the children of my enemies marry my friends!" And always – Sonya, Sonya, can't you hear it? – "Down with the czar! May he suffer for eternity!"' Delphi flushed. Her head was dizzy and she wondered if it might float away. When she opened her eyes, she saw Sonya holding her glass perfectly still with great effort in the cup of her hands. Her eyes were filled with tears. 'Sonya?'

'I am only thinking of your father again. How thoughts of him fill my mind . . . Do you remember his favorite toast?'

They nodded and held up their glasses toward one another, and the small crystal clash between them left a clear and perfect sound lingering in the room. Both of them spoke at once. 'May men envy my life and desire my death.' Silently, they finished the last of the wine. Sonya held up the empty wineglass a moment and then carefully placed it on the table beside her. She put her elbow on the arm of the chair and leaned her head into her hand, her eyes firmly on Delphi's face. 'I regret the leaving of my life, but not the life itself. You are exactly as I always hoped you would be, Delphi Stern. Exactly.'

Coming home the next week, she saw him walking toward the house. She was directly across the street and there was no time to walk to the corner to the path cut into the snow bank, and so she turned and climbed over the wall of snow in front of her. The blackened crust at its top gave way under her, and she lost her feet in snow as the cuff of her coat sleeves shoveled up more of it. But still Delphi ran, dodging cars, sliding and nearly falling but going ahead, running crazily toward the front door of the house through another snow bank, screaming his name. 'Tolchin! Papa!'

He had his hand on the door. He bowed slightly but stood there, not moving an inch toward her and waiting until she was next to him, breathless, soaking wet, pure panic in her face. She could not speak at first, there was no air left in her lungs. She leaned against the door because she could hardly stand. He took a step forward and kissed both her cheeks.

'You never change,' she said, her words little gasps.

'Nor you,' he said, kissing her again, this time on the forehead. Under his cashmere coat, magically content to stay just at his shoulders, he was wearing a pin-stripe suit, matchlessly tailored, his shirt so freshly laundered it still smelled of starch.

'I have written you everywhere. Wired you everywhere. Everywhere.' Her voice was so tired.

'I know,' he said, offering no explanation. Instead he touched her cheek just at the corner of her mouth, lightly rubbing his fingertip along it. His hand dropped and he took a breath. 'Is she very ill?'

Delphi sighed, looking down at her caked boots. The snow on them was slowly melting in puddles around her. 'The operation is tomorrow. I was just coming home to see my daughter, and then I must go back to the hospital.'

'I see,' he said. His face was set in an acquired expression of thoughtfulness, but his eyelids fluttered slightly. 'I would have liked to have had time to speak with her doctor, but . . .' He shrugged. 'I shall go with you.'

'Perhaps it is better if you didn't . . . She is very peaceful now, very accepting of her death. You know . . . you cannot change anything.'

'But I have no intention of changing anything. I have come to see Sonya so that nothing will change.'

'Oh, Tolchin, I think you will break her heart in the last.'

'Delphi, I am surprised at you.' He looked at her sadly. 'And disappointed.'

'But it is the only time in her life when she does not need you. It is a victory for her. Oh, Papa, it is really true. She does not need you anymore.' Delphi's tears were warm on her frozen cheeks.

'She never needed me. But she is waiting for me.'

In the hospital, Delphi followed her father down the hall. At the door to Sonya's room, Delphi braced herself for Sonya's shriek, not daring to look at Sonya, staring at the floor and holding fast to the door frame. But there was only silence and then, God, there was such a sound of sweetness, such a small, quiet voice, the voice of a young girl.

'Gregory Andreivitch. Oh, Grisha! I have been waiting so long.'

Delphi saw him walk to the bed and stand there, looking down at Sonya. Her face had transformed, had brightened, had widened. A thread of tears came down her cheeks soundlessly.

'How ridiculous you are to have gotten ill,' he said. His

voice was a lullaby.

'I have always been ridiculous. You see, I did not want to die until you came. Not even that. How you torture me.'

He sat on the bed and gathered her up into his arms, and her arms went up until her hands had settled at the sides of his face. Her eyes, even in the dusty yellow light, were luminous. Delphi stared at them both and backed away, once more a child too young to see this union. She walked slowly down the hall and sat in the deserted waiting room. She had no idea how long it was before Tolchin came to sit beside her.

'She is sleeping now,' he said. 'It will do no good to worry. Everything is up to God.'

* * *

Sonya   September 22, 1945

A new life, a new journal. I walked again today in the park at Washington Square. The trees are still so green and full, the air filled with summer. I laugh, thinking of myself reborn, naked on a seashell, a scarred and aging Venus. I did not believe them at first, but it is more than a year now. The world and I are healing together.

Delphi tells me this second life will be just a continuation of the first. Let us hope so! Contradicting the voices of doom, among which my own has always been loudest, it is possible to have everything. I have had everything. I have ridden horses to battle, stormed citadels, been slain on the field. It is all I have wanted. Delphi will miss that part of life I would not now relinquish for my soul. Let her be great. How I admire her. She has chosen a man's life and she has succeeded. But my Annushka, may she be as proud as I of her woman's strength, her woman's passion, so much greater than any man's.

How long, I wonder, can a second life last?

THE END

ABOUT THE AUTHORS

DORA LANDEY was born and raised in Manhattan. Currently a student at Sarah Lawrence College, she lives in the country with her husband and three daughters.

ELINOR KLEIN was born and educated in Massachusetts and was graduated from Smith College. With her son, her husband, and her three dogs, she commutes between an apartment in Manhattan and a donkey farm in the country